MUSIC THROUGH THE CENTURIES

The organ of St. Thomas Church in Leipzig where Bach served for many years

MUSIC THROUGH THE CENTURIES

Nick Rossi
LaGuardia Community College
City University of New York

Sadie Rafferty

University Press
of America™

University Press of America, Inc.™

P.O. Box 19101, Washington, DC 20036

ISBN: 0-8191-1499-5 Perfect
0-8191-1498-7 Case
Library of Congress Number: 80-9066

PREFACE

SINCE the distinguishing characteristic of music is tone, and tone is perceived through the ear, listening is the one indispensable activity in music education. Furthermore, it is not enough merely to hear music. It must be listened to with a focus of attention upon its most significant characteristics.

The listener needs help in knowing what to listen for. If he is to understand the nature, structure, and meaning of music he will require help in investigating the constituent elements of music and the inter-relationships which exist among them. The verbalizations in a book have meaning only in relation to music which the learner has experienced perceptually. Every music educator knows that this is accomplished best through direct contact with music itself. The use of this book, therefore, will be more effective when its content is used in a manner which builds upon previous aural experiences.

A volume of this type can help the learner listen for the things that are most important for him to hear in order to develop generalized concepts which result from his inquiry into the components which comprise music.

Moreover, such a book can help the learner to relate the music he hears to the total culture from which it came. This, of course, is a less musical purpose, but nevertheless a valuable one in many instances.

Books which can perform these functions for young people at the high school level are too few in number. This volume, therefore, is welcomed for the unique contribution it may be able to make to the musical understandings of young people. That it was prepared by authors of such insight and experience is cause to expect that it will serve its purpose with distinction.

WILLIAM C. HARTSHORN
Supervisor in Charge, Music Section
Los Angeles Board of Education

The Bayreuth Festspielhaus. Its corner-stone was laid on May 22, 1872, by Richard Wagner on his fifty-ninth birthday; he then conducted a performance of Beethoven's *Symphony No. 9* at the ceremony. At the first festival, in 1876, the *Ring des Nibelungen* had its first complete performance.

ACKNOWLEDGMENTS

The authors would like to express their sincerest thanks to Mrs. Geraldine Smith Healy, Supervisor of Music, Los Angeles City Schools, without whose enthusiasm and encouragement this book would not have come into being. Special thanks go to Mr. William C. Hartshorn, Supervisor in Charge of Music Education, Los Angeles City Schools, who patiently helped the authors discover a manner of writing "about" music. The authors also wish to thank Mr. Virgil Thomson for help in re-writing and in proofreading, and to Mr. Dominick Di Sarro, Los Angeles City College, and Mr. Joel O. Harry, U. S. Grant High School in Van Nuys, for help in the selection of compositions to be included in this book. For reading through certain sections on contemporary music and for typing a somewhat illegible manuscript, gratitude is extended to Mr. Rafael Kianowsky and Mrs. Lillian Wilson, respectively. The authors are also deeply indebted to the following for help in biographical sketches and analyses of compositions: Mrs. Arnold Schoenberg, Mr. Igor Stravinsky, Dr. Darius Milhaud, Sir William Walton, Mr. Benjamin Britten, Mr. Walter Piston, Dr. Howard Hanson, Mr. Virgil Thomson, Mr. Roy Harris, Mr. Aaron Copland, Mr. Paul Creston, Mr. Samuel Barber, Mr. William Schuman, and Mr. Gian-Carlo Menotti.

The authors wish to make grateful acknowledgment to the following publishers, authors, and composers for permission to quote from copyrighted materials:

Associated Music Publishers, Inc., New York, for permission to quote the composer's comments on *Sonata #4* by Charles Ives as they appear on the score.

The quotations from *Mathis der Maler* are printed with the permission of B. Schott's Söhne, Mainz, Germany and its United States representative, Associated Music Publishers, Inc., New York. Copyright 1934.

Basil Blackwell & Mott, Limited, for "L'Apres-Midi d'un Faune" by Aldous Huxley.

Boosey & Hawkes, Inc. for permission to quote the composer's description of *Appalachian Spring* by Aaron Copland as it appears on the score.

Durand & Cie, from *Suite #2* of *Daphnis and Chloe* by Maurice Ravel, and from *Bolero* by Maurice Ravel. Used by permission of the publisher, Durant & Cie, Paris.

E. C. Schirmer Music Company from *Alleluia* by Randall Thompson. Copyright, 1940, by E. C. Schirmer Music Company, Boston, and used with their permission.

G. Schirmer, Inc. from *Amahl and the Night Visitors* by Gian-Carlo Menotti. Copyright, MCMLI, MCMLII, by G. Schirmer, Inc. *Symphony No. 3* by Roy Harris. Copyright, 1939, 1940, by G. Schirmer, Inc. *The White Peacock* by Charles Griffes. Copyright, 1917, by G. Schirmer, Inc. Copyright renewal assigned, 1945, by G. Schirmer, Inc. *Symphony No. 1* by Samuel Barber. Copyright, 1943, by G. Schirmer, Inc. *Acadian Songs and Dances* by Virgil Thomson. Copyright, 1948, 1951, by Virgil Thomson. All reprinted by permission of the publisher, G. Schirmer, Inc.

ACKNOWLEDGMENTS

Holt, Rinehart and Winston, Inc. from *Toscanini and Great Music* by Lawrence Gilman. Copyright, 1938, by Lawrence Gilman. Reprinted by permission of Holt, Rinehart and Winston, Inc.

Howard Hanson from *Second Symphony* by Howard Hanson. Copyright, 1932, by Eastman School of Music. International Copyright secured. Copyright renewed 1959. Reprinted with the permission of Dr. Hanson.

J. & W. Chester, Ltd. from *Sombrero des Tres Picos* by Manuel de Falla. Copyright, 1942, by J. & W. Chester. Ltd.. London. and reprinted with their permission.

Alfred A. Knopf, Inc. for excerpts from *The Book of Modern Composers* by Merle Armitage. Copyright, 1942, by Alfred A. Knopf, Inc. *Masters of Russian Music* by Michel D. Calvocoressi and Gerald Abraham. Copyright, 1936, by Alfred A. Knopf, Inc. *My Musical Life* by Nikolay Rimsky-Korsakoff, translated by Judah A. Joffee. Copyright, 1923, by Alfred A. Knopf, Inc. *Charles T. Griffes* by Edward Maisel. Copyright, 1943, by Alfred A. Knopf, Inc. *The Book of Modern Composers* by David Ewen. Copyright, 1942, by Alfred A. Knopf, Inc. *The Life of Richard Wagner* by Ernest Newman. Copyright, 1946, by Alfred A. Knopf, Inc. *Giuseppe Verdi: His Life and Works* by Francis Toye. Copyright, 1931, by Alfred A. Knopf, Inc. Quotations are reprinted with permission of the publisher, Alfred A. Knopf, Inc.

Leeds Music Corporation, from *Suite Française* by Darius Milhaud, © Copyright, MCMXLVI, by Leeds Music Corporation, 322 West 48th Street, New York 36, New York. All Rights Reserved. Used by permission. Study scores of this work may be purchased from the publishers, Leeds Music Corporation.

Oxford University Press, Inc. from *Charles Ives and His Music* by Henry Cowell. Copyright, 1954. Reprinted by permission of the publisher, Oxford University Press, Inc., New York.

Oxford University Press, London, from *Symphony No. 8* by Ralph Vaughan Williams. © Copyright, 1956, by Oxford University Press, London, and from *Belshazzar's Feast* by William Walton. © Copyright, 1931, by Oxford University Press, London. Reprinted with the permission of the publishers, Oxford University Press, London.

Templeton Publishing Company, from *Symphony No. 3* by Paul Creston. Copyright 1957, Templeton Publishing Co., Inc., Delaware Water Gap, Pa. Used by special permission.

Theodore Presser Company from *New England Triptych* by William Schuman, and the composer's comments as they appear on the score. Copyright, 1957, by Marion Music, Inc. Used by permission of Theodore Presser Company.

Gertrud Schoenberg and Universal Edition A. G., Vienna, from *Pierrot Lunaire* by Arnold Schoenberg. Used by permission of Gertrud Schoenberg.

Universal Edition (London) Ltd. from *Hary Janos Suite* by Zoltan Kodaly. Used by permission of Universal Edition (London) Ltd.

CONTENTS

The musical Mozarts are pictured in this engraving by Delafosse after a watercolor by Carmontelle painted in Paris in 1763 during the Mozarts' visit to that city. Mozart's father plays the violin, young Wolfgang (then 7) is at the keyboard, and his 11-year old sister Nannerl sings.

LIST OF ILLUSTRATIONS

xiv

xv

xvi

MUSIC THROUGH THE CENTURIES

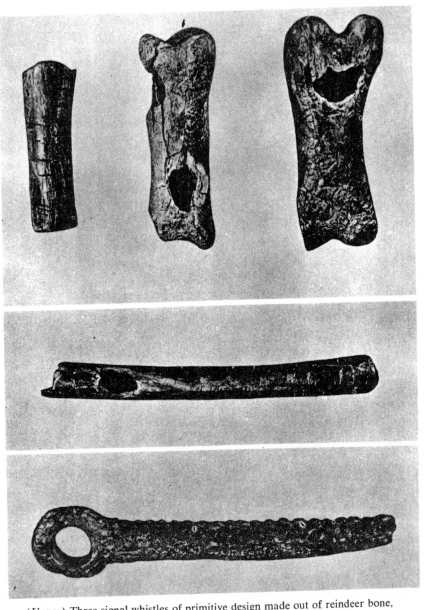

(*Upper*) Three signal whistles of primitive design made out of reindeer bone, found in a cave in Moravia

(*Center*) An ancient whistle found in the Pekárna cave, dated by paleontologists as coming from the Paleolithic era (Old Stone Age)

(*Lower*) A scraper found in the Pekárna cave from the Paleolithic era

THE BEGINNINGS

IN THE BEGINNING WAS MUSIC. Just how it sounded or in what order its early development took place will never be known, since music is an art that occupies time, not space. The pictures drawn on the walls of the caves by primitive men may indicate what their instruments looked like, but these give no hint as to how the music sounded or what its melody was.

Undoubtedly *rhythm* was one of the first discoveries in music. The walking or running of early cave men must have established in their minds some kind of rhythm, and it is known from primitive peoples in the remote corners of today's world that with the aid of drums, messages can be communicated over many miles of terrain by certain recognized rhythmic patterns. The Indians of North America used a rhythmical sequence to send their smoke signals, a system of long and short puffs.

Melody must have entered music quite early as the primitive peoples discovered that in talking the voice moves along at various pitches. Sometimes it could denote a question with a rising inflection at the end of a sentence, or at lower pitches it could sound ominous and foreboding. When these people discovered they could make sound through a ram's horn or a bamboo pipe, or by vibrating two willow reeds together, they had discovered tone quality or *timbre*. Eventually by repeating certain fragments of a tune, they discovered *form*.

Hundreds of centuries later, they tried having two or more voices sing or play different melodies at the same time and thus finally discovered what was known first as counterpoint and later as harmony, the *texture* of music.

The modern family of orchestral instruments are all descendants of very early, primitive instruments. Since rhythm was probably one of the first discoveries of man, it may be assumed that the percussion family was the first to be established. Anything that could be hit or pounded would form sounds, some more resonant or more mellow than others, but with a variety of timbre even though the pitch was indeterminate.

From the time of Moses in the history of the Jewish people, there is a record of the ram's horn (shofar) being blown at the time of certain religious festivals. This gave way in later generations, when metals came to be used, to the making of horns of brass. Pictures on ancient Greek vessels show many instruments of hollow wood pipes, or instruments with vibrating reed-like leaves of plants, thus foreshadowing the modern flute and reed instrument families. Stringed instruments (lutes and kitharas) were illustrated both on ancient Greek and Egyptian vessels and on bas reliefs.

It is assumed that most early music was vocal. Several factors lend authority to this statement: instruments were not very highly developed and thus had a limited range or number of pitches that they could sound; it required a trained player to perform on any of these instruments; and even these early instruments in their crude forms were not always accessible. In the hundreds of references to music, in the Old Testament of the Bible, there are only two in which voices are not mentioned along with the instruments.

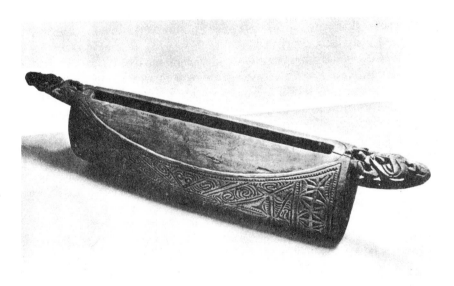

Slit drum from New Guinea

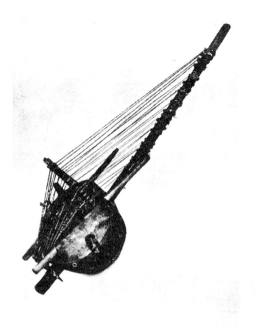

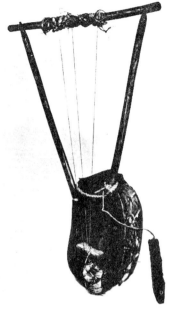

Harp-lute type of instrument known as *kasso* (from Senegambia)

An instrument resembling the ancient Greek lyre. known as a *kissar* (from Nubia)

This painting on an old Egyptian tomb in Thebes shows (from left to right) an Egyptian arched harp, a lute, a double oboe, and a lyre

An aulos on a Greek vase from about the fifth century B.C.

Greek notation of music from 1st century B.C., found on the side of a tomb

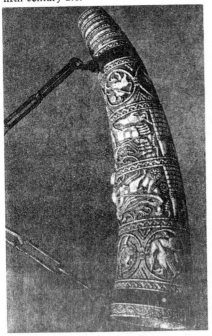

The famous hunting horn sounded by Roland, nephew of Charlemagne

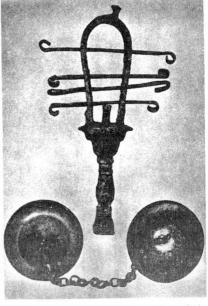

A sistrum or rattle and a pair of cymbals excavated from Pompeii

MUSIC OF THE GREEK ERA

Not too much is known about the music of the great classical civilization of the Greeks. Only eleven fragments of the music of ancient Greece remain and these can give no accurate picture of the music of this great civilization that lasted for hundreds of years.

The Greek civilization placed great importance on the study of music, making it for the educated man as important as the study of mathematics. The very term *music* comes from the Greek word *Muses,* the nine goddesses of song and poetry. Some of the best known Greek gods were those associated with music: Apollo, god of manly youth and of poetry and music; Orpheus, his son, who overcame the powers of Hades with his singing and poetry.

Largely through the work in acoustics of the Greek mathematician Pythagoras. the numerical ratios corresponding to the principal intervals of the musical scale were discovered: the octave, the fifth, and the fourth.

THE EARLY CHRISTIAN ERA

An accurate study of ancient music must start with that of the early Christian church since available records do not go much further back. Fortunately the monks of the Middle Ages recorded in their books a fairly accurate story of civilization in that period of history. All early Christian music was vocal. St. Clement of Alexandria said around 200 A.D. that "We need one instrument: the peaceful word of adoration. not harps or drums or pipes or trumpets."

Until a system of noting pitches was developed, the only way a melody could be preserved was for one generation to sing it for the next. Even though this was seldom accurate, the base melody *could* remain unchanged. It is known that some of the early melodies of the Christian church were derived from the Jewish cantorial music of an earlier generation, and there is some indication that it was also influenced by melodies from the Greek civilization.

The melodies of the early Christian church were sung in unison, women being excluded from singing in the church, and had a single melodic line (monophonic). Apparently many of the early churches (Roman Catholic) employed all types of melodies including secular ones. A codification was started so that only appropriate melodies were approved. Largely responsible for instigating this work on behalf of the Church was Gregory I, Pope from 590 to 604 A.D. Although this codification took considerable time to accomplish, these melodies have since been named after the Pope and called *Gregorian chants*. To this day they are the official, approved music of the Roman Catholic Church. Since chants are sung in unison and have no rhythm other than that dictated by the words, they are also known as *plainsong*.

The following is an example of Gregorian chant in the notation developed around the thirteenth century, and then a translation into modern notation by the monks of the Abbey Solesmes:

The Greeks established a series of four-note scales (*tetrachords*) on which melodies were built; and then they started building one tetrachord on top of another, thereby obtaining scales of eight notes, the first and last of which were an *octave* (from *octo* meaning "8") apart. Because there were thirteen half-tones within the octave range, four had to be eliminated. By eliminating different ones in different scales, the Greeks established *modes* on which melodies could be built.

These same modes were used by the Church for the Gregorian chants, but the Church seldom referred to them by name. Unfortunately, medieval scholars attempted to name them after the Greek modes, using the same names. Their information was incomplete so that although the medieval modes (or Church modes as they are sometimes called) used the same patterns as the Greeks, and although they used the same names for the modes as the Greeks, the medieval scholars attached these to the wrong modes. Thus what had been the Phyrgian mode to the Greeks was known as the Dorian mode to the medieval scholars, and what had been the Dorian mode to the Greeks was known to the Middle Ages as the Phrygian mode.

Today in references to the modes, the medieval names are employed:

Note that what is now known as the *major scale* is the same pattern of half steps and whole steps as the Ionian mode, and that the Aeolian mode is the same as the *melodic minor* in a descending pattern.

All Gregorian chant was built on one of these modal patterns as was the secular music of the time. These modes were in general use up to the time of the Baroque era (starting about 1600) when they were gradually replaced by the *major* and *minor* scale patterns. Although replaced, many melodies of a later era still followed the modal patterns rather than the contemporary scales; for example: Chopin's *Mazurka No. 15* with a melody in the Lydian mode; the first theme of the second movement of Brahms' *Symphony No. 4* which combines the Phrygian with the Mixolydian; and the *Symphony No. 2* of Sibelius in which the first theme of the second movement is Aeolian.

ORGANUM

Up to the ninth century all music was sung in unison. From the ninth to the thirteenth century a method of combining two melodic lines called *organum* was employed. The old Church melodies or plainsongs were sung by one voice called the *tenor* (from *tenore* meaning "to hold") or *vox principalis* (principal voice). To this was added a second voice called *duplum* or *vox organalis*. The second or duplum voice appeared at an interval of a fourth or fifth below the given plainsong of the tenor. The Latin term for this practise was *punctus contra punctum,* hence the later term *counterpoint* or note against note. This second voice moved parallel to the tenor except at the beginning and ending of lines at which time it could start and end in unison.

Here is an example of organum from the ninth century, a sequence *Rex Coeli Domine:*

(Plainsong)

(Organum Voice)

1. Rex coe- li   Do- mi- ne   ma- ris   un- di-   so-   ni
2. Ti-   ta- nis   ni- ti- di   squa- li-   di- que   so-   li,

3. Te hu- mi- les fa- mu- li mo- du- lis ve- ne- ran- do pi- is
4. Se ju- be- as fla-gi-tant va- ri- is li- be- ra- re ma- lis.

1. *King of the Heavens, Lord of the sounding sea,*
2. *Of the shining sun and of the squalid earth,*
3. *Thy humble servants, venerating Thee with pious accents,*
4. *Entreat Thee that Thou wilt order them freed from manifold ills.*

In this example the tenor voice sings the Gregorian chant (plainsong) as it had been used for centuries. To this has been added the duplum or second voice which parallels the tenor a 4th below except at the beginning and ending of each line at which points it starts and ends in unison. This example is taken from the ninth century *Musica Enchiriadis* (Musical Handbook) which contains the first discussion of music with more than one melodic line, *polyphony*. Some attribute the authorship of this work to Hucbald (c. 840 to 930 A.D.).

RHYTHMIC MODES

Although first described in the ninth century, the use of *rhythmic modes* to denote different rhythmic patterns was widespread from about 1230 A.D. onward, reaching its maximum use later in the same century. These "modes" or patterns were adopted from classical prosody and went by similar names. The basic rhythmic modes were:•

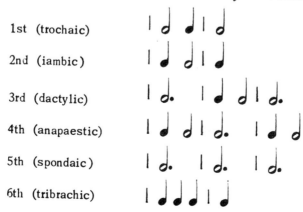

1st (trochaic)

2nd (iambic)

3rd (dactylic)

4th (anapaestic)

5th (spondaic)

6th (tribrachic)

The upper voices of polyphonic compositions were usually in the 1st, 2nd, or 6th modes, while the lower voices were in the 3rd or 5th mode. The use of the 4th mode was rare. All accents were by words as there were no bar lines. The triple figures were called "perfect" while any subdivision into two was called "imperfect."

Rhythmic modes were employed in folk music previously to their advent in sacred music and are still in use in the folk music of Iceland.

SOLMIZATION

Having established a method of writing pitch relationships with Gregorian chant notation, it was necessary to devise a method of reading the notation so that the intended melody could be quickly called to mind or reproduced by the voice. Guido d'Arezzo (980 to 1050) is credited with having established the method of *solmization*. Based on a method similar to that employed by the East Indians, Arabs, and Persians, names were assigned to the notes of a given composition: ut, re, mi, fa, sol, la. The word solmization comes from the combination of the syllables *sol* and *mi* — *sol-mi*-zation. Guido, in a letter, reports that this association of the syllables with each of the six degrees enabled the choir boys to learn in a few days what formerly required many weeks to master.

This system remained unaltered until the sixteenth century. In 1600 the French used *ut* for *C* and added the syllable *si* to complete the scale. In 1650 the syllable *ut* was changed to *do* to make it more singable. In the French system, *do* always represents *C, re* always represents *D, mi* represents *E,* etc.

The syllables were derived from a hymn, *Ut quetant laxis,* the poem by Paul Deacon written around 770 A.D.:

Ut qué-ant lá- xis Re-so-ná-re fib-ris Mi- ra ges-tó- rum Fá-mu-li tu-

ó- rum Sol- re pol- lú-ti lá-bi-i re- á-tum, San-cte Jo-en-nes

That with enfranchised voices
Thy servants may be able to proclaim
The wonders of thy deeds,
Remove the sin of polluted lips,
O holy John.

NOTATION

A series of neumes started to develop around the eighth century and were used for the notation of music through the fourteenth century. These neumes indicated melodic motion only; they did not indicate exact pitch or time value. Their early use was as an aid for someone already familiar with a given chant or melody, the neumes indicating melodic direction enough to recall the already known tune.

Some of the neumes included:

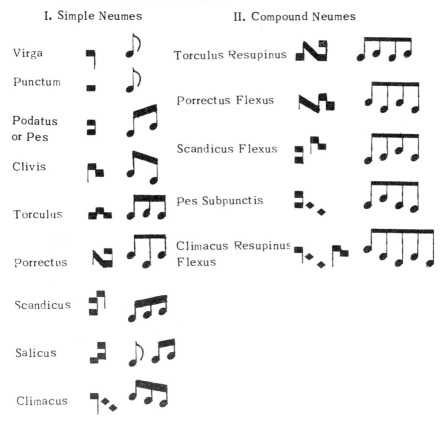

I. Simple Neumes   II. Compound Neumes

Virga

Punctum

Podatus or Pes

Clivis

Torculus

Porrectus

Scandicus

Salicus

Climacus

Torculus Resupinus

Porrectus Flexus

Scandicus Flexus

Pes Subpunctis

Climacus Resupinus Flexus

Around 1100 the first indication of pitch was established in written notation. This system of relative pitch notation was adopted around the thirteenth century and was used for notating Gregorian chants and the melodies of the troubadours and trouvères. The system is used to the present day in the official notation of the chants of the Roman Catholic Church.

At first colored lines were used to indicate pitch: from the eleventh century a red line was used to indicate F; later a yellow line (sometimes green) was added to represent C. The transition to a three- or four-line staff was then quite easy. Once the four-line staff had been adopted, its use has continued to this day for notating Gregorian chant.

With the advent of polyphony, music with more than one melodic line, an additional staff line was added, making what is known today as the five-line staff. This was accomplished around 1200.

This twelfth-Century manuscript shows the monk Luitherus offering St. Gallus the chants of the Gradual. The type of neume appearing in the *Alleluia* above the figures is known as the St. Gall *hook* or *round neume,* as it has an appearance of a hook or half-round circle. The word *neume* is derived from the Greek *neuma* which means something like a "nod" or "a sign." probably referring to a written representation of a manual sign as to whether the melodic line moved up or down. As written, neumes indicate the direction of the melody only, the rhythm being dictated by the text.

A page from a collection of masses (of Flemish origin) celebrating the Emperor Maximilian I's marriage in 1493. The Kyrie is noted on a five-line staff with mensural notation (indicating time values with hollow and solid lozenges, with and without stems).

CHAPTER II

MUSIC OF THE MIDDLE AGES

THE MIDDLE AGES in general history extend from the disintegration of the Roman Empire in the fifth century for about a thousand years thereafter. A period of this length must necessarily encompass vast changes in both politics and the arts. The medieval era was marked by the ruin of Paganism and encompassed vast migrations. Its most marked influence was from the Church of Rome.

Up to the Middle Ages, the peoples of the German areas were pagan barbarians; but through the Middle Ages they became Christian subjects. In the process, the civilization of the Romans became less than it had been; but at the same time the Germans ascended to new peaks of culture and religion. The period incorporated many feudal anarchies, each duke and prince fighting for more power and independence. The Church, however, was in ascendancy, building new monasteries, and gaining in power and influence.

The Crusades were an evidence of the power of the Church. In the eleventh century, records remain of over 116 separate pilgrimages to Jerusalem, involving from hundreds to thousands of people on each one. There was, during this time, a growth in the monastic orders as well as in the temporal powers of the Pope.

The Middle Ages were the ages of chivalry. The clergy and nobles formed an aristocracy. They were concerned with the power and influence of their own churches, castles, and fortresses. The worship of women, and in particular, the Virgin Mary, was supreme.

In this period, music occupied a unique position. With the advent of the first book on music, by Boethius, the theory of music was outlined and its importance in the quadrivium — which included arithmetic, geometry, and astronomy — was clearly emphasized. The book dealt with *ethos,* the spiritual qualities of music.

The musicians were concerned with more earthly matters — the training of musicians to sight-sing by reading notes and correctly negotiating the proper intervals between them. While the emphasis remained on liturgical music, some secular forms were in evidence: the *goliard* songs of the eleventh and twelfth centuries were named after Golias, their mythical patron. These are among the oldest preserved secular songs; but only their Latin texts remain, for they had no way of notating the melodic line. The persons that sang them were either students or footloose clerics. These songs celebrated their vagabond way of life. The texts frequently were concerned with wine, women, or satire.

The *conducti* were originally part of the worship service, meant to be sung as a priest made his entrance (from the Latin *conducere* meaning "to lead, to escort"). Eventually the conductus became associated with the liturgical dramas of the period, and then became divorced from the Church altogether. The texts were metrical verses. By the end of the twelfth century they were strictly non-liturgical, but still remained serious songs.

One of the earliest forms in the vernacular was the *chanson de geste,* an epic narrative which recounted the deeds of important heroes; the *Song of Roland,* of France, is a classic example of this form. The music for the chansons was very simple, the same melody frequently being repeated for each line of the poem. They were sung by *jongleurs.* The jongleurs were professional musicians who first appeared about the tenth century. They were either men or women, who wandered from village to village, from castle to castle, earning their precarious living by singing, playing their instruments, performing tricks, and exhibiting trained animals. They were social outcasts, often denied both the protection of the law and the Sacraments of the Church. Of themselves, they were neither poets nor composers, merely performers.

The jongleurs paved the way for an important movement in medieval music — the *troubadours.* The troubadours of southern France — whose very name came from the Provençal meaning "to invent" — created their own music as well as performed it. The *trouvères* of northern France, and later the *minnesinger* of Germany, were part of this movement. There are preserved today over 2600 troubadour poems and music for 260 of them; there are in collected editions some 4000 trouvère poems and 1400 melodies. These musicians were of the aristocracy, highly regarded by society. Their poems and music were preserved in beautiful medieval manuscripts in the most famous castles.

During the Middle Ages, instruments were being further modified and developed for accompanying the singing and dancing. The principal instruments of the era included lutes, shawms, trumpets, drums, and members of the vielle or viol family. Rhythmic modes developed, as did a polyphonic, two-voice form known as organum. At the end of the era, polyphonic conducti in three voices were quite universal.

With the fourteenth century, the *ars nova* (new art) led the way to the Renaissance. Corruption in the Church, with as many as three men claiming the papacy at once, lessened the influence of the Holy See. The slackening economic progress, along with the Black Plague (1348-1350) and the One Hundred Years War (1338-1453), changed both the cultural and economic pattern of Europe. There were peasant insurrections and there was urban discontent. Cities increased in local power. This was the period of the first "modern" literature — Dante's *Divine Comedy,* Boccaccio's *Decameron,* Chaucer's *Canterbury Tales.* The music of this final stage tended to become one of the solo song with accompaniment.

THE TROUBADOURS

The troubadours and the trouvères were not wanderers like the jongleurs of the Middle Ages. In the early years of the troubadours, especially, they were persons of rank: noblemen, princes, occasionally ladies of high position. Richard the Lion-Hearted (who died in 1199) was an example of a nobleman directly concerned with this musical movement. The troubadours flourished for 200 years, from the end of the eleventh century to the end of the thirteenth century (the so-called "Age of Chivalry").

This movement was brought about by a change in the knightly concept of life. Where life had been spent before in a rough fashion — fighting, hunting, drinking — it turned to the worship of the Virgin, to the idealization of mortal women, to elaborate chivalrous ethics, stylized manners, and an appreciation of poetry and music.

The songs of these troubadours dealt with conditions and events in the social and political world. Many of them were concerned directly with the Crusades (the first Crusade was proclaimed by Pope Urban II in 1095). The texts of these songs fell easily into natural groupings:

> *sirventes* — songs of service, usually political contests
> *planh* — songs of mourning
> *albas* — songs of dawn
> *tenson* — song contest (like the contest in the second act of Wagner's *Tannhäuser*)

Adam de la Halle, born in Arras about 1230 and died in Naples about 1288, is depicted here in a miniature from the Chansonier d'Arras. He was the last, and greatest of the trouvères.

Tannhaüser, in the white cloak of the Knights of the German Order, is shown at the famous Wartburg singing contest.

Pommers (a double reed instrument) and trumpets in an illumination from the Richenthal Chronicle

Henrich Frauenlob, one of the founders of the Meistersingers, is shown with a group of musicians

Almost all the songs are within the range of an octave and they do not seem to follow the church modes, using on occasion B-flats and F-sharps. These songs anticipate all the later song forms.

Because these songs were noted in plainsong notation, no exact rhythm was indicated. To this day scholars disagree about interpreting their rhythm, although most agree that they were subdivided into patterns of three units.

An example of one of the twelfth century songs of the troubadours is *A l'entrade del tems clar:*

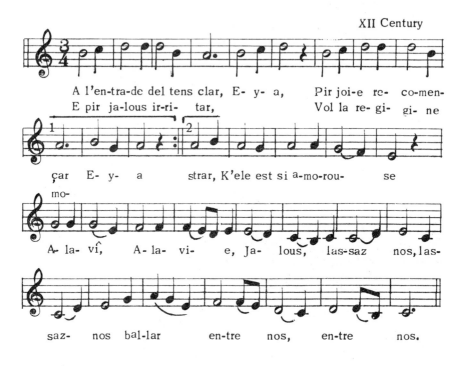

When the spring returns again
     E-y-a
Sadness can no more remain
     E-y-a
Queen of May has come to stay
     E-y-a
Come let us our homage pay,

For she is Queen
Long may she reign!
Far away must care now flee
Let sorrow come another day
So leave your work
And merry be
A-dancing 'round the Queen
     of May.

Following the pattern set in southern France by the troubadours, a movement known as the *trouvères* took place in northern France. This movement lasted little longer than a hundred years, from about 1170 until 1275 or 1285. The music of this northern group was more formal than that of its southern progenitor.

THE MINNESINGER

The *minnesinger* in Germany lagged behind the troubadour movement in France by about 100 years. The term comes from the German word "minne" meaning "chivalrous love" and the common noun "singer."

The *minnesinger* came principally from southern Germany and included many from Austria. The early movement started around 1150 to 1190 and gathered momentum before there was any influence from France. The texts of the German minnesinger tended more to the religious side than did those of the troubadours, while the melodies tended to be less popular and dance-like. Most of the compositions were closer to the style of Church melodies. One of the best known minnesinger was Walter von der Vogelweide (c. 1170-c. 1230), one of whose melodies has been preserved in current usage as a Protestant hymn, *Old Hundreth*.

Johannes de Grocheo, who lived at the end of the thirteenth century, recommended that some of these songs "be sung before old people, working burghers, and low-caste men when they rest from their toil, so they might, on hearing about the misery of others, better stand their own depressing condition and with more cheerfulness resume their occupations. Hence this kind of song is important for the conservation of the state."

Youths were required to sing some of them in order "that they may not entirely get lost in idleness." One of the forms, the *stantipes,* was so hard to perform that "it kept the minds of the boys and the maidens busy and took away from evil thoughts," while another type, the *ductia,* "protected the hearts of girls and boys from vanity and, as they say, from the kind of passion that they give the name of love."

An example of the music of the minnesinger is a composition by Neihart von Reuental who lived up to about the year 1245. Here is his *Mayenzeit one neidt:*

MENSURAL NOTATION

The accurate recording of music on paper was delayed until a system could be devised that not only would indicate pitch but could also accurately convey the relative length of each note, *mensural notation*. Around 1225 a system of notation that denoted time values started to evolve from the plainsong notation. The first distinction came between a stemmed square (known as a *longa*) and a stemless square (the *breve*). These served only to indicate long and short notes, comparable to our quarter and eighth notes, and were adequate only for the first and second modes.

Around 1250 the *semi-brevis* developed, a diamond-shaped note. This then gave the musical manuscript the equivalent of the modern

At the end of the century, Pierre de la Croix subdivided the breve into. four and later into nine semibreves which led to the next smaller time unit, the *minima*.

Franco of Cologne, who lived from about 1250 until sometime after 1280, was a practical musician who gathered together the various ideas concerning mensural notation and codified them. It became known as "Franconian notation." Franco's supply of single notes are:

double long, long breve semibreve

SECULAR POLYPHONY

One of the earliest known bits of secular *polyphony* (a composition with more than one melodic line) is an old English canon which dates from around 1310 to 1325 (although it was previously dated as early as 1240). *Sumer Is Icumen In* is an advanced canon in four voices ("canon" meaning that each voice exactly duplicates the others although each voice enters at a different time) with a *pes* or two-voice bass part that keeps repeating itself over and over again (as in a ground bass).

The melody of the canon is:

Su-mer is i- cu- men in,   Lhu-de sing cuc- cu,

Grow-eth sed and blow-eth med, and springth the w-de nu; Sing cuc-

cu;   Aw-e ble-teth   af-ter lomb,Lhouth af-ter cal-ve   cu;

Bul- loc stert-eth,buck-e ver-teth,Mur-ie sing cuc- cu.   Cuc-cu,

Cuc-cu, wel singes   thu cuc- cu,   Ne swik thu na-ver   nu.

The first voice starts out; when it reaches 2 , the second voice starts at the beginning; when the first voice reaches 3 , the third voice enters, etc. Underneath this four-voice canon is the *pes* (literally meaning "foot") which is the droned bass. One voice sings *pes no. 1* over and over again, while a second voice sings *pes no. 2* over and over again, making a total of six voices. The *pes:*

Pes I

Sing cuc- cu nu   sing cuc- cu;
Pes II

Sing   cuc- cu,   Sing cuc- cu nu.

A translation into more modern English:

Summer is a-coming in,
Loudly sing cuckoo!
Groweth seed and bloweth mead
And springeth wood anew.

Sing, cuckoo!

Ewe now bleateth after lamb,
For calf now loweth cow,
Bullock rouseth, buck he browseth,
Merry sing, cuckoo!

Cuckoo! Cuckoo!

Well thou singest, cuckoo,
O ne'er be silent now.

BIBLIOGRAPHY

Bukofzer, Manfred. *Studies in Medieval and Renaissance Music.* New York: W .W. Norton and Company, 1950.
Reese, Gustave. *Music in the Middle Ages.* New York: W. W. Norton and Company, 1940.

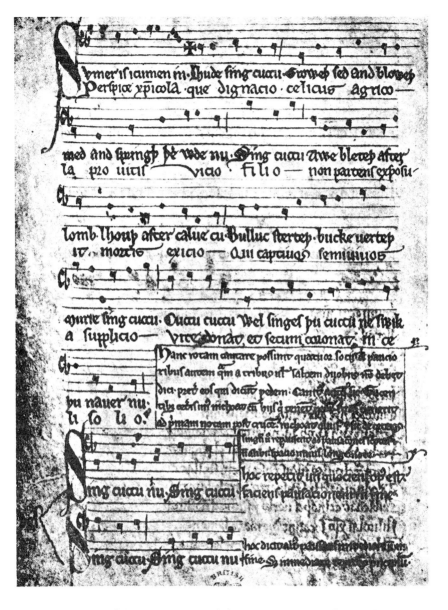

The first page of the English canon, *Sumer is icumen in,* usually dated about 1240 (although one authority believes that to be seventy years too early)

MUSIC OF THE RENAISSANCE

THE TERM *Renaissance* as applied to music was borrowed from art history. Musical historians have in turn divided it into two periods: the Early Renaissance, which begins with the early years of the fifteenth century, and the Late Renaissance, which extends through the sixteenth century into the first years of the seventeenth.

The literal meaning of *Renaissance* is "re-birth." Through the rediscovery of the ancient works of art and literature from the glorious days of Greece and Rome, the artists of the Renaissance regarded themselves as rivals of the classical masters. Erasmus said, "The world is coming to its senses as if awakening out of a deep sleep."

For the first time in centuries, art forms were developing and prospering outside the realm of the Church. Secular plays were being produced on the stages of court theatres; artists felt free to paint nudes. It was a time of artistic achievement — Michelangelo, Leonardo da Vinci, Raphael, Botticelli, Titian, and Cellini were of this era. The influence of ancient Greece was evidenced by the large number of scholars who learned to read the ancient language so that they could understand its literature.

The arts flourished because of patronage. The development of trade and industry supplied the rival merchant princes and the city-kingdoms with funds for the endowment of art. They became rivals not only in business, but for the services of the very best artists. Although the Renaissance was not exclusively an Italian phenomenon, the greatest concentration of artists in a thousand years centered in Italy.

The era witnessed the downfall of Constantinople, the last stronghold of the eastern Roman empire. The invention of printing from movable type and the discovery and colonization of the New World took place during these years.

Musically, major developments occurred in the Renaissance. *A cappella* singing, vocal music without instrumental accompaniment, became important; polyphonic settings for four or more voices became common; a counterpointing of rhythm between voices became as important as the melodic counterpoint between them. With the development of art forms outside the aegis of the Church, secular musical forms started to develop — the chansons, the frottole, and the madrigals. Polyphonic writing existed along side homophonic music; modality started to give way to tonality (major and minor) as this is known today.

The Protestant Reformation led to the development of new styles of sacred composition, for the Lutheran *choral* and the French *Psalter* were established. In answer to the secularization of the music of the Roman Catholic Church, the counter-reformation, and more particularly the Council of Trent, through such composers as Palestrina, reorganized the music acceptable to that religious body.

Instrumental music came into prominence during the Renaissance. Undoubtedly there were many fanfares and dances performed in the early days of the era. Later, instruments must have come into their own, for starting with the publication of the first book on music, in 1511, a number of books described the important instruments and had woodblock illustrations showing what they looked like. These books were written, not in Latin for the theorist, but in the vernacular for the practising musician. Books of keyboard music were published for the virginals and spinet. Numerous lute books came from the printing presses of Europe. The recorder (forerunner of the flute) and the viol (ancestor of varying size of today's bass viol) were frequently represented in drawings and paintings of the Renaissance. The development of the pipe organ led to its use in religious compositions.

Although there is no sharp line of demarcation between the Middle Ages and the Renaissance, and even though characteristics of the Renaissance lasted past 1600 (theoretically the beginning of the Baroque era), one of its most remarkable characteristics from the Early to the Late Renaissance was the writing of vocal lines all similar in style and equal as to expressive importance.

BIBLIOGRAPHY

Reese, Gustave. *Music in the Renaissance.* New York: W. W. Norton and Company, 1954.
Abraham, Gerald, and Dom Anselm Hughes. *The New Oxford History of Music,* Vol. III: *Ars Nova and the Renaissance, 1300-1540.* London: Oxford University Press, 1960.

MUSIC PRINTING

The development of music printing was a significant achievement in music history. Through the Middle Ages and in the Early Renaissance, copies of music were tediously reproduced by hand. Monks in the abbeys spent hours copying them note by note, producing books that were as beautiful to the eye as was the music when sung. With this method, however, a wide distribution of any one composition was impossible. In the Middle Ages and in the emerging Renaissance, with music largely of a sacred nature, this practice sufficed.

With the Renaissance trend toward music of a secular nature, it was imperative that a method of reproducing music be found. Although he was not the first to "print" music, Ottaviano de' Petrucci of Venice is regarded as the Gutenberg of music printing. His first publication appeared on May 14, 1501 — *Harmonice Musices Odhecaton* (literally "One Hundred Musical Harmonies" — actually there were only 99), which was followed by two more volumes in 1502 and 1504. Most of the compositions in these collections were by composers of the Franco-Netherlands group who were residing in Italy; the books included *chansons* and *frottole* (see Josquin) and were issued in part-books for family use. Part-books have never completely disappeared from the European continent although they have not been in use in the United States for many years. Each part-book includes only the music for one voice-part rather than the standard "score" form in which, for a four-voice composition, they all appear one above another: bass, tenor, alto, and soprano.

These early publications of Petrucci were printed by a double impression and from moveable type. Earlier examples of music printing used other devices. The music printers had been faced with three different problems: a method of reproducing (1) monophonic Gregorian chant; (2) polyphonic music; and (3) short musical examples in theoretical works. The first category was the last to be solved, for choirs continued to sing from hand-inscribed choir books long after Petrucci's volumes of chansons and frottole were being used by secular musicians. The third category offered a limited challenge, for usually quotations in theoretical works were quite short. The most common solution was to print the staff from a woodcut and later to enter the notes on the staff by hand.

The double impression method used by Petrucci and others was not without its pitfalls. Ordinarily the paper was put through the press for a first impression of red staff lines. It was then printed a second time, superimposing the notes in black ink on the staff. The difficulty lay in what the printer calls "registering" — having the second impression fall exactly into the proper place so that each note appears on the line or space on which it belongs.

Another method that had been tried by printers was the use of wood blocks. Since the discovery of this method for printing illustrations, musicians wondered if musical scores could not be carved into wood and thus printed. The first example of this method comes from the press of Nicolaus Burtius and Ugo de Rugeriis, printed at Bologna in 1487 — *Musices opusculum*. Because of the very nature of wood carving, it was difficult to carve straight lines for the staves and the whole process was necessarily very crude.

Printing from copper plates (later from pewter) started with the work of Sadeler of Antwerp in 1584; the first music in English was printed by this method in 1611 — *Parthenia,* containing *"the first Musicke that ever was printed for the Virginalls Composed by three famous Masters William Byrd, Dr. John Bull and Orlando Gibbons."* This was a more economical method of printing, the staff lines being scribed on to the metal plates, and then the notes, rests, text (if there was one) inscribed over the staff lines. A later development was the use of punches, small metal dies whose heads contained hollow notes, solid notes, stems with and without flags, rests, etc., that when punched over the staff lines on the plates made the notes of uniform size and shape. This method (with some later refinements) is to this day still the most common method of music reproduction. Paul Revere was one of the first music engravers in the United States.

Although in manuscript round notes were the custom, in music printing all the early manuscripts of measured music used angular (diamond or lozenge shaped) notes through most of the sixteenth and seventeenth centuries.

In 1789 a new discovery, that of lithography, was made by Alois Senefelder. While lithography is used in all branches of printing today, its invention was the result of a need to reproduce music more inexpensively than from hand-engraved plates. It is interesting to note that the composer von Weber (see his biographical sketch) was active in this field as a boy, working as an apprentice for Senefelder.

JOSQUIN DES PREZ

BORN: circa 1450, in the province of Hainault, now in Belgium.
DIED: August 27, 1521; Condé-sur-Escaut, France.

Josquin des Prez was honored as one of the greatest composers of his own day; and even now, some four hundred and fifty years later, musicians give him credit for being one of the great composers of all time. Donald J. Grout says in *A History of Western Music:*

Out of the extraordinarily large number of first-rank composers living around 1500, one, Josquin des Prez, must be counted among the greatest of all time. Few musicians have enjoyed higher reknown while they lived, or exercised more profound and lasting influence on those who came after them. Josquin was hailed by contemporaries as "the best of the composers of our time," the "Father of Musicians." "He is the master of notes," said Martin Luther.

Little is known of the life of Josquin, and even the dates of his service at various chapels and courts are confused, since the dates of his service at the Papal Chapel were incorrectly recorded. He was born in the Hainault area, then ruled by Burgundy, and served as a chorister at the Collegiate Church at St. Quentin (now in northwestern France). Josquin later became a canon and choirmaster there.

When he was about twenty-five, Josquin served as a chorister at the court of Duke Sforza in Milan, Italy. About eleven years later he served as a singer in the Papal Choir at the Vatican. By this time he had gained universal admiration. Adriaen Petit Coclico, in his *Compendium musices* of 1552, gives an account of Josquin's method of teaching:

My teacher Josquin . . . never gave a lecture on music or wrote a theoretical work, and yet he was able in a short time to form complete musicians, because he did not keep back his pupils with long and useless instructions, but taught them the rules in a few words, through practical application in the course of singing. As soon as he saw his pupils were well grounded in singing, that they had a good enunciation, that they knew how to embellish melodies and how to fit the text to the music, then he taught them the perfect and imperfect intervals and the different methods of inventing counterpoints against plainsong. If he discovered, however, pupils with an ingenious mind and promising disposition, then he would teach these in a few words the rules of three-part, and later of four-, five-, and six-part writing, always providing them with examples to imitate. Josquin did not, however, consider all suited to learn composition; he judged that only those should be taught who were drawn to this delightful art by a special natural impulse.

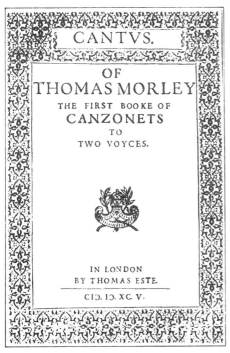

GIOVANNI DA PALESTRINA

Title page from *The first Books of Canzonets to two voyces* by Thomas Morley, London, 1595

Title-page of Victoria's *Cantiones sacrae* published by Johann Meyer at Dillingen in 1589. The cover indicates that the sacred motets are for four, five, six, eight, and nine voices.

Josquin des Prez (his name appearing in Latinized form under the picture) from a woodcut after the portrait formerly in St. Gudule, Brussels.

From Rome, Josquin traveled back to France where for a time he served at the Court of Louis XII. Several examples of his music from this period reveal his sense of humor. Apparently Louis XII had offered a position at one of the local churches in return for Josquin's services at his own court. When such a position was not forthcoming, the composer wrote a motet based on the 119th Psalm and had it performed in the presence of the king. The first line of the text was repeated in the music so many times that the king could not miss the point: "Deal bountifully with thy servant that I may live."

At another time the king requested Josquin to compose a little piece in which he might sing a part. The completed work was a canon for the two upper voices, the part for the king (*vox regis* or tenor line) was a single continuous note held throughout the composition; and the bass line that the composer sang consisted of an alternating root and fifth of the chord so that on every other note he reinforced the pitch of the king to help hold His Majesty true to his part.

Having served at numerous courts, including those of Ferrara and Florence, Josquin returned to northern France toward the end of his life, and died in Condé-sur-Escaut.

ET INCARNATUS EST

from *Missa Pange Lingua*

JOSQUIN DES PREZ

This Mass has been characterized by A. W. Ambrose as "one of those art works which shine like stars through all the following periods of time." The first edition was printed in 1539, eighteen years after Josquin's death.

The Mass is set *a cappella* (literally "in chapel style" — meaning without the accompaniment of instruments) for four voices: soprano, alto, tenor, and bass. It is a good example of the existence of polyphony side by side with homophonic music, for the excerpt quoted below is a fine example of homophonic music while the rest of the Mass is set polyphonically.

The Mass is titled *Pange Lingua* since it is based on the Gregorian chant (in the Phrygian mode) Pange Lingua:

Pan-ge lin-qua glo-ri- o-　si cor-　po-ris my-ster-i- um

The *Et Incarnatus Est* is the central section of the Mass; three precede it (*Kyrie, Gloria,* and *Credo*) and three succeed it (*Crucifixus, Sanctus, Agnus Dei*). Originally and usually the *Et Incarnatus Est* was part of the *Credo* ("I believe") of the Mass, but Josquin has treated it in this Mass as a separate section and, as has already been mentioned, set it differently (homophonically) from any other movement.

	("I believe . . . in one Lord, Jesus Christ . . .
Et incarnatus est,	Who) was incarnate
De Spiritu Sancto	By the Holy Ghost
Ex Maria Virgine:	Of the Virgin Mary,
Et homo factus est.	And was made man.

Notice that the ear perceives the upper voice (the soprano in this example) as the melody while the other voices provide a harmonic or chordal accompaniment to it, thus establishing a homophonic setting. The *Harvard Dictionary of Music* defines *homophonic* as a "designation for music in which one voice leads melodically, being supported by an accompaniment in chordal style."

ET INCARNATUS EST

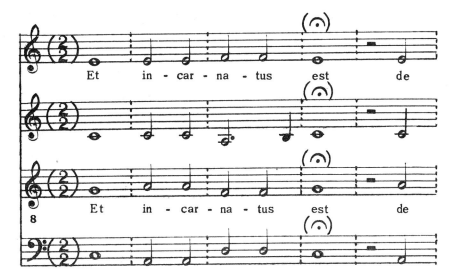

EL GRILLO

Josquin des Prez

El Grillo (The Cricket) is a frottola. The frottola was one of the first secular forms of music that was artistic in nature. Frottole were a product of the Late Renaissance, and were composed mostly by musicians living in and around northern Italy. Between 1504 and 1514, with the invention of a satisfactory method of printing music, eleven books of frottole were published in Venice.

A frottola could be in duple or triple time (triple was the more common), and was usually composed for four voices, with a prominent melody and a strong harmonic bass. The two middle voices were of less significance and filled in the harmony. The four voices moved in a square-cut manner, the rhythm always being precisely balanced with the meter of the text. The texts were frivolous or humorous poems written by the leading poets of northern Italy. Some musical historians believe that frottole were meant to be sung with instrumental accompaniment, probably with the lute.

Tenor, alto, and soprano *viola da gamba* and a *lute* as they appear in a painting dated 1641 on part of a wooden ceiling in the former Pauline Monastery in Prague

As in the case of *El Grillo*, the poems were usually stanzaic. Repetitions of rhymes and stanzas of the poem usually were set similarly by the composers. As the century progressed, the frottola gave way to new forms: the canzone (which were frivolous also) and madrigali (very noble in character).

EL GRILLO

El gril - lo, el gril-lo buon can-to-re Che
The crick - et, The crick-et's a good sing-er who

tie - ne lon-go ver — — — — so.
sings for such a long ——————————— time.

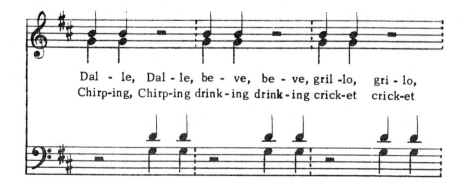

Dal - le, Dal - le, be - ve, be - ve, gril -lo, gri - lo,
Chirp-ing, Chirp-ing drink-ing drink-ing crick-et crick-et

can - ta,   can - ta Dal - le,   dal - le,   be - ve,   be - ve,
sing -ing   sing -ing, Chirp-ing, Chirp-ing, drink-ing, drink-ing,

gril - lo, gril - lo   can - ta. El   gril -
crick-et crick-et   sing - ing. The   crick -

Fine

lo,   El gril - lo`e buon can-to - re. Ma non fa
et,   The crick-et's a good sing-er. But un-like

co - me gl'al-triuc-cel - li, co-me li han can-ta-to un
birds of all des-crip-tions No-ble crick-ets for fun keep

po - co, Van' de fat - to in al - tro
sing-ing. But un-like man - y birds which

lo - co, sem - pre el gril-lo sta pur sal - do.
go 'way when they've sung crick-ets keep on sing-ing.

El gril - lo, El gril- lo e buon can-to - re.
The crick - et, The crick-et's a good sing-er.

Quan - do la mag - gior el cal - do Al -
When the heav - y heat is great-est, He

- hor can - ta sol per a - mo -
sings a - lone then, For love he

re,   can - ta   sol   per   a - mo   re.
sings, sings   for   love   for   love.

D.C. al Fine

THE PROTESTANT CHORAL

In the year 1517, Martin Luther nailed a series of ninety-five theses on the door of his church in Wittenberg, Germany — a series of objections and recriminations against the Catholic Church. By this act, a separation of the church in western civilization took place — a separation into Roman Catholics and Protestants. This was the *Reformation.*

In establishing a "protesting" church, Martin Luther had the responsibility of organizing its services. One of the most important aspects of the "new" service was the participation by the congregation in community singing, a logical outgrowth of the evangelical idea. A well-trained musician himself — he played both the lute and the flute — Luther was able to set several of the Psalms in a forceful manner in the vernacular (in German, rather than the Church Latin). He associated himself with two excellent musicians, Conrad Rupff and Johann Walter, who proceeded under his direction to select the best Latin chorals for use in the church and set them with German texts. Many well-known Gregorian hymns were translated and used in the German service. An edition of the Lutheran hymnal which was published in Wittenberg in 1524 contained thirty-eight German and five Latin songs. Where necessary, words were changed in the texts as they were translated if they did not agree with the creed of the new church, such as references to the Virgin Mary. Some of the secular tunes popular among the middle-class folk of Germany also were used with appropriate sacred texts in the early hymnals. Protestant church music, centered largely around the choral, did not assert its individual nature until around the sixteenth century. Except for the language of the texts, the early Protestant hymns are musically indistinguishable from the hymns of the Roman Catholic Church.

The reformation of the church in Switzerland came under the influence of Calvin. He had an entirely different outlook on music's place in the worship service. He banned all musical instruments from the church, and contemporary accounts describe renowned organists of that country who stood with tears streaming down their faces as the pipe organs in their churches were demolished. Calvin regarded the Psalms as the only fit text for use in the service, and *Psalters* were developed for this purpose (in the tradition later followed by the Puritans who emigrated to the United States). As Charles Burney has said in his *General History of Music* published in 1789:

The only amusement which Calvin seems ever to have allowed his followers was *Psalmody*, and that of the most unmeaning and monotonous kind; without harmony, variety of accent, rhythm, and most of the constituent parts of mere melody. Not a musical instrument was suffered within the walls of Geneva for more than a hundred years after the Reformation; and all Music, except this Metrical Psalmody, was proscribed wherever the doctrines of this reformer were received.

EIN' FESTE BURG IST UNSER GOTT

The text of this hymn is by Martin Luther, and although musical historians have never discovered a copy of the musical setting in Luther's own hand, there is little reason to doubt that he also composed the tune. That Luther was an excellent and accomplished musician is stressed by the noted musicologist Paul Henry Lang:

Nothing is more unjust than to consider him (Luther) a sort of enthusiastic and good-natured dilettante. The ultimate fate of German Protestant music depended on this man who, as a student in Eisenach singing all sorts of merry student songs, and as a celebrant priest familiar with the gradual and polyphonic Masses and motets, lived with music ringing in his ears.*

Ein' feste Burg (listed as Ein Veste Burg) is quoted in Charles Burney's music history published in 1789. He states of the work:

Hymn written, set to Music, and sung by Luther, at his Entrance into Worms, whither he was summoned to plead before the Emperor, 1521.

*Paul Henry Lang, *Music in Western Civilization*.

Ein' feste Burg is unser Gott,   A stronghold sure is God our Lord
Ein' gute Wehr und Waffen.   Whose strength will never fail us;
Er hilft uns frei aus aller Noth,   He keeps us free from all the horde
Die uns jetzt hat betroffen.   Of troubles that assail us.

Der alt' böse Feind,   Our old evil foe
Mit Ernst er's jetzt meint,   Would fain work us woe,
Gross Macht und viel List   With might and deep guile
Sein grausam Rüstung ist,   He plans his projects vile,
Auf Erd'n ist nicht sein's Gleichen.   On earth is not one like him.

(Translated by HENRY S. DRINKER)

A group of madrigalists around a table on which the music rests — from a painting by Sebastiano Florigerio C. 1540

GERMAN FLUTE. Transverse flutes came from Asia via Byzantium to the Austro-Hungarian area where they were widely used in folk music. In the middle ages Germany became the new center, hence the name.

FLUTE-A-BEC. Of tortoiseshell, this flute was known in English as a *recorder* (from the obsolete word *record* meaning "warble", referring to the bird-like quality of the instrument's tone.)

The first appearance of this hymn in print was probably in the lost *Geistliche Lieder* (Sacred Songs) of 1529, but was probably composed about 1527.

Ein ve-ste Burg ist un-ser Gott ein gut-te wehr und waf- fen.
Er hilft ung frey aus al-ter Noth die uns jetzt hat be-trof- fen.

Der al- te Bö- se feind, mit ernst ers jetzt meint, Gross

macht und viel list, sein crau-sam rüs-tung

ist, Auf erd'n ist nicht sein's glei-------chen.

GIOVANNI PIERLUIGI DA PALESTRINA

BORN: December 17 (?), 1525; Palestrina, Italy.
DIED: February 2, 1594; Rome, Italy.

Giovanni Pierluigi da Palestrina takes his name from his birth-place, Palestrina, a little hill-town not too distant from Rome. The family name was Pierluigi, but was frequently omitted in the writings of the composer, the name appearing as simply Giovanni da Palestrina. His exact birthdate is unknown as the official birth records of Palestrina were destroyed by a fire in 1577.

The composer's ancestors had provably lived for several genera-tions in Palestrina; his father, Sante Pierluigi, owned a little land and a home. Part of the house where the composer was born still stands and is marked with a plaque to designate it today. Giovanni, as a boy, probably sang in the choir at the local cathedral, Sant' Agapit. He later became the organist and choir director of the Palestrina cathedral. During his tenure there, he married Lucrezia Gori, receiv-ing as a dowry a household of goods, a vineyard, meadows, a house, and some cash. Two sons were born to the couple while they resided quite comfortably in Palestrina.

After the Bishop of Palestrina was elevated to the Holy See, becoming Pope Julius III, he requested Giovanni to move to Rome and appointed him director of the Julian Chapel choir. His first book of masses (1544) was printed at the composer's expense shortly after this move.

The Roman Catholic Church started a counter-Reformation, a setting in order of its own house. Much that was secular had crept into the music of the Church, and some authorities questioned whether polyphonic settings of the Mass obscured the text beyond recognition. Pope Julius III started some reforms which were carried on by his successor, Pope Marcellus II. The latter summoned the Papal Choir before him and directed that their music should be carried out "in a suitable manner, with properly modulated voices, so that everything could be both heard and properly understood." Palestrina seems to have been impressed with the artistic soundness of the Pope's direc-tive, and the untimely death of the Pope three weeks later led the composer to write a Mass since known as *The Pope Marcellus Mass*.

Pope Pius IV had organized the Council of Trent to survey the practices of musicians in the various churches to determine whether the plainsong ought to be the only acceptable music. A false legend has arisen that the Council listened to *The Pope Marcellus Mass* and thereby decided that polyphonic settings of the Mass could be used without obscuring the text. The title "Palestrina, Saviour of Church Music" was devised from this legend. Undoubtedly the Council did hear some of the works of Palestrina, but officially they did little more than reiterate the statements of Pope Marcellus.

Pope Paul IV succeeded Marcellus and started a reform within the laws and rules of the Church. He was surprised to discover that three married men, including Palestrina, served in the Papal Choir and they were immediately released. Palestrina found a position teaching music at a seminary and later served at the magnificent Villa d'Este; he also served at the Church of St. John Lateran in Rome for four years. Many of his motets date from these years.

Between the years 1572 and 1580 an epidemic killed his two sons, two of his brothers, and his wife. Grief-stricken, he applied for the Priesthood, but before the year was out, he met the well-to-do widow of a successful furrier and married her. In addition to managing the details relating to the fur business, he published between the year of his second marriage and his death four books of masses, three books each of motets and madrigals, a book of hymns, and a book of magnificats.

Palestrina returned to service in the Julian Chapel under a more liberal Pope and served in that capacity until his death. One of his duties on his return was to work on a revision of the plainsong, a hopeless task. He tried to discover the original melodies in use under Pope Gregory and eliminate copyist's errors and later additions, but the records were in such bad condition that it was impossible to discover the original chants.

The nature of Palestrina's final illness is unknown. His funeral service at St. Peter's was an acknowledgement of his stature in the musical world. He was buried under the pavement in the New Chapel which was later covered over by the new St. Peter's Cathedral, then in the process of being built. A later effort to locate Palestrina's remains was unsuccessful.

BIBLIOGRAPHY

Andrews, Herbert Kennedy. *An Introduction to the Technique of Palestrina.* London: Novello and Company, 1958.
Coates, Henry. *Palestrina.* London: J. M. Dent and Sons, Ltd., 1948.

AGNUS DEI I

From *The Pope Marcellus Mass*

GIOVANNI PIERLUIGI DA PALESTRINA

Today, one of the most frequently performed masses of Palestrina is *The Pope Marcellus Mass,* not because of the legend which surrounds it, but because of its own intrinsic beauty. The independence of the rhythmic line of each voice can be heard in the *Agnus Dei,* but still, when combined, the lines form a pleasing texture. Compared to the earlier mass of Josquin which was modal in nature, this work of Palestrina leads the way to the major-minor tonality of more modern compositions. While the Renaissance musicians would have termed it in the Ionian mode, the strong "key feeling" engendered is C major which is strengthened by frequent use of the root and fifth in the bass voice.

The *Agnus Dei* is set for six voices: soprano, alto, tenor I, tenor II, baritone, and bass. Its opening would at first seem to be a double canon, the sopranos imitating the tenors, and the altos imitating the baritone. Upon closer inspection it can be noted that each voice has its own melodic line (closely related to the others) as well as its own rhythmic pattern. Although the entire movement cannot be quoted here, it is interesting to note in listening to it that each new thematic idea is a logical outgrowth of the one preceding it.

TOMÁS LUIS DE VICTORIA

BORN: circa 1548: Ávila, Spain.

DIED: August 27, 1611; Madrid, Spain.

Tomás Luis de Victoria (frequently spelled Vittoria in Italian) was born in or near Avila in old Castile, Spain. He studied at Segovia and, when he was seventeen, obtained a grant from the King to study in Rome. He enrolled at the Jesuit Collegium Germanicum, not as a music student, but to study theology. The Collegium Germanicum had been founded by St. Ignatius Loyola to combat the Lutheran movement in Germany. Within a year after entering, Victoria was singing in the choir.

After leaving school he became the choir director and organist at the Santa Maria de Monserrato in Rome, the national church of the Spaniards of Aragon. He then succeeded Palestrina as musical director at the Roman seminary. His first published works, mostly motets, were printed in Venice when he was twenty-four. At twenty-seven, he was ordained a priest and shortly after that came into the service of the widowed Empress María, daughter of Charles V and a sister to Philip II of Spain. He served as her chaplain, but it was some time before either of them moved from Rome back to Spain. With such royal patronage, many of Victoria's works were published in handsome editions.

Although Victoria acknowledged Spain as his home when he was forty-six, accounts are not clear as to his actual activities after that year. It is known that he made some trips back to Rome, but spent the latter part of his career as a chaplain in the seminary where the Empress María's daughter was located.

Victoria composed no secular music. His works were largely unaccompanied polyphonic church music, although one of his last compositions included an organ part. His music was touched by a mysticism from his Spanish background. His music was well-known in his lifetime, and his works were printed in Italy, Germany, and Spain. He left a legacy of about twenty masses, sixteen magnificats, antiphonal choruses, thirty-two four-voice hymns, and two settings of the Passion. One of his best known compositions is the motet, *Ave Maria*.

AVE MARIA

Tomas Luis de Victoria

The *motet* was a popular form for about five hundred years, from about 1250 until about 1750 — a leading form in both the Middle Ages and the Renaissance. A motet is an unaccompanied work based on a Latin sacred text, intended for use in the Roman Catholic Church service, frequently for Vespers.

Originally the motets were in two voices, a set of words being added to the duplum or second voice which were different from the Latin text used with the Gregorian chant of the first voice. The name *motet* came from the Latin word *mot* meaning "word" and appearing as *motetus* in Latin. The polytextual nature of the early motets gave rise to this name. The second voice (or duplum) was a paraphrase of the thought suggested by the Gregorian chant.

Over the years, many variations and changes were made in this form. Additional voices, with additional texts, were added. They were almost always polylingual since the original voice sang the Gregorian chant with its Latin text and the other voices sang their words in the vernacular. The French motets were the most extreme examples of the use of texts, for they superimposed secular texts against the Gregorian chants.

In the fifteenth century two characteristics of the medieval motet were no longer frequently used: the use of more than one language for the text became extremely rare, and the cantus firmus or Gregorian chant ceased to be employed except on rare occasions.

Victoria's *Ave Maria* is one of the few Late Renaissance motets based on a Gregorian chant. It is quoted in the opening of the motet, a chant for the Vesper of the Annunciation:

A-ve Ma-ri-   a, gra-ti-a ple-na: Do-mi-nus te-cum

The tenor voice, unaccompanied, introduces the Gregorian chant and then is joined by the other voices in polyphonic style:

The tenor and bass carry the next line of the text, "in mulieribus." The upper three voices repeat the text.

All four voices join, polyphonically, in "et benedictus, fructus ventris tui, Jesus Christus."

The section, starting with "Sancta Maria," is forceful and in block style:

San— cta Ma— ri— a, ma— ter De— i.

After this harmonic section, the soprano voice has a descending phrase that leads to the final "Amens" in the lower voices.

Ave Maria, Gratia plena	Hail Mary, full of grace,
Dominus tecum,	The Lord is with thee,
Benedicta tu in mulieribus,	Blessed art thou among women,
Et benedictus, fructus	And blessed is the offspring of
ventris tui,	thy womb,
Jesus Christus.	Jesus Christ.
Sancta Maria, Mater Dei,	Holy Mary, Mother of God,
Ora pro nobis peccatoribus,	Pray for us sinners,
Nunc et in hora mortis nostrae.	Now and in the hour of death.
Amen.	Amen.

INSTRUMENTAL MUSIC

Instrumental music had first achieved independence in the Middle Ages by providing dance music. As instruments further developed, they became more independent. The late Middle Ages had seen improvements in the pipe organ with the replacement of the old wooden sliding bars by actual keys to activate the sound of the pipes. A stringed keyboard instrument known as the *clavichord* was developed with as many as nineteen strings.

During the Renaissance further progress was made in the development of instruments. The clavichord (from the Latin *claves* for "keys") had wire strings stretched from one side to the other of a small, shallow, rectangular box about three feet long and one foot deep. Each key had on its end an upright metal tangent which would gently touch the string when a key was depressed, producing a very faint tone.

The *harpsichord,* nearest relative to the clavichord, was a larger instrument which gradually grew to the size and shape of our modern grand piano. The strings of the harpsichord, however, were plucked by tiny, thornlike pieces of quills which projected from the jacks. The word harpsichord did not appear before the seventeenth century; the term *virginal* was used for this instrument in the Renaissance, whether the instrument was in the shape of a grand or in the square, box-like form. In those days people referred to a single instrument as virginals (in the pleural) or "a pair of virginals." The square form was also referred to as *spinetta* (spinet) in Italian.

Pictures and paintings from the Renaissance show scenes of ballrooms with three-piece bands. The band consisted of two shawms (a strident form of an oboe) and a slide trumpet (not unlike the modern trombone).

Probably the most common instrument of the era was the lute. This instrument had been brought from Persia somewhere around 1000 A.D. and was originally confined to the Arabian and Moorish parts of Spain. From Spain, it spread slowly across continental Europe. During the Middle Ages it had been played with a quill plectrum and therefore only a single melodic line could be played. During the Renaissance the quill had been abandoned and the lute was able to play more than one melodic line at a time, enabling it to play polyphonic music.

Around 1510 the bowed instruments started to divide themselves into two principal families: (1) the *viole da braccio* (later developing into the modern violin, viola, and cello); and (2) the *viole da gamba* (which was a fretted type of instrument). Frets were bars or bands across the fingerboard to establish the divisions of half-steps on the strings, similar to our modern fretted guitars, banjos, and ukeleles.

Cross-flutes and recorders are also to be seen in many of the paintings of the Renaissance. Lasso relates in his writings that five *zinken* (cornets or short wooden horns with finger holes) and two trombones played one of his motets.

In Elizabethan England, *consorts* made their appearance in the homes of the nobility and the rising middle class. The word consort was a misspelling of the word "concert." It referred to a collection of various sizes of bowed, stringed instruments that were frequently kept in a decorative chest and then brought out for musical amusement and enjoyment during periods of relaxation. If all the instruments in the consort were bowed, it was known as a "whole consort." If recorders, flutes, or other instruments appeared in the collection with bowed instruments, they were known as "broken consorts."

THE MADRIGAL

Today the most frequently performed type of Renaissance music is the *madrigal*. This form had originated in fourteenth century Italy and then had completely disappeared. The term made its reappearance in the sixteenth century, but its title was the only thing it had in common with the fourteenth century madrigals.

In the Renaissance, the madrigal was based on choice literary taste. It was a revolt against the frottola (see Josquin des Prez) which used humorous poetry. As has already been stated, the Italians were so busy in the field of the visual arts — painting, architecture, sculpture — that the madrigal which developed in Italy was largely the work of Netherlandish composers residing in Italy. They were sparked on to creative efforts by the excellence of the Italian poets.

The madrigal was an outgrowth of Italian secular forms, the French chansons, and sacred music. General characteristics included an equality of voices, each line or part written with equal care, and the use of the same text for all parts. Other important traits were:

(1) the music was composed for a specific text of literary quality rather than a text being written specifically for music;

(2) the music was intended to express the content of the text;

(3) as a result, a non-strophic (or through-composed) form was most common;

(4) the individual voices were of equal importance both melodically and harmonically;

(5) the texture of the madrigal could be either polyphonic or chordal in nature.

The Renaissance madrigal went through three general stages. The early period was characterized by a homophonic setting with three or four voices in a quiet and restrained type of music. In the classic stage, the time of Willaert, Lasso, Palestrina, the writing was for four to six (usually five) voices. The texture was usually polyphonic and imitative, and the expression deepened. The music of this stage is a pleasure for singers as each vocal line and part is of interest.

The late period of madrigal writing included chromaticism, word-painting, and coloristic effects. (Word-painting in the sense that if the text stated "an angel ascended to heaven," the music must likewise rise.) The virtuosity of the solo singer became important in the late madrigals as they strived for dramatic effects. The personality of the composer dominated this last stage and the individual voices sank to become only part of the organic whole. The chromaticism led to a breakdown of the modal tonality, and modulations were introduced which sound strange to present-day ears.

The madrigal form moved to England shortly after 1550. William Byrd (1543-1623) was one of the first English composers ot madrigals along with Thomas Morley (1557-1603). The English adopted a pattern close to the classic Italian style with adaptations allowing for the peculiarities of the English language.

The English madrigal flourished alongside the great Elizabethan poetry. It was less esoteric and more popular than its Italian counterpart, always sung by non-professionals in England in contrast to the professional madrigalists of Italy. Much use of madrigals was made by the new gentry and the rising middle class. In England the madrigal had a solid tonal structure (no chromaticism) and the compositions were a more unified whole. A "songfulness" pervaded them with good melodic writing throughout. In general, the top voice carried the principal tune in the English madrigal.

Examples of both the Italian and English madrigal schools follow.

ORLANDO DI LASSO

BORN: 1532; Mons, Belgium.
DIED: June 14, 1594; Munich, Germany.

Orlando di Lasso (or Roland de Lassus) was the greatest representative of the Flemish school. As a youth, he was a chorister at the Church of St. Nicholas and apparently possessed such a beautiful voice that three times he was kidnapped to sing in other choirs. While still a child, he was taken to Sicily to sing, and from there went to Milan. After his voice broke, he went first to Naples and then to Rome where he became choir director for the Church of St. John Lateran.

After two years with the Church of St. John, he returned home because of the illness of his parents. Unfortunately he was too late, for they had passed away by the time he got home. It is thought that he then went on a very quick visit to England and France before settling in Antwerp. He was established in Antwerp when his first work entitled *First Book of Madrigals á 5* (for five voices) to poems of Petrarch was published in Venice (1555). In these madrigals he made use of chromatic modulations.

A year later Lasso moved to Munich with the court of Albert V of Bavaria and remained in Munich for thirty-eight years until his death. In Munich he married an aristocratic lady. His fame while he was in Munich was so great that he traveled as a guest to the French courts.

Lasso was a versatile composer who wrote in the most elevated style and was equally at home in the popular idiom. He wrote Italian madrigals, German lieder, French chansons, and Latin motets, a total of over 2000 works.

O LADY FAIR

From *Libro di Villanelle,* Paris, 1581

ORLANDO DI LASSO

Lasso has set this madrigal in a harmonic style that makes use of chromaticism. The opening line is repeated:

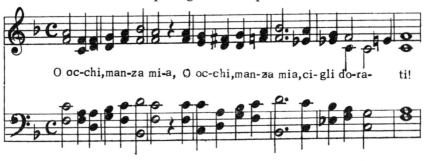

The second melodic section:

d'un- a lu- na stra- lu- cen- ti!

The third melodic section is repeated:

Tie- ne-mi men- te, gio- ia mia bel- la, guar - da-m'un po- ca

a me   a me

me, a me,   a me

a me   a me

O occhi, manza mia,	O lady fair, thy sweet smile
O occhi, manza mia,	O lady fair, thy sweet smile
Cigli dorati!	My soul entrances.
O occhi, manza mia,	O lady fair, thy sweet smile
O occhi, manza mia,	O lady fair, thy sweet smile
Cigli dorati!	My soul entrances.

O faccia d'una luna,	Thy face like silver moonrays,
O faccia d'una luna	Thy face like silver moonrays,
Stralucenti!	Beauty sends forth.

Tienemi mente,	In thy sweet mind
Gioia mia bella,	And memory fair love
Guardam' un poc'a me.	Keep but one thought for me,
A me, a me, fa mi contiento.	Ah me, ah me, and give me contentment.

Tienemi mente,	In thy sweet mind
Gioia mia bella,	And memory fair love
Guardam' un poc'a me,	Keep but one thought for me,
A me, a me, fa mi contiento.	Ah me, ah me, and give me contentment.

HANS LEO HASSLER

BORN: October 25, 1564; Nuremberg, Germnay.
DIED: June 8, 1612; Frankfurt, Germany.

As a child, Hassler studied music with his father and early achieved a reputation as a competent organist. When he was twenty years of age, he went to Venice to study with Andrea Gabrieli. Hassler was the first notable German musician to go to Italy. A year after arriving in Venice, he was recalled to Augsburg where he remained as an organist until the year 1600.

Hassler's first works were published in 1588 in a collection of Italian music printed in Nuremberg. His first madrigals for four to eight voices were published in 1596. After the death of his patron in Augsburg in 1600, Hassler applied for the position of conductor of the town band. This position did not particularly interest him, so he turned to the manufacture of musical clocks. During his association with this venture, he wrote very little music. His time was largely spent in trying to work out the many legal entanglements that involved his clock business.

In 1602 he was appointed Court Organist in Prague, but he seldom made an appearance there and the position was largely an honorary one. Two years later he moved to Ulm, where he married. Later he became organist to the Elector of Saxony in Dresden.

Three years after joining the Elector, he journeyed with him to Frankfurt for the Imperial Elections. Long troubled by tuberculosis, he was stricken while in Frankfurt and died there.

The style of Hassler was greatly influenced by that of Andrea Gabrieli and his nephew Giovanni Gabrieli in spite of the fact that Hassler spent very little time in Venice. Hassler was one of the founders of a national musical art in Germany.

DANCING AND SPRINGING

HANS LEO HASSLER

This madrigal is set in chordal style with the uppermost of the five voices carrying a distinct melody of more importance than the lower four voices. The opening section:

Example 1

This section is repeated.

The second section is more lyrical:

Example 2

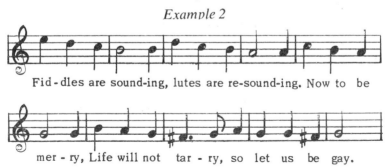

This section is repeated.

The third verse is based on Example 1, while the fourth verse is based on Example 2.

Tanzen und springen,	Dancing and springing,
Singen und klingen,	Singing and ringing,
Fa la la la,	Fa la la la,
Fa la la.	Fa la la.
	(repeated)
Lauten und Geigen	Fiddles are sounding,
Soll'n auch nicht schweigen:	Lutes are resounding,
Zu musizieren	Now to be merry
Und jubilieren steht	Life will not tarry,
Mir all mein sinn.	So let us be gay.
Fa la la la, etc.	Fa la la la, etc.
(repeated)	
Schöne Jung frauen	Lovely young maidens,
In grüner laden,	Hearts lightly laden,
Fa la la la, etc.	Fa la la la, etc.
(repeated)	
Mitihm spazieren	Together walking,
Und konversieren,	Laughing and talking,
Freundlich zu scherzen	Happy when nearer
Freut mich im Herzen	Friends that are dearer
Für silber und gold.	Than silver and gold.
Fa la la la, etc.	Fa la la la, etc.
(repeated)	

CLAUDE LE JEUNE

BORN: 1528; Valenciennes, Flanders.

DIED: September 25, 1600; Paris, France.

Comparatively little is known about the life of Claude le Jeune. It is known that most of his musical activity centered in Paris. He served as a musician at the Sainte Chapelle in Paris and at the Royal Private Chapel. He was also associated with the Académie de Musique which had been founded to encourage the growth of the new style of music known as *musique mesurée*, in which music was made to follow the rhythm of the text in conformity with the rules of classical prosody.

Le Jeune was known as one of the first composers to achieve a mating of ancient rhythm with a more modern harmony. He wrote French chansons, Italian madrigals, and Latin motets.

Claude le Jeune as portrayed in an engraving from *Le Printemps*

Orlando di Lasso as pictured on the cover of his *Faithful Unto Death*

An engraving of Hans Leo Hassler made by Domenico Custos

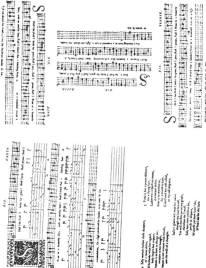

Dowland's *Shall I Sue*, printed with the parts facing different directions so that singers could each read their own music as they stood around the table on which it was placed.

He was attached to the Huguenot cause and set several of the Psalms; some found their way into the early American New England Psalm book. In 1588, during the siege of Paris by Henri III and the wars of the Catholic League, Le Jeune tried to escape, carrying his manuscripts with him. Huguenot Le Jeune was arrested by Catholic soldiers and would have been condemned to death if a Catholic fellow-musician by the name of Mauduit had not intervened.

THE RETURN OF MAYTIME

CLAUDE LE JEUNE

Opening with a refrain for five voices, the return of the refrain is each time interrupted by a verse; the first time for two voices, the second time for three, the third for four; and the final verse is for five voices.

The opening refrain:

Example 1

The first verse is set for two voices, soprano and alto. Its first melody:

Example 2

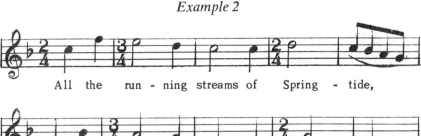

The second verse continues with another melody:

Example 3

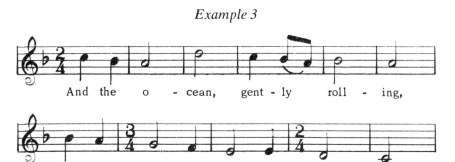

And the o - cean, gent - ly roll - ing, calms the an - gry storm of win - ter.

A third melody follows in the second verse:

Example 4

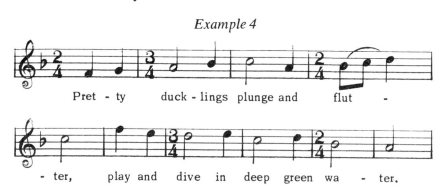

Pret - ty duck - lings plunge and flut - ter, play and dive in deep green wa - ter.

A fourth melody concludes the second verse:

Example 5

And the cranes, in turn - ing home - ward, re - tra - verse the skies and van - ish.

The refrain, Example 1, is repeated.

The second verse is set for three voices, soprano, alto, and tenor. It opens with the melody of Example 2. The melody of Example 4 follows and leads to a repetition of the last half of Example 3. The return of Example 5 concludes the second verse.

The refrain, Example 1, is once again repeated.

The next verse is set for four voices, soprano, alto, tenor, and bass. It opens with the melody of Example 2. A new melody is then introduced:

Example 6

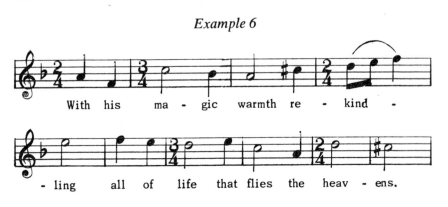

With his ma - gic warmth re - kind - - ling all of life that flies the heav - ens.

The last half of Example 4 is heard next, leading to still another melody:

Example 7

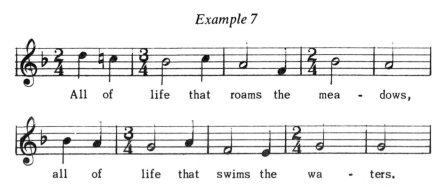

All of life that roams the mea - dows, all of life that swims the wa - ters.

This verse concludes with ten additional measures of new melodic material.

The refrain, Example 1, is repeated.

The final verse is set for five voices, there being two sopranos. It opens with Example 6 and concludes with Example 7.

The refrain, Example 1, is heard twice to complete the madrigal.

(Refrain)   (Repeat the refrain twice)
Revecy venir du printans,   Here returns once more the Maytime,
L'amoureuz et belle saison. Playful love and lovely playtime.

(Verse 1)
Le courant des eaus recherchant

    All the running streams of springtide,
Le canal d'èté s'eclaircît   Seeking summer fields, grow limpid
Et la mer calme de ses flots And the ocean, gently rolling,
Amolit le triste courous.   Calms the angry storm of winter.
Le canard s'égay' se plonjant Pretty ducklings plunge and flutter,
Et se lave coint dedans l'eau. Play and dive in deep green water.
Et la grû qui fourche son vol And the cranes, in turning homeward,
Retraverse l'air et s'en va. Retraverse the skies and vanish.

(Repeat the refrain)

(Verse 2)
Le soleil éclaire luizant   Now the sun, serenely shining,
D'une plus séraine clairé.   Floods the land in warmth and brightness.
Du nuage l'ombre s'enfuit   From the clouds the silent shadows
Qui se ioû'et court et
    noircit.   Swiftly pass and change and darken.
Et foretz et champs et coutaus

    All the meadows, woods, and hillsides,
Le labeur humain reverdît   With the aid of man, are fertile
Et la prê' découvre ses fleurs.

    And the fields uncover flowers.

(Repeat the refrain)

(Verse 3)
De Venus le filz Cupidon   Love-born Eros, child of beauty,
L'univers semant de ses trais Yearly sows his flaming nature,
De sa flamme va rechaufer   With his magic warmth rekindling all
    animaus,   of life

Qui volet en l'air,   That flies the heavens,
Animaus qui rampet au chams,
                      All of life that roams the meadows,
Animaus qui naget auz eaus All of life that swims the waters.
Ce qui mesmement ne sent pas
                      Even those who never knew him,
Amoureux se fond de plaizir. Being lovers, melt with pleasure.

(Repeat the refrain)

(Verse 4)
Rions aussi nous, et cherchons
                      Let us laugh, we too, and savor
Les ébas et jeus du printans. The diverting games of springtide.
Toute chose rit de plazir,   All the world, discarding reason,
Sélébron la gaye saison.   Greets with joy the happy season.

THOMAS MORLEY

BORN: 1557; England.
DIED: October, 1602, England.

    Thomas Morley was a pupil of Byrd and received his Bachelor of Music degree from Oxford University in 1588. He served as an organist at St. Paul's Cathedràl in London where he was undoubtedly heard by Queen Elizabeth I. Morley also served as a Gentleman of the Chapel Royal.

    The works of Morley are unusually melodious. In addition to his church music, motets, anthems (the English derivative of the motet meant for use in the Anglican church), and madrigals, he wrote the first theoretical work on music in England. It was published in 1597 as *A Plaine and Easie Introduction to Practicall Musicke.*

    Morley was the composer of at least two of the songs in the original productions of Shakespeare's plays and was undoubtedly acquainted with the great bard.

    Little else is known of his life. Church records reveal that he was married once, possibly twice, and that he probably had three children, two girls and a boy.

NOW IS THE MONTH OF MAYING

THOMAS MORLEY

This madrigal is set for five voices. The opening line with its "fa la la" after-phrase is:

Example 1

Now   is   the month   of   May-ing, When mer-ry lads are

play-ing. Fa la la la la   la   la la la la Fa la la la la la la

This opening section is repeated.
A second melody is introduced:

Example 2

Each with his bon-ny lass, Up-on the green-y grass. Fa la la la la

The third and fourth verses are set respectively to Examples 1 and 2.

The fifth and sixth verses are also set respectively to Examples 1 and 2.

> Now is the month of Maying,
> When merry lads are playing.
> Fa la la la la la la, etc.   :

Each with his bonny lass,
Upon the greeny grass.
Fa la la la la la la, etc.   :

The Spring, clad all in gladness,
Doth laugh at Winter's sadness.
Fa la la la la la la, etc.   :

And to the bagpipes' sound
The nymphs tread out their ground.
Fa la la la la la la, etc.   :

Fie then, why sit we musing,
Youth's sweet delight refusing?
Fa la la la la la la, etc.   :

Say, dainty nymphs, and speak,
Shall we play barley break?
Fa la la la la la la, etc.   :

CHAPTER IV

THE BAROQUE ERA

IN MUSIC it is generally assumed that the Baroque era started around the year 1600 with the birth of *opera* and lasted until around 1750 (the year of Johann Sebastian Bach's death). It is impossible to hold these dates as exact, however, for both the beginning and ending of the era are obscure. While the style developing around 1600 was called *stile moderno* (or *Nuove Musiche* — New Music), the older style of the Renaissance, the *stile antico,* was still being utilized by major composers. This latter was the *a cappella* style of writing brought to its height by Palestrina. The composer of the early seventeenth century had his choice of the two styles in which he could compose — either was equally acceptable. The end of the era faced a different situation. Musicians today generally agree that the music of Johann Sebastian Bach represents the highest achievement in composition of the Baroque era; but at his death in 1750, the music of his sons was far better known — that of Johann Christian Bach, Johann Christoph Bach, and Karl Philipp Emanuel Bach. The music of the father was regarded in 1750 as being "old-fashioned" and a bit out of style.

The term *baroque* was borrowed from art history, and when first applied to the works of this era by the next generation, it was used as a term of derision. The word probably came from the Portuguese *barrocco,* meaning a pearl of irregular shape. They applied it to the work of the Baroque masters which they thought was grotesque, corrupt in taste, and over-ornamented. A glance at the illustration will show the abundance of decorative figures in architecture. No period in music placed a greater importance on decorations or figurations of the melodic line — mordents, trills, turns, and shakes.

The Baroque era was one of style-consciousness. Many forms developed during the era. Opera was the cornerstone of the period, and its development of the *recitativo* or *recitative* affected all vocal forms. The Baroque composer Caccini spoke of recitativo as "speaking in music," and Peri said it was "to imitate a speaking person in song." Monumental forms of the era included, in the field of vocal music, the *oratorio* (see Handel), the *cantata* (see Bach), and the *Passion* (see Schütz). Instrumental forms included the *solo sonata*, the *fugue* (see Bach), the *concerto grosso* (see Corelli and Bach), the *solo concerto* (see Vivaldi), and the *suite* (see Bach).

As can be seen from the forms just mentioned, a unique development in the Baroque era was the trend toward a difference in the style of writing for instruments and voices. Whereas instruments and voices were interchangeable in the music of the Renaissance, the Baroque composers developed styles of writing for the different instruments and voices that were characteristic of their idiom. Another important development was the departure from the *tactus* (the regular flow of beats) of the previous eras; composers of the *stile moderno* departed from this and moved toward rhythmic extremes. Monteverdi at times discarded the beat in recitative passages, marking the music *senza battuta* (without measure).

Manfred Bukofzer, in *Music in the Baroque Era*, states that "the most striking difference between Renaissance and Baroque music comes to light in the treatment of dissonance." Where the Renaissance composer had accepted dissonance on weak beats, or suspensions over strong beats, the Baroque musician achieved it harmonically on the strong beats (see Gabrieli for a good example).

The characteristic most frequently associated with the Baroque is the affinity between the soprano and bass voices. Most music of the Renaissance had four or more voices of equal importance. Not so the Baroque. The music of the latter period kept the melody usually in the upper or soprano voice, but of almost equal significance was the bass voice. This gave rise to the designation of the era by some scholars as the *thorough-bass* or *basso continuo* period. This *continuo* was always written out (even though the inner voices were not in some of the instrumental compositions). The cello played the *continuo* part as written, while a keyboard instrument (the harpsichord for secular works, the organ for sacred works) played the given bass line and improvised chords above it. (See Corelli for a detailed explanation and an example.)

While early Baroque music lacked tonal direction, the *continuo* helped lead toward the establishment of chordal progressions (in the Renaissance these occurred as a result of linear writing rather than vertical consideration) and the foundation of our modern concept of two-scale patterns — the major scale and the minor scale.

To recapitulate, the Baroque era represented musically a new treatment of dissonance, a greatly increased importance for the bass line, a harmony that developed into the major and minor tonalities known today, a texture that was dominated by the soprano and bass lines, and a specific style of writing that was idiomatic and differed in instrumental compositions and vocal works.

BIBLIOGRAPHY

Bukofzer, Manfred. *Music in the Baroque Era*. New York: W. W. Norton and Company, 1947.

GIOVANNI GABRIELI

BORN: Usually given as 1557; Venice, Italy.
DIED: August 12, 1612; Venice, Italy.

It is a paradox that Giovanni Gabrieli initially set out to publish all of his famous Uncle Andrea's compositions as his main project in life; and, by including some of his own compositions at the end of each volume, became more famous than his uncle.

The original creations of Gabrieli emphasized the traits of a new era in music. During his days at St. Mark's Cathedral in Venice, he composed works in the new *concertante* style, scoring his liturgical works for several choirs and spatially placing them in various balconies of the Cathedral when the works were performed. He was one of the first composers to indicate, in many instances, which instruments of the orchestra he wanted to play specific melodic lines. He composed in bold harmonies in contrast to the earlier polyphonic style. He made use of dissonances on occasion, and was one of the first to employ his instrumental forces independently from the vocal lines.

Very little is known of Gabrieli's life before he arrived at St. Mark's Cathedral. He undoubtedly received most of his musical education from his uncle, Andrea Gabrieli, who was a famous composer in his own right. At eighteen, Giovanni traveled to Munich where he became a musical assistant to the composer Lasso at the court chapel. He remained in the German city for four years, and his first two works (madrigals) were published there.

Gabrieli returned to Venice where he served for a time as a substitute for the first organist at the Cathedral. He was appointed second organist in 1585 at the same time his uncle Andrea was appointed first organist. On his uncle's death in 1586, Giovanni became the first organist, a post he occupied for twenty-six years, until his own death.

BIBLIOGRAPHY

Bedbrook, G. Stares. *The Genius of G. Gabrieli. Music Review*, VIII. 1947.

IN ECCLESIIS

From *Symphoniae Sacrae*

Giovanni Gabrieli

The *Symphoniae Sacrae* (Sacred Symphonies) of Giovanni Gabrieli were settings of the liturgy that he made for special days of celebration at St. Mark's Cathedral in Venice. Because of the arrangement of the church, numerous choirs and choral forces could be arranged on various balconies overlooking the central square of the church. A contemporary account relates: "organs, . . . there are seven faire paire in that room, standing al in a rowe together." Some of these, undoubtedly, were the earlier portable reed organs, but even this is a sizeable number.

It was only natural that under these conditions, and with a musician of the ability of Gabrieli, St. Mark's should become the center of the Baroque concertante music. This unique style embodied the use of various bodies of sound, both instrumental and choral. Throughout *In Ecclesiis,* contrasting groups of choirs are heard in opposition to each other. The same is true of the instrumental forces, and in many places the choral and instrumental groups are pitted one against the other. This is the epitome of the concertante style of composition.

There are five verses in Gabrieli's setting of *In Ecclesiis,* each concluding with the same refrain — an *Alleluia* set in quick triple rhythm. The entire work is preceded by an organ *Intonazione* (the intoning of the pitch on which the work is based). There are differing opinions as to how the *Intonazione* should be executed, since the music for this portion of the work is lost. At least two different versions have been recorded, therefore it would be futile in this book to try to discuss the *Intonazione*.

Verse I

The women's chorus intones the first verse:

Example 1

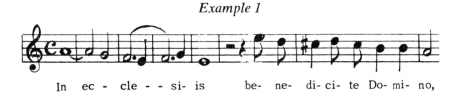

In   ec - cle - - si- is   be- ne- di- ci- te Do- mi- no,

In ecclesiis	In the congregation
Benedicte Domino,	Praise the Lord,
Benedicte Domino.	Praise the Lord.

Alleluia

The first *Alleluia* is an antiphonal setting (singing with alternating choirs) for a women's chorus and a four-part mixed choir. Both the *Alleluia* and the Verse 1 are accompanied only by the organs. The opening of the *Alleluia:*

Example 2

Verse 2

The second verse is for men's chorus in unison accompanied by the organ:

Example 3

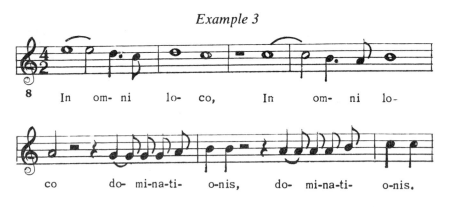

In omni loco, dominationis,   In all the places of His dominion,
Benedic, anima mea, Dominum. Bless the Lord, O my soul.

Alleluia

Example 2 is repeated exactly. On the last chord of the *Alleluia*, the instrumental forces enter brilliantly:

Example 4

Verse 3

The third verse is scored for the altos and tenors of the first mixed choir. All six instruments — 3 *cornetti* (a straight tube of wood with finger-holes and a cup-shaped mouthpiece), *violino,* and 2 *tromboni* — plus the organs, accompany, sometimes divided three against three, four against two, one against five. The opening of Verse 3:

Example 5

In Deo, salutari meo,	In God is my salvation,
Et gloria mea.	And my glory.
Deus, auxilium meum	O God, my help;
Et spes mea in Deo est.	My hope is in God.

Alleluia

The sopranos and contraltos of the women's chorus (in two parts) are contrasted with the second mixed choir in the *Alleluia*. The instruments at first accompany the women's chorus, then accompany the second mixed choir.

Verse 4

A duet between the sopranos and the tenors of the first mixed choir presents the text of this verse. At first the sopranos introduce the text and are answered by the tenors; in the latter portion, the the tenors introduce the text. The opening line of the fourth verse:

Example 6

Deus meus, te invocamus,	My God, we call upon Thee,
Te adoramus. Libera nos,	We adore Thee; deliver us,
Salva nos, vivifica nos.	Save us, quicken us.

Alleluia

This *Alleluia* is essentially the same as the first, Example 1, except that the women's chorus is divided into two parts, the lower singing in organum at the fifth to the upper voice. (For a description of organum, see Chapter I.)

Verse 5

Both mixed choirs are heard in this verse. After the initial four chords, combinations of various voices from both choirs are heard, but never one four-voiced choir against the other four-voiced choir. All six instruments of the orchestra join the organs in accompanying. The opening:

Example 7

| *Deus, adjutor noster,* | God, our refuge |
| *In aeternam.* | In all eternity. |

Alleluia

The final *Alleluia* is similar to the first, Example 1. It is heard as presented in Example 1 except that the upper chorus line is sung by the other four-voiced mixed choir in an harmonic setting. The *Alleluia* starting at the * in Example 1 is repeated. An additional *Alleluia* is added to bring the work to a full close. All the instruments of the orchestra and all the organs accompany the final *Alleluias*.

CLAUDIO MONTEVERDI

BORN: May 10 (?) 1567; Cremona, Italy.
DIED: November 29, 1643; Venice, Italy.

Monteverdi was one of the most important composers of the Baroque era, for he took the newly popular *opera* and was able to infuse into his works in this genre, principles that led to its great growth and success in the following decades. In addition to his operas, Monteverdi also wrote some of the most beautiful madrigals as well as many sacred works.

Claudio Monteverdi was the son of a physician of some standing in Cremona. As a boy, Claudio studied music at the Cathedral of Cremona where he learned to play the pipe organ and the viol. His first compositions were published when he was fifteen — three volumes that included motets, canzionettas, and madrigals.

From Cremona the composer moved to Mantua where he served the ducal court of the art-loving, spendthrift Vincenzo Gonzaga (I) for twelve years. He was employed as a violist, a madrigal singer, and later became an assistant conductor. The Duke was fond of Monteverdi and took the composer with him when he traveled to the Danube River to see how his war against the Turks was progressing. Later trips took the two of them to Flanders and Hungary.

Monteverdi married Claudia Cattaneo, a singer and harpist at the ducal court. She died when she was very young, leaving Monteverdi with two infant sons to rear. While at Mantua, Monteverdi's Books III and IV of madrigals were published. Some of the public were shocked at the "modern" innovations the composer had made in this form. His first opera, *La favola d'Orfeo* (The Legend of Orpheus), was commissioned by the Duke's two sons and produced in 1607. Many more operas followed, culminating in the production of *Arianna* (May, 1608, all of which is lost except the Lament), and *Ballo dell' Ingrate* (The Ungrateful's Ball). Monteverdi's first liturgical work was a setting of the Mass in the old tradition. He took this to Rome with him, apparently to see if he could locate a position there. He was unsuccessful.

After the Duke's death, his successor released the composer from his duties at the court. Monteverdi returned to his father's house in Cremona and remained there a year until an appointment came for him to serve as the choir director at St. Mark's Cathedral in Venice.

For the first time Monteverdi knew financial security. He produced a large quantity of church music for use at St. Mark's during his thirty-year tenure. He did not, however, abandon his favorite, opera. His stage works written in Venice included two novelties in the use of instruments — *pizzicato* (plucking the strings of the viols rather than bowing) and *tremolo* (a quick reiteration of the same note accomplished by fast up and down bowing).

The first public opera house in the world opened in Venice, the Teatro San Cassiano, in 1637. This undoubtedly rekindled Monteverdi's interest. *Arianna* was revived successfully, and more than twelve new operas were written. It was in these later works that the composer revolutionized the field: he introduced beautiful melodies and brilliancy of performance; he employed the *da capo* aria; and in his last opera, *Poppea,* he introduced a historical subject in place of the Greek legends used exclusively before.

BIBLIOGRAPHY

Ferdinand, Hans. *Claudio Monteverdi: His Life and Works,* trans. Kathleen Redlich. New York: Oxford University Press, 1952.
Schrade, Leo. *Monteverdi: Creator of Modern Music.* New York: W. W. Norton and Company, 1950.

ARIANNA

(An Opera)

CLAUDIO MONTEVERDI

Monteverdi's opera *Arianna* was based on the story from Greek mythology of Ariadne (*Arianna* is the Italian form of the name). Ariadne fell in love with Theseus as he was engaged in killing the

CLAUDIO MONTEVERDI

ARCANGELO CORELLI

ALESSANDRO SCARLATTI

FRANCOIS COUPERIN (le Grand)

The pipe chambers of the Baroque organs were not only functional but served as a center for the decorative efforts of the architect. The organ of the Holy Hill, Czechoslovakia, is by Sieber and Richter.

Procession of the Guild of St. John the Evangelist in St. Mark's Square in 1496, a painting by Gentile Bellini (1427?-1507)

Minotaur. She provided him with a thread which guided him out of the cave after he had slain the monster. In gratitude, Theseus took Ariadne with him when he departed for the Isle of Naxos, but then deserted her there.

The *Lament* of Ariadne, as she remains forsaken on the island, is the only remaining example of Monteverdi's most popular opera. Apparently the *Lament* was so well-liked in its own time for its poignant melody, that the composer later set it as a five-voice madrigal and extended its length. Both the original aria and the madrigal are still performed.

ARIA: *Lasciatemi Morire* (Abandon me to death)

This short aria is in terse ternary or three-part form. There are three melodic phrases; the first and the third are the same.

The first phrase of the aria:

Example 1

The second phrase follows without pause or interlude:

Example 2

Both the music and the text of Example 1 return to conclude the aria.

Lasciatemi morire!	Abandon me to death!
Lasciatemi morire!	Abandon me to death!

E che volete che mi conforte	What comfort can you give?
In così dura sorte,	I have lost all I cherish,
In così gran martire?	I suffer here, love's martyr.
Lasciatemi morire,	Abandon me to death,
Lasciatemi morire.	Abandon me to death.

HEINRICH SCHÜTZ

BORN: October 8, 1585; Köstritz, Germany.
DIED: November 6, 1672; Dresden, Germany.

Heinrich Schütz received his early musical education in Italy and returned there during the middle years of his life to learn of the new trends in composition. In both cases, he returned to Germany and employed the best of the Italian techniques in music that was, through his own artistic ability, still German in style. Although there were other well-known composers in his day, and composers who made their contributions too, he is acknowledged as the founder of the German tradition in music. There is no question that he composed the first German opera, and his settings of the Passion established a pattern which inspired Johann Sebastian Bach about one hundred years later.

Schütz was born of a family with a good social position. At fourteen he became a choir boy in the Landgrave's chapel and received not only a thorough musical education at the choir school, but also an excellent general education in the arts and sciences of that day. His scholastic ability led him to the University of Marburg where he studied law. During a visit to the University by the Landgrave, Schütz' musical abilities became evident to the ruler. The Landgrave offered to underwrite a trip to Venice so that Schütz could study with the famous Giovanni Gabrieli.

After two years in Venice, Schütz' first group of compositions was published — a book of five-part madrigals. Following the death of Gabrieli, Schütz returned to Germany; and possibly because he was not yet convinced he should follow a career in music, he moved to Leipzig to pursue further the study of law.

The composer had not been in Leipzig long when he was appointed organist to the Landgrave of that city. His ability must have been well-known, for soon the Elector of Dresden started bargaining with the Landgrave to release Schütz for service in his court. The ruler of Dresden finally won out. Schütz moved to that city, where, with visits elsewhere from time to time, he continued to live the balance of his life. At the wish of the Elector, he reorganized the musical activities in the Italian style. He sent his instrumentalists to Italy to study the latest performance techniques on their respective instruments, and he composed a number of works in the new *concerted* manner learned from Gabrieli — the scoring for groups of performers. Some of his settings of the Psalms called for two, three, and even four choirs of voices. He also made much use of brass choirs in the accompaniments, as had his teacher.

Schütz married in Dresden, but it was an unhappy experience for him as his wife died within six years. Probably to divert his mind from grief, he obtained a leave and made a second trip to Italy where Claudio Monteverdi was then the leading figure. While there, Schütz completed a set of Latin motets.

On his return to Germany, Schütz composed and produced the first German opera, *Dafne*. Little is known of this work as the score is lost; the extant libretto can give no idea as to the composer's treatment of it.

The start of the Thirty Years' War disrupted activities at the Dresden court, and salaries for the musicians were soon in arrears. Schütz obtained another leave so that he could visit Denmark at the invitation of King Christian IV. For six years the composer wandered among various courts — Copenhagen, Hanover, and Dresden.

When the composer finally settled down in Dresden again, he was not as successful as he had been the first time in setting the musical standards. Salaries for the musicians were still irregular, Schütz sometimes paying them out of his own allowance. Some of the younger Italian musicians employed there had new ideas and techniques that were in conflict with the composer's intentions. Schütz's own works written during these years would seem to indicate that he was more or less living in retirement, for they were simple four-part settings of portions of the liturgy: Glorias, the Nicene Creed, etc.

When the composer was in his eightieth year, he composed some of his finest music: at least three settings of the Passion, and a Christmas oratorio. He suffered, however, from a loss of hearing and seldom went out. Most of his time was spent at home reading the Scriptures, particularly the Psalms. His last musical setting was of Psalm CXIX: "Thy statutes have been my songs in the house of my pilgrimage."

PASSION ACCORDING TO ST. MATTHEW

HEINRICH SCHÜTZ

Portrayals of the *Passion* (from the Latin *passio* — "to suffer"), the sufferings of Jesus from the Feast of the Passover until His crucifixion, come from the earliest days of Christianity. Musical settings of it were the logical outgrowth of early mystery plays to which music had been added, and to the services of the Roman Catholic Church in which, since the twelfth century up to the present day, the story was recited in semi-dramatic form, one priest singing the narrative portions, another the words of Christ, and a third the words of the crowd (*turba*).

After the late fifteenth century, composers started setting the *turbas* in motet style in contrast to the plainsong solo parts. It was in this manner that Heinrich Schütz made his four settings of the Passion. This tradition allowed only two additions to the text as found in one of the four Gospels, an *introitus* and a *conclusio* — a prologue and an epilogue to the narrative. Schütz' setting, particularly in the St. Matthew, is a severe one: the entire Passion is scored to be sung *a cappella,* without the use of any instruments; except for the introitus (a motet) and the conclusio (a free setting of a Passion choral), the text is directly from the German Vulgate Bible. Later settings, such as the great Bach *St. Matthew Passion,* came closer to oratorios than to the work under discussion, using double choruses, double orchestras, and inserting a great number of chorals throughout as well as many arias based on non-Biblical sacred texts.

Schütz scores the *Passion* for the following solo voices:

Evangelist (*St. Matthew*)	tenor
Christ	bass
Judas	contralto
Peter	tenor
Two false witnesses	tenors
Caiphas	bass
The two Marys	soprano and contralto
Pontius Pilate	tenor
Pilate's wife	contralto

The assignment of a tenor voice for the Evangelist and a bass voice for the part of Jesus was in the oldest tradition of musical settings of the Passion. The recitatives (the connecting descriptive passages which move at the tempo of spoken words) are patterned after Gregorian chant and are in the Dorian mode. (See Chapter I for a description of Gregorian chant and modes.) The text is from verses 26 and 27 of the Gospel of St. Matthew in the Bible.

CONCLUSIO: *Ehre sei dir, Christe*

The *conclusio,* or epilogue, is a free setting of the Passion choral, *Ach wir armen Sünder* (Ah, We Poor Sinners). The choral (sometimes used in English with its foreign spelling, *chorale*) was established by Martin Luther as an integral part of the church service to be sung by the congregation. In order for them to hear the melody better (the chorals were generally sung in unison) the melody was moved from the tenor voice (where it had been in earlier polyphonic music) to the upper or soprano voice. The newly perfected organ that was used in the Evangelical or Lutheran churches gave harmonic support by the addition of chords underneath the melody, thus making it a monodic (single melody) setting. In order for the congregation to stay together, the music was also measured in contrast to the earlier free flowing style.

In the *Ehre sei dir,* Schütz has kept the melody in the soprano and used a harmonic setting that is chordal and measured. At the ends of the short phrases, he allows the inner voices to move more freely as in the older contrapuntal style. The choral opens:

Example 1

Eh- re sei dir　Chri-　ste, der du lit- test Not

Ehre sei dir Christe,	Glory to Thee, Christ,
Der du littest Not,	Who suffered a bitter death
An dem Stamm des Kreuzes	On the wood of the Cross
Für uns den bittern Tod,	For our sake.

and continues:

Example 2

Und herrschest mit dem Vater And Thou reignest in Heaven
Dort in Ewigkeit. With God the Father forever.

The next line of text, *Hilf uns armen Sündern zu der Seligkeit* (Help us sinners toward blessed happiness), is started by the sopranos and altos, then stated in full by the lower three voices. It is repeated in full by the four-part chorus.

The final text of the *conclusio* is from the opening of the Mass: *Kyrie eleison, Christe eleison, Kyrie eleison* (Lord have mercy, Christ have mercy, Lord have mercy). Schütz' setting of these lines, while basically harmonic, is more florid than the earlier part of the conclusio and is reminiscent of polyphonic settings. The sopranos introduce the melody of the first Kyrie:

Example 3

Ky-   ri- e e- lei-   son,

Chri- ste e- le- i-   son, e- lei-   son.

ARCANGELO CORELLI

BORN: February 17, 1653; Fusignano, Italy.
DIED: January 8, 1713; Rome, Italy.

Although the total number of compositions that Arcangelo Corelli wrote is comparatively small, his impact on the course of music cannot be underestimated. As one of the finest violinists of his day, he established a technique for playing the instrument that led directly to all later developments: correct bowing, the use of double stops (two notes at once), and chords. His contribution to the field of composition includes not only the establishment of the *concerto grosso* form, the most important instrumental one of the era, but also the solo violin *sonata*. He is also responsible for the establishment of tonality as it is now known, the adherence of a composition to basic chords built on a major or minor scale.

Arcangelo was the youngest of four children born to a family of culture. He received his early education at Faenza, and was thirteen when he went to Bologna to take his first violin lessons. He was in the latter city four years before he entered the Accademia Filharmonica as a violinist.

From Bologna he moved to Rome and served as violinist in the orchestra of the French Church when he was twenty-two. He next served as a violinist in the orchestra of the Teatro Capranica. He may have served the Elector of Bavaria in Munich for a time, but there is no evidence to support this legend.

Corelli was definitely settled in Rome in 1685 (he was then thirty-two) when his first published compositions were released, a set of twelve sonatas. He soon had a great reputation in the Holy City and moved in the highest circles of society. When the Queen of Sweden took up residence in Rome, Corelli performed in her palace several times. The King of Naples invited Corelli to move to that city and become a royal musician. The composer had, however, been befriended by Cardinal Ottoboni and lived in his palace the rest of his life except for a short stay in Modena. The Cardinal sponsored orchestral concerts in his palace every Monday night at which Corelli was in charge. These concerts were considered the most important and interesting event taking place in Rome.

Arcangelo Corelli was a very simple and unpretentious man who dressed in shabby clothes and would never hire a carriage, preferring to go on foot. His fame became international during his lifetime; students arrived from all over Europe to work and study with him. His compositions were published not only in Italy, but in Amsterdam, Antwerp, Paris, and London.

After a short trip to Naples, where he played some of Alessandro Scarlatti's compositions for the composer, he returned to Rome in failing health. After his death in the latter city, he was buried in princely style in the Parthenon.

BIBLIOGRAPHY

Pincherle. Marc. *Corelli: His Life and His Work,* trans. Hubert E. M. Russell. New York: W. W. Norton and Company, 1956.

CONCERTO GROSSO

Opus 6, No. 8

("The Christmas Concerto")

ARCANGELO CORELLI

The *concerto grosso* was a development of the latter part of the Baroque era, but it was an outgrowth of elements in evidence earlier. The *concertante* style of Gabrieli, the use of a large instrumental ensemble in contrast to a very small ensemble, paved the way. The concerto grosso as a specific form was the creation of Arcangelo Corelli. It consisted of a number of separate movements, usually four or five alternating between slow and moderately fast ones; the orchestra was spatially separated into two groups: a large ensemble known as the *tutti* (Italian for "all") and a small group (usually two violins and a continuo of its own) known as the *concertino* (*ino* is a diminutive Italian suffix). Just as the sonatas were specified for church or secular use, so he grouped his concerti grossi: *concerto da chiesa* (*chiesa* — "church") and *concerto da camera* (*camera* — "chamber"). His first eight concerti were of the first group, the last four of the latter classification.

This concerto is the last of his group of church concerti, and is known as "The Christmas Concerto" because of the composer's inscription on the title page: *Fatto per la notte di natale* (composed for Christmas Eve). The concertino is composed of two violins and continuo; the tutti is a string orchestra with continuo. There is a short introduction followed by five movements.

The *continuo* mentioned in the above paragraphs is a short form of the Italian expression *basso continuo* (literally, "continued bass") and sometimes called by its English name *thorough-bass* ("thorough" being an old English manner of spelling "through" for throughout). The music for the continuo is written on a single bass clef (see Example 1), sometimes with numbers and/or accidentals (sharps and flats) written underneath the melody (known then as *figured bass*). The continuo is played by two instruments, a cello and a harpsichord or organ. The cello plays the melody as written; the harpsichord or organ employs the melody as the bass line of a full keyboard part. The upper voices or chords are created by the performer from either the numbers under the clef, which represent specific chords, or in the absence of such indications by the composer, creates a harmonic accompaniment from the harmonies indicated in the melodic lines the other instruments are playing. This art of improvising on the keyboard from a given bass line is known as *realizing the continuo*. Example 1 below is the continuo part of the first Allegro of this concerto:

Example 1

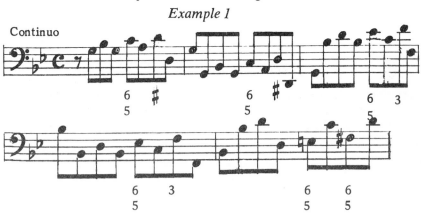

FIFTH MOVEMENT: Pastorale ad libitum. *Largo.*

The *ad libitum* in the title of this movement indicates that it is an optional movement. Since it is in the rhythm of a *Siciliano* (an Italian dance from Sicily), which suggests "soft rural scenes," this movement is usually more associated with the Nativity scene than the other movements.

The flowing, dance-like melody in 12/8 meter is stated by the two violins of the concertino:

Example 2

The tutti support the soloist with a harmonic accompaniment.

The middle section is based on a theme introduced by the combined concertino and tutti:

Example 3

Violins

Although this movement resembles the ternary form, the return of Example 2 is not exact and the section is considerably shorter than its initial appearance.

ALESSANDRO SCARLATTI

BORN: May 2, 1660; Palermo, Sicily.
DIED: October 24, 1725; Naples, Italy.

Alessandro Scarlatti is known principally for his contributions to the field of opera, and is frequently denoted as the "founder of the Neopolitan school" of opera composers. He wrote around one hundred and fifteen operas, of which about fifty examples are extant today. In addition to the stage works, he composed a large number of sacred cantatas as well as oratorios, motets, and other sacred works.

The history of the Scarlatti family is obscure, but it is known that Alessandro was born in Palermo. It is supposed that his father was a musician as were all of his children. The family was probably poor, so that the children were sent off to live with relatives in areas where they could receive an education, either from the "free" schools of Naples, or through the help of relatives in other cities. At twelve Alessandro went to Rome with two of his sisters; two younger brothers joined them there later. The first record of Alessandro's activities in that city relates that he was commissioned to write a Latin oratorio for the season following Lent. He was probably in his mid-teens about this time.

Alessandro Scarlatti married when he was eighteen. A year later his first opera was performed in Rome and won the attention of Queen Christina of Sweden who was in residence there at the time. By the time Scarlatti's second opera was given, a note in the program informed the public that he was "Director of Music" to the Queen of Sweden. Other operas of his were soon performed in Naples, and by the time he was twenty-two, he had moved to Naples and been appointed "Director of Music" to the Royal Chapel by the Spanish viceroy who governed the Kingdom of Naples.

Scarlatti's famous son, Domenico, was born during this stay in Naples (he was one of nine children). Domenico later became an equally famous composer. Unlike his father, Domenico's claim to renown was largely through his compositions for the solo harpsichord.

After a number of Alessandro's operas had been performed at both the Royal Palace and at the Royal Theater (he was also constantly in demand at the aristocratic entertainments), he revolted against the poor salary and the mediocre tastes of the Spanish viceroy. He and Domenico traveled to Florence where they came under the patronage of Prince Ferdinando de' Medici. The elder Scarlatti created a number of new operas for the Prince's private theater. The Prince, however, did not offer the Scarlattis any official or permanent post, so they departed for Rome.

In Rome, Alessandro assumed the not too important post of an assistant music director for the church of Santa Maria Maggiore, later becoming the director. Most of his compositions of this period were sacred works as the Pope looked with disfavor on the "immorality" of most of the opera plots. The flow of operas from Alessandro's fertile mind could not be stopped, and soon new ones were being produced in Naples. Once again Scarlatti took up residence in Naples. By this time he was at the height of his fame, and the operas he composed were on a larger scale than the earlier ones. He was knighted and also awarded the Order of the Golden Spur by the Pope.

Scarlatti returned to Rome for a brief period of time during which he produced more operas. He composed some sacred music for the installation of the new Pope, and then returned to Naples. An old man by this time, he lived in virtual retirement. He died in Naples and was buried there in the church of Montesanto.

BIBLIOGRAPHY

Dent, Edward. *Alessandro Scarlatti: His Life and Works.* London: Edward Arnold, 1960.

The Palazzo Pitti, in Florence, Italy, from an engraving made by J. S. Müller. It was in this palace and in similar ones in Florence that opera was born.

EXULTATE DEO

ALESSANDRO SCARLATTI

While Alessandro Scarlatti was the leader of the "new" Neopolitan style of opera composition, many of his sacred works followed the "old" *a cappella* style and have no instrumental accompaniment. One of the most frequently performed of these is *Exultate Deo*. It is polyphonic throughout, and contrapuntal imitations abound in it. The work is scored for a chorus of four groups of voices: sopranos, altos, tenors, and basses. It is in four sections, the second and fourth sections being the same.

The opening section is based on the Latin text, "Exultate Deo, Adjutori nostro" (Magnify the God of our salvation). The four voices enter in quick succession, starting with the highest and moving to the lowest. The sopranos and tenors have the same melodic subject, while the altos and basses share another:

Example 1

The sopranos continue with another melodic figure which appears frequently throughout the first section, passing from voice to voice:

Example 2

The second section is an *Alleluia*. The sopranos introduce a melodic subject that is imitated in inversion (turned upside down) by the altos, and in its original form by the tenors. The basses have a more sustained line:

The third section is based on the text, "Jubilate Deo Jacob" (Make a joyful noise unto the God of Jacob). The altos, tenors, and basses start in almost harmonic fashion before they break into their separate polyphonic lines; the sopranos are immediately independent:

Example 4

Ju-bi-la-te De- o, ju-bi-la-te De- o,

Ju-bi-la- te De-o, ju-bi-la-te De- o,

Ju-bi-la- te De-o, ju-bi-la-te De- o,

Ju-bi-la- te De-o, ju-bi-la-te De- o,

The second section, the *Alleluia,* is repeated.

FRANÇOIS COUPERIN ("le Grand")

BORN: November 10, 1668; Paris, France.
DIED: September 12, 1733; Paris, France.

The name Couperin was famous in French musical circles. François Couperin's father and two uncles were famous organists, violinists, and probably composers. His grandfather also had been a well-known musician in Paris. One of the uncles was also named François, so the Parisians, in order to distinguish the younger Couperin from the uncle, dubbed him François Couperin "le Grand."

François received his first musical instruction from his father, and soon was studying with the organist of the King's Chapel. It was from the latter that he probably learned the technique of polyphonic composition. ·Couperin's father died when the boy was eleven, and young François was appointed to fill the organist's post at the Saint-Gervais Church vacated by his father's death. A deputy was appointed to play until the youth was old enough to assume the full responsibility, but the boy and his mother continued to live in the "organist's house" maintained by the church (similar to parsonages furnished by today's churches for their ministers).

At eighteen, Couperin officially assumed the full duties as organist. Four years later he married Marie-Anne Ansault, about whom little is known. His first compositions date from the year of his marriage, several organ masses composed in the old tradition.

In 1693, Louis XIV personally chose Couperin as one of the four organists of the Royal Chapel. Their duties included, in addition to playing for services for three months of the year, providing new music for the chapel services and conducting the performance of it. A year later the King appointed Couperin the official harpsichord instructor. Among his pupils were the Duke of Burgundy and most of the royal children.

It was not long before the composer also assumed charge of the instrumental music of the court, although he had to wait a number of years before he received the official title that went with the position (until the death of the incumbent who was so ill that he occupied the post in name only). By the time he was forty, Couperin was a well-known figure in France. In 1713, with the permission of the King, his first book of compositions was published, a series of harpsichord solos that he had written over a period of ten or fifteen years.

Couperin wrote a text on the art of keyboard technique, known as *L'Art de toucher le clavecin* (The Art of Harpsichord Technique) which, although not the first such text, was the first serious study, one that Johann Sebastian Bach read thoroughly.

After the death of Louis XIV, Couperin continued in royal favor with Louis XV. With the gradual increase in his remuneration from the Court, the composer kept moving his wife and children to better homes. Early in his service to Louis XV, he moved to a luxurious home on the Rue Neuve des Bons Enfants, not far from the home of Rameau.

Almost nothing is known of the last ten years of Couperin's life in spite of his great reputation, by that time, in France. He was in correspondence with Bach, but their letters were used by a descendant as covers for some jam pots. Nothing is known of any other correspondence of Couperin. It is known that he was in failing health after he reached forty, and in 1723 handed over his duties as organist at Saint-Gervais. In 1730, his daughter Marguerite-Antoinette took over his responsibilities for supervising the music at the court, the first woman ever to occupy that position.

BIBLIOGRAPHY

Brunold, Paul. *François Couperin*, trans. J. B. Hanson. Monaco: The Lyrebird Press, 1949.
Mellers, Wilfred H. *François Couperin and the French Classical Tradition*. New York: Roy Publishers, 1951.

LES BARRICADES MYSTÉRIEUSES

(The Mysterious Barricades)
Rondeau

François Couperin ("le Grand")

Although Couperin composed music for other media, it is by his harpsichord works that he is remembered. He utilized largely the same keyboard forms that were then in style in Italy and Germany, particularly the *dance suite* (see section on Bach), but he always gave his works programmatic titles. He said, "I have always had some object in mind when composing these pieces, and have furnished the titles to suggest what it was."

Many Baroque compositions were written that could be, and were, performed on either the harpsichord or the lute. *Les Barricades Mystérieuses* was written for the harpsichord, but it is reminiscent of the style of lute compositions. Frequently when it is performed, one or more sections of it are played on the harpsichord with the "lute" stop (a drawbar, that when "pulled" makes one manual of the instrument sound like a lute).

Speaking of *Les Barricades,* the famous harpsichordist, Wanda Landowska, said:

In the *Barricades Mystérieuses,* Couperin reveals his love for the mysterious play of crossed keyboards, the interlacing of voices on the same level. Thus brought together, the voices murmur voluptuously, flash tenderly and flare out of the double keyboards in tiny, dancing flames.*

*Copyright, 1958, RCA-Victor.

The French subtitle, *rondeau*, is the equivalent of the more generally used Italian expression, *rondo*. It is a sectional work in which the principal melody is introduced in the first section and recurs in between each new melody of the succeeding sections.

Les Barricades Mystérieuses opens with the principal, or recurring, melody:

Example 1

A repetition of Example 1 is indicated in the music (although not always observed).

A second theme is introduced:

Example 2

Example 1 is heard again.
A new theme, Example 3, follows:

Example 3

The melody of Example 1 returns for a full statement.

The final theme of the composition is somewhat longer than the others; its opening is quoted in Example 4:

Example 4

The principal melody, Example 1, is heard for the final time, bringing the work to a close.

ANTONIO VIVALDI

BORN: March 4, 1678; Venice, Italy
DIED: July 27 (?), 1741; Vienna, Austria.

An appreciation of the immense contribution of Antonio Vivaldi to the field of music is only becoming apparent in the last half of the twentieth century. Although Johann Sebastian Bach claimed that much of his knowledge concerning the concerto was learned from the works of Vivaldi (Bach arranged twenty-one of them), most of Vivaldi's works were little known to the musicians of the nineteenth century. It has only been since around 1960 that they have been published and available to the general musical public.

Little is known of the life of Antonio Vivaldi. He was the son of one of the finest violinists at St. Mark's Cathedral in Venice, but the name of his mother and the details of his childhood are unknown. His father provided the boy with his first violin lessons.

Vivaldi received the first of the minor orders of the Roman Catholic Church in 1693, and was ordained a priest about ten years later. He was known as *il prete rosso* (the red priest) because of his red hair.

From 1704 until 1740 he was employed at the Conservatory of the Pietà Hospital for foundling girls, one of four such institutions in Venice. These were known for their outstanding concerts, with great rivalry between schools. Musicians of importance traveled from all over Europe to hear their programs. An account written in a letter of 1739 by Charles de Brosses gives some idea of their quality:

The Ospedali have the best music here. There are four of them, all for illegitimate or orphaned girls or whose parents cannot support them. These are brought up at state expense and trained exclusively in music. Indeed they sing like angels, play the violin, flute, organ, oboe, cello, and bassoon. . . . The performances are entirely their own and each concert is composed of about forty girls.

Antonio Vivaldi, an engraving made by I. Caldwall in 1725

Johann Sebastian Bach, painted by Haussmann, considered the most faithful likeness by the Bach family

Viola d'amour (made in Prague around the eighteenth century)

The Metropolitan Museum of Art, gift of Mrs. Rudolph Keppler, 1897

GEORGE FRIDRIC HANDEL

It must have been during Vivaldi's days at the Conservatory that he spent three years as the music director to the governor of Mantua. Apparently the directors of the Pietà appreciated his services enough that they allowed him time to make frequent trips, even to the extent of providing a regular carriage assigned to him. In turn, it is recorded, they expected Vivaldi to compose two concerti a month. For a time they also anticipated his writing two motets a month, plus Masses and Vespers for Easter. The composer speaks in a letter of 1737 of his travels, saying, "for over fourteen years we have traveled together to many European cities." During these trips he probably visited both Germany and France.

In 1737 he was about to leave Venice to go to Ferrara to produce an opera of his when he was forbidden to enter the latter city by the ecclesiastical leaders since he was a priest who did not say Mass. Vivaldi replied to this insinuation:

I have not said mass for twenty-five years nor shall I ever again, not on account of any prohibition or order, but by my own choice, because of an illness [asthma] suffered from birth and which still troubles me. After I was ordained priest I said mass for a little over a year, and then gave it up, as three times I had to leave the altar before the end on account of my illness. I nearly always live indoors for this reason and never go out except in a gondola or a carriage, as I cannot walk on account of the pain or constriction in my chest. No gentleman has ever asked me to go to his house, not even our Prince, as everyone knows about my weakness. I can go out usually after dinner but never on foot. This is the reason I never say mass. As Your Lordship knows, I have been to Rome three times to give opera there at Carnival time, but I never said mass there. . . . I was three years at Mantua . . . but never said mass. My journeys have always cost me a great deal because I have always taken four or five people to assist me. Anything that I can do that is worthwhile, I do at home at my desk. . . . I have been Maestro della Pietà for over thirty years with never a scandal.

In 1740 Vivaldi left Venice permanently and traveled to Vienna where he expected to enjoy the many opportunities offered to musicians and performers at the court of Charles VI. He failed to prosper, however, and died destitute in that city.

The records are not complete as to the total number of works that Vivaldi composed, but it is known that he wrote over forty operas, two oratorios, twenty-four cantatas. The concerti, by which he is principally known today, occupy five pages in the catalogue of the famous Italian publisher, G. Ricordi.

BIBLIOGRAPHY

Pincherle, Marc. *Vivaldi, Genius of the Baroque.* New York: W. W. Norton and Company, 1957.

CONCERTO IN D MINOR

For Viola d'Amore and String Orchestra

(Instituto Italiano Vivaldi, Book 196, F. 2, No. 2)

ANTONIO VIVALDI

During Vivaldi's most active period at the Ospitale della Pietà in Venice, he was expected to compose two concerti per month. For centuries the manuscripts of these numerous concerti lay scattered in various libraries of the world, unpublished — in Dresden, Berlin, Siena, London, New York, and elsewhere. The largest body of them reposed in the Mauro Foà Collection of the Turin Library in Italy. During the 1950's, the Italian publishing firm of G. Ricordi started publishing them for the first time. The *F.* number attached to the title refers to the categorization by Antonio Fanna into concerti for violins, violas (No. 2), celli, concertino of strings, mandolins, flutes, oboes, bassoons, trumpets, horns, etc.

The *viola d'amore* was a stringed instrument which was gradually disappearing from the orchestra during Vivaldi's time, although the composer seemed to have an affection for the instrument as demonstrated by his numerous concerti for it. The viola d'amore seems to have been a rather special member of the ancient family of viols. It was a rather large instrument, about 32½ inches in length, played across the body in the same way as the treble viols and violin. The characteristic of the instrument was its "sympathetic strings" — strings lying below those that were actually bowed and vibrating "sympathetically" with the bowed strings. This gave it a richness of tone rare in the upper stringed instruments.

The concerto form became standardized by the works of Vivaldi into a cycle of three movements. The composer extended the number of entrances of the full orchestra within a movement, and his unique contribution was the use of solo melodies distinct from those played by the full orchestra (although they are closely related in rhythmic patterns and are in the same key).

THIRD MOVEMENT: *Allegro.*

The full string orchestra is heard in the ritornello theme (a theme that reappears almost each time the full orchestra is heard):

Example 1

(Ritornello)

The first solo theme of this movement is closely related rhythmically to the ritornello theme. It employs double-stops (two strings sounded simultaneously):

Example 2

The ritornello, Example 1, returns in the full orchestra, a third higher in pitch this time.

The soloist is heard in a passage of sixteenth-note sequences based on the chords appearing in the orchestral accompaniment:

Example 3

A very brief passage for full orchestra is based on a sixteenth-note imitation of the solo passage, Example 3, just completed.

Rhythmical variety is offered in the next solo theme which utilizes a triplet figure:

Example 4

A brief restatement of the ritornello, Example 1, in its original key is played by the full string orchestra.

A new solo theme is introduced by the viola d'amore:

Example 5

After this extended solo passage, the ritornello, Example 1, is heard in the full orchestra and brings the concerto to a close.

GEORGE FRIDERIC HANDEL

BORN: February 23, 1685; Halle, Germany.
DIED: April 14, 1759; London, England.

George Frideric Handel (the common English spelling of his name which in German appears as Georg Friedrich Händel) was truly a cosmopolitan musician, for he was born a German, became a British subject, composed music in the Italian tradition, and his most famous work, *Messiah,* was premiered in Ireland.

Handel's father was a barber-surgeon who had been appointed surgeon and valet to the Prince of Saxe-Magdeburg in Germany. George was born of his father's second marriage, his mother being a pastor's daughter. The elder Handel had little training in music and was against his son following it as a profession. He had no objection, however, when George was seven, to arranging for the boy to have some music lessons for his own amusement. Through his step-brother, George was able to take lessons and practice on the organ in the Prince's chapel. As his talent became evident, the boy was also given lessons on the oboe, the harpsichord, and studied counterpoint and fugue. By the time George was twelve, he was appointed assistant organist at the Cathedral. He had already composed six sonatas for oboes and bass, and had written several motets.

George's father died soon after. In fulfillment of his parents' wishes, the boy entered the University of Halle as a law student. He remained at the University one year; then in desperation, he gave up the study of law. He moved to Hamburg where he secured a position as a violinist at the opera house. He composed two operas while he was employed at Hamburg.

By the time Handel was twenty-one, he had saved a small amount of money which enabled him to make a trip to Italy, the opera center of Europe. During his visit to Florence, he composed an opera which was presented there. Another opera, written and produced during his visit to Venice, was a big success with the public. In Rome he completed two oratorios that were given their first performance under the direction of Corelli. When he traveled south to Naples, he met both Alessandro and Domenico Scarlatti. He had a keyboard "contest" with the latter. According to the judges, Handel won for his ability on the pipe organ, Domenico Scarlatti for his ability on the harpsichord.

After having spent four years in Italy, Handel returned to Germany and was appointed Court Musician to the Elector of Hanover. During the latter part of that year, Handel made his first visit to London where an opera of his was presented with success at the Haymarket Theatre. Handel returned for a second visit to England two years later and presented a *Te Deum* and a *Jubilate,* which were so well-received that he was awarded a royal annuity. The enthusiasm of the British public for his works caused him to overstay his leave from Germany. During this time Queen Anne died leaving no direct heir to the throne, and the Elector of Hanover (Handel's patron) was crowned King George I of England. With his old patron on the throne, Handel decided to remain in England, and in 1727 became a British subject.

Soon after his coronation, King George planned a wonderful party for the members of his court. He arranged to have barges drawn up the Thames River on which his guests were to travel. On an adjoining barge, fifty musicians were to provide the entertainment. Handel was asked to compose music for this fête; it is known today as *The Royal Water Music.* The King and his court liked it so well they asked Handel to have the musicians play it a second time.

Handel enjoyed the royal favor, teaching both the Prince of Wales and Princess Anne. He was appointed the director of the new Royal Academy of Music, his chief function being the production of

Italian operas. In a period of a little over ten years, the composer produced eighteen of his operas. Oxford University conferred upon him the honorary degree of Doctor of Music. He then became the sole director of the Covent Garden Opera House, producing nine of his own works in three years there.

Italian opera was so popular in the British capital that a second opera company soon started producing works. The rivalries and jealousies that occurred in the business world were too much for Handel, and he lost most of his money with the decline in popularity of his own works. A stroke, which resulted in the paralysis of one hand, led his friends to encourage him to take a much-needed rest. After a recuperative period in Aix-la-Chappelle, he returned to London in far better health. Once again he turned to directing Italian opera, creating five more operas that were produced within a period of three years, but he could not achieve the popularity he had once enjoyed.

Handel then turned almost exclusively to the field of oratorio. He had written thirteen oratorios, including *Saul* and *Israel in Egypt*, when the Viceroy of Ireland invited him to that country to give the premiere performance of his newest oratorio, *Messiah*. It was well-received in Ireland and then produced in London.

By the time Handel had completed his oratorio, *Judas Macca-baeus* (in 1747), he was acknowledged once again as a popular composer by the British public. For the third time in his life he acquired financial security. A few years later, during work on *Jeptha*, he was afflicted with failing eyesight. After three unsuccessful opera-tions, he was totally blind. In spite of this, he continued to accompany his oratorios from the organ console. On April 6, 1759, his *Messiah* was given its final performance of the season with the blind composer at the organ. Less than a week later, on the Saturday between Good Friday and Easter, he passed away.

Handel, honored composer of England, was buried with royal ceremonies in Westminster Abbey alongside the former Kings and Queens of England, a magnificent monument marking his crypt.

BIBLIOGRAPHY

Flower, Sir Newman. *George Frederic Handel: His Personality and His Times*.
    London: Cassell and Company, 1959.
Weinstock, Herbert. *Handel*. New York: Alfred A. Knopf, 1959.

MESSIAH

(*An Oratorio*)

GEORGE FRIDERIC HANDEL

The *oratorio* and the *cantata* were the two most important vocal forms of Baroque music performed without scenery, costumes, or action. The oratorio was the larger form, usually written for soloists, a large chorus, and a good sized orchestra. The text, usually sacred, was non-liturgical, and frequently of extended length. The form developed in Italy (where Handel learned of it), and was in its earlier form acted out upon the stage similar to the operas. In its later development, scenery and costumes were eliminated; musically it was separated from the opera category (in general) by its heavier reliance on large choral movements, and by the fact that there were no quick question-answer sequences between two soloists as in the dramatic action of an opera. The oratorio was generally preceded by an orchestral overture. The dramatic text was divided into movements which were assigned by the composer to either solo voices (including ensembles) or to the chorus. As in opera, recitatives frequently were used for narrative purposes.

At the invitation of the Viceroy of Ireland, Handel journeyed to Dublin and produced the first performance of *Messiah* on Good Friday, April 13, 1741. It was received most successfully and additional performances of it were soon scheduled for London. The work is cast by the composer in three main sections: the first relates of the advent and birth of a Messiah; part two is concerned with Jesus' ministry on earth; and the final part concerns the death and resurrection of Jesus. By omitting all of the third part, and about half of the second, *Messiah* is most frequently performed in the United States, not as an Easter oratorio, but as a Christmas oratorio.

The text of *Messiah* is taken entirely from the Bible. It is subdivided into fifty-three separate movements, and is scored for four solo voices, a four-voiced choir, and a large orchestra with continuo. Five of these movements are described below, the number before the title indicating their position in the complete oratorio.

No. 12: CHORUS: *For unto Us a Child Is Born*.

The text of this chorus, cast in fugal form, is from the ninth chapter of Isaiah, verse six. The subject of the fugue is introduced in turn by sopranos, tenors, altos, and an incomplete statement by the basses. The subject of the fugue:

Example 1

For un-to us a Child is born   Un-to us   a Son is

giv-en,   un-to   us   a Son is   giv-en

For unto us a Child is born,
Unto us a Son is given.

Immediately after the entrance of the tenors with the subject, the sopranos are heard with a second melody derived from Example 1:

Example 2

For un-to us a Child is born———

A melodic phrase is introduced by the tenors and imitated by the sopranos, then the combined basses and altos:

Example 3

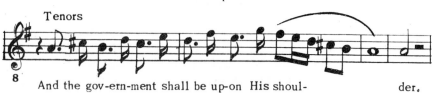

And the gov-ern-ment shall be up-on His shoul-   der.

And the government shall be
Upon His shoulder;
And His name shall be called

A bold chordal passage follows:

Example 4

Won-der-ful,   Coun-sel-lor,   The might-y God, The

ev-er last-ing Fa-ther, The Prince of Peace

Wonderful, Counsellor,
The Mighty God,
The Everlasting Father,
The Prince of Peace.

A polyphonic passage occurs in which the tenors are heard with Example 2, the altos entering a measure later with fragments of the fugue subject, Example 1. The altos then turn to the episodic melody, Example 3.

The harmonic passage, Example 4, is repeated by the chorus.

A fugal passage is heard in which the tenors announce the subject, Example 1, followed in turn by the sopranos and basses. The altos enter with Example 2.

Example 3 is heard again and leads to Example 4 in harmonic form.

A development of the subject, Example 1, in the men's voices is in counterpoint to the development of Example 2 in the women's voices.

Example 3 leads to the final phrase of the chorus, Example 4. No. 20: ARIA: *He Shall Feed His Flock Like a Shepherd.*

The aria is introduced by a contralto recitative using a text from Chapter XXXV of Isaiah, verses 5 and 6:

> *Then shall the eyes of the blind be opened,*
> *And the ears of the deaf unstopped.*
> *Then shall the lame man leap as an hart,*
> *And the tongue of the dumb shall sing.*

The aria is in two parts, the first sung by the contralto soloist, and after a two-measure modulation (a chordal progression leading to another key), the soprano soloist sings the second verse to the same melody with very slight rhythmic and melodic variations.

The contralto portion of the aria is in *binary* or *two-part* form: the same melody is used for the first two lines, and a new one is introduced for the concluding lines. The opening:

Example 5

The second melody is derived from the first:

Example 6

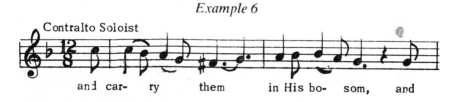

and car- ry   them   in His bo- som,   and

gen - tly lead those   that   are   with young,

Contralto:

> *He shall feed His flock*
> *Like a shepherd,*
> *And He shall gather*
> *The lambs with His arm,*
> *And carry them in His bosom,*
> *And gently lead those*
> *That are with young.*
> > (Isaiah 40: 11)

Soprano:

> *Come unto Him,*
> *All ye that labour,*
> *Come unto Him,*
> *Ye that are heavy laden,*
> *And He will give you rest.*
> *Take His yoke upon you,*
> *And learn of Him,*
> *For He is meek*
> *And lowly of heart,*
> *And ye shall find rest*
> *Unto your souls.*
> > (Matthew 11: 28, 29)

No. 44: CHORUS: *Hallelujah!*

This chorus closes the second part of the oratorio. The tradition is that audiences always stand when this chorus is performed.

The movement is cast in the mixture of polyphonic and harmonic writing that characterized *For Unto Us* already described. The opening phrase of this chorus is in harmonic style:

Example 7

A Subject, which will later be treated fugally, is introduced by the chorus in unison:

Example 8

The chorus responds with four *Hallelujahs*, and then the three lower voices restate Example 8.

The fugal passage is introduced by four harmonic *Hallelujahs*. Example 8 is heard entering first in the sopranos, followed in turn by the basses and tenors in unison, then by the altos and tenors in unison.

A soft harmonic passage follows in which the chorus sings the text:

> *The kingdom of this world*
> *Is become the kingdom of our Lord*
> *And of His Christ.*

A fugal section occurs based on a new Subject:

Example 9

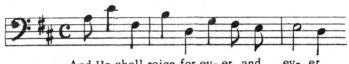

And He shall reign for ev- er and　　ev- er

Successive entrances of the Subject are by: basses, tenors, altos, and sopranos.

The women's voices declaim the words, *King of Kings; and Lord of Lords* on sustained pitches, rising a step each time they repeat it. The men repeat the words, *for ever and ever, Hallelujah!*

The fugal Subject, Example 9, returns in the basses who are imitated by the sopranos. Altos and tenors have a counter-subject.

The tenors this time intone the words. *King of Kings* on sustained pitches as the other three voices respond with, *for ever and ever . . .*

The concluding passage is a contrapuntal treatment of Example 9, stated first by the basses and entering two beats later in the alto. The basses repeat Example 9 and lead to the concluding measures in which the chorus triumphantly proclaims, *King of Kings, and Lord of Lords, Hallelujah!*

No. 45: ARIA: *I Know That My Redeemer Liveth.*

This soprano aria introduces the third section of *Messiah.* The text is taken from Job 19: 25-26 and I Corinthians 15: 20.

An eighteen measure orchestral introduction is based on Example 10. The soprano then enters:

Example 10

Soprano Soloist

I　　know　that　　my　Re- deem- er　liv-eth,

I know that my Redeemer liveth,
And that He shall stand
At the latter day upon the earth.

The opening phrase, Example 10, and its after-phrase are repeated both in text and melody, although the after-phrase is somewhat extended in the repetition.

The second melody of this aria follows a nine measure orchestral interlude:

Example 11

And though worms de-stroy this bod-y   yet in my

flesh shall I   see God,

And though worms destroy this body,
Yet in my flesh shall I see God.

A section is heard which starts and finishes with a variation of Example 10 and its text; the middle is a variation of Example 11 and its text.

The concluding section is based on the melody of Example 12:

Example 12

For now is Christ ris-en   from the dead,

For now is Christ risen from the dead,
The first fruits of them that sleep.

No. 53: CHORUS: *Worthy Is the Lamb That Was Slain.*

The oratorio concludes with this mighty chorus, the text from the fifth chapter of Revelation. It opens with bold chords:

Example 13

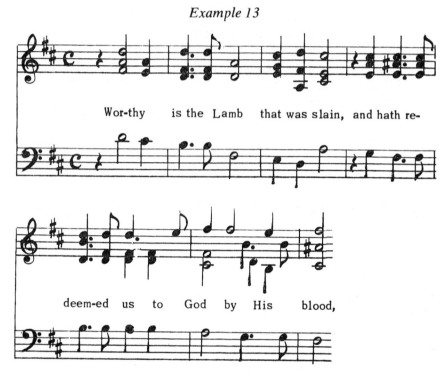

A fugal passage follows, the Subject being announced by the tenors and basses:

Example 14

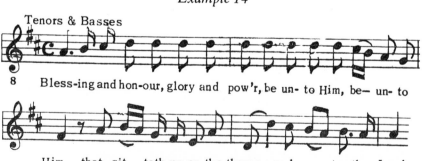

Example 14 is sung, in turn, by sopranos, altos, then basses.

After a cadence, Example 14 is heard again, this time in *stretto* (the second statement entering before the first is finished). It appears, in turn, sung by basses, altos, sopranos, and tenors. Example 14 then passes freely between the voices in an extended section.

The section based on Example 14 ends with a full cadence. A new fugal Subject is introduced by the basses:

Example 15

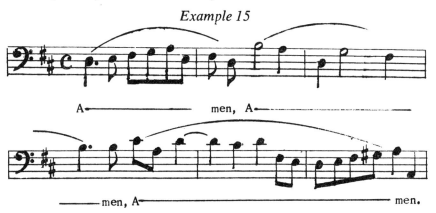

Example 15 enters polyphonically in each higher voice: after the basses, the tenors, next the altos, and finally the sopranos.

A ten measure orchestral interlude leads to the final section of the chorus. Example 15 is stated by the basses and then moves freely throughout the voices as the music builds to the final cadence.

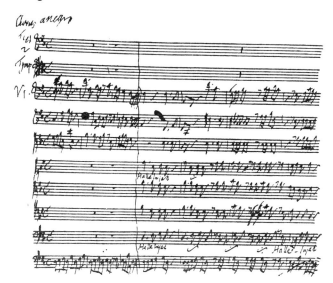

A page from Handel's original manuscript of *Messiah*

JOHANN SEBASTIAN BACH

BORN: March 21, 1685; Eisenach, Germany.
DIED: July 28, 1750; Leipzig, Germany.

The name of Bach is a legend in the musical history of Germany. As Ernest Newman says, "the known history of the tribe extends over seven generations, and members of it still flourish, though the direct male line of the composer died out in the nineteenth century. The stock was pure German of the sturdiest physical and mental type; and a surprisingly large proportion of it was musically gifted."*

Johann Sebastian Bach's father was the town musician of Eisenach, and probably was also the Court Musician to the Duke. Johann Sebastian received his elementary education at the Gymnasium (or school), while he learned the violin and viola from his father. When Johann was nine, his mother died. Although his father remarried, he died within a year. The ten-year-old Johann was sent to Ohrdruf (some thirty miles from Eisenach) to live with his elder brother Johann Christoph who was the organist at St. Michael's Church in that town. From his brother, Johann received his first keyboard lessons and probably his first lessons on the pipe organ.

When he was fifteen, Johann Sebastian had to find a means of earning his own living. He became a chorister at St. Michael's Church in Lüneburg, some 200 miles from his brother's home. It is likely that he walked this distance to take the position. He spent three years at the Lüneburg church, making several trips to nearby cities to hear more music. He walked thirty miles to Hamburg to hear the famous German organist Reinken (then eighty) play, and also made several trips to Celle where the court orchestra played music from the French repertoire. What schooling Bach had in the formal art of composition, he received from the Lüneburg organist, Georg Böhm.

At eighteen Bach joined the staff of Duke Johann Ernst in Weimar as a string player and organist. After five months in this position, he was appointed organist for St. Boniface Church in Arnstadt where a newly completed pipe organ attracted him. He encountered difficulty there with both the ministerial staff and the congregation because of his improvisations and original compositions which they did not appreciate. He took a leave from this position to travel to Lübeck to hear the famous organist Buxtehude play, and failed to return to Arnstadt until commanded to do so.

*In Oscar Thompson's *Cyclopedia of Music and Musicians*.

Resigning his position at Arnstadt, Bach became the organist at Mühlhausen where he stayed for a year. He married during his tenure there and felt that the salary was not sufficient to support a family. He next took a position as an organist and chamber musician to Duke Wilhelm Ernst of Sachsen-Weimar. During the nine years that he occupied this post, he composed some of his finest organ works and a number of church cantatas. Bach, his wife, and four children, then moved to Cöthen where he served the Prince as a musical director. The Prince was of the "reformed" faith and thus no cantatas were used in the church services. The few cantatas Bach composed while at Cöthen were secular. The Prince particularly took delight in orchestral music and was proud of his own eighteen-piece orchestra. Concentrating mainly on instrumental works during his days in Cöthen, Bach composed six *Suites* for orchestra, six *Brandenburg Concerti,* six *French* and six *English Suites* for the harpsichord, his violin concerti, the two- and three-part *Inventions* and the first part of the *Well-Tempered Clavier.*

The death of his wife left him with the added responsibility of rearing and looking after his children, one daughter and four sons. A year and a half later he married the daughter of the court trumpeter, a girl named Anna Magdalena. His household was always a happy one, and Anna Magdalena did much to further her husband's music, even to copying parts. In addition to the five surviving children of his first marriage (the twins born to his first wife died shortly after birth), they raised seven daughters and six sons of their own. Many of Bach's compositions were written as educational pieces; the two- and three-part *Inventions* are a fine example.

On Good Friday of 1723, Bach applied for the position that was vacant at the church in Leipzig, conducting his recently completed *Passion According to St. John* as a trial. He was accepted and assumed the duties of caring for the music in both Leipzig churches, St. Thomas and St. Nicholas, in addition to superintending the training and performance of both the vocal and instrumental students associated with the churches. He remained with this position the balance of his life. During this "Leipzig" period, he composed 265 church cantatas, several secular cantatas, five settings of the Mass (including the *B Minor Mass*), four Passions (including the *Passion According to St. Matthew*), both a Christmas and an Easter oratorio, and the last part of the *Well-Tempered Clavier.* In 1736 he edited the hymns published in Schemelli's *Musikalisches Gesangbuch* (Musical Songbook), adding eighteen original tunes.

During his lifetime, Bach's fame was principally that of a fine organist. All of his compositions were written in the traditional forms of the Baroque era, and they were already becoming slightly out-moded by the newer school of composition which was paving the way for the Classical era. Several of his own sons were more famous than their father during his lifetime because they were writing com-positions in the new style. Few of Johann Sebastian's compositions were published during his lifetime, and a great many manuscripts of his cantatas were lost before a later generation undertook the publi-cation of all of his music.

One of his last compositions was the *Art of the Fugue*. As a master of the contrapuntal forms, Bach endeavored in this work to demonstrate all the possibilities of development of one fugal Sub-ject. It remained in open score at his death (four lines simply indi-cating the four voices, but not specifying the performing medium) and today it is usually performed by either an organ or a string quartet.

In his last years, Bach's eyesight started to fail rapidly, and an operation was arranged with the English surgeon-oculist, John Taylor, who had treated Handel's blindness. The operation was unsuccessful and total blindness ensued. His last composition, the choral prelude *Vor deinen Thron tret' ich hiermit* (I Tread Before Thy Throne), was dictated. His sight was suddenly restored on July 18, 1750, but he was then struck by apoplexy and died ten days later of a paralytic stroke.

BIBLIOGRAPHY

Schweitzer, Albert. *J. S. Bach.* 2 vols. New York: The Macmillan Company, 1950.
Spitta, Philipp. *Johann Sebastian Bach.* 3 vols. New York: Dover Publications, 1951.

FUGUE IN G MINOR
("Little")

JOHANN SEBASTIAN BACH

A fugue may be vocal or instrumental, and is written for two or more voices (the independent lines are called voices regardless of whether they are vocal or instrumental). The voices enter inde-pendently, and in a sequence of the composer's choosing; on their initial entrance, each is heard with the melody on which the fugue is based, known as the *Subject*. The accompaniment one voice pro-vides for another is known as the *counterpoint,* since the melodies run counter to each other. During the initial section of the fugue, known as the *exposition,* the first voice plays an accompaniment to the statement of the Subject by the second voice; if this second melody is reproduced faithfully each time a new voice enters, it is known as the *Countersubject.* This latter term is also applied to new melodies occurring later in the fugue. The passages separating the entrances of the Subject are called *episodes.* The second statement of the Subject usually occurs on the dominant (fifth tone of the scale), and is known as the *Answer* to the Subject which was heard in the tonic, or root of the scale.

This fugue was composed for the pipe organ while Bach was the organist at Weimar, written somewhere around the year 1712. He wrote two fugues in G minor, so musicians refer to this one, which is the shorter, as "The Little" to distinguish it from the longer one, known as "The Great."

This is a four-voice fugue built on the following Subject:

Example 1 (Subject)

figure A

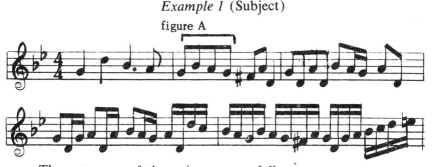

The entrances of the voices are as follows:
   in G minor
   in D minor, below the first voice (short episode)
   in G minor, one octave below the first voice
   in D minor, one octave below the second voice

After the *exposition,* in which all four voices have stated the Subject, the second melody of this fugue, known as the *Countersubject,* a four-note figure, is heard:

Example 2 (Countersubject)

The Subject returns in G minor, but only the first part is heard before it appears an octave higher (known as *stretto,* an overlapping of entrances).

A brief episode occurs.

The Subject is presented twice in B-flat major, first in the middle voice, then in the bass.

The Countersubject, Example 2, is heard again.

The Subject, Example 1, appears in C minor, and is followed by an episode based on the rhythmic figure of Example 2, the Countersubject.

A rising sequence (a pattern repeated over and over) occurs, built on Figure A of the Subject, Example 1. This builds to a climax.

A final statement of the Subject, Example 1, occurs in the bass voice.

SUITE NO. 3

In D Major

Johann Sebastian Bach

One of the most popular genres of the Baroque composers was the *Suite.* It generally consisted of an overture, followed by a number of independent dance movements. Bach called his orchestral suites by the French title, *Ouvertures.* In this one (which English speaking people call a *suite* to distinguish it from the more popular conception of *an* overture) he follows the overture with four French dance movements — an *Air,* a *Gavotte* (actually two gavottes), a *Bourrée,* and a *Gigue.* The orchestra consists of strings, two oboes, three trumpets, and timpani.

AIR

The term *air* was derived from usage in the French ballets of pre- and early Baroque times. In the Baroque suites, an *air* is distinguished from the other dance movements by the song-like nature of its melody, and lacks the strong rhythmical aspects of the others. One of Johann Sebastian Bach's most lyrical themes is the basis of this movement. It was rewritten for solo violin in 1871 by August Wilhelmj and transposed down to the key of C major so that the melody could be played on the low, or G string, of the violin. It is frequently heard in this version, known as the *Air on the G String.*

The theme is a slow but continuously flowing melody played by the violins:

Example 1

The bass accompaniment is a continuous patter of eighth-notes in octaves:

Example 2

The inner voices move in counter-melodies, moving when the principal melody, Example 1, is sustained.

GAVOTTE

The Gavotte movement is actually two separate gavottes, numbered by Bach as *Gavotte I* and *Gavotte II*. The first is repeated after the second gavotte, thus forming the pattern: I—II—I. The gavotte is a French dance which originated with the peasants from the Pays de Gap region, known as "gavots." It is a robust dance in 4/4 meter.

The *Gavotte I* begins with a melody in the oboes, violins, and trumpets:

Example 3

The second melody of this gavotte is an inversion of the first melody:

Example 4

Gavotte II opens with a melody played by the full orchestra:

Example 5

Violins

The second part of this gavotte begins with Example 5, this time heard in A major, with a brilliant trumpet counter-melody accompanying it.

After a modulation back to D major, *Gavotte I* is repeated.

BOURRÉE

The bourrée is a rhythmic dance that probably originated in the Auvergne. It is in quick duple meter and begins on the up-beat.

The first theme is introduced by the oboes and violins:

Example 6

Violins

The first section, eight measures in length, is repeated and modulates to the key of A major.

The second section, which is also repeated, is based on Example 6 heard in A major.

In a transitional section, a new theme is introduced:

Example 7

Violins

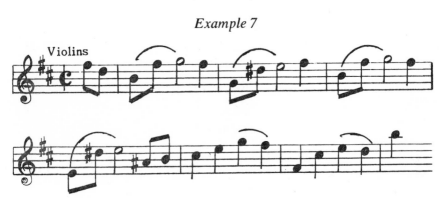

After a modulation which returns the tonality to D major, Example 6 is heard again.

GIGUE

The gigue is an exuberant dance in triple meter, usually based on one of two rhythmic figures:

The violins and oboes introduce the main theme:

Example 8

A second theme, based on the repetitive triple eighth-note figure, is announced by the violins:

Example 9

Example 8 returns, this time in the key of A major, followed by a repetition in B minor.

After a modulation through F minor, Example 8 returns to G major.

The tonality of D major is reached through another modulation, and leads to a final cadence in this key.

BRANDENBURG CONCERTO NO. 2

In F Major

JOHANN SEBASTIAN BACH

Bach composed six concerti grossi which are all known as *Brandenburg Concerti*. A meeting took place between Bach and the Margrave, Christian Ludwig of Brandenburg (son of the Great Elector), at which the Margrave invited the composer to write a set of concerti grossi for his own private orchestra. Bach obliged by completing six such works.

The *concerto grosso* form was the principal medium of composition for orchestral music of highest stature in the Baroque era, comparable to the position of the *symphony* in the later Classical era. The word *concerto* derives from a Latin verb, *concertare,* meaning "to fight side by side." In all concerti, there are two different groups of sound: the orchestra, and either a solo instrument or a small group of instruments. They "play" side by side the same musical material as equals, not as a solo and an accompaniment. In the concerto grosso (*grosso* meaning "large"), the orchestra is contrasted with a *group* of instruments, originally two violins and a cello. The term concerto grosso was employed to differentiate such works from the *solo concerto* in which the orchestra was contrasted with a single, solo instrument.

The concerto grosso originally emerged from the dance suites of the period and consisted of numerous movements, all in dance form, and alternating between slow and fast tempi. By Bach's time, the concerto grosso pattern had become well established as a three movement form, the first and third movements being *allegros,* and the second movement being slow. Frequently the slow movement was played only by the small group of instruments, and in cases such as Bach's *Brandenburg Concerto No. 1,* was written for only three instruments, hence the title *trio* for the middle section.

The Bach *Brandenburg Concerto No. 2* is scored for an orchestra of strings (known as the *tutti,* i.e., the full group), and a small ensemble (known as the *concertino,* or "little" concertising group) consisting of a flute, an oboe, a violin, and a high trumpet (now played by the *D trumpet* or *Bach trumpet,* and obsolete after the Baroque era).

FIRST MOVEMENT: *Allegro.*

The concerto opens with both the tutti and the concertino playing the principal theme of this movement:

Example 1

Example 2 is heard four times as outlined below:

Example 2

Example 2 — concertino violin
Example 1 (two measures) — tutti
Example 2 — concertino oboe
Example 1 — tutti
Example 2 — concertino flute
Example 1 — tutti
Example 2 — concertino trumpet

After a contrapuntally developed section, the trumpet of the concertino restates Example 2.

The tutti once again appears with Example 1, and a new counter-theme is introduced by the trumpet:

Example 3

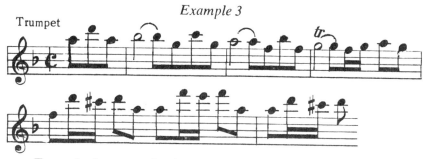

Example 2 returns in the concertino, but successive statements of it are not interrupted by tutti passages. Example 2 is heard, in turn, played by flute, violin, oboe, and trumpet.

The concluding section of the movement is played by both the tutti and the concertino and is based on Example 1. It is heard first in the tutti violins, then the solo trumpet.

The counter-melody, Example 3, is heard briefly in the solo oboe and imitated two beats later by the solo trumpet.

The trumpet is heard twice more with Example 1, the tutti following with rhythmical developments from it.

A short coda based on Example 1 concludes the movement.

JESU, JOY OF MAN'S DESIRING
From *Cantata No. 147*

JOHANN SEBASTIAN BACH

Bach composed five sets of cantatas, each set containing a cantata for every Sunday of the liturgical year, a total of 295 cantatas, of which 202 have survived. The cantata (from the Italian verb *cantare,* "to sing," as opposed to *sonare,* "to play") was one of the most frequently used vocal forms of the Baroque era, and could be either secular or sacred. It usually consisted of a number of movements which were linked by a narrative or descriptive text. The various movements were set as soli, duets, recitatives, and choruses. Some of the Bach cantatas are for solo voices only, although most of them are for one or more solo voices and chorus. The instrumentation of the accompaniment varies widely throughout the series.

Chorals, the congregational hymns, were the heritage of the Lutheran church, going back to the earliest days of the Reformation. Practically all of Bach's sacred cantatas were based on chorals. Sometimes he used only the melody, and at other times he employed both the music and text. Many of the cantatas end with the choral in its original form.

Cantata No. 147, "Herz und Mund und Tat und Leben" (Heart and Mouth and Soul and Spirit), was written for the fourth Sunday in Advent. It was composed about 1716 and then reworked into its present form about 1727. It is divided into two parts, there being six movements in the first and four in the second. The cantata is scored for four solo voices, chorus, and an orchestra of strings, trumpet, oboes, bassoon, and continuo.

The cantata is divided as follows:

Part I: chorus
        tenor recitative
        alto aria
        bass recitative
        soprano aria
        choral
Part II: tenor aria
        alto recitative
        bass aria
        choral

The text is non-Biblical (only the earliest of Bach's cantatas made use of texts from the Bible), written by Salomo Franck, who, along with Erdmann Neumeister, supplied most of the texts for the church cantatas. The same choral appears at the end of the first and second parts; the first verse is used the first time, the second verse at the end of the cantata. This choral is frequently performed by itself.The melody of the choral, as in the majority of Bach chorals, is not original with the composer. The melody, titled *Werde munter, mein Gemüthe* (Come Awake, My Mind), is by Johann Schop and was found in a hymnal published in 1642. Bach liked this melody so well that he employed it in three different settings (he frequently used the same melody in more than one work). The original choral, as Bach harmonized it, appears below:

Harmonized by J. S. Bach   Johann Schop (1642)

This choral consists of eight lines. The principal melody (which may be designated by the letter A) is the first line, while a variation of it (A_1) with a more definite ending (on the tonic) is the setting for the second line. These two melodic lines (A and A_1) are repeated for the third and fourth lines of the text. The fifth and sixth lines are set with a different melody (B and B_1), the second of these two lines being only slightly altered from the first to bring that pair to a more definite ending. The concluding two lines of the choral are similar to the first two (A and A_1). This is known as a *ternary* or three-part form in which the first and third parts are nearly identical.

These pairs of lines are separated by orchestral interludes. The pattern for the interludes is established in the introduction in which the violins and oboe play a flowing melody in triplets:

Example 1

The flowing violin-oboe melody is continuous throughout the composition with the exception of the first line (and its repetition) of the choral:

Example 2

Je- su, Joy of   man's de- sir-ing.

Jesu, Joy of man's desiring
Holy Wisdom, Love most bright;

Six measures of the orchestral interlude are heard before the first two melodic lines of the choral are repeated (this is the custom with chorals, to repeat the first two lines melodically with a different text):

Drawn by Thee, our souls aspiring
Soar to uncreated light.

After the next orchestral interlude, a new melody (closely related to the first and developed from it) is heard:

Example 3

Word of   God, our   flesh   that fash-ion'd.

Word of God, our flesh that fashioned,
With the glow of faith impassioned,

A two measure interlude leads to the return of the first melody
(Example 2):

Striving still to Truth unknown,
*Life attaining near Thy throne.**

A ten measure orchestral postlude concludes the setting.

---

*This is the text generally used when this composition is sung in English.
It is a free translation of verses 6 and 17 of Martin Jahn's poem. written in 1661.
"Jesu, meiner Seelen Wonne" (literally, Jesus, My Soul's Delight) which is used in
place of the text from the cantata that starts:

It is well for me that I have Jesus.
Oh, how firmly I hold to Him.
That He will refresh my heart
When I am sad and ill.

CHAPTER V

MUSIC OF THE CLASSICAL ERA

THERE IS NO WORD IN MUSIC that has more connotations and is more misused than the word *classic*. It has three separate and distinct meanings: (1) to the musician, it refers to music composed in the last part of the eighteenth and very early nineteenth centuries (and it is in this sense that this book uses the word); (2) by the definition in the dictionary, it refers to a work of the "first class or rank; a work, especially in literature or art, of the highest class and of acknowledged excellence"; and (3) to the average layman, the term is used in contradistinction to the term *popular* which refers to commercial and dance music.

The term *classic* was first applied around 1820 in reference to music of the late eighteenth century to suggest that it had abandoned the ornateness and over-decoration associated with the earlier Baroque era. A return had been made to the ideals of the classic culture of ancient Greece with its formal beauty within unity, its clarity of purpose and self-control in expression. It was an intellectual approach rather than an emotional one.

It was a product of a cosmopolitan age. Foreign rulers were to be found throughout Europe — German kings in England, Sweden, and Poland; a Spanish king in Naples; a German princess as Empress of Russia. Artists were associated with capitals far removed from the lands of their birth: the Frenchman Voltaire was at the Prussian court; the Italian poet Metastasio at the Viennese court; Italian opera composers were in residence in Paris and London. It was because of the cosmopolitan atmosphere that the Viennese Haydn was hailed in London, the German Gluck at the capital of France.

Princes and their courts were to be found throughout Europe, but they were rapidly declining in power and influence. It was still possible for Haydn to be an employee of a court on the same level as all the other household servants. This was not considered disagreeable, because everyone was in the service of the princes except other

The home in Salzburg in which the Mozarts lived; Wolfgang was then about seventeen

The chamber orchestra of Frederick the Great

princes. Musical concerts and operatic performances were still governed and sponsored by the courts; public concerts had not yet developed.

This was called the age of *Enlightenment;* but art must not be complicated as it had been in the Baroque! Rousseau, the noted French philosopher, wrote that music was "the art of pleasing by the succession and combination of agreeable sounds, . . . the art of inventing tunes and accompanying them with suitable harmonies; to sing two melodies at once [as in the polyphonic style of the Baroque] is like making two speeches at once in order to be more forceful."

The musicians that have been associated with this period are Gluck, Haydn, Mozart, and the early Beethoven. For many years it was believed that Haydn created some of the forms in use, such as the symphony. More recent research has revealed that the concepts of the Classical era were already in progress before the Baroque era was finished. While Johann Sebastian Bach was busy composing some of the greatest masterpieces in the Baroque idiom, four of his sons were busy developing the forms, including the symphony, that were to be the highlights of the later era.

Musicians in and around the court at Mannheim, Germany (known as the "Mannheim school" of composers), were at work establishing the *sonata* and the *symphony* as the cornerstones of the new style. Polyphonic writing was no longer supreme; the emphasis was placed on the melody which was to be accompanied by simple chords. A formal structure for compositions was established — the *sonata-allegro* form (see Haydn for a description), and the *rondo*. The dominating tradition of the Classical era, opera, was reformed.

The invention of the pianoforte (now commonly known simply as "the piano") was by its very name to change the style of keyboard composition. Because of its different action, this new instrument could play both soft (*piano*) and loud (*forte*), and all the shades of dynamics between the two. Gradual dynamic changes within a phrase became possible and were indicated in the later music of the Classical era. The instruments of the orchestra became more standardized, so that the average court orchestra had a full complement of strings (discarding the old Baroque members of the viol family except for the bass), and woodwinds and horns were regularly employed. Instrumental music could then grow without relying on choral forms. With the age of Enlightenment, society detached itself from a close association with the church, and secular forms of music came into prominence.

One caution must be mentioned, however. The over-generalization that music of the Classical era was all form without emotion, and that music of the later Romantic era was all emotion without form is completely false. Music of the Classical era was a portrayal of emotion within restricted limits, a controlled expression. Music of the Romantic age expressed emotion much more freely, and liberties were taken with form to serve this purpose, but form was never abandoned.

BIBLIOGRAPHY

Bukofzer, Manfred. *Music of the Classical Period, 1750-1827*. Berkeley: University of California Press, 1955.

FRANZ JOSEPH HAYDN

BORN: March 31, 1732; Rohrau, Austria.
DIED: May 31, 1809; Vienna, Austria.

The life of Joseph Haydn refutes the old adage that all musicians are financially poor and die young. He was the last of the famous musicians to have a patron, the Prince of Esterházy. From the Prince, he received a handsome fixed income, to which was added considerable profit from the sale of his compositions. Born the same year as George Washington, Haydn lived to be seventy-seven at a time when the average life span of a man was several decades shorter.

Joseph Haydn was the second son of a wheelwright who served as sexton and organist of the village church. His father was also a fine tenor, and music was performed in their home every Sunday. When Joseph was five years old, his musical talent was noticed by his cousin, a choir director and school teacher. The cousin took the boy home with him and gave him musical instruction in singing, the violin, and other instruments, as well as lessons in Latin. The musical director of St. Stephen's Cathedral in Vienna had his attention called to this precocious lad of eight and was so impressed that he found a spot for him in the choir at the Cathedral.

As was the custom of the time, singing in the Cathedral choir also provided board and room as well as instruction in both music and academic subjects. Haydn's later accounts of life at the Cathedral school make several references to the scarcity of both food and a good education in his case. When Haydn's voice broke, the Cathedral no longer had use for his services, so he was released. His only possessions were "three poor shirts and a threadbare coat."

A friend provided him with a temporary bed and soon loaned him 150 florins so he could rent a room of his own, one that had a rickety old harpsichord. Haydn supported himself by giving music lessons to children, playing in serenades that were then so popular in Vienna, and by becoming an accompanist for an Italian singing teacher. By the time Haydn was twenty, he had composed sonatas, trios, a mass, and a musico-dramatic work that had been performed at the state theater.

Haydn's first position of official stature was at the castle of Count Fürnberg, where he played chamber music and for whom he composed a number of works. Through the Count, Haydn became acquainted with Count Morzin who appointed him his music director. In his new position, Haydn wrote his first symphony in his twenty-seventh year. It was during his tenure with the Count that the girl whom Haydn had fallen in love with took the veil, so he married her older sister, Anna Keller. This was the most unfortunate move of his entire life. Anna cared nothing for the arts, was extravagant, and the marriage caused Haydn nothing but trouble.

Count Morzin experienced some financial difficulties and had to dismiss his employees, but saw to it that Haydn was introduced to Prince Paul Anton Esterházy. The Esterházy estate at Eisenstadt had been completed only a few years earlier, a spacious estate modeled after Versailles. The owners were among the richest and most influential families in all of Europe. Haydn received an appointment from the estate, an association that was to last for forty-eight years.

The fact that Haydn's status in the household was the equivalent of any servant did not bother him at all, for this was the custom of the time and was to be expected. His duties were many and varied: he handled many administrative matters, he was in charge of both music and instruments, he had to take care of the personal needs of the musicians employed by the court, he conducted the orchestra, he directed the opera presentations given in the theater of the castle, he took part in chamber music performances, and he was expected to compose new works for all these functions. The Esterházys did a great deal for the cause of music, and, when Prince Niklaus succeeded his deceased brother in 1762, the status of music and the musicians greatly improved. The new Prince requested, in addition to daily music, two weekly operatic performances and two formal concerts. While in the service of Prince Niklaus, Haydn composed eighty symphonies, forty-three quartets, and nearly all of his many operas.

Anton succeeded Niklaus on the latter's death in 1790 and the activities of the castle, including music, were greatly curtailed. Haydn's stipend was increased; but, since regular performances were no longer required, he was free to travel. In Vienna, he met Mozart and the two became good friends and helped each other in music: Haydn helped Mozart in the composition of quartets, while Mozart helped Haydn in the creation of operas.

An impressario from London by the name of Salomon passed through Vienna and became acquainted with Haydn. He encouraged the composer to travel to London and write some music for the orchestras there. Haydn spent eighteen months in England, and was so well received by the public that the University of Oxford conferred upon him the honorary degree of Doctor of Music. On this and his following visits to London, Haydn wrote a series of symphonies known either as the "Salomon symphonies" or the "London symphonies."

He returned to Vienna with a little over $10,000 he had made in Great Britain and with 768 pages of new compositions. Emperor Franz II was crowned shortly after Haydn returned to Austria, and it was during this period that Haydn gave lessons to Beethoven. He returned to England in 1794. The King insisted that the composer make London his permanent home. Haydn declined the invitation. He returned to the Esterházy estate to organize music for still another new Prince that had succeeded to the title.

The following years were filled with some of Haydn's most important compositions. In London, he had heard Handel's *Messiah* for the first time and became greatly interested in choral composition. He composed the Austrian national hymn in 1797; *The Creation,* an oratorio, in 1798; and another oratorio, *The Seasons,* in 1801.

His health began to fail and he lived in a small home in Vienna in retirement. With a friend, he started cataloguing all the many compositions that he had written over a long and full life-time. His death was hastened by the bombardment of Vienna by Napoleon and the French army.

BIBLIOGRAPHY

Geiringer, Karl. *Haydn: A Creative Life in Music.* New York: W. W. Norton and Company, 1946.

Landon, H. C. Robbins. *The Symphonies of Joseph Haydn.* London: Universal Edition and Rockliff Publishing Corp., 1955.

The change from the harpsichord to the piano as the principal keyboard instrument was largely effected during the Classical Era. All photographs on pages 141, 142, and 143 courtesy of The Metropolitan Museum of Art, The Crosby Brown Collection of Musical Instruments, 1889.

Clavichord. A direct descendant of the monochord and one of the first keyboard string instruments. With a compass of 28 notes, its keys are fitted with blades of brass called "tangents" which strike the string and divide it; several pitches are produced by any one string.

Spinet or Virginal. It has a compass of a little over four octaves. The "Plectra" or quills fitted into the jacks set the string in vibration by plucking them.

Harpischord — the most important keyboard instrument during the Baroque and the early years of the Classical Eras. With a compass of 4½ octaves, there were two or three strings for each key. A jack with a quill gave individuality of tone, and with the use of stops (draw bars or foot pedals), the player could change the number of strings sounded by each key, thus giving a change in the dynamic level. Most harpsichords had two manuals (keyboards) so that contrasts in volume could be effected between notes played on the upper and lower manuals.

Piano Forte. The dulcimer was the prototype of the piano, and the invention of the hammer action by Bartolomeo Cristofori about 1710 gave this instrument more power and a wide dynamic range.

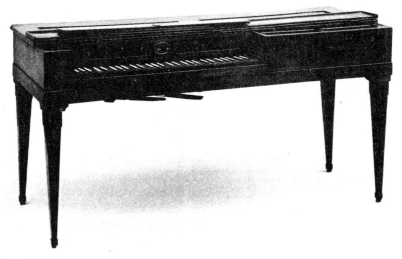

PIANO made by Anton Vatter in Vienna, in the late 1700's. The light, primitive hammer action of the Viennese piano makers (Stein, Streicher, Vatter) gave performers an opportunity to develop an even, light, and facile touch. Mozart was very fond of this early type of piano.

PIANO made by André Stein of Vienna early in the 1800's. The need to play repeated notes on the piano fostered the invention of the double escapement action, which also gave the performer further possibilities in touch and tone. Mozart and Beethoven used pianos embodying these developments.

SYMPHONY NO. 88

In G Major

Franz Joseph Haydn

Although Haydn is known as "the father of the symphony," the statement is not correct in its original intention. Now that many works of the "Mannheim" school, which included two of Bach's sons — Johann Christian and Karl Philipp Emanuel — are known, it is evident that the symphony, and the patterns of the individual movements, were well established by Haydn's time. The "father of the symphony" statement is correct in the sense that Haydn was able to infuse into the form such artistry as had not been heard before.

The symphonic pattern established in the Classical era was of four movements, usually in the sequence outlined below:

First movement: *sonata-allegro* form
Second movement: a slow movement, usually quite lyrical
Third movement: *Minuet and trio* form
Fourth movement: usually a *rondo,* sometimes in the *sonata-allegro* form

The characteristics of the separate movements and their forms will be discussed movement by movement.

FIRST MOVEMENT: *Adagio-Allegro.*

The first movement form, known as the *sonata-allegro* form, was a unique development of the Classicists from trends evident at the end of the Baroque era. Its chief characteristic is the use of two separate melodies or subjects; another important element is a middle section in which a development of one or both themes takes place.

The name of the form is perhaps confusing to the musical novice. The hyphenated word is derived from the general use of this form as the first movement (usually in an *allegro* or "cheerful" tempo) of *sonatas* (works to be played by instruments in contrast to works meant to be sung, *cantatas*).

Below, in outline form, is the standard pattern of the *sonata-allegro* form, with its key relationships and indicated repetitions.

Introduction   slow; either in chordal style or with a theme of its own.

EXPOSITION

Principal Subject	the more important of the two themes, usually bold — sometimes quite lyrical.
bridge	a passage in which a modulation takes place to prepare the proper key for the Second Subject.
Second Subject	the less important of the two themes; in either the dominant key (if the symphony is in major), or the relative minor (if the symphony is in minor). Frequently this theme is quite lyrical in contrast to the Principal Subject.
Closing episode	a passage which definitely brings the exposition to a close, and in which a modulation back to the tonic key of the symphony takes place.

(At this point a repeat to the beginning of the Exposition is always indicated, so that the two themes on which the movement is based will become firmly implanted in the listener's mind. Unfortunately many phonograph performances, and occasionally concert performances, ignore the repeat in the interest of time.)

DEVELOPMENT	in this second main section, the composer treats the Principal Subject, and sometimes the Second Subject, in variations and fragmentary sections. Usually these appear in a number of different keys, some far removed from the tonic key.

RECAPITULATION

Principal Subject	this is repeated in its entirety, in its original key, and usually with little change in the orchestration.
bridge	this passage resembles the first bridge, but this time does not modulate.

Second Subject

this is repeated in its entirety, but in the tonic key. Whatever changes are made in it either melodically or in its instrumentation are usually dictated by the difference in the key from its initial presentation.

Coda

the counterpart of the Introduction. This section brings the movement to a full, and usually bold, conclusion. It is generally based on thematic material already presented, most commonly fragments of the Principal Subject.

Haydn opens the *Symphony No. 88* with a slow introduction (marked *Adagio*), based on its own theme, Example 1. The introduction is sixteen measures in length.

Example 1 (Introductory Theme)

The *exposition* opens with the Principal Subject (eight measures in length) stated by the violins. It is quite rhythmical in nature.

Example 2 (Principal Subject)

The Principal Subject, Example 2, is stated a second time by the strings and woodwinds.

A thirty measure bridge modulates from the key of the Principal Subject, G major, to its dominant key, D major, for the Second Subject.

The Second Subject is presented by the violins (note that even though it is in a different key, the *key signature* does not change; the *accidentals* are written in to effect the change):

Example 3 (Second Subject)

The closing episode of the *exposition* is thirty-two measures in length, and modulates up to the point where the next down-beat will be a G major chord (the G major chord will either be the first in the repeat of the entire *exposition,* or the first chord of the *development* after the repeat has been made).

The *development* is concerned primarily with the Principal Subject, Example 2. After an eighth-note figure for four measures, the Principal Subject appears in A-flat major. Following a ten measure modulation, it is then repeated in A major. Fragments of it are then heard in several other keys.

Figure A of Example 3, the Second Subject, appears briefly in the violins and flutes. Two measures later, the Principal Subject reappears in the oboe and strings.

The *development* closes with a fourteen measure episode in which the music modulates back to the tonic key of G major.

The *recapitulation* starts coincident with the return of the Principal Subject, Example 2, as it was first heard. A slight change in orchestration is made with the addition of a flute obbligato. The theme, Example 2, is played a second time, with the woodwinds playing the melody and strings accompanying.

The bridge passage returns, but this time stays in the key of G major.

The Second Subject, Example 3, is recapitulated in the key of G major by the violins.

The *coda* which brings the movement to a close is based on the opening figure of the Principal Subject, Example 2.

SECOND MOVEMENT: *Largo.*

The second movement is based on a single lyrical theme which is introduced by an oboe and a solo cello:

Example 4

A series of variations on Example 4 follows; the first three start out almost identically to Example 4 and then develop differently:

Variation 1: by the flute and solo cello.
Variation 2: by oboe and solo cello.
Variation 3: by flute and violins in A major.
Variation 4: by oboe and solo cello in D major.
Variation 5: by first violins and celli in F major, then D minor, and returning to A major.
Variation 6: by oboe, first violins, and celli (opening phrase only) in D major.

A *coda* crescendos to a *fortissimo;* the movement ends *pianissimo.*

THIRD MOVEMENT: Minuetto and Trio. *Allegretto.*

The minuet (or *minuetto,* a small minuet) was the only dance form of the Baroque suites that did not become obsolete at the end of that era. It was employed as the third movement of the Classical symphony.

The minuet is in 3/4 meter, and usually a very stately tempo (although since it was not written to accompany the dance, it became faster as the Classical era progressed). It is divided into three parts, the first and third being the same. The middle section, known as the *trio,* was a contrasting section both in themes, and frequently in key. Its name is derived from the Baroque *trio-sonatas* in which only three instruments played the middle section for contrast. Although the full orchestra participates in the *trios* of the *minuet and trio* form, it is usually a thinner instrumentation than the minuet, and frequently softer and more delicate in texture.

The *minuet and trio* is based principally on two themes — one each for the minuet and trio. Each has a subordinate theme derived from the principal one. This form, if outlined, would appear as follows, assuming that a number affixed to a letter (as in A_1) stands for a melodic derivation of the original theme.

MINUET	A theme
	A theme repeated
	A_1 theme (usually twice the length of A)
	A_1 theme repeated
TRIO	B theme (generally more lyrical in nature than the A theme)
	B theme repeated
	B_1 theme (usually twice the length of B)
	B_1 theme repeated
MINUET	A theme
	A_1 theme

The return to the minuet is seldom written out in music, the symbol *D.C. al fine* being used to indicate that the first section is to be repeated. *D.C.* stands for *da capo,* meaning "from the beginning to the end," *fine* (or "end") being previously indicated in the music at the end of the minuet. This form is therefore occasionally referred to as a *da capo* form, meaning a three-part form in which the first and third sections are the same, musicians understanding that on the repetition of the first section, none of the individual repeat signs are observed.

Haydn's *minuet* of the *Symphony No. 88* opens with its theme played by the violins and flute:

Example 5 (A theme)

A repetition of this ten measure melody is indicated.

The second part of the minuet is based on a theme derived from A, played by the woodwinds and strings:

Example 6 (A₁ theme, derived from Example 5)

A repetition is made of the second part of the Minuet.

The *trio* is based on a second theme which is played by the oboe and violins:

Example 7 (B theme)

The first part of the trio is repeated.

The second part of the trio is based on a variation of the B theme:

Example 8 (B$_1$ theme, derived from Example 7)

The second part of the trio is repeated.

A return is made to the minuet. The A theme, Example 5, is heard once.

The second part of the minuet based on Example 6 is heard once and concludes the movement.

FOURTH MOVEMENT: *Allegro con spirito.*

The *rondo* form is the one most frequently employed for the final movement of Classical symphonies, although others are used. It was originally derived from the rondel in verse, and became one of the first established "forms" in music. It consists of a principal or rondo theme which alternates with several episodes based on secondary themes. The name *rondo* implies at least two such episodes.

In the Haydn symphony under discussion, there are eight episodes (the principal theme appearing between each one) based on five secondary themes. Outlined, it would appear as follows:

Principal theme, repeated
   Sub-theme A
Principal theme
   Sub-theme A
Principal theme
   Sub-theme B
Principal theme (in a variation)
   Sub-theme C
Principal theme
   Sub-theme A, repeated

Principal theme (in a second variation)
    Sub-theme D
Principal theme
    Sub-theme A
Principal theme
    Sub-theme E
Principal theme

The Principal Theme is stated by the violins, a melody similar to a Viennese folk tune:

Example 9 (Principal Theme)

Example 9 is repeated.
The first Sub-theme is introduced by the violins:

Example 10 (Sub-theme A)

The Principal Theme, Example 9, is heard again, followed by a repetition of the Sub-theme A, Example 10.

The violins repeat the Principal Theme, Example 9, and then introduce the second Sub-theme:

Example 11 (Sub-theme B)

A variation of the Principal Theme, Example 9, is followed by the third Sub-theme:

Example 12 (Sub-theme C)

The Principal Theme, Example 9, returns and is followed by the first Sub-theme, Example 10, played twice.

A second variation of the Principal Theme, Example 9, is heard. A new Sub-theme is introduced:

Example 13 (Sub-theme D)

The Principal Theme (Example 9), the first Sub-theme (Example 10), and the Principal Theme (Example 9) are heard in succession.

The last Sub-theme is heard:

Example 14 (Sub-theme E)

The final statement of the Principal Theme, Example 9, concludes the symphony.

WOLFGANG AMADEUS MOZART

BORN: January 27, 1756; Salzburg, Austria.
DIED: December 5, 1791; Vienna, Austria.

A contemporary letter by Friedrich Grimm describes Mozart's travels and abilities:

We have just now seen Herr Mozart, who during his stay in Paris in 1764, had so great a success. He has been in England eighteen months, and six months in Holland, and has of late [come] back here, on his way to Salzburg. All over, there has been but one opinion, he has astonished all connoisseurs. . . . As early as two years ago, he has composed and edited sonatas; and since then, he has had six sonatas printed for the Queen of England; six for the Princess of Nassau-Weilburg; he has composed Symphonies for a large orchestra, that have been performed and were acclaimed with great praise. He has even written several Italian arias, and I am not giving up hope that he will [soon] have written an opera for some Italian theater.

This letter ends with a revealing fact, "this curious boy is now nine years old!"

Never before or since has there been such a precocious child in the field of music. Of the seven children born to Leopold Mozart and his wife, only two survived: Maria Anna (known to the family as Nannerl) and Wolfgang. Leopold Mozart was an excellent violinist who not only was the assistant concertmaster of the Court orchestra at Salzburg, but was the court composer and the author of a book on violin technique. Young Wolfgang, in bed for his nap, could hear the piano lessons his sister Nannerl received in the parlor. He was so interested in the keyboard that at three he could pick out many chords and melodies, and with instruction, he could play the piano well by the time he was four. His first compositions, short works for the keyboard, were written when he was five.

Leopold Mozart was a sensitive and appreciative musician. He recognized the exceptional talent that both Nannerl and Wolfgang exhibited at the harpsichord. He took both children and presented them in a recital at the Court of Munich when Wolfgang was six. He then took them to Vienna, the capital of the Holy Roman Empire, and presented them in a concert for the Empress Maria Theresa and her court. They did so well and were accepted by the Empress with such enthusiasm that the two children were soon playing in all the homes of the Viennese nobility.

Wolfgang's first compositions were published when he was seven.

Josef Haydn in his sixtieth year, painted during a visit to London

The mature Mozart

Haydn's "musical" calling-card

(Translation: "Gone is all my strength, old and feeble am I.")

In the same year someone gave him a half-size violin which he learned to play exceptionally well without formal lessons. He also learned to play the pipe organ without instruction, once the function of the pedal-board was explained to him.

Later that year, Leopold decided to take his children on an extended tour that led them to Munich, Heidelberg, Frankfurt, Cologne, Brussels, and to Paris where they played at the Court of Louis XV. In London, they played for King George III, Wolfgang reading at sight various works that the King placed before him — compositions by Johann Christian Bach and Handel. The Mozarts were so well accepted in Great Britain that they spent many months there. It was during an illness of Leopold, when the children were forbidden to play any instrument for fear of disturbing their father's rest, that Wolfgang composed his first two symphonies. These were frequently played during the next few months. Several of Wolfgang's compositions, largely keyboard works, were published during their stay in England.

The Mozarts returned to Austria via The Hague and Bern, only to arrive home during a smallpox epidemic. Wolfgang caught the dread disease and for nine days was sightless. The Emperor Joseph II of Austria invited Mozart to write an opera, and *La Finta Semplice* (The Simple Fake) was soon completed, followed by another, *Bastien and Bastienne*. Wolfgang returned with his father to Salzburg when the Archbishop appointed him concertmaster of the court orchestra (without salary!). The boy spent his time composing masses and symphonies.

Leopold Mozart decided that a trip to Italy was necessary for Wolfgang to have a well-rounded education. Actually there were three separate trips to that country, the first when Wolfgang was thirteen. They traveled through and gave concerts in several Italian cities, proceeding as far south as Naples. The following description of Wolfgang's concert in Mantua, when he was fourteen, is quoted to show what was expected of him:

A symphony of his own composition; a harpsichord concerto, which will be handed to him, and which he will immediately play from sight; a Sonata handed to him in like manner, which he will provide with variations, and afterwards repeat in another key; an Aria, the words for which will be handed to him, and which he will immediately set to music and sing himself, accompanying himself on the keyboard; a Sonata for harpsichord on a subject given him by the leader of the violins; a Strict Fugue on a theme to be selected, which he will improvise on the harpsichord; a Trio, in which he will improvise the violin part; and finally, the latest Symphony composed by himself.

In Rome, during Holy Week, he heard a performance of Allegri's *Miserere,* copies of which were not permitted outside of the Vatican. Wolfgang went home and wrote out all the parts from memory. Years later (after Mozart's death), when copies of the original score were available to musicians, they checked Mozart's copy made from memory against it and found not one mistake! Pope Clement XIV was so fascinated by the boy's playing that he conferred on him the Order of the Golden Spur. In Milan, Mozart wrote and had produced a new opera. Leopold and his son then returned home, having in their possession two commissions for new operas.

Wolfgang's last trip to Italy was made when he was seventeen, but he did not raise the furor that he had on his first two. No longer was he a phenomenon, a child prodigy. After this venture, he returned to Salzburg and his father started to look for a court position for his son, hoping that he might become permanently attached to one of the wealthier courts and never have need to worry about financial matters. With this in mind, Leopold sent Wolfgang with his mother off on a trip to Paris via several other cities. Paris failed to welcome the twenty-two year old musician as it had earlier. He was offered a position as Court Organist at Versailles at an insignificant salary, but he wisely refused it. His mother became ill in Paris and passed away. This was Wolfgang's first experience of not being under the direct guidance of either his father or mother. He stayed on in Paris for some time and renewed his acquaintance with Johann Christian Bach whom he had first met in London as a child. On his journey home, he stopped in Mannheim where he became acquainted with the Weber family, a family of four lovely girls, all of whom were fine opera singers. Wolfgang thought he had fallen in love with the oldest, but bid her a fond farewell and returned to Salzburg.

Home again, Mozart was appointed the Court and Cathedral Organist by the Archbishop of Salzburg. Relations between the two became strained, and when the Archbishop refused to let Mozart go to Vienna to play in a benefit concert, a permanent break in their relationship occurred. Wolfgang moved to Vienna; now twenty-five, he was free of all commitments for the first time in his life. He found lodging with the Weber family that he had earlier met in Mannheim and who had now moved to the Austrian capital so that the girls could sing in the opera house.

Mozart enjoyed the musical climate in Vienna; he met the famous Haydn, and also participated in a contest with Clementi, well-known for his keyboard *sonatinas*. His first operatic creation in this new city was *The Abduction from the Seraglio*. His keyboard works were written exclusively for the piano which had become familiar in all the concert halls and in private homes, supplanting the earlier harpsichord.

Mozart married Constanze Weber in spite of objections from his father. Although she was a fine singer, her temperament did not make her an ideal wife. The house was frequently in a state of disorder, she managed money poorly, and spent what income her husband made very foolishly, so that Wolfgang never again knew freedom from financial worries or debts.

Mozart turned to intensive creative work, turning out in a short period of time: *Le Nozze de Figaro* (*The Marriage of Figaro*) produced in Vienna in 1786; *Don Giovanni* (*Don Juan*) produced in Prague in 1787; his last three symphonies, numbers 39, 40, and 41 in one year — 1788; *Così fan Tutti* (*Women Are Like That*) produced in Vienna in 1790; and *Der Zauberflöte* (*The Magic Flute*) produced in Vienna in 1791.

Mozart made a trip to Berlin and visited Dresden and Leipzig along the way. He played on the organ at Johann Sebastian Bach's church, the Thomaskirke, in Leipzig, remarking, "Here is one man from whom we can all learn." On his return, his health showed signs of giving way. His final illness has never been diagnosed by the medical profession.

It was during this illness that a gentleman, wishing to remain anonymous, appeared and gave him a commission for a *Requiem Mass for the Dead*. In his semi-delirious state, Mozart imagined him to be an envoy from death giving him a commission to write his own funeral music. Months after Mozart's death the mystery was solved: a Count Franz von Walsseg was in the habit of commissioning great composers to write works which he would pay for, sign, and exhibit as his own creations.

Mozart started to work on the *Requiem,* quite frequently being unable to leave his bed. He was working on the "Lacrymosa" on the morning of December 4 when partial paralysis set in. A priest was called and extreme unction given. He died a little past midnight that same evening. His wife Constanze was completely overcome, and not one friend of theirs showed up to comfort the distraught wife. On the following day, one friend did arrive, but he limited his help to telling Constanze how she could arrange for the least expensive funeral service, a third class one. That day the service was held for Wolfgang Amadeus Mozart, a third class service. The unaccompanied hearse left afterwards for a common grave for paupers. To this day, no one has any knowledge of exactly where Mozart is buried.

BIBLIOGRAPHY

Biancolli, Louis L. *The Mozart Handbook: A Guide to the Man and His Music.* Cleveland: World Publishing Company, 1954.
Einstein, Alfred. *Mozart, His Character and His Work.* New York: Oxford University Press, 1945.

SYMPHONY NO. 40

in G Minor

WOLFGANG AMADEUS MOZART

Mozart's last three symphonies, Nos. 39, 40, and 41, were completed in three months' time in 1788, one each in June, July, and August. The one under discussion, No. 40, did not, in its July, 1788, manuscript call for clarinets, and many miniature scores are published from that copy. Mozart later revised the orchestration and included two clarinets which took over many of the parts originally assigned to the oboe. Since most conductors perform from the later, revised score, this analysis follows that instrumentation.

Three of the movements of this symphony are based on the sonata-allegro pattern — the first, second, and fourth. The third movement is in the Minuet and Trio form.

FIRST MOVEMENT: *Allegro molto.*

The movement opens with the Principal Subject played by the violins, accompanied by the lower strings:

Example 1 (Principal Subject)

Example 1 is repeated.

A bridge passage modulates to the relative major key, B-flat. The Second Subject begins in the violins with a little figure by the clarinet and bassoons:

Example 2 (Second Subject)

Example 2 is repeated.

The closing portion of the *exposition* is based on Figure A of Example 1, which is repeated several times by clarinets and bassoons, against an augmentation of it in the violins.

The *development* treats only the Principal Subject, Example 1. At first, most of the theme is heard as it moves from key to key, then only Figure A of it is heard. This section ends as finally only the first three notes of Figure A are heard, sometimes inverted.

In the *recapitulation,* the bassoon joins in a counter-melody as the strings repeat the Principal Subject, Example 1.

The Second Subject, Example 2, appears twice, the first time in G major (it was originally in the major mode), and the second time in G minor.

Figure A of Example 1 is heard again and again as the *recapitulation* closes.

The opening portion of the Principal Subject, Example 1, is heard twice in the *coda.* The second violins are heard first with it, and before they finish it, the first violins play it in counterpoint to the second violins. A series of final chords concludes the movement.

SECOND MOVEMENT: *Andante.*

The Principal Subject appears softly in the strings:

Example 3 (Principal Subject)

It is repeated.

After a transitional section modulates to the dominant key, B-flat major, the Second Subject is introduced by the violins:

Example 4 (Second Subject)

The *development* is based on Figure A of Example 3, which is repeated several times, each time in a different key; it also alternates between the strings and the woodwinds.

The Principal Subject, Example 3, returns to open the *recapitulation*.

After a rather extended bridge, in which fragments of Example 3 are heard, the Second Subject, Example 4, is repeated in E-flat.

The movement closes with a few chords immediately after the Second Subject has been heard.

THIRD MOVEMENT: Minuetto and Trio. *Allegretto.*

The first theme is played by the violins:

Example 5

Example 5, which is fourteen measures in length in its entirety, is repeated.

The second part of the *minuetto* is based on a theme derived from Example 5. It is played by the woodwinds:

Example 6 (Derived from Example 5)

The second part of the *minuetto* is twenty-eight measures in length and is repeated.

(Trio)

The first theme of the trio is presented by the first and second violins in thirds:

Example 7

This section of eighteen measures is repeated.

The second part of the trio is based on a theme derived from Example 7:

Example 8 (Derived from Example 7)

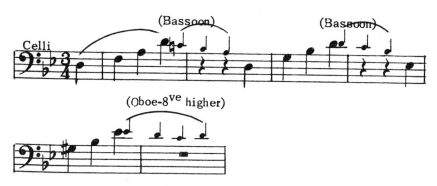

The French horns are heard prominently in the last portion of this section which is also repeated.

Both parts of the *minuetto* are heard again, but this time neither section is repeated.

FOURTH MOVEMENT: Finale. *Allegro assai.*

The Principal Subject is introduced immediately. It starts with upward leaps for the strings (the tonic chord), answered by the full orchestra:

Example 9 (Principal Subject)

The Second Subject is less energetic and more lyrical:

Example 10 (Second Subject)

The *exposition* closes with repetitions of Figure B of Example 9.

Once again Mozart is concerned only with the Principal Subject, Example 9, in the *development*. Figure A from Example 9 appears first in the strings and is then echoed one measure later by the woodwinds. Each time this dialogue is repeated, it is done in a different key.

After a brief pause, the Principal Subject, Example 9, is *recapitu-, lated*.

The Second Subject, Example 10. returns in G minor.

Figure B of Example 9 returns in the *coda* and leads to the final chords of the symphony.

CHAPTER VI

MUSIC OF THE ROMANTIC ERA

THE ROMANTIC era in music began to emerge in the early nineteenth century and reached its peak just before the last quarter of the century started. The name "Romantic" is derived from the German literary school of the late eighteenth century. The Teutonic writers tried to avoid the formalism of the earlier Classical School, and turned for inspiration and ideals to the Middle Ages with its valiant knights and gracious ladies. The German term *romantisch* originally referred to the Romanesque era (about the eleventh and twelfth centuries) and it was this term they adopted to suit their purposes.

A political as well as artistic revolution started in the late eighteenth century with the assertion of the "natural rights of man" by the philosopher Jean Jacques Rousseau. The men of the early eighteenth century accepted the rules of symmetry, static rules of order, established conventions and rules of conduct expected of several castes of society. Harold Nicolson says in an article, "The Romantic Revolt," in *Horizon,* the Romantics "preferred freedom to order, adventure to conformity, surprise to recognition, imagination to correctness, the natural to the artificial, the irregular to the regular, individual expression to tradition."

The French Revolution was a logical outgrowth of the desire of men to be considered as individuals and as equals — "liberty, equality, fraternity" was the motto. What started in France as the action of one country within its own borders, soon spread throughout Europe as Napoleon declared himself Emperor. As his forces captured country after country, their life, even after Napoleon's defeat at Waterloo, never returned to the formalism of the old aristocracy. Nationalistic pride and an insistence on the rights of the individual became of prime importance.

In the arts, too, the assertion of the individual became important; subjection to styles and forms of the past was put aside. Where art had been formal and perhaps artificial, "the bleeding heart" was now

HECTOR BERLIOZ CONDUCTING

A contemporary German cartoon which pokes fun at the excesses Berlioz used in the size and instrumentation of his orchestra.

exposed. As C. H. H. Parry has said in *The Evolution of the Art of Music,* the movement "expresses the complete emancipation of human emotion and mind, and attempts to give expression to every kind of mood and of inner sensibility which is capable and worthy of being brought into the circuit of an artistic scheme of design."

In the German literary school mentioned in the first paragraph, certain characteristics became noticeable in its effort to avoid the formalism of the earlier age. It became interested in legends and fairy tales; a new interest in folk lore and folk songs took place. It attempted an emotional interpretation of nature. The old tales of knight errantry and the chivalrous worship of women were revived from the Romanesque era. Sentimentality and the extremes of personal emotion were vividly portrayed.

Musically, the change from Classicism to Romanticism was gradual. Von Weber's opera, *Der Freischütz,* was one of the first examples in Germany of the new era. It not only flattered the pride of the Germans to see an opera based on one of their old legends, but they were happy to see the portrayal on stage of the common man, the peasant, where earlier operas had dealt with nobility exclusively. It paralleled the literary movement in its story, for it included the supernatural as well as the extremes of personal emotion. In France a new path was forged by Hector Berlioz with his early work, *Symphonie Fantastique.* Although the older Classical form of a symphony is visible throughout, he attempted to paint a musical picture of his own life.

He portrayed, musically, his "Beloved One" and her debasement as an individual. In the final movement, she appears as the most grotesque figure in *The Witches' Sabbath.* Probably Beethoven's name is associated with the early Romantic era more than any other. His own personal life was an assertion that he considered himself the equal of any and all nobility. His philosophy of the right of the common man found itself realized in the motto of the French Revolution. Napoleon's reversal of all this when he declared himself Emperor is graphically illustrated by Beethoven. His *Symphony No. 3* bore the dedication on its title page to *Napoleon Bounaparte,* but it was scratched out with a pen knife by the composer and replaced by a new dedication, "To the memory of a great man" — to the memory of what he had stood for. Beethoven's first two symphonies are excellent models of the Classical symphony in their symmetry and adherence to the formal pattern. With *Symphony No. 3* much of this is pushed aside to let the artist create his own personal expression. Form is not abandoned, but it is subjugated to the needs of the artist.

With Schubert, the development of the *lied,* or Romantic art song, was a personal expression. With the excellence of the new Romantic poetry, he was able to fuse text, melody, and accompaniment to a unified creation that expressed the extremes of human emotion. It perhaps helped pave the way for the short piano pieces (the *Harvard Dictionary of Music* calls them "character pieces") that were so much a part of this epoch. At first these short pieces had names of little meaning — *Bagatelles* by Beethoven; *Moments Musicales* by Schubert; *Songs Without Words* by Mendelssohn. Robert Schumann, who gave each short piano work a descriptive title, was musically able to present the subjective mood.

The association of programmatic elements with music led to the creation of the symphonic poems of Franz Liszt and the tone poems of Richard Strauss. The music dramas of Richard Wagner encompassed the same idea on a more extensive scale. The formal aspects of Classicism, however, were never lost. Johannes Brahms was able to take the best elements of Romanticism and utilize them in the old patterns, thereby earning the name of a "Romantic Classicist."

In the beginning of the twentieth century, the excesses of the Romantic era had reached an extreme. The orchestra had grown in size from the Mozartian orchestra of thirty-five, to a thousand performers (in several choruses and orchestras) in Gustav Mahler's *Symphony No. 8.* So much personal emotion had been portrayed in both music and literature that it was now accused of being over-emotional. Music, as an abstract art, had gone as far as it could in its programmatic implications. What was left of the Romantic school in the twentieth century, when it merged into Impressionism and New Music, was largely a combination of the legacy left by Brahms in absolute music and Richard Strauss in the tone poem. The last vestiges of Romanticism were in evidence in the music of Rachmaninoff, Sibelius, and Strauss.

BIBLIOGRAPHY

Barzun, Jacques. *Romanticism and the Modern Ego.* Boston: Little, Brown and Company, 1943.

Einstein, Alfred. *Music in the Romantic Era.* New York: W. W. Norton and Company, 1947.

CARL MARIA VON WEBER

BORN: November 18, 1786; Lübeck, Germany.
DIED: June 5, 1826; London, England.

The von Weber family at one time had been landed gentry with estates throughout Germany. Franz von Weber, Carl's father, inherited only the "von" of petty nobility, for the estates had disappeared from the family possessions. After Franz was mustered out of the army at the end of the Seven Years' War, he married and started a traveling theatrical troupe which consisted mainly of his relatives. Two sons were born to him and his wife as they moved from village to village, staying as long in each location as the public was willing to buy tickets. Frau von Weber couldn't take the rigorous life and passed away, a thoroughly wretched and worn-out individual. Franz decided that his boys should become musicians, hoping that they might be child prodigies such as Mozart had been. He took them to Vienna where he enrolled them for lessons with Haydn. Franz became enamored of the daughter of the proprietor of the boarding house where he placed the two boys, and married her. Carl Maria was their first child, born so sickly that he could not walk until he was four years old. He was troubled with a disease of the right hip bone that later in life left him permanently lame.

Carl's father once again took to the theatrical trail, taking both his wife and Carl with him. The boy was prevented by this constant travel from obtaining any kind of a formal education, but in its place received a first hand knowledge of plays and the theater that no other composer had ever had. Disappointed that his first two sons did not show much musical aptitude, Franz was determined to have a musician in the family and started to teach Carl music at an early age. The boy learned to play the piano well, had a good singing voice, and composed profusely in an amateurish way. Carl also had lessons in harmony and composition. At eleven the father enrolled him for lessons with Michael Haydn (Joseph's younger brother).

Aloys Sennefelder, a friend of Franz von Weber, was a prolific author, and in an effort to get some of his works published, invented the process of lithography. Sennefelder needed help in his shop and inquired of Franz about young Carl's helping him. The father saw this as an opportunity for his son not only to learn the new process, but a chance for the boy, then thirteen, to publish inexpensively some of his many compositions.

FELIX MENDELSSOHN-BARTHOLDY

HECTOR BERLIOZ

CARL MARIA VON WEBER

ROBERT SCHUMANN

Probably the best-known likeness of the composer

The unrelenting father was able to arrange for a performance of his son's *The Forest Maid* at a little theater the following year. The work made no impression on the audience whatsoever. A similar fate befell *Peter Schmoll and His Neighbors* which his father staged three years later. Franz then decided that the boy needed a more comprehensive knowledge of music and took him to Vienna to study with Abbé Vogler — a musician and composer whom some Viennese praised highly and whom others thought a charlatan Through his work with Vogler, Carl was appointed the conductor of the Breslau Opera House when he was barely seventeen and a half.

Carl remained at the Breslau theater for two years, during which he raised their standards of performance. It was not easy, as the opera company resented having a mere youth as their director. When he left that position he was installed by the Duke and Duchess of Carlsruhe in Silesia as the director of their court theater. It was the custom at that time for nobility with vast estates to maintain their own court theaters, orchestras, and opera companies. The Duke was most cordial to Carl, and allowed him to bring both his father and an aunt to live on the estate. The Napoleonic wars, at their height in central Europe, necessitated the Duke leaving to serve in the army. The Duchess kept the court musicians on as long as she could, but the economies of war finally forced her to close the theater. She introduced Carl Maria to Duke Ludwig of Wüttenberg who was in need of a personal secretary.

Weber's duties for Duke Ludwig had nothing to do with music, and for the two and a half years Carl remained in this position, he handled only clerical details. A rather unfortunate series of circumstances ended this service. Duke Ludwig's brother was King Frederick of Stuttgart (married to the daughter of George III of England). The King maintained a very large court and extracted as much money in taxes and liens as he could from the people in his kingdom so that he and his court could enjoy all the pleasure that life had to offer them. The King, however, had no use for his brother, Duke Ludwig, Carl's employer.

Carl discovered one day that his father had borrowed quite a large sum of money which he couldn't possibly repay. Carl assumed this debt but did not have the ready cash to settle the account. A friend of the Duke's court offered to loan Carl the money, saying he could obtain it from a gentleman by the name of Huber. A short time after the money was borrowed and his father's debt paid off, Huber approached Weber and told him that he had paid the money in good faith so that Weber, as private secretary to the Duke, would see that his son wasn't drafted into the army. That week a summons had arrived for his son to report for duty. It became clear to Weber that he had been tricked by his friend, but couldn't convince Huber that he was under the assumption that the money was a loan, not a bribe to keep Huber's son out of the army. Huber went immediately to King Frederick with his story. For some time Frederick had been seeking a way in which he could embarrass and degrade his brother, the Duke. He had also known for some time that quite a number of men had been evading service in the large armies being raised to fight Napoleon. This had been possible through bribery at the court. Here was his first evidence of it. He lost no time in having Weber placed in jail and the facts, as he believed them, made known throughout the kingdom.

"Since with the 26th of February a new epoch in my life began," wrote Weber on his release from prison, "God has indeed given me many vexations and adversities to contend with . . . Truly I can say in these ten months I have grown *better:* my sad experiences have taught me; I have at last become regularly industrious."

During the years 1813-1814, Napoleon's power was declining and a new wave of nationalistic feeling swept across Germany, the people having aspirations for independence. Theodor Körner, a poet, had written many works based on this theme, and when he was killed by a bullet while fighting the Napoleonic forces, his works enjoyed a new popularity. Weber set one of Körner's poems, *Kampf und Sieg* (*Conflict and Victory*), as a patriotic cantata to celebrate Napoleon's defeat at Waterloo.

It was shortly after this that he resigned his position with the Prague Opera, stating, "It seems to me a higher thing in art to work as a composer for the whole world than to labor as musical director for the pleasure of a particular public; I must not let the years in which my strength may still remain in me slip by unused."

He tried first for a position in Berlin, but the Italian tradition was so well established there that the public wanted nothing to do with this composer of patriotic German cantatas. Weber was appointed to a post at the Dresden Opera; he thought he had been appointed as the principal director, but when he arrived, he found that they insisted an Italian had to be the director. Italian opera and artists had reigned supreme for over a hundred years and the public was completely satisfied with the status quo. Weber discovered that all the best singers and musicians were used by the Italian director, and that as part of his "German" staff he had inferior artists. He struggled bit by bit to improve the German staff.

Weber married one of the sopranos from this company. Their first child, a girl, lived only a few months. Their second was a boy whom they named Max (he later became a famous railway engineer and his father's biographer). It was soon after Max's birth that Weber recalled a story he had read many years before in Apel's *Gespenter Geschichten* (Ghost Stories) entitled *Der Freischütz*. He decided it was the basis of a good opera libretto and had his friend Kind write one. The premiere of the finished opera was scheduled for Berlin, but even this had to give way for the Italian tradition. The first performance of *Der Freischütz* was moved later in the week so that the premiere of an insignificant Italian opera could take place first. Although the opera house was full for the presentation of the Weber opera — Heinrich Heine, Mendelssohn, novelist E. T. A. Hoffman were there — the members of the Court were conspicuous by their absence. They wanted no part of a German opera. The Overture was enthusiastically received and had to be repeated. The first act went by with little interest since no women appeared in it. From the start of the second act, however, enthusiasm mounted and a thunderous ovation followed the final curtain.

On his return to Dresden, a second son was born. Weber's health began to fail; in fifteen months he composed only one insignificant song. He received a commission for a new opera. His doctor warned him that consumption had gone so far that there was no hope of a cure. If he rested and did no more work, he might live for six or seven years; if he kept at the pace he was then working, he could expect only a few more months. Weber decided to accept the London commission, hoping through it to obtain enough money for his wife and two sons to live on after his death.

With a flutist from his orchestra to help him move about, Weber left for England on February 16, 1826. He had hopes that his new opera, *Oberon*, would make his name well known in England and that he would be invited to the fancy salons as Rossini had been in London, thereby receiving additional sums of money to send his family. He was disappointed in this, for the sickly von Weber had little to offer society in competition with the genial and talkative Italian. He conducted the premiere of *Oberon* and eleven additional performances. It was obvious to him that if he were ever to see his family again, he must sail hurriedly for home. Arrangements were made to that end, and on the evening of March 5, he retired for bed at 10 P.M., for he was to leave early the following day. His host discovered the next morning that Weber had passed away during the night.

A funeral service was held and he was buried in London. Some eighteen years later, having become the national hero of German opera, funds were raised to have his body brought back to Germany. Memorial services were held when Weber was interred in a specially designed marble tomb. Richard Wagner gave an oration at the service, and composed special music for the occasion.

BIBLIOGRAPHY

Saunders, William. *Carl Maria von Weber.* New York: Pellegrini and Cudahy, Inc., 1940.
Weber. Max Maria von. *Carl Maria von Weber,* trans. J. P. Simpson. London. 1868.

DER FREISCHÜTZ

CARL MARIA VON WEBER

Der Freischütz is a unique work in the history of German opera. Up to the time of its appearance, Germany had been dominated by Italian opera, and although the last two Mozart operas had been written in German, no true break with the Italian tradition was in evidence. With *Freischütz,* not only was the way paved for Germanic opera that culminated in the works of Wagner, but the break between the older Classical era and the new Romantic movement was more clearly delineated.

In three acts, *Der Freischütz* relies on spoken dialogue rather than recitative. Infused in its set pieces are works of native origin such as the *Hunters' Chorus* which could never be mistaken for an Italian *brandisi* or drinking song. The spirit of Romanticism pervades its story of peasant life, with hints of the supernatural in the *Wolf's Glen Scene,* and its portrayal of the gamut of emotion: love, hate, jealousy.

The title first suggested for the opera was *The Trial Shot* and later changed to *The Huntsman's Bride.* When it was already in rehearsal, Weber changed to the present title, *Der Freischütz,* for which the English translation, *The Free Shooter,* means little.

Cast of Characters:

Max, *a forester* .... tenor
Agathe, *in love with Max* .... soprano
Cuno, *Chief Forester and Agathe's father* .... bass
Prince Ottokar .... baritone
Caspar, *a forester* .... bass
Killian, *a young peasant* .... bass
Zamiel, *the Black Huntsman* .... spoken
Annchen, *Agathe's cousin* .... soprano
Hermit .... bass

The scene is Bohemia after the Seven Years' War.

Overture

The *Overture* itself is a departure from the earlier tradition, for with few exceptions (one thinks of the theme from the Supper Scene in *Don Giovanni*), it was not customary to use in the Overture any of the melodies or themes from the opera proper.

An *Adagio* prelude introduces the Overture. It is based on a theme played by the strings and woodwinds:

Example 1

The French horns are heard with the next theme, one characteristic of the hunting horn so closely associated with German forests (and in Weber's day played on an orchestral horn not far removed from the ones used in the hunt):

Example 2

As the horn call fades away, the strings take up a tremulant figure, and double basses and timpani repeat low A, making the over-all effect quite sinister.

The tempo changes to *molto vivace,* and a theme from Max's aria ("What evil power is closing round me?") of the first act is heard:

Example 3

Example 3 merges into Example 4 which is played by full orchestra. It is a theme from the Wolf's Glen scene of the second act when Max cries out in terror at the horrors around him:

Example 4

This section culminates in another sinister string tremulo, followed by a clarinet melody:

Example 5

After a transitional passage, Agathe's aria (in which she speaks of eventual happiness with Max) from the second act is heard:

Example 6

The composer has now given a dramatic foreshadowing of what is to transpire: the setting in the German woods, the intrusion of evil powers, the horror and despair of Max, the trustfulness of Agathe, and the final triumph of simplicity and goodness. The balance of the Overture is developed from thematic fragments already quoted. The timpani and string bass repeated notes are heard again in their suggestion of the sinister.

After a dramatic silence of two measures, there is a single pizzicato note in the celli and double basses. After a second pause, a long crescendo in full orchestra leads to a final statement of Agathe's melody, Example 6, associated with her belief in ultimate happiness for Max and herself.

ACT I

SCENE: *An open space before an inn in the forest.*

The opera is based on an old folk legend known in Germany for many years before this work was written. It concerns the magic power of Zamiel, known also as the Black Huntsman or Evil One. Any hunter who knows the proper incantations and the right time and place to invoke them, can summon Zamiel. He may then bargain with Zamiel to cast seven bullets, known as "free bullets" (*Freikugeln*). The first six of these will hit any target that the hunter wishes; the seventh will hit the target that Zamiel wills. The huntsman who obtains these magic bullets is known as a "freeshooter" (*Freischütz*). The price that he pays for them is his own soul, to be delivered to Zamiel at the end of three years; or, a "stay of execution" may be obtained by supplying Zamiel with the soul of a third party in a similar bargain.

As the curtain rises on the first act, Max is seen seated at a table, tankard in hand, looking very dejected. He is supposed to be an outstanding forester with uncanny ability with a rifle, but in a contest just completed, he has lost to a peasant, Killian, without once hitting the target. All this just before the most important shooting event of his life! It is the custom on Prince Ottokar's estate that each new Chief Forester be appointed by winning a trial Contest. Cuno, the present Chief Forester, is about to retire and the contest has been announced. Not only does Max wish to be appointed to this high position, but Cuno has promised him his daughter Agathe's hand in marriage if he wins. Max is in love with Agathe, and she not only returns his affection, but expects him to win the contest and her hand.

The Wolf's Glen Scene in *Der Freischütz* designed by Wilhelm Reinking for the Hamburg Staatsoper, West Germany

Photo by Reinking

Caspar mixes the magic bullets in a cauldron over the fire. The apparition of the ghost and the wheel can be seen in the upper right.

Photo by Elizabeth Speidel

Caspar, another forester, is also in love with Agathe, but she is completely uninterested in him. In discouragement, he made the fateful bargain with Zamiel. It is through this pact with the Black Huntsman that he is able to throw a magic spell over Max so that he cannot hit anything. All of this is in preparation for a plan that Caspar has, for his three years of grace are up the following day.

As Caspar and Cuno approach the Inn, Max can no longer take the taunts that Killian has been throwing at him since winning the contest. Max leaps from his seat and is about to fight Killian when he sees Cuno and Caspar. Cuno is surprised to learn of Max's failure, and reminds him of the important contest coming up. Caspar furthers his plan by pouring a magic elixir in the cup of wine he draws for Max, but which has little effect. After the crowd and Cuno have departed, Caspar reminds Max that there is a certain way for him to win the contest: he can summon Zamiel and obtain magic bullets. Startled at the proposition, yet beside himself in desperation, Max agrees to meet Caspar in the Wolf's Glen at the stroke of midnight.

ACT II

SCENE 1: *A room in the ancient hunting lodge occupied by Cuno and his daughter. It is evening.*

Annchen is seen hanging up an old portrait that has fallen down and scratched Agathe on the forehead. As the two girls converse, Agathe tells of her visit to the old hermit that morning and his warning of danger. She assumes that the falling picture was the danger of which he spoke. As Annchen leaves, Agathe steps out onto the balcony of her room and raises her hands in a sign of prayer:

LEISE, LEISE, FROMME WEISE

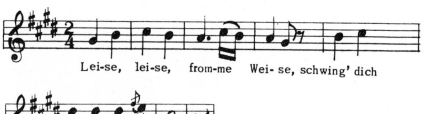

Lei-se, lei-se, from-me Wei-se, schwing' dich

auf zum Ster-nen krei-se!

In Act II of *Der Freischütz,* Annchen can be seen hanging up the old portrait in the ancient hunting lodge

Jürgen Simon, Theaterfotografie

The Huntsman's Chorus opens the final scene which takes place before the tents of Prince Ottokar.

Hamburgische Staatsoper, Peyer Foto

Leise, leise, fromme Weise,	Softly, softly, in a pious way,
Schwing' dich auf zum Sternenkreise!	
	My song wings heavenward!
Lied, erschalle, feiernd walle	May my prayer to heaven
Mein Gebet zur Himmelshalle!	Bring a blessing on our celebration!

SCENE 2: *The Wolf's Glen. It is approaching midnight.*

The scene is a weird, craggy glen, surrounded by high mountains down the side of which is a waterfall. To the left is a blasted tree on the knotty branch of which sits an owl. To the right is a steep path beneath which is a cave. The moon throws a lurid light over the scene. A few wind-battered pine trees are scattered here and there. Caspar, in shirt-sleeves, is making a circle of black stones; a skull is in the center. Nearby is a ladle, a bullet mold, and an eagle's wing. Thunder is heard in the distance.

A chorus of Invisible Spirits is heard in the background singing "poisoned dew the moon has shed, Spider's web dyed with red blood, ere tomorrow's sun has died, Death will wed another bride!"

A clock in the distance strikes twelve; Caspar turns around three times with the skull held high in his hands. He calls for Zamiel to appear. As he replaces the skull in the circle, Zamiel suddenly appears. Caspar pleads with Zamiel to grant him three more years, to which the Black Huntsman says no. Caspar offers this very night to bring a young forester here to offer his soul to Zamiel as a ransom for his own. The latter inquires why such a youth would come to this evil spot, and is told that it is because he needs the magic bullets. "Six shall make him, seven break him," says Zamiel. "The seventh is yours," answers Caspar eagerly. "Direct it from his own gun to his bride, and so drive both him and her father mad!" Over Agathe, says Zamiel regretfully, he has no power. He agrees to grant another three years of grace to Caspar if he can encourage Max to submit. "Tomorrow, it must be him or you!" and Zamiel disappears.

As a crash of thunder is heard, the skull in the circle disappears and in its place a small bonfire is seen for heating the solution for the bullets. The owls and birds flap their wings to fan the flames. By the light of the fire, Max is seen starting to descend the path. He inquires of himself why he should feel as though he were descending into hell, why the moon disappears, why he sees ghostly forms. Caspar mutters softly as he sees Max, "Thanks, Zamiel, my ransom is won!"

Caspar fans the flame with the eagle's wing that was resting beside the cauldron. Max sees an apparition; it is his dead mother. "In robes of her death, there stands my mother's ghost," he calls. "She warns me to flee." The ghostly figure disappears, and in its place Max sees Agathe. She seems about to throw herself off the cliff, and Max rushes the rest of the way down the path to try and save her. As he reaches the bottom, her figure disappears.

Caspar removes some items from his hunting pouch and throws them into the cauldron. "First the lead; some broken glass of church windows; some quicksilver; three bullets that have hit their mark. The right eye of a lapwing, the left of a lynx." He again calls on Zamiel for help, and the cauldron ferments with a green flame. A cloud passes over the moon and only the light of the fire can be seen.

As each of the magic bullets is cast, new phantasma take place. Caspar cries "One!" as he moulds the first, and nightbirds fly out of the forest and gather around the fire. "Two!" and a black boar dashes wildly across the glen and disappears. "Three!" — a hurricane rises, bends and breaks the tops of the trees. Four wheels on fire roll across the glen at the cry of "Four!" Huntsmen on horseback followed by hounds dash through mid-air at the cry of "Five!" The Invisible Chorus then intones another mysterious refrain. Total darkness obscures the sky as Caspar calls "Six!" Flames start up from the earth and meteors descend from the heavens.

So angry is the final tempest as Caspar calls "Seven!" that he falls in convulsions; Max has to seize the branch of a dead tree to keep from falling. They both cry out the name of Zamiel who appears instantly. He reaches for Max's hand, saying, "I am here!" Caspar becomes senseless as Max crosses himself. As the distant clock strikes one, Zamiel vanishes and Max falls prostrate to the ground.

Act III

Scene 1: *Agathe's room in the old hunting lodge of her father. It is the day of the contest which is to be followed by her wedding to the winner.*

Agathe is alone, dressed for her wedding. She kneels at the little altar at the side of the room and offers a prayer:

UND OB DIE WOLKE

Und ob die Wol- ke sie ver- hül-le, die

Son- ne bleibt am Him- mels- zelt

Und ob die Wolke sie verhülle,	Although a cloud has covered the sky,
Die Sonne bleibt am Himmelszelt,	The sun shines in splendor above it;
Es waltet dort ein heil'ger Wille,	We are not governed by chance alone,
Nicht blindem Zufall dient die Welt.	But by a loving Father in heaven.

At the end of the prayer, Annchen enters to help her cousin make final preparations for the wedding. Agathe sends her downstairs to fetch the bridal wreath that is in a box. When her cousin comes back with it, Annchen says that she almost didn't return, for the portrait has fallen from the wall again and she tripped over it. Agathe senses this as an evil omen, recalling the hermit's earlier warning. Annchen calms her by stating that it was only natural that such a thing could happen on a night like the past one when the very heavens shook with thunder and lightning.

Agathe opens the box to remove the floral wedding wreath, but stands aghast as she removes the top. In the place of a wedding wreath there is a funeral wreath of silver leaves. Once again Annchen calms the frayed nerves of the bride, saying that undoubtedly the servant handed her the wrong box. In desperation, Agathe takes the white roses from the little stand on the altar for her wedding bouquet, the roses that the little hermit had given her on her earlier visit.

SCENE 2: *The tents of Prince Ottokar and his nobility are seen at one side, the hunters are at tables feasting on the other.*

The call of hunting horns is heard from the orchestra:

The hunters join in a rousing chorus:

The Hunters' Chorus

Was gleicht wohl auf Er-den dem Jä-ger ver- gnü- gen.

Was gleicht wohl auf Erden dem
 Jägervergnügen,
Wem sprudelt der Becher des
 Lebens so reich?
Beim Klange der Hörner im Grünen
 zu liegen,
Den Hirsch zu verfolgen durch
 Dickicht und Teich.

The joy of the hunter surpasses
 all joy on earth,
The fountain of pleasure runs
 rich for the sport;
Through wood and through flood
 where the stag passes,
He flies in pursuit while the
 horns gayly sound.

Prince Ottokar inquires about the bride-to-be, Agathe, whom he says he has never had the pleasure of meeting. Cuno tells him that his daughter will be arriving shortly, but perhaps it would be best to have the trial shot before she gets there since Max has had so much trouble of late with his marksmanship. If he were to see his bride before the trial shot is fired, he might become unnerved. Ottokar agrees to this and commands that Max be summoned.

Caspar and Max have already divided the seven magic bullets, Caspar giving Max four and keeping three for himself. Earlier Max had to use three of his to impress Prince Ottokar who was watching him practice his marksmanship. He demanded more of Caspar, who pulled two magpies out of his hunter's pouch, stating that two of his went for those. Max asked for the one remaining bullet that Caspar had in his possession, but Caspar loaded his gun and fired at a fleeting fox.

Now that the trial shoot is about to take place, only the fateful seventh bullet remains. Caspar climbs a tree to get a better view of the occasion. The Prince spots a white dove on a branch and calls to Max that that shall be his target. Just as Max is about to pull the trigger, Agathe and Annchen appear directly behind the dove as they descend the trail to the scene of the festivities. "Don't shoot!" calls Agathe. The startled dove flies to the tree in which Caspar has climbed just as Max fires the gun. Both Caspar and Agathe fall to the ground at the sound of the gun, it has all happened so quickly.

The crowd rushes to Agathe's side and exclaims, "She lives! She lives!" Caspar, on the other side, is struggling in his own blood to reach his feet. "I saw the hermit beside her," he mutters. Suddenly Zamiel appears in front of him as he says, "You, Zamiel, here already? Is this how you keep your promise to me? Take your prey then, I defy my doom." As Caspar falls lifeless to earth, Zamiel disappears.

The Prince orders some of the hunters to take Caspar's body and throw it in the Wolf's Glen. He demands to know of Max what this is all about. After Max has explained it all, including the magic bullets, the Prince banishes him forever and forbids him ever to look on Agathe again. The hermit, who is now realized to be a holy man of God, comes forward to talk to the Prince. He explains that all humans make mistakes. "Which of us has the right to throw any stone at a sinner?" He suggests that the trial shooting be abolished in the future. He reminds the Prince that Max, with the one exception just witnessed, has always been an honest and upstanding youth as well as an expert marksman. "Put the boy on a year's probation, and if he is seen to be the person he used to be, then let him take Agathe's hand in marriage." The Prince agrees to do this as the crowd rejoices.

LUDWIG VAN BEETHOVEN

BORN: December 16 (?), 1770; Bonn, Germany.
DIED: March 26, 1827; Vienna, Austria.

At No. 20 Bonngasse in Bonn, Germany, stands a little house, now the Beethoven Museum, in whose garret apartment Ludwig van Beethoven was born in December of 1770. Today in the upstairs

LUDWIG VAN BEETHOVEN

Portrait made by Steiler

LUDWIG VAN BEETHOVEN

Crayon sketch made by Kloeber

HEILIGENSTADT

It was in this home in Heiligenstadt that Beethoven wrote his famous testament in 1802.

apartment in which his family once lived, rest momentos of one of the greatest composers the world has ever known. Among the original scores of several Beethoven works — including the *Symphony No. 6* and the so-called Moonlight sonata — repose other things associated with the master: quill pens, his seal, even an old pipe organ console on which he played as a boy. The most tragic part of the entire display is a table given over to pathetic reminders of Beethoven's tormented life on earth — innumerable ear trumpets and crude hearing devices. One is almost the size of a French horn, so large it would require the bearer to wear the tubing leading to the bell or "trumpet" across the top of his head to support its great size and weight.

It was in this house that, as a child, Beethoven received his first musical instruction on the keyboard from his father, a trumpeter in the village band. The family lived in poverty, due in large part to the father's addiction to drink. He was in a drunken stupor much of the time, and most of his meager income went to buy alcohol. By the time Ludwig was eight, he could play the violin well and shortly mastered J. S. Bach's *Well-Tempered Clavier* on the keyboard. In 1781 or 1782 Beethoven wrote his first compositions, three piano sonatas.

When Beethoven was thirteen, he was appointed harpsichordist for the opera house orchestra, and a year later accepted the position of assistant organist for his church at a salary of 150 florins (now about $63). He held the position for eight years and continued his duties with the theater orchestra. At seventeen, Beethoven visited Vienna for the first time, playing before Mozart, who exclaimed, "He will give the world something that is worth listening to."

Beethoven returned from Vienna to Bonn just as his mother lay fatally ill with tuberculosis. After her death, his father took to even heavier drinking and soon lost his voice. Young Ludwig had to assume the position as head of the family, and took care of money matters as well as looking after his brother's welfare. Life was so wretched for him that he turned for comfort to the family of Frau von Breuning, whose son and daughter he taught. In the refined atmosphere of their home, Beethoven first developed a taste for the best in English and German literature. Through this association, he also became acquainted with young Count Waldstein who became his lifelong friend, admirer, and benefactor.

In 1792 Haydn passed through Bonn and highly praised a cantata of Beethoven's that he heard performed there. Probably influenced strongly by Haydn's praise, the Elector of Bonn financed a trip to

Vienna for Beethoven, along with a monthly stipend. Vienna, then the musical center of Europe, heard Beethoven perform at many *soirées* and *musicales.* Through these, Beethoven became acquainted with some of the best families of that city. His chief fame during this period was as a keyboard artist rather than as a composer.

Prince and Princess Lichnowsky installed Beethoven in their household during his second year in Vienna. The composer was treated more as a son than as a servant, and almost all the old traces of the master-servant relationship as known in the Esterházy-Haydn period of servitude, were unknown. Through long association with the aristocratic and titled families, Beethoven came to think of himself as an equal.

Beethoven was scheduled to study music with Haydn, but so great were the demands on the latter's time, many of the lessons were given by Haydn's assistants. Most of Beethoven's musical education in composition was received from his study with the Italian, Salieri. His early Viennese compositions included several piano sonatas (including the *Pathétique*), string quartets, and trios.

From about 1802, the malady, which later resulted in total deafness, made Beethoven's life miserable. He became morose and suspicious of friends. He removed himself entirely from society, taking long walks in the parks and countryside, filling notebooks with musical sketches. He stated, "How could I . . . bring myself to admit the weakness of a *sense* which ought to be more perfect in me than in others?" In October he visited a little house in Heiligenstadt on the outskirts of Vienna and contemplated suicide. His frame of mind is vividly depicted in a will written in his own hand at this time, known as the *Heiligenstadt Testament:*

Consider that for six years I have been in an incurable condition, aggravated by senseless physicians, year after year deceived in the hope of recovery, and in the end compelled to contemplate a *lasting malady,* the cure of which may take years or even prove impossible. Born with a fiery, lively temperament, inclined even for the amusements of society, I was early forced to isolate myself, to lead a solitary life. If now and again I tried to forget all this, how rudely was I repulsed by the redoubled mournful experience of my defective hearing; not yet could I bring myself to say to people, "Speak louder, shout, for I am deaf!" . . . I must live like an exile; if I venture into company, a burning dread falls on me — the dreadful risk of letting my condition be perceived . . . What humiliation when somebody stood by me and heard a flute in the distance, and *I* heard *nothing* . . . Such occurrences brought me to despair, a little more and I would have put an end to my own life — only it, *my art,* held me back! It seemed to me to be impossible to quit the world until I had

produced all I felt it in me to compose; and so I reprieved my wretched life —
truly wretched . . . To my art, my thanks are due that I did not end my life
by suicide.

The death of Beethoven's brother Karl in 1815 left a nephew in
his charge. The composer undertook this task with zeal, but the
nephew was a scamp and made his uncle's life even more miserable.
Beethoven lamented about his poverty, and inferred that all his asso-
ciates were taking advantage of him in financial matters. Probably
because of his suspicious nature resulting from deafness, he accused
many people unjustly of cheating him. Had he been a better manager
of funds, he could have lived a life free from financial worries.

Increasing deafness plagued the composer as he worked on the
scores of his symphonies. Through numerous notebooks preserved
from this period of his life (his only method of communication), there
is a fairly accurate record of his career. His keyboard appearances
became less frequent, and he records that at times when he was conducting an orchestra the only way he could tell they were even playing was to watch the violinists' bows. On several occasions, according
to contemporary accounts, the orchestra was several measures ahead
of Beethoven's beat. After 1819, Beethoven was totally deaf. Following the performance he conducted of his mammoth *Symphony
No. 9,* the concertmaster had to tug on the composer's sleeve to get
him to turn around and acknowledge the thunderous applause. Other
great works of this period of total deafness include the choral master-
piece, the *Missa Solemnis,* the last five piano sonatas, and the last six
quartets.

Beethoven was not without fame in his own time. Many of his
compositions were published during his lifetime, and his name was
known throughout Europe. In Paris, by the King's command, a medal
of gold was struck in his honor; from St. Petersburg, Prince Galitzin
sent him a request for string quartets; the Philharmonic Society of
London played an important part in the composer's life; his name and
some of his music had reached the United States, then a country in
its infancy. In 1815 he received the "Freedom of the City of Vienna."

In December of 1826, Beethoven caught a violent cold which
resulted in an attack of pneumonia; dropsy supervened, and after several operations he succumbed on March 26, 1827. The cause of death
in the opinion of modern doctors was cirrhosis of the liver.

Beethoven's funeral was attended by hundreds of people, and
the edges of the pall were borne by eight well-known conductors. The

procession was accompanied by twenty-six torch bearers with sprays of flowers attached to their sleeves. Among the torch bearers was Franz Schubert. Acknowledging one of the great masters of music, many titled nobility followed the procession until Beethoven was interred in a hero's grave.

BIBLIOGRAPHY

Grove, Sir George. *Beethoven and His Nine Symphonies.* London: Novello and Co., Ltd., 1896.
Thayer, Alexander Wheelock. *The Life of Ludwig van Beethoven.* Original in German. 1879. English translation by Henry Edward Krehbiel, 1921. Reprinted, Southern Illinois University Press, 1960. 3 Vols.

SYMPHONY NO. 3

in E-flat Major

"Eroica"

LUDWIG VAN BEETHOVEN

The original manuscript of this symphony bore the inscription in Beethoven's handwriting: *Sinfonia grande, Napoleon Bounaparte, 1804 in August: del Sigr. Louis van Beethoven. Sinfonia 3, Op. 55.* Beethoven, who considered himself the equal of the landed gentry and the nobility, was very much impressed by Napoleon and the French Revolution with its motto of "Liberty, equality, fraternity." After work had progressed on the symphony, Napoleon rejected a democracy for France and declared himself Emperor. A copy of Beethoven's manuscript in the musical archives of Vienna shows the composer's reaction to this announcement. The original dedication was scratched out with a pen knife, and below it appeared the new dedication: *Sinfonia eroica, composta per festeggiare il sovvenire di un grand' Uomo dedicata* (Composed to celebrate the memory of a great man).

This symphony marks a radical departure from the established Classical symphony then in vogue in Germany; in fact, it is immensely different from Beethoven's own first two symphonies. It was the genesis of the Romantic symphony. The most obvious differences between the work under discussion and the older Classical symphonies include: the use of more than two themes in the sonata-allegro form (the first movement uses a transition theme, two parts to the Second Subject, and a closing theme); the extension and enlargement of the development section (in the Classical symphony, the *development* was seldom more than 2/3 the length of the *exposition;* in this symphony the development is 2/3 *longer* than the exposition); the use of a funeral march for the second movement was unusual; and the introduction of the form known as the *scherzo* to replace the older *minuet* which had served the classical symphony changed the pattern for all future works in this genre.

FIRST MOVEMENT: *Allegro con brio.*

After two loud chords, the Principal Subject is stated (note that it is based on the tonic chord):

Example 1 (Principal Subject)

With the use of more than two themes in this movement (as already described) it becomes difficult for the music analysts to agree on exactly which one is the Second Subject and which ones serve other purposes. For the sake of discussion, the following three themes in this analysis will all be considered the Second Subject: the first part, a transition, and the second part. The first part is played by the woodwinds and violins alternating with a three-note motive:

Example 2 (Second Subject — part one)

A transition to the second part of the Second Subject is introduced by the violins:

Example 3 (Second Subject — transition)

The clarinets play the final portion of the Second Subject:

Example 4 (Second Subject — part two)

The closing episode of the *exposition* is based on a theme of its own:

Example 5 (Closing Theme)

The *development* opens with the Principal Subject, Example 1, appearing in fragments, modulating through several keys and arriving at C major.

Fragments of Example 2, the first part of the Second Subject, are heard, followed by Example 1 now in C minor.

Example 1 and 3 are combined, moving through several keys to a *fortissimo* passage.

Beethoven's boldest stroke of all is to introduce a new theme in the *development,* Example 6. It is repeated:

Example 6

Example 1 returns in C major in a bold statement, followed by Example 6 in E-flat minor.

Example 1 appears in stretto and leads to the close of the *development*. After an abrupt pause, a transition leads back to the tonic key of E-flat. Note the dissonance of the horns sounding Example 1 on the tonic of E-flat, while the strings sound the dominant of the same key.

Example 1 (the Principal Subject) is heard in its original form to open the *recapitulation*.

Example 2 (the Second Subject — part one) is *recapitulated* in E-flat.

Example 3 (Transition theme) appears in C minor.

Example 4 (the Second Subject — part two) is heard in E-flat major.

The Closing theme (Example 5) closes this group of themes.

The *coda* is based principally on Example 1. After it has been heard once, Example 6 (the theme from the development section) appears, and is followed by the return of Example 1, which leads to the brilliant closing measures.

Second Movement: Marcia funebre. *Adagio assai.*

The second movement is of *march and trio* design, a three part form in which the first part is repeated after the second — march, trio, march. The term *trio* is misleading, for it also must be in the nature of a march in order not to disturb the continuity of the movement as a whole. It is really a misnomer which descended from the Baroque era (see that chapter) and has been in use ever since when large three part forms are discussed, i.e., minuet and trio; scherzo and trio; march and trio.

A theme of great pathos is played by the violins over the march rhythm established by the lower strings:

Example 7

The oboe mournfully echoes Example 7.
The second theme of the march is introduced by the violins:

Example 8

The *trio* is in the tonic major. In practically all funeral marches, after the intense grief represented in the first section, the trio theme is in major — perhaps offering a ray of hope for the bereaved. The C major theme is played first by the oboe:

Example 9

The flute and bassoon in turn play Example 9.

After an episode in which the violins introduce a subordinate theme, the trio closes with a restatement of Example 9 by the French horns and oboe.

The march returns, the strings presenting eight measures of Example 7.

A four-voiced fugue whose subject is Example 10, is introduced at this point:

Example 10

The entrance of voices in the fugue are as follows:
second violins
first violins
violas and celli
celli and double basses
upper woodwinds (*fortissimo*)
clarinets and horns (*fortissimo*)

Example 7 is played by the oboe and clarinet in octaves.

The strings are heard playing Example 8, followed by a repetition of Example 7 in the oboe and clarinet.

A *coda* closes the movement.

THIRD MOVEMENT: Scherzo. *Allegro vivo.*

In place of the traditional *minuet,* Beethoven has marked a *scherzo.* It is in the same meter as the minuet (3/4) and is in the same form (three part — scherzo, trio, scherzo); but the tempo is changed to a fast *Allegro vivo* which changes the whole nature of the movement. The term *scherzo,* Italian for joke or jest, had been used infrequently in music since the early Baroque era. It was first applied to a symphonic movement in this symphony and the change from the minuet was adopted by many composers after this pioneer usage. Actually, the stately minuet of the early Classical era had already disappeared although the name remained in use. In many of the Haydn symphonies, and in Beethoven's own *Symphony No. 1,* the tempo had become so fast and the nature of the music so light, that it bore little resemblance to the true minuet.

Musically, the term "jest" is more appropriate than the frequently used translation of "joke," for there is no broad, laughable joke displayed in a scherzo. It is, rather, a lighter movement, one that at times can be considered humorous.

The lightness and the rapidity of the scherzo is heard immediately in the string introduction:

Example 11

The oboe introduces a short melody which is repeated in a somewhat lengthened form:

Example 12

The introductory theme, Example 11, is heard one step higher in pitch, with the oboe theme, Example 12, entering in the key of the dominant.

The climax of the first thematic idea, Example 12, comes with descending syncopated accents which were a bold innovation in this work:

Example 13

Repetition is made of the entire theme, Example 12, and a slight development of it follows.

The trio is based on a horn call:

Example 14

After a development and a repetition of Example 14, a flute theme follows:

Example 15

A return of the first section, the scherzo, occurs. It is introduced by the strings with Example 11.

A surprising *alla breve* climax occurs:

Example 16

A *coda* is introduced by a short timpani solo ending with an eighteen measure flourish built on the introductory theme, Example 1.

FOURTH MOVEMENT: Finale. *Allegro molto.*

Again Beethoven departs from the Classical tradition. In place of a fourth movement based on either the *rondo* or *sonata-allegro* patterns, he has written one that almost defies categorization. Tovey refers to it, quite simply, as "a Bass, a Tune, and a Fugue." It is perhaps easiest for the student to hear it in reference to a "theme and variation" pattern.

A sweeping passage for strings, *fortissimo,* leads to a series of chords for full orchestra. The "bass" theme is introduced by the strings, *pizzicato.* It is in two-part form, each of eight measures, and each repeated. The essence of the theme:

Example 17 (Theme)

(Variation 1)

The theme, Example 17, appears *legato* in the second violins, with added figures in the first violins and celli:

Example 18

(Variation 2)

The theme appears in the first violins with a contrapuntal second voice in third species (three notes to one):

Example 19

(Variation 3)

A new melody is introduced by the oboe, clarinet, and bassoon, with the theme, Example 17, accompanying it contrapuntally:

Example 20

(Variation 4)

Example 17, the theme, becomes the Subject of a fugue with successive entrances moving down through the strings; the motive of Example 18 is used for embellishment.

Example 21

(Variation 5)

The new theme of Example 20 is played by the flutes and violins; the second part of the theme, Example 17, appears with an accompaniment of three notes to one.

(Variation 6)

A second new melody is introduced in counterpoint to the theme:

Example 22

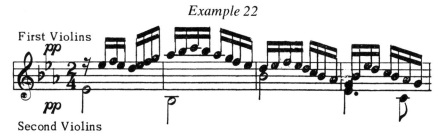

(Variation 7)

The melody from Example 20 is repeated softly.

(Variation 8)

Another fugal passage is heard. The theme, Example 17, is inverted and a new countersubject in sixteenth notes appears. Eventually all the orchestra enters into this.

Example 23

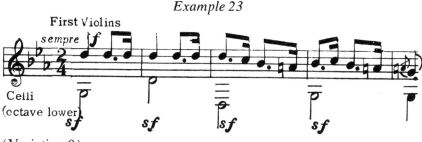

(Variation 9)

A variation of the melody of Example 20 is announced by the woodwinds and answered by the strings:

Example 24

(Variation 10)

The brass enter *fortissimo* with the theme of Example 20. It is an extended passage that reaches great sonority.

A coda brings the symphony to a close.

FRANZ SCHUBERT

BORN: January 31, 1797; Vienna, Austria.
DIED: November 19, 1828; Vienna, Austria.

Vienna is a city famous for the many coffee houses that line its streets. Had one looked in on the Bognerschen Coffee House on Singerstrasse early in the nineteenth century, Schubert could have been seen having coffee with his friends, reading the afternoon newspapers, and heard in a discussion of the art and politics of the day. At the end of the coffee hour, the friends would adjourn to one of their homes where they would hold a *Schubertianer,* an evening during which Vogl, a famous singer, would sing some of Schubert's latest lieder, followed by Schubert at the keyboard playing his piano works. The evening would then be climaxed by dancing and perhaps a game of charades. Each of the members of this close circle of friends had a nickname. Schubert's was "Tubby" (*Schwammerl* — literally "a little mushroom") because of his short stature — 4' 11" — and his stocky build.

Of the many famous Viennese composers, Franz Schubert was the only one born in the city of Vienna. He, however, had no Viennese blood in his veins, for his father was of Moravian extraction and his mother of Silesian descent. His father was a school teacher who envisioned the same occupation for his son Franz. The elder Schubert was an amateur cellist and taught his son to play the violin when he was eight. A little later the boy studied the piano, receiving lessons from his older brother Ignaz. (The Schuberts had fourteen children, of whom nine died in infancy. Franz was their twelfth child.)

Young Franz had a fine soprano voice and when his father saw an announcement of two vacancies at the Imperial Chapel choir school (Convict), he immediately submitted an application for his son. Should the boy be accepted, it meant free tuition, board, and lodging; and should he do well in "morals and studies," he could remain for a time at the school after his voice changed. Franz passed the entrance examination and was enrolled at the Convict (middle and high school)

SCHUBERT'S BIRTHPLACE

Now Nussdorfer Strasse 54 in Vienna

SCHUBERT at age sixteen

The steel engraving that appeared on the title page of the first published edition of Schubert's *Der Erlkönig* showing the Erl king hovering over the father with his sick boy.

OIL PORTRAIT OF SCHUBERT

By W. A. Rieder

to serve as an Angelic Chorister. What formal training in music Schubert had was gained during his years at the Convict. He played violin in the orchestra which gave a concert every evening, playing a different symphony and an overture each time. Schubert was soon playing second stand. The boy that played first stand, Spaun, became a lifelong friend. Spaun later wrote in his *Memoirs* concerning Schubert's original compositions during the Convict days: "He wrote music extraordinarily fast and the study hours he devoted unremittingly to composition." The composer's first song, *Hagars Klage,* a rather long ballad telling the lament of Hagar lost in the desert with her dying child, comes from this period. His *Symphony No. 1* was written for the orchestra at the school.

Eventually Schubert's voice broke and his days at the school became numbered. It was the policy for all young men of those days to be conscripted into the Austrian army for a period of fourteen years if they could not "buy their way out" or use political influence to avoid it. Schubert was able to miss military service by enrolling for a year at a Normal School for the training of teachers. Upon graduation, Franz became an assistant instructor at the school in which his father taught. He was most unhappy as a teacher, and found that the students interfered with his train of thought as he sat at his desk working on a composition. Some of his finest lieder date from these days — *Der Erlkönig* (The Erlking) and *Die Forelle* (The Trout). By the time Schubert was eighteen, he had written over one hundred and forty-four songs, plus some works for the stage and five symphonies. A year later Schubert sold his first composition, a cantata entitled *Prometheus,* for 100 florins (about $20 today).

When he was twenty, Schubert took a leave of absence from the school and left his father's house in disgrace. From this date onward, the composer never had a steady income or a permanent place of residence. He lived first with one friend and then another. He continued to compose prodigiously. Usually he was to be found in whatever room he was occupying at the time in his shirt sleeves from sunrise until noon, composing. Stories circulated that he slept with his glasses on at night so that he could start to work immediately on awakening in the morning. After noon, he would adjourn to the coffee house with his friends. Evenings were spent either in the *Schubertianer* or else at the theater. Many times the composer spent what few florins he had to purchase tickets for concerts, those of Paganini being among his favorites. The stage so fascinated him that he probably spent more time writing operas and operettas than any other form of composition. He composed at least eighteen works for the lyric stage, many of them mounted unsuccessfully during his lifetime. None of them is known or performed today. Compositions continued to flow from his pen, not all necessarily written during the morning hours. One of his famous songs was scribbled down on paper at midnight when the melody first entered his head. Tired when the task of setting down the notes was completed, the sleepy Schubert grabbed the ink well instead of the jar of sand as he went to blot the wet ink of the manuscript. To this day, the manuscript has a large ink smudge on the title page.

During Schubert's twenty-third year, a large social gathering was held in Vienna to usher in the Christmas season. As part of the evening's entertainment, *Der Erlkönig* was sung most successfully. The publisher Diabelli was in the audience and offered to publish the song. It was Schubert's first work to be accepted by a publisher and was assigned the misleading opus number of one.

Schubert's health took a turn for the worse, as he had contracted an incurable disease. He was hospitalized in 1823 for several months. Following his release, he had the opportunity of going to Hungary as a music teacher and conductor for the famous Esterházy family. Several years earlier he had spent a short vacation there and found that he was homesick for his beloved Vienna. He hoped this time to spend a pleasant and relaxing summer. Unfortunately he enjoyed himself no more than the first time, and longed to return to his friends and the old familiar coffee houses of Vienna.

A year later he experienced a more pleasant trip with his friend, the singer Vogl. They traveled through upper Austria and to Salzburg. This was the most extensive trip Schubert ever made. While stopping in Gastein, he composed a symphony. Although he and Vogl both refer to this "Gastein" symphony in their correspondence several times, the music for it has never been discovered.

On his return to Vienna, Schubert sold some of the songs from his cycle, *Die Winterreise* (Winter's Journey) for 20¢ apiece to add to his meager finances. He turned to work on a symphony in B minor (*Symphony No. 8*), followed by some piano works. Early in 1828 he started on a symphony in C major (*Symphony No. 9*) which was handed back to him by the Vienna orchestra when completed as "too difficult to play."

Not long after this Schubert's health broke down completely. Already weakened by the incurable disease, an attack of typhus found little resistance. He moved in with a friend whose house was damp and this aggravated the illness. From October 13 onward, he was unable to retain any food, but tried to act as if all were well. By the beginning of November, he had decided that he did not have the mastery of form that he desired so made arrangements to study fugue and counterpoint with Simon Sechter, the Court organist. He never had the opportunity of taking his first lessons. On November 12 he wrote to one of his friends, "I am ill. For eleven days now I have neither eaten or drunk anything. I totter from the bed to the sofa." On November 16 the doctors diagnosed abdominal typhus caused by impure water. On the 18th, Schubert became delirious, and on the following day, at three in the afternoon, he passed away.

Schubert was buried in the Währing cemetery one grave removed from Beethoven, the adjoining site having been previously committed. It had been Schubert's final desire to be buried as close as possible to his musical hero, Ludwig van Beethoven.

BIBLIOGRAPHY

Brown, Maurice J. E. *Schubert: A Critical Biography*. London: Macmillan and Company, Ltd., 1958.
Einstein, Alfred. *Schubert: A Musical Portrait*. New York: Oxford University Press, 1951.

SYMPHONY NO. 8
in B Minor

Franz Schubert

In the year 1822 Schubert composed two movements of a symphony in B minor and sketched out ten measures of a scherzo movement. The same year he received one of the few awards of his life, an honorary membership in the Musikverein of Styria. In a letter of gratitude, the composer said, "In order to express my liveliest thanks in music, I will be so bold as to present your honored Society at the earliest date with the score of one of my symphonies."

He gave to Anselm Hüttenbrenner, president of the Society, the score for the B minor symphony (two movements) for delivery to the society. Anselm, who had been a friend of the composer and had championed Schubert's music to the general public, for some reason never delivered the manuscript but put it among a pile of old manuscripts in his home.

Some forty-three years later (thirty-seven after Schubert's death) the conductor of the Vienna Musikfreunde orchestra learned of a symphony in B minor and further discovered that it had been given to Hüttenbrenner by the composer. The conductor immediately made a trip to Graz where Hüttenbrenner lived. He had to work obliquely to come across the manuscript of the Schubert work. The conductor cordially suggested that he schedule one of Hüttenbrenner's compositions for an early Vienna concert. Once this had been done, he inquired discreetly about any old Schubert manuscripts Hüttenbrenner had around his home. When the latter produced a pile of manuscripts yellow with age, the original Schubert draft of a symphony in B minor was located. It was premiered in Vienna that year (along with the ignoble work by Hüttenbrenner!).

The title "Unfinished" was immediately affixed to it since it had only two movements. A number of would-be composers have attempted to complete the scherzo from the ten measure fragment, and have even supplied a fourth movement out of thin air. Noted musicians, conductors, and Schubert biographers agree, however, that "Unfinished" is a complete misnomer. Schubert was in the habit of writing out his compositions hurriedly, almost in one sitting, and complete in the first draft. Had he wished to add a full scherzo and a fourth movement, he had ample time, for he lived another six years after the B minor symphony was composed.

FIRST MOVEMENT: *Allegro moderato.*

An introductory theme is played in octaves by the celli and double basses:

Example 1

The *exposition* opens with the oboe and clarinet, in unison, playing the Principal Subject:

Example 2 (Principal Subject)

The Principal Subject ends with a short *sforzando* chord, and is then played a second time by the clarinet and oboe in a shortened version which builds to a crescendo.

The celli announce the Second Subject:

Example 3 (Second Subject)

The violins repeat the Second Subject, Example 3, ending abruptly with a full measure of silence.

Two short, loud chords by the full orchestra are heard, followed by an ascending string tremolo in the violins and violas with full orchestral accompaniment.

Fragments of the Second Subject, Example 3, are played by the first violins, imitated canonically by the second violins, then the celli.

The *development* is concerned almost exclusively with a development of the introductory theme, Example 1. A sustained chord in the brass and woodwinds, to which the strings add a descending pizzicato scale, leads to a repetition of Example 1 by the celli and double basses.

Variations of Example 1 are then heard in the violins, echoed by the violas and bassoon. It is expanded into a powerful *fortissimo* by full orchestra.

The *recapitulation* begins with the strings playing the Principal Subject, Example 2, extended by repetition and in a slightly heavier orchestration.

After a sustained tone held by the bassoons and horns, the Second Subject, Example 3, is played by the celli and violins. It is repeated several times, ending in a passage of canonical imitation.

The *coda* is a balance to the introduction. Example 1, the theme of the introduction, is expanded slightly to serve as the close for the movement.

SECOND MOVEMENT: *Andante con moto.*

As the low strings play a descending pizzicato scale, the strings present the first theme:

Example 4

Following a short bridge passage, a theme played by the clarinet, accompanied by the strings, is heard:

Example 5

Example 4 reappears in several different keys: E major; G major; and A major.

The oboe, then the clarinet, repeat Example 5.

The *coda* is built on Example 4. It is heard first in the flutes and oboes, then in the bassoons, horns, and clarinets.

Fragments of Example 4 lead to a final statement of Example 4 in its entirety by flutes, clarinets, and horns. A quiet ending follows.

DER ERLKÖNIG

(The Erlking)

Franz Schubert

Many books claim that Schubert was the *"creator of the lied."* This statement is both true and false. It is false in the sense that the Germanic word *lied* means "song," for songs had been sung since the Renaissance throughout Europe. It is true in the sense that the manner in which Schubert united music with artistic poetry established a new model that changed the course of the solo song for all time. So important was this new wedding of text and music that *lied* ceased to be just the Germanic word for song, and was adopted into all languages as referring to Schubert's works and those of his successors and imitators.

In the classical Italian art song, and other later derivations, the melody of the vocal line was of supreme importance; the accompaniment was incidental. The rise of a school of great poetry in Germany at the beginning of the Romantic era naturally attracted composers who wished to write vocal works. The importance of an artistic text, coupled with a beautiful vocal line, and enhanced by an equally important accompaniment, changed the entire nature of the song. Paul Henry Lang in his book, *Music in Western Civilization,* states the case well:

Schubert who recognized the new order of things, the new relationship of poet and musician, was far more creative in the purely musical sense than any other song writer, with the occasional exception of Schumann and Brahms. Had he accepted the romantic dictum of the poet's absolute supremacy, merely providing music to the text, he would not have created the modern song; but by consciously elevating such purely musical elements as harmony and instrumental piano accompaniment to equal importance with the poem and melody, he brought to bear an atmosphere of the song the force of an overwhelming musical organism, a force sufficient to establish a balance between poetry and music.[*]

Der Erlkönig was one of Schubert's early *lieder.* Although it was written when he was seventeen, it was by no means his first. It was published six years after it was completed (no one at first wanted to publish such an involved song with a very difficult accompaniment)

---

[*] Paul Henry Lang, *Music in Western Civilization.* W. W. Norton Co.

and listed by the publisher as Opus 1. It was composed, as many of Schubert's songs, in a sudden burst of inspiration. One of Schubert's friends, Spaun, relates in his *Memoirs* how one afternoon he went to see Schubert and found him "all aglow, reading the *Erlkönig* aloud from a book. He walked up and down the room several times, book in hand, then suddenly sat down, and, as fast as his pen could travel, put the splendid ballad on paper. As he had no piano, we hurried over to the . . . school, and there the *Erlkönig* was sung the same evening and received with enthusiasm."

The text is by one of the greatest German Romantic literary figures, Johann Wolfgang Goethe. It describes the night journey of a father who is returning home with his child ill with marsh fever. As the child rests in his father's arms, he becomes delirious and thinks he sees the Erlking, a mythological goblin that exercises a fatal influence upon children with alluring promises or visions. The story, except for the first and last verses, is told by the characters themselves.

In Schubert's setting the pitch of the father's speech is low, that of the boy, high. The unearthly Erlking exceeds both in range and in the "lightness" of the melodic line.

Throughout the song, a repeated octave figure in the piano accompaniment represents the galloping of the horse, which stops just before the end when the father and child reach home. An ominous figure in the left hand of the accompaniment adds tension and mystery to the atmosphere. The distress of the child's cry to the father is sharpened by biting dissonance, and his increasing fear by a rise in pitch, each appeal a tone higher. The Erlking's entreaties are accompanied almost as though they were dance tunes, for indeed the Erlking invites the child to "come dance." At the end of the song, when the fatal ride is finished, the music comes to a halt. The words *"war todt"* are then sung without accompaniment, followed by two final chords (dominant — tonic) that musically write *finis* to the ballad as no other chords could do. The opening portion of the introduction:

Piano

In the fifteenth measure, a voice inquires:

Wer reitet so spät durch Nacht und Wind?

Who rides so late at night through the wind?

Es ist der Vater mit seinem Kind;

It is a father with his child;

Er hat den Knaben wohl in dem Arm,

He has the boy safe in his arms,

Er fasst ihn sicher, er hält ihn warm.

He holds him tightly and keeps him warm.

The father speaks:

,,*Mein Sohn, was birgst du so bang dein Gesicht?*"

"My son, why do you hide your face?"

The child replies:

,,Siehst Va - ter, du den Erl - ko - nig nicht?''

,,*Siehst, Vater, du den Erlkönig nicht?*
Den Erlenkönig mit Kron' und Schweif?"
,,*Mein Sohn, es ist ein Nebelstreif.*"

"O Father, don't you see the Erlking there?
The Erkling with his crown and robe?"
"My son, it is but a fantasy of the mist."

The Erlking then speaks to the feverish child:

,,Du lie - bes Kind, komm geh' mit mir!''

,,*Du liebes Kind, komm, geh' mit mir!*
Gar schöne Spiele spiel' ich mit dir;
Manch' bunte Blumen sind an dem Strand,
Meine Mutter hat manch gülden Gewand."
,,*Mein Vater, mein Vater, und hörest du nicht,*
Was Erlenkönig mir leise verspricht?"

"My dearest child, come with me!
I'll play many games with you
Where the flowers bloom along the street.
My mother has a golden robe for you."
"My father, my father! Don't you hear it,
What the Erlking whispers in my ear?"

,,*Sei ruhig, bleibe ruhig, mein Kind;*
In dürren Blättern säuselt der Wind."

"Be quiet, be quiet, my child.

It is only the dead leaves stirred by the wind."

„Willst, feiner Knabe, du mit mir gehn?
Meine Töchter sollen dich warten schön;
Meine Töchter führen den nächtlichen Reihn
Und wiegen und tanzen und singen dich ein."

"Come, my child, come with me,
My daughter shall wait on you,
My daughter will lead you in a merry dance every night.
She'll sing and dance, and rock you to sleep."

„Mein Vater, mein Vater, und sichst du nicht dort
Erlkönigs Töchter am düstern Ort?"
„Mein Sohn, mein Sohn, ich seh' es genau:
Es scheinen die alteng Weiden so grau?"

"My father, my father, don't you see
The Erlking's daughter in that gloomy spot?"
"My son, my son, I see and I know
It is only the reflection of light on the old willow tree."

„Ich liebe dich, mich reizt deine schöne Gestalt;
Und bist du nicht willig, so brauch' ich Gewalt."

"I love you; I'm entranced with your appearance.
And willing or not, I'll carry you off with me."

„Mein Vater, mein Vater, jetzt fasster mich an!
Erlkönig hat mir ein Leid's gethan!"

"My father, my father! He's grabbed my arm!
The Erlking has seized me and is hurting me!"

Den Vater grauset's, er reitet geschwind,
Er hält in den Armen das ächzende Kind,
Erreicht den Hof mit Mühe und Not;
In seinen Armen das Kind war todt!

The father shudders and rides like the wind,
He clasps the pale, sobbing child tighter.
He reaches home with fear and dread.
In his arms, the child was dead!

STÄNDCHEN
(Serenade)
Franz Schubert

The *Serenade* is one of the last songs that Schubert composed, written in the final year of his very short life. The text is a poem by Ludwig Rellstab. The accompaniment may seem at first over-simple as compared to the last lied, *Der Erlkönig,* but on closer inspection it will be noted that it is most appropriate. The idea of a serenade has passed down through the centuries as sung by a gentleman to his young love, accompanying himself on a stringed instrument. It will be noted that it hovers, particularly in the interludes, between major and minor, a characteristic frequently found in the songs of Schubert.

The song is cast in the *binary* or two-part song form. The first part, which may be referred by the letter A, consists of thirty-two measures that are repeated (A — A) and a concluding section of twenty-two measures (B). The overall two-part form would then be: A — A — B.

There is a four measure introduction:

Piano

The opening measures of A:

Lei - se fle - hen mei - ne Lie-der durch die Nacht zu dir;

Leise flehen meine Lieder   I am pleading with my song
Durch die Nacht zu dir;   Through the night to you;
In den stillen Hain hernieder,   Through these woods where nothing is stirring,
Liebchen, komm zu mir!   My dearest, come to me!

The second melodic phrase of A:

Flü sternd schlan-ke Wip-fel rau-schen in des Mon-des Licht,

Flüsternd schlanke Wipfel rau-
schen   Here the slender tree-tops whisper
In des Mondes Licht;   In the moonlight;
Des Veräters feindlich Lauschen   No eavesdropper is lurking here,
Fürchte, Holde, nicht!   Be not afraid, my love!

The next two quatrains are sung to the same melodic line as the first two:

Hörst die Nachtigallen schlagen?   Do you hear the nightingales singing?

Ach! sie flehen dich,   Ah! They plead to you,
Mit der Töne süssen Klagen   They sing with such sweet tones;
Flehen sie für mich.   Beloved, they plead for me.
    They can understand love's longing,

Sie verstehn des Busens Sehnen,   Know the lover's smart,
Kennen Liebesschmerz,
Rühren mit den Silbertönen   They can stir with silver voices
Jedes weiche Herz.   Every tender heart.

The opening portion of B is more agitated:

Lass auch dir die Brust be-we-gen, Lieb-chen, hö-re mich!

Lass auch dir die Brust bewegen,   Listen then and let my pleading,
Liebchen, höre mich!   Stir your breast, beloved!
Bebend harr' ich dir entgegen!   I stand before you trembling
Komm, beglücke mich!   Come and favor me!
    Beglücke mich!   And favor me!

HECTOR BERLIOZ

BORN: December 11, 1803; La Côte St. André, France.
DIED: March 8, 1869; Paris, France.

Hector Berlioz' courtship of his first wife sounds for all the world like the most romantic novel of its day. Berlioz, who was fascinated by the plays of William Shakespeare, attended a performance one evening of *Hamlet*. He became entranced by the young Irish actress playing the role of Ophelia. He discovered that her name was Henrietta Smithson and learned the shops and cafés that she frequented. Eventually, he was successful in "accidentally" running into and meeting her, but she showed no interest whatsoever.

He became obsessed with her beauty and had difficulty putting her from his mind. When he started on his autobiographical symphony, *Symphonie Fantastique,* she became the central figure and inspiration for the work. In the earlier movements, she was "the Beloved." As the work progressed, Berlioz was piqued by her lack of interest in him. By the time he got to the final movement of the symphony, he depicted her, musically, as the most grotesque and common type of woman.

After Berlioz spent some time in Italy (on the Prix de Rome), he returned to Paris to resume his courtship of Miss Smithson. By this time she had her own theatrical troupe which was playing at the Théâtre Italiens. A stormy courtship of ten months was necessary before she agreed to marry him. The ceremony took place at the British Embassy on October 3, 1833. They settled in a home in Montmartre, where their son Louis was born a year later. Their married life was turbulent, filled with tangled nerves, jealousies, and bitter quarrels.

This romantic young composer, the son of a country doctor, was baptized Louis Hector Berlioz. His father's fondest hope was for the boy to follow in his own footsteps and practice medicine. From an early age, the lad showed a natural aptitude for music. Before he was twelve, he had learned to sing at sight, played the flute and flageolet, and later mastered the guitar. He never studied the piano, and in later years he wrote that he was glad that "under necessity he could compose silently and freely." He studied the rudiments of composition from a book and then tried writing a number of works. By the time he was fifteen, he was trying to have some of them published.

Berlioz' father was adamant about the boy studying medicine, and at sixteen saw that he was enrolled for beginning courses in medicine. Two years later, he was enrolled in the Paris Medical School. The school, in general, and the dissection room in particular, were too much for Berlioz. He was determined to quit school, and all the pleadings of his family could not make him change his mind. "I am convinced that I shall distinguish myself in music," he wrote to his father, and added, "Within me the voice of Nature is stronger than the strictest objections of reason." His father thereupon cut off most of his son's monthly allowance.

Anxious to hear one of his compositions performed, Berlioz borrowed a considerable sum of money from one of his friends in order to have his recently completed *Mass* performed at the Church of St. Roch. He also tried to enter the Prix de Rome contest; on hearing of this, his father threatened to stop what was left of his allowance. He finally convinced his father that he should enroll at the Conservatory as a full-time student. He subsisted some days on only raisins or bread and salt as he tried to repay the loan he had obtained for the performance of the *Mass*. When his father learned of this, he paid off the balance of the loan and then stopped what was left of Hector's monthly allowance. Berlioz then found a position as a singer in a very small theater which paid very little. The seven years at the Conservatory were very difficult ones for him, for not only was he in disgrace with his family, he disliked most of the professors at the school and detested the old-fashioned (to his way of thinking) Cherubini who was the director. His objection to the instructors was their habit of teaching in the academic forms and styles of fifty or a hundred years before. Young Berlioz wished to blaze new paths into the future of music.

The year 1830 was a memorable one for him (he was then twenty-six). Early in the year he completed the work for which he is best known, *Symphonie Fantastique, Episode de la Vie d'un Artiste* (Fantastic Symphony, An Episode in the Life of an Artist) which, as previously described, was inspired by the young lady he had seen playing in *Hamlet*. This year was also the one in which he won the Prix de Rome after five tries, with the cantata *Sardanapale* (which depicted a king who refused to abdicate and perished in a fire set by his own hand). The cantata was publicly performed in October, and in December a performance was given of the *Symphonie*. Franz Liszt was present at this latter concert and became greatly enthused by the work. It was the start of a long friendship between the two. A brilliant piano arrangement of the *Symphonie* was made by Liszt and performed by him throughout Germany. It was through this that the German public became familiar with the name Berlioz.

Once in Italy on the Prix, Berlioz became restless and was thwarted in a second love affair (he had temporarily given up on Henrietta Smithson). He requested of the Parisian authorities that he be permitted to terminate his stay in Rome six months before the stipulated period of two years was up. Permission was granted, and the twenty-nine-year-old composer returned to France with a revised score of the *Symphonie* and resumed his courtship of Miss Smithson.

After his marriage, Berlioz discovered that he could not rely on his pupils and concert appearances for a sufficient income, so he turned to journalism. He became the music critic for the important *Journal des Débats*. He loathed the position, although his writings were excellent and to this day prove very interesting reading. Three years later he received his first substantial funds from his compositions. The famous violin virtuoso, Paganini, paid him 20,000 francs for *Harold in Italy,* a programmatic work for solo viola and orchestra based on Byron's *Childe Harold's Pilgrimage*. He received 10,000 francs for his *Symphonie Funèbre et Triomphale:* In addition, the French government offered him 4,000 francs to write a *Requiem*.

The composer contemplated a tour of Germany to conduct his own compositions, since his opportunities in Paris were limited (Paris had only its opera houses; concerts had to be given at the composer's expense). His wife objected to the trip. Coming as it did after years of a turbulent marriage, the objection precipitated Berlioz's separation from his wife. Although he supported her financially until her death in 1854, there was no longer any affection between them. The tour was quite successful in spite of the fact that the German orchestras had difficulty in meeting the demands of the music. The following year he toured central Europe — Vienna,

Prague, Budapest — then traveled to Russia. London was next on his list, and he conducted a series of concerts there including his opera *Benvenuto Cellini* at Covent Garden. The latter was a complete failure.

After his third tour to London, Berlioz was honored by the French government on his return to Paris. They conferred upon him a seat in the French Académie and commissioned him to write a *Te Deum* and a cantata for the Paris Exposition. In the same year, Berlioz married a singer by the name of Marie Recio whom he had met the year of his separation from his first wife. The second marriage was only terminated by Marie's death seven years later.

Berlioz composed a lyric drama based on the *Aeneid*. Because the completed work took six and a half hours to perform, it was divided into two parts of which *Les Troyens à Carthage* (The Trojans at Carthage) was produced at the Théâtre-Lyrique in November, 1863 and ran for twenty-two performances.

After the death of his second wife, he was a very lonely man. He composed one more work, *Béatrice et Bénédict,* based on Shakespeare's *Much Ado About Nothing.* Although the work was well-received both when it was produced at Baden-Baden and at Weimar under Liszt, the death from yellow fever of his son Louis in Havana, Cuba, while in the service of the French navy, was a severe blow. He renewed his strength enough to make one more tour of Russia, but returned to Paris completely exhausted. He traveled to the Riviera for rest and recuperation, but twice fainted there and badly bruised and cut himself. He returned to Paris and informed his friends that the doctors had numbered his days. In his last note he wrote, "I feel I am dying; I no longer believe in anything." He fell into a partial coma, and died at half-past twelve that afternoon.

BIBLIOGRAPHY

Barzun, Jacques. *Berlioz and His Century* (Revised edition). New York: Meridian Books, 1959.
Newman, Ernest, editor. *Memoirs of Hector Berlioz.* New York: Tudor Publishing Company, 1947.

SYMPHONIE FANTASTIQUE

Episode in the Life of an Artist

HECTOR BERLIOZ

Hector Berlioz was twenty-six when he wrote this symphony which he intended to be autobiographical. He had fallen in love with Henrietta Smithson (see the biographical sketch) and represented her in the *Symphonie* by a melody stated directly after the introduction of the first movement. He called this theme his *idée fixe* or fixed idea. Throughout the work it represents the "Beloved One" but melodically does not always appear in its original form. The timbre of the *idée fixe* is changed, and in the last movement it is completely debased by the addition of appogiaturas and changed rhythm.

The "program" is stated in Berlioz' own words in the orchestral score:

A young musician of unhealthy, sensitive nature, and endowed with a vivid imagination, has poisoned himself with opium in a sudden, violent outburst of lovesick despair. The narcotic dose he had taken was too weak to cause death, but it has thrown him into a long sleep accompanied by the most extraordinary visions. In this condition, his sensations, his feelings, and his memories find utterance in his sick brain in the form of musical imagery. Even the Beloved One takes the form of a melody in his mind, like a fixed idea which is ever returning and which he hears everywhere.

In spite of this detailed program, the *Symphonie Fantastique* is a true symphony and not a rhapsodic, rambling type of creation. The first movement is in the sonata-allegro form, a waltz takes the place of the scherzo, a sonata-form is the slow movement, and the finale combines the characteristics of variations and rondo. The "program" itself is very vague at the beginning of the work, and becomes more specific and graphic as the work progresses to its wild conclusion.

Hector Berlioz was known in his own day as a brilliant orchestrator and, to this day, his treatise on orchestration is a student's bible of information. Several of his innovations came from this work: two harps in the ball scene; the English horn and oboe duet in the shepherd's scene; the use of the timpani in chords for the distant thunder; the employment of the shrill E-flat clarinet; and the use of the wood of the violin bows in the grotesque finale. Berlioz' enthusiasm over the instrumentation of this work actually led to a delay in its premiere performance. He went out and hired so many musicians (approximately 130) that there were neither enough chairs nor stands when they all reported to the symphony rehearsal!

The quotations in the following paragraphs are from Berlioz' printed remarks in the score; the running commentary relates the formal structure of the symphony.

FIRST MOVEMENT: Reveries, Passions. *Allegro agitato e appasionato assai.*

At first he thinks of the uneasy and nervous condition of his mind, of somber longings, of depression and joyous elation without any recognizable cause, which he experienced before the Beloved One had appeared to him. Then he remembered the ardent love with which she suddenly inspired him; he thinks of his almost insane anxiety of mind, of his raging jealousy, of his reawakening love, of his religious consolation.

A rather lengthy introduction of some seventy-one measures involves several thematic fragments which never appear again. It perhaps suggests the "reveries" of the young musician.

The *exposition* starts with the Principal Subject, Example 1, which is also the *idée fixe* that represents the Beloved One.

Example 1 (Principal Subject — *Idée fixe*)

After several measures of *fortissimo,* a secondary theme appears in the woodwinds, and the *fortissimo* episode returns.

The Second Subject is introduced by the strings:

Example 2 (Second Subject)

The Principal and Second Subjects, Examples 1 and 2, answer each other three successive times.

The Principal Subject, Example 1, is heard several times in the lower strings at the beginning of the *development,* each time at a higher pitch; the first measure of Example 2 is interjected by the woodwinds in octaves after each statement.

A staccato figure in the strings, moving upward by the chromatic scale, rises almost as if in billows, sweeping to an unexpected end.

A sustained French horn tone serves as the bridge to the *recapitulation.*

The Principal Subject, Example 1, returns in G major, and is played by the violins and woodwinds.

The bridge is made up of new thematic material which subsides in intensity and then builds to large, sonorous chords in full orchestra.

The Second Subject, Example 2, is heard twice; first it is played by the celli, then by the full orchestra.

The *coda,* like the introduction, is of extreme length (almost two hundred measures). Example 1, the Principal Subject, eventually is heard as the celli and violas contrapuntally imitate each other, then much later appears in the flute, clarinet, oboe, and horn in succession.

SECOND MOVEMENT: A Ball. *Allegro non troppo.*

In a ballroom, amidst the confusion of a brilliant festival, he finds the Beloved One again.

This movement is essentially a waltz, preceded by a thirty-eight measure introduction, and succeeded by another lengthy coda (this time of one hundred measures).

The introduction opens with the strings and harp predominating, then the woodwinds join to build the music to a dynamic climax.

The rhythm of the waltz is suggested in the lower strings accompaniment, the violins play the theme:

Example 3

Violins

p

dolce e tenero

sf

The violins continue in prominence, introducing two additional sub-themes. They eventually restate Example 3, with a new accompaniment in the harp and woodwind on the second and third beats of the measure. It builds to a climax.

The middle episode is built on a theme derived from the *idée fixe*, Example 1. Example 4, the derivative, is first played by the flute and oboe in unison (in F major) and is repeated by the flute and clarinet (in C major).

Example 4 (Idée fixe — second version)

The woodwinds predominate throughout the middle episode, the strings providing only a light harmonic background. A dialogue between the strings and woodwinds leads to a return of the first section of the waltz.

The low strings again establish the waltz rhythm as the strings play Example 3. The sub-themes are heard again, leading to the return of Example 3 as the woodwinds play it in octaves.

In the very long *coda,* two new sub-themes are introduced and lead to a final statement of the *idée fixe* as used in this movement — Example 4. It is almost like a dream as the clarinet plays Example 4, accompanied by a single note on the flute, one on the horn, and three chords on the harp.

With a swirl and a crash the dance continues its mad pace, leading to a brilliant conclusion.

THIRD MOVEMENT: In the Country. *Adagio.*

It is a summer evening. He is in the country, musing, when he hears two shepherd lads who play, in alternation, the *ranz des vaches* [the tune used by Swiss shepherds to call their flocks]. This pastoral duet, the quiet scene, the soft whisperings of the trees stirred by the zephyr wind, some prospects of hope recently made known to him — all these sensations unite to impart a long unknown repose to his heart, and lend a smiling color to his imagination. And then she appears once more. His heart stops beating, painful forebodings fill his soul. Should she prove false to him! One of the shepherds resumes the melody, but the other answers him no more . . . Sunset . . . distant rolling of thunder . . . loneliness . . . silence . . .

This movement is in rhapsodic form (*i.e.,* follows no standard form, but is free in nature). It is in this movement that the music starts more graphically to represent the story.

The movement opens with a short passage of alternating calls by the English horn and the oboe off stage:

Example 5

After a few measures the main theme of the movement is introduced by the flute and violins with practically no accompaniment:

Example 6

Example 6 is repeated with flutes and violins in thirds in a more intense statement.

A short, transitional theme in the woodwinds leads to another statement of the main theme, Example 6, played by the violas and celli.

After a figure for low strings and bassoons, a version of the *idée fixe* (Example 1) is heard several times:

Example 7 (Idée fixe — third version)

Following a clarinet melody, the main theme, Example 6, returns in the second violins.

After a climax has been reached, the main theme, Example 6, and the *idée fixe,* Example 7, are heard simultaneously between pairs of instruments: first, between flute and first violins; then, between clarinet and second violins.

Sounds of the impending storm arise from the orchestra, then the mood of the introduction returns as fragments of Example 5 are heard.

The sounds of the distant storm are heard played by timpani again, and then disappear.

FOURTH MOVEMENT: March to the Gallows. *Allegretto non troppo.*

He dreams that he has murdered his Beloved, that he has been condemned to death and is being led to the execution. A march that is alternately somber and wild, brilliant and solemn, accompanies the procession . . . The tumultuous outbursts are followed without modulation by measured steps. At last the fixed idea returns, for a moment a last thought of love is revived — which is cut short by the death blow.

This movement is cast in the *march with trio* form. An introduction establishes with muffled drums the nature of this march.

After the introduction, the theme of the march is played by the celli and basses:

Example 8

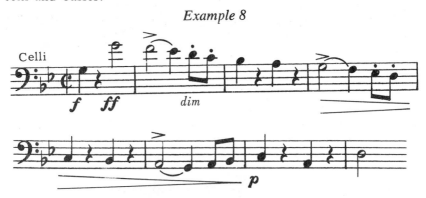

Example 8 is repeated by the violins, and the rhythm of the drum becomes more persistent.

The *trio* is based on a lighter, though still martial, theme:

Example 9

The *march* is repeated, this time with Example 8 played by the trombones and tuba. It is repeated by the full orchestra *fortissimo*.

In the *coda* the strings play an agitated melodic figure of alternating dotted-eighths and sixteenth notes, which is interrupted.

The clarinet plays the *idée fixe* (Example 1) or "dream of the Beloved":

Example 10 (Idée fixe — fourth version)

A few chords conclude the movement.

FIFTH MOVEMENT: Dream of the Witches' Sabbath. *Larghetto.*

He dreams that he is present at a witches' revel, surrounded by horrible spirits, amidst sorcerers and monsters in many fearful forms, who have come together for his funeral. Strange sounds, groans, shrill laughter, distant yells, which other cries seem to answer. The Beloved melody is heard again, but it has lost its shy and noble character; it has become a vulgar, trivial, grotesque dance tune. She it is who comes to attend the witches' meeting. Riotous howls and shouts greet her arrival . . . She joins the infernal orgy . . . bells toll for the dead . . . a burlesque parody of the *Dies Irae* [the Latin mass for the dead] . . . the witches' round dance. The dance and the *Dies Irae* are heard together.

Repeated notes by the upper strings provide an eerie introduction.

The theme of the Beloved (*idée fixe* — Example 1) is played by the clarinet in a debased and vulgar version:

Example 11 (Idée fixe — fifth version)

The full orchestra takes up the theme of the Beloved in its vulgar version, Example 11.

The swirl of the dance reaches a climax and the brass sustain a loud chord. The midnight bell is heard.

The bells continue to sound as the bassoons and tuba announce the *Dies Irae:*

Example 12 (Dies Irae)

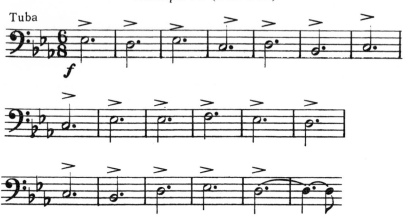

Example 12, the *Dies Irae,* is repeated twice as fast by the horns and trombones in a passage of mock solemnity. It is then repeated four times as fast by the woodwinds.

The bassoons and tuba then announce the last portion of the *Dies Irae.* It is, in turn, repeated twice as fast by the horns and trombones, then four times as fast by the woodwinds.

Accompanied by gong and pizzicato strings, Example 12 returns as it appeared the first time. The repetition of this theme at double and quadruple tempo is heard again.

A crescendo is made by the gong and timpani leading to the dance of the witches. The theme of the "round" dance is introduced in canonic imitation:

Example 13

A watercolor painted by Mendelssohn in 1847 during his stay in Switzerland. Throughout his life the composer made pencil sketches and watercolors of scenes during his travels.

A fanciful painting by Joseph Danhauser showing Franz Liszt and his friends: Musset, Victor Hugo, George Sands, Paganini, Rossini, and Countess d'Agoult.

The horns and violas are heard with fragments of the *Dies Irae*, Example 12.

The witches' dance theme, Example 13, returns in imitative style, starting in the lower strings and rising higher and higher. It is then played in unison by the strings.

As the composer stated in the preface, the two tunes are now combined: the witches' dance, Example 13, and the *Dies Irae*, Example 12, the first by the strings, the latter by the brass and woodwinds. This leads quickly to an ending of complete abandon.

FELIX MENDELSSOHN-BARTHOLDY

BORN: February 3, 1809; Hamburg, Germany.
DIED: November 4, 1847; Leipzig, Germany.

For over twenty years, thanks to the cooperation of professional musicians, concerts of exceptionally high caliber were given in the home of Abraham Mendelssohn each Sunday. Many were conducted by his son Felix. An account describes the setting for the orchestra programs:

The large and noble old house in the Leipzigerstrasse was well suited to recitals of music. An immense *salon* was connected by a colonnade to another room, a sort of annex for theatrical performances. Behind the house . . . there stretched a courtyard, lawns, a park, magnificent avenues of trees and a private forest, a peaceful retreat and a paradise for birds. Beneath a leafy dome there stretched a summer house, the main body of which was an entrancing arbor which served as a sort of concert hall . . . Distinguished foreigners, ·Berlin's high society, poets, artists, painters, sculptors, scientists, philosophers and. well-known writers met in this *salon de musique* which was soon famous throughout all Germany.*

Young Felix (for he was then a boy of only fourteen) not only conducted this semi-professional orchestra, but composed a great many works for the concerts. It was a unique experience for him to have an orchestra at his disposal for the purpose of learning both composition and conducting technique.

Abraham Moses was the grandson of Mendel, a poor Jew of Dessau who spent his time transcribing the Pentateuch and other sacred writings. Mendel's son Moses (who took the name Mendelssohn according to Jewish tradition) rose from obscurity to become the leading scholar of Germany, known in his day as the "German Sophocles." His second son, Abraham, married Leah Salomon, the

* Jacques Petitpiere, *The Romance of the Mendelssohns.*

daughter of a Berlin banker, and they became Protestant Christians at the time of their marriage. In order to distinguish their branch of the family from the Jewish, they added the name *Bartholdy* to their own.

Abraham Mendelssohn-Bartholdy was a banker of Hamburg; his wife was a talented person who played the piano and sang well, painted water-colors, and spoke German, French, Italian, English, and read Greek. She started giving both Felix and his older sister Fanny daily piano lessons when they were four. Fanny evidenced as much musical talent as did Felix, and she also composed music (her father warned her, however, that for a young lady, music could be nothing more than an avocation). The Mendelssohns left Hamburg for Berlin when Napoleon's forces overtook the former city.

In their new home, the Mendelssohn children (there were two besides Fanny and Felix—Rebecca and Paul—who also had musical ability) were expected to do well in their academic subjects. They were up at five in the morning and had to be at their studies immediately after breakfast. The children were closely supervised by both parents as they learned Greek and mathematics. The services of a professional piano teacher were secured for Fanny and Felix who studied together. Felix became a member of the Singakademie when he was ten as an alto (he remained with this group after his voice changed, singing as a tenor). He composed and had performed a setting of *Psalm XIX* the first year he belonged.

When he was fourteen, Felix' father took him to Paris to meet the famous Cherubini who was head of the Conservatory there. Cherubini assured Abraham Mendelssohn that what other musicians had told him about his son were indeed true, that the boy had an exceptional talent. So enthusiastic was Cherubini, he offered to teach the boy. The father decided, however, that the home influence would be better and took young Felix back to Berlin with him.

One of Mendelssohn's (it is in this abbreviated form that his name is generally seen) most famous compositions was completed when he was only sixteen, the *Overture* to *A Midsummer Night's Dream*. Although other movements were added to this incidental music for Shakespeare's play seventeen years later, the *Overture* shows as much skill and maturity in its composition as the later movements. The same year that the *Overture* was completed, Mendelssohn enrolled at the University of Berlin. He probably received a better formal and general education than any other composer. In addition to his classical studies there, he learned how to ride, swim, dance, play billiards, and participated actively in the social life of the school. As a student, he completed his first volume of *Songs Without Words* and a concert overture, inspired by a work of Goethe, *Calm Sea and Prosperous Voyage.*

In reading through various musical scores, Mendelssohn came across the *Passion According to St. Matthew* by Johann Sebastian Bach, a name almost unknown in Germany at that time. After much effort, the twenty-year-old Felix was able to persuade the Singakademie to perform the work. This was the first time it had been heard since Bach's death seventy-nine years before. The performance was responsible for a revival of all the music of Bach. So successful was the performance of the work, that over a thousand people had to be turned away from its first rendition, and two more performances were scheduled.

Abraham Mendelssohn decided that an extensive tour was a fitting climax to his son's completion of a formal education at the University. Felix traveled first to London where he conducted orchestral concerts and gave piano recitals. His *Symphony No. 1* was premiered in England. He traveled to Scotland where a phenomenon of nature known as Fingal's Cave inspired a concert overture which he so named. He then traveled leisurely to south Germany, then on to Austria, Italy (where both the *Scotch* and the *Italian* symphonies were completed), to Switzerland, Paris, and back to London again. The English city again gave him an enthusiastic reception. It was his first opportunity to have a work published — the first six *Songs Without Words* for piano.

On his return to Germany, he was called to the Lower Rhine Music Festival held at Düsseldorf and, from the quality of his conducting at the festival, he was invited to become the Musical Director there. In this position, he headed the church music, opera, and two singing societies as well as the orchestra.

Mendelssohn next received an appointment as the director of the Leipzig Gewandhaus Orchestra. His work with this orchestra influenced the musical life of that city tremendously. He worked long and hard to build the orchestra into one of the finest performing organizations in Germany. During his Leipzig days, he composed both his oratorio *St. Paul* and the *Concerto in E Minor for Violin and Orchestra.* He met a young lady by the name of Cécile Charlotte Sophie Jeanrenaud, the daughter of a Protestant clergyman, and fell in love with her. They were married on the twenty-eighth of March, 1837, at the French Reformed Church in Frankfurt. The oratorio *Elijah* was started shortly after this.

Frederich Wilhelm IV tried to found a school of the arts in Berlin and offered Mendelssohn the position of director of the School of Music. After many letters were exchanged between the two, Mendelssohn reluctantly left his Leipzig position to become the Royal General Director of Music at the new institution. Two years later, he returned to Leipzig to found a Conservatory and invited his friend Robert Schumann to join him on the staff. Mendelssohn taught piano at the Leipzig school as well as handling the directorial responsibilities.

Mendelssohn soon made his tenth trip to London. He conducted six performances of his *Elijah* and gave a two-hour command recital for Queen Victoria and Prince Albert. On his return to Germany, he resigned his position at the Conservatory for he felt that he had been overworked for several years. He retired to Frankfurt, but had hardly arrived there when he received word of the death of his beloved sister Fanny who had been a partner in so many of his musical activities. He was prostrated, falling senseless from a rupture of a blood vessel in his head. He rallied enough to move his wife and five children to Switzerland for rest, but four months later had to return to Leipzig. His strength ebbed steadily and he finally passed away after a period of twenty-four hours of unconsciousness.

BIBLIOGRAPHY

Seldon-Goth, G., editor. *Felix Mendelssohn Letters.* London: Cole and Co., Ltd., 1946.
Petitpiere, Jacques. *The Romance of the Mendelssohns,* trans. G. Micholet-Coté. London: Dennis Dobson, Ltd., 1947.

CONCERTO FOR VIOLIN AND ORCHESTRA
in E Minor

Felix Mendelssohn

Felix Mendelssohn had made several attempts to compose a violin concerto, but the *E Minor* is the only one he ever completed. Ferdinand David was one of the most important violinists of the nineteenth century and had been a close friend of Mendelssohn's since their childhood days in Hamburg. When Mendelssohn was appointed the director of the Gewandhaus Concerts in Leipzig, he immediately requested his friend David to serve as concertmaster. Two years after David assumed this position, Mendelssohn started talking about a concerto in E minor, but it was another six years before the work was completed. The composer made a special effort to consult with David numerous times to evaluate the technical difficulties of the solo part. He wanted it to be easy enough to "be executed with the greatest delicacy." The *Concerto* is not without its difficulties, yet is one that is particularly rewarding for the soloist.

Up to the time of the Mendelssohn *Concerto for Violin*, it had been the custom in the first movement (based on the sonata-allegro form) to have a double exposition: the full orchestra (tutti) first introduced the themes in a bold manner, and then, in order for the soloist to be heard above the orchestral forces, the dynamics would suddenly drop to a piano and the soloist would state the themes. All this changed with this concerto. Mendelssohn introduces the solo violin in the second measure playing the Principal Subject.

Another problem that had long bothered composers was the *cadenza*. The virtuosi demanded this opportunity to display their technical skill and bravura, yet the cadenza had little connection with the thematic development of the composition. Up to Beethoven's time, most soloists composed their own cadenzas and simply inserted them at the point marked in the music: CADENZA. Beethoven could not tolerate what he heard interpolated in artistic compositions, so he became the first to write out the exact cadenza he wanted the performer to play. The custom was for the cadenza to occur at the end of the *recapitulation* leading directly to the *coda* and the culmination of the movement. This kept the artist's fiery display fresh in the public's mind so that a large burst of applause could follow. Mendelssohn in the *Concerto for Violin* instituted a tremendous change, one that was imitated many times after his daring. The position of the cadenza was moved to the end of the *development,* or at the dramatic crisis of the *recapitulation* after the *development.* (He avoided the problem in his piano concerti by omitting the cadenza altogether.)

The composer also insisted that the three movements be played without a break, writing artistic bridges to cross from one movement to the next. Unfortunately, the public is seldom educated to this, and they break the continuity by applause between movements.

FIRST MOVEMENT: *Allegro molto appassionato.*

After a measure and a half of introduction, the solo violin announces the Principal Subject:

Example 1 (Principal Subject)

The soloist elaborates on this theme, Example 1, and then the orchestra becomes prominent, arriving shortly at a restatement of Example 1

The violins and oboe play an energetic transitional theme which is repeated by the solo violin:

Example 2 (transitional theme)

The solo violin has many figurations and runs in an extended episode. The music then becomes more tranquil, and the solo violin descends in an arpeggio a three octave span, sustaining a low, open G at its conclusion.

Over the sustained solo violin G, the flutes and clarinets play the Second Subject:

Example 3 (*Second Subject*)

Example 3 is repeated by the solo violin.

The solo violin takes up Example 1, this time in D major. As the music builds in intensity, trills and tremolos are heard in the full orchestra as Example 1 is brilliantly declaimed by the soloist.

The *development* begins with the transition theme, Example 2. It moves quickly to the opening figure of Example 1, constantly shifting keys.

It is at the return to the tonic key that Mendelssohn introduces the cadenza. It is dramatic and most logical in this position.

As the solo violinist's arpeggios from the end of the cadenza continue, the *recapitulation* opens with the Principal Subject, Example 1, softly played by the flutes, oboes, and violins.

The transition theme, Example 2, enters dramatically in the full orchestra, *fortissimo,* and is repeated by the solo violin, fading away to *pianissimo.*

As the solo violinist fades away with Example 2 (see above) it sustains an E as the Second Subject, Example 3, is recapitulated in the tonic major. This is an extended section.

The orchestra resumes Example 1 over which the soloist plays some bravura passages. The *recapitulation* ends as did the *exposition,* the solo violin expands Example 1 as the orchestra supports with tremolos and trills.

The *coda* begins with Example 2 as the tempo accelerates and leads to the conclusion.

ROBERT SCHUMANN

BORN: June 8, 1810; Zwickau, Germany.
DIED: July 29, 1856; Endenich, Germany.

The marriage of Clara and Robert Schumann is one of the most ideal recorded in the annals of music history. She was the daughter of Robert's piano teacher, and, as children, they regarded each other affectionately as brother and sister. As a youthful composer, he confined himself exclusively to the writing of piano music. But as he became aware of his love for Clara, he turned to expressing himself in beautiful songs. During the year in which he was married, he composed over one hundred and thirty-eight! As a sensitive musician herself, Clara encouraged her husband and soon suggested he try the field of orchestral composition. His *Symphony No. 1* was completed the first year of their marriage. Clara outlived her husband

ROBERT AND CLARA SCHUMANN

A daguerreotype taken in 1850

FRANZ LISZT

Painted when the composer was twenty-seven

Liszt-Museum, Weimar

FRÉDÉRIC CHOPIN

The earliest known portrait, painted by Ambroise Miroszewski

The famous painting of Chopin by Eugène Delacroix in the Louvre

by many years and, after his death, she traveled the length and breadth of Europe giving recitals of her husband's music. One of her final concerts bears the date 1896 — forty years after Robert's death.

Robert Schumann was the youngest son of a bookseller and editor. His first music lessons with the town organist started when Robert was eight. He had tried his hand at composition the year before. By eleven, the boy was writing both instrumental and choral compositions without instruction. When he was sixteen, his father wished him to study with Carl Maria von Weber, but unfortunately von Weber died before the arrangement could be completed. Schumann's father passed away shortly afterward. Robert graduated from the Zwickau Gymnasium (high school) where his principal interest had been in the Romantic writers, Byron and Jean Paul Richter. He enrolled in Leipzig University to pursue a course in law.

Schumann was soon attracted to the University of Heidelberg where he studied both law and music. While there he heard a concert by the famous violinist, Paganini, and decided to make music his career. He wrote to his mother requesting permission to move to Leipzig so that he could devote his full time to the study of music. After receiving her permission, he moved into the home of Friederick Wieck who was to be his piano teacher. At first he regarded his teacher's daughter, Clara, as a very charming sister.

Not being acquainted with the physiology of the hand, Schumann developed a device that made use of a sling and some weights whereby he could strengthen his fourth finger, always the pianist's weakest. The finger, unfortunately, could not take the gruelling exercise and torture and became paralyzed. Schumann then turned his attention from a career as a pianist and concentrated on piano compositions.

When he was twenty-four, Schumann founded a new journal, the *Neue Zeitschrift für Musik*. The paper was dedicated to the promotion of new music and opposed the "decadent Italian music" then heard frequently. He was the sole editor for nine years and contributed many valuable and important articles to it. It was through this publication that the music world first became acquainted with a new Polish-French pianist by the name of Frédéric Chopin. Much later, the *Neue Zeitschrift* was the first to hail Johannes Brahms as a composer of talent.

Having been kept from visiting Clara at the insistence of her father, Robert traveled to Vienna in the hopes that he could publish his paper there. No one seemed to be interested in the project. He returned home and convinced Clara that if she could not get her father's permission to marry, they should apply to the legal authorities for a permit. The two were married on September 12, 1840. This was the year Robert composed one hundred and thirty-eight songs.

Settled in their new home, Clara inquired of her husband why he had written both piano music and lieder, but had never tried instrumental compositions. He turned immediately to this genre and soon completed his first symphony, the *Spring*. He recorded in his writings concerning this first year of marriage: "Few events, much happiness."

The following year Robert turned to chamber music, completing three string quartets, a piano quintet, and a piano quartet. An invitation was extended by Felix Mendelssohn to join the staff of the newly founded Leipzig Conservatory. Schumann became the professor of piano and composition and, while there, introduced a practice piano with footpedals for organ students (it was ten years before the Conservatory had its own pipe organ).

The Schumanns went on a tour of Russia during which Robert conducted many concerts. They returned from the trip to Dresden where Robert started giving private piano lessons, continuing work on his compositions (the *Piano Concerto* and *Symphony No. 2*), and frequently appeared as a guest conductor. He tried to make a move for his family to Vienna or Berlin, but was unsuccessful.

Schumann was such an intense person that he did not make an especially good piano teacher. Sometimes the entire lesson would pass without a word of comment from him. He felt that he was an ineffectual conductor. Once during a rehearsal, when the French horns had trouble with a passage, his only solution was to have the whole orchestra go back and play the passage again. The French horns made the same mistake; Schumann turned to the concertmaster and said, simply, "Poor fellows, they've made a mistake again."

An offer was extended to him, however, in 1850 to go to Düsseldorf on the Rhine River and become the conductor. The town had a better than average orchestra and a rather good choral society, so the Schumanns moved to the Rhenish city. He and his wife both looked forward to this change of residence and they seemed completely happy in their new home. Robert started work on another symphony which was completed in nine months — the *Rhenish Symphony*.

After three years in Düsseldorf, the strain of the past twenty years seemed too much for him to bear. All his life he had had the problem of learning to adjust to new situations and had never quite mastered it. He was quiet when in public and he never had any physical diversion from his intensive work with music — writing about it, conducting, and composing it. He felt the burden of family responsibility which kept growing larger. His income had never been good because he had been a poor piano teacher and an ineffective conductor. His compositions were still too "new" in style and manner to have a wide following, and thus little income was realized from them.

Mental depression, an affliction that had bothered him before, returned. He heard a constant pitch of A in his inner ear and became frightened. There were times when he became lost in a reverie and was completely oblivious to the outside world. Suddenly on the morning of February 6, 1854, he left the room which was occupied by a few of his friends and threw himself into the Rhine River. Whether he was lucid at the time and tried to commit suicide to prevent harm to his family, or whether this was part of one of his hallucinations, no one is certain.

He was rescued by the friends from the river, but it was necessary to place him in an institution just outside Bonn. His faithful wife was frequently at his bedside. After almost two years, during which time the hoped-for recovery had not taken place, he was less and less in the world of reality. Visiting him one day, Clara said, "he smiled at me." She wrote later that "with a great effort he clasped me with one of his arms. I would not give up that embrace for all the treasures on earth." Six days later Schumann passed away in mid-afternoon.

BIBLIOGRAPHY

Bourourechliev, André. *Schumann,* trans. Arthur Boyars. New York: Grove Press, 1959.
Young, Percy M. *Tragic Muse: The Life and Works of Robert Schumann.* London: Hutchinson and Co., Ltd., 1957.

SYMPHONY NO. 3

in E-Flat Major

"RHENISH"

Robert Schumann wrote to his publisher that this symphony "mirrors here and there something of Rhenish life." At another time, he said: "In my symphony I hoped to portray joyful folk life along the Rhine, and I think I have succeeded."

It was during Schumann's first winter at Düsseldorf that he composed the *Symphony No. 3,* between November 2 and December 9. During the span of those thirty-seven days the composer was called upon to make a trip to Cologne. While there he witnessed the installation of the Archbishop at the Cologne Cathedral. It was this solemn ceremony which inspired the fourth movement, sometimes called the "Cathedral" movement.

SECOND MOVEMENT: Scherzo. *Sehr mässig* (Very moderate).

This movement was originally titled "Morning on the Rhine."

It is more a ländler, a peasant folk dance of Germany, than a scherzo, although it loosely follows the traditional *scherzo with trio* form. If the principal melody of the movement is not an old peasant drinking song, as claimed by some critics, it is identical in character to a Rhineweinlied (a Rhenish wine song).

The movement opens with a melody full of good nature and reminiscent of the lumbering ländler. It is played by the violins, bassoons, and celli:

Example 1

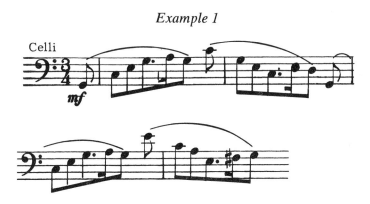

The first eight measures are repeated, then the violins and upper woodwinds play Example 1 and repeat it.

The second theme, also played by the strings, moves more lightly and quickly in the style of a true *scherzo:*

Example 2

In the closing portion of the first section, fragments of the first melody (Example 1) are heard in the celli, horns, and bassoons, against the rhythm of the second melody (Example 2) played by high strings.

The *trio* opens with the French horns playing Example 3 to the accompaniment of clarinets and bassoons:

Example 3

This is accompanied by the rhythm of the second theme (Example 2).

After the first theme, Example 1, reappears, the opening measures of the *trio* are repeated. (This use in the *trio* of a melody from the first section is unorthodox. The movement as a whole departs from tradition in that its third section is not a repetition of the first since the second theme, Example 2, does not appear at all in it.)

The third section (supposedly the recapitulation of the first) begins with the first theme, Example 1, which predominates until the end:

      in the low woodwinds and celli
      in the strings
      in the French horn with a new woodwind accompaniment
         which builds to a rousing climax

A French horn call boldly announces the brief *coda*. The *coda* closes with a final statement of the first theme, Example 1, by the celli.

THIRD MOVEMENT: *Nicht schnell* (Not fast).

The third movement is in ternary form and opens with the clarinets, bassoons, and violas playing the theme of the first section:

Example 4

The second part of this first theme follows one measure later in the first violins:

Example 5

The middle section is based on a melody introduced by the bassoons:

Example 6

Only fifteen measures later the first section returns; the clarinet introduces Example 4 and then is joined by the bassoons.

A short *codetta* brings the movement to a close.

DIE BEIDEN GRENADIERE

(*The Two Grenadiers*)

ROBERT SCHUMANN

Both Robert Schumann and Richard Wagner composed settings for this poem of Heinrich Heine, and both introduced the melody of the *Marseillaise:* Schumann as the climax of it, and Wagner as a general motive. Schumann's was written in 1840, the so-called "year of song" in which he composed over one hundred and sixty-eight lieder.

The poem is a ballad which tells about two soldiers of the *Grande Armée* who, freed from a Russian prison camp, were returning to France. En route they heard about the Battle of Waterloo, the defeat of their army, and the capture of Napoleon.

After a two measure piano introduction which establishes a martial atmosphere, Example 1 is heard:

Example 1

Nach Frank-reich zogen zwei   Grena - dier',   die

wa - ren   in Russland   ge - fangen.

Nach Frankreich zogen zwei Grenadier',	Toward France there journeyed two grenadiers,
Die waren in Russland gefangen.	Who had been captured in Russia;
Und als sie kamen in's deutsche Quartier,	And they hung their heads, and their eyes had tears
Sie liessen die Köpfe hangen.	As they came to the border of Prussia.

A second melody is introduced, accompanied by grave-sounding half-notes in the piano accompaniment:

Example 2

Da hör - ten sie Bei - de die trau - ri - ge Mähr': dass

Frankreich ver - lo - ren ge - gan - gen,

Da hörten sie Beide die traurige Mähr':	They heard the terrible news again
Dass Frankreich verloren gegangen,	That France had been lost and forsaken;
Besiegt und geschlagen das tapfere Heer,	Her armies were beaten, her captains were slain,
Und der Kaiser, der Kaiser gefangen.	And the Emperor, the Emperor was taken!

The melody of Example 1 is repeated and moves on to a variation of Example 2, almost in the style of a recitative:

Da weinten zusammen die Grenadier'	Together they wept, these two grenadiers,
Wohl ob der kläglichen Kunde.	To one thing their thoughts kept returning —
Der Eine sprach: ,,Wie weh' wird mir,	"Alas," cried one, half-choked with tears,
Wie brennt meine alte Wunde!"	"Once more my old wound is burning."
Der Andre sprach: ,,Das Lied ist aus,	The other said, "The tale is told:
Auch ich möcht' mit dir sterben,	I'd welcome Death about me,
Doch hab' ich Weib und Kind zu Haus,	But I've a wife and child to hold;
Die ohne mich verderben."	What would they do without me?"

Example 1 returns for the next verse with a feeling of increased speed and tempo achieved by rhythmical variations within the melody:

,,*Was schert mich Weib., was schert mich Kind,*	"What matters wife? What matters child?
Ich trage weit besser Verlangen;	With far greater cares I'm shaken;
Lass sie betteln gehn, wenn sie hungrig sind —	Let them go and beg with hunger wild —
Mein Kaiser, mein Kaiser gefangen!	My Emperor, my Emperor is taken!

A variation of Example 2 accompanies the next verse, but becomes more intense as the accompaniment is changed from half-notes to an agitated triplet figure:

Gewähr' mir, Bruder, eine Bitt':	"And this, oh friend, my only prayer
Wenn ich jetzt sterben werde,	When I am dying, grant me:
So nimm meine Leiche nach Frankreich mit,	You'll carry my body to France, and there
Begrab' mich in Frankreichs Erde.	In the sweet soil of France you'll plant me.

An agitated melody, marked *faster,* is heard:

Das Ehren kreuz am rothen Band	"The cross of honor with crimson band
Sollst du auf's Herz mir legen;	Lay on my heart to cheer me;
Die Flinte gieb mir in die Hand.	Then put my musket in my hand
Und gürt' mir um den Degen.	And strap my sabre near me.

At the climax, the *Marseillaise* in the major mode is introduced:

Example 3

So will ich lie - gen und hor - chen still, wie

ei - ne Schildwach', im Gra - be

So will ich liegen und horchen still,
Wie eine Schildwach' im Grabe

Bis einst ich höre Kanonen gebrüll
Und wiehernder Rosse Getrabe.

Dann reitet mein Kaiser wohl über mein Grab,
Viel Schwerter klirren und blitzen,
Dann steig' ich gewaffnet hervor aus dem Grab
Den Kaiser, den Kaiser zu schützen!"

"And so I will lie and listen and wait,
Like a sentinel down in the grass there,
Till I hear the roar of the guns, and the great
Thunder of hoofs as they pass there.

"And the Emperor will come, and his columns will wave;
And the swords will be flashing and rending —
And I will arise, full-armored from the grave,
My Emperor, my Emperor attending!"

(Poem by Heinrich Heine; English translation by Louis Untermeyer)

DICHTERLIEBE

(*Poet's Love*)

A Song Cycle

ROBERT SCHUMANN

The term *song cycle* was first employed by Beethoven, and was later used by Schubert. Robert Schumann composed several, of which *Dichterliebe* is an outstanding example. It is a setting of sixteen songs based on the poems of Heinrich Heine. Schumann extracted from Heine's *Buch der Lieder* (Book of Songs), a collection of seventy-five poems, the first four in sequence, and then skipped among the others for twelve more. The original series had no plot, no action; rather, they were poems of love, frequently tinged with hints of faithlessness and anguish. Schumann added the title of "Poet" to these love songs.

The cyclical nature of this work derives not only from the poetry, which is from one source and itself somewhat cyclical, but from the musical treatment. The cadence at the end of *Im wunder-*

schönen Monat Mai (see below) is not complete, for it leads directly to the second song. Similarly, song follows song without jarring changes of keys, even though the subject matter and melodic treatment might be quite different from that of the preceding one. A repetition of one epilogue (from No. 12 to the last song) also gives a unity to the cycle. Three of the sixteen songs are discussed below.

(No. 1) Im Wunderschönen Monat Mai

This short, little miniature (but twenty-six measures in length) is strophic — its two verses are set to the same melodic line.

Im   wun-derschönen   Mo - nat   Mai,   als

al - le Knos - pen   sprangen,

Im wunderschönen Monat Mai,	In the wonderful month of May,
Als alle Knospen sprangen,	When all the buds were breaking,
Da ist in meinem Herzen	There was within my heart
Die Liebe aufgegangen.	An awakening of love.

Im wunderschönen Monat Mai,	In the wonderful month of May,
Als alle Vögel sangen,	When all the birds were singing,
Da hab' ich ihr gestanden	I did confess to her
Mein Sehnen und Verlangen.	My longing and my yearning.

(No. 3) Die Rose, Die Lilie

This short, fleeting lied sung *mezzo voce,* is marked *Sprightly* (*Munter*) by the composer. It seems as though it is one uninterrupted melodic line from beginning to end; it is however composed of three phrases, which, if designated by letters, would prove to be in binary form: A A' B.

Die Ro-se, die Li - lie, die   Tau-be, die Son-ne,

Die Rose, die Lilie, die Taube, die Sonne — The rose and the lily, the sun and the dove,
Die lieb' ich einst alle in Liebeswonne. — I loved them all once with the joy of love.

Melodic line A is repeated.

Ich lieb' sie nicht mehr, ich liebe alleine — I love them no more, I love only one,
Die Kleine, die Feine, die Reine, die Eine; — The little one, the fine one, the pure one, the only one!

B

sie sel - ber, al - ler Lie - be Won - ne,

Sie selber, aller Liebe Wonne, — She, herself, the joy of all love,
Ist Rose und Lilie und Taube und Sonne. — Is the rose and the lily, the sun and the dove.
Ich liebe alleine die Kleine, — I love only one, the little one,
Die Feine, die Reine, die Eine! — The fine one, the pure one, the only one!

(No. 7) ICH GROLLE NICHT

This lied is in contrast to the two just discussed, for it displays a picture of heartbroken misery. Heine wrote the poem out of great grief, for his beloved married another for money. Schumann has to be able to sustain this tragic feeling musically. The piano serves this purpose, for half-notes in the bass seem to proclaim a solemn march, while repeated chords in the right hand give the music a sense of urgency. The vocal line consists of short phrases, indicating such grief that one cannot continue.

Both verses start with the same nine measures, and then finish differently.

Ich grolle   nicht, und wenn das Herz   auch bricht,

Ich grolle nicht, und wenn das Herz auch bricht,
Ewig verlor'nes Lieb! Ich grolle nicht.
Wie du auch strahlst in Diamantenpracht,
Es fällt kein Strahl in deines Herzens Nacht,
Das weiss ich längst.

I bear no grudge, even though my heart may break,
Eternally lost love! I bear no grudge.
Though you are shining in your diamonds' splendor,
No ray falls into the darkness of your heart,
I've known it well for a long time.

Ich grolle nicht, und wenn das Herz auch bricht.
Ich sah dich ja im Traume,
Und sah die Nacht in deines Herzens Raume,
Und sah die Schlang', die dir am Herzen frisst,
Ich sah, mein Lieb, wie sehr du elend bist.
Ich grolle nicht, ich grolle nicht.

I bear no grudge, even though my heart may break.
For I saw you in my dream,
And I saw the darkness in your heart,
And saw the snake that feeds upon your heart,
I saw, my love, how utterly wretched you are.
I bear no grudge, I bear no grudge.

FRÉDÉRIC CHOPIN

BORN: February 22, 1810; Zelazowa Wola, Poland.
DIED: October 17, 1849; Paris, France.

In the days just before the Second Empire in France, Frédéric Chopin could frequently be found playing the piano in the grandest salons of the Parisian aristocracy. He was the toast of the city and was in demand at all the social gatherings of the cultured families. He lived in style with his own carriage and servants, gave receptions of his own, and was able to dine with his friends at the Café de Paris or at the Maison Dorée. He was witty, elegant, and just a bit of a snob.

Chopin was not born into the aristocratic life. He was born in Poland of a French father and a Polish mother. His father had moved to Poland as a young man and served for a time as a book-keeper in a tobacco firm run by a Frenchman. After this position, he twice tried to return to France, but was not able to effect the move. In financial desperation, he accepted a position as a French tutor in one of the wealthier homes. He fell in love with the housekeeper of the estate, a Polish girl, and they were married. Frédéric was the second child of this marriage.

Young Frédéric would spend hours crouched underneath the piano as his mother played. When he was six, his parents decided that he should receive lessons on the instrument. A Czechoslovak named Zwyny became Frédéric's piano teacher, actually the only piano teacher he ever had. Two years after the lessons started, the boy tried his hand at composition for the first time, writing a *polonaise*. It was at about this time that the young lad gave his first recital, playing a piano concerto at a charity benefit. He was hailed by his family and friends as another child prodigy like Mozart.

The Chopin family moved to Warsaw so that the boy could complete his general education at the Lyceum (high school) and then attend the Warsaw Conservatory. He studied both harmony and counterpoint with the head of that institution. Although Frédéric received no private lessons after his twelfth year, he continued to practice the piano as well as work on original compositions. When he was fifteen, he was presented a diamond ring by the Czar for his pianistic ability. In the same year, he prepared his first opus for publication, *Rondo in C Minor*. His feverish work in getting the manuscript ready for the publisher showed a strain on him, for he was of delicate health.

When Chopin was nineteen, he went with three of his friends for a visit to Vienna, Munich, and Paris. As he left his friends in Vienna, they insisted that he return soon, so great was the public's reception of his piano recitals. Chopin moved on to Paris where he settled. At the end of a year he returned to Vienna with great expectations, but his reception was not the same as on his first visit. In addition, he had a long argument with a Viennese publisher who had offered to publish two of his manuscripts. Bothered again with his health, he was shocked to hear that Poland had declared war on Russia. Persons of Polish extraction were then shunned in Vienna, and, between this and his concern for his family back in Warsaw, his days were most unhappy. Chopin's funds were at a low ebb and he decided to give a concert to raise enough money to return home. The concert was a failure, as the Viennese refused to attend a program given by a Pole. Finally enough money arrived from his family so that he planned to travel to London. En route, he learned that Warsaw had fallen. His trip to Great Britain was never completed; he stopped in Paris and decided to make that friendly city his home.

There he met Cherubini and Rossini. Later he became acquainted with Mendelssohn, Liszt, Meyerbeer, and Bellini. He made his Paris debut as a pianist when he was twenty-two. Up to this point, he had never been self-supporting and he realized that, with the war, he could no longer count on the stipend from his father. His concert appearances and piano lessons for children of middle class families could not possibly bring in enough money to support him either securely or in the style that he desired. He had about decided to emigrate to the United States where he was certain that parents paid more for their children's music lessons, when a chance encounter changed the course of his life. He met a friend one day during a walk down a Parisian boulevard who invited him to a soirée to be given that evening at the home of the Baron de Rothschild. Chopin's excellent manners, good grooming, and obvious refinement caught the eyes of many of the wealthy ladies there. When they heard the young man play the piano, they became convinced that he was the person who should teach their children.

For the next ten years Chopin was supremely happy. The lessons to the children of the aristocracy gave him an excellent income, and he greatly enjoyed being a guest in their homes and playing the piano for their social gatherings. (He never did enjoy giving a "public" concert.) These were also some of the most fertile years as far as his compositions were concerned, for he completed a number of *Preludes, Mazurkas,* and *Waltzes.*

Robert Schumann, who had been one of the first to acknowledge Chopin's ability as a composer, wrote in his journal, the *Neue Zeitschrift* in 1839: "He is indeed the boldest and proudest poetic spirit of the time." As Chopin's fame as a composer rose, his ability as a pianist declined. He much preferred composition to playing the piano. He disliked technical exercises and hours of practice at the keyboard. When he was twenty-five, he renounced a career as a pianist. He only appeared three times after that in a public recital.

His health, never good, started to decline. During the first winter after this, he met the famous writer George Sand (the pen name of Madame Dudevant) through their mutual friend, Franz Liszt. She had a son about the same age as Chopin who was also quite ill. She suggested that the composer join them in a trip to Majorca off the Spanish coast for recuperation. Chopin borrowed some money on the *Preludes* he was preparing in order to make the trip.

Majorca did nothing to improve his health. There were no adequate hotels, the rooms that were rented were poorly furnished, the food not edible, and the rains were incessant. Chopin's cough turned to bronchitis and the people of Majorca treated him as an infected person, forcing him to leave the village. The custom officials refused to release his piano and he could not complete the *Preludes*. Knowing that he had to finish them so that he could obtain enough money to pay for the trip, he found an old piano in the basement of the house they were renting. The three, Sand, her son, and Chopin, finally left Majorca for Barcelona and then moved on to Marseilles where Chopin underwent a medical examination. The doctor claimed that he did not have tuberculosis even though he complained of coughing "bowls full of blood."

The trio returned to Paris. Madame Sand had become tired of nursing her "patient" so arranged for them to live in adjoining houses. Chopin shortly had many of his old piano students back again and started publishing new works so that his financial status improved tremendously. Unfortunately his health did not make the same recovery, and in 1842 he wrote a friend, "I have to stay in bed all day I have so much pain in my beastly face and glands." The news of his father's death greatly depressed him. He was already too ill to walk up the stairs to his own room, and his cough became even worse.

The following spring his friendship with George Sand was ruptured. Her son, Maurice, had never liked Chopin in spite of their common bond of poor health, had always resented the composer's presence in his mother's home. The mother sided with her son, while her daughter sided with Chopin in this disagreement. After the friendship ended, Chopin composed no more.

When the revolution hit Paris for the second time, Chopin was forced to flee to London in spite of his health. There he found it necessary to spend many hours making social calls and meeting new people. He gave a command performance for Queen Victoria as well as several other recitals. He tried to support himself by giving private piano lessons, but complained that the British refused to pay the teacher adequately. On an excursion to Scotland, he caught a cold and was forced to return to London where he was confined to his bed. He recovered sufficiently to make the return trip to Paris which was again a peaceful city. Home once more, his health rapidly deteriorated and he passed away on the seventeenth of October in his thirty-ninth year.

His funeral was held at the Madelaine church where the Mozart *Requiem* was sung at his request; the organist played the *Funeral March* from Chopin's own *Sonata*. He was buried at Père-Lachaise cemetery between Cherubini and Bellini. The small bit of Polish soil that he had carried with him ever since he had left home in his early twenties was thrown across his casket.

BIBLIOGRAPHY

Cortot, Alfred. *In Search of Chopin,* trans. Cyril and Rena Clarke. London: Peter Neville, Ltd., 1951.

Weinstock, Herbert. *Chopin: The Man and His Music.* New York: Alfred A. Knopf, Inc., 1949.

BALLADE NO. 3
Opus 47, in A-Flat Major

The term *ballade* (French form of the noun "ballad") was used by Chopin in a new sense. Ballads originally were dance-songs, and later the dance part was abandoned, leaving it as a vocal form. In its turn, the epic or "romantic" ballad was a song in which an heroic story was sung — sometimes dealing with feats of knightly gallantry, or perhaps with miraculous or gruesome deeds. Chopin was familiar with the poetic ballads of early Romanticism — *The Erlking* (a poem by Goethe, later set as a lied by Schubert), *The Two Grenadiers* (a poem by Heine, later set as a lied by Schumann), and many others.

Although some authors have attempted to attach certain ballads or stories with the four Chopin *Ballades,* there is no evidence whatsoever to support their claim. It seems, rather, that Chopin intended to convey through his piano music the flavor of romantic feeling. He usually employed a first theme which was heroic and epic in line, contrasted with a second theme which was lyrical.

The *Ballade No. 3* employs two such contrasting themes.

The first eight measures introduce the first theme:

Example 1

mezza voce

After a seventeen measure development of the first theme, a transition motive is introduced:

Example 2

The first theme, Example 1, is then heard again, ending with a long-sustained tonic chord.

The second theme, lyrical in nature, is ushered in with broken octaves:

Example 3

There is a constant shifting of the key center throughout the following section as harmonies float about in an unanchored way. After a development of Example 3, it returns for ten measures in its original form.

A transitory figure (derived from Example 2 in inversion) appears:

Example 4

A low, fast-moving figure appears in the bass as the key changes to C-sharp minor:

Example 5

A repeated G-sharp in the upper voice accompanies the melodic development of this section.

The heroic first theme, Example 1, returns, first in fragments, then in a full statement with a greatly altered accompaniment. An impressive climax builds, and then is interrupted by Example 4. A cadence closes the *Ballade*.

ETUDE

Opus 10, No. 12 in C Minor

Etudes are frequently called "Studies" in English. This is a literal translation from the French. Studies have been written by many keyboard virtuosi to develop a technique and skill in the manipulation of the hands across the keyboard. No one, however, was able to invest his Studies with such melody and harmonic development as Chopin. His became selections for the concert hall rather than just exercises to be practiced at home.

The Chopin *Etudes* employed several techniques that were new and unique. Some of these in the *Twelve Etudes* of Opus 10 are: extension of the hand, covering the keyboard with arpeggios across many octaves (No. 1); attacks and a quick passing over weak fingers (No. 2); study entirely on the black keys (No. 5); training for the thumb in a manner never employed before (No. 8); chords of the broken sixth requiring the wrist to be levered up and down some six hundred times (No. 10); and arpeggio chords for both hands (No. 12). In addition he quite frequently required rapid successions of parallel thirds and sixths in unexpected keys. The performer of Chopin *Etudes* must be careful that these difficult technical feats are well learned so that the performance does not become mechanical, but can bring out the musical elements in the music.

This *Etude* is frequently listed on concert programs as the "Revolutionary" etude, although the composer never appended such a title.

Some fanciful writers have said that it was inspired by the fall of Warsaw, but musically it seems much more an heroic statement of faith with its broad, choral-like theme. The composer intended one to know only that it was to be played *con fuoco* (with fire!).

A brilliant, descending arpeggio for the left hand is punctuated by chords played by the right hand.

After the nine measure introduction, the main theme is introduced in octaves in the right hand, accompanied by arpeggios in the left:

Example 1

After a restatement of this theme, fragments of it are heard as the music modulates through several keys.

A new theme is heard:

Example 2

A descending arpeggio in octaves, played by both hands, returns the music to the original bass accompaniment over which Example 1 is heard again. The opening three notes are expanded to four and five notes which embellish the principal melodic line; these become part of a triplet figure.

As the embellishments to the opening notes of Example 1 appear in another form, a climax is built, at which point Example 2 returns in a bold manner.

The volume quickly subsides, although the descending bass arpeggio continues.

Suddenly, the descending arpeggio in octaves is repeated *fortissimo ed appassionato* (loudly and passionately) and ends the composition after four chords in C major, a most deceptive ending.

FANTAISIE-IMPROMPTU

Opus 66 (Posthumous)

The *Fantaisie* in the title was not prefixed by Chopin, but by the first publisher. Another curious point is the fact that of the four *Impromptus,* this one was written first, but not published until fifteen years later, after the composer's death.

The *Impromptu* of the title comes from the French adjective meaning "unprepared" or "unpremeditated." The four Chopin *Impromptus* are basically in ternary form. The famous pianist of the early twentieth century, Alfred Cortot, sums it up very nicely in his edition of Chopin's *Impromptu:* "The music should appear in some way to be born under the fingers of the performer."

The first section of the ternary form opens with a fast figure in the right hand, Example 1, over a rolling bass arpeggio:

Example 1

After an extended presentation of Example 1, it is repeated.

After a downward series of octaves in quarter notes is played by the left hand, the tempo changes to *Moderato cantabile* for the introduction of the theme of the middle section. The second theme is so lyrical that it once became the theme of a popular Broadway song.

Example 2

Example 2 is repeated once, and then developed in an extended passage.

The key and tempo of the first section returns, and Example 1 is recapitulated. It is repeated as it was the first time; the descending octaves in the left hand lead to the coda.

The coda quickly moves from a *fortissimo* to a *pianissimo* as an arpeggio pattern is established in the right hand. Underneath this, the melody of Example 2 returns in extension in the bass and leads to an ending marked *ppp*.

MAZURKA

Opus 7, No. 3 in F Minor

Chopin composed over fifty *Mazurkas*, probably his favorite of the many characteristic piano genre in which he composed. His last two works before his death were mazurkas. Too ill to play the piano, he stated, "I must work, I must draw these mazurkas out of my lacerated heart!"

The mazurka is a lively peasant dance that originated in the plains of Mazovia and later became identified with the history of Poland. The dance is in triple meter (3/4 or 3/8) with the accent on the second or third beat of the measure. Franz Liszt called it a dance that was "proud, tender, provocative."

Chopin was the first to use the mazurka as an art form. Liszt stated that Chopin "released the unknown poetry which had only been hinted at in the original themes of the Polish mazurkas. Retaining their rhythm, he has ennobled their melody, enlarged their proportions."

The opening theme gives evidence of its folk origin, both in melody and rhythm. The triplet that sets off the phrase is very characteristic of Polish dances. A guitar-like bass provides a unique accompaniment.

Example 1

Another dance theme is introduced:

Example 2

Large, solid chords are heard in a section that begins on the dominant, D-flat:

Example 3

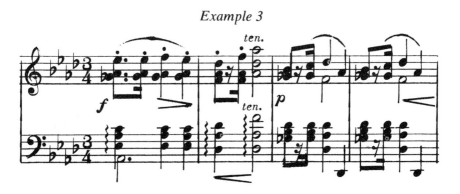

Following the development of Example 3, the left hand appears with a new melody:

Example 4

The *Mazurka* ends with a return to the melody of Example 1.

NOCTURNE

Opus 15, No. 2 in F-sharp Major

The first nocturnes were written by an Irishman, John Field, from whom Chopin adopted the name and idea. Field's works by this name were full of arpeggio chords, ornamentation, great climaxes, and sweet melodies that swept ladies of the salons of Paris into an "enthusiasm impossible to describe."

That night and night-pieces had an appeal for the nineteenth century Romanticists is undeniable. Hector Berlioz wrote of the evening rites at one of Chopin's homes (in Nohant with George Sand) when all the lamps were put out and everyone fell silent: "when the big salon butterflies had gone, when the scandal-mongers had come to an end of their stories, when all the traps were laid, all the treacheries committed, when everyone was all too weary of prose, then, in answer to the prayer of some beautiful, intelligent pair of eyes, Chopin became the poet."

While Berlioz' account might seem verbose and highly romantic, this was the very essence of the period into which the nocturne entered. Chopin in his nineteen *Nocturnes* was able to avoid the hollow indulgences of the earlier Fields, and instill his compositions with both an emotional and musical content never quite equalled.

The F-sharp major *Nocturne* opens with a melancholy melody over a broken bass accompaniment:

Example 1

Example 1 becomes hard to distinguish as it is ornamented with arabesques and figurations.

The tempo doubles as a more lively theme is heard:

Example 2

Example 2 is repeated and developed.

The first theme, Example 1, returns — starting just about as it did the first time — for two measures, and then a smooth, cadenza-like passage intrudes. The balance of the theme is highly decorated with trills and triplets.

The music quickly fades at the end.

POLONAISE

Opus 53 in A-Flat Major

Frédéric Chopin's first composition at the age of eight was a *polonaise;* at twelve, and again at sixteen, he composed polonaises. Yet this form took time for the composer to master; it did not leap from his pen in inspiration and complete mastery of the genre, as did the *Etudes,* for example.

The polonaise is a slow dance, twice as slow as the mazurka, the rhythmic structure in a triple meter being:

By origin, it was the dance of the nobility, a procession in grave and majestic rhythm, of princes before their king. In its popular form, the polonaise retains the character of a dance that one walks or, better, glides.

The A-flat major *Polonaise* opens with an introduction based on a series of first inversion chords which move quickly up the chromatic scale:

Example 1

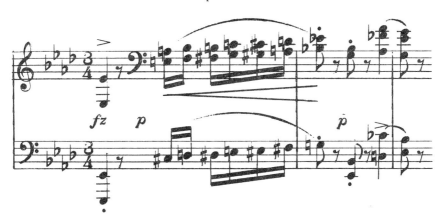

The main theme is heard immediately after the introduction, accompanied by octaves in the left hand based on the tonic chord:

Example 2

After an extension of Example 2, it is repeated more forcefully in octaves.

A new section is built on a figure which keeps moving within the initial octave span:

Example 3

A more lyrical theme is introduced:

Example 4

Example 4 is played in octaves and decorated with trills and runs, and leads immediately to a return of Example 2 in octaves, *fortissimo.*

A new section is introduced. The accompaniment pattern is heard first: after a series of rolled E major chords, the left hand takes up a pattern of four descending notes in octaves (E, D-sharp, C-sharp, B). The melody appears over this continually repeated bass pattern:

Example 5

The music modulates to E-flat major briefly, then returns to E major as Example 5 is heard again.

Once again a modulation to E-flat major occurs, this time more boldly. As the force of the passage subsides, a new and lighter theme is introduced in D major:

Example 6

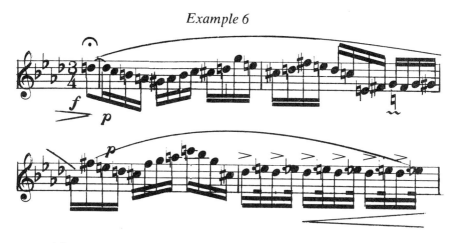

After Example 6 has been expanded and developed, a crescendo leads to the return of the melody of Example 2 in octaves, *fortissimo.*

A powerful, five octave scale moves upwards across the keyboard, leading to the final statement of Example 2 in the upper octaves of the piano.

A series of chords concludes the polonaise.

PRELUDE

Opus 28, No. 15 in D-Flat Major

The Chopin *Preludes* are the most miniature of the short character pieces of the Romantic piano literature; one is thirteen measures in length. They are a miracle of conciseness, yet these sketches abound in lyricism and inspiration. They are set out according to the scheme devised by Johann Sebastian Bach in his *Wohl Tempiert Clavier* (The Well Tempered Keyboard) in which he composed a *Prelude* and *Fugue* in each of the major and minor keys. Chopin has used only the *Prelude,* and in the twenty-four of them, examined each of the major and minor keys; he appends the relative minor immediately after the major: *i.e.* C major by A minor; G major by E minor, and so on.

Frédéric Chopin felt that Bach was the epitome of economy in form, and said, "Bach will not age. The structure of his work resembles perfectly drawn, geometrical figures, in which everything is in its proper place, in which no line is too much."

The age of Romanticism could not accept this explanation of a reversion to the earlier, more absolute form of music. The Romantics in their enthusiasm had to attach a programmatic idea to everything. Since many of the *Preludes* of Chopin were composed while he lived on the island of Majorca, this seemed to be the logical area in which to search for "titles" and programmatic allusions. The D-flat major *Prelude* described below was christened by them the "Raindrop" since it was learned it had rained a good portion of the time Chopin was in Majorca. Other foolish titles or ideas that Romantics attached to these little gems of absolute music include, among others: "A Young Girl's Desire," "Feverishly awaiting the loved one," "Blood, voluptuousness and death!"

Although the left hand accompaniment is based on the tonic chord, a constant reiteration of A-flat is predominant; the melody, a beautiful and lyrical theme, appears immediately:

Example 1

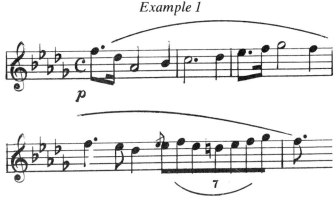

At the end of twenty-seven measures based on Example 1, the repeated A-flat is pivotal in a key change to E major: the A-flat of the old key (D-flat major) continues to be repeated and enharmonically is transformed into a repeated G-sharp (actually the same key on the piano, but regarded by two different names, depending whether one is in flats and calls it A-flat, or in sharps and calls it G-sharp). The repeated G-sharp is taken over by the right hand, the second melody appearing underneath it in the bass:

Example 2

After forty-eight measures, all centered around the repeated G-sharp and based on Example 2 and developments of it, the music returns to the original key of D-flat measure via the same enharmonic change.

The first melody, Example 1, returns briefly to conclude the *Prelude*.

WALTZ

Opus 18 in E-Flat Major

The history of the *waltz* as a dance form is veiled in obscurity. It is known that it was a developed dance form before the start of the nineteenth century and that it bears close resemblance to the German folk dance, the *ländler*. It was a dance in moderate triple meter (usually 3/4) and consisted of many sections, each with its own melody. Both Beethoven and Schubert composed waltzes, although they frequently sound more like the peasant *ländler*. Carl Maria von Weber, in his *Invitation to the Dance*, was the first to represent the waltz as a concert selection rather than an accompaniment to the actual dancing of the waltz itself.

Chopin, in his *Waltzes*, moved far away from the type of music that could actually accompany dancers. "I have nothing of what is needed for Viennese waltzes," he acknowledged. The Chopin *Waltzes* retained, of course, the triple meter, and are for the most part sectional, each with its own melody. They have, however, in addition, a grace and charm that was never infused into the form by any other composer.

The E-flat major *Waltz* (sub-titled "Grande Valse Brillante") is sectional. The first waltz melody starts after a rhythmical repetition of B-flat:

Example 1

The second section is based on a melody that appears in either thirds or sixths:

Example 2

The third section is marked *con anima* and makes use of appogiaturas:

Example 3

The fourth section centers around a more lyrical melody:

Example 4

After a series of repeated B-flats, a return is made to the melody of Example 1.

A pause, followed by a ritard and another pause, leads to the coda. The left hand establishes the waltz rhythm and the key of E-flat. The right hand enters with a series of descending chromatic intervals preceded by appogiaturas. A brilliant series of flourishes concludes the waltz.

FRANZ LISZT

BORN: October 22, 1811; Raiding, Hungary.
DIED: July 31, 1886; Bayreuth, Germany.

Born the son of a steward on perhaps the wealthiest estate in Hungary, Franz Liszt became acquainted with the leading composers of his day: Beethoven, Schubert, Schumann, Chopin, Berlioz, Grieg, and became Richard Wagner's father-in-law. He was the idol of the aristocratic families of Europe and played command performances for such royalty as Queen Victoria. In addition to his musical prominence, he also had several questionable "flirtations" which involved both society matrons and royalty. He finally took refuge from the world in a minor order of the Roman Catholic Church, donning the tonsure and clerical robe.

Liszt's father was one of the stewards on the Esterházy estate in Hungary, and remembered when both Haydn and Cherubini had been employed there. An amateur pianist of considerable ability, the father gave young Franz his first keyboard lessons. At nine years of age, the boy gave his first public performance at the Esterházy estate and later played before Niklaus Esterházy himself. Niklaus was so impressed that he arranged for a concert in Pressburg. In turn, the nobility were so awed at the child's precocity at the Pressburg affair, they provided him with 600 Austrian gulden a year for the next six years to enable him to study with professionals. With this money the boy was enrolled for studies with Czerny in Vienna. Beethoven, who had been in the audience for the boy's second public performance in Vienna, kissed him on the forehead afterward. Through another piano teacher with whom Liszt studied, he was able to meet Franz Schubert.

Franz Liszt left Vienna and traveled to Paris where he hoped to enroll in the famous Conservatory. He was denied admission by Cherubini, the Director, who objected to child prodigies. Liszt then secured the services of private piano teachers, but did a great amount of study on his own. When he was fourteen, an operetta, one of his first works to be publicly performed, was given at the Académie Royale de Musique.

From the age of twelve until he was twenty-four, Liszt was a resident of Paris. During this time he became acquainted with the literary figures of that city — Victor Hugo, Lamartine, and George Sand. He also knew Berlioz and Chopin and their music. In his twenty-second year he met Madame d'Agoult, a lady of twenty-eight who was estranged from her husband. After they had become good friends, they eloped to Geneva where a daughter was born to them. From Geneva they moved to Lake Como in Italy where a second daughter, Cosima, was born. Cosima later became the wife of Richard Wagner.

Liszt was at this time at the height of his power and popularity as a piano virtuoso. He was welcomed with an enormous response in all the musical centers of Europe. With the money from these concerts, he was most generous. He offered to pay out of his own pocket the balance due on the Beethoven monument being erected in Bonn.

When the city of Pest in his native Hungary (now united with Buda in the modern city of Budapest) was inundated by the waters overflowing the banks of the Danube, Liszt gave three concerts to help raise funds for the needy. The poor of his home town, Raiding, never ceased to give thanks for the composer's munificence.

His concert tours took him to Paris, Vienna, London, Spain, Portugal, Turkey, Poland, Denmark, and Russia. Two of his greatest triumphs took place in St. Petersburg and in Moscow.

At the conclusion of these extensive tours, he was appointed the musical director at Weimar where he served for thirteen years. Having broken with Mme. d'Agoult several years earlier, Liszt became enamored of Princess Carolyne of Sayne-Wittgenstein. Together they settled in Weimar and their home became a mecca for musicians from all over Europe. They indulged in literary works which included a *Life of Chopin* and several pamphlets on the music of Richard Wagner.

Part of Liszt's contract at Weimar was to aid the cause of new music. He was responsible for producing the first performance of several outstanding stage works: Richard Wagner's *Lohengrin, Tannhäuser, The Flying Dutchman;* Hector Berlioz' *Benvenuto Cellini;* Schumann's only operatic venture, *Genoveva;* and the neglected Schubert work, *Alfonso und Estrella.* His own most famous orchestral works stem from this period of activity, including the development of the *symphonic poem.*

In addition to his duties as a conductor, Liszt opened his home each afternoon to work with pupils in composition and piano. Seldom were there fewer than twelve students grouped around the piano playing their works for each other. On rare occasions, the master himself would be seated at the keyboard and extemporize for them.

On his fiftieth birthday, Liszt and the Princess Carolyne went to Rome to be married, but at the last minute the Vatican postponed the ceremony because of some details having to do with her separation from her Russian husband. Liszt then continued to live in Rome in semi-musical retirement, making preparations to enter one of the orders of the Church. Four years later Pope Pius IX conferred upon him the dignity of Abbé. This minor order did not allow the composer to say Mass or listen to confession, but he was awarded the position of honorary canon of St. Albano in Rome.

Traveling in his clerical garb, he divided his time between Rome, Weimar, and Budapest. In his seventy-fifth year, he undertook a "Jubilee Tour" and traveled to Paris and then London, where he played before Queen Victoria. On the return trip, he visited Antwerp, Jena, and Luxembourg. He intended to stop at Bayreuth for only a short visit, but discovered that the rigors of the tour had greatly taxed his strength. He was, however, able (with help) to watch from Cosima's box at the Festspielhaus a performance of *Parsifal* and returned another night to witness a production of *Tristan und Isolde* which was outstanding. On his return home from the last performance, he was prostrate.

The chill which he had caught developed into pneumonia and the end was inevitable. The tour had sapped every bit of his reserve energy, and he passed away during the night.

BIBLIOGRAPHY

Rousselot, Jean. *Franz Liszt.* London: Jonathan Cape Ltd., 1960
Sitwell, Sacheverell. *Liszt.* London: Cassell and Co., 1955.

LES PRÉLUDES

Symphonic Poem No. 3

FRANZ LISZT

The *symphonic poem* was the creation of Franz Liszt and occupied an important area in late Romantic music. It was no new form; rather it was an attempt to produce a musical paraphrase of the thought, feeling, and color of a literary poem — to say in the language of music what the poet says in words. Whether it did, or could, accomplish this is open to question. The symphonic poem is programmatic music in its purest form. It is in one movement in contrast to "program" symphonies of several movements, and at first relied heavily on the sonata-allegro pattern for its formal outline. Deviations were made in the form to portray better the *feeling* and *color* of the inspirational literary poem; at its height, the symphonic poem (or tone poem — *tondichtung,* as Strauss called it) became quite literal in its attempt to convey a story. Not all symphonic poems relied on literary works for their program. Some were inspired and based on paintings; a great many of the works of the Nationalist composers (see the next chapter) attempted to sound-paint landscapes, as in Bedrich Smetana's *The Moldau* (a river of his native Bohemia) and *Mà Vlast* (My Fatherland).

Les Preludes was written by Liszt in 1848 as an introduction to the choral work, *Les Quatre Éléments* (The Four Elements) from which the themes are derived. It was revised by the composer two years later and fitted to Lamartine's poem. The poem, also called *Les Préludes,* was the fifteenth of the *Méditations Poétiques* written by Liszt's friend, Alophonse Lamartine, in 1822.

In a preface to the score, the composer gives the gist of the material in the poem. The following is a translation of Liszt's paraphrase:

What is life but a series of preludes to that unknown song whose initial solemn note is tolled by Death? The enchanted dawn of every life is love; but where is the destiny on whose first delicious joys some storm does not break? — a storm whose deadly blast disperses youth's illusions, whose fatal bolt consumes its altar. And what soul, thus cruelly bruised when the tempest rolls away, seeks not to rest its memories in the pleasant calm of rural life?

Yet man allows himself not long to taste the kindly quiet which first attracted him to Nature's lap: when the trumpet gives the signal, he hastens to danger's post, whatever be the fight which draws him to its lists, that in strife he may once more regain full knowledge of himself and all his strength.

This symphonic poem, as in several others of Franz Liszt, is based on the sonata-allegro form.

Les Préludes opens with an introduction whose theme is derived from the Principal Subject, Example 2. The opening theme, Example 1, is played by the violins:

Example 1

The *exposition* opens in a majestic *Andante maestoso* with the bassoons, trombones, and tuba loudly declaiming the Principal Subject:

Example 2 (Principal Subject)

Bassoons, Trombones, Tuba

A variation of Example 2 appears in a lyrical variation played by the second violins, then by a solo French horn:

Example 3

Second Violins

A French horn quartet introduces the lyrical Second Subject with harp and muted string accompaniment:

Example 4 (Second Subject)

French Horns

The *exposition* closes with a codetta based on both the Principal and Second Subjects, Examples 2 and 4, and reaches a forceful climax.

Two variations of the Principal Subject, Example 2, open the development. The first employs many chromatics and a more forceful rhythmic intensity; the second is even more forceful, based on sycopated accents.

A rhythmic figure is introduced in the trumpets, followed by the oboe with fragments of the variation, Example 3, of the Principal Subject.

The *development* closes with the introduction of a new theme played first by the horn, then by the oboe, and a third repetition is made by the clarinet:

Example 5

French Horn

dolciss.

This symphonic poem has followed the sonata-allegro pattern quite closely up to this point, but with the *recapitulation,* the first major deviation occurs. The *recapitulation* is based entirely on the Second Subject, Example 3. Its first appearance is a peaceful one, but it is repeated twice, each time with a more brilliant orchestration.

The *coda* opens with the brass playing a rhythmical variation of the Principal Subject, Example 2.

Example 4, the Second Subject, is treated in a martial fashion, followed by the most brilliant presentation of the Principal Subject, Example 2, heard in the work.

GIUSEPPE VERDI

BORN: October 10, 1813; Le Roncole, Italy.
DIED: January 27, 1901; Milan, Italy.

Giuseppe Verdi is one of the greatest operatic composers Italy has ever known. Born of peasant stock, he failed the entrance examination to the famous Milan Conservatory. Despite great personal tragedy early in his professional life, he rose to fame and

An autographed photograph of Giuseppe Verdi taken in 1897 when the composer was in Genoa; he was working at this time on his *Stabat Mater*.

wealth by middle age. The gift of originality stayed with him so that at eighty he was able to compose one of his greatest masterpieces.

Verdi was born at Le Roncole, just a few miles from the village of Busseto, then in the Duchy of Parma, ruled by France under Napoleon. His father was an innkeeper in the smallest of village inns who augmented his income by selling wine, coffee, sugar, and tobacco. Little Giuseppe was seven, when, serving as an acolyte during Mass, he heard the church organ for the first time and became fascinated by it. So insistent was the boy in his desire to study music that his father purchased an old spinet piano without pedals, the hammers and keys almost unusable. ·A friend, familiar with piano repair and aware of the interest of the boy in studying music, repaired the instrument and left a written report: "The key-hammers were renewed and lined with leather, and I fitted pedals which I give as a present . . . seeing the excellent disposition the young Giuseppe Verdi shows to learn how to play this instrument."

The boy started studying with the village organist, and soon was filling in for him when the organist was called out of town. Giuseppe's progress was so extraordinary that after three years of lessons (when he was twelve), he was appointed the regular organist for the church on salary. Several compositions date from these early years, largely works written for use at the church. The quality of these works is well delineated by Verdi's biographer, Francis Toye:

As a matter of fact, Verdi's early compositions prove conclusively that he possessed none of the miraculous facility of a Mozart or Mendelssohn. Like Wagner he attained musical power by the sweat of his brow. There can be no doubt, however, that this spinet played the leading part in the first scenes of life's drama. It was the great friend of his childhood. Seated at the miserable instrument when tired of working the fields or the inn, when bored with playing the inevitable game of bowls with the village children, he dreamed . . . dreams [there].*

Giuseppe's father arranged for him to live with a shoemaker friend of the family in Busseto so that he could further his musical studies. The boy not only studied music, but he enrolled for a general education at the local school. He continued to trudge three miles each way on Sundays and Feast days to play the organ at Le Roncole. Giuseppe became acquainted with Antonio Barezzi, a grocer, who was deeply interested in music. Barezzi played the flute as well as several other orchestral instruments, and the local Philharmonic So-

* Francis Toye, *Giuseppe Verdi: His Life and Works* (New York, 1946).

ciety orchestra met in one of the large rooms of his home. Within two years after the boy arrived in Busseto, he moved in with the Barezzis. Here young Verdi learned the fundamentals of music, copied parts for the Philharmonic, in addition to pursuing his general education and helping with the groceries. As though these activities were not enough along with his piano practicing, the boy read avidly everything he could borrow from the library.

It was through the encouragement of Barezzi that a stipend became available for Verdi to travel to Milan and apply for entrance at the Conservatory there. On his arrival in the large city, Verdi filed a formal entrance application, including a request that the age requirement be waived, since he was then nineteen. The Conservatory was largely meant for students about fourteen who would stay until they were twenty. The Conservatory's refusal to accept Verdi has become a legend, some attributing it to the lack of pianistic ability, some to his still somewhat peasant bearing and lack of the social graces. There is no doubt it was a bad mistake on the part of the Conservatory, but here was a boy applying for admission at an age when most of their students were ready to depart. In their letter of refusal, the staff suggested that Verdi study with a private teacher and they suggested the names of two such persons. Wisely, Verdi followed their advice and enrolled with one of them, Vincenzo Lavigna, who was the chief pianist for the opera house. For two years Verdi studied counterpoint, harmony, and became acquainted with the music of Palestrina, Marcello, and especially Mozart. So much Mozart, in fact, that Verdi later said he hated to hear the works of that composer.

Verdi returned to Busseto after his studies and assumed the duties of choir director, organist for the church, and became the conductor for the Philharmonic orchestra. Shortly after his return he married the girl with whom he had long been in love, Margherita, the daughter of Barezzi.

He completed his first opera, *Oberto,* in Busseto and traveled to Milan to hear the work presented with success at La Scala Opera House. The trip to Milan was one filled with tragedy, for the Verdis lost their first child, Virginia, just before leaving Busseto; their baby son, Icilio, died the year they arrived in Milan. Just a year later, while working on the comic opera *Un Giorno di Regno* (King for a Day), his beloved wife died. Tragedy was added to grief when *Un Giorno* was presented at La Scala and was a failure.

The composer was ready to move back to Busseto and give up composition, but his great and good friend, Merelli — the Impressario — encouraged him to try his hand at another opera. The Impressario persuaded Verdi to read a libretto based on the life of the Biblical character, Nebuchadnezzar. It not only interested the composer, but he started to work immediately on it. *Nabucodonosor* (or as it is commonly known, *Nabucco*) was a tremendous success at its premiere.

His next two operas were well accepted: first came *I Lombardi* (The Lombards), which dealt with events of the First Crusade; then *Ernani*, based on Victor Hugo's romantic novel concerning the outlaw Hernani. The latter opera was presented in fifteen different opera houses within the year after its first presentation. Verdi's fame as an opera composer was firmly established, and not only La Scala, but many other opera houses, looked forward to presenting new Verdi operas.

A series of operas, almost forgotten now, continued to flow from his pen. He traveled to London, spent some time in Paris, and then returned to Italy. During these travels he showed an acute business sense, and was able to see that impressarios and publishers paid him his just dues. In Paris, he became acquainted with Giuseppina Strepponi, who encouraged the musical talents of the master and later became his wife.

Verdi purchased the Villa Sant' Agata just outside of Busseto which became his home for the balance of his life. Giuseppina traveled with him to his new home where they became engaged in making repairs and developing the vineyards and kitchen-garden. Most of Verdi's operas that are in the current repertoire date from this period: *Rigoletto* (Venice, 1851); *Il Trovatore* (The Troubadour; Rome, 1853); *La Traviata* (The Courtesan; Venice, 1853); *Simon Boccanegra* (Venice, 1857); *Un Ballo in Maschera* (A Masked Ball; Rome, 1859). The latter work fell into problems with the official censor. Italy was then starting on its second campaign for independence, and as originally written, *Un Ballo* concerned King Gustav III of Sweden and an attempted assassination. Napoleon III had recently been the object of just such an attempted assassination, and the similarity was thought politically dangerous. Verdi was finally convinced, and changed the action to the United States; the object of the plot became Riccardo, the English governor of Boston!

While Verdi did nothing overt to aid the fight for Italy's independence, he was definitely heart and spirit a part of it. The old cry of "Viva Verdi" took on a new meaning as Victor Emanuel was championed as the first king of an independent Italy, for the cry stood for "Viva V(ictor) E(manuel) R(e) D'I(talia)" (Victor Emanuel King of Italy). When the Italians won their campaign, Verdi was appointed a member of its first senate.

Four commissions from four cities were extended to the composer. For St. Petersburg, Verdi prepared *La Forza del Destino* (The Force of Destiny); for London, a cantata (not well accepted); for Paris, *Don Carlos;* and for Cairo, *Aïda*. Shortly after this Verdi wrote his *Requiem* in memory of a writer friend, Alessandro Manzoni. The public assumed that with this last named work the composer had retired from the operatic field. He was in his seventies, had a handsome income from his operas, and longed to spend his time at Villa Sant' Agata. An introduction to the composer of the opera *Mefistofele,* Arrigo Boïto, changed all this. At the request of Verdi's publisher, G. Ricordi of Milan, Boïto prepared a libretto based on Shakespeare's *Othello*. Verdi was seventy-four when *Otello* was premiered, an advanced and well integrated opera without the former "set pieces" separated by recitatives.

Boïto long suggested *Falstaff* based on Shakespeare's *The Merry Wives of Windsor*) as a fine libretto. Verdi was reluctant to start for fear he would not live long enough to complete it, but in his eighty-first year he was able to enjoy the success with which the public accepted this comedy.

In November, 1897 his beloved wife, Giuseppina, died quite suddenly even though she had been ailing for several years. Verdi built a home for aged musicians, *Casa di Riposa Musicisti,* in Milan in memory of her. Now alone in the world, unable to see well, the composer lost his will to live. One day, four years after Giuseppina's death, while dressing in a Milan hotel room, Verdi suffered a stroke. Six days later, in his eighty-eighth year, he died.

BIBLIOGRAPHY

Bonavia, Ferruccio. *Verdi*. London: Dennis Dobson, Ltd., 1947.
Toye, Francis. *Giuseppe Verdi: His Life and Works*. New York: Alfred A. Knopf, 1946.

AÏDA

(Opera in Four Acts)

Giuseppe Verdi

A new Italian opera house was opened in Cairo, Egypt, in November, 1869, and the Kedive, Ismail Pasha, invited Giuseppe Verdi to compose an opera for it, to be performed in connection with the opening ceremonies of the Suez Canal. Twice Verdi refused the invitation. A friend of the composer sent him a four-page sketch of a possible opera plot. The sketch was by the famous French Egyptologist, Mariette, who had served as Inspector-General of Monuments in Egypt and had been given the title of Bey. Verdi became interested in it, and worked up the sketch in French prose. He called in his friend Ghislanzoni to complete a libretto in Italian. It was planned that the new opera would be produced in Cairo in January, 1871; the premiere performance was delayed until December of that year, however, since the costume and scenery designs were in the possession of Mariette who had become imprisoned in Paris during the Franco-Prussian War.

CAST OF CHARACTERS

Aïda, *an Ethiopian slave in the service of Egypt*   soprano
The King of Egypt   bass
Amneris, *his daughter*   mezzo-soprano
Radamès, *Captain of the Guard*   tenor
Amonasro, *King of Ethiopia, and Aïda's father*   baritone
Ramfis, *High Priest*   bass

The action takes place at Memphis and Thebes, during the epoch of the Pharaohs.

ACT I

Scene 1: *Palace of the King*

The palace of the King of Egypt in Memphis is the setting of the first scene of Act I. Imposing colonnades flank either side of the square, and in the background the temples and palaces of Memphis can be seen, with the Pyramids visible in the far distance. Radamès, an Eypgtian soldier, and Ramfis, the High Priest, are in conference. They are concerned that Egypt is once more being invaded by the Ethiopians who have already captured a large part of the Nile valley. Ramfis discloses that the goddess Isis has already decreed who is to

Act I, Scene 1 of the Chicago Lyric Opera's production of *Aïda*. The King of Egypt stands on the steps of the temple, having announced that Rhadames shall lead the Egyptian forces against the invading Ethiopians.

The triumphal scene of Act II. The slaves kneel in front of the victorious Egyptian soldiers as the Egyptian King proclaims to Rhadames, "Saviour of the country, I salute you!"

Photos by Nancy Sorenson

lead the Egyptian army in routing the invaders. Ramfis is on his way to the King to disclose who it will be.

As Radamès is left alone, he dreams of being the one chosen to lead the victorious Egyptian forces, returning as a hero, and laying the laurels of the victor at the feet of his beloved Aïda. He also muses that, with such honor, he would be able to free her from her slave bond and restore her to her native land.

CELESTE AÏDA (Heavenly Aïda)

A recitative precedes the aria:

Se quel guerrier io fossi!	What if I am the chosen one!
Se il mio sogno si avverasse!	What if my dreams come true!
Un esercito di prodi da me guidato	If I am chosen leader of the glorious army
E la vitoria e il plauso di Menfi tutta!	And the victory is received by Memphis in triumph!
E a te, dolce Aïda, tornar di lauri einto	And to you, dearest Aïda, I return with the laurel crown,
Dirti: per te ho pugnato,	I'll tell you; it was for you I battled,
Per te ho vinto!	For you I conquered!

After a brief martial fanfare, the aria proper begins:

Celeste Aïda, forma divina,	Heavenly Aïda, my beautiful one,
Mistico serto di luce e fior;	Radiant beauty, bright as a flower,
Del mio pensiero tu sei regina,	You are the queen of my dreams,
Tu di mia vita sei lo splendor.	You are the splendor of my life.

Amneris, daughter of the Egyptian King, and in love with Radamès, interrupts his reverie. She suspects that Radamès and Aïda are secretly in love, and her jealous hatred is aroused as she notices how the two look at each other as Aïda enters. At this moment a messenger arrives to report that the enemy, led by King Amonasro, is marching on Thebes. At the mention of the name Amonasro, Aïda gasps, "My father!" Excitement mounts as the King of Egypt preceded by guards, and followed by Ramfis, the priests, the ministers of state, and other officers arrives. The King announces that Isis has chosen Radamès to lead the army, and in the following ensemble, the ecstatic crowd gives their approval of the choice.

Su! del Ni — lo al sa — cro li — do

ac- cor — re—te, E- gi — zii e roi

Su! del Nilo (Guard the Nile!)

The King

Su! del Nilo al sacro lido	Guard the Nile's sacred shores
Accorrete, Egizii e roi,	Do this for Egypt and her King.
Da ogni cor prorompa il grido,	Until each heart breaks forth in screams,
Guerra e morte, morte allo stra-nier!	War and death, death to the strangers!

Ramfis

Gloria ai Numi! ognun rammenti	Glory to the Gods! Always remember
Ch'essi reggono gli eventi,	That the outcome is carried
Che in poter d'e Numi solo	In the hands of the gods alone;
Stan le sorti del guerrier.	It is the destiny of the war.

Chorus of Ministers and Captains

Su! del Nilo al sacro lido . . .	Guard the Nile's sacred shores...

The crowd leads the way to the sacred Temple of Vulcan where Radamès will receive his sacred armor. Aïda is left alone, and she reflects that she, too, urged Radamès on to victory. She is appalled, for the enemy is her own people, and their leader, Amonasro, her father. Torn by her love for Radamès and her love for father and country, she cries out:

Aïda

RITORNA VINCITOR (Return Victorious)

Ritorna vincitor!	Return victorious!
E dal mio labbro uscì l'empia parola!	What are these wicked words I speak?
Vincitor del padre mio,	Victorious over my father,
Di lui che impugna l'armi per me,	The one who leads the army for me
Per ridonarmi una patria, una reggia,	That I might be restored to my country
E il nome illustre che qui celar m'è forza!	And my title which I now keep in hiding;
Vincitor de' miei fratelli!	Victorious over my own brothers!

She continues, envisioning her father in chains, a captive; but, can she wish that her beloved Radamès be slain? In despair, she falls on the mercy of the gods in a poignant ending to her aria:

Numi, pietà del mio soffrir!

Speme non v'ha pel mio dolor.
Amor fatal, tremendo amor,
Spezza mi il cor, fammi morir!

O gods, have mercy on my suffering!
There is no hope for my sadness.
Fatal love, dreadful love,
Break my heart, let me die!

SCENE 2: *Interior of the Temple of Vulcan*

The Temple of Vulcan is bathed in a mysterious light, and statues of the gods surround it. With incense burning in huge tripods, Radamès appears below the great altar in the center to be invested with the sacred rites. A silver veil is placed over his head, and Ramfis challenges him as the one chosen by Isis to defend Egypt's honor. The chorus intones the name of the powerful god Fthà.

ACT II

SCENE 1: *Amneris' Apartment*

Princess Amneris, surrounded by her slave girls and young Moorish dancers, is being attired for the triumphal feast. As the slaves go about their tasks, they tell how the Egyptian forces, led by Radamès, have defeated the Ethiopians and are returning with them as their prisoners. As Aïda enters, Amneris greets her and dismisses the other attendants. In her intense desire to find out if her suspicions about Aïda and Radamès are true, she tricks Aïda by suggesting that Radamès was killed in the battle. Immediately Amneris sees the intense grief written on Aïda's face that leaves no doubt as to her love for Radamès. Amneris changes her tactics and states that she was only joking, that Radamès not only lives, but is the hero of the battle. When Aïda falls on her knees with a cry of gratitude to the gods, all question about the relationship of the two is dispelled from Amneris' mind. Amneris then reveals herself as Aïda's rival for the affection of Radamès, she, a daughter of the Pharaohs. Aïda is on the verge of stating that she, too, is a princess, but checks herself in time.

As Aïda pleads for mercy, trumpets are heard in the distance heralding the arrival of the victorious forces. Amneris ends the interview with a threat to humiliate Aïda during the approaching festivities.

SCENE 2: *An Avenue to the City of Thebes.*

The scene opens with a Triumphal March as crowds of people gather to celebrate the glorious victory over the Ethiopians. The King, followed by officials, priests, priestesses, captains, fan-bearers, and standard-bearers, take their places. The King is seated on the royal throne with Amneris at his left side.

TRIUMPHAL MARCH

Glori — a all' E— git — to ad I — si — de

che il sa— cro suol pro — teg — ge!

Gloria all'Egitto, ad Iside	Glory to Egypt by Isis
Che il sacro suol protegge!	Our sole sacred protector!
Al Re che il Delta regge	To the King who rules the Delta
Inni festosi alziam.	We raise our festive hymns!

After an extended chorus, the Egyptian troops, preceded by trumpets (the straight trumpets generally employed in this scene have been called *Aïda trumpets*) defile before the King. A martial melody is proclaimed; each time it is repeated a half-step higher, making it more brilliant:

Radamès, last to enter in the procession, receives the crown of the victor from Amneris. The King offers him any prize that he desires. Radamès requests that the Ethiopian prisoners be brought forward. As they approach, Aïda spots Amonasro and rushes to him, crying, "My father!" "Do not disclose my name or rank," he cautions her as they embrace fondly. Amneris, watching all this, comments, "Her father, and in our power!"

Radamès, reminding the King of his promise, asks that the prisoners be released. The priests protest against this act of clemency, fearing that the Ethiopians will again war against Egypt. Radamès defends his request, saying that with the Ethiopian king Amonasro dead, no one has the power to rally them to battle again. The High Priest then suggests to the King that if the prisoners are released, Aïda's father ought to be kept prisoner as a hostage. Amneris couldn't be more pleased with the suggestion. The King then grants Radamès' request and frees the prisoners except for Aïda's father, whose identity as Amonasro is not suspected. The King goes further in his gifts to the victorious Captain; he grants his daughter Amneris' hand in marriage to Radamès.

The scene closes as Amneris exults in her two-fold triumph; Radamès laments his miserable fate, for he has won a kingdom but lost Aïda.

ACT III

SCENE 1: *The Temple of Isis on the bank of the Nile; it is moonlight.*

Amneris approaches the Temple of Isis, accompanied by Ramfis, in a bark on the river. She has come, veiled for her vigil, to spend the night in the temple praying for her marriage which will take place on the next day.

After Amneris and Ramfis have entered the temple, Aïda stealthily arrives for her secret and final farewell to Radamès. She reminisces of her homeland:

O PATRIA MIA (Oh My Native Land)

O patria mia,	Oh, my native land,
Mai più ti rivedrò!	Never shall I see it again!
O cieli azzurri, o dolci aure native,	Oh skies of blue, oh gentle breezes,
Dove sereno il mio mattin brillò!	Where the light of my youth shone in tranquillity!

Aïda has no sooner finished her reminiscing than she is interrupted, not by Radamès whom she expects, but by her own father. He has evaded his captors, and tells his daughter that he knows she is to meet Radamès in secret at this spot. It will be her opportunity, he tells her, to gain revenge on Amneris and at the same time restore Ethiopia's glory. In a passage of tender beauty, he recalls the beauty of their homeland. He tells her that the forces of Ethiopia are ready to move again; only one thing is lacking, he must know what route the Egyptian enemy will take. He is certain that Radamès must know this, and bids his daughter ask him about it. She recoils in anger; she cannot betray the one she loves. Amonasro then paints a distasteful picture of desolation that will spread across the face of their homeland if the Egyptian forces are successful. "The Egyptians will destroy our cities with fire, they will spread terror, carnage, and death," he tells her. "Rivers of blood will engulf us; from black whirlpools the dead will arise and point to you, 'Through you your native land has perished.'" Aïda still refuses to be a part of this subterfuge. Amonasro then casts her off, saying that she is no longer a daughter of his, no longer a princess, but a slave of the Egyptians.

Aïda falls at her father's feet and recants: "Have mercy, father! I am not their slave. Do not curse and revile me. You will still be able to call me your daughter. I will be worthy of my homeland."

Amonasro, seeing Radamès approaching, takes cover among the palms. As Aïda and Radamès embrace, they again declare their love for each other. Radamès tells her that Ethiopia and Egypt are at war again, and he must leave on the morrow to lead the Egyptian forces. Once he returns from this battle, he will tell the King of his love for Aïda and be released from his obligation to Amneris. Aïda has a better plan. They could flee this very night, together, to a happier land. Radamès is too much the soldier to accept this escape, and refuses. Aïda bids him enter the temple, then, where Amneris is waiting; "let the axe fall on me and my father!"

In a passionate duet, Radamès accepts Aïda's plan. She asks him, though, how they can escape when the Egyptian forces are marshalled to march upon the enemy. "By the route already chosen for us to march upon the enemy," replied Radamès. "And where is that?" she questions. "The mountain gorge of Nàpata," he says. At hearing this information, Amonasro steps from his hiding place with a cry of "There will I post my men — I, Aïda's father and Ethiopia's King!"

Amneris and Ramfis step from the temple; they have heard it all. Amneris shouts "Traitor!" as Amonasro draws his dagger and rushes at her. As the guards advance on him, Radamès begs them to let Amonasro and Aïda take flight and he himself will surrender to the High Priest.

ACT IV

SCENE 1: *A hall in the King's palace.*

Amneris is in despair: the two whom she hated have escaped, and the one that she loves stands condemned to death for betraying his country. She commands the guards to bring Radamès to her, for if she can persuade him to love her, she can perhaps obtain a pardon for him.

She addresses him in tender tones:

GIÀ I SACERDOTI (Already the Priests)

Già i sacerdoti adunansi	Already the priests, the arbiters
Arbitri del tuo fato;	Of your fate, are assembling;
Pur dell' accusa orrible	But from this horrible charge
Scolparti ancor t'è dato;	You may yet exculpate yourself;
Ti scolpa, e la tua grazia	Apologize, and I will
Io pregherò dal trono.	Plead for you before the throne.

The music modulates from E-flat minor to F-sharp minor, and Radamès replies to the same melody:

Di mie discolpe i guidici	Words of excuses the judges
Mai non udran l'accento;	Will never hear from me;
Dinanzi ai Numi, agli uomini	In the sight of the gods and mankind
Nè vil, nè reo mi sento.	I feel myself neither a coward nor guilty.

Radames continues by saying that it was love that parted his lips to reveal the secret, but his honor remains unsmirched. "Save yourself," Amneris pleads, but he replies that all the pleasures of living have been taken from him. Amneris makes one final plea:

Amneris

Ah! tu dei vivere!	Oh, you must live!
Sì, all'amor mio vivrai;	Yes, for my love you shall live;
Per te le angoscie orribili	For you the terrible anguish
Di morte io già provai;	Of death have I endured already;
T'amai, soffersi tanto	I loved you, I suffered so much
Vegliai le notti in pianto	At night I have lain awake in tears
E patria, e trono, e vita,	And my country, and throne, and life,
Tutto darei, tutto, tutto, darei per te.	All this, all, all of this I would give for you.

Radamès

Per essa anch'io la patria	For her, too, I betrayed
E l'onor mio tradia.	My country and my honor.

The duet continues as Amneris pleads with Radamès to forget Aïda and take her in his arms. He refuses to do this, preferring to die for the one he loves.

Radamès is returned to the subterranean cell by the guards as Ramfis and the court follow to pronounce judgment on the traitor. Amneris' love has now changed to jealousy, and she reviles herself for having delivered him to the hands of the priests, "the white robed ministers of death."

From below, Amneris hears the judgment: "Beneath the altar of the god you have betrayed, you will be buried alive!" Amneris, now regretting her anger, decries a curse on the priesthood for their sentence.

SCENE 2: *The stage is divided into two levels: on the upper is seen the Temple of Vulcan; on the lower, the gloomy crypt in which the colossal statue of Osiris supports the temple above.*

Radamès is led by the priests to the steps that descend into the crypt. As he proceeds into the dark, living tomb, the priests move the fatal rock to the stairway. In the semi-darkness, Radamès perceives a form; it is Aïda, who has come to be with him in death if not in life. Radamès hails her, lovingly:

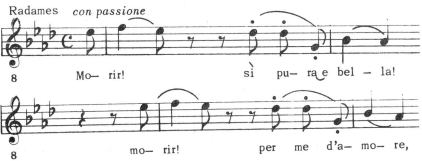

Radames *con passione*

Mo— rir!   si   pu— ra̱ e bel – la!

mo— rir!   per   me   d'a— mo— re,

Morir! sì pura e bella!	To die! So pure and lovely!
Morir per me d'amore;	To die for love of me;
Degli anni tuoi nel fiore	In the flower of your youth
Fuggir la vita!	To fly from life!

Radamès exclaims that heaven created her for love, and he is killing her through love. She replies that "death's radiant angel carries us to eternal joy."

The chant of the priestesses above is heard and the priests seal the fatal stone:

Priestesses

Im – – men – so, im—men—so   Fthà,

Immenso, immenso, Fthà.	Almighty, almighty Fthà.

Radamès tries to move the stone, but his strong arms are unable to budge it. The priests continue their chant, as Aïda remarks that "All is finished."

Radamès and Aïda join their voices in a final farewell:

Aïda

O terra, addio.	Oh earth, farewell.
Addio, valle di pianti,	Farewell, vale of tears,
Sogno di gaudio	Dream of joy
Che in dolor svanì.	Which in sorrow faded.
A noi si schiude il ciel,	For us heaven opens
E l'alme erranti	And our errant souls
Volano al raggio dell'eterno dì.	Fly to the light of eternal day.

Radamès

O terra, addio;	Oh earth, farewell,

As the voices of the couple fade away, the chanting of the priests concludes above them; Amneris makes a final plea; "I beg peace . . . peace . . . peace."

RICHARD WAGNER

BORN: May 22, 1813; Leipzig, Germany.
DIED: February 13, 1883; Venice, Italy.

When Richard Wagner was twenty-two, he bought a notebook and started writing the details of the life of "one of the world's greatest geniuses." The book was his own autobiography, *Mein Leben* (My Life). At the time he purchased the sketch book, he was the conductor of a very poor, small opera house orchestra and the composer of two unproduced operas. The next forty-eight years evidenced a fantastic life. Wagner's biographer Ernest Newman sums up the composer's character during those years in contrasts:

Wagner is one who stands . . . equally capable of great virtues and of great vices, of heroic self-sacrifice and the meanest egoism, packed with a vitality too superabundant for the moral sense always to control it; now concentrating magnificently, now wasting himself tragically, but always believing in himself with the faith that moves mountains, and finally achieving a roundness and completeness of life and a mastery of mankind that makes his record read more like romance than reality.*

Wagner's father, who died six months after the boy was born, was a clerk in the Leipzig police court. His mother married Ludwig Geyser soon after her first husband's death. He was an actor and playwright who did some painting. Although Geyser died when Richard was eight, the effect of a cultured home in which there were good books and plays had an influence on the boy. After the death

* Ernest Newman, *The Life of Richard Wagner* (New York, 1933).

RICHARD WAGNER

The best-known portrait, painted by F. von Lenbach for the Wagner family

of his step-father, Richard transferred from the school in Leipzig to Dresden where he studied among other things Greek tragedies in their original language. During these student days, his interest was in literature and writing; music had not yet attracted him. His favorite authors included Shakespeare, Goethe, and Schiller.

When Richard was eleven, he became acquainted with the operas of Weber which greatly interested him. It was in the same year that his sisters, Clara and Rosalie, made their debut as opera singers. He started taking piano lessons and as he learned simple exercises, he tried unsuccessfully to play the piano scores of Weber operas. He later took up the violin and did as poorly on that as he had done with piano. He composed several works, including a string quartet and a piano sonata. Wagner was left alone in Dresden when his family moved to Prague (he was thirteen at the time) and started writing a tragedy. He rejoined his family in Leipzig a year later where he entered St. Nicholas' School and finished his tragedy. He also completed a piano arrangement of the *Symphony No. 9* of Beethoven. While at St. Nicholas, his *Overture in B-Flat* was performed and "evoked ridicule."

Wagner enrolled at the Leipzig University when he was eighteen. He completed the libretto for his first opera and started to compose the music for it. *Die Hochzeit* (The Marriage) was destroyed before completion as its gore shocked his sister Rosalie. After a year at the University, he accepted an appointment, arranged through his brother Albert, as chorus master at the Würzburg Theater. During this time he completed his first opera, *Die Feen* (The Fairy). It showed the influence of his favorite composers, Weber and Beethoven.

The composer joined, as conductor, an opera company of which Minna Planner was a member; two years later they were married. It was a union that Wagner regretted almost as soon as the ceremony was over, for although Minna had beauty, she lacked the cultural background compatible with a person like Wagner. Many family quarrels and separations occurred over the period of their marriage. The first separation took place after Wagner assumed the position of conductor in Königsburg; Minna joined him as he left for Riga, Russia, to serve as a conductor. While in Russia he completed the libretto for *Rienzi* and started to compose the music. He was unhappy with his position in the Riga opera house, objecting to both the choice of operas and the policies. One day, when he showed up for a rehearsal, he discovered that he had been replaced and his passport taken away. With the music for two acts of *Rienzi* in his possession, he and Minna fled by ship via Norway and England. The sea was rough on the trip, and some suggest that it was this that inspired his next opera, *Der Fliegende Holländer* (The Flying Dutchman), the story of a sailor condemned to sail the ocean for eternity.

The Wagners settled in Paris where the composer hoped to write a production for the Paris Grand Opera. With little income (he sold the libretto for *Der Fliegende Holländer* and later used it himself), he was twice imprisoned because of the debts he had incurred in living far beyond his means. Finally the Dresden Court Theater accepted *Rienzi* for performance and Richard and Minna, on borrowed money, returned to that city. The opera was accepted with success; *Die Fliegende Holländer* was premiered a year later, but was not as successful as the earlier opera.

Wagner was appointed Director of Music at the Royal Court of Saxony, and during his first year in this position completed *Der Venusberg* (The Land of Venus). When presented at its first performance, Wagner changed the name to *Tannhäuser*. It was hailed variously as pornographic, unsingable, or unplayable. The composer then turned to work on sketches for both *Die Meistersinger* (The Mastersingers) and *Lohengrin*. He also gave some thought to setting a Norse legend, the opera to be called *Siegfried's Tod* (Siegfried's Death). It was during these years that Wagner met and became close friends with both the composer Franz Liszt and the most famous German conductor of the time, Hans von Bülow. He also became a member of a radical political organization. During the May uprising of 1849, he wrote tracts that he distributed, gave revolutionary speeches, and after a night on the Kreuz tower as an observer, had to flee from a political warrant for his arrest.

He fled first to Franz Liszt in Weimar who was unable to help him; after visiting a professor-friend in Jena, he was loaned the friend's own passport so that he and his wife could travel to Switzerland. The composer spent thirteen years in exile in Zürich. The premiere of *Lohengrin* was given in Weimar by Liszt, but because of his exile, the composer was unable to attend. In Switzerland Wagner started to work on what later came to be known as *Der Ring des Nibelungen* (The Ring of the Nibelungs). His original opera based on the Norse legend, *Siegfried's Tod*, did not completely tell the story and needed a preface. A second opera describing Siegfried's youth and called *Siegfried* was an attempt to prepare the audience for the events in *Siegfried's Tod* which Wagner now called *Die Götterdämmerung* (The Twilight of the Gods). Yet a third opera seemed necessary to explain events leading up to *Siegfried* and *Die Götter-*

dämmerung, so *Die Walküre* (The Valkyrie) was composed. It in turn, however, did not seem to reveal all the details necessary for the development of future events, so that a prelude was written: the opera *Das Rheingold* (The Rhine Gold). This cycle of four operas occupied the composer for over twenty-five years.

In Zürich Wagner had become acquainted with Otto Wesendock and his wife and was a frequent visitor in their home. Otto offered the Wagners the use of one of the homes on his estate, and it was while they lived there that Richard Wagner became enamored of Wesendock's wife. Minna Wagner could take no more; she returned to Germany as Richard moved to Venice. In Italy, Wagner completed the opera *Tristan und Isolde,* based on an old Irish legend concerning the love of Tristan for Isolde. The composer wrote to Frau Wesendock after its completion: "That I wrote *Tristan,* I thank you from the depths of my soul forever and ever." Critics disagree as to whether Wagner was inspired to compose *Tristan* because of his relationship with Frau Wesendock, or because of *Tristan* he needed to find a kindred spirit.

Wagner then settled in Paris where Tannhäuser was revived, and where he started work on his comic opera *Die Meistersinger von Nürnberg* (The Mastersingers of Nurenburg). In the meantime a pardon had been extended the composer so that he could re-enter Germany. His stay in Germany was short, for he traveled to Vienna to arrange for a performance of *Tristan,* which was shelved as unplayable after seventy-seven rehearsals. Once again rising debts and a lack of funds were catching up with him, and he fled from Austria back to Germany.

Stopping in Stuttgart, Wagner perhaps had the most fortunate experience of his life. It was there that he met King Ludwig II of Bavaria, who immediately took a liking to the composer and who had great admiration for his music. The King, who provided Wagner with adoration and encouragement, also granted him living expenses and paid all his back debts. Wagner again started work on the *Ring* and was able to see *Tristan* premiered. Ludwig then suggested Wagner complete his autobiography, *Mein Leben,* already mentioned, and employ von Bülow's wife Cosima (the daughter of Franz Liszt) to take dictation.

A political upheaval forced Ludwig to stop his underwriting of Wagner's expenses and necessitated both the King and Wagner leaving Germany again. The composer fled with Cosima Liszt von Bülow to Geneva, where in 1870 she became his wife after obtaining an annulment of her first marriage. They had three children: Isolde, Eva, and Siegfried (names of three leading characters in three different Wagner operas — *Tristan und Isolde, Die Meistersinger,* and *Siegfried*). This was a happy marriage for the composer, as evidenced by his birthday present for his wife one year. He had a chamber orchestra gather outside her bedroom door and play a composition written especially for the occasion, the *Siegfried Idyll.*

King Ludwig of Bavaria once again was financially able to help Wagner. The composer returned to Munich where *Die Meistersinger* was completed in 1867 and presented a year later. The sketches for *Siegfried* and *Die Götterdämmerung* were then completed. In 1872 Wagner and Cosima moved to Bayreuth where an excellent site for an opera house had been given to the composer. After two decades of dreaming of a radically different type of theater, one in which the orchestra would be under the stage so as not to bar the audience's view of the stage, it became a reality. The cornerstone of the new *Festspielhaus* (Festival Hall) was placed on Wagner's fifty-ninth birthday. The opera house opened on August 13, 1876, with the first complete performance of the *Ring* (it was the premiere performance of both *Siegfried* and *Die Götterdämmerung*). A distinguished audience attended and included the composers Tchaikovsky, Saint-Saëns, Gounod, Grieg, and Liszt. The critics outdid each other in their attacks on the cycle and on its creator, and because of this the second performance was poorly attended. The opera house was temporarily closed until the premiere there of Wagner's last opera, *Parsifal,* based on the legend of the Holy Grail as found in the legends of King Arthur.

The same year the Wagners traveled to Venice, since Richard's health was greatly undermined. While at work on a literary epistle, he suffered a heart attack and passed away a few moments later. He was cremated and buried at his beloved home in Bayreuth.

BIBLIOGRAPHY

Newman, Ernest. *The Life of Richard Wagner,* 4 vols. New York: Alfred A. Knopf, 1933.

Stein, Jack M. *Richard Wagner and the Synthesis of an Art.* Detroit: Wayne University Press, 1960.

DER RING DES NIBELUNGEN

(*The Ring of the Nibelungs*)

RICHARD WAGNER

Although referred to as a *trilogy,* there are actually four operas (called *music dramas* by the composer) in his unparalleled stage work. After completing what are now the second, third, and fourth operas in this cycle, Wagner felt compelled to write one more as a *prelude,* hence a *trilogy* with a *prelude.*

When performed in its entirety, the *Ring* is given on four successive nights, taking a total performance time of about fourteen hours. It is the longest musical work of sustained story and thematic material in existence. The four operas which comprise the *Ring* are (in chronological order): *Das Rheingold* (The Rhine Gold); *Die Walküre* (The Valkyrie); *Siegfried;* and *Die Götterdämmerung* (The Twilight of the Gods).

The four operas constitute a continuous story and employ the same characters and musical motives. The term *leit motiv* (leading motive) was used by Wagner to identify musical motives, usually of quite short length, which were used continuously throughout the work, but which were always to be associated in the listener's mind with either a specific character, an important object (*i.e.,* sword, god, etc.), or with a characteristic (*i.e.,* love, a curse, etc.). Although the composer makes minor variations in the timbre, rhythm, or sometimes even the melodic line, these motives can always be recognized as derivatives of the initial presentation. Wagner did not devise the idea of the *leit motiv,* but was the supreme master of its use.

The story of this trilogy is based on an old Norse legend, the libretti being fashioned by Wagner himself. As with many folk legends, a large cast of characters appears, and the sub-plots as well as the main plot become, at times, quite complicated. The following *Cast of Characters* should be used as a reference when one momentarily forgets the relationship of one character to another.

CAST OF CHARACTERS

Wotan, *King of the Gods (he later disguises as Wälse and the Wanderer)*   bass-baritone
Fricka, *his wife and Goddess of Marriage and Home*   mezzo-soprano
Brünnhilde, *Wotan's daughter by Erda; Chief of the Valkyries* soprano

Sieglinde ⎫ *twins of Wotan's on earth* ⎫ soprano
Siegmund ⎬   ⎬ tenor
Hunding, *Sieglinde's husband*   bass
Siegfried, *son of Siegmund and Sieglinde*   tenor
Gods ⎧ Donner, *God of Thunder*   baritone
     ⎩ Loge, *God of Fire*   tenor
Goddesses ⎧ Freia, *Goddess of Youth*   soprano
          ⎩ Erda, *Goddess of Earth*   mezzo-soprano
Giants ⎧ Fasolt, *a giant*   baritone
       ⎩ Fafner, *his brother*   bass
Nibelungs ⎧ Alberich, *a dwarf*   baritone
          ⎩ Mime, *his brother*   tenor
            ⎧ Gunther, *Chief of the Gibichungs*   baritone
Gibichungs ⎨ Hagen, *his half-brother; Alberich's son*   bass
            ⎩ Gutrune, *Gunther's sister*   soprano

DAS RHEINGOLD

(*The Rhine Gold*)

This opera serves as a prelude to the *Ring*. It is the shortest of the music dramas, and was written to be performed without intermissions — one scene changing into the next while the music continues.

Three maidens are seen afloat in the Rhine River where they guard the gold from the dwarf Alberich. This gold is unique, for whoever forges a ring from it will be all-powerful providing he also renounces all love. Alberich is finally able to steal the gold from the Rhinemaidens, and immediately fashions just such a ring; he thereby renounces love.

With his new-found power, Alberich forces his brother Mime to fashion a helmet or *tarnhelm* (*tarn:* camouflage; *helm:* helmet) out of the gold. The power of the tarnhelm is such that whoever wears it can either become invisible or transform himself into any form of animal life. The cave of the dwarf echoes with the laughter of Alberich at his latest acquisition.

Wotan, the King of the Gods, is having a new home built for these gods to be called Valhalla. He has contracted with two giants, Fafner and Fasolt, to create it, promising them the Goddess of Youth, Freia, as payment. When the two giants approach him after completing the project, Wotan realizes what an awkward position he is in, for without Freia, the keeper of the golden apples of youth, he will no longer be able to remain young.

To work his way out of this situation, Wotan sends Loge, one of the lesser gods, to earth to see if he can find something as a substitute payment for the two giants. On his trip to earth, Loge meets Alberich and learns of the gold, the ring, and the tarnhelm. He rushes back to tell Wotan of his discovery and suggests that perhaps the gold would satisfy Fafner and Fasolt. Wotan thereupon departs for the land of the Nibelungs.

Knowing that acquisition of the gold, the ring, and the tarnhelm will not be easy, Wotan devises a tricky plan. When he meets Alberich, he questions the dwarf about his possessions. As Alberich greedily explains the power of the tarnhelm, Wotan acts amazed and says that he doesn't believe the helmet has the power to transform its wearer into various forms of animal life. He challenges Alberich to put it on and transform himself into something very, very large — perhaps a dragon. The dwarf immediately becomes an enormous dragon. When Alberich has once again taken up his own identity, Wotan urges him on. "Transform yourself into something very, very small — say a toad!" No sooner said than done, and Alberich becomes a small toad. Wotan immediately grabs the small toad and binds him up, powerless. The King of the Gods is then able to help himself to all the gold, the ring, and the very tarnhelm itself. As Wotan makes off with it, Alberich places a curse on the ring: whoever owns it will come to a tragic fate.

Wotan finally comes to an agreement about the payment of the two giants for their work on Valhalla. Fafner and Fasolt agree to accept gold as a substitute for Freia, but the pile of gold must be high enough to hide Freia completely from their view as she stands a short distance away. Gold is piled on top of gold until Freia seems to have disappeared, but the giants discover that a bit of Freia's blond hair can be seen over the pile. Wotan has no gold left, and finally parts with the tarnhelm which he wishes to keep, along with the ring, for himself. Hesitatingly he places the tarnhelm on top of the pile of gold hiding Freia. The giants then discover one little hole in the pile just large enough to see one of Freia's eyes. There is nothing left with which to plug the hole except the ring which is begrudgingly set in the opening by Wotan.

The curse of the ring is evident, for no sooner do the giants possess it than they start fighting over it. Fasolt is killed in the fight by Fafner. Fafner then uses the power of the tarnhelm to transform himself into a huge dragon, and carries off the gold to a cave where he can guard and protect it.

Das Rheingold — In the subterranean caves of the Nibelheim

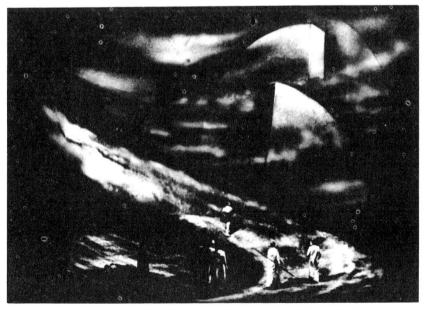

Das Rheingold — After Donner has struck his hammer a vivid flash of lightning is seen and thunder heard.

Photos by Foto Festspiele Bayreuth/Siegfried Lauterwasser

Having completed the transaction, Wotan prepares to enter Valhalla along with the lesser gods and goddesses. He summons Donner, the God of Thunder, to create a storm, and with it a rainbow over which the gods can walk as a bridge to their new home. Their journey over the rainbow bridge is interrupted by the three Rhinemaidens who plead with Wotan to return the gold to them, but Wotan refuses.

THE ENTRANCE OF THE GODS INTO VALHALLA

As Donner mounts a high crag and swings his mighty hammer, the motive of Donner is heard:

Example 1 (Donner)

Rushing arpeggios in the strings accompany this motive which is repeated by the horns, then by tubas, trumpets, and trombones.

When the clouds are at their darkest, a single hammer stroke dispels them in lightning and thunder. A rainbow appears:

Example 2 (The Rainbow)

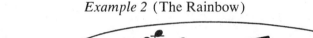

This melody is played by celli, horns, bassoons, and bass clarinets to the accompaniment of the upper strings and six harps with arpeggios. The flutes, oboes, and clarinets sustain a G-flat harmony.

The Valhalla motive replaces the Rainbow motive as the string accompaniment continues:

Example 3 (Valhalla)

Wotan considers the events of the day: the ring with its curse, the prophecy of disaster. Although nothing is said on stage, he plots a plan for the protection of Valhalla and the recovery of the ring by a race of heroes. His idea is expressed in the music through a motive which is here called the motive of Wotan's Idea and later becomes the Sword motive:

Example 4 (Wotan's Idea — later, The Sword)

As Wotan and the gods pass over the bridge, the Rhinemaidens make their final plea for the return of the gold. First the motive of the Rhinemaidens is heard:

Example 5 (The Rhinemaidens)

Rhein—gold! Rhein—gold! rei – – nes Gold!

The Valhalla motive returns momentarily, and is followed by a repetition of the motive of the Rhinemaidens.

Wotan tells Loge to bid the Rhinemaidens stop their pleas; the gods continue their procession over the rainbow bridge. The music' culminates and *Das Rheingold* closes as three themes are superimposed in the orchestra: the motive of Valhalla; the motive of Wotan's Idea; and the motive of the Rainbow.

DIE WALKÜRE

(*The Valkyrie*)

The action of this music drama takes place quite some time after the close of *Das Rheingold*. At first it will appear as though it is hardly a continuation of the same story, but after the start of *Siegfried*, and particularly in *Die Götterdämmerung*, all the loose threads of the story will be "pulled together" and the overall legend becomes apparent.

A rather crude hut is seen, built around a large ash tree; a fierce storm is raging outside. A man stumbles inside, escaping from the violent weather. The stranger is greeted by Sieglinde. She offers him food and drink, and suggests that, since he is obviously tired and worn, he is welcome to spend the night.

Hunding, Sieglinde's husband, enters and joins them at the table. He notices how much his guest resembles his wife, and inquires of the stranger's life. The latter explains that he has roamed the woods since his mother was killed and his twin sister abducted. His father also disappeared shortly after that. Ever since, misfortune has followed him everywhere, and for this reason his name is *Wehwalt* (Woeful). Urged on by Sieglinde, he tells of his last fight, the one from which he has just fled. It, too, ended in disaster and the stranger was unable to help the maiden who was in distress. Hunding recognizes the locale and people involved in this story of the fight, and discovers from the description that the stranger's adversaries are his own kinsmen. Hunding tells the stranger that by ancient custom the stranger can rest here peacefully for the night, but on the morrow he will be challenged to a fight.

Hunding and his wife retire for the night, leaving the stranger brooding by the fire. "My father promised me a weapon in my hour of direst need," he muses. He calls his father by the only name by which he knows him, "Wälse, Wälse!" The fire in the open hearth burns a little brighter, throwing a ray of light on the handle of a sword buried to the hilt in the ash tree; the fire soon dies down.

Sieglinde enters, saying that she has drugged her husband's nightly cup. She has returned to show the stranger the sword that is buried in the tree. She explains that on the night of her wedding to Hunding against her wishes, an old man with only one eye had walked in, glared fiercely at Hunding's kinsmen, and then had smiled at her as he buried the sword in the trunk. He told her that only the one who could save her would be able to withdraw it. All Hunding's relatives had tried the night of the wedding to withdraw it, but none could budge it. If only the stranger would try, she remarks, perhaps he is the one sent to redeem her honor.

Suddenly the door of the hut bursts open; moonlight streams in — the storm has passed. The stranger is enraptured of Sieglinde and explains his feelings in *The Spring Song:*

Die Walküre — Act I: Siegmund draws the sword from the tree as Sieglinde watches.

Die Walküre — Act III: Brünnhilde has led Sieglinde to the summit of a rocky mountain which the Valkyries use as a meeting place.

WINTERSTÜRME (Siegmund's Spring Song)

The stranger sings of spring and of love; the opening Spring Song Motive is relatively unimportant as far as the balance of the story is concerned:

Example 6 (Spring Song)

Win— ter— stür—me wi—chen dem Won—ne—mond,   in

mil— dem Lich—te leuch-tet der   Lenz;

Winterstürme wichen dem Won-nemond,	Winter storms have waned in the moon of May,
In mildem Lichte leuchtet der Lenz;	With tender radiance sparkles the spring;
Auf linden Lüften, leicht und lieblich,	On balmy breezes, light and lovely,
Wunder webend er sich wiegt;	Weaving wonders, on it floats;
Durch Wald und Auen weht sein Athem,	O'er wood and meadow wafts its breath,
Weit geöffnet lacht sein Aug':	Always with joy and laughter,
Aus sel'ger Vöglein Sange süss ertönt,	In blithesome song of birds re-sounds its voice
Holde Düfte haucht er aus:	Sweetest fragrance it breathes forth:
Seinem warmen Blut entblühen wonnige Blumen,	From ardent blood bloom out joy-giving blossoms,
Keim und Spross entspringt sei-ner Kraft.	Bud and shoot spring up by spring's might

An instrumental interlude before the stranger completes the song is based on the motive of Siegmund's Love:

Example 7 (Siegmund's Love)

As the pair embrace, Sieglinde looks carefully into the stranger's face, for she feels she recognizes him. It dawns on her that the face resembles the one she saw in the pond as she bent over the water, using it as a mirror to comb her hair. "You are the picture that lays hidden within me," she says. Then she recalls that he also resembles the stranger that appeared with the sword at her wedding feast. She asks if his name is really "Woeful." It is no longer "Woeful," he replies, since he has fallen in love with Sieglinde. "Give me a name to your own liking," he requests. "If Wälse was your father and you a Wälsung, if it is his sword that was struck into the tree for you, I name you as I love you — Siegmund!"

Siegmund, wild with delight, approaches the tree and grabs the hilt of the sword, exclaiming: "Siegmund my name, Siegmund I am; witness this sword which I fearlessly grasp." He thereupon wrests the sword from the mighty ash tree and names it *Nothung* (Needful). It is to be his bridal gift to his beloved, freeing her from the bondage of this hut; let them flee far away into the spring. She frees herself from his embrace to tell him, "I am Sieglinde, who have longed for you: your own twin sister you win with the sword." "Bride and sister!" shouts Siegmund. "Let the blood of the Wälsungs prevail!"

In the following act, a mountain pass surrounded by rough crags is seen. Wotan is awaiting the battle he knows must come between Hunding and Siegmund. He is anxious for Siegmund, his own son on earth, to win. Beside him stands Brünnhilde, his favorite Valkyrie daughter. Since it is the Valkyrie maidens that are charged with the duty of watching over the battles on earth, bringing to Valhalla the bodies of the truly heroic, Wotan counsels Brünnhilde: "Now bridle your horse, warrior maid; soon a fierce battle will rage. Brünnhilde, hasten to it and shield the Wälsung in the fight. There let Hunding go where he belongs; I do not want him in Valhalla. Ride to the field!" Brünnhilde then springs from rock to rock up on the heights, shouting her Battle Cry as she goes about this happy charge.

Brunnhilde   *Example 8* (War Cry of the Valkyries)

Ho— jo— to— ho!   Ho— jo— to— ho!   he —ia—

ha!   he—ia — ha!

As soon as Brünnhilde has disappeared on her horse, Fricka approaches Wotan. She tells him that Hunding has approached her as the Goddess of Marriage and the Home to protect him in battle. She has agreed to do this. Wotan explains that it is not his fault that Siegmund and Sieglinde have fallen in love, and that the girl will be much happier with Siegmund than she would have been in her loveless marriage to Hunding. Fricka protests that this goes against the sacred vows of marriage, and that the relationship of Sieglinde to Siegmund is already irregular. Finally she is able to persuade Wotan to stop Brünnhilde from protecting Siegmund and to protect Hunding instead, "or else the law of the gods means nothing." As Fricka departs, Brünnhilde returns to Wotan's side.

Brünnhilde immediately senses that all is not well with her father and questions what is troubling him, stating that his every wish is her command. He tells her of his past and how it has led to the present problem: "When the first delight of my youthful love faded away, my spirit longed for power. Urged by wild desire, I won the world. Loge enticed me into evil undertakings, which I supported by faithless compacts. Yet, in my might, I would not abandon love, while Alberich, by renouncing it, gained riches and mastery. The ring he wrought I stole from him by guile, but instead of returning it to the Rhinemaidens, I paid it to the giants for Valhalla, where I now rule. Wise old Erda cautioned me against the ring and foretold disaster. Bent on knowing more of the threatened doom, I sought her in the innermost earth, and, troubling her wisdom by love, I received counsel from her, and by me she bore you, Brünnhilde, who with your sisters peopled Valhalla with an army of heroes. They now protect me from the swarthy Nibelungs, but Erda predicted that if ever Alberich recovered the ring, Valhalla would be lost; through its magic he would corrupt my defenders. In deep care I thought how to regain the ring, but the bond I closed with Fafner, who now guards it, fettered me. Helpless myself, I imagined another, fighting against gods and men, yet my unconscious champion, accomplishing the deed denied to me. But in all I create, my own image repeats itself. The true freeman must create himself; I produce only slaves. Siegmund I incited to defiance of the gods; against them he holds my only sword. How could I so delude myself? Fricka detected me with ease; in shame I must bow to her demand. I coveted Alberich's ring, and the curse that I fled will not flee from me. Perish then the glittering pretense of godhood's splendor and pomp! I abandon my work, and look only for the end. And Alberich will bring about the doom, for now I grasp the hidden sense of Erda's prophecy: 'When the foe of love in hate begets a son, the downfall of the gods will not delay.' Lately I heard a rumor that the dwarf had depraved a woman with his gold. She has conceived and bears the fruit of his malice. Take then my blessing, son of the Nibelung! Inherit the empty glory of the gods which I now loathe, and destroy it with thy envy."

Brünnhilde asks, simply, "What must I do now?" Her father replies, "Fight for Fricka; her choice is also mine, Fell Siegmund! And look well to it, for with the sword he wields he is no easy prey."

After Wotan has departed, Brünnhilde sees Siegmund and Sieglinde approaching, arm in arm. She warns Siegmund of his fate in the coming battle and summons him to Valhalla. He protests, and states that dead or alive he wishes to dwell in the same realm as his beloved Sieglinde. This love of the two overwhelms Brünnhilde, and coupled with her desire to do what her father *wishes* done, rather than what he *says* must be done, convinces her to disobey her father's order.

Horns announce the arrival of the furious Hunding. The battle between him and Siegmund starts immediately, and it is obvious from the results of the first encounter that Brünnhilde is protecting Siegmund and not Hunding. Wotan himself is forced to interfere, using his spear to break Siegmund's sword. The latter is then killed instantly by the revengeful Hunding. As Hunding recovers the spear, Wotan addresses him: "Go, slave! Kneel before Fricka, and tell her that my spear has avenged her wrong. Go!" At a contemptuous wave of the god's hand, Hunding falls dead.

Brünnhilde recovers the pieces of the broken sword, Nothung, which Siegmund had carried and returns to Sieglinde. She bids Sieglinde join her and travel far away from this spot so that she can give birth to Siegmund's son in peace and quiet.

The third and final act of this opera takes place at "Brünnhilde's Rock" where the Valkyrie maidens are gathered, awaiting Brünnhilde's return. The music that starts just before the curtain goes up, and continues while the Valkyrie maidens appear, is known as *The Ride of the Valkyries:*

THE RIDE OF THE VALKYRIES

A continuous measured trill in the woodwinds, preceded by a flourish in the strings, is heard.

A repeated motive is played by the horns, bassoons, and celli:

Example 9 (Riding)

French Horns

The motive of the Valkyries appears in the horns and trombones:

Example 10 (The Valkyries)

French Horns

The motive of the Valkyries is repeated several times, each time in a more forceful manner with more low brass and woodwinds joining in its statement.

Fragments of Brünnhilde's Battle Cry, Example 8, are heard in the violins:

Example 11

Violins

The motive of the Valkyries, Example 10, is treated with a cumulative effect, appearing first in the horns and trumpets in unison, next (at the rise of the curtain) in octaves by the trombones, and at the climax, by the addition of the bass tuba making the statement in three octaves and changing to the major key.

Descending figures are heard in the strings and woodwinds.

The Riding motive, Example 9, appears in counterpoint to the descending figures.

The Valkyries motive, Example 10, returns and is repeated and developed, leading to a mighty climax.

Brünnhilde soon joins her eight Valkyrie sisters, but in her hurried approach they notice that, instead of a hero, she bears Sieglinde with her on the horse. Brünnhilde explains what has happened and why she has brought Sieglinde to this spot of refuge, but none of her sisters will aid her. Sieglinde states that she wishes to die, but this Brünnhilde will not accept. She tells Sieglinde she must live to bear Siegmund's son, a child who shall be called Siegfried.

Brünnhilde sees Wotan arriving in the distance and tells Sieglinde to flee into the woods where she can bear Siegfried undisturbed; she gives directions to a spot near Fafner's cave, a spot that Wotan is afraid to approach. As Wotan reaches the rock, Brünnhilde hides behind her sisters. The Valkyrie maidens attempt to pacify Wotan, but are unsuccessful. He calls Brünnhilde forward; she replies, "Here I am, father, pronounce my sentence!" The terrified Valkyrie sisters flee, leaving Brünnhilde and Wotan alone. Brünnhilde asks her father if her crime "was so shameful?" She has only carried out his wish, if not his orders. She tells him that she knew how much he loved the Wälsung, and that when she talked to Siegmund, his selfless grief touched her heart, that the love she had learned from her father moved her to rebel against his command. Wotan comments that he has had to overthrow his entire plan and bury his dreams. Since Brünnhilde has followed the call of love rather than her father's command, she must continue to follow the course of love. She will no longer be a Valkyrie, but a mere mortal. Wotan will cause a deep sleep to fall upon her; the first man to pass by and awaken her will be her earthly partner in this pursuit of love.

Fervently Brünnhilde begs her father to surround her with defenses that only a hero, undaunted by god or man, will be able to pierce. Wotan's love for Brünnhilde wells in his heart; this last request is the least he can do in meting out this punishment which he is already reluctant to do. He decrees that as she sleeps, hungry tongues of fire shall lash out all around the rock to repel cowards; that a mortal, a hero, will some day traverse the flames and recall her to mortal life. Wotan bids a fond farewell as the flames of the magic fire start to encircle the rock:

WOTAN'S FAREWELL AND MAGIC FIRE MUSIC

The motive of Slumber is heard in the woodwinds and strings:

Example 12 (Slumber)

"Farewell, my valiant, glorious child!" cries Wotan. "You, blessed pride of my heart, farewell." With regret Wotan muses, "Must I forsake you, will you never be able to ride again as my comrade, nor eat with me at the banquet table, must I never again hear your laughter?" Resolutely he declaims, "A bridal fire shall be kindled for you such as has never burned for a bride! Threatening flames shall flare around the rock; let cowards fly from Brünnhilde's Rock. For one alone shall win you as his bride, one freer than I."

As Wotan sings, "one alone shall win you," the Siegfried motive is heard in the horns and trumpets:

Example 13 (Siegfried)

The motive of Brünnhilde's love for the Wälsungs is heard in the upper woodwinds:

Example 14 (Brünnhilde's Love for the Wälsungs)

Example 14 merges into the Slumber motive, Example 12.

Over an extended development of Example 12, Wotan bids a final farewell to his beloved daughter.

Strings, *pianissimo*, play the motive of Charmed Sleep:

Example 15 (Charmed Sleep)

Woodwinds (repeated by Strings)

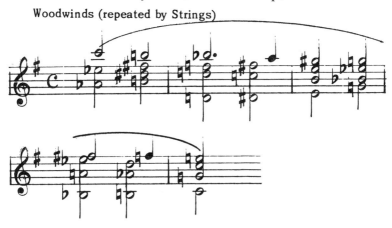

Wotan clasps her head in his hands; he gives her a longing kiss on the eyes. She sinks back with closed eyes, unconscious, in his arms. He gently bears her to a low mossy mound, which is over-shadowed by a wide-spreading fir tree, and lays her upon it. He looks upon her and closes her helmet, his eyes rest on the form of the sleeper, which he now completely covers with the great steel shield of the Valkyrie. He turns slowly away, then again turns around with a sorrowful look.

Extending his spear commandingly, he calls on Loge to build a magic fire around the rock. The motive of Loge is heard forcefully declaimed by the trombones and tuba:

Example 16 (Loge)

Trombones

f

A quivering in the low strings is heard. Wotan strikes the rock three times with his spear, and a first stream of fire gushes from the rock. Soon the Magic Fire is heard in the harps and piccolos:

Example 17 (Magic Fire)

The motive of Charmed Sleep returns. Wotan sings to the Siegfried motive (Example 13), "He who fears the sharp point of my spear shall never break through the wall of fire."

The music, based on the Slumber motive (Example 12), gradually fades away as Wotan takes a final look at the slumbering Brünnhilde, now completely surrounded by the magic flames. The curtain slowly closes on the scene.

SIEGFRIED

A number of years have elapsed since the second music drama, *Die Walküre*. The cave of the dwarf, Mime, is seen as he sits at his forge hammering away at a sword. He laments that he is capable of making swords for giants, but that every one he makes is smashed to bits by Siegfried who has now grown to manhood under his care. The dwarf mumbles to himself that if he could only forge a sword out of the pieces of Nothung, then Siegfried could slay Fafner and retrieve the ring.

Siegfried enters, leading a bear. The frightened Mime is able to talk Siegfried into sending the animal out into the woods again. He then tells the young man that he has forged another sword, one that shall surely be strong enough to serve Siegfried this time without breaking. Siegfried accepts the proffered weapon and strikes it against the anvil. It immediately shatters to bits. As Siegfried rails the dwarf for his incompetence, Mime reminds the youth that he has spared no effort in raising him and that after all this, the boy is still ungrateful. Siegfried replies that he has, indeed, learned a great deal from Mime, but not how to love him. The dwarf tries to convince Siegfried that

Siegfried — Act I: Mime's cave in a forest; the anvil on the left and the forge right center

Götterdämmerung — Act I: The hall of the Gibichungs on the Rhine river

Photos by Foto Festspiele Bayreuth/Siegfried Lauterwasser

deep in his heart the boy does love him, that he, in fact, *must* love him as the nestling loves the parent bird. As Siegfried recalls the forest animals that he knows, he asks where is the mother that bore him if Mime is his father. Mime's claim that he is both Siegfried's father and mother is called a lie by the youth. The boy further recalls that of all the forest animals he has seen, they all resemble their parents; he has seen his own face reflected in a pool of water, and it bore no resemblance to Mime's ugly face. As he grabs the dwarf by the throat, he demands to know who his parents were.

Mime hesitatingly tells Siegfried that one day in the woods he found Sieglinde about to give birth to a baby. The dwarf was able to learn from the dying woman that she had named the child Siegfried and that the boy's father was killed in a battle. The dwarf asked for proof of this, and Sieglinde produced the pieces of the broken sword Nothung.

Siegfried demands that Mime immediately forge a sword from the pieces of Nothung. Armed with this all-powerful weapon, he has visions of entering the world, free and happy, and never seeing this miserable dwarf again.

Mime attempts to forge the sword as soon as the youth leaves, but is unable to accomplish the task. Wotan, disguised as the Wanderer, enters the cave and greets Mime courteously. Realizing that he can no longer control the course of events, Wotan hopes that through Siegfried they will shape themselves favorably to the gods.

Mime is anxious to be rid of this stranger. The Wanderer relates how in his varied travels many have shown him hospitality in exchange for his great wisdom. Mime replies that he, himself, possesses quite a fund of knowledge and does not need any more. The Wanderer is not to be put off so easily! He sits on the hearth and makes himself at home. He challenges the dwarf, stating that he will gamble his head against the answers to any three difficult questions the dwarf might pose. Mime accepts this, and for his first question tries to find something that does not relate to everyday existence, something that would prove hard to answer. The dwarf asks the Wanderer, "What race dwells in the depths of the earth?" The stranger immediately replies that it is the Nibelung, that their home is Niebelheim, and that Alberich was once their lord by the power of a ring he had fashioned. The dwarf tries a second question, "What race inhabits the rocky heights of the earth?" "The giants," answers the Wanderer, "and Riesenheim is their home. Fafner and Fasolt won the ring and the treasure and quarreled over them. Fafner slew Fasolt and now, in the form of a dragon, guards the horde." Mime thinks hard for a third question that will stump his guest and rid his cave of the unwanted visitor. "What race lives in the cloudy heights?" he inquires. "On the cloudy heights reside the gods; Valhalla is their home. They are spirits of light ruled by Wotan. Once he shaped an ash tree into which he thrust a sword. With that sword the world shall be ruled; Nibelungs and giants alike shall obey its eternal power."

As the Wanderer finishes answering the last question, he unconsciously taps his spear against the cave's floor, causing a low rumble of thunder. Mime then recognizes the Wanderer as Wotan, and pleadingly asks him to leave. Wotan replies that he has fulfilled his part of the agreement; he has answered Mime's three questions with the correct answers. Now the dwarf is not fulfilling his part, for he has not extended hospitality but has bid his guest to leave. Wotan tells Mime that now he will ask three questions, the answers to be gambled against the dwarf's head.

Wotan asks first, "What is the race opposed by Wotan and still most dear to him?" Mime is overjoyed, for he knows the answer! "It is the Wälsungs. Siegmund and Sieglinde were the children of Wälse, and their child was Siegfried." Wotan proceeds to ask his second question. "Siegfried's guardian is a wise Nibelung who plans Fafner's death by the hero's hand, and he hopes later to gain the treasure for himself; now, what sword must Siegfried use to accomplish this task?" Mime is quite at home with this question. "It is Nothung, struck into an ash tree by Wotan and later withdrawn by Siegmund. It was later shattered to pieces by Wotan's spear. The pieces are now in the possession of a clever smith who knows that this is the sword Siegfried must wield." Wotan laughs at the dwarf's wisdom. "Who will forge the sword from the fragments?" is Wotan's final question.

Mime shrinks in terror. This was the very question he had wanted to ask the Wanderer, but had forgotten to do so. Wotan then wills the head of the dwarf, Mime's forfeit for being unable to answer the three questions, to him who will forge Nothung — that is, to him that knows no fear. Mime collapses in despair as Wotan leaves.

Siegfried returns and demands to know if Mime has fashioned the sword. Mime mumbles about his latest troubles, and finally, in an effort to save his own head, tells Siegfried that acccording to his mother's wish, the dwarf must teach him fear before he can go out into the world. He inquires of Siegfried if ever, in his many trips into the woods, he has not, even for a moment, been struck by sudden fear.

The reply is negative. Mime then tells the youth that he will lead him to the entrance of the cave of Fafner, an enormous dragon, and there he will learn fear. Siegfried's only reply is a demand for the sword; since Mime admits he cannot forge it, Siegfried seizes the pieces and starts to work upon it himself. He sings of the sword: NOTHUNG! NOTHUNG! (Bellow's Song)

After a brief orchestral introduction, Siegfried calls out the name of the sword to the Nothung motive, which was first heard as Siegmund withdrew the sword from the ash tree in *Die Walküre:*

Example 18A (Nothung)

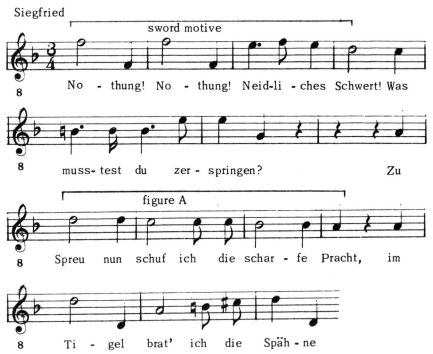

Nothung! Nothung! Neidliches Schwert!
Was musstest du zerspringen?
Zu Spreu nun schuf ich die scharfe Pracht,
Im Tigel brat' ich die Spähne.

Nothung! Nothung! Conquering sword!
What blow has served to break you?
To shreds I shattered your shining blade;
The fire has melted the splinters.

Example 18B

Ho-ho! Ho-ho! Ho-heil! Ho-heil! Ho-hei! Ho-ho!

Bla - se Balg! Bla - se die Gluth!

Ho-ho! Ho-ho!
Ho-heil! Ho-heil!
Ho-ho! Bellows blow!

The melody of the second stanza is derived from Figure A, Example 18A:

Wild im Walde wuchs ein Baum, A tree grew in the wild woods,
Den hab' ich im Forst gefällt: And I felled it there;
Die braune Esche brannt' ich zur I burned the ash tree's trunk to
 Kohl', charcoal,
Auf dem Herd nun liegt sie ge- It now lies heaped on the hearth.
 häuft.

For the third stanza, the melodic line of Figure A, Example 18A is embellished:

Des Baumes Kohle, wie brennt The blackened charcoal, how
 sie kühn; bravely it burns,
Wie glüht sie hell und hehr! How bright and fair the flames!
In springenden Funken sprühet With showering sparks they
 sie auf: shoot aloft;
Zerschmilzt mir des Strahles And I fuse the splintered steel!
 Spreu.

Ho-ho! Ho-ho!
Ho-heil! Ho-heil!
Ho-ho! Bellows blow!

Mime, sitting at a distance from the forging scene, muses to himself: "The sword will be forged and Fafner vanquished; the gold and the ring will fall to the boy. How then shall I win the prize for myself?"

The crafty dwarf then schemes to offer Siegfried a drugged drink after the battle; when he is in a stupor, Mime will kill the boy with his own sword. No sooner has the dwarf concocted this, than Siegfried brandishes the completed sword in the air, decrying, "Show to all villains your sheen! Strike at the traitor, cut down the deceitful! See, Mime, your smithy, what Siegfried's sword sunders!" With a powerful blow, Siegfried brings Nothung down upon the anvil and rends it in twain.

In the following scene, the cave in which Fafner, still transformed as a dragon, guards the horde of gold is seen. Alberich guards the entrance to it, and sees Wotan approaching. He warns Wotan that by the early agreement he made with Fafner, Wotan himself cannot try to recover the treasure. Wotan assures the dwarf that he will be only an innocent bystander watching the one that is coming to slay the dragon.

By the first light of morning Mime and Siegfried arrive at the entrance to the cave. Mime tells Siegfried that it is here that he will learn fear. Mime then leaves Siegfried alone to battle the dragon, hoping that they will slay each other. Confident of his ability to kill the dragon, Siegfried stretches out under a linden tree for a rest. An orchestral interlude known as *Forest Murmurs* is heard while Siegfried dozes.

WALDWEBEN (Forest Murmurs)

A quiet movement begins in the lower strings, starting in F major and soon modulating upward to E major, moving from celli to violas:

Example 19 (Forest Murmurs)

As Siegfried falls into a reverie, he wonders who his father really is, for he still does not know his name; he wonders also about his gentle mother who died in childbirth. Soon the call of the birds of the forest are heard (there are four distinct bird call melodies):

Example 20 (Bird Calls)

A particularly haunting bird call is heard:

Example 21 (Bird Song)

Siegfried suddenly realizes how lonely he has been; his only companion has been the miserable, ugly dwarf Mime. The boy longs to commune with the birds, and recalls that the dwarf told him that the bird calls had a meaning, if only man had a way to understand them. Siegfried springs up, withdraws his sword and cuts a reed with it to try and imitate the birds, and perhaps converse with them. The results are bad (Siegfried's attempt is played by an off-stage English horn very sadly out of tune). Disappointed Siegfried takes the hunting horn from his side and plays a call upon it.

The results are most unexpected, for the dragon, awakened by the noise, appears in the mouth of the cave. The two battle, and soon Siegfried buries his sword in Fafner's heart. As the youth withdraws it, blood from the blade falls on his hands. He attempts to lick it off, and in so doing, tastes the blood and gains the power to understand the speech of the birds. The birds tell Siegfried about the treasure hidden in the cave; Siegfried enters and comes out with the ring and the tarnhelm which he decides to keep as souvenirs of the fight. The birds warn him about the tricky Mime and tell him that the taste of the dragon's blood will enable him to know Mime's thoughts in addition to understanding his spoken words.

Mime returns and approaches Siegfried, the dwarf's eyes held in fascination by the ring and the tarnheim that the youth holds. While Mime speaks compassionate words, Siegfried understands his thoughts and learns that the dwarf plans to cut off his head while he is in a drugged sleep. Siegfried slays the dwarf and throws the body into the cave.

Siegfried then turns to the birds, telling them of his loneliness and lack of companionship. They tell him of a beautiful maiden who sleeps on a high mountain peak, surrounded by a wall of fire. Guided by the birds, Siegfried starts for the mountain precipice.

In the next scene, as dawn is breaking, Siegfried approaches Brünnhilde's Rock. The Wanderer blocks his path, and the birds, seeing the old man, fly away. Wotan, anxious to talk with his grandson, asks him of recent events. Siegfried relates the slaying of the dragon, but becomes impatient at the delay in finding the woman the birds had described. He tells the Wanderer that all his life his path had been blocked by an old man. Upon looking closer, Siegfried discovers that underneath the hat pulled down over his forehead, the Wanderer has but one eye. Relentlessly agitating the Wanderer, Siegfried commands him to show him the way to the magical rock. Wotan becomes angry when his authority is questioned. Wotan informs the youth that he himself is the protector of the wall of flame around the woman, and that Siegfried shall approach no closer to the rock. Fearlessly Siegfried bids the old man step aside. Once again Wotan's spear encounters the sword Nothung in battle. This time the spear is broken in two as Siegfried proceeds on the trail to Brünnhilde's Rock; Wotan's rule is finally at an end, the fate of the world is now in Siegfried's hands.

Siegfried pierces the magic wall of flame, and, on removing the helmet and shield of the body reclining on the rock, is surprised to discover that it is a woman. With strange palpitations of the heart, he thinks perhaps he knows fear for the first time. In order to conquer this, he boldly kisses the dormant figure. Brünnhilde slowly awakens, and in doing so realizes that she is now only a mortal, that the weapons at her side and the sleeping horse, Grane, are no longer of use to her. The fire that Siegfried traversed to reach Brünnhilde now burns in his heart, and the two lovers fondly embrace. At the height of an extended scene, they pledge themselves to each other through life and death.

GÖTTERDÄMMERUNG

(*The Twilight of the Gods*)

In a prologue to this music drama, three Norns, daughters of Erda, sit before the cave below Brünnhilde's Rock and weave the thread of fate. They sing as they weave under the cover of darkness. The first Norn recalls how a brave god once came to the holy ash tree and paid with one of his eyes to drink from the nearby well of wisdom; he cut a branch from the tree and fashioned a spear from it, the tree then died. As she throws the thread of fate to the second Norn, the second Norn continues the narrative. She tells how the spear, inscribed with compacts, was shattered by a young hero, and that Wotan had thereupon ordered the holy ash tree cut into logs. "These logs are now placed around Valhalla," continues the third sister. When they catch fire and burn Valhalla, it will mean the end of the gods. One day Wotan will have Loge, who has placed a ring of magic fire around Brünnhilde, light the splinters of his broken spear and will throw them into the logs heaped around Valhalla. Just as the Norns are about to inquire the fate of the Rhinegold and the ring, the thread of fate breaks. They realize that their hour has struck and return forever to Erda.

Brünnhilde and Siegfried enter from the cave just beneath Brünn-hilde's Rock. It is just before daybreak. Siegfried pledges his love and presents her with the ring as a token of his love. Brünnhilde in return gives Siegfried her horse Grane to carry him on to new vic-tories; she also gives him all her wisdom as protection. She then sends her hero down the Rhine in quest of new honors.

DAWN AND SIEGFRIED'S RHINE JOURNEY

Frequently on orchestral programs, the music immediately pre-ceding the scene of Brünnhilde and Siegfried is coupled with the music succeeding this scene, the Rhine journey. The following is an outline of the orchestral excerpt:

(DAWN)

Over a low timpani roll, the Fate motive is heard:

Example 22 (Fate)

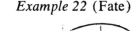

A rising arpeggio in the celli hails the birth of a new day.

The French horns proudly proclaim the motive of Siegfried as Hero:

Example 23 (Siegfried as Hero)

The Brünnhilde motive follows immediately in the clarinet:

Example 24 (Brünnhilde as a Mortal)

Götterdämmerung — Act II: Hagen has mounted a rocky cliff and blown a great horn; the vassals have assembled; he bids them greet Brünnhilde's arrival.

Götterdämmerung — Act II: Hagen, on watch outside the hall of the Gibichungs, is approached by his father, Alberich, and urged to try and recover the ring.

Photos by Foto Festspiele Bayreuth/Siegfried Lauterwasser

Example 24 is developed, rising higher and higher in the register of the clarinet, until at the climax, daylight breaks forth.

Siegfried's motive, Example 23, returns *fortissimo* in the full brass.

The Valkyrie motive (Example 10 — repeated here) accompanies Siegfried and Brünnhilde as they *enter from the cave; he is fully armed; she leads her horse by the bridle:*

Example 10 (Valkyrie)

(In the orchestral excerpt, a cut is made from this point to the end of the Siegfried-Brünnhilde scene, starting at the point where the two pledge eternal love.)

(Siegfried's Rhine Journey)

Brünnhilde's motive, Example 24, is repeated.

A motive heard before in the *Ring* (although not in the excerpts quoted previously in this book) is repeated boldly: the motive of Siegfried's Wanderlust:

Example 25 (Siegfried's Wanderlust)

This is followed immediately by Brünnhilde's motive, Example 24. (It is at this point that Siegfried bids Brünnhilde farewell.)

A variation (Example 26) of Siegfried's Horn Call (Example 27) is heard in the full orchestra as Siegfried leads his horse down the slope:

Example 26

The Wanderlust motive, Example 25, follows immediately.

As Brünnhilde watches Siegfried disappear from view, Brünnhilde's motive, Example 24, returns in the violins and is repeated by the horns.

From a distance Siegfried's Horn Call is heard:

Example 27 (Siegfried's Horn Call)

The bass clarinet repeats Example 24, Brünnhilde's motive; the Horn Call, Example 27, is heard again.

An augmentation of the motive of Flight is heard *fortissimo* in full orchestra:

Example 28 (Flight — in augmentation)

The celli respond with the motive of Love's Resolution:

Example 29 (Love's Resolution)

Siegfried's Horn Call, Example 27, is then combined with the Magic Fire mótive, Example 17.

The motive of Love's Resolution (Example 29) appears in the low register of the orchestra.

The Rhine motive, Example 30, signifies that Siegfried has arrived at the river:

Example 30 (The Rhine)

Wagner then interweaves singly and contrapuntally several important motives heard earlier in the cycle:

Example 31 (Rhinemaidens' Greeting to the Gold)

and

Example 32 (Rhinegold)

Trumpet

The motive of the Ring returns:

Example 33 (The Ring)

Oboes

The *Rhine Journey* concludes with statements of the Rhinegold motive, Example 32.

As the *Rhine Journey* music fades away, the castle of the Gibichungs is seen. The Gibichungs are the children of Gibich. The king is Gunther, who has a sister Gutrune, and a half-brother, Hagen. Hagen is the child of the loveless union between Alberich and Grimhilde, the mother of Gunther and Gutrune.

Gunther and Gutrune both realize that as the last two people of their race, they must either marry and bear children, or the race will die out. Hagen tells Gunther of a beautiful woman, Brünnhilde, who sleeps on a near-by mountain top surrounded by flame. He tells Gutrune of a handsome hero, Siegfried by name, whom she should marry. Hagen, a selfish, gloomy individual, then devises a plot whereby a special potion can be made which will make Siegfried forget that he had seen any woman before Gutrune.

A horn call (Siegfried's Horn Call) is heard in the distance announcing the arrival of the hero. Hagen leaves to prepare the magic elixir. Siegfried meets Gunther, and they are soon joined by Gutrune who bears a cup from which she suggests Siegfried drink after his long journey. The potion goes to work immediately, Siegfried becoming so attracted to Gutrune that he immediately asks her to be his bride.

Gunther tells Siegfried that he is still without a wife. He tells the hero that he knows of a woman that dwells on a high mountain peak not far from there, but she unfortunately is surrounded by a wall of flame that he is afraid to cross. Siegfried shows no sign that he recognizes the description of Brünnhilde and her magic home; the potion has done its work! The hero comes forth with a suggestion to help his new friend: with the aid of the tarnhelm that he has brought with him, he can transform himself into anything in the living world. He will transform himself into Gunther's likeness, cross the flames of which he is not afraid, and lead the maiden to a waiting boat that will contain the real Gunther; Siegfried, in his disguise, will then disappear from her sight and she will never know the difference. To this pact, Siegfried and Gunther pledge their blood brotherhood.

In the following scene, again by Brünnhilde's Rock, one of the Valkyrie maidens approaches Brünnhilde. She asks Brünnhilde to return the ring that is on her finger to the Rhinemaidens, for, alas, Wotan no longer seems to care what becomes of the world. He sits all day dreaming. The Valkyries are no longer sent to battle; Wotan has had the ash tree of life cut down and chopped into firewood and placed around Valhalla. Wotan even returned from earth with his spear shattered to bits. Should Brünnhilde return the ring to the Rhinemaidens, the curse on the gods would be lifted. The Valkyries plead with Brünnhilde to give up the ring and save Valhalla. Brünnhilde replies that Wotan banished her from the world of the gods, and she no longer cares what happens to them. The ring was Siegfried's sacred pledge to her, and to no one will she yield this symbol.

No sooner has the Valkyrie left Brünnhilde than the theme of Siegfried is heard in the orchestra. The person who steps through the flames, however, appears to be Gunther. In his role as Gunther, Siegfried proposes marriage to Brünnhilde. She shows the false Gunther the ring on her finger and states that she is already married. He then wrenches the ring from her and forces her to follow him.

The hall of the Gibichungs is seen again, and Siegfried, no longer disguised, tells Hagen and Gutrune of his experiences in the mountains. Hagen commands the vassals to prepare a feast for the coming marriage of Brünnhilde to Gunther. When Brünnhilde arrives, she immediately sees the ring on Siegfried's hand and realizes that it was he who betrayed her. All Siegfried can recall of the ring's history is that he obtained it from Fafner, for the magic potion still blocks his memory of any other experience with it. Siegfried then swears an oath of loyalty to Gunther. Brünnhilde rushes forward and cries that it is a false oath and vows vengeance on Siegfried.

Crafty Hagen soon devises a new plan to obtain the ring. He decides that Siegfried will accompany them all on a hunting trip, and while on the trip he will be killed and the ring taken from his finger. Fortunately for Hagen, Brünnhilde, in her wrath against the hero, discloses that the only place Siegfried is vulnerable is in the back. Hagen then continues his scheme, planning to tell Gutrune on their return that Siegfried has been killed by a wild boar.

In the next scene, Siegfried is seen standing beside the Rhine, dejected because he has lost the track of the wild boar. The Rhinemaidens appear and offer to show him the wild boar if only he will toss them the ring which he wears. Siegfried replies that he had to kill a mighty dragon to get it, and he will not throw it in the river.

Hagen and Gunther soon arrive. As they pause to eat, Hagen leads Siegfried into telling the story of his life. Hagen, releasing the spell of the magic potion, asks Siegfried if he can really understand the call of the birds. When the hero replies in the affirmative, Hagen suggests that Siegfried turn around and listen to what the ravens are saying and then translate it for him and Gunther. As Siegfried turns his back, Hagen thrusts his spear into it. Gunther strikes Hagen on the arm, but it is too late. Siegfried swings his shield on high with both hands and tries to crush Hagen, but his strength fails him. He falls on it with a crash.

The horrified vassals ask Hagen why he did this evil thing. He replies, "Death for a broken oath!" and leaves the scene. Gunther, grieved and stricken, bends down to support the dying man. For a brief moment, Brünnhilde's love motive is heard in the orchestra. Siegfried opens his eyes. Now that the effects of the magic potion have been dispelled, he recalls once more his beloved. He then sinks slowly back, and dies.

Gunther orders the vassals to raise Siegfried's body and carry it in a solemn procession over the rocky crags back to the castle.

SIEGFRIED'S FUNERAL MUSIC

A soft, solemn roll on the timpani is heard.

The violas and celli play the motive of the Funeral:

Example 34 (Funeral)

The French horns, tenor and bass tubas sound the motive of the Wälsungs:

Example 35 (Wälsungs)

The clarinet, bass clarinet, and bassoon continue the Wälsung motive.

The rhythm of the funeral procession becomes more persistent.

The Wälsung motive returns to the tenor, bass, and double bass tubas.

The English horn, followed by the clarinet, play the motive of Pity, while the motive of the Wälsung's Suffering is heard in the celli and double basses:

Example 36 (Pity — Wälsung's Suffering)
English Horn

This is followed without pause by the motive of Love:

Example 37 (Love)
Oboe

The motive of the Wälsung's Suffering appears in the bass clarinet, bassoon, bass and double bass tubas:

Example 38 (Wälsung's Suffering)
Bass Tuba

The trumpet boldly proclaims the sword motive:

Example 4 (Sword)

The music builds in intensity, then fades away as the motive of Siegfried is played by the French horns:

Example 13 (Siegfried)

Bass Trumpet

The Siegfried motive, Example 13, builds to a forceful, dynamic climax.

As the Funeral motive (Example 34) is heard in the strings, the trumpet repeats Siegfried's motive, Example 13.

The brass repeat Siegfried's Horn Call, Example 27:

Example 27 (Siegfried's Horn Call)

Trumpets

Example 27 builds to another powerful climax.

Brünnhilde's Love as a Mortal motive is played by the English horn and clarinet:

Example 24 (Brünnhilde's Love as a Mortal)

English Horn

The Rhinemaidens' Greeting to the Gold, Example 31, appears in the woodwinds:

Example 31 (Rhinemaidens' Greeting to the Gold)

Oboe & Clarinets

As the *Funeral Music* comes to an end, Siegfried's Horn Call, Example 27, is heard a final time as played by the French horns.

The funeral procession has carried the scene back to the hall of the Gibichungs. Gutrune, who has been having bad dreams, awakens when she hears Hagen's voice outside. He enters and heartlessly tells her to welcome her husband home; the body of Siegfried is then borne into the room. Gutrune falls on the corpse with shrieks of horror. She blames Gunther for the death of the hero. He throws the blame on Hagen: "There stands the accursed boar which gored the noble hero!"

Hagen admits his crime and claims his is the right of booty — the ring on Siegfried's hand. Gunther angrily asserts his own right to the prize, and the two fall to fighting over it. The curse of the ring claims another victim; Gunther falls dead.

Hagen reaches for the ring, only to fall back in horror when Siegfried's arm is miraculously uplifted. As all stand amazed, Brünnhilde approaches. She bids them stop their weeping, for it is she, Brünnhilde, who has been betrayed by those present. Gutrune, now realizing that Brünnhilde was Siegfried's love until blinded by her potion, moves away from Siegfried's body and laments over the corpse of her brother Gunther.

BRÜNNHILDE'S IMMOLATION

The concluding scene, starting at this point, is known as *Brünnhild's Immolation.*

Almost all the motives heard in the *Immolation* have been heard previously in the cycle, though they are not necessarily quoted in the excerpts in this book. Where a previous quotation of a motive has occurred, the original Example number has been assigned so that it can be compared to the earlier statement. (*Italics* indicate the composer's stage directions.)

The French horns sound the motive of Fate, Example 22, twice, separated by a rhythmical timpani figure reminiscent of the *Funeral Procession:*

Example 22 (Fate)

The motive of the Pyre is heard:

Example 39 (Pyre)

Brünnhilde commands the vassals:

Example 40

Star - ke Scheite   schichtet mir   dort

am   Ran - de des Rhein's zu Hauf'!

Starke Scheite schichtet mir dort I command you to pile the
                                      mighty logs

Am Rande des Rhein's zu Hauf'! High on the river's shore!
Hoch und hell lod're die Gluth, Kindle a hot and fierce fire;
  The Fire motive is then heard in the orchestra:

Example 17 (Fire)

  Brünnhilde continues:
Die den edlen Leib des hehresten   Let the noblest hero's body be
  Helden verzehrt.   consumed in its flames.
Sein Ross führet daher,   His steed bring here to me,
Dass mit mir dem Recken es   That he with me may follow:
  folge:

To Siegfried's motive (Example 13) she sings:

Example 41

denn des Hel - den hei - lig - ste Eh - re zu

thei - len ver - langt mein ei - ge - ner Leib.

Denn des Helden heiligste Ehre   For my hero's highest honor
Zu theilen verlangt mein eigener   My body burns with longing.
  Leib.

The vassals *raise a huge funeral pyre of logs before the hall, near the bank of the Rhine; the women decorate this with coverings on which they strew flowers. Brünnhilde becomes absorbed in contemplating the lifeless hero's face.*

The motive of Rapture is heard:

Example 42 (Rapture)

To Love's Greeting, Brünnhilde continues:

Example 43 (Love's Greeting)

Wie Son - ne lau - ter strahlt mir sein Licht:

Wie Sonne lauter strahlt mir sein Licht:	Like the rays of the sunshine streams his light:
Der Reinste war er, der mich verieth!	The purest was he who betrayed!
Die Gattin trügend treu dem Freunde,	Deceived as wife, but true in friendship,
Vor der eig'nen Trauten einzig ihm theuer,	From his heart's only true love
Schied er sich durch sein Schwert.	He was barred by his sword.

(The Sword motive, Example 4, appears here in the accompaniment.)

Ächter als er schwur Keiner Eide,	Truer oaths than his were never spoken,
Treuer als er heilt Keiner Verträge;	No more faithful than he ever sealed a promise.
Lautrer als er liebte kein And'rer:	Purer love than his was never given;
Und doch, alle Eide, alle Verträge,	Yet oaths he has scorned, bonds he has broken,
Die treueste Liebe,	The most faithful love —

A dramatic pause in her singing is punctuated by the Oath of Fidelity:

Example 44 (Oath of Fidelity)

Trog Keiner wie Er!	He has not betrayed!

The Prophecy motive, Example 45, follows immediately as an orchestral introduction to Brünnhilde's question: "Do you know why that was?"

Example 45 (Prophecy)

The Valhalla motive, Example 3, in the orchestra accompanies Brünnhilde's plea to the gods:

Example 3 (Valhalla)

Oh ihr, der Eide ewige Hüter!	O you, the guardians of heavenly vows,
Lenkt euren Blick auf mein blü-hendes Lied;	Turn your gaze on my sad song;
Erschaut eure ewige Schuld!	Behold your eternal disgrace!
Meine Klage hör', du hehrster Gott!	Give your ear to my plea, you mighty god!
Durch seine tapferste That,	Through his most valiant deed,
Dir so tauglich erwünscht,	By you so dearly desired,
Weihtest du den, der sie gewirkt,	You condemned him to endure
Dem Fluche dem du verfielest,	The doom that had fallen on you,
Mich musste der Reinste Verra-then	He, truest of all, must betray me,
Dass wissend würde ein Weib!	That I might become a wise woman!

The Fate motive, Example 22, is heard in the orchestra as Brünnhilde asks, "Do I know your need?"

Example 22 (Fate)

Alles ward mir nun frei.	All is revealed to me.
Auch deine Raben hör' ich rau-schen;	Wings of the ravens flutter around me;
Mit bang ersehnter Botschaft send' ich die Beiden nun heim.	With the long desired message I send them home.

(According to mythology, ravens were to fly around all day, listening, and then fly home at nightfall to tell their master what they had learned.)

The Rhine Gold motive, Example 5, accompanies Brünnhilde's "Rest, rest, Oh god!"

Example 5 (Rhine Gold)

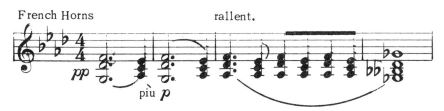

She makes a sign to the vassals to lift Siegfried's body on the pyre; at the same time she draws the ring from Siegfried's finger and looks at it meditatively.

The Ring, Example 33, is heard as Brünnhilde remarks about it:

Example 33 (The Ring)

Verfluchter Reif!	Accursed charm!
Furchtbarer Ring!	Terrible ring!
Dein Gold fass' ich,	My hand grasps you,
Und geb' es nun fort.	And gives you away.

The Rhinemaidens' Song appears in the accompaniment:

Example 45 (Rhinemaidens' Song)

Des Rheines schwimmende Töchter,	Listen, daughters of the **Rhine**,
Dank' ich redlichen Rath:	I give you honest counsel:
Was ihr begehrt	What you desire
Ich geb' es euch.	I leave to you.
Aus meiner Asche nehmt es zu eigen!	From my ashes take your treasure!
Das Feuer, das mich verbrennt,	Let fire, burning this hand,
Rein'ge vom Fluche den Ring!	Cleanse, too, the ring from its curse!

She has put the ring on her finger and now turns to the pile of logs on which Siegfried's body is stretched. She takes a torch from one of the vassals.

Example 16, Loge, is heard:

Example 16 (Loge)

Brandishing the torch in the air (the Magic Fire, Example 17, is heard), she commands the ravens to "Fly home! Fly home you ravens!"

Example 17 (Magic Fire)

She throws the torch on the wood-pile which quickly breaks out in bright flames. The two ravens fly up from the rock and disappear.

As two vassals lead in her horse, Grane, Brünnhilde's Battle Cry (Example 8) is heard, followed immediately by the Valkyrie motive (Example 10):

Examples 8 and 10 (Battle Cry — Valkyrie)

"Grane, my steed, I greet you!" As she unbridles him, the Valkyries motive, Example 10, is repeated.

Weisst du auch, mein Freund,	Do you know, my friend,
Wohin ich dich führe?	To whom I lead you?
Im Feuer leuchtend,	In brilliant fire,
Liegt dort dein Herr, Siegfried!	Lies there the master, Siegfried!
Mein seliger Held.	My beloved hero.

To the Redemption by Love motive, Brünnhilde continues her song:

Example 46 (Redemption by Love)

Fühl meine Brust auch, wie sie entbrennt,	Feel, too, my bosom, how it burns;
Helles Feuer das Herz mir erfasst,	Glowing flames now lay hold on my heart;
Ihn zu umschlingen, umschlossen von ihm,	Embraced and enfolded by his arms,
In mächtigster Minne,	In the strength of our love,
Vermählt ihm zu sein!	We are made one!

Example 8 (Brünnhilde's Battle Cry)

With her Battle Cry, she mounts Grane and heads for the flames:

Brünnhilde

Sieg - fried! Sieg - fried! Sieh!
Sieg - frieg! Sieg - fried! See!

Se - lig   grüsst dich dein Weib.
Loved   one,   greet   then your wife!

The music now moves swiftly to its final climax, incorporating first one motive, then another:

She makes her horse leap into the burning pile of logs. (Example 8, Battle Cry)

The flames immediately blaze up so that they appear to seize the castle itself. (Example 17, Magic Fire)

The glow suddenly subsides, so that only a cloud of smoke remains which is drawn to the background, and there lies on the horizon as a dark bank of clouds. (Example 15, Charmed Sleep)

At the same time, the Rhine overflows its banks in a mighty flood which rolls over the fire. (A Rhine motive not previously quoted, a rippling figure in the low strings.)

On the waves the three Rhinemaidens swim forward, and now appear on the place of the fire. (Example 22, Fate)

One Rhinemaiden *holds up the regained ring joyously.* (Example 45, Rhinemaidens' Song)

The Rhine has gradually returned to its natural bed. (Example 46, Redemption by Love)

The growing firelight in the heavens |reveals| *the interior of Valhalla.* (Example 33, The Ring)

The gods and heroes [are seen| *assembled in Valhalla.* (Example 3, Valhalla)

Bright flames appear to seize the hall of the gods. (Example 47, Twilight of the Gods)

Example 47 (Twilight of the Gods)

As the gods become entirely hidden by the flames, the curtain falls. (Example 46, Redemption by Love, followed by the theme of the Rhine)

JOHANNES BRAHMS

BORN: May 7, 1833; Hamburg, Germany.
DIED: April 3, 1897; Vienna, Austria.

During the last years of his life, Brahms frequently could be seen in the woods and parks of Vienna taking long walks. Dressed in a cheap suit that had probably not been pressed since it was purchased, his head crowned with a derby, he would walk along the pathways, smoking a black cigar, and watch the children at play.

Brahms had been raised in a household on intimate terms with poverty, and although he had amassed a moderate sum of money by this later period of his life, his habits did not change. He always traveled by third (tourist) class railway, bought the least expensive clothes he could find (and then wore them until they were threadbare), brewed his own coffee (no one else made it strong enough), and ate at modest restaurants. He was shrewd in his business dealings, but probably was unaware of exactly how much money he did have since it filled the pockets of many suits and was placed in paper sacks hidden in various places around his home. Brahms' life was truly a paradox, for in spite of the disorderly personal habits and condition of his home, his musical creations were the paragon of orderliness and design.

Johannes Brahms was born of an extremely poor family that lived in the slum area of Hamburg. His father was a double bass player in the Hamburg City Theater Orchestra, and his mother earned additional money for the family by taking in sewing. Johannes started learning the elements of music from his father when he was six, studying also the cello and piano. His parents managed to spare enough money so the boy had an opportunity to attend a private school and receive a general education. As 'Hannes (the family nickname) progressed on the piano, the services of a private teacher were obtained for him. By the time he was eleven, he gave his first private concert.

'Hannes' pianistic ability was used to further the family income. At thirteen he started playing in taverns for dances and the back stage piano for several small theaters. Through a friend of his father's, he was able to spend two summers away from Hamburg at the little town of Winsen where he conducted the male chorus of the village and tried his hand at composition. Johannes arranged a number of folk songs for male voices in addition to the creation of some original works. A piano composition, *Fantasy on a Favorite Waltz,* also dates from his summer visits to Winsen. The first public performance of this work was given when Brahms returned to Hamburg. In addition to this original work, the fifteen-year-old Brahms included a fugue by Bach and Beethoven's *Waldstein Sonata* in this first public recital.

When he was seventeen, Brahms had the good fortune to meet the famous Hungarian violinist Reményi who, forced to leave his native land because of his political activities, had settled in Hamburg. The violinist became extremely interested in Johannes' musical talent. The latter was anxious to become acquainted with the world of music, and was eager to get away from writing hack works for a local publisher under an assumed name in order to increase his income. Reményi finally decided on an extended tour and asked Brahms to make the trip with him and serve as his accompanist. This trip, made during Brahms' twentieth year, was a decided turning point in his career. On the tour he met the world famous violinist Joachim at Göttingen, Franz Liszt at Weimar, Robert Schumann at Düsseldorf (after this meeting Schumann made an entry in his diary, "Brahms to see me — a genius"), and Hector Berlioz at Leipzig.

The visit to the Schumann household at Düsseldorf was probably the most important single factor in Brahms' life. The former was the editor of a musical newsletter, the *Neue Zeitschrift für Musik* (The New Journal for Music) which championed the cause of new music. Robert Schumann wrote an often-quoted article for the newsletter after he had heard Brahms and hailed him in the article as a composer who "did not need training and experience." He said the young Brahms had been thrust into the world "in musical maturity from the beginning." The article made Johannes' name known throughout Europe, but later acted as a stumbling block to the acceptance by the public of his music. Since the newsletter's avowed purpose was to

CÉSAR FRANCK

JOHANNES BRAHMS

PETER ILYITCH TCHAIKOVSKY

GEORGES BIZET

further the cause of "modern music," the public was surprised to hear in the works of Brahms a heavy reliance on the old *classical* forms.

Brahms became intimately acquainted with both Clara and Robert Schumann, and when the latter first had a breakdown, it was Johannes who stood by and comforted the distraught wife. For a year Brahms stayed at Düsseldorf and taught so that he would not be far away from Clara. After Robert's death a year later (Brahms was only twenty-three), he helped pull Clara out of the depths of despair. The mutual friendship of Clara and Johannes enabled them both to reach new musical heights. Johannes played most of his new works for her critical comment, and dedicated a number of them to her or her children. Clara, in turn, was urged to return to the concert stage and champion the piano music of her late husband. This mutual friendship lasted throughout both their lives, for it was at Clara's funeral that Brahms' health was impaired, leading to his own death a few months later.

After Robert Schumann's death, Brahms spent several years traveling. For three years he served in the town of Lippe-Detmold where he was the princess' piano instructor, served as conductor of the local choral society, composed his *Piano Concerto No. 1,* and during summers, conducted the Women's Choir at Hamburg.

In 1862, Brahms visited Vienna and, later in the year, accepted an appointment as conductor of the Singakademie. From this point, Vienna became his permanent home. The *German Requiem* was composed there, followed five years later by another choral composition, *Triumphlied,* written to celebrate the German victory in the Franco-Prussian War of 1871. The *Variations on a Theme of Haydn* followed.

Brahms was forty-two when he started to work on his *Symphony No. 1.* It was premiered in November, 1876. Its acceptance was mixed, many having expected a more "modern" type of work. Liszt was already a well-known composer and the public was most enthusiastic about the works of the Liszt-Wagner-Bruckner school. Brahms had, however, several years previously participated in a manifesto against the "new German school of Liszt." Although Brahms had met Wagner, and actually purchased scores of his new works and studied them with interest, the general public divided themselves into two groups. The first accepted Wagner and rejected the works of Brahms, the others reversed their allegiance. Although the works of these two masters are admittedly different, it is hard for the present generation, who can easily admire the works of both masters, to realize the violent attitude of the late nineteenth-century public in accepting either one or the other — becoming either Wagnerites or Brahmsians.

An honorary Doctorate was extended to Brahms in 1877 by Cambridge University in England, but the composer refused to accept the award. Soon after this his *Symphony No. 2* was completed, and the composer left for one of many visits to Italy. On his return, his *Violin Concerto* was premiered in Leipzig by Joachim.

The year 1881 proved to be a busy one for the composer. His two concert overtures, the *Tragic Overture* and the *Academic Festival Overture* (written as a token of gratitude for an honorary Doctorate from the University of Breslau which he did accept) were completed early in the year. A concert tour led him to visits in both Holland and Hungary. He moved next to Budapest where he again met Franz Liszt. The spring he spent in Sicily, returning later in the year to play the premier performance of his *Piano Concerto No. 2* in Stuttgart.

Two years later, the *Symphony No. 3* was completed and given its first performance in Vienna, followed shortly by his last work in this genre, the *Symphony No. 4*. During further visits to Italy, he met Tchaikovsky for the first time.

In 1896 Clara Schumann, his beloved friend and musical compatriot, died. He attended her funeral on March 24 and caught a severe cold. This affected a complaint he had had for some time, cancer of the liver. His health steadily declined, and on the seventh of March of the following year, attended his last concert, a performance of his *Symphony No. 4*. The audience paid him a glowing final tribute (although at the time they did not know it was to be final), standing and applauding at the end of each movement, and continuing the applause after the performance until Brahms came forward in the artist's box to acknowledge it. Less than a month later, the composer succumbed to the cancer. He was buried in the cemetery in the heart of Vienna, not far from the graves of Beethoven and Schubert.

BIBLIOGRAPHY

Brahms, Johannes, and Clara Schumann. *Letters of Clara Schumann and Johannes Brahms,* ed. Litzmann. New York: Longmans, Green and Co., 1927.
Geiringer, Karl. *Brahms, His Life and Work,* 2nd ed. London: Oxford University Press, 1947.

SYMPHONY NO. 2
in D Major

Johannes Brahms

First Movement: *Allegro non troppo.*

The first movement, which is in sonata-allegro form, opens with the Principal Subject:

Example 1 (Principal Subject)

This theme, Example 1, is passed through the woodwinds and strings; then a short but lyrical theme (derived from Figure A, Example 1) appears in the violins:

Example 2

Figures A and B from Example 1 are passed back and forth among the woodwinds and strings.

The Second Subject is introduced by the violas and celli:

Example 3 (Second Subject)

The Second Subject, Example 3, is repeated by the flutes, oboes, and bassoons.

As the music builds to a dynamic climax, another short theme is introduced:

Example 4

In the closing measures of the *exposition,* fragments of the Principal Subject, Example 1, are followed by fragments of the Second Subject, Example 3. This leads to a double bar at which point Brahms indicates a repeat of the entire exposition.

The *development* commences with the violins enlarging upon the Principal Subject, Example 1. Figure A of Example 1 soon becomes the Subject of a fugal passage. Fragments of Example 1 then appear throughout an extended section.

The clarinets and bassoons play the bridge theme, Example 2, in counterpoint to Example 1. Figure B of Example 1 is heard in various sections of the orchestra, bringing the *development* to a close.

The oboes play the Principal Subject, Example 1, to open the *recapitulation,* and are followed by a passage for violins and celli which leads to a repeat of the Second Subject, Example 3.

A counter-statement of the Second Subject, Example 3, is made by the oboes and violins.

A repetition of Example 4 leads to the *coda.*

The *coda* is based on both the Principal and Second Subjects, Examples 1 and 3. The French horns play a lyrical melody above the strings in the closing moments of the movement which leads to this final theme, Example 5, built from Figure A of Example 1:

Example 5

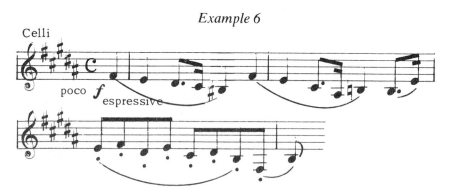

Second Movement: *Adagio non troppo.*

The second movement is essentially in ternary form. The first section opens with a slow, lyrical theme played by the celli:

Example 6

A counter-statement of Example 6 is made by the violins.

In the middle section the meter changes to 12/8, and a new theme, much lighter in character, appears:

Example 7

The first section is melodically recapitulated, with the insertion of a slight episode in the center of it.

THIRD MOVEMENT: *Allegretto grazioso (quasi Andantino).*

The scherzo appears to be in second rondo form (a form in which the first, or principal melody returns between new themes — *second* rondo meaning that there are two themes in addition to the principal one).

The "rondo" theme is heard immediately as played by the oboe (in folk song style) accompanied by the clarinets, bassoons, and pizzicati celli. It is repeated once with an alteration in the after-phrase.

Example 8

The meter changes from 3/4 to 2/4, and the first sub-theme (built out of Example 8) is played in a rhythmic fashion by full orchestra. It is repeated by the strings softly.

Example 9

The meter returns to 3/4 and the principal melody, Example 8, is repeated by the oboe, this time with a different harmonic accompaniment.

The second sub-theme is also rhythmical in nature; the fore-phrase is played by the strings, the after-phrase (an inversion of Example 8) is played by the flutes:

Example 10

The principal melody, Example 8, returns for a final time as played by the strings. It is expanded somewhat to form a codetta.

FOURTH MOVEMENT: *Allegro con spirito.*

Another sonata-allegro, the fourth movement opens with the Principal Subject:

Example 11 (Principal Subject)

A counter-statement of Example 11 is made by full orchestra in expanded form.

The tempo slows to a *Largamente* for the introduction of the Second Subject, a broad and sweeping melody played in majestic manner by the violins:

Example 12 (Second Subject)

The Second Subject, Example 12, in altered form, is repeated with the melody played in thirds.

A passage of quickly moving thirds played by the woodwinds over pizzicato strings brings the *exposition* to a close.

The *development* opens with Figure A of Example 11, followed by an inversion (the melodic intervals turned upside down) of the Principal Subject. Example 11, in the strings and woodwinds:

Example 13

The Principal Subject, Example 11, returns in C-sharp minor, followed by a development of Figure B of this example.

A return to the original key for the *recapitulation* leads to the repetition of the Principal Subject, Example 11, by the strings in unison, *pianissimo*.

The Second Subject returns, this time in the tonic key of D major.

The *recapitulation* ends with the return of the running scale-like passage in thirds.

The *coda* is based primarily on the Second Subject, Example 12, which builds to a fast and moving climax — the theme appearing in the lower voices in majestic manner, over which a very rhythmical accompaniment is heard in full orchestra.

MINNELIED
(*Love Song*)

JOHANNES BRAHMS

One of the many beautiful Brahms lieder is this setting of the poem of Ludwig Hölty. It is the fifth of five songs from the composer's Opus 71, written in the year 1877, a year filled with the creation of many of his finest songs and the *Symphony No. 2.*

The setting is an excellent example of ternary, or three-part song form. Each of the stanzas has two four-measure phrases, separated by piano interludes. The first, second, and fourth phrases are similar in contour and may be outlined as *A, A', * and *A''.* The third phrase is a contrasting one which can be called B. In other words, the simple ternary form of this song is: A A' B A''. In addition to this basic form, there is a flowing introduction for piano marked by the composer to be played "with much tenderness, but not too slowly." The song ends with a repetition of the last line which builds to the final emotional climax.

Note that during the words *"Ohne sie ist alles tot"* (without her all things are dead), there is a pedal point (the same note repeated over and over again) on a low G. The pedal point lasts throughout the third stanza.

PHRASE A

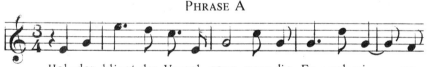

Hol - der klingt der Vo-gel-sang, wenn die En - gel-rei - ne,

I

Holder klingt der Vogelsang,	Lovelier sounds the singing of the birds
Wenn die Engelreine,	When she, the pure angel
Die mein Jünglingsherz bezwang,	Who had conquered my youthful heart,
Wandelt durch die Haine.	Strolls through the woods.

II

Röter blühen Tal und Au,	Redder bloom valleys and fields,
Grüner wird der Wasen,	Greener grows the grass,
Wo die Finger meiner Frau	Where the fingers of my lady
Maienblumen lasen.	Gathered the flowers of May.

PHRASE B

Oh-ne sie ist al-les tot, welk sind Blüt' und Kräu - ter;

III

Ohne sie ist alles tot,	Without her all things are dead,
Welk sind Blüt' und Kräuter;	Faded are flowers and herbs,
Und kein Frühlingsabendrot	And no spring sunset
Dünkt mir schön und heiter.	Seems to me fair and serene.

IV

Traute minnigliche Frau,	Sweet and lovely lady,
Wollest nimmer fliehen,	Never flee from here,
Dass mein Herz, gleich dieser Au,	That my heart like these fields,
Mög' in Wonne blühen!	May blossom with joy!

(Ludwig Hölty)

CÉSAR FRANCK

BORN: December 10, 1822; Liége, Belgium.
DIED: November 8, 1890; Paris, France.

In August, 1885, the sixty-three-year-old César Franck received his first public recognition: he was presented with the ribbon of Chevalier of the French Legion of Honor. Strangely, this award was not made to him as a composer, but as a teacher at the Conservatory. Recognition as a composer had to wait until the last year of his life, when he was in his sixty-ninth year! Probably no other famous composer waited until so late in life for the acceptance by the general public of his talent as a composer!

César Franck was born into a family that had an artistic background, for several of his forebears had been well-accepted painters (César himself enjoyed drawing and painting). His father was a banker in Liége, Belgium, and decided that both César and his brother Joseph should become musicians (Joseph later became an organist-teacher, a minor composer, and an author of musical textbooks). Hoping that César would become a virtuoso in the grand manner, his father enrolled him at the Liége Conservatory at a very early age. The boy won first prize for singing when he was nine, and a little later won the first prize for his pianistic ability. When the boy was eleven, his father withdrew him from the Conservatory and sent him on a concert tour.

When the concert tour was finished, the entire family moved to Paris so the two boys could study at the Paris Conservatory. César was given private lessons in harmony and counterpoint to qualify him for the Conservatory which he entered when he was fifteen. At the end of his first year in this school, Franck won second prize in the fugue contest; but his father, always pushing the boy's career, reprimanded his son for not having worked harder and taken more care in the fugue so that he could have won first prize. Franck won in successive years: first prize in piano, first prize in fugue, second prize in organ.

His father, not satisfied with the boy's progress at the Conservatory, and worried because of his proclivity for playing the pipe organ and writing compositions, withdrew him in his twentieth year as César was preparing for the Prix de Rome contest. Liszt was then at the height of his virtuoso career, and Franck's father had not yet given up the idea that it was this type of career his son César should follow. The family moved back to Liége and César spent hours at the keyboard practicing; the only opportunity he had for composition during this period was for showy works to be presented at his piano recitals. His father arranged a special concert for the King of Belgium, hoping that through this his son's career could be furthered. Nothing came of the venture.

The family moved to Paris again, and César became immersed in work on four trios and a Biblical eclogue, *Ruth*. The latter was his first attempt at a composition that was neither for piano nor embodying the use of the piano (as in the piano *Trios*). The family fortune was almost depleted by this time and they were dependent upon what César and Joseph could earn from giving music lessons. Things continued to grow worse as the war clouds hovered over Paris and many of the wealthier families, including those from which their pupils came, moved out of the city.

At the height of the Revolution of 1848, César married. The bridal party had to climb over a barricade in order to enter the church for the ceremonies. Franck's bride had been an actress and in those days the women of that profession were not accepted by society. The combination of his wife's former occupation, and the fact that what money César earned would be needed to support his own house, strained the relationship with his father beyond repair.

Franck and his wife settled in a small house in Paris which was to be their home for the balance of their lives. He became a naturalized French citizen. Winter and summer he rose at half-past five, beginning his long day by giving private lessons. The balance of the morning was given over to composition, which he referred to as "reserving time for thought." In the afternoon he would go to the Sainte Clothilde Church to practice organ. He had been appointed organist-choir director at that church in 1858 and served in that position until his death some thirty-two years later.

The Sainte Clothilde had a magnificent organ, and it was here that his friends and fellow musicians came to visit him, learn from him, and worship him as the master. Franz Liszt, after having heard Franck play, compared him to the immortal Johann Sebastian Bach.

When he was fifty, Franck was appointed Professor of Organ at the Paris Conservatory. This appointment surprised not only the composer, but also the members of the Conservatory staff who regarded Franck with suspicion since he would never involve himself with any of the many intrigues and political machinations of the Parisian musicians. He was even less liked by his colleagues after his appointment because he spent much of his organ class teaching composition, his pupils doing far better in the composition competitions than those enrolled in the composition classes.

About the time of his Conservatory appointment, he began work on a choral composition, *Les Béatitudes,* based on the Sermon on the Mount. After ten years of work on it, a private performance was to be given in his home. Most of the invited guests (including the Minister of Arts and the Director of the Conservatory) declined; of the few that attended, only two remained until the end. The first public performance of this work followed fourteen years later, three years after the composer's death, and the cantata was well received.

After the Legion of Honor award, already described, had been made, Franck's pupils, who included d'Indy, Duparc, and Pierné, became so incensed because he was acknowledged as a teacher and not as a composer, that they organized a concert devoted to their master's compositions. The concert took place, but the rehearsals and performance were so poorly conducted that the *Variations Symphoniques* was chaotic, and d'Indy described the *Béatitudes* as "a deplorable affair." Franck was oblivious to all this, however, and was extremely grateful for this tribute by his pupils.

The last years of his life saw his major compositions take form: the *Symphony in D Minor* (his only venture in this genre), the *String*

Quartet in D Major, and the *Three Chorales for Organ.* The *Symphony in D Minor* was first performed by the Société des Concerts des Conservatoire just one year before Franck's death. The orchestra and the patrons had objected to this work in the concert series and, when it was performed, it was not welcomed by either the musicians or the audience. One critic violently objected to Franck's use of an English horn to introduce the melody of the second movement; Haydn and Beethoven had not used this instrument, why should Franck? Gounod, who attended this performance, said it was "the affirmation of impotency carried to the point of dogma."

On April 18, 1890, seven months before Franck's death, a public performance of his *String Quartet* was accepted by the public with enthusiasm, his first composition to win popular acclaim. Vincent d'Indy wrote of this episode: "The next day, filled with pride at his *first success* (in his sixty-ninth year!) he said to us quite naïvely. 'There, you see, the public is beginning to understand me.' "

A short time later, Franck, while crossing a Paris street, was hit by a bus. Although he fainted after the accident, he attached no importance to it and proceeded to an engagement he had to play in a two-piano rendition of his *Variations Symphoniques.*

By autumn an attack of pleurisy was complicated by the injuries sustained in the bus accident. He climbed to the organ loft of Sainte Clothilde to try his final composition, *Trois Chorales.* The score of this work lay on his bed as a parish priest administered the last sacraments of the Church.

BIBLIOGRAPHY

Demuth, Norman. *César Franck.* New York: Philosophical Library, 1949.
Vallas, Léon. *César Franck,* trans. Hubert Foss. New York: Oxford University Press, 1951.

SYMPHONY IN D MINOR

CÉSAR FRANCK

The following is Franck's analysis in a free translation by the author.

THIRD MOVEMENT: *Allegro non troppo.*

The third movement opens brilliantly in contrast with the somberness of the two preceding ones. The principal theme is stated by the celli and bassoons:

Example 1

After the development of Example 1, a new theme appears in the brasses and continues in the strings:

Example 2

Another new theme occurs, this time in the basses, followed in its turn by a theme from the second movement:

Example 3

After a development of Example 2 in the violins, a ritard is followed by a suggestion of Example 3 in the oboe.

After a pause, development of previous materials leads to a climax, the full orchestra recapitulating Example 3.

The *coda* follows with suggestions of themes from the first movement.

The movement closes with its principal subject, Example 1.

GEORGES BIZET

BORN: October 25, 1838; Paris, France.
DIED: June 3, 1875; Bougival, France.

The myth has arisen that Georges Bizet died at the early age of thirty-six as the result of a broken heart over the failure of the opera *Carmen*. Both portions of this myth are incorrect. Bizet suffered most of his life from a throat ailment, a severe chronic ulceration thought by many doctors from the evidence to have been a case of neglected tonsilitis. Every time Bizet's health was affected by any common ailment, the throat trouble accompanied it. During his final illness, Bizet suffered a feeling of "suffocation" for three days before finally succumbing. His death occurred not long after the final curtain had come down on the thirty-first performance of *Carmen* in Paris. That *Carmen* reached the thirty-first consecutive perform-ance is proof that it was not a failure. True, the ·public and press were not overly receptive. It was only after its premiere in England a few years later that it became an outstanding success.

Bizet was born of a musical family: his father was an excellent singing teacher. and his mother a distinguished pianist who had taken prizes during her student days at the Conservatory. Georges was baptized at the Church of Notre-Dame-de-Lorette, on the south slope of Monmartre the area in which he lived during all his days in Paris. The home was a happy one, and Georges received his first music lessons from his mother when he was four. The boy was encouraged in music by his father who never questioned that Georges would become a musician. There were times when, as a student, Georges' books on literature and other subjects were hidden by his father so that he wouldn't neglect his musical studies for subjects of lesser im-portance.

When Georges was nine, his father enrolled him as a student at the Paris Conservatory where the boy spent nine years. He studied piano, organ, and composition there; the composers Charles Gounod (known for his opera *Faust*) and Jacques Halévy (the composer of the opera *La Juive*, The Jewess) were his instructors. During his stu-dent days, he completed a *Symphony in C Major* (1855) which was not performed until 1935, some seventy years later (it is now an established symphony in the standard repertoire). At the Conserv-atory Bizet won several prizes, first prize in piano when he was fourteen, at seventeen (the year of the *Symphony*) a first prize in both fugue and organ. At nineteen Bizet won the coveted Priz de

Rome which entitled him to four years at the Villa Medici in Rome with all expenses paid. He won this prize the same year that he tied for first place in a contest sponsored by Jacques Offenbach who hoped to raise the status of the operetta, then the current rage of Paris. All contestants used the same libretto, *Le Docteur Miracle* (The Miracle Doctor). The two winning compositions were produced at a small Paris theater.

Once in Italy under the auspices of the Prix, Bizet fell in love with the country and its people. He particularly enjoyed travelling about Rome and witnessing the glorious works of the past — both art and architecture — standing alongside the rubble and decay of the present. As part of the award, he was required to send back to Paris several works; the first was to be a setting of the Mass. In lieu of this, Bizet returned an opera in two acts!

Returning to Paris at the end of his tenure in Rome, Bizet considered teaching at the Conservatory or perhaps becoming a concert pianist. He decided against both and resolved to stay in Paris and pursue a career as an opera composer. In order to support himself, he gave private piano lessons, usually to students who only wanted to learn for social purposes. He also arranged countless opera scores for piano. Bizet was even known to have composed some third rate dance music to help himself financially.

His first major operatic venture after this was *La Guzla de l'Emir* which was accepted by the Opéra-Comique for production. It was withdrawn before it could be presented, speculation being that only one work by any composer could be underwritten by a grant of money used for producing new operas. Subsequently Bizet submitted *Les Pêcheurs des Perles* (The Pearl Fishers) which was also based on a story of the East (in this case, Ceylon), and in which he used some of the melodies from *La Guzla*. The second opera was accepted and presented; the composer was twenty-four at the time. The reception of the opera by both public and press was cold, although Berlioz stressed in his newspaper report the very high quality of many of the passages in it. Although the work was dropped after eighteen performances, it has been in the permanent repertoire of the Paris Opéra-Comique since 1932.

Bizet's father purchased some land a few miles down the Seine River from Paris and had two bungalows constructed on it; one he occupied, the other Georges lived in. It was here that Bizet started work on an opera to be called *Ivan the Terrible*. For many years it was thought that the composer had destroyed the score before completing it, but a version (how far from the original is impossible to ascertain) was given in Mühringen in 1946. He next turned to another opera, *La Jolie Fille de Perth* (The Fair Maid of Perth). While this opera was in rehearsal, Bizet announced his engagement to Genevieve Halévy, daughter of the composer who had served as Bizet's instructor during the Conservatory days. *La Jolie Fille* was the only opera by Bizet that received a good press and reception by the public at the premiere performance.

After several other works, the next major composition with which the contemporary public is familiar was the incidental music (twenty-seven different selections) for the *mélodrame*, *L'Arlesienne* (The Girl from Arles). The revival of the *mélodrame* form at the Vaudeville Theater was short-lived, but the music composed by Bizet in the short period of six months was so well liked that the composer made an orchestral suite from it. (The original suite became known as *L'Arlesienne Suite No. 1;* a later suite known as *No. 2* was completed after the composer's death by others.)

After a rather serious bout with his throat trouble (he had had trouble with it first during his Prix de Rome days in Italy, and it had recurred several times since), he turned to the play by Prosper Mérimée, *Carmen*. The opera was prepared for presentation at the Opéra-Comique and in the tradition of that theater included spoken dialogue. The reception of this opera at its premiere has already been mentioned.

It is interesting to note that with the exception of one very minor opera, the published vocal scores of Bizet's operas all include vast changes from the composer's original intentions, changes which were never authorized by him. *Carmen* is a case in point. (See the analysis of *Carmen*.)

BIBLIOGRAPHY

Cooper, Martin. *Georges Bizet* London: Oxford University Press, 1938.
Curtis, Mina. *Bizet and His World*. New York: Alfred A. Knopf Co., 1958.

CARMEN

(*An Opera in Four Acts*)

GEORGES BIZET

Carmen, as produced in opera houses since Bizet's death, differs considerably from the work as premiered at the Opéra-Comique in Paris on March 3, 1875. The original version (the only one written

The Lyric Opera of Chicago's setting for Act I of *Carmen*. In front of the cigarette factory in which she works, Carmen sings the *Habanera* and flirts with Don Jose.

Photos by Nancy Sorensen

In the closing scene of Act IV, Carmen is indifferent to the pleas of Don José

by Bizet) included spoken dialogue, some of which was taken from the original Mérimée story. When *Carmen* was produced in Vienna four months after the composer's death, Ernest Guiraud (a French operatic composer born in New Orleans, Louisiana), substituted recitatives for the original spoken dialogue. Because the recitatives took longer to deliver than spoken dialogue, many cuts in the original libretto had to be made. Unfortunately, this process eliminated some lines essential to a full appreciation of the characters and the motivation behind certain scenes. The story as related in the following paragraphs is based on Bizet's original libretto and therefore gives a few more details than the published score now in use. The practice of using the recitatives in place of the spoken dialogue seems to be universal nowadays with the exception of the Royal Opera House of Sweden.

Bizet clearly indicated in his score that the melody of the *Habanera* was not an original tune, but he thought it to be a Spanish folk melody. Actually it was the work of Sebastian Yradier (a Spanish-born composer who later lived in both Cuba and Paris, writing among other works, *La Paloma*). Bizet kept the original Habanera accompaniment, alternating the melodic line to fit the French text.

CAST OF CHARACTERS

Carmen, *a Gypsy girl*	mezzo-soprano
Don José, *Corporal of the Dragoons*	tenor
Micaëla, *José's childhood sweetheart*	soprano
Escamillo, *Toreador*	baritone
Frasquita, *a Gypsy friend of Carmen*	soprano
Mercédès, *another Gypsy friend*	soprano
Zuniga, *Captain of the Dragoons*	bass
Moralès, *an officer*	baritone
Le Dancaïre, *a smuggler*	tenor
Le Remendado, *a smuggler*	baritone

Dragoons, Gypsies, smugglers, cigarette girls, and street boys.

PRELUDE

The *Prelude* is full of the animation and excitement of a Spanish celebration, and is based upon three themes from the opera. The "Procession of the Toreadors" from Act IV is heard first:

Example 1

After a modulation, the "Toreador's Song" from Act II appears, first *piano*, then *fortissimo:*

Example 2

Another modulation returns to the original key and Example 1 is heard again.

In the final twenty-seven measures of this short *Prelude,* a menacing note is introduced. It is the melody associated with Carmen (or some call it the "Fate" motive — the fate of which Carmen was the instrument):

Example 3

The *Prelude* ends with this foreboding theme.

ACT I

Time: 1820.

Scene: *A square in Seville, Spain. On one side, the door of the tobacco factory; on the other, the guard house. At the back is a bridge. The soldiers are lounging about the door of the guard house, watching the people as they come and go.*

A pretty girl, Micaëla — apparently a stranger to this square — approaches timidly. She inquires of Corporal Moralès if he knows where Don José might be found. Moralès answers that Josè is a member of the guard who will come on duty shortly, and offers her the use of the guard house where she can wait for him. She declines the offer, stating that she will return later.

A cornet fanfare is heard in the distance, and soon the relief guard is seen entering. Don José and Zuniga follow the guard, and they are in turn followed by a group of boys carrying broomsticks with which to mimic the march and the changing of the guard. Before the retired guard leaves, Moralès tells José of the girl who inquired of his whereabouts. José exclaims that it must be Micaëla, a childhood sweetheart, an orphan girl whom his mother has raised. José confesses that he is in love with Micaëla.

As the lunch bell rings in the factory, the soldiers gather around to watch the cigarette girls as they come out. Eagerly they await Carmen, a Gypsy girl who works in the factory. Finally, she leaves the factory, bouquet in hand and a rose clenched between her teeth (the motive of Example 3 is heard as she appears). The soldiers joke with her about when she'll fall in love with them. Carmen replies, "I do not know, perhaps never, perhaps tomorrow." With a glance toward Don José, she sings the *Habanera:*

HABANERA

L'amour est un oiseau rebelle	Love is like a wild bird
Que nul ne peut apprivoiser,	That none can ever hope to
Et c'est bien en vain qu'on l'ap-	tame;
pelle,	And it is in vain to call his name
S'il lui convient de refuser.	If he feels like flying elsewhere.

Carmen ends her solo with a warning: "If you love me not, I will love you! and if I love you, then beware!"

As the bell signals the end of the lunch hour, the girls hurry back to the factory. Carmen remains behind, hesitating, then she boldly flings the flower that she has been holding to Don José and runs into the factory. It hits him in the forehead and then falls to the ground. José pauses a moment, then picks up the flower. The soldiers return to the guard house and José is left alone. He muses, "This little flower gave me a start, like an arrow aimed at my heart. The fragrance of the flower is strong; and the woman? If there are really witches, she is surely one of them."

His meditations are interrupted by the return of Micaëla who tells him that she brings a message from his mother along with a small gift of money and a kiss, which she proceeds to give him. A tender duet follows:

Don José

PARLE MOI DE MA MÈRE (Tell Me of My Mother)

JOSÉ

Ma mère je la vois!	I can see my mother now!
Qui, je revois mon village!	Again I see my village home!
Ô souvenirs d'autre fois,	O happy memories of other days,
Doux souvenirs du pays!	Sweet memories of the country!

MICAELA

Sa mère, il la revoit!	His mother he now beholds!
Il revoit son village.	Again he sees his village home.

Micaëla tells José that she is leaving Seville that evening and will carry any messages back to his mother. José instructs her to tell his mother that her son will always be worthy of her; then gives Micaëla a kiss to return to his mother.

After she leaves, José meditates once again. He vows to follow his mother's wish and marry Micaëla; then he withdraws from his tunic the flower that Carmen had thrown to him, ready to toss the whole Carmen episode off with a shrug of the shoulder. Suddenly a great commotion is heard inside the factory. The girls hurry down the steps to the square shouting that it was "la Carmencita!" Zuniga enters from the guard house to try and discover what has caused the disturbance. Everyone is so excited that he can get no answers to his questions. He sends José inside the factory to locate the source of the trouble.

José leads Carmen from the factory, and as the soldiers hold the crowd back from the steps, he announces that it is more serious than they had at first suspected. A factory girl has had a cross scored on her cheek with two knife-cuts made by Carmen! The soldiers finally get the square cleared of people, and Zuniga calls for a rope with which to bind Carmen's hands. Zuniga leaves to prepare the report of the incident.

Carmen and José are left alone. In the *Séguidilla* which Carmen sings, she flirts with José; she tells him of a meeting place where the two of them can rendezvous under much happier circumstances, if only he will loosen the rope ever so slightly on her wrists.

SÉGUIDILLE

Près des remparts de Séville,	Near the walls of Sevilla,
Chez mon ami Lillas Pastia,	At the place of my friend Lillas Pastia,
J'irai danser la Séguidille,	I'll soon dance the Seguidilla.
Et boire du Manzanilla!	And I'll drink Manzanilla.

José, completely under her spell, loosens the rope with which her hands are tied. Zuniga brings the order for Carmen's arrest and orders José to guard her well. Carmen whispers to José that on the road she will push him very hard; he must fall, and she will escape; he knows where to meet her. She laughs derisively at the Captain, then marches off with José. As they arrive at the bridge, she pushes him aside and escapes, laughing loudly.

ACT II

Time: *A month later.*
Scene: *The tavern of Lillas Pastia, near the city walls of Seville.*

The rustic tavern of Lillas Pastia is seen, a meeting place for a large band of smugglers of which Carmen is one of the leading members. Army officers are sitting around the tables drinking with the Gypsy girls, obviously a place the army men frequent on their off-duty hours. The rhythm of a Gypsy dance is heard, and Carmen, sitting at a table with Zuniga, leaves him momentarily to join in the dance. As Carmen sings each succeeding verse, it is at an even faster tempo so that by the end of the song and dance she falls back into her chair, exhausted.

Carmen

GYPSY SONG AND DANCE

Les tringles des cistres tintaient
Avec un éclat métallique,
Et sur cette étrange musique
Les Zingarellas se levaient.
Tambours de Basque allaient
* leur train,*
Et les guitares forcenées,
Grincaient sous des mains obsti-
* nées*
Même chanson, même refrain,
Tra la la la la la la la, . . .

The bars of the sistrum* jingle
With a metallic sound,
And with this strange music
The Gypsies spring forth.
Tambourines establish the
  rhythm,
And the mad guitars
Grind out under these obstinate
  hands
The same song, the same refrain.
Tra la la la la la la la, . . .

* An instrument of Egyptian origin consisting of a handle and a lyre-shaped frame with jingling metal cross bars.

Zuniga now tells Carmen that Don José is a free man once more, after being imprisoned for a month and degraded for having allowed his prisoner to escape. Just as the crowd is about to leave the tavern, voices are heard in the distance heralding the arrival of the torero, Escamillo. As Escamillo enters Lillas Pastia's, he immediately launches into a toast:

TOREADOR SONG

Votre toast, je peux vous le ren-
* dre,*
Señors, car avec les soldats
Oui, les Toréros, peuvent s'en-
* tendre;*
Pour plaisirs, ils ont les combats!

Let me offer a toast to you,

Senors, because with the soldiers,
Yes, with toreros, we join to-
  gether
For pleasure in a fight!

Escamillo

To - ré - a - dor, en gar - de!

To - ré - a - dor! To - ré - a - dor!

Toréador, en garde! Toréador,　　Toreador, en garde! Toreador,
　Toréador!　　　　　　　　　　　Toreador!
Et songe bien, en combattant　　And the dream of combat
Qu'un oeil noir te regarde　　　Is to have a pair of black eyes
Et que l'amour t'attend.　　　　Watch and wait in love for you.

As Lillas Pastia tries to clear the tavern, for he tells them it is after the legal closing hour, Escamillo wanders over to Carmen's table and inquires her name. She replies that it is Carmen or Carmencita, whichever he prefers. Gallantly he declares that it is her name he will speak, according to the torero custom, when he kills his next bull. "And what if I say I am in love with you," asks Escamillo. Carmen replies that it is all right with her, but that she won't love him in return. Escamillo says that he will wait. Perhaps in time she will fall in love with him. Carmen shrugs her shoulders and tells him to go ahead and wait.

As the last of the crowd leaves the tavern, Zuniga tells Carmen that he will return to her in an hour, after roll call at the barracks has been taken. She tells him not to bother, but he assures her that he will come back.

After the tavern is closed, only Pastia, Carmen, Frasquita, and Mercédès are left. Frasquita inquires of Pastia why he was so anxious to get rid of the crowd. He replies that Dancaïre, the leader of the smugglers, and Remendado are expected so that they may discuss some contraband business. Pastia opens a side door and beckons them to enter. As Dancaïre outlines the plan, Carmen tells him that she will not be able to participate for she is in love. Her friends tell her that this is nothing new, and that when "business" calls, love must come second. Carmen assures them that this time "business" will be a bad second to love.

José's voice is heard in the distance singing a military tune. As the smugglers open the window shutters to see what Carmen's new friend looks like, they remark that he looks like a likely prospect for their band of smugglers. They then leave the room so that Carmen and her new friend can be alone.

Carmen taunts José, for she tells him that other officers were at the café that evening and she danced for them; one of them even told her that he would return later to meet her. As José shows signs of jealousy, Carmen agrees to dance for him, too. Just as she finishes her dance, the military call of *retreat* is heard in the distance. José rises, stating that it is time to return to the barracks. Carmen is furious that José should consider leaving her, not aware of the strong instinct he has for doing what is right and what is expected of him. In her frenzy, Carmen accuses José of not loving her. He withdraws from his tunic the flower that she threw to him outside the cigarette factory and relates how this flower kept up his hopes during the long month in jail:

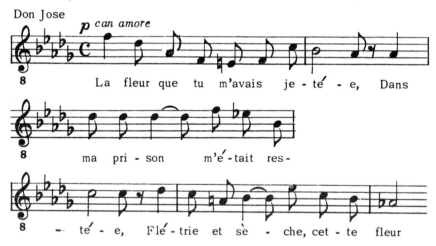

FLOWER SONG

La fleur que tu m'avais jetée	The flower that you threw to me
Dans ma prison m'était restée,	I have cherished in my prison cell,
Flétrie et sèche, cette fleur	For me it still retained its perfume
Gardait toujours sa douce odeur;	Though its beauty had perished long ago;

Et pendant des heures entières	And through many a silent hour
Sur mes yeux, fermant mes pau-	On my closed eyes lay the flower,
pières,	This rare perfume was my de-
De cette odeur je m'enivrais	light.
Et dans la nuit je te voyais!	And in the night I saw your face,
Je me prenais à te maudire,	And I began to curse your name,
A te détester, à me dire:	And detest you and exclaim:
Pourquoi faut-il que le destin	Why must it be, that destiny
L'ait mise là sur mon chemin!	Would have you pass my way?

Carmen says again that he does not love her, for if he did, he would follow her to the Gypsy camp. "You would take me up on your horse and, as a brave man, ride like the wind. There you would be free as air. No officers, no bugle calls. The wide sky, the whole world — and for law, whatever you please. Above all — the best thing — we are free." José breaks away from her. "No, I will not listen to you. To desert my flag is dishonor! I cannot do it!" Furiously, Carmen bids him leave. As José is saying farewell, Zuniga breaks in. He taunts Carmen for falling in love with José who is now a private when she might have a captain. Zuniga orders José to return to the barracks, but José defies him. Swords are drawn and Zuniga and José start to fight. Carmen signals Dancaïre and Remendado, who have returned at the sound of a fight. They seize Zuniga, disarm him, and lead him out the door at pistol point. José realizes that his fate has been sealed, for he must now follow the Gypsies — he will be an outlaw and a smuggler.

ACT III

Scene: *A wild, picturesque rocky place in the mountains; the rendezvous of the smugglers and the Gypsies.*

A few smugglers are seen here and there in the darkness, lying on the ground, wrapped in their cloaks; gradually others become visible, carrying bales of smuggled merchandise. José is seen as one of the group now, his appearance changed immeasurably. Gone is the handsome uniform; in its place he wears the old tattered clothing of a smuggler; he is unshaven and he looks haggard. He tells Carmen of a village only a few miles away in which his mother lives, believing her son still an honest man. Carmen scornfully advises him to return to her, for obviously the life of a smuggler isn't meant for him. When José threatens her, she replies, "Perhaps you will kill me? Very well, I have often read it in the cards that you and I will die together."

Carmen's two companions, Frasquita and Mercédès, are frivolously telling each other's fortunes at cards, dreaming of the handsome men with whom they are going to fall in love. Carmen joins them, but such light-hearted activities are not part of her fate. Turning the cards, she exclaims, "Diamonds! Spades! To die. First to me, then to him, then both of us to the grave!"

Carmen

En vain pour e´ - vi - ter les re´ - ponses a -
— mères,   En vain tu mê - le - ras,

Card Song

En vain pour éviter les résponses amères,	Vain it is to shun the answer,
En vain tu mêleras,	Vain it is to mix the cards!
Cela ne sert a rien, les cartes sont sincères	It is to no avail, the cards still remain sincere,
Et ne mentiront pas!	They can never lie!

Dancaïre and Remendado return from their patrol down the mountainside. They tell the crowd that the breach in the town wall is protected by three guards whom they must eliminate. They will leave José posted on a rock from which he will have a good view of the surrounding countryside. His job is to guard the contraband they will leave behind until the smugglers have a chance to make a second trip. As they all leave, José follows them to the start of the path to bid farewell. No sooner is the cave empty than Micaëla arrives by another path. She has paid a guide well to lead her to this hideout where she hopes to find José. The guide having departed, Micaëla, alone and frightened, sings of her plight and prays to heaven for courage.

MICAËLA'S ARIA

Je dis, que rien ne m'é-pou-van-te, Je dis, hé-las! que je re-ponds de moi,

Je dis, que rien ne m'épouvante,	I say, nothing shall deter me,
Je dis, hélas! que je réponds de moi,	I say, I am able to play my part.

She catches sight of José on a rock above her and calls to him, but apparently he does not hear her. Suddenly he fires a shot at someone approaching up the mountain path; Michaëla quickly hides.

Escamillo enters from the path, looking at his hat which the bullet has pierced. José demands to know who this stranger is. Escamillo identifies himself as a torero from Granada, and states that he is in love with a Gypsy by the name of Carmen and is in search of her. As each man realizes who the other is, a quarrel follows and they start to fight. Escamillo fells José, but spares his life. The fight continues, and just as José has Escamillo at his mercy, Carmen suddenly appears with the returning smugglers and intervenes. Dancaïre announces that there is no time for a fight for there is work to be done. Escamillo departs with the invitation to all the Gypsies and smugglers to visit him at the bull ring at Seville where he will do his best to earn their approval.

José tells Carmen that he has endured just about all he can take on her account; she merely shrugs her shoulders and walks away. Remendado appears with Micaëla whom he has discovered hiding. José recognizes her immediately; she begs him to return to his mother. Carmen bids José to follow the girl's advice and leave the Gypsies. José accepts this proposal as an insult, refusing to leave "even though it costs my life. The chain that binds us will endure to death."

José's spirit changes only when Micaëla finally has to tell him that his mother is dying, and that her last wish is to see her son again. "She will forgive all." The curtain falls as José and Micaëla are seen leaving together, but José turns back and warns Carmen that they will meet again!

Act IV

Scene: *A square in Seville, at the back of which is the amphitheater where the bull fight will take place.*

A crowd of people wait for the procession to the arena. There are vendors of fans, oranges, cigarettes, water, and programs. Zuniga enters and the girls crowd around him to sell him oranges and fans. Suddenly there are shouts, "Here they come! Here comes the procession! Hats off!" First comes the Constable whom the crowd mocks. Next are the assistants to the bull fighter — the banderilleros, with gallant bearing and bright costumes; then the picadors whose pointed lances will tease the bull. Finally Escamillo appears with Carmen at his side. He promises her that she will be proud of him today. The Mayor then arrives in the procession and the crowd follows him into the arena, leaving Carmen and Escamillo alone for a moment.

Waiting until most of the crowd is in the arena, Escamillo turns to Carmen and sings:

Escamillo

Si tu m'ai-mes, Car-men,   si tu m'ai-mes, Car-men,

Si tu m'aimes (If you love me)

Si tu m'aimes Carmen,	If you love me, Carmen,
Tu pourras, tout à l'heure,	Then at this moment you may be proud,
Être fière de moi!	If you love me.

As Escamillo enters the arena, Carmen's two Gypsy friends approach to tell her that they have seen Don José lurking in the crowd. She should not remain there alone if she values her life. Carmen refuses to leave.

After the Gypsy girls have left, Don José comes out of hiding and accosts Carmen. His clothes are even dirtier and more tattered than when Carmen last saw him, and he has the look of a hunted man. He pleads with her to come back to him, stating that he will do anything if only they can be together again. Carmen replies, "Free I was born, and free I shall die!"

Carmen keeps watching the arena and smiles as shouts go up from the crowd for Escamillo's feats. José forbids her to enter the arena and accuses her of loving the torero. Carmen replies, "I'd say, even if it were my last breath, even in the face of death, that I love Escamillo!"

Once again José vows that Carmen shall go with him, and once more Carmen says no. José replies, "No more threats, I am tired of them!"

"Then come, strike me at once, or let me go to him!" With that Carmen throws José's ring at his feet. This is too much for José. As a fanfare in the arena is heard signalling Escamillo's victory, José pulls a knife and stabs Carmen.

As the crowd emerges from the arena, José throws himself on the lifeless body with a cry, "It was I who killed her! Oh, my Carmen, my adored Carmen."

PETER ILYITCH TCHAIKOVSKY

BORN: May 7, 1840; Votkinsk, Russia.
DIED: November 6, 1893; St. Petersburg, Russia.

When the famous Carnegie Hall in New York city was opened on May 5, 1891, Tchaikovsky was brought from Russia to conduct at the dedicatory concert. The program included his *Marche Solennelle;* subsequent programs in the opening week listed the composer's *Suite No. 3,* two a cappella choruses, and the *Concerto No. 1 for Piano and Orchestra.*

The gala opening of this hall is part of the musical legend of the United States, but the path that led Tchaikovsky to the conductor's podium for it was a long and difficult one. Since early childhood the composer had suffered from moods of greatest depression; he had an indomitable fear of conducting; he disliked meeting new people, yet was afraid to be alone; and he had had several nervous breakdowns. In spite of these handicaps, original works flowed from his pen over the years in an almost uninterrupted series. Throughout his brief visit to the United States, he appeared in the best of spirits.

Peter Tchaikovsky was born in a little mining town in the Ural Mountains of Russia; his father was a mining engineer. Peter was the second of a family of five boys (two of them twins) and one girl. Peter became quite attached to his only sister, Alexandra, and one of the twins, Modest, who later furnished the libretti for some of his operas and wrote his official biography. Peter received a good education; a French governess, and later a music teacher, supervised his training. Although he started piano lessons when he was four and had tried his hand at composition by the time he was ten, neither he nor his family attached any significance to music or suspected that his ability in this field was anything other than average.

Tchaikovsky was sent to the School of Jurisprudence in St. Petersburg to study law. Concurrently he continued his music lessons, but still showed no more than average ability at either the keyboard or composition. Upon graduation from the law school, he obtained a position as a minor clerk in the Ministry of Justice. He continued to take a few classes in music while he served at the Ministry (where he was barely an "efficient" worker). When the Russian Music Society opened its new Conservatory of Music with Anton Rubinstein as its director, Tchaikovsky enrolled for additional classes. He had already come to the conclusion that sooner or later "I shall exchange the civil service for music. Don't imagine that I dream of becoming a great artist, I only want to do the work for which I feel I have a vocation. Whether I become a celebrated composer or a poor music teacher — it's all the same . . . My conscience will be clear . . . Of course, I won't resign my post until I'm quite sure that I'm not an official but an artist."

In less than six months Tchaikovsky resigned from the Ministry and concentrated on music. It was a risky step since his father's financial condition was so poor that he could only provide a very meager board and room allowance for his son. Peter found it necessary to give music lessons to help augment his income. He studied harmony, counterpoint, and composition, the latter with Anton Rubinstein. He graduated in 1865, winning a silver medal for his cantata *Hymn to Joy* based on Schiller's text.

The following year, Nicholas Rubinstein (brother of Tchaikovsky's composition teacher) invited Tchaikovsky to join the staff at the Moscow Conservatory of Music. The composer moved to Moscow and started work on his first symphony, later subtitled *Winter Dreams*. It was labor for him: he stayed awake nights worrying about it; he bordered on a nervous breakdown over its completion; and almost gave up composition as too strenuous for his delicate nerves. When completed, the *Symphony No. 1* was to have been performed at the St. Petersburg Conservatory by Anton Rubinstein, but the latter refused the work, alienating the close friendship between Tchaikovsky and his teacher. The symphony was performed the following year in Moscow.

The Russian "nationalists" were at work about this time trying to develop music that was not only Russian in spirit, but which made liberal use of Russian folk melodies and Russian legends. The group, known as the "Mighty Five" (for further details, see Chapter VII), centered their activities in St. Petersburg. They tried to encourage Tchaikovsky to join their ranks. Not only did Tchaikovsky refuse, but he had some vitriolic words about them — they were uncouth, barbaric, untrained. Only Rimsky-Korsakov had any talent, said Tchaikovsky. The Russian element is quite strong in Tchaikovsky's music, and he did make use on occasion of Russian folk songs, but this nationalistic spirit is instinctive rather than consciously cultivated.

Tchaikovsky's sensitive feelings suffered two serious blows when he turned to the concerto form. Upon completion, his *Concerto No. 1 for Piano and Orchestra in B-Flat Minor* was dedicated to the celebrated pianist and close friend, Nicholas Rubinstein. After looking over the score, Rubinstein declared that it was unplayable and refused to touch it. The concerto was given its world premiere in Boston with the conductor-pianist Hans von Bülow as the artist. Greatly hurt by this incident, Tchaikovsky crossed out Rubinstein's name in the dedication and substituted Hans von Bülow's. The *Violin Concerto in D Major* was dedicated to the internationally famous violin virtuoso Leopold Auer, who refused to accept the honor, declaring that the concerto was impossible to perform. Both Rubinstein and Auer later acknowledged their misjudgments, for they respectively played the piano and the violin concerti.

Following the completion of the piano concerto, Tchaikovsky embarked on an extensive trip that took him to Berlin, Paris, Munich, Italy, and Vienna. He served as a part-time music critic and sent some reviews back to his paper. On his return to Moscow, a most unusual friendship developed. Nadja von Meck, the wealthy widow of a railroad engineer, was a great patroness of music and learned that a young composer of talent, Peter Tchaikovsky, was in difficult straits financially. At first she commissioned several works for which she paid him quite well. At the end of the first year, Madame von Meck gave the composer an annual stipend of 6000 rubles on which he could live quite securely. She also made available for his use several of her villas in Russia and Europe. The one condition of this mutual arrangement was that the two should never meet. Except for a chance encounter in the crowd at a concert, the two knew each other only by correspondence.

The year 1877 was an important one in the life of the composer, for not only did he become acquainted with Madame von Meck that year, but it was the year in which he entered into an ill-advised marriage that ended disastrously shortly after it had taken place. Completely demoralized by this experience, Tchaikovsky traveled to Switzerland, Italy, Paris, and then Vienna to recuperate. During these months he completed his *Symphony No. 4* and his most frequently performed opera, *Eugene Onegin.*

Having established his reputation as a composer throughout Europe, and with an adequate income from the von Meck stipend, Tchaikovsky resigned his position at the Moscow Conservatory. The *Symphony No. 5* was completed along with another opera, *La Pique Dame* (The Queen of Spades). An extensive tour on which Tchaikovsky was to be a guest conductor with many different orchestras was planned. On these travels he met Brahms and Grieg in Leipzig, Dvořák in Prague, and Gounod and Massenet in Paris.

Shortly before his departure for the United States for the opening of Carnegie Hall, his friendship with Nadja von Meck was ruptured. Fortunately his compositions now provided sufficient income so that the loss of his annual stipend was not catastrophic, but the loss of the friendship deeply affected Tchaikovsky's sensitive nature. His stay in the United States was short; from New York he traveled to Philadelphia and Baltimore to conduct and then returned to Russia.

He worked on two greatly different compositions at the same time, the somewhat morose *Symphony No. 6* (subtitled by his brother the *"Pathétique"*), and the spritely ballet, *The Nutcracker.* The composer traveled to St. Petersburg to conduct the premiere of the *Symphony No. 6.* Four days after this performance had taken place, Tchaikovsky dined with a group of people, including his brother Modest, went to the theater afterwards, and then sat drinking in a restaurant until two in the morning. The next day he complained of indigestion and insomnia, and at lunch he ate nothing, but incautiously drank a glass of unboiled water, scoffing at his brother's fear of cholera (from which their mother had died). He felt worse after lunch, but declined to see a doctor. That evening he was confined to bed and the doctor called. It was diagnosed as cholera and Tchaikovsky succumbed to it three days later.

BIBLIOGRAPHY

Abraham, Gerald. *Tchaikovsky*. New York: A. A. Wyn, Inc., 1949.
Weinstock, Herbert. *Tchaikovsky*. New York: Alfred A Knopf, 1943.

SYMPHONY NO. 4

Peter Ilyitch Tchaikovsky

Second Movement: *Andantino in modo di canzona.*

The second movement, "in the style of a song," is in ternary form. The opening section introduces a theme in the oboe against a pizzicato string accompaniment:

Example 1

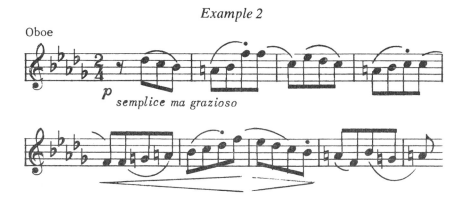

The celli repeat Example 1.
A second theme is introduced in the opening section by the strings:

Example 2

Examples 1 and 2 are repeated in turn.

The middle section is based on a rhythmical theme stated by the clarinet and bassoon:

Example 3

Clarinets

The first section is repeated. As the strings restate Example 1, decorative figures are played by various woodwinds.

Example 2 is restated by the strings.

The *coda* features the individual woodwinds with short melodic fragments, ending with a statement by the bassoon of Example 1 accompanied by a countermelody in the violins.

Third Movement: Scherzo. *Pizzicato ostinato.*

This is a unique scherzo, for the strings play pizzicato throughout. The strings announce the first theme:

Example 4

Violins

The oboe and bassoon introduce the theme of the center section:

Example 5

Oboe

The transition that prepares for a return to the first section alternates the opening figures of Example 4 and Example 5.

The first section is repeated exactly.

A *coda* based on Example 5 brings the movement to a close.

GIACOMO PUCCINI

BORN: December 22, 1858; Lucca, Italy.
DIED: November 29, 1924; Brussels, Belgium.

Giacomo Puccini, while a shy man in public, thoroughly enjoyed life and living. He celebrated the success of *La Bohème* by buying an expensive bicycle; *Tosca* by the largest and noisiest automobile he could find; and his American triumph with an imported speedboat. He was a man that fell head-over-heels in love with each heroine he created. Yet beneath it all, he loved the Tuscan soil, his home on the Torre del Lago, his hunting trips into the mountains around the lake, and the little café on the waterfront, Club Bohème.

In the Italian town of Lucca the name of Puccini was very well known when Giacomo was born, for starting with his great-great-grandfather, every one of his male forebears had served the town as musicians, most of them as church organists. Even though Giacomo's father passed away when he was very young, his mother never questioned the profession her son would follow. Actually Signora Puccini was probably the only person who didn't question her son's future, for the boy did very poorly in school and had to repeat the last grade in grammar school; he was full of mischievous pranks. The boy's uncle accused him of stealing a few pipes from the church organ and selling them! As the uncle told the story, Giacomo and a friend requested the local sexton to let them use the church organ for practice. The name "Puccini" being well known in Lucca as a family of organists, the boys were admitted to the church, where, according to his uncle, Giacomo and his friend removed the pipes which they later sold.

Giacomo's mother never lost faith, and with the few meager coins she was able to muster, saw to it that the boy received music lessons. Although Giacomo apparently wasn't interested in music at all, he did write a few compositions during his student days. He became the choir director and organist at the Church of San Martino, and studied at the Instituto Musicale of Lucca. His graduation thesis was the *Messa di Gloria,* written when he was eighteen, a work which lay dormant for seventy-two years until some biographical research uncovered it in 1951. Since its rediscovery, it has been frequently performed by high school and college choirs in this country.

Late in his student days, a performance of Giuseppe Verdi's *Aïda* in Pisa became a turning point in Giacomo's career. Interested in hearing this famous work, the boy had no money to pay for either coach fare or a ticket. He walked both ways to Pisa, a distance of some thirteen miles over a rather steep mountain road. Once at the theater, he used the famous Puccini name to obtain a free pass. It was largely this moving performance that convinced the boy that he, too, wished to become a composer of operas.

When Puccini had learned all that Lucca had to offer in music, he was able to enter the Conservatory in Milan (the center of Italian opera) by putting together some money his mother had saved, some money from a well-to-do relative, and a special grant from Queen Margherita of Italy to the heir of the Puccini name.

Puccini studied first with the opera composer Bazzini in Milan, but soon changed to lessons with Amilcare Ponchielli who was already famous as the composer of *La Gioconda*. Puccini did well in the Conservatory and completed a *Capriccio Sinfonico* for his graduation requirement. His teacher, Ponchielli, thought Giacomo's talents better suited for opera than for symphonic writing and tried to encourage him in that direction. He went so far as to offer the student a libretto for an opera, a libretto he had originally secured for his own use. Ponchielli hoped that Giacomo could complete the opera in time to submit it to a contest being held by a music publishing company, a contest for a one-act opera. Puccini completed the opera, *Le Villi,* in time but lost to Pietro Mascagni who had submitted his first opera, *Cavalleria Rusticana.* Arrigo Boïto, composer of the opera *Mefistofele* and librettist for Verdi's *Otello* and *Falstaff,* saw the score of *Le Villi* and was so impressed with it that he raised money to mount a production. Even though the opera was produced at a small opera house, it was well-received by the public, and the music publisher Guilio Ricordi thought the composer had enough talent to warrant a commission from his firm for another opera.

The stipend of 300 lire a month for two years while Puccini completed his second opera, *Edgar,* was hardly enough on which to live. Puccini's later excess of expenditures on luxury items after he became rich was probably a revolt against the years he labored long and hard over music, never quite certain when the next check from Ricordi would arrive or whether there would be enough food.

Edgar was a complete failure at its first performance, largely due to a preposterous libretto. From this experience, Puccini was very careful in the selection of libretti, laboring many hours over each selection, writing to the authors with many suggested changes. When he started to work on his third opera, *Manon Lescaut,* practically none of the original libretto remained, as he and Guilio Ricordi rewrote almost every line; the original author does not even have his name on the published score.

Manon Lescaut, which was first produced in Turin, was immediately accepted by the public as a successful opera. The local paper, *Gazetta,* said the audience "was stunned and overcome by emotion." With this opera, the composer's fame spread throughout the opera world.

With the money earned from *Manon Lescaut,* Puccini moved to Torre del Lago where he enjoyed country life to the fullest. He began, at this lakeside home, to work on a libretto taken from Murger's novel *Vie de Bohème.* The composer was undoubtedly helped in his appreciation of the characters in the story by his recollection of his own rather bohemian days as a Conservatory student, and also by the people he met almost daily at the little café across the lake, the Club Bohème. The opera, *La Bohème,* was conducted by Arturo Toscanini at its world premiere. The first night audience was rather apathetic, and it took many more performances throughout Italy before its popularity became unquestioned.

Puccini witnessed a performance by the famous actress Sarah Bernhardt, in Paris, of Sardou's play *Tosca* and was very impressed with the story. Wishing to use it as the subject for an opera, he learned from the author that someone else had already purchased the rights. Puccini convinced his competitor that *Tosca* was indeed the worst possible subject for an opera, that a work based on it was doomed to failure from the start. The option was cancelled by its owner and Puccini subsequently obtained the rights. When completed, it added greatly to Puccini's international reputation.

In London Puccini saw a work by the American playwright David Belasco, *Madam Butterfly*. He immediately secured the rights and had a libretto prepared. At its premiere, *Madama Butterfly* was hissed. The conductor, Arturo Toscanini, encouraged Puccini to make certain alterations in it that he felt were necessary. The composer thereupon made the two acts in three, dividing the second into two parts at the point where Madama Butterfly takes up her all-night vigil. A tenor aria, the *Addio,* was introduced into the final scene. In its new version, *Butterfly* was an instant success. When Puccini traveled to New York to witness the premiere in this country he also visited the dramatic theaters. He saw David Belasco's play, *The Girl of the Golden West,* based on Bret Harte's novel of western life in a gold mining town. The Metropolitan Opera House commissioned him to write a new opera, and for its story Puccini chose this one of the West. The opera was never the success in the United States that the other operas had been; perhaps the idea of a "western" (as known in the movies and on television) was too much for the public when sung in Italian.

During World War I, Puccini completed *La Rondine,* which was originally to have been a Viennese-type operetta, but which ended as a full opera. Later during the war he completed his *Triptych,* three one-act operas: *Il Tabarro* (The Cloak), *Gianni Schicci,* and *Suor Angelica* (Sister Angelica).

Puccini next started to work on a libretto with a Chinese theme, *Turandot.* The work was slow in developing since Puccini's health had begun to fail. When he traveled to Brussels for an operation for cancer of the throat, he took the final duets of the opera with him to complete there. The cancer operation was a success, but unfortunately his heart could not stand the shock. His death on November 29, 1924, was from a heart attack. *Turandot* was completed from sketches by his friend and fellow musician Alfano. At the premiere in 1926, Toscanini conducted the opera up to the last scene, then laid his baton on the music stand, turned to the audience and said, "This is where the Master stopped."

BIBLIOGRAPHY

Carner, Mosco. *Puccini: A Critical Biography.* London: Gerald Duckworth and Company, Ltd., 1958.

Fiorentino, Dante del. *Immortal Bohemian: An Intimate Memoir of Giacomo Puccini.* New York: Prentice-Hall, Inc., 1952.

LA BOHEME

(*An Opera in Four Acts*)

GIACOMO PUCCINI

La Bohème is sometimes labeled as a *verismo* (literally — "realism") opera. Verismo works deal with scenes of everyday life, in contrast to the mythological or historical libretti of earlier operas.

Frequently the action in a verismo work was violent, as in the earlier *Cavalleria Rusticana* (1890 — dealing with peasant life and loves in Sicily) and *I Pagliacci* (1892 — dealing with circus life). *La Bohème* (1896) can be considered as a somewhat modified type.

Many verismo operas are without a prelude or overture, the composers feeling that this destroys the illusion of realism. Most of Puccini's operas are without preludes or overtures; in *La Bohème,* the curtain goes up quickly with the first note of music.

The recitative, as such, disappeared in verismo operas as unrealistic and, as in *La Bohème,* the story line is continued either during an "aria" or by a melodic line of its own.

The time of *La Bohème* is given as "about 1830." Although this date is sixty years before Puccini started to work on the opera, it does not make it a "historical" story, for the Bohemian artists occupied the Latin quarter of Paris through World War I in much the same manner as they are depicted in Henri Murger's *Scènes de la Vie de Bohème* (1847-— Scenes of Bohemian Life) upon which Puccini's libretto is based. It might be noted that although Puccini dropped the term "Scenes from" in his opera's title, the opera is, essentially, four separate "scenes" of Bohemian life; there is no real "dramatic action," nor is there any real character development.

In the original score Puccini quoted Murger's novel in his description of the Bohemians:

Mimi was a charming girl specially apt to appeal to Rodolfo, the poet and dreamer. Aged twenty-two, she was slight and graceful. Her face reminded one of some sketch of highborn beauty; its features had marvelous refinement . . .

Gustave Colline, the great philosopher; Marcello, the great painter: Rodolfo, the great poet: and Schaunard, the great musician —— as they were wont to style themselves — regularly frequented the Café Momus, where, being inseparable, they were nicknamed the four musketeers. Indeed they always went about together, played together, dined together, often without paying the bill . . .

CAST OF CHARACTERS

The Bohemians	⎧ Rodolfo, *a poet*	tenor
	⎨ Marcello, *a painter*	baritone
	⎬ Schaunard, *a musician*	baritone
	⎩ Colline, *a philosopher*	bass
Mimi, *a seamstress and flowermaker*		soprano
Musetta, *a singer and sometime sweetheart of Marcello*		soprano
Benoit, *the Bohemians' landlord*		bass
Alcindoro, *a Councilor of State*		bass

ACT I

Time: *About 1830.*

Scene: *The garret apartment of the Bohemians in the Latin Quarter of Paris.*

It is a cold and snowy Christmas Eve. Rodolfo, a struggling poet, and Marcello, an equally struggling painter, are trying to work in their icy garret. Marcello is about to feed a chair to their idle stove when Rodolfo remembers the rejected manuscript lying on the table and decides it would make better fuel than literature. The two friends applaud the "performance" of the play while they warm themselves around the short-lived fire. Colline enters, having unsuccessfully tried to pawn his precious books. Suddenly Schaunard bursts in with porters bearing fuel and food, and the gloom is lifted. An English lord has paid him handsomely for his music, so he is going to treat them all to a joyous Christmas Eve.

The hilarity is interrupted as Benoit, the landlord, tries to collect the long over-due rent. The young men invite him in for wine which loosens his tongue. They induce him to boast about his love life, and then, pretending to be horrified by such immorality, they hustle him out of the room. Then the four friends decide to go to the Café Momus and start the evening's celebration. Rodolfo tells them to go ahead while he finishes an article that is due for a newspaper. They leave, urging him to finish quickly.

Alone in the room, Rodolfo waits for inspiration to move his pen. He is surprised by a knock at the door. Opening it, he discovers Mimi with an unlighted candle in her hand. The draft in the stairwell has blown her candle out and she has come seeking a light. As he bids her come in, she is seized by a coughing spasm and falls fainting into a chair. When she has recovered, she asks him to light her candle, and then shyly hastens to leave. At the threshold she realizes that she has dropped her key. As she comes back to search for it, her candle goes out again. In hurrying to help her, Rodolfo puts his own candle out, and together they grope in the dark for the lost key. When Rodolfo finds it, he quickly puts it in his pocket. Suddenly their hands meet:

Rodolfo *dolcissimo*

Che ge - li - da ma - ni - na, se la la - sci riscal - dar.

CHE GELIDA MANINA (Your tiny hand is frozen)

Che gelida manina,	Your tiny hand is frozen!
Se la lasci riscaldar.	Here, let me warm it in mine.
Cercar che giova?	Why search any further?
Al buio non si trova.	We won't find it in the dark.
Ma per fortuna è una notte di luna,	But, fortunately, the moon will be out soon
E qui la luna l'abbiamo vicina.	And we can look for it in the moonlight.
Aspetti signorina,	Wait a moment, mademoiselle.
Le dirò con due parole	Let me tell you in a few words
Chi son, chi son	Who I am, who I am —
E che faccio, come vivo.	What I do, and how I live.

Rodolfo goes on to explain that though he lives in poverty, he's a millionaire in spirit; that he is a poet and writes rhymes and songs of love. He then inquires of Mimi, "What of yourself? Please tell me."

Mimi replies:

MI CHIAMANO MIMÌ

Sì.	Yes.
Mi chiamano Mimì,	I am called Mimi,
Ma il mio nome è Lucia.	But my name is Lucia.
La storia mia è breve.	My story is brief.
A tela o a seta ricamo in casa e fuori.	I embroider silk and satin at home or away.
Son tranquilla e lieta,	I am peaceful and happy,
Ed è mio svago far gigli e rose.	I pass the time by making lilies and roses.

As Mimi finishes, the other Bohemians are heard outside the window beckoning Rodolfo to join them. Rodolfo replies that he is not alone, but tells them "to get a table at Momus, we'll follow soon."

Rodolfo turns and sees Mimi bathed in the soft glow of the moonlight. A tender duet closes the scene (the two pass out the door at the final notes of the duet, en route to the Café Momus):

O SOAVE FANCIULLA

RODOLFO

O soave fanciulla	O lovely maiden
O dolce viso	O sweet face
Di mite circonfuso alba lunar,	Surrounded by soft moonlight,
In te, ravviso il sogno	As I now see you,
Ch'io vorrei sempre sognar!	This is what I have dreamed of.

ACT II

Scene: *The Café Momus.*

The Café Momus, in the heart of the Latin Quarter, is gaily lighted for the evening's festivities. Tables are set outside, and the street is crowded with milling people and hawkers. Schaunard buys an ill-tuned horn and Colline a huge overcoat which is a little worse for wear. They find a table with Marcello and order supper.

Rodolfo and Mimi enter; Mimi admires a pink bonnet, and Rodolfo buys it for her. Then they see the others and join them. Rodolfo introduces Mimi to his friends with a flowery speech, and they propose a toast to the lovers. Suddenly Musetta, who has recently quarrelled with Marcello, bursts in upon the scene attracting as much attention as possible. Marcello ignores her with disdainful contempt. She is with a rich old man, Alcindoro, who is some sort of public official. He nervously tries to keep Musetta quiet, but she is determined to make Marcello notice her. She begins to sing:

QUANDO ME'N VO'

Quando me'n vo'	As through the streets
Quando me'n vo' soletta per la via	I wander onward merrily,
La gente sosta e mira . . .	I wander on daintily,
E la bellezza mia	See how the people look around
Tutta ricerca in me,	Because they know
Ricerca in me da capo a piè; . . .	I am a very charming little girl.

As Musetta sings, she decides to rid herself of Alcindoro. She purposely breaks the heel of her shoe and screams in supposed pain. Alcindoro hastily removes the damaged shoe and hurries off to find a suitable replacement.

Before Musetta is finished with her song, Marcello has weakened and goes over to her table. As the Bohemians are about to leave, the waiter brings their bill. They all protest poverty. Schaunard wonders where his fortune has gone. As they talk, the bugle call of an approaching guard of soldiers is heard. The children and street crowds line up to watch the parade. Musetta calls for her bill, then grandly tells the waiter that Alcindoro will pay both bills. Since she has only one shoe, the Bohemians lift her on their shoulders and leave. Alcindoro comes back with a new pair of shoes only to be confronted by an empty table and not one, but two bills. He falls back in his chair in bewilderment, as the curtain falls.

ACT III

Scene: *A Gate to the city of Paris.*

It is early one morning the following February. Near a tollgate at the edge of the city there is a tavern where Marcello and Musetta have been working; he paints portraits of the customers and she entertains them and teaches singing. (His picture of "The Red Sea" has now become a sign advertising the tavern.) It is quite cold and snow is everywhere. Mimi enters the little square outside the tavern; she is coughing badly, weakened not only by her consuming illness, but by unhappiness. Rodolfo has been a jealous lover, full of suspicions and anger, and though they love one another, they cannot seem to get along. The day before, Rodolfo left Mimi vowing that their affair was over. Desperately, Mimi has come to Marcello, hoping through him to locate Rodolfo. She asks a serving girl to fetch Marcello from the tavern. He comes out and, fearing for Mimi's health, begs her to come in. Mimi declines the offer, and tells him that she has come in search of Rodolfo. She knows he loves her very much, but being such a jealous person, he is always accusing her of being in love with another.

Marcello counsels Mimi, saying that two who fight as bitterly as Rodolfo and Mimi should not be together, that it would be better to part. Mimi finally concedes, and begs Marcello to help make this parting as easy as possible.

Rodolfo, who stumbled into the tavern an hour before dawn and fell asleep on a bench, is heard inside looking for Marcello. Mimi tells Marcello that Rodolfo must not find her here.

Mimi hides behind a tree as Rodolfo comes out of the tavern. He, too, has decided that they should part, and has come to confide in Marcello. He says he suspects that Mimi flirts with other men, but Marcello refuses to believe him. Then Rodolfo says that the real reason he wants Mimi to leave him is that she is dying of tuberculosis and he is powerless to help her. She needs rest and care, and he does not even have the money to heat his garret. He says he loves her desperately, but that she needs more than love to save her life. Mimi, overhearing the men talking, begins to weep and cough, thus revealing her presence to Rodolfo. He tries to make light of his morbid conversation and bids Mimi to come inside out of the cold. Mimi says that the heat would suffocate her, and Rodolfo embraces her sadly. Marcello, hearing Musetta laughing brazenly in the tavern, hurries in to investigate. Mimi turns to Rodolfo and says goodbye. "What!

You are going?" he replies. "Back to the simple life I knew before your love called me," she says, "back all alone goes Mimi to her lonely nest to make paper flowers!"

In a tender duet, they bid each other goodbye:

Mimi

Ad - di - o, sen - za ran - cor. A - scolta, a-
- scol - ta. Le po - che ro - be a - du - na che la - sciai spor - se.

ADDIO, SENZA RANCOR

MIMI

Addio, senza rancor	Goodbye . . . without anger.
Ascolta, ascolta.	Listen, listen.
Le poche robe aduna	These few old things
Che lasciai sparse	I've left behind me —
Nel mio cassetto stan chiusi	In my trunk I've left
Quel cerchietto d'or	That bracelet of gold,
E il libro de preghiere.	And my prayer-book.
Involgi tutto quanto	Wrap them all
In un grembiale e manderò	In my apron, and I'll send
Il portiere.	A porter to fetch them.
Bada sotto il guanciale	Wait, under my pillow
C'è la cuffietta rosa.	Is that pink bonnet.
Se vuoi, se vuoi,	Who knows, perhaps . . .
Se vuoi serbarla	Perhaps you would want to keep it,
A ricordo d'amor!	To remind you of our love!
Addio, addio, senza rancor.	Farewell, farewell . . . without anger.

Before the duet is finished, Musetta and Marcello can be heard inside the tavern having another one of their arguments. They call each other vile names, and finally agree to part, also, but it is in bitterness and anger. Mimi and Rodolfo continue their tender good-byes, completely oblivious of the commotion inside the tavern. The moment to depart has come; the curtain slowly descends.

ACT IV

Scene: *The garret apartment as in Act I.*

Several months have passed; flirtation and jealousy have taken their toll, and both pairs of lovers have been parted for some time. Marcello and Rodolfo are seen in the apartment trying to work, but it isn't easy for them.

Rodolfo casually remarks that he accidentally saw Musetta riding by in a carriage one day. Marcello, trying to force a laugh, replies, "I'm glad! Truly glad!" He then adds that he happened to see Mimi one afternoon riding past, dressed very well. Rodolfo forces an acknowledgement.

The men try to work, but it is obvious that their minds are with the two young girls. Rodolfo throws down his pen in disgust; Marcello's paint brush receives a curse. Rodolfo sings of days gone by:

O MIMÌ TU PIÙ

O Mimì tu più non torni.	O Mimi, you won't return,
O giorni belli, piccole mani.	O beautiful days, little hands,
Odorosi capelli.	Fragrant hair . . .
Collo di neve!	Lovely neck.
Ah, Mimì, mia breve gioventù!	Ah, Mimi, where is my lost youth.

MARCELLO

Io non so come sia	I don't know how
Che il mio pennella lavori	My brush works
E impasti colori contro voglia mia.	And paints completely wrong colors.

La Boheme — Act III: The "farewells" of Act III in the San Francisco Opera production. At the right, Mimi and Rudolfo; at the left and center, Marcello and Musetta.

La Boheme — Act IV: The Garret apartment of the Bohemians. The ailing Mimi reposes on the chaise lounge as Rudolfo kneels at her side.

The reveries of these unhappy young men are interrupted as Schaunard and Colline come in with some long-awaited food. The feast turns out to be four rolls and a salted herring, but the carefree artists pretend it is an elegant supper. There will be dancing after supper, so the "gentlemen" ask the shy "ladies" to dance. Someone's toe is trod upon, and a sword-fight with fire-tongs ensues. In the midst of all this nonsense, Musetta suddenly appears, out of breath and obviously upset. She has found Mimi wandering the streets, dazed and confused. Mimi is mortally ill and has begged to be taken to Rodolfo. As Musetta informs them that Mimi is below but does not have the strength to climb the stairs, Rodolfo rushes out after her, followed by Marcello. Together they bring her back to the apartment and let her recline on the little bed. Mimi says she is so happy to be back with Rodolfo; Musetta looks about for some coffee or wine to give the ailing girl, but can find nothing. Mimi requests a muff to keep her hands warm, but alas, there isn't even that in the barren garret.

Musetta gives her earrings to Marcello and tells him to go and sell them, and with the money bring back a doctor and some medicine. She then dashes out to get her own muff for Mimi's hands. Colline, greatly shaken by the scene, decides to sell his overcoat, his favorite possession, in order to buy some delicacies for Mimi:

Vec-chia zi-mar-ra, sen-ti, io re-sto al pian, tu a-

—scen-de-re il sa-cro mon-te or de-vi.

Vecchia Zimarra

Vecchia zimarra, senti,	Sentimental old overcoat,
Io resto al pian,	I rest with a tear in my eye,
Tu ascendere il sacro monte or devi	Faded friend, so tried and true,
Le mie grazie ricevi.	We must part, you and I.

Colline folds his overcoat and is about to depart. When he passes by Schaunard, he pats him on the back. He says to Schaunard, "Our methods may possibly differ, but two kindly acts we'll do. Mine's this (pointing to the overcoat he is about to sell), and yours is to leave Mimi and Rodolfo alone."

After they have gone, Mimi tells Rodolfo that she was only pretending to sleep because she was hoping that they would leave the two of them alone:

Mimi

SONO ANDATI?

Sono andati?	Have they left us?
Fingevo di dormire	I only pretend to sleep
Perchè voli con te sola restare	For I wanted to be alone with you, love.
Ho tante cose che ti voglio dire	So many things there are I would tell you;
O una sola, ma grande come il mare,	There is one, too, as spacious as the ocean:
. . . . .	
Sei il mio amore e tutta la mia vita!	You are my love and all my life.

Mimi recalls her melody of yesteryear: "They call me Mimi." She sings and Rodolfo remembers the time they went shopping and shows her the bonnet he has kept all this time. They recall how they fell in love, and Rodolfo confesses he really found the key that first night but hid it in his pocket.

Just as a coughing spell bothers Mimi, the Bohemians return with food and medicine; Musetta presents Mimi with a muff. But it is too late; the gentle little Mimi falls back as if asleep and life passes from her. Rodolfo finally senses the hushed atmosphere and asks what is wrong. When he sees that his beloved Mimi is dead, he cries out, "Mimi!" Marcello replies, "Courage! Courage!"

RICHARD STRAUSS

BORN: June 11, 1864; Munich, Germany.
DIED: September 8, 1949; Garmisch-Partenkirchen, Germany.

Richard Strauss was a genial man who loved his wife, money, and art. His home in Garmisch was filled with paintings by such famous artists as El Greco, Tintoretto, and Rubens. He particularly liked to play cards and drink beer, but he usually had to sneak away from his strong-willed wife, Pauline, to enjoy these diversions (he humorously said that of his operas, his favorite was *Intermezzo* — the story of a musician and his termagant wife). Strauss loved to make money and hang on to it. According to one story, he once invited many Parisian celebrities to a post-premiere feast at a leading restaurant, and after he had been praised and cheered for his work, and after all had thanked him for being a genial host, he had each guest handed a separate check!

Strauss was the son of the first horn player of the Munich Opera orchestra; the Strauss home was always filled with music. Richard was given his first music lesson when he was four, and at six had composed a little *Polka in C* for piano. His first published work, Opus 1 (*Festival March*), was written when he was ten; the same year he wrote a *Serenade for Wind Instruments,* published as Opus 7. Most of the other compositions of this period are either in manuscript form or else have been destroyed. Strauss was sixteen when the first public performance was given of one of his works, a *Symphony in D Major.*

After an academic course at the Gymnasium (high school), Strauss enrolled during his eighteenth year at the University of Munich where he majored in philosophy and esthetics. It took three years at the University before he made up his mind that music would be his profession. He traveled to Berlin where he had hopes of finding some good music teachers, but he had no sooner arrived there than he received word from the famous conductor, Hans von Bülow, requesting him to become an assistant conductor. Strauss accepted and became acquainted through this new post with Alexander Ritter, a poet and musician. The latter persuaded Strauss to give up the traditional style of composition and encouraged him to follow a new path. Strauss said later of Ritter: "His influence was in the nature of a wind storm. He urged me on to the development of the poetic, the expressive in music, as exemplified in the works of Liszt, Wagner, and Berlioz. My symphonic fantasy 'Aus Italien' is the connecting link between the old and the new method."

The *Aus Italien* was completed after Strauss had made a visit to Italy. When it was premiered, the public was shocked and accused the composer of vulgarity because he had used the popular tune *Funiculi, Funicula* in it (although this melody was an authentic folk tune long before it was made into a popular Neapolitan song).

In August, 1886, when Strauss was twenty-two, he was appointed sub-conductor at the Munich Opera, a post he held for three years. While there, he completed two of his best known works: *Don Juan* and *Tod und Verklärung* (Death and Transfiguration). Both were symphonic poems that followed the form established by Liszt; Ritter's poem that had inspired the latter work was printed in the score.

Richard Strauss moved to Weimar to serve as a conductor, and while there was invited by Richard Wagner's widow, Cosima Wagner, to conduct *Tannhäuser* at the Bayreuth Festspielhaus. After a year in Weimar, Strauss became seriously ill with lung trouble. He took leave of his conducting activities and toured the Mediterranean, visiting Greece, Sicily, and Egypt. On this voyage he completed most of his first opera, *Guntram*. The opera was produced in May, 1894 with Pauline de Ahna as the leading lady. Strauss fell in love with her and they were married in June of the same year.

Strauss resigned his post at Weimar to succeed von Bülow as conductor of the Berlin Philharmonic after the latter's death. During his first four years of association with this orchestra, four famous symphonic poems were completed: *Till Eulenspiegels Lustige Streiche* (Till Eulenspiegel's Merry Pranks); *Also Sprach Zarathustra* (Thus Spoke Zarathustra); *Don Quixote;* and *Ein Heldenleben* (A Hero's Life). After the premiere performances of these works, the public reacted in diverse ways: those that admired Strauss' work praised him highly, the traditionalists damned him violently. The latter group had been shocked when they discovered *Ein Heldenleben* to be an autobiographical composition and wondered at his audacity in flaunting it in front of the public. They further questioned such devices as a gadget to imitate bleating sheep and the wind machine he had used in *Don Quixote*.

The composer turned from the symphonic poem to a more traditional form, that of the symphony, for his next major works. He, however, took great liberties in this established pattern. The *Domestic Symphony* was written in 1903 and performed a year later at Carnegie Hall, New York, on Strauss' first visit to the United States. It was followed by the *Alpine Symphony* written in 1915, both works making use of unusual devices in the percussion section to make the music more expressionistic.

In the field of opera, Strauss had shocked the world with *Salome* in 1903. It was based on Oscar Wilde's French play taken from the Biblical story, a psychological tragedy of "shattering impact." This opera was followed by *Elektra* based on Greek mythology, a story full of gloom and the horrors of matricide. As if not to alienate the opera public completely, the composer turned next to an opera whose story concerned an eighteenth century comedy, *Der Rosenkavalier*. Many other operas, infrequently performed in this country, followed; *Ariadne auf Naxos* (Ariadne of Naxos); *Die Frau ohne Schatten* (The Woman Without a Shadow); and *Arabella* are some of them. His last opera, *Capriccio* was completed in 1941.

On November 15, 1933, Dictator Adolph Hitler appointed Richard Strauss the President of the Reichs-Musikkamer (The National Music Council) for the Nazi regime. Although Strauss claimed to be no politician, he held this post until 1935 when a difference in viewpoints led him to resign.

Most of World War II he spent at his home in Garmisch, but in the final days of the war (1945), fled to Lausanne, Switzerland, just ahead of the Allied invasion of southern Germany. At the end of the war he returned to his home, leaving it in 1947 to tour England as a guest of the British government, conducting his own works.

On September 8, 1949, he succumbed to a chronic heart disease at eighty-five years of age. At his bedside was his wife who almost fifty years earlier had been the leading lady in his first opera. She followed her husband in death a few months later.

BIBLIOGRAPHY

Finck, Henry T. *Richard Strauss: The Man and His Works*. Boston: Little, Brown, and Co., 1917.
Strauss, Richard. *Recollections and Reflections*. London: Boosey and Hawkes, Ltd., 1953.

TILL EULENSPIEGEL'S MERRY PRANKS
AFTER THE OLD-FASHIONED ROGUISH MANNER, IN RONDO FORM

Richard Strauss

The name of Eulenspiegel literally means "Owl-glass" and is said to come from the old German proverb: "Man sees his own faults as little as a monkey or an owl recognizes his ugliness on looking into a mirror." The original Till was a wandering artisan of Brunswick, the hero of a legend attributed to Dr. Thomas Murner, written about the end of the fifteenth century. Till may have lived a hundred years earlier.

The composer has provided in his own words the following program of episodes in this symphonic poem:

Prologue. "Once upon a time there was a rogue by the name of Till Eulenspiegel." He was a mischievous sprite. Away for new pranks. Wait! You hypocrite! Hop! On horseback through the midst of the market women! With seven-league boots he makes off. Hidden in a mousehole. Disguised as a monk, he overflows with unction and morality. But the rogue peeps out from the big toe. Before the end, however, a secret horror takes hold of him on account of the mockery of religion. Till, as a cavalier, exchanging tender persiflage with pretty girls. With one of them he has really fallen in love. He proposes to her. A polite refusal is still a refusal. He turns away in rage. Swears to take vengeance on the whole human race. Philistine's motive. After proposing a couple of monstrous theses he abandons the dumbfounded ones to their fate. Great grimace from afar. Till's street song. He is collared by the bailiff. The judgement. He whistles to himself with indifference. Up the ladder! There he is swinging; his breath is gone out — a last quiver. All that is mortal of Till is ended. Epilogue. What is immortal, his humor, remains.

The tone poem opens with the "Once Upon a Time" theme:

Example 1

Two measures later the French horn plays the "Till" theme:

Example 2 (Till himself)

This melody (Example 2) is repeated by the horn and then its opening measures are played in turn by the oboe, the clarinet, and low strings and woodwinds.

After a series of chords in the strings, the "Prank" theme is heard (a rhythmical variation of Example 1):

Example 3 (Prank theme)

After a sharp, rhythmical jerk there is a rising glissando (suggestive of Till mounting his horse) and then the trotting rhythm of a horse is heard.

In an extended passage which includes many repetitions of Example 2 and Example 3, the melody of Example 1 is heard very quietly in the low strings.

A crash of cymbals, followed by great confusion both rhythmically and melodically, suggests that Till has upset the pots and pans in the market place.

A choral-like passage is heard. Till, disguised as a monk (Figure A), tries to fool the public:

Example 4

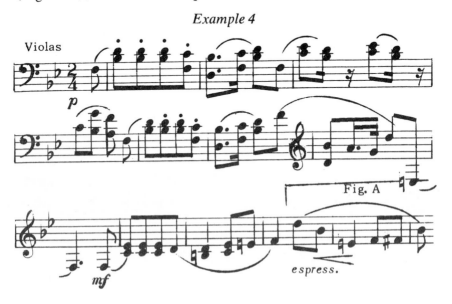

Till's amorous adventures are introduced by a long glissando on the violin. Both the "Till" theme (Example 2) and the "Prank" theme (Example 3) appear, but in altered form. The "love" theme (Example 5) is a variation of Till's theme.

Example 5

Angered when the young lady to whom he proposes turns him away, the "Prank" theme becomes bold in augmentation (the value of each note is extended, compare Examples 3 and 6).

Example 6

Till meets a group of Philistines, a rather dull group of academic people. In this passage Example 1 starts in the style of a canon, a rather "academic" form. It soon departs, however, from the strict form and is little more than a "mock" canon!

Example 7

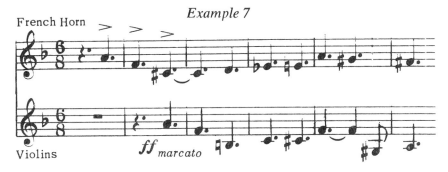

"Till's street song" is a light and happy melody played by the violins and clarinet:

Example 8

Example 1 returns as Till has a moment of doubt about his life filled with pranks, but soon his original theme (Example 2) returns to prove that he is the same roguish Till.

"Till's theme" is played by the horns (Example 9) in such a bold manner (like a march) that it becomes obvious that Till does not intend to change his ways.

Example 9

French Horn

The horns then play "Till's theme" (Example 2) in combination with the first four notes of the "Prank" theme (Example 3).

Example 10

GIACOMO PUCCINI

JEAN SIBELIUS
Courtesy Finnish National Travel Office

SERGEI RACHMANINOFF

RICHARD STRAUSS

A loud timpani roll indicates the capture of Till by the bailiff. Solemn chords suggest their judgment, but a high clarinet solo (Till's motive) suggest his indifference.

Example 11

A dramatic downward leap of a 7th in the horns, bassoons, and trombones indicates that the trap on the gallows has been sprung. Till is dead!

Example 12

The high clarinet starts an upward arpeggio, perhaps depicting Till's departing soul leaving for heaven, but something happens! The arpeggio turns around and descends downward and tumbles hurriedly to the bass notes of the orchestra.

EPILOGUE

In a section marked by the composer "Epilogue," the "Once Upon a Time" theme (Example 1) returns to close the tone poem serenely.

Suddenly the "Prank" theme (Example 3) returns *fortissimo* in full orchestra and ends the composition suddenly in one final prank!

JEAN SIBELIUS

BORN: December 8, 1865; Tavastehus, Finland.
DIED: September 20, 1957; Järvenpää, Finland.

For many years the villagers who wandered the birch-covered slopes near Lake Tuusula in Finland were accustomed to seeing an old man of massive size, dressed in a business suit, a homburg on his head, walking slowly along the shaded lanes, easing his weight on a heavy cane. Invariably they saluted him, for they knew they were in the presence of greatness. Jean Sibelius never traveled far from his home near the lake during his years of retirement. When he wasn't wandering about on the many footpaths, he was at home listening to concerts from all over the world on his powerful short wave radio.

Sibelius came of pure Finnish stock: his father, an army surgeon, was a peasant by birth; his mother came from a clerical family. Jean was given piano lessons when he was nine years of age, and when he was fifteen he started studying the violin. He played in amateur chamber ensembles and was so enamored with the violin that until he was twenty-five, he kept toying with the idea of becoming a concert violinist. He received an excellent general education at the Hämeea Lyseo (high school), the center of Finnish culture. In the Lyseo, Sibelius acted in dramatic productions and received a thorough training in classic Latin and Greek. He excelled in both literature and mathematics, and found astronomy fascinating; music remained, however, his first love throughout these school days. On vacations from school he spent his time hunting in the mountains and forests of southern Finland.

After graduation from the Lyseo, Sibelius entered Helsinki University as a law student and in addition took special courses in music at the Conservatory. During his second year at the University he decided to give up law and become a musician. He subsequently enrolled as a full time student at the Conservatory. Although he had dabbled in composition earlier, the Conservatory provided him with his first courses in music theory.

At his graduation from the Conservatory, two of his compositions were performed: a *Suite for Strings* and a *Quartet*. Through these performances he was able to obtain both a scholarship and a government grant which allowed him to study in Berlin. From Berlin he moved on to study composition with Carl Goldmark in Vienna.

Returning to Finland four years later, Sibelius married Aino Järnefelt. The country was in the throes of a nationalistic furor. Finland, under the political rule of Russia, was about to have its Assembly abolished, thereby leaving the Finns without representation in government. Sibelius became imbued with the patriotic fervor the country was then demonstrating and composed a work for soli, chorus, and orchestra in five movements which he titled *Kullervo*. This work was based on the national folk legend of Finland, *Kalevala,* a literary work that was to serve as the basis for many more of his compositions. The legend itself, some 22,800 verses long, was a collection made in 1835 of folk poetry from all over Finland, and although it lacks a central plot, it maintains its popularity with the Finns because of its vivid imagery.

Sibelius was appointed to the staff of the Helsingfor Conservatory to teach violin and theory. A request was made by the school for a work that was not too difficult for the Conservatory orchestra. For this purpose Sibelius wrote a work titled *A Saga* (frequently performed in orchestral concerts in this country; the Swedish article *En* is usually used in place of the English *A* in the title).

The composer completed one of his most frequently performed works next, *The Swan of Tuonela,* based on the story of the swan that glides majestically across the black river of death in the *Kalevala* legend. The Finnish Senate (under Russian rule) thereupon granted the composer an annual pension of 2000 marks (it was substantially increased in 1926) so that he could devote all of his time to composition. From this date onward, Sibelius lived a rather uneventful life except for frequent trips.

During the last year of the nineteenth century he traveled to Italy and then visited Munich and Bayreuth. On his return to his native country, Sibelius was requested to write a tone poem for a patriotic demonstration to be called *Tableaux of the Past.* The work which he composed for this pageant, *Finlandia,* was so popular with the public, and so patriotic in nature, the Russians had to ban its performance.

Sibelius purchased a home at Lake Tuusula where he and his wife reared five daughters. In this home, not far from Helsinki, one of the first works he completed was his *Symphony No. 4.* In 1914 he was invited to come to the United States to guest conduct the Litchfield County Choral Union concert. The composer made the trip and included on his program *Finlandia, Pohjola's Daughter* (another work based on *Kalevala*), the *King Christian Suite,* and a work composed especially for the occasion, *The Oceanides.* While in this country he taught a season at the New England Conservatory of Music and was granted an honorary Doctor of Music degree by Yale University.

Shortly after his return to Finland, Europe became enmeshed in World War I. During the war years Sibelius completed his fifth, sixth, and seventh symphonies. Once while working on a composition, the sounds of Russian cannon could be heard distinctly in the distance. By 1920 Sibelius had composed thirteen tone poems (five based on *Kalevala*), seven symphonies, over eighty songs, ten chamber works, and a quantity of music for violin and piano.

In 1929 Sibelius announced that he was retiring from active composition. In spite of this announcement, Serge Koussevitsky, conductor of the Boston Symphony, hoped to premiere a *Symphony No. 8* of Sibelius. Friends kept informing the conductor that the symphony was almost ready to go to the publisher, but the work never materialized, nor were any sketches for it found after the composer's death.

National celebrations were held in Finland on Sibelius' eightieth and ninetieth birthdays. In his ninety-first year, Jean Sibelius died of a cerebral hemorrhage several hours after rising and taking a final look at the wooded countryside that had nourished his art.

BIBLIOGRAPHY

Johnson, Harold E. *Jean Sibelius.* New York: Alfred A. Knopf, 1959.
Ringbom, Nils-Eric. *Jean Sibelius; A Master and His Work,* trans. G. I. C. de Courcy. Norman, Oklahoma: University of Oklahoma Press, 1954.

SYMPHONY NO. 2
in D Major

JEAN SIBELIUS

This symphony was first performed in Helsingfor, Finland, in March, 1902, and dismissed by the critics as "beneath serious notice." Gradually it kept reappearing on concert programs until today it is one of the works of the standard repertoire.

In this symphony, Sibelius sometimes works backwards, as it were, giving first fragments of themes and juggling them around until finally at the dynamic climax, he presents the theme in its entirety.

FOURTH MOVEMENT: Finale. *Allegro moderato.*

For the Finale, Sibelius turns to the sonata-allegro pattern. Starting with fragments of the Principal Subject, Example 1, a dynamic climax is built before the theme is stated in full by the violins:

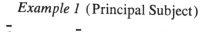

Example 1 (Principal Subject)

con forza

A transitional theme appears in the upper register of the flutes:

Example 2

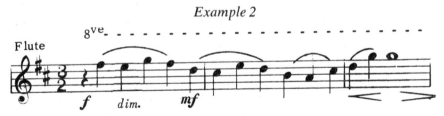

The Second Subject, Example 3, is presented first by the oboe, repeated by the clarinet, then developed by the woodwinds over a continuously moving accompaniment in the violas and celli:

Example 3 (Second Subject)

A closing theme is introduced by the trombones in the final measures of the *exposition:*

Example 4

The *development* opens with an orchestral dialogue alternating between the Principal Subject, Example 1, and the closing theme, Example 4.

The celli expand the Principal Subject, Example 1; they are answered by the bassoons with Example 4. First oboes, then clarinets, repeat this dialogue between the two themes.

The trombones play Example 4, followed by the Principal Subject, Example 1, in the French horns, competing with each other until a climax is reached.

A long, sustained bass note accompanied by a timpani roll, leads to a final statement of the Principal Subject, Example 1.

The *recapitulation* opens with the Principal Subject, Example 1, this time with a new woodwind accompaniment. The brass join in as the strings repeat Example 1.

The trumpet announces the Second Subject, Example 3. The oboe echoes it, and then a development of it occurs in the woodwinds.

The violins and clarinets repeat Example 3; the trumpets join in. The *recapitulation* aptly closes with the closing theme, Example 4.

The *coda* is based on the Principal Subject, Example 1, first presented by the basses, celli, and bassoons. The brass choir repeats it over full orchestra to close the symphony.

SERGEI RACHMANINOFF

BORN: April 1, 1873; Oneg, Russia.
DIED: March 28, 1943; Beverly Hills, California.

During the Romantic era, music had become a specialized field; one was either a composer, a performer, or a conductor. Rarely was one person equally competent in two fields (one thinks of Liszt and Chopin as exceptions), almost never in all three. Sergei Rachmaninoff was the exception to this. No one who had the privilege of hearing a piano recital by him could ever forget either his virtuosity at the keyboard or his artistic interpretations. On the conductor's podium, he was master of the orchestra and in complete command of the music. These two phases of his career can only be judged now by the legacy of phonograph records that he made, which, as with all phonograph records, cannot convey the sparkle, the spontaneity of a live performance. The merit of his compositions remains for all to enjoy; his *Symphony No. 2* and his *Concerto No. 2 for Piano and Orchestra* seem to be among his most frequently performed works.

Sergei was the son of a Captain of the Imperial Guards of Russia, and the lad probably would have followed in his father's footsteps had not the liberation of the serfs in 1861 decreased the wealth of the Rachmaninoff family. Reduced to one estate, the family was further impoverished by the elder Rachmaninoff's penchant for gambling. Dissention between Sergei's father and mother over financial as well as other matters caused them to separate. Sergei moved with his mother to St. Petersburg.

The boy had shown indisputable signs of musical ability by the time he was four years of age, for he had not only perfect pitch, but he was able to pick out melodies on the piano. When he and his mother arrived in St. Petersburg, he was enrolled at the Conservatory. Music came so easily for him that he did not really apply himself. At the end of three years he was transferred to the Moscow Conservatory (he was then twelve) in the hope that he would realize his full potential. His piano teacher was Zvereff, and it was in his home that Rachmaninoff boarded.

From Zvereff, Rachmaninoff learned the piano technique that was later to make him such a virtuoso at the keyboard. It was in this home that he had an opportunity to meet Tchaikovsky, a good friend of Zvereff. After three years a bitter quarrel developed between Sergei and his teacher-landlord. Since there were other piano students residing in the Svereff home, it was necessary to post a schedule of when each student could use the family piano for practice. Anxious to spend more time at the keyboard, and at hours of his own choosing, Rachmaninoff asked Zvereff to provide a piano for his private room. What started as a simple request ended in a bitter quarrel; Rachmaninoff moved.

The problem of where to move was a real one. Low on funds, it would have been logical for Sergei to return to St. Petersburg to live with his mother and study again at the Conservatory. Sergei frowned on this suggestion as he did not wish to become involved in the St. Petersburg musical circle that included Borodin, Mussorgsky, and Rimsky-Korsakov who were bent on establishing a Russian nationalistic school of composition. Rachmaninoff wished to stay in Moscow where the musical scene was dominated by Tchaikovsky and Anton Rubinstein who followed in the footsteps of the German Romantic tradition.

A great-aunt of Rachmaninoff's opened her home in Moscow to him and provided both board and room for the student. It was here that he met his bride-to-be, the daughter of his great-aunt. After looking for a new teacher at the Conservatory, Rachmaninoff enrolled for work with Arensky, and through the later became acquainted with Arensky's pupil, Alexander Scriabin.

Rachmaninoff's *Prelude in C-Sharp Minor* was written when he was twenty; the composition was so well liked that soon the composer's name was known all over Russia. The work's fame spread outside Russia and led the London Philharmonic Orchestra to invite the composer for a concert appearance in London. While Rachmaninoff was in England, his *Symphony No. 1* was given its premiere in St. Petersburg and proved to be a failure with the public, partially due to a poor and inept performance, and partially to a bad review by Cui who was prejudiced against the "Moscow" composers. Once back in Russia, he received another invitation from London requesting him to return the following year and present a piano concerto. The composer was already in doubt as to his field of endeavor, and since he didn't consider his *Concerto No. 1 for Piano and Orchestra* a worthy work, and since his *Symphony No. 1* had proved to be such a dismal failure, he decided to give up completely the field of composition.

Rachmaninoff's friends and fellow musicians finally talked him into visiting a famous Russian doctor, Dr. Dahl. Dr. Dahl worked with the composer in the field of auto-suggestion. Through his work, the doctor was eventually able to convince Rachmaninoff that he could not only create good, new music, but that he could do it quickly and easily. The composer thereupon turned to writing a piano concerto for the London engagement. When the *Concerto No. 2 for Piano and Orchestra* was presented in England, its title page bore a dedication to Dr. Dahl.

On his return to Russia, Rachmaninoff was engaged as a conductor at the Imperial Grand Theater of Moscow where he conducted the operas of Tchaikovsky as well as the popular non-Russian operas. Dresden, Germany, sent the composer an invitation to conduct in that city. This charming city had caught Rachmaninoff's eye when he was there on his honeymoon and he quickly accepted the invitation. Both his *Symphony No. 2* and *The Isle of the Dead* were completed there.

In 1909 Rachmaninoff was invited to make a concert tour of the United States. For this the composer wrote the *Concerto No. 3 for Piano and Orchestra* which he performed throughout the tour. When he returned to Russia, he was appointed the First Vice-President of the Imperial Russian Musical Society, and soon became the conductor of the Philharmonic Concerts.

The death in 1915 of his friend and fellow composer, Alexander Scriabin, led Rachmaninoff to vow that he would tour all the important cities of the world and familiarize the concert public with the piano works of Scriabin. This marked Rachmaninoff's first appearance in piano recitals playing music other than his own, and launched him on a long career as one of the greatest piano virtuosi. During World War I Rachmaninoff continued to concertize in Russia, giving benefit performances for Russian soldiers.

When the war was over, Russia turned to a revolution for which Rachmaninoff had no sympathy. The world of Imperial Russia was at an end and the Soviet government of Lenin was establishing itself. Completely out of sympathy with both the revolution and the new Communistic government, Rachmaninoff scheduled a concert tour of Scandinavia and crossed the border into Finland on Christmas Day, 1917, never to return to Russia again.

Although Rachmaninoff lived for almost a quarter of a century in the United States, he could never forget his homeland as he knew it. No matter whether he lived on Riverside Drive in New York City, or in Beverly Hills, California, he continued to celebrate the Russian holidays, he ate Russian cuisine, and he continued to observe Russian traditions. It made him, in the midst of a great crowd, a very lonely man.

By 1940, his failing health and the severe winter weather of New York led him to the purchase of a small home in Beverly Hills. Rachmaninoff gave up concertizing when he moved to California. After a few years' rest he wanted to make one more tour upon which he embarked on February 8, 1943. He got as far as New Orleans when he became so ill that the balance of the tour had to be cancelled. Returning to his home in Beverly Hills, he died on March 28 in his seventieth year.

BIBLIOGRAPHY

Bertensson, Sergei and Jay Leyda. *Serge Rachmaninoff: A Lifetime in Music.* New York, New York University Press, 1956.
Seroff, Victor I. *Rachmaninoff.* London: Cassell and Co., 1952.

CONCERTO NO. 2 FOR PIANO AND ORCHESTRA
in C Minor

SERGEI RACHMANINOFF

The first movement of the *Concerto No. 2* is based on the sonata-allegro pattern, but melody is its predominating element. Sabaneiev describes the musical demand placed on a composer in Russia in the late-Romantic era: "It was not form or harmoniousness, or Apollonic vision that was demanded of music, but passion, feeling, languor, heartache."

This concerto was dedicated to Dr. Dahl in gratitude for the help extended to the composer in auto-suggestion (see the biographical sketch). Its fine reception by the audience at the Philharmonic Society Concert in Moscow (1901), with the composer at the piano, helped restore Rachmaninoff's confidence in the field of composition.

FIRST MOVEMENT: *Moderato*

The piano, unaccompanied, plays a series of chords which grow in volume from a *pianissimo* to a *fortissimo con passione.*

The piano continues with an accompanying figuration while the violins, violas, and clarinet state the Principal Subject:

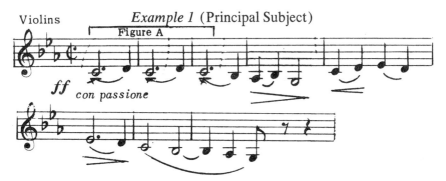

Example 1 (Principal Subject)

Example 1 is repeated.

A transitional theme appears in the celli:

Example 2

Example 2 is repeated, in turn, by the violin and piano.

A bold, rhythmical figure derived from Figure A of Example 1 is heard in the piano and full orchestra.

A viola solo, *espressivo,* introduces the piano which plays the Second Subject:

Example 3 (Second Subject)

The piano repeats Example 3 and develops it.

A dialogue, based on Example 3, is heard between the oboe and the clarinet, and the piano.

The *development* opens with some quickly moving passages for the piano which leads to a development of the Principal Subject, Example 1, by the woodwinds.

The viola and bassoon are heard with a variant of Example 1, and then the violins take it up.

The Second Subject, Example 3, eventually emerges from the strings to be followed by a development of the transitional theme, Example 2.

After building to a dynamic climax, the orchestra is heard with the Principal Subject, Example 1, in a march tempo. The piano introduces a new theme over the string melody:

Example 4

The transitional theme, Example 2, makes its return in the piano and then appears in the orchestra.

The Second Subject, Example 3, is recapitulated by the French horns in augmentation (the time value of each note is doubled).

The transitional theme, Example 2, returns briefly and leads to the *coda*.

The piano plays some fiery passages in the coda as the tempo accelerates. The movement ends with crashing chords for piano and orchestra.

NATIONALISM

NATIONALISM is a movement which grew out of the main stream of Romanticism in the last half of the nineteenth century. It reached its peak between 1875 and 1885, and around the turn of the century merged with the trends in both Impressionism and New Music.

An awakening of national pride, and an awareness of the rich heritage of folk music, legends, and history, was evidenced in the music of this school. The great change in the political-social life of Europe, which started with the French Revolution, championed the cause of the common man and gave him equality and independence. In Russia, where the *Nationalistic* movement started, the freeing of the serfs in 1861 gave impetus to a national pride. The desire for political independence in Czechoslovakia, under Hapsburg Austrian-Hungarian domination since 1620, was the stimulus there. Nationalism was not in evidence in the countries that had a musical tradition of their own, such as France, Italy, and Germany.

The Russian composer Glinka (1804-1857) wrote the opera *A Life for the Czar* in 1836, probably the first nationalistic work. He was followed by another generation of Russian composers who are known as "The Mighty Five": Alexander Borodin (1833-1887); César Cui (1835-1918); Mily Balakirev (1837-1910); Modest Mussorgsky (1839-1881); and Nicholas Rimsky-Korsakov (1844-1908). Nowhere else did Nationalism acquire the intensity it did in Russia, nor the aggressiveness that was in evidence there. It existed in Russia alongside the mainstream of Romanticism. The "Mighty Five" centered their activities in St. Petersburg and created such intensely Nationalistic operas as *Prince Igor* (Borodin), *Boris Godunov* (Mussorgsky), and *The Czar's Bride* (Rimsky-Korsakov). Rimsky-Korsakov was appointed to the staff of the St. Petersburg Conservatory, and, over a period of many years, devoted himself to furthering the cause of Russian Nationalism. In Moscow, Anton Rubinstein and Peter Tchaikovsky continued to follow the universal tradition of Romanticism. Rubinstein was appointed director of the Moscow Conservatory and staffed it mostly with German professors of music.

He was also responsible for selecting the programs of the orchestral concerts, and he devoted most of each concert to works of the German Romantics.

In Czechoslovakia, Bedřich Smetana was one of the early leaders of Nationalism in that country, which culminated in the building of an opera house dedicated to the production of only native Czech operas. In the northern countries of Europe, there were trends toward Nationalism, but the split with the main Romantic tradition was not nearly as great. Evidences of Nationalism influenced the music of Edvard Grieg in Norway, especially in his vocal compositions, although to a certain degree in his piano and orchestral works. Jean Sibelius of Finland was quite Nationalistic in his early works; he returned to the absolute music of post-Romanticism in his later works, but never quite obliterated the traces of his great patriotic spirit.

In several areas, Nationalism was linked with other major developments. Manuel de Falla of Spain relied heavily on Spanish rhythms and even local color, but his music was largely written in the Impressionistic idiom. Zoltán Kodály and Belá Bartók of Hungary did more extensive research into the true folk melodies of their native land than any other composers have ever done. It was only natural that some of these melodies and rhythms would appear in their compositions, yet Bartók is not a Nationalistic composer; rather, he forged a unique idiom in New Music.

An exact definition of what makes a musical work *Nationalistic* is almost impossible. One needs to know the stimulus of the composer in writing the work, for Nationalism is not so much a matter of fact, as it is of *intention*. The composers consciously used folk melodies and stories *because* they were representative of their patriotic fervor for their country. Since this act was largely external, no new forms were developed by the Nationalistic schools; instead, a heavy reliance was placed on programmatic music — the tone or symphonic poem, and opera in particular.

BIBLIOGRAPHY

Vaughan Williams, Ralph. *National Music*. London: Oxford University Press, 1934.

Costumes for the Borodin opera, *Prince Igor*

The *Polovetsian Dances* from *Prince Igor*, as produced in Moscow. Both dance and music were inspired by the folk element; the story of the opera is based on Russian history.

MODEST MUSSORGSKY

BORN: March 21, 1839; Karevo, Russia.
DIED: March 28, 1881; St. Petersburg, Russia.

Mussorgsky had graduated from the Army Cadet School at seventeen years of age when he was assigned to the Second Military Hospital. Bored with his duties there as Officer of the Day, he fell into conversation with a doctor at the hospital who was also bored with the routine activity. They liked each other and happened to meet again that evening at the home of the Chief Medical Officer who, having a young daughter of marriageable age, entertained frequently. After two or three such meetings between Mussorgsky and the bored doctor, the doctor (Alexander Borodin) wrote this description of Mussorgsky at seventeen:

A smallish, very elegant, dapper little officer, brand-new, close-fitting uniform; shapely feet; delicate, altogether aristocratic hands. Elegant, aristocratic manners; conversation the same, somewhat affected. Some traces of foppishness, but very moderate. Unusually polite and cultured. The ladies made a fuss of him. He sat at the piano and coquettishly throwing up his hands, played excerpts from "Trovatore," "Traviata," etc., very pleasantly and gracefully, while the circle around him murmured in chorus, "Charmant! Délicieux!" and so on.

Modest Mussorgsky was born in the village of Karevo where his father was a well-to-do landowner of over forty square miles to which he had retired from government service. It was here, according to Mussorgsky's not too reliable autobiographical sketch, he first learned the folk legends of Russia from his nurse and received his first piano lessons from his mother. By the time the boy was seven he was able to play some small pieces by Liszt and, two years later, gave a concert for friends in his home.

Modest's father was greatly interested in his son's musical education and, when the boy was ten, sent him to St. Petersburg to study piano and receive a general education. Three years later Modest entered the Cadet School of Guards, his chief interest at that time being in German philosophy and history. Unfortunately, the Cadet School was a bad influence on Mussorgsky. The morals of the cadets were extremely low and they considered it beneath their dignity to study. They made fun of Modest when they discovered him studying and frequently encouraged Mussorgsky to join them in their drinking bouts. Mussorgsky composed a little polka while at the school and dedicated it to his comrades. This miniature work so pleased his father that the elder Mussorgsky arranged to have it printed.

At seventeen Mussorgsky left the Cadet School and was assigned to the Preobrajensky Guards a year after his brother had received the same assignment. Bored with the Guards, he tried his hand at writing an opera based on Hugo's *Han d'Islande,* but nothing came of it. The following spring he made the acquaintance of Dargomyjsky whose opera *Russalka* had recently been produced. Through Dargomyjsky, Mussorgsky met César Cui who was dabbling in composition and considering work on an opera. These two friends introduced Mussorgsky to Mily Balakirev. From association with these musicians, Mussorgsky became interested in increasing his own knowledge of music and composition and made arrangements with Balakirev for instruction. Of his pupil, Balakirev later said:

> Not being a theorist, I could not — unfortunately — teach Mussorgsky harmony, as Rimsky-Korsakov teaches it now. But I used to explain the form of composition to him. We played through all Beethoven's symphonies in four-hand arrangements as well as many other compositions by Schumann, Schubert, Glinka, and others. I explained to him the technical construction of the pieces we played, and he himself analyzed their form. However, as far as I remember, there were not many paid lessons, for some reason or other.

Some excellent songs were composed by Mussorgsky after these lessons were started, but soon a nervous disorder started to manifest itself and he resigned from the military service. When traces of this disorder seemed to recede for a while, he arranged for a trip to Moscow. He was very much impressed with this large city and wrote back to Balakirev his enthusiasm for the sights in the capitol: "The Kremlin, the marvelous Kremlin! St. Basil's [cathedral] worked on me so pleasantly and yet so strangely that it seemed as if at any moment a boyar might appear in long smock and high cap . . . Moscow has taken me into another world, the world of antiquity, a dirty world, but one that none the less affects me pleasantly — I don't know why . . . You know I have been a cosmopolitan, but now — I have undergone a sort of re-birth; I have been brought near to everything Russian."

Returning to St. Petersburg Mussorgsky continued to work on several compositions, one of them a symphony, but apparently did not get very far with any of them. An Imperial decree which was issued about this time ordered the emancipation of all serfs during

the next two years, and all except the wealthiest of land-owners suffered great financial losses. It meant that Modest and his brother
were eventually to lose their own family estate and finally to come
to desperate straits. Modest, however, seemed to approve of this
decree and had respect for the peasants, for his brother wrote of him:
"throughout his life [he] showed a peculiar affection for the peasants,
considering the Russian serf a genuine human being — in which he
was sadly mistaken."

Modest's creative talents were just starting to mature when this
decree necessitated his visit to the family estate to arrange financial
matters. When he returned to St. Petersburg he was forced to find
employment and entered the government service in the engineering
department of the Ministry of Communications. Two years later his
mother's death greatly affected him and his reliance on liquor became
greater. Delirium tremens forced him to move in with his brother
and his wife for three years to recuperate.

A few of Mussorgsky's compositions had been played publicly,
but the composer seemed inclined to work on several different ones
at the same time and he could never quite get around to finishing any
of them. When the staff of the Ministry in which he worked was
reduced in size, he was let go. Having more time to devote to music,
he completed *Night on Bald Mountain* which was a musical picture
of the witches' sabbath on St. John's Eve (July 5). This was his first
notable composition and one which was daring in conception. Well
aware of this, he said:

> The general character of the thing is warmth; it doesn't drag; its structure
> is concise without any German padding, which makes it remarkably refreshing
> . . . I feel [it] is something new and is bound to produce a favorable impression
> on intelligent musicians. I am aware that there are things in it which would
> make César [Cui] send me to the Conservatoire for lessons in respectable
> composition, for which they would turn me *out* of the Conservatoire. [Never-
> theless,] I'm not going to start altering it; with whatever shortcomings it was
> born, it will have to live.

Mussorgsky became enthralled with the prospect of composing
an opera and cast about for a good libretto. He spoke of his hopes
for the opera: "I'll tell you what I'd like to do; to make my characters
speak on the stage as living people really speak . . . and my music
must be an artistic reproduction of human speech in all its finest
shades. That's my idea." After several experiments with other subjects, he became enthused with the history of Czar Boris Godunov,

his rise to the throne of Russia through intrigue and murder, and his eventual overthrow by a false Pretender. After long struggles with the composition of this great work, and two refusals of the score by the opera house, most of it was finally performed in 1874 when Mussorgsky was thirty-five. It was accepted by the public with moderate success, but César Cui served as the music critic for the leading newspaper and gave the opera as bad a review as could be written.

More songs were composed by Mussorgsky and he worked simultaneously on two operas (later completed from Mussorgsky's sketches by Rimsky-Korsakov): *Khovantchina* and *The Fair at Sorochnsk.* The death of his friend Victor Hartmann, a painter, upset Mussorgsky greatly. After a memorial exhibit had been held of the paintings of Hartmann, Mussorgsky felt a burst of creative energy and completed his piano work, *Pictures at an Exhibition,* in as short a period of time as anything he ever composed.

Although Mussorgsky had been employed again by the government, this time as a clerk in the Forestry division, he was obliged to leave that office early in 1880 because of his increasing problem with alcoholism. Destitute, his friends came to his aid in providing lodging and food. By the following year his condition had become so bad he had to be moved to the Military Hospital after several attacks of alcoholic epilepsy. In his brief period there he was painted by the artist Repin, the picture by which most people know Mussorgsky — a picture frightening as it shows the man in the last stages of alcoholism. Ten days after the painting was completed Mussorgsky died.

BIBLIOGRAPHY

Calvocoressi, Michael. *Mussorgsky.* London: J. M. Dent and Sons, Ltd., 1946.
Leyda, Jay and Bertensson, ed. and trans. *The Mussorgsky Reader: A Life of Modeste Petrovich Mussorgsky in Letters and Documents.* New York: W. W. Norton, 1947.

BORIS GODUNOV

(An Opera in Four Acts)

MODEST MUSSORGSKY

The libretto of *Boris Godunov* was based largely on a play by Pushkin with certain deviations, changes, and additions made by Mussorgsky. He composed the music between October, 1868 and May of the following year, and had completed the scoring of it by

December, 1869. He submitted it to the Imperial Theater of St. Petersburg in the summer of 1870 and it was rejected. The composer spent two years making corrections, changes, and additions and then re-orchestrated it. The first production of it took place at the Marjinski Theater of St. Petersburg in January of 1874. It received limited praise from the public and a bad press. A vocal score of the work was published at that time.

The opera was little known even in Russia when in 1896 Rimsky-Korsakov reworked the score, changed some scenes and completely re-orchestrated it. It was in this latter version that it achieved a rousing success with the public, press, and musicians alike throughout both Russia and Europe.

When the "original" vocal score of 1874 was reprinted around 1925, several vital differences in the sequence of scenes in Act IV were in evidence. In the vocal score (1874) the scenes were in this order:

(1) the meeting of the Council of Boyars in the Kremlin and death of Boris

(2) the revolutionary scene in which the people protest against Boris

In Rimsky-Korsakov's revision of 1896 (the one most frequently performed nowadays) the scenes were in this sequence:

(a) the revolutionary scene in the forest

(2) the triumphal entry of Dimitri

(3) the lament of the village idiot

(4) the meeting of the Council of Boyars and death of Boris

Many felt the sequence of the "original" Mussorgsky version of 1874 was the better and historically more accurate. Some thought it was truer to the story since the Russian people were left on stage at the end and they were the real protagonists in it.

In 1928, however, the *true* original score was published from Mussorgsky's original manuscript copy. This edition had only two scenes in Act IV: (1) the square of the Cathedral of St. Basil in which the Russian people give vent to their grievances and the idiot laments; and, (2) the Council meeting and death of Boris. To further complicate matters, the Metropolitan Opera House decided in 1953 to lay aside the Rimsky-Korsakov version which it had produced for half a century and return to Mussorgsky's original. After the decision had been made, however, it was obvious that there were two originals and both in the composer's own hand, the 1874 version and the one published in 1928. The Metropolitan compromised, using largely the

The Czar's apartment as seen in the San Francisco Opera Company production of *Boris Godunov*

The Kromy Forest in the same production. The Kremlin can be seen in the distance through the trees.

1928 version, but moving the scene of the village idiot (which did not appear in the 1874 version) to the very end of the opera.

The foregoing is mentioned, not to confuse the reader which it well could, but to clarify why there are a number of different performances of the opera available on phonograph recordings in which the sequence of scenes varies. Also, on both recordings and in stage performances of the opera, cuts are frequently made because of its length. Most cuts are generally in the third act and scenes that take place in Poland. The following outline follows the Rimsky-Korsakov revision in which the opera is most frequently heard.

THE CHARACTERS

Boris Godunov, *Czar of all Russia*	bass
Xenia, *his daughter*	soprano
Feodor, *'his son*	mezzo-soprano
Prince Shuisky, *a boyar*	tenor
Marina, *daughter of a Polish nobleman*	mezzo-soprano
Gregory, *a novice, later the Pretender Dimitri*	tenor
Varlaam, *a vagabond monk*	bass
Pimen, *a monk and chronicler*	bass
The Village Idiot	tenor
The People of Russia	

The action takes place in Russia and Poland from 1598 to 1605.

Prologue

Scene 1: *The courtyard of the Monastery of Novodievich, near Moscow; February 20, 1598.*

The courtyard is filled with people largely there at the official command of the boyars, the old Russian nobility. The boyars want Boris Godunov to become the Czar of Russia, but he has been reluctant to accept the crown. While Boris is in the monastery meditating, the boyars encourage the people in the square to raise their voices in a plea to Boris to accept the throne.

Chorus

Why do you a- ban- don us, your peo-ple, oh fath-er?

Why do you abandon us, your people, O Father?
Unto whom do you leave your people, O Father?
If you desert us, poor orphans, we shall be helpless.
We entreat you to hear our cries and to heed our weeping.

Having finished their chorus, the people fall to gossiping, and then, being tired, they become silent. The boyars are in evidence again, whip in hand, commanding the people to kneel and raise their voices even louder so that Boris can hear them and heed their demand.

A boyar emerges from the monastery and bids the people to stand. "Your prayers are in vain, he will not yield," he announces. "Boris declines the kingdom. Oh, woe to our land, woe to all Russia!"

As the rays of the evening sun shine across the people in the courtyard, a group of Pilgrims are heard singing in the distance. As they approach the monastery, the people refer to them as "messengers of God." The curtain descends on this scene as they enter the monastery.

Scene 2: *The courtyard of the Kremlin; at the left and right are the Cathedrals of the Assumption and the Archangels. In the center, in back of the Cathedrals, is the Red Staircase which leads to the Terem or Czar's apartment. September 1, 1598.*

Boris has finally decided to accept the crown and this is the day of his coronation. A procession of boyars is seen entering the cathedral; Prince Shuisky announces from the steps, "Long life to you, Czar Boris Feodorovich!" As bells from both cathedrals toll, the assembled crowd in the square echoes the salutation.

Chorus

As the sun is to heav- en its high-est glor-y, glor-   y,

As the sun is to heaven its highest glory,
Sing the glory of Czar Boris in Russia!
Long life and glory, Czar, our Father!

Boris emerges from the cathedral and it is apparent that he is both happy and yet greatly troubled.

Boris

My soul is sad!   a-gainst my will strange trem- ors, and

e-vil pre- sen- ti- ments op-press my spir- it

My soul is sad!
Against my will strange tremors and evil presentments oppress my
    spirit.
O saint long dead, oh you my royal Father,
Thou see'st in Heaven Thy faithful servant's tears !
Look down on me and send a blessing from on high.
May I be true and merciful as Thou,
And justify my people's praise.

    As Boris leaves for the Terem, the people respond with cries of
"Glory, glory!"

ACT I

Scene 1: *A cell in the Monastery of the Miracle; 1603.*

    In a dark cell, illuminated only by candlelight, the old monk
Pimen has been chronicling the history of Russia. He has been writing
all night while the young novice, Gregory, has been asleep on his bed.
When Gregory finally awakens, Pimen tells him that he has about
finished his life work, the history of Russia. In a talkative mood,
Pimen further tells Gregory that he himself was in the same town
when Dimitri, the heir to the throne, was killed at nine years of age.
He saw the murderers and heard them confess that Boris Godunov had
instigated the plot.
    When Gregory questions him as to what age the Pretender Di-
mitri would have been had he lived, Pimen figures that he would be
about the same age as Gregory now is and would now have been
Czar of Russia instead of Boris Godunov.
    The bell sounds, summoning the monks to the morning mass. As
chanting is heard through the vaulted passageways, Pimen leaves for

the morning service. Gregory, alone now, shouts aloud: "Boris —
Boris — you will be called before your earthly judges, nor can you
flee the judgment of the Lord!"

Scene 2: *An Inn on the Lithuanian border.*

Gregory, who thinks he has been divinely chosen to expose Boris,
has escaped from the monastery, and, en route to Lithuania, pretends
to be the murdered heir Dimitri ready to raise an army and claim the
Russian throne. He stops with Varlaam and another monk at an inn
on the Lithuanian border. The monks, disguised as peasants, order
a round of drinks. All except Gregory keep drinking heavily, and
Varlaam lunges into a lusty song about the fighting at Kazan when
forty thousand Tartars were slain.

Varlaam

Long a- go   at Ka- zan where I was   fight- ing,

Czar I-   van sat a- feast-ing with his lead-ers.

Long ago at Kazan where I was fighting,
Czar Ivan sat afeasting with his leaders.
There the Tartar horde he harried.
Spared he not a man!
It was then that Russia knew good times.

While the men of grace continue to get drunker, Gregory draws
aside the proprietress and discovers that all roads to the Lithuanian
border are guarded because a monk has escaped from the monastery.
He does learn, however, that there is one footpath open.

Guards enter the Inn with a warrant for the arrest of Gregory,
but since they are illiterate, they hand the warrant to Gregory to read
aloud. As he reads the document, which assures death for the victim,
he omits the description of himself and in its place "reads" a descrip-

tion of the drunken monk Varlaam. Varlaam, alarmed, sobers himself enough to grab the document and read the true description. This
forces Gregory to produce his knife and forcefully escape through the
window.

ACT II

Scene 1: *The sumptuous apartment of the Czar in the Kremlin.*

Xenia is weeping over a picture of her dead sweetheart as the
family nurse tries to comfort and distract her by singing a tune in
folk-song vein about a gnat. Feodor is busy reading "The Book of
Great Plans" as his father, the Czar, enters the apartment. Boris
tells his son that some day he will be Czar of all Russia and will rule
all this land and all its people.

After the children leave, Boris appears troubled. Since he has
been Czar, famine and pestilence have spread across the face of
Russia. He recalls how he gets no rest at night because he blames
these evil things on himself.

Boris

I have at- tain'd the pow- er. Six years have

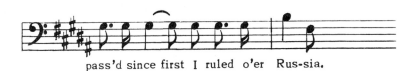

pass'd since first I ruled o'er Rus-sia.

I have attained the power,
Six years have passed since first I ruled o'er Russia,
But still no peace returns to my remorseful soul.
In vain the soothsayers promised
Long life and long reign, unmolested.

. . .

Impenetrable darkness enfolds me,
If only there were a ray of comforting light.

Prince Shuisky enters and tells Boris of a person in Lithuania
who claims to be the Pretender Dimitri and is raising an army, claim-

ing that he will capture the throne of Russia. Shuisky further relates that this "false" Dimitri has the support of both Poland and the Roman Pope.

Boris is shaken by the news and inquires of Shuisky if the real Dimitri was indeed murdered as he had arranged. After Shuisky tells him of the fatal scene in most sanguine and gory detail, Boris is forced to order the Prince from the room as he cannot stand the bloody description.

The clock strikes. Boris gasps for air. He is in a frenzy. His guilty conscience pictures the murdered Dimitri, his throat dripping blood. "I am guilty of your murder!" cries Boris. "Not I! Not I! It was the people's will!"

Boris

Ouf!   I suf- fo cate! Scarce can I draw my breath!

I suffocate! Scarce can I draw my breath!
I feel that all my blood has rushed into my brain;
It stays there and still throbs.
Oh conscience, remorseless, how sternly do you chastize me!

O Lord, have mercy upon me;
Yes, on me, the guilty Czar Boris.

ACT III

Scene 1: *The room of Marina in the Polish castle of Sandomir.*

After a chorus of maidens sings of the beauty of Marina, she sends them from the room. Bored with life in spite of her jewels and riches, she sings of a young man recently arrived from Moscow who hopes to wreak vengeance on Boris. She decides to use her wealth to raise an army for this Pretender, and then she sings, "I will stifle all his scruples with ardent kisses . . . Marina longs for glory, Marina craves power! On the royal throne of Moscow I could sit so proudly!"

Scene 2: *A garden with a fountain at its center in the castle of Sandomir. It is moonlight.*

Dimitri (Gregory uses this name exclusively now) enters the garden from the castle where a ball is in progress. He murmurs of his anticipated rendezvous, " 'Meet me tonight in the garden near the fountain.' With what fond rapture this voice fills my heart!"

A polonaise is heard as a crowd of guests come out of the ballroom.

Violins

As Dimitri finds Marina he pours out his heart to her, but she gives him to understand that she cannot return his love until he is of more noble rank, until he is the Czar of Russia.

ACT IV

Scene 1: *The woods with the town walls of Kromy in the distance.*

A crowd of vagabonds are seen dragging a boyar bound hand and foot. After gagging him, they set him upon a fallen tree trunk, make fun of him, and insult him because he has upheld the reign of Boris. The village idiot stumbles into the scene. A pitiful figure, clothed in rags, he sits on a rock and sings a meaningless song.

The crowd voices their hope that the fate of Russia will be better with the coming of the liberator Dimitri. "Death to Boris! Death to the murderer!" they shout.

Martial music heralds the approach of Dimitri's troops followed by Dimitri himself on horseback. The crowd hails him as the rightful Czar and follows him as he heads toward his ultimate goal, the Kremlin. Only the village idiot remains. The simpleton muses:

The Idiot

Flow, ah, flow, my bitter tears!
Weep, lament, all you true believers!
Soon the foe will come, all the world grow dark,
Dark as blackest night ne'er a star shines through.
Woe and sorrow always!
Let the tears flow, poor, starving Russia!

Scene 2: *The Council Chambers of the Boyars in the Kremlin; April 13, 1605.*

The boyars are in the process of issuing a proclamation denouncing the false Dimitri and threatening death to all who support him, when Shuisky arrives. The Prince relates to the Council how he had recently seen Boris in a bad state, trembling, and having hallucinations. His story is interrupted by the entrance of Boris himself who is again in a trance and cries out: "I am no murderer!"

Regaining control of himself, Boris mounts the throne and tells the boyars that he requested this meeting so they could advise him on the difficult times through which Russia was passing. Shuisky interrupts Boris and brings in Pimen who has a story he wishes to tell the Czar. Pimen relates how an old shepherd, blind from childhood, had heard a voice bidding him to pray at the tomb of the murdered Dimitri who was now a saint in heaven. The old shepherd had done just that and his sight had been restored!

Boris shrieks: "Help! Light! Air!" Tortured beyond comprehension, he collapses into the arms of the boyars. He begs them to leave him alone and to send him his son and the vestments of the church, for it was the custom of the Czars to prepare for death by being received into a holy order of the church.

As Feodor enters, Boris addresses him.

Boris

Fare-well my son!   I   am   dy-ing.

'Tis you will reign when I am gone.

Farewell, my son! I am dying.
'Tis you will reign when I am gone.
Inquire not how your father came to the Russian throne,
For it does not concern you.
You are the true and lawful Czar.

After he has counselled the boy how to rule wisely and justly,
Boris embraces and kisses his son. The sound of bells and of chanting
choristers is heard. Boris cries:

(Boris)   It is the funeral knell!
(Chorus)

Chorus

All ye peo-ple weep, la-ment!   For he

breathes no more!   Wrap him in   monk's at- tire

Weep, weep, people,
For he breathes no more.
(Boris)   The funeral dirge!
(Chorus)   Wrap him in monk's attire
And bear the Czar away.
Forever his lips are sealed
And no answer may he give.
Weep. Alleluia!

            .   .   .

(Boris)   While I have breath I am still Czar!
I AM STILL CZAR!!
God! Death! Forgive me!
Here! (*pointing to Feodor*) Here is your Czar ...
Forgive me. Forgive me.
(Boyars)   (*in a whisper*) He is dead!

MODEST MUSSORGSKY

George London as Czar Boris Godunov

NICHOLAS RIMSKY-KORSAKOV

ALEXANDER BORODIN

ALEXANDER BORODIN

BORN: November 12, 1833; St. Petersburg, Russia.
DIED: February 27, 1887; St. Petersburg, Russia.

Alexander Borodin was a man of contrasts. A chemist by profession, he was exacting in his scientific research. A musician by inclination, he was genial, easy-going, and most unconcerned about unessentials. A sense of humor pervaded all his work, whether scientific or musical. This trait is characterized by his composition *Paraphrases*. One day his adopted daughter wanted him to sit down and play duets on the piano with her, but, she confessed, her knowledge of the piano was limited to the ability to play *Chopsticks* with one finger of each hand. The genial father sat at the keyboard with her and improvised a polka accompaniment to the only melody in her repertoire. When Borodin told Rimsky-Korsakov about this with enthusiasm, the latter decided to compose some variations of the tune also. Cui and Liadof were persuaded to join in the fun, and when the work was published it was brought to the attention of Franz Liszt. He was so fascinated by it that he wrote a prelude to the *Paraphrases* for its second edition.

Alexander Borodin was the illegitimate son of Prince Luke Ghedeanof, a sixty-one year old descendant of former Kings of the Caucasus, and Eudoxia Kleineke, a middle-class girl of twenty-four. As was the custom of the time, the child was christened for propriety's sake as the son of one of the Prince's serfs, Porphyri Borodin. The Prince died when Alexander was seven and he was raised by his mother, a woman of culture and intelligence. With tutoring, the boy was soon proficient in English, French, and German, and a little later, in Italian. The boy had keen interests in both music and the natural sciences.

Alexander's first musical experiences were in listening to band concerts. At nine he thought he had fallen in love with a grown woman and composed a polka dedicated to her. According to musical authorities, this composition is more striking for its originality than for its childishness. Because of the polka and the boy's interest, music lessons were quickly arranged. His teacher was the flutist in the military band; shortly Borodin was to receive piano lessons as well as those in flute. He became acquainted with another piano student, Michael Shchiglef, and together they discovered the music of Haydn, Beethoven, and Mendelssohn. They started learning without help to play, Shchiglef the violin and Borodin the cello, in order to play chamber music. The two boys attended many orchestra concerts also.

By the time Borodin was fourteen, both his interest in music and in science were well in evidence. He had composed a number of chamber works, and his room at home had been converted into a laboratory in which he experimented with chemicals, making his own fireworks. Other hobbies included modelling and painting. He made his own pigments for the latter.

At seventeen Alexander Borodin entered the Academy of Medicine and Surgery where he specialized in botany and chemistry, eventually limiting his studies to chemistry only. While in attendance at the Academy, he studied the art of the fugue at home and played in a string quartet. The quartet met some seven miles from his home and he trudged on foot carrying his cello with him to the rehearsals in fair weather and foul because he could not afford cab fare. During these days he composed more chamber works and a few songs.

After completing his training at the Academy, he was appointed an assistant to the Professor of Pathology and Therapeutics and traveled to Belgium to deliver in public his thesis: "The Analogies Between Arsenious Acid and Phosphorous Acid." He received his doctorate of medicine degree shortly after this, having served as a house physician in a hospital that treated serfs. The dressing of wounds displeased him so much that once graduated he restricted himself to laboratory work.

His journeys for scientific research took him to Heidelberg for a winter, thence to Italy and Switzerland for a summer, then back to Heidelberg via Paris. During his stay in the German city, he heard many concerts and met the young lady who was later to become his wife, Catherine Protopopova. She was a fine pianist and through her Borodin became acquainted for the first time with the piano works of Chopin and Schumann. Together they traveled to Mannheim to hear some of the operas of Richard Wagner. While in Heidelberg, he completed eight papers on chemistry and composed more chamber music, none of which is published.

On his return to St. Petersburg, Borodin met Balakirev and became his pupil. Balakirev said of Borodin:

> Until [this time] he regarded himself as a mere amateur, and ascribed no importance to the impulse that drove him towards musical composition. I believe I was the first to tell him that composition was his real business. He

eagerly started work on his symphony in E-flat major. Every bar of it was criticised and overhauled by me — which may have contributed to develop his critical sense, and finally determined his musical tastes and sympathies.

Borodin was appointed an Assistant Professor of Organic Chemistry at the Academy and shortly afterward married Catherine Protopopova. His musical interests continued and he soon became acquainted with Rimsky-Korsakov who had just returned from a long naval voyage. Borodin's debut as a composer came at a concert in 1869 of the Russian Music Society at which Balakirev conducted his *Symphony No. 1*. The same year the composer started on an opera to be called *Prince Igor*, but he put it aside to work on his second symphony. Rimsky-Korsakov tried to encourage Borodin to complete the opera, but the latter was busy with activities at the Academy and his home was occupied almost every day by ladies soliciting funds and endorsements for charity drives. All spare space in his home was devoted to providing living quarters for relatives that could not afford a boarding house (space, that is, not occupied by the countless stray cats his wife was in the habit of acquiring and providing a home for). There were days he couldn't even play the piano for fear of disturbing someone's sleep or rest. Students were always calling at his home for advice and help.

The year 1880 was an important one for Borodin. During this year he completed his musical sketch *In the Steppes of Central Asia*, and his *Symphony No. 2* was premiered in Moscow. The symphony received a warm welcome by the public but did not receive a favorable response from the press. In Baden-Baden his *Symphony No. 1* was performed with great success and his reputation outside Russia was becoming established. He continued to work on sketches for the opera *Prince Igor*, but again he put it aside, this time to compose his *Quartet No. 2*, which he dedicated to his wife.

A bout with cholera four years later made him push work on the opera aside, and Rimsky-Korsakov volunteered to finish it. "Borodin, strange to say," stated Rimsky-Korsakov in his *Memoirs*, "was not annoyed, but delighted."

Early in 1887 Borodin's wife had to go to Moscow because of her health. One day while she was gone, Borodin worked intensively on his third symphony, but put it aside as evening approached so that he could attend a dance given by the professors of the Academy which he was expected to attend. At the dance Borodin suddenly collapsed and died immediately from a burst of aneurysm without even uttering a sigh. His body was buried at the Alexander Nevsky cemetery close to Mussorgsky's burial spot. Borodin's wife survived him by only a few months.

BIBLIOGRAPHY

Abraham, Gerald. *Borodin the Composer and His Music.* London: William Reeves, Ltd., 1927.

QUARTET NO. 2

ALEXANDER BORODIN

SECOND MOVEMENT: Scherzo. *Allegro.*
The first scherzo theme is played immediately by the first violin:

Example 1

A tempo change to *Meno mosso* occurs as the second theme, a very lyrical one, is introduced:

Example 2

The first section of the scherzo closes with a codetta based on Example 1.
The middle section does not introduce any new thematic material.

It is based entirely on Examples 1 and 2; first the melody of Example
1 is varied, then the opening pattern of Example 2 is inverted.

Example 1 appears in the first violin while a variation of Example
2 appears in the viola.

The first section of the scherzo returns.

The *coda* is based on Example 1.

THIRD MOVEMENT: Notturno *Andante*.

The first theme of the nocturne, a lyrical theme, is introduced
by the cello:

Example 3

Example 3 is repeated by the cello, then twice by the first violin.

The tempo changes to *Più mosso* as a faster, more rhythmical
theme is heard.

Example 4

Examples 3 and 4 are heard alternately.

Example 3 is then heard four times in a canonic passage: twice the cello in its upper register starts the melody and is imitated an octave higher by the first violin one beat later; twice the melody begins in the first violin and is repeated an octave lower by the second violin.

Fragments of both themes, Examples 3 and 4, are then heard, "dying away" at the end.

NICHOLAS RIMSKY-KORSAKOV

BORN: March 18, 1844; Tikhvin, Russia.

DIED: June 21, 1908; Lyubensk, Russia.

There were three influences or inspirations that remained dominant throughout the career of Rimsky-Korsakov: folk songs, the Orient, and the sea. His early life as a sailor and his love for the sea are reflected in both his opera *Sadko* (a wandering minstrel who becomes acquainted with the Princess of the Sea) and the symphonic suite *Scheherazade*. Rimsky-Korsakov's fascination with things Oriental is represented musically by his *Symphony No. 1 (Antar)* which he later referred to as his "Oriental suite." His interest in folk songs led him to the monumental task of assembling, editing, and harmonizing native Rusisan tunes for the collection called *One Hundred Russian Folk Songs*.

In his autobiography, *Chronicle of My Musical Life*, Rimsky-Korsakov described his early years:

From early childhood I manifested musical abilities. We had an old piano; my father played by ear rather decently, though with no particular fluency. His repertory included a number of melodies from the operas of his time . . . Rossini and Mozart . . . My father sang frequently, playing his own accompaniments.

The first indications of musical talent appeared in me at a very early age. I was not fully two years old when I clearly distinguished all the tunes my mother sang to me. Later, when three or four years of age, I beat a toy drum in perfect time, while my father played the piano. Often my father would suddenly change tempo and rhythm on purpose, and I at once followed suit. Soon afterward I began to sing correctly whatever my father played . . . I could, from an adjoining room, recognize and name any note of the piano. When I was six, or thereabouts, they began to give me piano lessons . . .

It cannot be said that I was fond of music at that time: I endured it and took barely sufficient pains with my studies . . . I was eleven years old when I conceived the idea of composing a duet for voices with a piano accompaniment . . . I succeeded [and] I recall that it was sufficiently coherent . . .

I was not studying music with any particular diligence, and was fascinated by the thought of becoming a seaman.

Coming from an aristocratic family, Rimsky-Korsakov was limited to two professions that he could follow, of which a Naval career was one. As he himself stated, he was fascinated by the sea, and it was in the best family tradition for he had a great-grandfather and an uncle who were Admirals, and his older brother had already entered the Navy. At twelve years of age he was enrolled by his parents in the Naval College at St. Petersburg.

Rimsky-Korsakov remained there for six years. On Sundays and holidays he found time to take both cello and piano lessons, and it was during his early days at the College that he heard his first opera and attended his first symphony concert. Having become acquainted with the music of Glinka through his piano studies back in Tikhvin, the appearance of some of Glinka's orchestral music on the programs in St. Petersburg renewed his interest in the music of this Russian composer. Rimsky-Korsakov was soon spending all his pocket money purchasing scores of Glinka's works.

The year before Rimsky-Korsakov graduated from the Naval College, he met Balakirev who was then twenty-four and the center of a group of *nationally* inspired composers who included Cui, Borodin, and Mussorgsky. Rimsky-Korsakov was just beginning to get seriously interested in music through conversations and meetings with this young group, when he graduated. The Navy assigned him to the ship *Almaz* which was scheduled for a three-year voyage around the world. He took leave of his friends and sailed from Russia. Aboard the ship he started work on his *Symphony No. 1*, a work that proved difficult for him, for he had had no theoretical training. Section by section he sent the work back to Balakirev for criticism and corrections. When the voyage was over, he returned to St. Petersburg and learned that a performance of the symphony had been scheduled by Balakirev and was to be conducted by the latter at the Free School of Music. It was well received by the public. The audience was surprised to see a young naval officer in uniform take the "composer's bow" at the end of the performance.

Rimsky-Korsakov remained in St. Petersburg where his naval duties became largely clerical. He renewed his musical acquaintances. The circle of Russian nationalists (Balakirev, Cui, Borodin, and Mussorgsky, along with Rimsky-Korsakov, soon to be known as "The Mighty Five") encouraged each other in the use of Russian folk lore, folk songs, Russian history, and above all, dramatic truth. The operas *Sadko* and *The Maid of Pskov* stem from this period.

In 1871 Rimsky-Korsakov was appointed Professor of Composition and Instrumentation at the St. Petersburg Conservatory of Music. Nobody was more aware of his shortcomings for this position than the composer himself. He had never studied theory and was completely unacquainted with the names of chords, counterpoint, or form. Once he assumed the professorship, however, he studied furiously to learn the fundamentals so that he could adequately teach others. Two years after assuming this position, he resigned from the Navy and was thereupon appointed Inspector of Naval Bands, a post he occupied until it was abolished eleven years later. Many think that Rimsky-Korsakov's success in orchestration stems from his many visits to the bands and his careful scrutiny of the ranges and timbres of the various instruments.

Rimsky-Korsakov became attracted to a fine young pianist, Nadezhda Puregold, and in 1873 they were married. Shortly after their marriage, he succeeded Balakirev as Director and Conductor of the Free School Concerts, serving in that post until 1881. Five years later Rimsky-Korsakov was appointed the conductor of the Russian Symphony Concerts, a post he occupied until 1900. His *Capriccio Espagnol* and the *Russian Easter Overture* were composed during his tenure with the Russian Symphony Orchestra.

Mussorgsky's early death in 1881, and Borodin's in 1887, left Rimsky-Korsakov with additional burdens. At the time of his death, Mussorgsky's last opera, *Khovantchina,* was incomplete and he had not had time to finish his reworking of his earlier opera, *Boris Godunov.* Rimsky-Korsakov assumed the task of completing *Khovantchina* and completely orchestrated the entire opera. He also completed *Boris* from sketches left by Mussorgsky and re-orchestrated it, although Mussorgsky had left nothing to indicate he wanted the work rescored. In Borodin's case, the opera, *Prince Igor,* was in even worse shape. Borodin had worked on it for over a decade — some parts were complete, some parts half-finished, and there were gaps where he had written nothing to accompany the libretto. Once again the faithful Rimsky-Korsakov took up the work of one of his colleagues and completed it.

In March, 1905, a letter of Rimsky-Korsakov's was published in the newspaper in which he advocated autonomy for the St. Petersburg Conservatory so that it would not be under the dictatorial powers of the Imperial Russian Music Society. This was so displeasing to the Society, that he was immediately dismissed. Respected music professors Glazunov and Liadov resigned in protest. By autumn of that year, the atmosphere had cleared, and with some concessions to the St. Petersburg school, Glazunov was appointed director. He immediately reinstated Rimsky-Korsakov in his position at the Conservatory. Pupils of Rimsky-Korsakov during his long tenure at the Conservatory included: Liadov, Ippolitov-Ivanov, Gretchaninov, Glazunov, Stravinsky, and the Italian, Respighi.

In 1907 Rimsky-Korsakov went to Paris to conduct many of his own works at a festival of Russian music. This was his last public appearance. In April of the following year, he suffered a heart attack. Although the attack was not immediately fatal, it prevented his attending the marriage of his daughter two months later. He died four days after the wedding.

BIBLIOGRAPHY

Calvocoressi, Michel D. and Gerald Abraham. *Masters of Russian Music.* New York: Alfred Knopf and Co., 1936.

Rimsky-Korsakov, Nicholas. *My Musical Life,* trans. J. A. Joffe. New York: Alfred Knopf and Co., 1942.

SCHEHERAZADE
Symphonic Suite

Nicholas Rimsky-Korsakov

Speaking of the titles of the four movements, the composer states in his autobiography:

In composing *Scheherazade* I meant these hints to direct but slightly the hearer's fancy on the path which my own fancy had traveled, and to leave more minute and particular conceptions to the will and mood of each listener. All I had desired was that the hearer, if he liked my piece as symphonic music, should carry away the impression that it is beyond doubt an Oriental narrative of some numerous and varied fairy-tale wonders, and not merely four pieces played one after another . . . This name [*Scheherazade*] and the subtitle. *After the Thousand and One Nights,* connote in everybody's mind the East and fairy-tale wonders.

The score published during Rimsky-Korsakov's lifetime has on its cover a general story of the incidents that inspired the music:

The Sultan Schahriar, convinced of the duplicity and infidelity of all women, vowed to slay each of his wives after the first night. The Sultana Scheherazade, however, saved her life by the expedient of recounting to the Sultan a succession of tales over a period of a thousand and one nights. Overcome by curiosity, the monarch postponed from day to day the execution of his wife, and ended by renouncing altogether his blood-thirsty resolution.

The titles of the movements are the ones the composer specified.

THE SEA AND SINBAD'S SHIP

Two themes are introduced immediately; the first, played by the trombones, tuba, strings, and low woodwinds, is associated with the Sultan:

Example 1 (Sultan)

The second theme, played by the solo violin, is associated with Scheherazade:

Example 2 (Scheherazade)

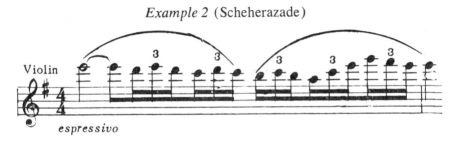

A rhythmic variation of Example 1, suggestive of the rolling sea, is introduced by the violins (Example 3), and later repeated in a more sonorous orchestration.

Example 3

A new theme, a series of chords, appears in the woodwinds and is repeated without pause an octave higher:

Example 4

Clarinets, Bassoon

The French horn plays Figure A of Example 1 and is answered by the flute with Example 5:

Example 5

Flute   8^{ve}

Figure A of Example 1, followed by Example 5, is repeated twice:

> Example 1, Figure A: French horn; Example 5: oboe
> Example 1, Figure A: French horn; Example 5: clarinet

The Scheherazade theme, Example 2, returns in the solo violin.

The *exposition* of themes in this movement ends with a modification of the Sultan theme, Example 1.

A *recapitulation* of thematic material already presented is made.

> Example 3
> Example 4
> Celli with Figure A, Example 1, answered successively by:
>   clarinet, oboe, then flute with Example 5
> Example 2, Scheherazade theme, played by the solo violin
> Example 3 developed by the winds

In the *coda,* the Sultan's theme, Example 1, is played successively by flute, oboe, then violins with rich harmonic support from the French horns.

The *coda* ends with variations of Example 4.

STORY OF THE KALENDAR PRINCE

(A Kalendar was one of an order of poor, begging Mohammedan religious persons who carried on unusual observances of their religious rites such as dancing, shouting, whirling, or howling. They were also fakirs, and it is probably to this type that Rimsky-Korsakov has reference.)

The solo violin with the Scheherazade theme, Example 2, introduces the movement.

The principal theme of this movement is announced by the bassoon with harp and muted string accompaniment:

Example 6

dolce ed espressivo

The oboe plays Example 6 accompanied principally by the harp.

The violins take up Example 6, followed by the woodwinds with a rhythmic variation of it.

This first section of the movement ends with an oboe statement of Example 6 and elaborations on it.

Suddenly the trombone sounds a fanfare-type theme, echoed by muted trumpet:

Example 7

con forza

An elaborate series of variations on the fanfare theme, Example 7, follows.

The clarinet interrupts wtih a variation of Example 2, the Scheherazade theme:

Example 8

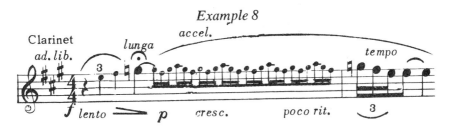

The fanfare motive, Example 7, is further developed and varied, ending in a march-like variation.

A bassoon states Example 8.

This movement ends as Example 6 reappears, in an extended section, followed by the Sultan's theme, Example 1.

THE YOUNG PRINCE AND THE YOUNG PRINCESS

A lyrical theme, associated with the Prince, is introduced by the violins:

Example 9 (Prince)

After two clarinets play a scale-like figure up and down the span of two octaves, the oboe and violins play the theme of the Prince, Example 9.

The flutes play the scale-like figure, followed by fragments of Example 9 in the second violins (the firsts take over the scale-like figure), clarinets, English horn, and oboe.

The tambourine establishes a dance rhythm; the clarinet introduces the melody associated with the Princess.

Example 10 (Princess)

A development of both Example 9 and 10 follows; the movement ends with the theme of the Princess, Example 10.

FESTIVAL AT BAGHDAD; THE SEA; THE SHIP GOES TO PIECES ON A ROCK SURMOUNTED BY A BRONZE WARRIOR; CONCLUSION

The strings and woodwinds play the Sultan theme, Example 1, *fortissimo.*

Scheherazade's theme, Example 2, is played by the solo violin.

Example 1 is heard again in an extended section, followed by Example 2.

A festive theme appears in the flutes:

Example 11

Flutes

Another festive theme is introduced, this one by the violins:

Example 12

Violins

un poco pesante

Themes from the second and third movements are heard.

A development of Example 11 takes place, followed by themes from other movements.

A variation of the Sultan theme (Example 1) is played by the trombones:

Example 13

Trombones

The theme of Scheherazade, Example 2, returns.

The Sultan's theme, Example 1, is heard as the movement ends quietly.

BEDŘICH SMETANA

BORN: March 2, 1824; Litomyšl, Bohemia.
DIED: May 12, 1884; Prague, Czechoslovakia.

When at age sixteen Smetana started to keep a diary, he said of his childhood days:

> I, Bedřich Smetana, born in Litomyšl on Tuesday, March 2nd, 1824, at ten o'clock in the morning, am the son of František Smetana, a master brewer, and of Barbora Smetana, née Lynek. I was not yet four when my father taught me how to keep time to music. At the age of five I started school, and I was taught the piano and violin as well. I was seven when I gave a performance of the Overture to "La Muette" [an opera by Auber] at an academy in Litomyšl.

This early manifestation of talent was hindered in its systematic development by his father's strong opposition to music as a profession. Although the boy frequently played quartets at home, the boy playing first violin and the father second, this was regarded by the older Smetana as only a diversion. Fortunately a friend of his school days, Katharina Kolař, introduced him to her piano teacher at the Conservatory in Prague and Smetana studied both piano and theory with the professor. The Director of the Conservatory procured a position for Smetana as a music teacher for the family of Count Thun. After four years, Smetana gave up this position and undertook a concert tour which resulted in a disastrous financial failure.

The nationalistic feeling of the Bohemian people reached fever pitch and resulted in the revolution of 1848 in which Smetana took part. The revolution was short lived, and after its failure Smetana needed to find an adequate source of income. He applied for a permit to open a piano school, and with funds supplied in a large measure by Franz Liszt, the project was a success. A year later Smetana married his friend of school days, Katharina Kolař, who had also become a fine pianist.

Smetana was not happy with his life in Prague and in October of 1856 moved to Göteborg, Sweden. There he served as both a teacher and as conductor of the Philharmonic Society Orchestra. Early presentations included Haydn's *Creation*, Mendelssohn's *Elijah*, and Mozart's *Requiem*. In addition to the private lessons and his duties as conductor, Smetana also gave piano and chamber music recitals. From these varied activities he fared well financially. Un-

BEDŘICH SMETANA

ANTONÍN DVOŘÁK

EDVARD GRIEG

ZOLTÁN KODÁLY

fortunately the climate did not agree with his wife's health, so he made plans to return to Prague. His wife died in Dresden as they were en route home.

On this sad journey, he detoured via Weimar in order to visit Franz Liszt. Smetana, who had already composed three symphonic poems, was anxious to discuss Liszt's ideas concerning this new form.

Smetana spent only a year in Prague, marrying Bettina Fernandi just before his return to Sweden. Although he conducted many successful concerts in both Göteborg and Stockholm, his second wife enjoyed the northern climate no more than the first. When, in 1860, Bohemia was granted its independence, the Smetanas returned home.

The nationalistic spirit was at its highest pitch. Smetana once again opened his piano school and later worked with the National Theater whose avowed purpose was to produce only Bohemian operas. The success of his first opera, *The Brandenburgers in Bohemia,* which had a weak libretto, was eclipsed by the success of his second opera, *The Bartered Bride.*

The National Theater soon appointed Smetana as its conductor. During his years in this capacity he continued to compose operas based on Bohemian stories: *Dalibor* (Dalibor was a legendary liberation hero of the Czech people) in 1867; *Libuše* (Libuše was the foundress of Prague) in 1872; and his comic opera *Dvě Vdoy* (The Two Widows).

Frequent headaches were an omen of total deafness which overtook Smetana in 1874. Forced by this malady to resign his position as conductor, he was granted a small pension which was not large enough to pay his family's living expenses. Friends from his Göteborg days raised enough money to pay for the services of an ear specialist who, after prolonged examination, pronounced the case incurable.

Despite this physical condition, Smetana continued to compose. His string quartet, *From My Life,* appeared, followed by the operas *Hubicka* (The Kiss) and *Tajemstvi* (The Secret). The deaf composer then turned to the composition of his best known work, *Má Vlast* (My Country), an orchestral composition of six parts of which *Vlatava* (The Moldau) is the second. Some Czechoslovakian dances were also written at this time.

The deafness was a prelude to hallucinations which he later experienced. He was encouraged by friends to enter a Prague asylum where he died two months later.

BIBLIOGRAPHY

Bartos, Frantisek. *Bedrich Smetana: Letters and Reminiscences,* trans. D. Rusbridge. Czechoslovakia: Artia, 1955.

Nejedly, Zdenek. *Frederick Smetana.* London: Geoffrey Bles, 1924.

THE MOLDAU

Bedřich Smetana

The Moldau is the second of a group of six symphonic poems by Smetana called *Má Vlast* (My Fatherland). They are dedicated to the City of Prague, and they tell not only of the composer's love of nature, but also of the strong patriotism and deep love for his country which are evident in practically all the music he wrote.

The composer includes the following programmatic notes in the score:

Two springs pour forth their streams in the shade of the Bohemian forest, the one warm and gushing, the other cold and more quiet. Their waves, joyfully flowing over their rocky beds, unite and sparkle in the morning sun. The forest brook, rushing on, becomes the river Moldau, which, with its waters speeding through Bohemia's valleys, grows into a mighty stream. It flows through dense woods from which come the joyous sounds of the chase, and the notes of the hunter's horn are heard always nearer and nearer.

It flows through green meadows and lowlands where a wedding feast is being celebrated with song and dancing. At night, in its shining waves, wood and water nymphs hold their revels, and in these waves are reflected many a fortress and castle — witnesses of bygone splendor, of chivalry and the vanished martial fame of days that are no more. At the Rapids of St. John the stream speeds on, winding its way through cataracts and hewing the path for its foaming waters through the rocky chasm into the broad river bed, in which it flows on in majestic calm toward Prague, welcomed by time-honored Vyšehrad, to disappear in the far distance from the poet's gaze.

The Moldau, although one continuous movement, has six sections designated by the composer. They are:

1. The source of the Moldau
2. The forest hunt
3. The rustic wedding
4. Moonlight; Dance of the Nymphs
5. The St. John rapids
6. The Moldau flows along its broad river bed; the Vyšehrad castle

THE SOURCE OF THE MOLDAU

The composition begins with a rippling figure in the flute, the phrases of which become longer as the music proceeds. The capricious character of the rhythm, the melody, and the instrumentation aptly suggest the first spring "warm and gushing":

Example 1

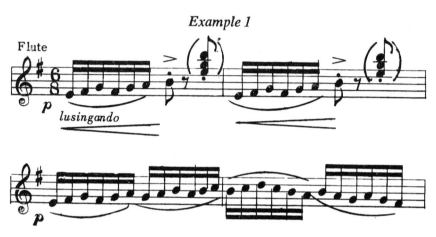

The flute is joined by the clarinet which plays a second melody, which at first moves in contrary motion to Example 1 (see Example 2). It uses a sequential motive of three notes moving downward, and can be associated with the second spring. Eventually the melody of the flute and the clarinet move in parallel thirds, suggesting the joining of the two springs:

Example 2

The broad, lyrical melody of the river emerges, played by violins, oboes, and bassoons:

Example 3

It is repeated once in the minor mode, then moves to its tonic major.

THE FOREST HUNT

Hunting calls are sounded by the horns, at first remote, but soon approaching in a steady crescendo while the music grows more spirited:

Example 4

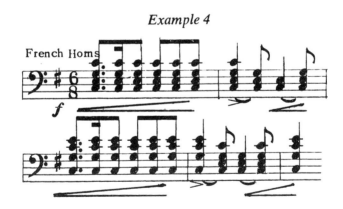

The sound of the hunters' horns diminishes in volume and finally disappears.

THE RUSTIC WEDDING

A rustic folk dance is now heard, a polka (a dance which originated in Bohemia). The dance is part of the peasant wedding festivities in the meadows along the river bank:

Example 5

The polka swells to a fortissimo, and then dies away.

MOONLIGHT; DANCE OF THE NYMPHS
The high strings suggest moonlight on the water:

Example 6

Horns, trombones, and tuba intone stately chords, as from afar, in the rhythm of a march — perhaps suggesting the castles of "bygone splendor, of chivalry, and the vanished martial fame."

Example 7

The melody of the Moldau (Example 3) returns in an extended passage in which strings and woodwinds are prominent.

THE ST. JOHN RAPIDS
Upward swirling figures in the upper strings are heard; Figure A (of Example 3, The Moldau theme) is heard in the low strings and woodwinds. The music and the river become violent with varied rhythmic patterns.

THE MOLDAU FLOWS ALONG ITS BROAD RIVER BED

The theme of the river (Example 3) returns in the triumphant major mode, having successfully passed the rapids. The harmonies increase in breadth and volume.

THE VYŠEHRAD CASTLE

A noble choral in the brass and woodwinds, designated by the composer as the "Vyšehrad" motive, is heard:

Example 8

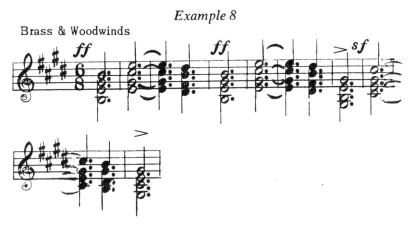

The climax passes. The music fades into soft, rippling arpeggios played by the strings as the river flows on in the distance, "beyond the poet's vision."

ZOLTÁN KODÁLY

born: December 16, 1882; Kecskemet, Hungary
died: March 6, 1967; Budapest, Hungary

During the years just before and after his graduation from college, Zoltán Kodály spent many months traveling the length and breadth of Hungary trying to unearth the true folk-music of that country. It became evident to him that Hungarian music had not only been influenced by the Magyars or Gypsies, but that most of the folk-song collections that had been made were really of Gypsy melodies and not the true Hungarian songs. He discovered that composers such as Brahms, in his *Hungarian Dances,* and Liszt, in his *Hungarian Rhapsodies,* had been fooled by these Gypsy melodies they had thought to be Hungarian. From village to village Kodály traveled, transcribing some of the melodies he heard on manuscript paper; others he recorded with a phonograph. These collections numbered between 3,000 and 4,000 separate authentic Hungarian folk songs.

During the years after his graduation from the University, he worked with fellow Hungarian Béla Bartók on this project. Bartók in later years went on to compose in the new musical idiom of the twentieth century, but Kodály adopted the post-romantic style and incorporated these bits of folk-lore background into his compositions. Of Kodály's music, his colleague Bartók said:

> Kodály's music . . . is not "modern" in the current sense of the word. It has nothing in common with atonal, bitonal, polytonal tendencies . . . yet his musical language is entirely new and expresses musical ideas never heard before.

Kodály's father was the stationmaster in the little Hungarian town in which he was born, and it was there that Kodály spent most of his first eighteen years. Like most rural villages, it did not have a stimulating musical life. Although his father was an amateur violinist and played string quartets, from which Zoltán learned the music of Haydn, the boy's early musical experiences were largely dependent on the performances of a Gypsy orchestra. Zoltán did learn the violin in his childhood and began some childish compositions at an early age.

While enrolled in high school Kodály sang in the choir, an experience which led him to compose a *Mass* and several *Ave Marias*. By the time he was fifteen the high school orchestra performed one of his compositions, a concert-overture. He also composed some chamber music which included a *Trio* for two violins and a viola.

At the turn of the century Kodály entered the University of Budapest to study science, enrolling simultaneously at the Conservatory. At the Conservatory he was first influenced by the music of Brahms and Debussy. He met Béla Bartók there and the two of them had many interesting musical discussions. These led, in 1905, to the travels of the two throughout Hungary already described. They discovered that the true Hungarian folk melodies were buried under an overlay of Gypsy melodies and influences. With this material Kodály prepared his doctoral dissertation entitled *Strophic Construction in Hungarian Folk Songs*.

After graduation he was appointed a professor at the Conservatory, and thirteen years later became its director. During his first year there he visited Paris and Berlin to broaden his musical horizon, and the following year completed sixteen songs on Hungarian folk texts. These waited fourteen years for publication as his Opus 1.

Around 1910 he became known in Budapest musical circles as a composer when some of his chamber music was listed on programs. Ten years later his international reputation developed and shortly thereafter his works appeared on the program at the Salzburg festival.

In 1923 Budapest celebrated the fiftieth anniversary of the union of the two cities, Buda and Pest. On a commission Kodály composed his *Psalmus Hungaricus,* based on a sixteenth century Hungarian text, for this celebration. So successful was this work that it was soon translated into eight different languages.

In 1926 he completed his first opera and had it produced at the Budapest Opera. *Háry János,* based on a folk legend, was almost a *singspiel* rather than a grand opera. A suite was made from the opera and first presented the following year in the United States by William Mengelberg and the New York Philharmonic Society Orchestra. His second opera, *The Spinning Room,* was even more of a folk opera than the first, as it had no continuous story. It formed a setting in which a variety of peasant choruses, arias, and dances could be performed.

Kodály's *Dances of Galanta* was written the following year. Of his many great choral works, the *Te Deum* was written in 1935.

During World War II the Nazis occupied Hungary and begged Kodály to divorce his Jewish wife. Not only did Kodály refuse, but he helped the underground smuggle many Jewish people out of the sphere of Nazi activity. The Gestapo apprehended Kodály and under the threat of physical violence tried to force him to give information. Steadfastly refusing to divulge any secrets, the Nazis finally released him as they did not want repercussions from his thousands of admirers throughout Hungary.

At the end of the war he had left "only two suits and a half wrecked apartment in Budapest." With the rebirth of musical activity in Hungary his fortune was partially rehabilitated and he resumed his duties as director of the Budapest Conservatory. In the winter of 1946 he visited the United States for the first time to guest conduct some of his works.

Most of Kodály's compositions since the war have been choral settings of Hungarian folk tunes, including a number of them for children's choruses. In 1959 he married for the second time, and in 1960 was awarded an honorary Doctor of Music degree by Oxford University.

HÁRY JÁNOS SUITE

Háry János, a comic opera based on a folk legend, was first presented on October 16, 1926, at the Budapest Royal Opera House. Kodály later arranged some of the music from this opera into a suite, and in this form it was first presented in the United States a year after the opera's premiere. *Háry János* was not presented in this country as an opera until 1960 when it was mounted by the Opera Workshop of the Juilliard School of Music.

On the occasion of the New York premiere of the Suite, the composer supplied the following description:

The story tells the adventures of Háry János, a national hero of folklore. A peasant and an ex-soldier, with great powers of imagination, old Háry sits in the village inn day after day telling of the wonderful exploits of his youth. In typical peasant fashion, these glorious products of his fancy are presented in terms of extreme realism and naïveté. yielding a curious mixture of comedy and pathos. Yet Háry is not viewed as merely a Hungarian Münchhausen. The apparent swaggerer is at bottom the type of enthusiastic dreamer, a born fanatic and rhapsodist. His stories are not true but that is unimportant! They are expressions of the beauty of his fantasy which builds for himself and others an artistic and absorbing world of the imagination. We all dream of these impossible deeds of glory and grandeur, only we lack the naïve courage of Háry, and dare not reveal them. A deeper significance is given to the story by regarding Háry as symbolic of the Hungarian nation, whose strivings and ambitions can be fulfilled only in dreams.

PRELUDE: The Fairy Tale Begins.

According to a Hungarian superstition, if a statement is followed by a sneeze by one of the listeners, it is regarded as confirmation of the truth of the assertion. The *Háry Suite* begins with a sneeze of this kind. One of Háry's group of faithful listeners, who sneezes at the wildest assertions of the old tale spinner, is equal to the occasion even when Háry declares that he once had to subdue Napoleon himself! With a suggestion of this sneeze "the tale begins."

With quickly rising chromatic scales in the upper winds and strings, the orchestral sneeze is started; suddenly the piano plays a downward glissando, completing this imitation of a sneeze. The theme of the introductory movement is then heard a few measures later in the celli and violas:

"The Viennese Musical Clock" scene from *Háry János* in the Juilliard School of Music production. Although the orchestral suite is well known in the United States, the opera has been mounted only once.

"The Emperor and His Court" from *Háry János*

Example 1

Celli

Example 1 is played in turn by the strings and the bassoon, then the strings, clarinet and French horn.

A development of this thematic material follows.

The French horn appears with the theme against a shimmering effect of the strings. The woodwinds join in and build to a *fff* climax.

The movement closes with a soft, sustained chord in the horns over which the flute and oboe appear with Figure A.

SECOND MOVEMENT: Viennese Musical Clock.

The scene is laid in the imperial palace in Vienna, where the ingenious Hungarian peasant is amazed and enraptured by the famous Musical Clock with its little soldier figures in their brave uniforms appearing and disappearing at every rotation of the marvelous machinery.

Kodály writes most ingeniously for orchestra in this section. He uses a large number of percussion instruments to imitate the clock and its movement: bells, chimes, triangle, snare drums, Chinese gong, bass drum, celesta, and the piano (for glissandi). The stringed instruments are not heard at all, the melodic development being carried entirely by the woodwinds with the trumpet and French horns added for climaxes.

The movement opens with the bells and snare drum, accented by the Chinese gong. The melody appears in the fifth measure high in the piccolos, flutes, and oboes:

Example 2

Oboes

THIRD MOVEMENT: Song.

Háry and his sweetheart are longing for their village home, its quiet evenings, musical with love songs (an ancient Hungarian melody is used).

The use of an authentic folk melody plus the use of the *cimbalo ongaress* or *cimbalom* makes this a truely "nationalistic" bit of music. The folk melody is in a Hungarian mode resembling the medieval Æolian Mode (the white keys between A and a, the g being natural). The cimbalom is an instrument of Eastern derivation which has long been associated with both Hungary and the gypsies. It is a close relative of the dulcimer, consisting of a series of strings stretched across a sound-board and played with wooden mallets.

The movement opens with the viola playing the folk song unaccompanied:

Example 3

The clarinet appears above the metallic sound of the cimbalom.

The oboe plays the theme with a string accompaniment which is punctuated by the sound of the cimbalom.

Although there is a slight tempo change, the melody is repeated a third time (as in the strophic form of folk songs) played by the French horn.

The oboe reappears above the strings with the melody.

In a codetta the flute is accompanied by the cimbalom, and the movement ends as the clarinet is accompanied by the strings.

FOURTH MOVEMENT: The Battle and Defeat of Napoleon.

Háry, as general in command of his hussars, confronts the French army. He brandishes his sword, and lo! the French begin to fall before him like tin soldiers! First, two at a time, then four — eight — ten, and so on. Finally there are no more soldiers left, and Napoleon is forced to engage in person the invincible Háry. Háry's fantasy pictures a Napoleon made in the image of his own burly peasant imagination — an immensely tall and formidable Napoleon who, shaking in every limb, kneels before his conqueror and pleads for mercy. The ironical French Victory March is transformed into a dirge.

The march opens with an appropriate introduction by the snare and bass drums. Three trombones in unison sound the theme representing Háry and his awkward peasant soldiers:

Example 4

The trumpets join the trombones against the rhythm of the percussion section (Kodály uses no strings in this movement).

A sad motive of two notes is sounded by the alto saxophone and answered by a trumpet call.

The trumpet resumes the melody as the rhythmic pulsation becomes more predominant. At the climax of this section, a trumpet call halts the music.

Now the drums are heard with the trombones and tuba sounding forth the theme of Napoleon's forces:

Example 5

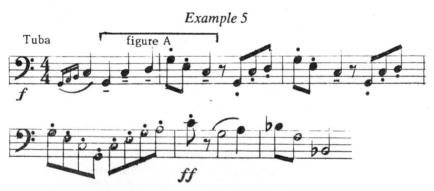

Notice that the theme representing the French forces quoted above has a hint of the Marseillaise in it by taking Figure A and repeating notes where necessary and altering the rhythm.

This "French" theme is answered by trumpets with the call to battle:

Example 6

Example 4 re-enters in the trombones and builds to a climax with a fluttering accompaniment by the piccolos and flutes, suggesting the French soldiers going down two by two, then four by four. As the music reaches the climax there is a pause, the tempo changes to that of a funeral march and the mournful tones of the alto saxophone sound a dirge, Example 7, based on Háry's theme, Example 4:

Example 7

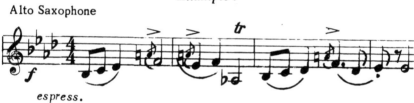

FIFTH MOVEMENT: Intermezzo.

Number five is an intermezzo without special significance.

This movement is a *czardas,* a wild Hungarian dance of fast rhythms almost always accompanied by the cimbalom. The first section opens with the melody in the strings and clarinet accompanied by fast passages for the cimbalom:

Example 8

A second theme is based on the first theme. The introductory measure is changed entirely, but notice that the melody that follows is in the same rhythm and melodically is almost an inversion of the first theme.

Example 9

The middle or trio section is based on a beautiful French horn solo in slow, lyrical style:

Example 10

This ternary movement comes to a close as the first section returns.

SIXTH MOVEMENT: Entrance of the Emperor and His Court.

An ironical march of triumph, in which Háry pictures the entrance of the emperor and the imperial court at Vienna: but it is not the Austrian nobility — only a Hungarian peasant's way of imagining the rich happiness of the celebrated Wiener Burg.

Again the drums establish the military rhythm of a march as the theme appears in the upper woodwinds and the xylophone.

Example 11

The horns follow this melody with a second one, derived from Example 11:

Example 12

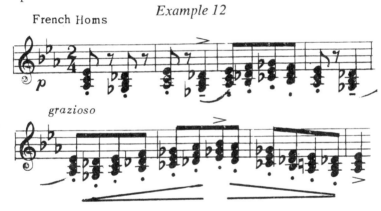

Example 12 is repeated, followed by Example 11.

A bridge theme is heard after the climax, a fanfare type theme in trumpets and trombones.

Example 13

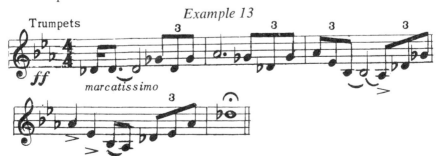

Immediately after the fanfare, the final theme is introduced in the shrill notes of the piccolo:

Example 14

Piccolos 8^{ve}

f

cresc.

A small development of this final theme builds up to a climax that ends the movement.

ANTONÍN DVOŘÁK

BORN: September 8, 1841; Nelahozeves, Czechoslovakia.
DIED: May 1, 1904; Prague, Czechoslovakia.

Dvořák, imbued with the spirit of Czech nationalism, tried during his three years in the United States to develop a national school of music. His ideas met with little success although he provided an example in his *Symphony No. 5* to which he referred as *From the New World*. In a letter written to Bohemia during the composition of this work he said: "I should never have written the symphony like I have, if I hadn't seen America." Accused of using Negro spirituals for his thematic material he replied in an interview for the New York *Herald* of December 12, 1893: "I did not make use of one of these melodies. I wrote my own themes embodying in them the qualities of Indian music and using these themes as subjects. I developed them with all the resources of modern rhythm, harmonization, counterpoint, and orchestral coloring."

Dvořák was the son of an amateur musician who played the violin, the zither, and was a member of the town band. His father both kept an inn and ran a butcher shop. As a boy of eight, Antonín played in his father's band and sang in the church choir. When he was twelve years old, his father sent him to the adjoining town of

Zlonice to learn German. While there he also learned the rudiments of music from the local schoolmaster who was both the village organist and the conductor of his own band.

When the financial situation at home took a turn for the worse, Dvořák served for a short time as a butcher. Fortunately, at sixteen, he was able to go to Prague to receive musical training at the Organ School. There he studied organ, theory, singing, and also became acquainted with the works of the classic masters. He played in the orchestra of the Society of St. Cecilia and became familiar with the music of Schumann and Wagner.

When Dvořák left school at eighteen he had no visible means of support, so he entered a concert orchestra as a violinist. He moved from this position to one with the National Theater Orchestra. In serving fourteen years with this ensemble, he became acquainted with the works of its conductor, Bedřich Smetana.

Few people knew of Dvořák's early efforts at composition except very intimate friends. It was toward the end of this period with the opera orchestra that his first works were publicly performed. He had written a *Hymnus* in honor of the "suffering mother-country." It brought him much success when performed because of its nationalistic nature. The excellent reception of this work induced him to resign from the opera orchestra so that he could devote most of his time to composition.

He met an attractive contralto at the opera house, one Anna Cermákova, and shortly after his resignation from the opera orchestra, married her. They spent a wonderful life together, raising a family of six children.

After Dvořák's association with Smetana at the opera, he resolved to follow the nationalistic pattern of composition. His next few works reflected this: his first *Symphony in D Minor,* an opera *King and Collier,* and a number of chamber pieces. His first song cycle was based on folk poetry and was followed by a set of duets, *Strains from Moravia.* Dvořák had trouble finding a publisher. Since Brahms was acquainted with the work of the young Czech, he wrote to a publisher in Berlin, saying: "I have taken much pleasure in the works of Dvořák of Prague. I have recommended him to send you his Moravian duets. If you play them through you will enjoy them as much as I have done . . . Dvořák has written in all possible styles: operas, symphonies, quartets, pianoforte pieces. Decidedly he is a very talented man. Besides, he is poor. Please take this into consideration."

Thanks to Brahms' effort, Dvořák saw his *Moravian Duets* published and received by the public with success. So much success, in fact, that other publishers started contacting Dvořák to see if he had something they might print. Dvořák had by now become a warm and close personal friend of Johannes Brahms, a friendship that endured all their lives.

There followed from Dvořák's pen the early *Slavonic Dances, Three Slavonic Rhapsodies,* and *Ten Legends* for the piano. The *Slavonic Dances* were played in both Germany and in London, being the works by which Dvořák was first known in those areas. Because of his increasing fame in London, Dvořák was invited in 1884 to visit there and to conduct his *Stabat Mater*. Having conducted that work at Royal Albert Hall, he moved across town to conduct his *Symphony in D Major* at the Crystal Palace. He was so well accepted in London as a composer of the first order, he visited England five times in two years to conduct his newest compositions. This popularity, of course, was most encouraging to the composer. In 1890 he toured Russia, Germany, and then back to England. From Cambridge University he received the honorary degree, Doctor of Music.

Dvořák purchased a home in the south of Bohemia, Vysoká, to which he returned after these travels. He received several honors in his own country: he received an honorary Ph.D. from the University at Prague; he was elected a member of the Czechoslovakian Academy of Arts and Sciences; and he received from the Austrian government the Order of the Iron Crown. Later Dvořák became Professor of Composition at the Prague Conservatory.

An invitation was received from Mrs. Thurber, founder of the National Conservatory of Music in New York, to become the Director of that school. Dvořák accepted the appointment and moved to the United States for three years.

Returning from the new world, Dvořák resumed his duties as Professor at the Prague Conservatory and was appointed its Director in 1901. He now turned exclusively to the composition of symphonic poems and opera.

Dvořák was appointed to the Upper Austrian House, the first musician to be so honored. In excellent health, he contemplated living to be quite old. His death on May 1, 1904, came suddenly. The funeral four days later took the form of a national ceremony of mourning.

BIBLIOGRAPHY

Robertson, Alec. *Dvořák.* New York: Pellegrini, 1949.
Šourek, Otakar. *The Orchestral Works of Antonín Dvořák,* trans. R. F. Samsour. Czechoslovakia: Artia.

SLAVONIC DANCES

ANTONÍN DVOŘÁK

Dvořák composed two sets of *Slavonic Dances,* each consisting of eight dances. These have become among the most popular of the nationalistic dances which were written during the last half of the nineteenth century. The two sets were not written successively; the first was written in 1878 and the second eight years later. Both sets were originally composed as piano duets and later orchestrated by the composer.

Dvořák composed these not only because of his love for the native dances of Bohemia, but also because of the encouragement he received from Brahms, whose *Hungarian Dances* were receiving wide acclaim. Unlike Brahms, Dvořák did not use the tunes of original folk dances. He made use of their rhythms as the most characteristic element, creating his own melodic material. He chose characteristic types of Czech dances: Numbers 1 and 8 are *furiants,* number 3 is a *polka,* numbers 4 and 6 are *sousedskás,* number 2 is a *dumka,* while 5 and 7 are *skočnás* (spring dances that resemble a jig).

SLAVONIC DANCE IN C MAJOR, Opus 46, No. 1.

This *Slavonic Dance* is a furiant, a fast and fiery Bohemian dance in 3/4 time with shifting accents. Dvořák and Smetana were responsible for bringing this dance to the attention of the symphonic audience.

After a crashing chord, the full orchestra launches into a vigorous *presto* theme which is repeated:

Example 1

This is followed by a quieter theme stated by the woodwinds. The derivation of this theme from Example 1 is easily recognizable:

Example 2

Example 1 is repeated by the full orchestra, and again by the strings and woodwinds.

The ·fury of the music subsides and leads to a middle section of much lighter vein and in a different key. The first theme in this section is stated by the pizzicato strings and staccato woodwinds:

Example 3

A more lyric theme, presented by the oboe, flute, and piccolo accompanied by the other woodwinds and strings is heard:

Example 4

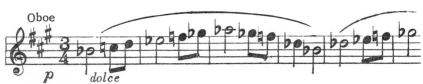

A recurrence of Examples 3 and 4 leads to the return of the first section of this ternary form in which Examples 1 and 2 are heard again.

A coda, composed of a combination of Examples 2 and 3, leads to the final presto statement of Example 1.

SLAVONIC DANCE IN A-FLAT, Opus 46, No. 3.

This *Slavonic Dance* is a polka, another Bohemian dance, in quick duple meter. This dance form was introduced into symphonic music by Smetana, and is a form that Dvořák used in many of his works.

The first section opens with a gay theme presented by the woodwinds against a counter-melody played by the viola and the second oboe:

Example 1

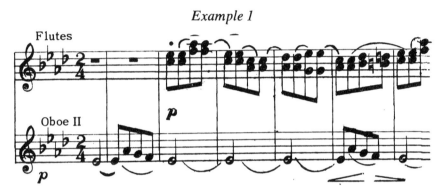

This is followed by a lively, vigorous theme by full orchestra:

Example 2

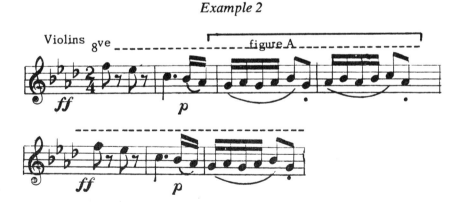

As Example 2 subsides and retards, a restatement of Example 1 is heard.

A new theme, in polka rhythm, is presented by the trumpets and continued by the woodwinds:

Example 3

This is repeated by the strings and bassoons.

The vigorous melody of Example 2 is presented again by the full orchestra. The force of this theme subsides and leads to an interlude which is built on Figure A of Example 2.

The first theme, Example 1, is repeated.

Example 2 appears again, this time extended by the use of Figure A of that theme. The dance finishes *accelerando molto sin' al fine* (accelerating as much as possible to the end).

EDVARD GRIEG

BORN: June 15, 1843; Bergen, Norway.
DIED: September 4, 1907; Bergen, Norway.

 Nestled in the rolling hills six miles from Bergen and overlooking the fjord is Troldhaugen, the home in which Edvard Grieg lived for over 20 years. In the little pamphlet issued to visitors to this place, now a museum, Sigmund Torsteinson says:

Grieg loved every nook of *Troldhaugen,* and characteristically allowed everything to grow wild. Nothing must be trimmed or chopped down on this little spot, everything must be granted the freedom of self-expression. In his time the garden was really quite a wilderness, with small, narrow footpaths leading down to the boathouse and the studio-hut. No fences obstructed the view either, — it was one's own duty to be careful on the cliffs. Nesting-boxes were hung up to attract song-birds. "Would that some of these wee folk would come to settle down with us!" [Grieg] writes in a letter. The front garden at *Troldhaugen* can easily be described as historic. Here on this little spot, the leading men and women of the artistic world met every summer for over twenty years. Here, Grieg's fellow-townsmen marched up, with their brass band ringing in the air, to honour him on his sixtieth birthday, and here festive tables were laid out for 150 guests which the house could not accommodate!

"Troldhaugen"

Home of Edvard Grieg, Bergen, Norway

A *cembalo ongarese* or *cimbalom*, a native Hungarian instrument of the dulcimer family used by Kodály in both the *Love Song* and the *Intermezzo*.

The Metropolitan Museum of Art; gift of Miss Agnes Kun, 1943

In Bergen, some forty-two years before the days of Troldhaugen, Edvard Grieg was born. His father served as the British Consul, but it was from his mother that young Edvard gained his musical background. His mother had been trained in music in both Hamburg and London and was frequently a soloist with the orchestra in Bergen. She gave Edvard his first piano lessons when he was six.

As a schoolboy Grieg was not particularly good. Known to play hookey frequently, he once took a piano composition of his marked *Variations on a German Melody for Pianoforte by Edvard Grieg, Opus 1* to school with him to show a boy friend. Unfortunately the teacher picked the work up before his friend had a chance to see it. The teacher told Grieg to take such trash home with him and not to bring it to school. The manuscript was then burned.

Although young Grieg loved music, he had no idea of becoming a musician, rather he wished to become a pastor. One evening the internationally famous violinist of Bergen, Ole Bull, was a guest in the Grieg household. Bull was impressed by the fifteen year old Edvard and Grieg later described the incident:

When he heard I had composed music, I had to go to the piano; all my entreaties were in vain. I cannot understand what Ole Bull could find at that time in my juvenile pieces. But he was quite serious and talked quietly to my parents. The matter of their discussion was by no means disagreeable to me. For suddenly Ole Bull came to me, shook me in his own way, and said: "You are going to Leipzig, and become a musician." Everybody looked at me affectionately, and I understood just one thing, that a good fairy was stroking my cheek and that I was happy. And my good parents! Not one moment's opposition or hesitation; everything was arranged, and it seemed to me the most natural thing in the world.

Grieg arrived at the Leipzig Conservatory after both Mendelssohn and Schumann had left, but the influence of these men, plus a good staff, gave Grieg a firm foundation for his music. Progress at first was slow. When requested in his harmony class to write an exercise over a figured bass, he wrote in his own harmonies rather than the ones suggested in the theory texts. His papers were always returned with the remark in big red letters drawn across them: WRONG. While at the Conservatory he worked so industriously night and day that his frail physique could not stand it. He broke down with a bad case of pleurisy two years after he had arrived. This completely destroyed his left lung, and his health remained impaired for the rest of his life.

His mother brought him back to Bergen where it took him about a year to recuperate. Then he returned to Leipzig and graduated with honors in 1862. He played four pieces on the piano at graduation which were later published as his Opus 1. Returning to Bergen, he spent one season there and then left for Copenhagen, a much larger city with more musical activity. Here he met Niels Gade, the acknowledged leader of the new "Scandinavian School" of music. Although Grieg did not study with him, he often asked advice from this friend. After one year in Copenhagen Grieg met another young Norwegian composer, Richard Nordraak. Nordraak was very anxious to form a Norse school of composition and, together with Grieg, formed the "Euterpe Society." Nordraak's premature death at twenty-two cut short their crusade, as Grieg put it, "against the effeminate Mendelssohn and Gade 'Scandinavianism,' turning with enthusiasm into the new, well-defined path along which the Northern school is now traveling."

It was during this time that Grieg met young Nina Hagerup, a fine young singer, to whom he became betrothed. Unfortunately his lack of ready finances to support a family delayed his marriage for three years. While betrothed to Nina he wrote a lovely song, *Ich Liebe Dich* (I Love Thee), to words by Hans Christian Andersen. Nina was to inspire many songs and sang a great many of them in concerts, appearing as late as 1898 in a London concert. Nina Grieg outlived her husband by some twenty-eight years, passing away in 1935.

In 1865 Grieg visited Italy and while there wrote his first orchestral composition, a concert overture entitled *In Autumn*. The next year he was appointed conductor of the Philharmonic Society of Christiania where he presented the first concert ever given of all Norwegian music. Franz Liszt happened about this time on a copy of a Grieg sonata and wrote him from Rome to come and visit him. Grieg went to meet Liszt in Weimar and the two became close friends.

The Griegs lost their thirteen-month-old daughter and their sorrow was intense. Edvard continued to work on his compositions valiantly and completed his *Concerto for Piano and Orchestra in A Minor*. The Norwegian government was soon to bestow upon him a life annuity of 1600 crowns (about $450) to enable him to spend all his time in composition. Fortunately that amount of money went much further in Norway than it does these days in America.

Grieg was at first tempted to turn down an offer by the great playwright, Henrik Ibsen, to compose incidental music for his play

Peer Gynt. The play did not throw a favorable light on the Norwegian people and Grieg further thought the play did not lend itself to incidental music. But Grieg needed the money that Ibsen offered so he turned to creating the music that was to make his name world famous. The play had to be repeated thirty-five times the first year of its existence.

In 1885 Grieg acquired his beloved home *Troldhaugen* and spent most of the balance of his life, some twenty-two years, there. Although frequently making guest appearances all over the world, he hated to leave the home where he and Nina were always entertaining friends, playing and singing for them.

In 1907 Grieg accepted an invitation to play at a festival in England, but instead of the festival he went to the hospital where he died of a heart disease on September 4, 1907. A state funeral was held and Grieg's ashes were placed in a niche in the hillside of Troldhaugen overlooking the fjord.

BIBLIOGRAPHY

Abraham, Gerald. *Grieg: A Symposium.* Oklahoma: University of Oklahoma Press. 1950.

Johansen, David Monrad. *Edvard Grieg.* New York: Tudor, 1945.

CONCERTO FOR PIANO AND ORCHESTRA

in A Minor

EDVARD GRIEG

The *Concerto,* written when the composer was but twenty-five, was dedicated to the pianist Edmund Neupart, who first played it in Copenhagen on April 3, 1869. Neupart wrote to Grieg after the world premiere: "On Saturday your divine Concerto resounded in the hall of the Casino. The triumph I achieved was tremendous. Even as early as the cadenza in the first movement the public broke into a real storm."

The keyboard idol of the time, Franz Liszt, was also impressed with compositions by the young composer. In Rome, in 1870, Liszt played the *A Minor Concerto* at sight. At the end he handed the music to Grieg and said: "Go on, I tell you, you have the right stuff in you! And don't let them scare you!"

FIRST MOVEMENT: *Allegro molto moderato.*
(Exposition)

The beginning of the movement is a brilliant outburst of chords played by the piano, based on the following theme:

Example 1

The solo introduction leads directly to the Principal Subject played by the woodwinds:

Example 2 (Principal Subject)

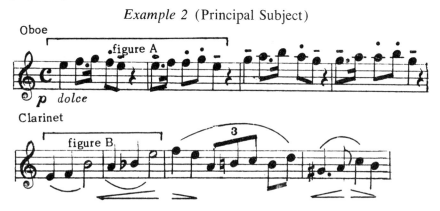

Figure B of the Principal Subject is played by the orchestra.

The Principal Subject is played by the solo piano, with a simple orchestral accompaniment.

The piano and orchestra play a faster rhythmical transition, which leads to the first part of the Second Subject:

Example 3 (Second Subject — first part)

The piano repeats this melody with embellishments and then continues with the second part of the Second Subject:

Example 4 (Second Subject — second part)

A modulation section in which the piano is predominant is based on the Second Subject. A climax is built by both the piano and orchestra.

(Development)

The orchestra plays a development section based on the introduction and Figure A of the Principal Subject.

The flute and horns alternately play Figure A of the Principal Subject accompanied by arpeggios on the piano; the orchestra interrupts with Figure B of the Principal Subject.

The full orchestra plays rhythmical fragments of the Principal Subject (Figure A) while the solo piano plays Figure B of it and parts of the introduction.

(Recapitulation)

The Principal Subject (Example 2) is stated by the solo piano.

Figure B of the Principal Subject is played by the orchestra.

The piano and orchestra again play a fast, rhythmical transition.

The Second Subject is played by the celli, and then by the piano.

A modulation section in which the piano is predominant is based on the Second Subject.

A climax is built by both the piano and orchestra.

The orchestra plays Figure A of the Principal Subject, ending with a sforzando chord.

The solo piano cadenza follows, based on the Principal Subject.

(Coda)

The orchestra plays the Principal Subject softly, followed by the piano with it in a bold presentation.

The movement ends with the same outburst of chords as were used in the introduction (Example 1).

CHAPTER VIII

IMPRESSIONISM

Impressionism was originally used as a term of derision in referring to the works of the French painters active in Paris at the end of the nineteenth century. It was first employed by Monet in a title he gave to one of his paintings in the Paris exhibit of 1863 — *Impression: Soleil levant* (Sunrise, An Impression). Rather than give a "photographic realism" to his subject, he attempted to suggest the "impression" of a sunrise, what one might see "at a glance." Contemporaries of Monet (1840-1926) — Manet (1832-1883), Degas (1834-1917), and Renoir (1841-1919) — revolted against the "realism" of Romanticism and concerned themselves with representing on canvas "fleeting glimpses" or first impressions. They preferred "common" subjects — still life, dancing girls, nudes, scenes of middle-class life such as picnics, boating and café scenes — as opposed to the grandiose and drama-packed scenes of their predecessors. They were concerned with color and light and shade; the actual subject of the painting was of secondary importance. The public at first was offended by this lack of definition; it objected to "grass that was pink, yellow, or blue."

A parallel revolt against realism occurred among the French poets during the 1880's. Known as *symbolists,* they attempted to suggest rather than describe; they abandoned rhyme and the traditional forms; they used a word for its color rather than its meaning. Important poets of the Symbolist school include the French Baudelaire (1821-1867), Mallarmé (1842-1898), Verlaine (1844-1896), and the Belgian Maeterlinck (1862-1949). They preferred to present the "symbol" rather than to state the thing; to experiment with new sounds and sonorities.

No true analogy can be made between poetry, painting, and music, for they are different arts, using entirely different media. In fact, Debussy — the leading exponent of Impressionism in music — objected to the use of the term as a "label" for his style. The public has, however, continued to use Impressionism to describe music that does have certain parallel goals and objectives to those of impression-istic painters and symbolistic poets. In music the movement centered largely in France and is best represented by the works of Debussy, really the only true impressionist in the sense of the definition now in common use.

Debussy's break with the Romantic tradition dates from 1892 with the *Prélude à l'Après-midi d'un Faune* (Prelude to the After-noon of a Faun) inspired by the symbolistic poem of Stéphane Mallarmé. Characteristic of Debussy is music that hints rather than states; music in which a succession of colors takes the place of dy-namic development; music that is vague and intangible.

A different view of form was one of the major breaks with Romanticism. Debussy had "form *in* music" but did not follow the traditional "form *of* music." The sonata-allegro pattern, the sym-phony, the sonata, the symphonic poem that musically related a story, binary and ternary forms were all abandoned. Themes or musi-cal subjects were no longer of conventional length and symmetry; rather, thematic fragments or short musical figures were used and became "patterns." Thematic development, as such, no longer oc-curred, and any contrapuntal use of themes was foreign to the new style.

New chordal combinations became common, chords with added 2nds, or chords of the 9th, 11th, or even 13th, were employed, chords with unresolved dissonances. Where contrary motion between voices had been a foundation-stone of Romantic tradition, parallel motion between voices derived from gliding chords became a chief character-istic of Impressionistic composition. The use of scales other than the traditional major and minor was common — Debussy used the whole-tone scale (c-d-e-f♯-g♯-a♯-c) which was alien to the most im-portant aspects of nineteenth century harmony. It eliminated the perfect fourth and perfect fifth as well as the leading tone, which earlier had required harmonic movement and had given the force to traditional harmony. The whole-tone scale, along with the use of medieval modes and Oriental scale patterns, imparted a "floating," non-directional quality to the music.

The ethereal quality of Impressionism is best in evidence in the many piano compositions by both Debussy and Ravel. In the major orchestral works, this quality is achieved by instrumentation — im-portant use of the harp, the discreet use of percussion instruments of color: the celesta, the triangle, the tambourine, the glockenspiel. The timbre of the woodwinds was featured, the flute is particular. Drums,

CHANSON D'AUTOMNE

PAUL VERLAINE (1844-1896)

The long-drawn sighs,
Like violin-cries
  Of autumn wailing,
Lull in my soul
The languorous shoal
  Of thoughts assailing.

Wan, as whom knells
Of funeral bells
  Bemoan and banish,
I weep upon
Days dead and gone
  With dreams that vanish;

Then helpless swing
On the wind's wing;
  Tossed hither and thither
As winter sweeps
From swirling heaps
  Worn leaves that wither.

(Translated by W. J. Robertson)

Rouen Cathedral
See Impressionistic painting of this
cathedral on page 485

CLAUDE DEBUSSY

The faun of Greek mythology

when used, were often muffled, and trumpets and trombones frequently muted. String parts were divided into four, eight, or even
ten sections. Human voices were used on occasion, usually singing
on a neutral syllable and employed as another orchestral instrument,
another tone-color in the orchestral palette.

As stated earlier, Claude Debussy was the only true exponent
of Impressionism. Maurice Ravel used many of the elements of it,
particularly in his earlier works, but his reliance on clear, metrical
rhythms, strong cadences, and his easily discerned phrase structure
and over-all form were not in keeping with the techniques of true
Debussy Impressionism.

Others who used certain aspects of Impressionism in their compositions included: in France, Roussel and Ibert; in England, Delius
and Cyril Scott; in the United States, Griffes and John Alden Car-
penter; in Spain, de Falla; and in Italy, Respighi.

When Stravinsky's *The Firebird* was first presented in Paris in
1910, the death-knell of Impressionism started to ring. Strangely
enough, the revolt against Impressionism was largely centered in
Paris, headed by Erik Satie and carried on by *Les Six,* a group of
six French composers of whom Milhaud is the best known.

Like Beethoven in an earlier era, Debussy is a pivotal figure.
Impressionism was rooted in antagonism to Romanticism, yet viewed
now from a distance, many critics and historians think of it as the
last phase of Romanticism, a *fin de siècle* movement. With the music
of Stravinsky, Schoenberg, and Bartók entering upon the musical
horizon between 1910 and 1920, and with Debussy's death in 1918,
Impressionism had reached its apex. In the words of French novelist
Cocteau: "After the music with the silk brush, the music with the ax."

BIBLIOGRAPHY

Cooper, Martin. *French Music.* London: Oxford University Press, 1961.
Hill, Edward B. *Modern French Music.* Boston: Houghton-Mifflin, 1924.

CLAUDE DEBUSSY

BORN: August 22, 1862; Saint-Germain-en-Laye, France.
DIED: March 25, 1918; Paris, France.

During Debussy's happiest days he was seen frequently in the
cafés of Montmartre: Chat Noir, the Chez Weber, or the Brasserie
Pousset. He could always be recognized by the flowing cape he wore,
his broad-brimmed hat, and his black beard. Many times the candles

on the café tables burned past midnight as he and his artist friends
— painters and writers — discussed both art and current events.

Although Debussy's piano compositions are among his best
known works, his friends claimed that in the evenings when Debussy
would sit at the keyboard and improvise for long periods of time, the
music far exceeded the beauty of his published compositions.

Debussy might have had a different career except for the per-
ceptiveness of his god-parents. Debussy was the son of a china shop
proprietor whose store in Saint-Germain-en-Laye went bankrupt
when Claude was three. The Debussy family then moved to Paris.
Although his father liked operettas and some operas, his son's talents
in music went unnoticed. Debussy's father was considering a naval
career for his son and had even inquired of admission requirements
at the nautical school. A friend of the family, a banker, paid for
Debussy's first piano lessons. Apparently Debussy never had a formal
education or attended any kind of a regular school; what little general
education he received was from his mother and his god-mother.

When Debussy was eight years old, he met Madame Mauté de
Fleurville, a piano student of Frédéric Chopin. Debussy studied
piano with her for three years during which time she prepared him
to take the entrance examination at the Conservatory. When Claude
was eleven years of age he was enrolled in the Paris Conservatory.
Debussy spent eleven years at the Conservatory, not all happy ones,
but he was always working toward his goal, the Prix de Rome. Debussy entered many of the various contests that were sponsored by
the school, contests in piano, in the writing of fugues and major
compositions for orchestra. He was the problem child of the Conservatory and had an erratic record in these contests because he
objected to the accepted theories of harmony and composition. His
fellow students found Debussy both uncouth and sarcastic.

At sixteen Debussy made his first visit to London. Two years
later he met Tchaikovsky's patroness, Nadja von Meck, and his
travels became far more extensive. She was a wealthy, middle-aged
widow and adored music. After she heard Debussy perform at the
keyboard, she became so entranced with his playing that she hired
him to join her group of household musicians. Madame von Meck
owned homes and villas in Switzerland, Italy, and Austria, and as she
traveled from one to another, she had the musicians move with her.
After Debussy's official tenure with her was finished, he traveled twice
to Russia.

Debussy became enamored of several young ladies during his

lifetime, the first of which was a Madame Vasnier who not only inspired one of his early groups of songs but was also kind enough to sing them in public.

Debussy still continued to work for the Prix de Rome at the Conservatory and in three years of tries, and as many compositions, netted, in order: a *no mention,* a *fourth place,* and a *second place.* On his fourth major attempt he finally won with his cantata, *L'Enfant Prodigue* (The Prodigal Son).

As part of this prize he was supposed to spend three years in Italy studying, and was obligated to send compositions back to the Conservatory to show his progress. Debussy was unhappy in Italy, he disliked Italian opera (although he did discover the music of Palestrina and di Lasso), and longed for his visits to Montmartre and his beloved Paris. While in Italy he met Franz Liszt, Giuseppe Verdi, Ruggiero Leoncavallo, and Arrigo Boïto. Debussy's only composition of his Roman days was *La Primavera* (Springtime), a suite for orchestra with wordless chorus.

On his return to Mŏntmartre and the Paris he loved, he wrote a work for solo voices, chorus, and orchestra entitled *La Damoiselle Elue* (The Blessed Damozel). In this work he first showed his many deviations from the "Romantic" school of the nineteenth century.

During his twenty-fifth year Debussy made another visit to London, this time in search of a publisher for his works. Returning unsuccessful, his writer friends of Montmartre encouraged him to compose an opera based on Maeterlinck's *Pelléas et Melisande.* While making sketches for this lyric-drama, his *String Quartet* was performed at the Sociétè Nationale. It was a success.

The following year Debussy had another composition performed at these concerts, the *Prélude à l'Après-midi d'un Faune* (Prelude to the Afternoon of a Faun). This composition had been inspired by a symbolistic poem and Debussy had originally envisioned three works to be based on the poem, the Prelude just mentioned, and a projected two additional movements which he never completed. His next major compositions were the three nocturnes: *Nuages* (Clouds); *Fêtes* (Festivals); and *Sirènes* (Sirens). These were first presented in 1900 at the Concerts Lamoureux. During his work on the nocturnes, Debussy married Rosalie Texier, to whom the nocturnes are dedicated.

Finally *Pelléas et Melisande* was accepted for performance at the Opéra-Comique. The author of the libretto, Maurice Maeterlinck, had expected his wife to be the leading lady of the production. When

"Rouen Cathedral' painted by Claude Monet (1840-1926) is an excellent example of Impressionistic artistry. Note that almost all detail has disappeared, and only the "impression" or suggestion of the outline of the cathedral with its sculptured façade is in evidence.

he learned that Mary Garden was to have the lead, he took pen in hand and wrote vile criticisms of the opera for the daily newspapers. Although many critics gave a bad report of the premiere, it was a success and the opera had many performances. Debussy received a decoration from the French government for it.

La Mer (The Sea) was Debussy's next great orchestral work, started in Burgundy while visiting his wife's parents, and finished in Eastbourne, England. *Ibéria* followed three years later. Debussy made two visits to London, in 1908 and 1909, to conduct his own works. It was there that he first learned of his incurable cancerous condition. Debussy decided not to let the public know of this affliction and hid his failing health behind successful conducting tours that took him to Vienna, Budapest, and Turin. In Turin, Debussy met both Richard Strauss and Sir Edward Elgar for the first time. His tours also took him to Amsterdam and Rome. He continued to compose during these travels, but most of the works of this period are not well known.

At the outbreak of World War I in 1914, Debussy was a semi-invalid at fifty-two. He wrote a couple of war-inspired works, and because his finances were at a low ebb, he contemplated another tour in the hope of earning additional money. He was too ill to travel, however. Debussy was finally taken to the hospital where two operations were performed for the removal of the cancer. While German long range cannons were shelling Paris at the height of the war, the final operation was performed. Debussy died shortly after it, too weak even to have been carried to the safety of the bomb shelter in the hospital cellar. So concerned was Paris with the war that his passing went practically unnoticed in the French newspapers.

BIBLIOGRAPHY

Lockspeiser, Edward, editor. *Debussy*. New York: Pellegrini and Cudahy, 1952.
Seroff, Victor I. *Debussy, Musician of France*. New York: G. P. Putnam's Sons. 1956.

PRELUDE À L'APRÉS-MIDI D'UN FAUNE
(Prelude to the Afternoon of a Faun)

CLAUDE DEBUSSY

Claude Debussy was inspired by a symbolistic poem (or eclogue) of Stéphane Mallarmé entitled *Prelude to the Afternoon of a Faun.* He wrote this prelude as the first of three projected works to represent the poem in music, and it could be supposed that this prelude (the only one of the three ever to be composed) does not attempt to depict the entire poem but serves only as a prelude to the main body of the poem.

As in all symbolistic literature there is much in this poem that is vague and obscure. The following excerpts are from Aldous Huxley's translation:

> I would immortalize these nymphs: so bright
> Their sunlit coloring, so airy light,
> It floats like drowsy down. Loved I a dream?
> My doubts, born of oblivious darkness, seem
> A subtle tracery of branches grown
> The tree's true self — proving that I have known,
> Thinking it love, the blushing of a rose.
> . . . Through this quiet, when a weary swoon
> Crushes and chokes the latest faint essay
> Of morning, cool against the encroaching day,
> There is no murmuring water, save the gush
> Of my clear fluted notes; and in the hush
> Blows never a wind, save that which through my reed
> Puffs out before the rain of notes can speed
> Upon the air, with that calm breath of art
> That mounts the unwrinkled zenith visibly,
> Where inspiration seeks its native sky.
> You fringes of a calm Sicilian lake,
> The sun's own mirror which I love to take,
> Silent beneath your starry flowers, tell
> How here I cut the hollow rushes, well
> Tamed by my skill, when on the glaucous gold
> Of distant lawns about their fountain cold
> A living whiteness stirs like a lazy wave;
> And at the first slow notes my panpipes gave
> These flocking swans, these naiads, rather, fly
> Or dive . . .
>
> But the unthinking soul and body swoon
> At last beneath the heavy hush of noon.
> Forgetful let me lie where summer's drouth
> Sifts fine the sand and then with gaping mouth
> Dream planet-struck by the grape's round wine-red star.
>
> Nymphs, I shall see the shade that now you are.

The *Prelude* opens with an unaccompanied flute solo suggestive of the faun. (A faun is a rural deity of Roman mythology with the ears, horns, hind legs, and tail of a goat, while the body and head are those of a man. Most pictures of fauns depict them playing reed flutes.)

Example 1

The flute solo is then repeated, this time with an accompaniment of strings.

When the flute theme is repeated a second time it is accompanied by arpeggios on the harp. This is an extended flute solo.

The clarinet next introduces a theme derived from the flute solo.

Example 2

The oboe then answers with another motive derived from the opening flute solo.

Example 3

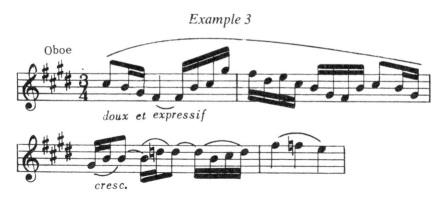

After an episode, the clarinet plays a motive which serves as a bridge.

Example 4

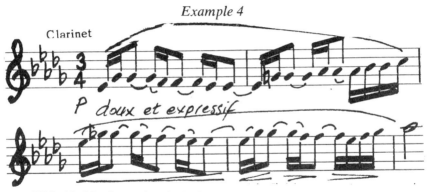

This "bridge" motive is followed immediately by a new theme in the woodwinds.

Example 5

The strings in octaves now take up this theme (Example 5) to an accompaniment of woodwinds.

A solo violin plays this last theme (Example 5).

The opening flute solo theme (Example 1) returns with sustained chords in the strings and harp arpeggios. This time the pitch is higher and the theme appears in extension.

At this point it seems as though Debussy has returned to the first section of the composition, for next two flutes play the opening theme (Example 1) against a background of shimmering strings.

This theme (Example 1) is repeated by the solo flute and a solo cello, but they do not finish the melody; instead, the oboe enters with the second half of the melody (although without careful attention it may sound like a new theme).

The music gradually fades away.

LA MER

(The Sea)

Claude Debussy

The composer's life-long interest in the sea has been suggested in his letters as well as in his composition, for he said in a letter:

Here I am again with my old friend the sea, always . . . beautiful. It is truly the one thing in nature that puts you in your place; only one does not sufficiently respect the sea . . .

You may not know that I was destined for the life of a sailor and that it was only by chance that I was led away from it. But still I have a great passion for the sea.

His finest achievement in a large work ultimately reflected this interest and love of the sea. One of the finest word pictures of *La Mer* was writen by the late music critic, Lawrence Gilman, who said:

The score of *La Mer* — those three linked tone-pictures that Debussy called "symphonic sketches" — contains no preface, motto, argument, or explanatory guide except the releasing words that designate the work as a whole, and the subtitles of the different movements: "From Dawn till Noon on the Sea"; "Sport of the Waves"; "Dialogue of the Wind and Sea."

This music is an incantation; a tonal rendering of colors and odors, of mysterious calls, echoes, visions, imagined or perceived; a recapturing and transcription through the medium of an art that is consumate sorcery, of "the most fantastical sports of light and of fluid whirlwinds." When Debussy suggests in the music such things as dawn and noon at sea, sport of the waves, gales and surges and far horizons, he is less the poet and painter than the mystical dreamer. It is not chiefly of those familiar aspects of the ocean's winds and waters that he is telling us, but of the changing phases of a sea unknown to mariners or airmen; a sea of strange visions and stranger voices, of fantastic colors and incalculable winds, at times full of bodement and terror, at times sunlit and dazzling. It is a spectacle perceived as in a trance, and evoked by a magician who could summon spirits from the vasty deep.

Yet, beneath these elusive and mysterious overtones, the reality of the sea persists; as we listen, its immemorial fascination lures and enthralls and terrifies; so that we are almost tempted to fancy that the two are, after all, incidental: the ocean that seems an actuality of wet winds and tossing spray and inexorable depths and reaches, and that unchartered and haunted and untraversable sea which opens before the magic casements of the dreaming mind.

DIALOGUE DU VENT ET DE LA MER (Dialogue of the Wind and Sea)

A timpani roll joined by celli and basses with Example 1 opens the movement:

Example 1

After the motive of Example 1 has been heard several times, a muted trumpet appears with Example 2:

Example 2

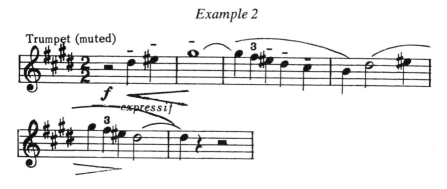

It is repeated without mute.

Example 3 is derived from a motive prominent throughout all three movements. It is played by the horns:

Example 3

Double reeds introduce Example 4 which is repeated:

Example 4

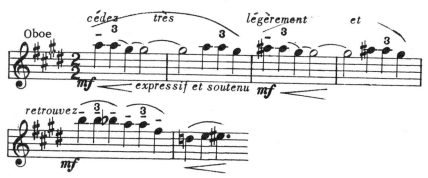

The celli and flute are heard immediately with example 5 (derived from an inversion of the opening figure of Example 3):

Example 5

A dramatic horn motive appears:

Example 6

The bassoon and string bass restate Example 2 (*mezzo-forte*) while the horn call (Example 6) appears at the terminal points of the phrases.

Cornets are heard with Example 3, and then at the end of the phrase echo it *pianissimo*.

The tonality changes as muted French horn chords are heard:

Example 7

There is a small crescendo based on the opening figure of Example 3, followed by a decrescendo. Example 4 then appears in the woodwinds.

The strings vary Example 4 slightly — shifting keys and building to a dynamic climax.

Example 5 is heard as an accompaniment to Example 2: first with the woodwinds above the strings, then with the woodwinds and celli under the second violins.

The double reeds again state Example 4.

As the closing measures of this movement approach, Example 4 builds to a climax and is followed by Example 7 in the trumpets.

Example 5 predominates as the music builds to its final, tremendous climax.

MAURICE RAVEL

BORN: March 7, 1875; Ciboure, France.
DIED: December 28, 1937; Paris, France.

Some composers led lives that were filled with fluctuations of artistic temperament in either political or amorous affairs; Ravel led a life that was in extreme contrast. Ravel was a quiet, dedicated man who wrote music for neither money nor fame, but because he "had to." He gave piano lessons and usually didn't want any payment for them. At concerts that included one of his works, he usually

stepped outside during its performance for a "cigarette libératrice."
He was neither poor nor was he wealthy; he only made enough money
from his musical activities to allow him to live the modest life which
was to his liking.

Accused first of being an imitator of Debussy and later hailed a
composer of originality with the creation of *Bolero,* Ravel had this
to say of his "style":

> I have never been a slave to any one style of composition. Nor have I
> ever allied myself with any particular school of music. I have always felt
> that a composer should put on paper what he feels and how he feels it —
> irrespective of what the current style of composition may be. Great music,
> I have always felt, must always come from the heart. Any music created by
> technique and brains alone is not worth the paper it is written on.
> This has always been my argument against the so-called "modern music"
> of the younger rebel composers. Their music has been a product of their
> minds and not of their hearts.

Maurice Ravel was born in the French-Basque seacoast town of
Ciboure. Shortly after his birth, his parents moved to Paris. His
father, an engineer as well as an amateur musician, saw to it that his
son was enrolled in the Paris Conservatory by the time he was fourteen.

At the Conservatory Ravel was a brilliant student in counterpoint, but ran into difficulty in harmony because he didn't care to
use the traditional chords of the "classical" style taught by the school.
As a student he wrote several short works including a *Habanera*
which was later incorporated into his *Rapsodie Espagnole.* It was
fortunate for Ravel that Fauré eventually became his composition
instructor. Fauré allowed for an individual approach to composition
in contrast to the pedantic masters who accepted only the forms of
late nineteenth century Romanticism.

Ravel, in his tries for the Prix de Rome, had almost as much
difficulty as Debussy. In 1901 he submitted a cantata, *Myrrha,* which
won second place; the next two years his compositions won nothing,
and on the fourth try he was eliminated in the preliminaries which
were held to remove those that had no competence.

When Ravel was twenty-seven he composed *Jeux d'Eau* (Play of
the Water) for the piano, and his *Pavane Pour une Infante Défunte*
(Pavanne for a Dead Princess). His first publicly acknowledged
work, *Quartet in F,* followed two years later.

Scene from *Daphnes et Chloë*. The nymphs lead Daphnis toward the rock and invoke the aid of the god Pan.

At the end of the ballet, Daphnis and Chloë are re-united and a general dance of rejoicing follows.

The premiere of his *Histoires Naturelles* in 1907 raised much musical commotion. Some criticized it because it was the story of animals in the zoo; others tried to accuse Ravel of cheaply imitating Debussy. In the next three years Ravel established a musical personality of his own with *Rapsodie Espagnole,* the *Mother Goose Suite,* and his opera *L'Heure Espagnole* (The Spanish Hour).

In 1910 Ravel was commissioned by the famous ballet impressario Diaghilev to prepare music for a ballet to be based on the story of Daphnis and Chloë of ancient mythology. After two years of work, it was presented to the public of Paris and earned great popularity.

During World War I Ravel served in the French army as an ambulance driver, but was discharged before the end of the war because of bad health. On returning to Paris he purchased a villa in Montfort l'Amaury, a few miles from Paris, where he was to live the rest of his life. One of his first compositions after settling down there was *La Valse.*

Another opera was written by Ravel, *L'Enfant et les Sortilèges* (The Child and the Sorcerer), which was presented at Monte Carlo in 1924 and a year later in Paris. In 1928 the famous dancer Ida Rubinstein commissioned him to write a dance for her. For this purpose Ravel wrote his famous *Bolero.* So successful was this work, and so popular, that arrangements were made for jazz bands, and Ravel's name was no longer known exclusively by the serious concert audience. Although he had for years lived quietly in his home near Paris and was known by only a few people, he now became the most famous musician in all of France. His international reputation also . grew because of the *Bolero,* and he had many invitations to guest conduct his own works.

Ravel's final works were two greatly different piano concerti that he worked on simultaneously. These occupied the years around 1930, one concerto being written for Paul Wittgenstein, a pianist who had lost one arm. This concerto grew to be known as the *Concerto for Left Hand* and was premiered in Vienna with Wittgenstein at the piano and Ravel conducting.

After 1932 Ravel was too ill to work on any compositions and died five years later from an unsuccessful operation on the brain.

BIBLIOGRAPHY

Myers, Rollo Hugh. *Ravel; Life and Works.* London: Duckworth and Co., Ltd., 1960.
Seroff, Victor I. *Maurice Ravel.* New York: Henry Holt and Co., 1953.

DAPHNIS ET CHLOE
Suite No. 2

MAURICE RAVEL

The story of the ballet is based on the legend written by Longus sometime between the beginning of the third century A.D. and the end of the fifth century. The quotations in the story given below are from the English translation made by George Thornley in 1657.

In the complete ballet, the opening tableau, which takes place in a vast meadow before the grotto of the sacred Nymphs (three figures carved in stone), the shepherd Daphnis exchanges vows of love with Chloé. Soon the peaceful fields are invaded by pirates who abduct Chloé.

In the following scene, Chloé is brought before the pirates in their lair. First, as they command, she dances for them, then begs her freedom. The pirate chief refuses. Creatures of Pan invade the place; the outlaws fall back in fear, and Chloé is liberated.

The final scene (from which this *Suite No. 2* is drawn) takes place again in the meadows at sunrise.

Daphnis . . . started up out of his sleep and, full of pleasure, full of grief, with tears in his eyes, adored the statues of the Nymphs and vowed to sacrifice to them . . . if Chloé should return safe. And running to the pine where the statue of Pan was placed. the legs a goat's, the head horned, one hand holding a pipe, the other a goat dancing to it . . . made a vow for the safety of Chloé . . .

That night seemed to him the longest of nights, but in it . . . wonders were done . . .

It was now the time . . . and Daphnis, having spied from a high stand Chloé coming with the flocks, crying out mainly, O ye Nymphs, O blessed Pan! made down to the plains, and rushing into the embraces of Chloé [fell] in a swoon . . .

Therefore the two . . . fell to dancing . . . Daphnis played Pan; and Chloé, Syrinx. He woos and prays to persuade and win her; she shows her disdain, laughs at his love, and flees him. Daphnis follows as to force her, and running on his tiptoes, imitates the hooves of Pan. Chloé, on the other side, acts Syrinx wearied in her flight, and throws herself into the wood . . . But Daphnis, catching up that great pipe . . . plays at first something that was doleful, and bewailing a lover; then something that made love, and was persuasive.

The music of *Suite No. 2* is divided by the composer into three sections that are played without pause. The first, *Daybreak,* represents the story from the awakening of Daphnis up to the point where he is reunited with his beloved Chloé. The second, *Pantomime,* accompanies the scene in the ballet in which Daphnis and Chloé mime the story of Pan and Syrinx. The concluding section is entitled *General Dance* and represents the "joyous tumult" because Daphnis and Chloé have been brought together again.

DAYBREAK (The quotations are from the score).

"No sound other than the murmuring of the pebbles gathered by the stream that runs over the rocks." This example is heard alternating between two flutes and two clarinets. The harps, with glissandi, and the muted strings provide a shimmering background.

Example 1

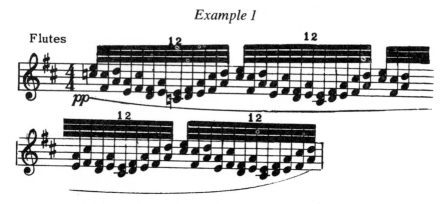

"Daphnis is stretched out in front of the grotto of the Nymphs. Little by little, day breaks." This next example begins in the lower strings and woodwinds and ascends.

Example 2

A quick little figure for three solo violins, echoed by the piccolo, announces the "singing of birds." The trills in the piccolo and violins, interrupted by fast little figures in the flute, continue the bird calls.

After a series of undulating passages for clarinets, flutes, and violins, the clarinet finally announces the main theme of this movement (from which Example 2 was derived).

Ravel studies a score of *Daphnis*

MAURICE RAVEL

MANUEL DE FALLA

OTTORINO RESPIGHI

Example 3

"In the distance a shepherd passes with his flock" and a short passage is heard from a solo flute.

The clarinets and violas announce the second theme of this movement:

Example 4

"Another shepherd crosses the scene" and another short melody is heard, this time played by a solo E-flat clarinet (a very high and shrill clarinet). Underneath the solo, Example 3 is heard arising from the basses.

Ravel introduces a wordless chorus with accompaniment by fast passages in the upper woodwinds and the harp. Underneath the wordless voices, the violins intone Example 3.

"A group of shepherds enter, looking for Daphnis and Chloé. They discover Daphnis and awaken him. Anguished, he looks about for Chloé." As the music builds to a climax in rising tremolo passages for the strings, "Chloé appears, surrounded by shepherdesses." The piccolo and strings anounce a new theme as Daphnis and Chloé "throw themselves into each other's arms":

Example 5

"Daphnis perceives the crown of Chloé. His dream was prophesied; Pan's intervention is made manifest." The low celli return with Example 1 which works its way up through the violas and then the violins; fast passages for clarinets and flutes are heard high above it.

At the climax, a triangle rings brilliantly as both harps play fast glissandi with a shimmering effect in the celesta, flutes, clarinets, and celli. The music quickly softens and dies away.

An "old shepherd, Lammon, explains that if Pan saved Chloé, it was because of his remembrance of Syrinx of whom he was enamored." At this point the oboe announces a short motive.

Example 6

This motive is repeated over and over again.

PANTOMIME

"Daphnis and Chloé mimic the story of Pan and Syrinx." A haunting melody in the oboe heralds "Chloé |who| plays the young nymph wandering in the open plains."

Example 7

"Daphnis mimes Pan, appearing and declaring his love for the nymph." A descending motive in the oboe is heard.

Example 8

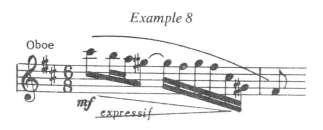

This indicates that Chloé "repulses him. Pan becomes more persistent" as an upward sweep in strings and flutes is heard.

Example 8 is repeated by the clarinet, indicating that Syrinx again repulses him.

With an ascending figure in the oboe "she disappears in the clumps."

Example 7 appears in the strings as "Pan, despaired, tears up some reeds in the form of a flute and plays a melancholy air."

Example 9

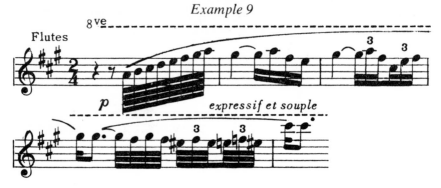

As the melody is being played by the orchestral flute, "Chloé reappears and mimes the mood of the flute." The flute melody continues in an extended solo.

"The dance becomes more and more animated" as the music reaches a climax; a descending figure is heard passing through the woodwind section and "Chloé, in a turn, falls into Daphnis' arms."

After a bridge made from the opening notes of Example 7, Example 5 emerges in the strings and woodwinds, the melody heard when Daphnis and Chloé originally fell into each others arms. It has added intensity this time for each few measures, as the music is about to reach a climax, the melody is interrupted by an upward glissando by both harps.

The solo violin and viola repeat Example 8.

The soft murmuring of the stream is heard again with the return of the rippling figure of Example 1.

"Before the altar of the Nymphs, Daphnis swears his faith." A solemn figure is heard in the orchestra, repeated more softly.

Example 10

The soft sound of the triangle, tambourine, and cymbals is heard as "young girls enter dressed as bacchanites and shaking tambourines."

The melody of Daphnis and Chloé's first embrace (Example 5) returns as Daphnis and Chloé "embrace tenderly. A group of young men fill the scene." There is "joyous tumult" as a new theme is heard in the violas.

Example 11

GENERAL DANCE

After a brief introduction of repeated thirds which appear successively in horns, flutes, and violins, the theme of the general dance is introduced by the E-flat clarinet.

Example 12

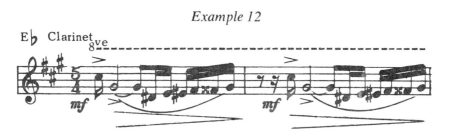

The fast moving chromatic runs of this theme are repeated by other members of the woodwind choir.

Strings repeat the moving chromatic scale passages in thirds used in the introduction to this movement.

Example 12 returns building to impressive climaxes.

The French horns burst in fortissimo with the repeated thirds, followed by a chromatic run as used in the introduction:

Example 13

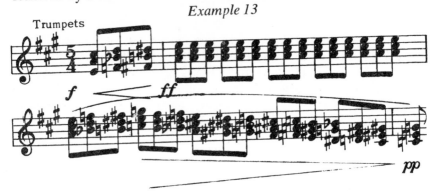

While woodwinds re-echo short segments of Example 13, the strings keep repeating the first two notes of Example 12.

The trombones enter as a climax marked *fff* is reached.

The orchestral voices start descending in chromatic runs and getting ever softer. Finally only the celli are heard, sustaining a chord. The bass drum and double basses accentuate a rhythmic pattern until the clarinet and some celli enter with Example 11. Chromatic passages keep interrupting this theme until finally the trumpet states it boldly.

As the music again rises to a climax, Example 12, followed by ascending chromatic scales, accentuate this final section.

After a *ff* climax, the music again rises from a *ppp* to another climax, drops in volume just as suddenly a second time, and builds in one grand, final surge.

BOLERO

Maurice Ravel

The "bolero" is not a true folk-form, although it probably was influenced by the earlier "zarabanda" (a lively successor of the stately sarabande), the chaconne, and the polonaise. The bolero was devised by the Spanish dancer Sebastian Cerezo around 1780, and was similar in style to the Andalusian cachuca. The bolero, in stately triple meter (the bolero in duple meter is of later Cuban origin), was used by Weber, Beethoven, and Chopin.

The first performance of *Bolero* was given by Ida Rubinstein, who had requested Ravel to compose a dance for her based on a Spanish motive. The setting was after the manner of Goya, the choreographer was Nijinski. The program of the ballet, like the music, was simple, direct, and violent. The setting represented the interior of an Andalusian inn, filled with gypsies in indolent poses, some of them half asleep. Only gradually did they become aware of the music appearing from out of nowhere, but as it increased in volume, they came to life, and watched in fascination the central figure of a woman who danced, first languidly, and then with more animation, upon a table in the center of the floor. As she responded to the insistence of the music, the other dancers worked themselves into a frenzy. Knives were drawn, the woman was tossed from arm to arm, and only when her partner intervened was quiet restored and the dance finished.

Of *Bolero* Ravel said to a Parisian music critic:

I am particularly desirous that there should be no misunderstanding about this work. It constitutes an experiment in a very special and very limited direction and should not be suspected of aiming at achieving anything different from or anything more than it actually does achieve.

Before its first performance I issued a warning to the effect that what I had written was a piece lasting seventeen minutes and consisting wholly of "orchestral tissue without music" — of one very long, very gradual crescendo. There are no contrasts, there is practically no invention except the plan and the manner of execution. . . . I have carried out exactly what I intended, and it is for the listeners to take it or leave it.

Ravel has used a single rhythmic figure throughout:

The composer has used two forms of the theme:

Example 1

Example 2

This is all there is to *Bolero*, an unvarying rhythmic pattern throughout and two forms of the theme — except, of course, Ravel's master hand at orchestration!

The following is the sequence of presentation:

1. Example 1 played by solo flute (pp).
2. Example 1 played by solo clarinet (p).
3. Example 2 played by solo bassoon (mp).

4. Example 2 played (p) by solo E-flat clarinet (higher and more piercing than the normal B-flat or A clarinet of the orchestra).

5. Example 1 played by solo oboe d'amore (mp) (a seldom used instrument, one third lower in pitch than the regular oboe, and more serene in timbre).

6. Example 1 played by the flute (pp) and muted trumpet (mp) in octaves.

7. Example 2 played by solo tenor saxophone (mp).

8. Example 2 played by sopranino saxophone (mp) (a fourth higher than the soprano saxophone. An instrument almost never used elsewhere. The melody drops too low in pitch for it and the end of the last phrase is played by the soprano saxophone).

9. Example 1 played by two piccolos in octaves (pp), the French horn (mf), and celesta in octaves (p).

10. Example 1 played by the oboe, oboe d'amore, English horn; and, clarinets in octaves (mf).

11. Example 2 played by solo trombone (mf).

12. Example 2 played by pairs of flutes, oboes, clarinets; and, a piccolo, English horn, and tenor saxophone, in triads of the second inversion (f).

13. Example 1 played by pairs of flutes, oboes, clarinets; a piccolo; and first violins in octaves.

14. Example 1 played by pairs of flutes, oboes, clarinets; a piccolo, English horn, tenor saxophone, and all first and second violins.

15. Example 2 played by pairs of flutes, oboes; a piccolo, English horn, trumpet, and all violins.

16. Example 2 played by pairs of flutes, oboes, clarinets, trombones; a piccolo, English horn, soprano saxophone, all violins, violas, and celli.

17. Example 1 played in triads (ff) by two flutes, piccolo, four trumpets (two are D trumpets), soprano and tenor saxophone, and first violins.

18. Example 2 played by two flutes, piccolo, the four trumpets, a trombone, soprano and tenor saxophones, and first violins.

A short coda closes the work with brilliant and lightning fast passages for all the orchestra with the slide trombone making use of a glissando that stands out above the entire force of the orchestra.

MANUEL DE FALLA

BORN: November 23, 1876; Cádiz, Spain.

DIED: November 14, 1946; Alta Gracia, Argentina.

Manuel de Falla was described by a friend as a "lover of peace and solitude." So quiet and self-effacing was he that during his seven-year stay in Paris, a time when he frequently did not have enough money to buy regular meals, he lost a wealthy student rather than reveal his identity. He had been given the name and address of a well-to-do Parisian family who wished to secure a good piano teacher for their child. De Falla discovered that the address was near the residence of his laundress, so he bundled his dirty clothes in a brown paper sack and set off to call first on his laundress and then on his prospective student. Arriving at the home of his laundress he discovered no one there, so he proceeded to the home of the would-be pupil, paper sack of laundry still under his arm. When the maid answered the door she saw the sack and mistook him for a tradesman. She reprimanded him for coming to the front door rather than the back servant's entrance, and requested him to go around to the proper door. As de Falla arrived at the back door, he was met by the mistress of the house who censured him again for having gone to the front door. Quiet, self-effacing de Falla apologized and immediately left the house rather than identify himself.

De Falla was born of well-educated parents, his mother being an excellent pianist. Manuel's first piano teacher was his mother, with whom, at the age of eleven, he took part in a public performance of Haydn's *Seven Last Words of Our Savior,* a work originally composed for one of the churches in Cádiz.

De Falla was later given professional piano lessons and also studied harmony and theory, writing some chamber works which he later destroyed. When de Falla was seventeen he heard his first orchestra concert, which included a symphony of Beethoven. It was at this point in his life that de Falla decided to make music his career.

He entered the Madrid Conservatory and studied both piano and composition. Although he was a pianist of remarkable talents, earning two piano performance awards while there, he was fortunate in working with a sixty-year old gentleman named Felipe Pedrell in composition. Pedrell had become convinced that there was much that was good in Spanish church music and old Spanish folk songs. He had endeavored to write music of his own that would incorporate these rich inheritances into them. Failing in his own attempt at composition, Pedrell had two gifted students whom he influenced enough to carry out his goal — Isaac Albeniz and Manuel de Falla. Working closely with de Falla, he was able to impress him with the fact that his talent was more important in the field of composition than it was in piano. De Falla stated, "It is to the lessons of Pedrell and to the powerful stimulation exercised on me by his works that I owe my artistic life."

Music has never been a very rewarding occupation as far as money is concerned and de Falla learned this lesson early. In order to earn living expenses, he gave private piano lessons, played piano with local chamber groups, and tried to earn money from his compositions. The only field of music that was open to original compositions in his early days was that of *zarzuelas*. A zarzuela was a native type of comic operetta frequently performed in Madrid. De Falla's first, *Los Amores de la Inés,* was a failure, while his second zarzuela was never performed. In 1905 he submitted an opera, *La Vida Breve,* to a contest sponsored by the Academia de Bellas Artes in Madrid. The opera won the prize, but unfortunately the contest had made no arrangements for a performance of the winning work.

Paris attracted the attention of de Falla, who saw it as the center of the musical life of Europe. Two years after winning the opera competition he was able to raise enough money for a seven-day trip to Paris. So fascinated and inspired was he when he reached Paris that the seven-day visit lasted for seven years. While there he became acquainted with Debussy, Dukas, and Ravel. A warm friendship developed between de Falla and Debussy, and de Falla discovered in the impressionistic works of Debussy much that he admired in style and technique. De Falla's days in Paris, although richly rewarding as far as musical experience was concerned, were days of meager fare. Scarcely did he know sometimes from where the next meal was coming. De Falla gave private piano lessons and appeared from time to time as a guest pianist to earn what little money he had. During his stay in Paris, the first performance of his earlier opera, *La Vida Breve,* was scheduled for the Casino at Nice (1913). De Falla saw it performed a year after its Nice debut at the Opéra-Comique in Paris, some nine years after it had won the contest.

At the outbreak of World War I de Falla returned to his native Spain where he completed the score of *El Amor Brujo.* His work for piano and orchestra, *Nights in the Gardens of Spain,* on which he had worked in Paris, was completed in 1916. These two works established de Falla as a composer of importance. In 1919 he met the ballet impressario, Serg Diaghilev, and played for him on the piano some sketches he had written for a work to be entitled *El Sombrero de Tres Picos* (The Three-Cornered Hat). These immediately took Diaghilev's fancy and he commissioned de Falla to complete the work so that he could mount it as a ballet. When presented, this work added to de Falla's reputation as the outstanding composer of Spain.

In 1921 de Falla moved to Granada, in the shadow of the Alhambra, where he lived a quiet and peaceful life for over seventeen years, leaving Granada only to appear as a guest on frequent tours of Europe. It was in Granada that he completed his *Concerto for Harpsichord*.

De Falla suffered from hypochondria, was fearful of drafts, and fully believed that the full moon was extremely harmful. In this frame of mind, his health grew worse. When the civil war broke out in Spain, de Falla, a religious man, aligned himself with Franco and his forces since he thought they would overthrow the anti-religious group that had taken over since the monarchy. De Falla was rewarded with an appointment as President of the Instituto España in 1938 but was too ill to go to Madrid to receive the official installation.

Soon disillusioned with Franco's government, de Falla decided a year later to leave Spain and travel to Argentina where he could live with his sister. He settled in Carlos Paz, near Córdoba in Argentina. Although his health was already bad, de Falla was able to live for almost seven years in this new environment. He died in 1946 just nine days before his seventieth birthday.

BIBLIOGRAPHY

Trend, J. B. *Manuel de Falla and Spanish Music.* New York: Alfred Knopf, Inc., 1929 (new ed. 1934).
Pahissa, Jaime, *Life and Works of Manuel de Falla.* London: 1954.

EL SOMBRERO DE TRES PICOS*

(*The Three-Cornered Hat*)

Suite No. 2

Manuel de Falla

The story of this ballet concerns the "eternal triangle." A young miller's wife attracts the attentions of the local Governor (Corregidor) who nicely eliminates his competition by having the miller put in jail. The faithful miller's wife dances for the Governor and so excites him that she has no trouble in getting him to follow her to the millstream where she leads him off the bridge and he falls into the water. Drying himself at the miller's home, he is discovered by the miller who then steals the Governor's clothes that have been set out to dry. He walks off with these, leaving the Governor to his fate.

In the orchestral Suite No. 2 from *The Three-Cornered Hat* three dances are included: *The Dance of the Neighbors, The Miller's Dance,* and finally, the *Jota.*

The Dance of the Neighbors

This dance opens immediately with its principal theme being sounded twice by the violins:

Example 1

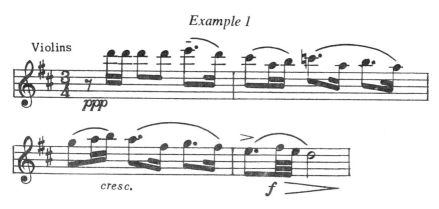

This is answered immediately by the subordinate theme:

Example 2

Violins

The trumpets respond brilliantly with Example 1. The Spanish rhythm of this dance is then played by the full orchestra.

The flute and then the piccolo are heard with Example 1.

The violins appear as they did at the opening with Example 1, played twice. The subordinate theme (Example 2) is heard next.

A slow coda in which the woodwinds state Example 1 for a final time closes the dance.

MILLER'S DANCE

This is a slower dance introduced by a French horn cadenza which is followed by an English horn cadenza.

The rhythm of the dance appears in the strings and percussion, an emphatic rhythm even if the tempo is slower than that of the other two dances.

The oboe states the theme of the dance:

Example 3

Oboe

The rhythmic pattern is heard again, followed by a development of the thematic material.

The French horn plays the first two measures of the theme (Example 3) and is answered by the strings. The French horn is heard with the next two measures of the theme and is answered by the strings with the rhythmic motive.

The strings keep up the rhythmic pattern and accelerate until the dance is brought to a close.

The stage setting of *The Three Cornered Hat*

The Corregador and the miller's wife

JOTA

The jota is a dance of northern Spain (Aragon) which is performed by couples in rapid triple time and usually accompanied by castanets. In this dance, de Falla opens with a brilliant principal theme sounded by the violins.

Example 4

After this principal theme has been exploited in quite an extended section, the second theme is introduced by the woodwinds.

Example 5

The third theme of the *Jota* is heard in the full orchestra.

Example 6

The fourth theme is heard predominantly in the woodwinds with the full orchestra behind it.

Example 7

The rhythm of the *Jota* is then heard in all its intensity in the orchestra until the principal theme (Example 4) is repeated for a final time with castanets predominating in the rhythmical accompaniment.

The coda is based on the rhythmic pattern established in the introduction to this dance with a xylophone added to the tonal color.

The dance closes with great crescendi for full orchestra bringing the movement to a powerful and dramatic climax.

OTTORINO RESPIGHI

BORN: July 9, 1879; Bologna, Italy.
DIED: April 18, 1936; Rome, Italy.

Although the roster of well-known Italian opera composers of the late nineteenth century is long, there is but one name that appears on the roster of serious symphonic composers, that of Ottorino Respighi. An expert craftsman at orchestration, having studied with Rimsky-Korsakov, he adopted many of the techniques of the impressionistic composers. In speaking of *The Fountains of Rome* he said that it was intended "to reproduce by means of tone an impression of nature." *The Pines of Rome,* he says, was an attempt to use "nature as a point of departure in order to recall memories and visions."

At one time Respighi was greatly influenced by the Gregorian melodies and ecclesiastical modes of the Middle Ages. During this period he wrote a *Concerto in the Mixolydian Mode,* for piano; the *Concerto Gregorino,* for violin; and a set of four impressions entitled *Church Windows.* Of contemporary schools and styles of composition, Respighi said:

> The future course of music? Who can say? I believe that every composer should first of all be an individual. As for dissonance, it has its place as a medium of tone-color. It is the same with polytonality. For its own sake it is abhorrent to me, but as a means to expression it has important uses.

. . . So far as modern Italian musicians are concerned — Pizzetti, DeSabata, Castelnuovo-Tedesco, Malipiero and others — they had their beginning in impressionism. We stem from this school, but for some years we have not been of it. The Italian genius is for melody and clarity. Today there is a noticeable return to the less sophisticated music of our past — in harmony to the church modes and in form to the suite of dances and other charming forms. This is no doubt good, providing we all cling to our own individualities and really express them.

Respighi was born of a musical family; his grandfather had been a choir director for all the churches of Bologna, and his father was a pianist and teacher at the Bologna Liceo Musicale. It was only natural that after piano lessons from his father, young Ottorino should be enrolled in his twelfth year at the Liceo Musicale. At the same time he was also taking violin lessons.

At nineteen Respighi started studies in composition, studying for two years in Bologna. His last year in Bologna saw him earning his diploma in violin. In order to enlarge his musical knowledge, he travelled in his twenty-first year to St. Petersburg in Russia where he secured a position as first violist with the orchestra of the Opera Theater. This same year his first composition, *Symphonic Variations,* was given a school performance.

After his first year in St. Petersburg Respighi was able to study both composition and orchestration with Rimsky-Korsakov. After five months of study with the Russian master, Respighi moved to Berlin, Germany, where he studied composition with Max Bruch. His studies were followed by a career as a concert artist. In 1905 his first work to be played publicly, *Notturno,* was performed in New York at the Metropolitan. Some of his compositions were published soon after this.

The next ten years were spent as a violinist and violist. He played with the Mugellini Quartet for a while, and then turned to piano work at a singing school in Berlin.

1910 heralded the performance of his first opera, *Semirama,* in Bologna. Three years later he was appointed an instructor of composition at the Academy of Santa Cecilia in Rome, and he became director some ten years later. His *Fountains of Rome* dates from 1916 and earned him such a reputation that he was invited all over Europe to guest conduct his own works. At the end of World War I, Respighi married a pupil of his, Elsa Olivieri-Sangiacomo, an accomplished composer and singer. She frequently sang some of his compositions when they went on concert tours. His last opera was not quite complete at the time of his death and she finished the work so that it could be mounted posthumously.

Respighi only served as director of the Academy for two years after his appointment in 1923 as it occupied too much of his time and involved too many absences from Rome. The season following his resignation, he paid his first visit to the United States and appeared with the New York Philharmonic in his *Concerto in the Mixolydian Mode*. Two years later the Metropolitan Opera premiered his opera *Sunken Bell*. Four years later Respighi made another visit to the United States.

Returning from his last concert tour of America, he was nominated to the Italian Royal Academy. Soon after this great honor from his native land he suffered a heart attack. Although confined to his bed, he continued to work on his opera *Lucrezia*. Fate was not kind to him, though, for he died in his beloved villa in Rome, "I Pini," shortly before the opera's completion.

THE FOUNTAINS OF ROME*

Symphonic Poem

OTTORINO RESPIGHI

Although the symphonic poem is in one continuous movement, it is subdivided into four parts: (1) The Fountain of Valle Giulia at Dawn; (2) The Triton Fountain in the Morning; (3) The Fountain of Trevi at Mid-day; and (4) The Fountain of the Villa Medici at Sunset. In the score the composer expresses his thoughts:

In this symphonic poem the composer has endeavored to give expression to the sentiments and visions suggested to him by four of Rome's fountains contemplated at the hour in which their character is most in harmony with the surrounding landscape, or in which their beauty appears most impressive to the observer.

The first part of the poem, inspired by the fountain of Valle Giulia, depicts a pastoral landscape: droves of cattle pass and disappear in the fresh, damp mists of a Roman dawn.

A sudden loud and insistent blast of horns above the whole orchestra introduces the second part, *The Triton Fountain*. It is like a joyous call summoning troops of naiads [in mythology, young nymphs who preside over

* All musical examples from *The Fountains of Rome* are used by permission of G. Ricordi & Co., copyright owners.

bodies of water] and tritons [a god of the sea who usually holds a trumpet made of a shell] who come running up, pursuing each other and mingling in a frenzied dance between the jets of water.

Next there appears a solemn theme borne on the undulations of the orchestra. It is *The Fountain of Trevi at Mid-day.* The solemn theme, passing from wood to the brass instruments, assumes a triumphal character. Trumpets peal: across the radiant surface of the water there passes Neptune's chariot, drawn by sea horses, and followed by a train of sirens and tritons. The procession then vanishes while faint trumpet blasts resound in the distance.

The fourth part, the "Villa Medici" fountain, is announced by a sad theme which rises above a subdued warbling. It is the nostalgic hour of sunset. The air is full of the sound of tolling bells, birds twittering, leaves rustling. Then all dies peacefully into the silence of the night.

THE FOUNTAIN OF VALLE GIULIA AT DAWN

A high harmonic in the first violins is sustained, while the muted second violins play a slow moving figure in the center of their range. Two measures after this pianissimo introduction, the oboe enters with a pastoral theme, suggestive of the shepherds and their pipes of old:

Example 1

An episode follows this with sustained chords in the strings; woodwinds sound above them with figures taken from Example 1.

The clarinet enters with Example 1 accompanied by a moving figure in the strings *ppp.* This is then repeated by the piccolo and bassoon playing the theme two octaves apart.

A lyrical theme is introduced by the oboe and solo cello:

The Fountain of Valle Giulia at Dawn

The Triton Fountain in the Morning

Example 2

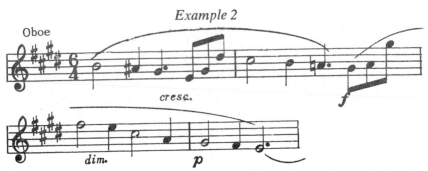

This theme is answered by descending chromatic triads in the flutes and celesta.

The clarinet enters with Example 2 over sustained chords in the muted trumpets and harp.

Chords, ascending chromatically, in woodwinds and celesta lead to a restatement by the flute of Example 1.

The afterphrase of Example 1 is repeated first by the oboe and then by the clarinet to bring this section to a close.

THE TRITON FOUNTAIN IN THE MORNING

The peaceful atmosphere surrounding the close of the first movement is broken by the French horns, a "sudden loud and insistent blast . . . above the whole orchestra." These are followed by ascending glissandi in woods, harp, piano, and upper strings. Three times the horns enter with this call. A shimmering climax is reached on the third one and the brilliant metallic sound of the triangle and orchestral bells is heard above the full orchestra *fff*.

The orchestra subdues and, over trilling violins, the flutes, clarinets, and two harps announce a dance-like theme:

Example 3

The stringed instruments repeat this theme, with little triplet figures in the woods punctuating it.

The theme returns a third time, started by the piccolo and oboe, then imitated by the clarinet, harp, and violins. It returns to the oboe for a full statement.

After an episode of trills for the strings over which the woodwinds play tremolos, the flute, oboe, and celesta introduce a variation of Example 3:

Example 4

Oboe

p

legg.

Example 4 is then accompanied by glissandi passages in both harps and celesta while the flutes and clarinets play diatonic scales. Finally all the strings enter with a repeated figure.

The orchestra builds to a climax during which the violins repeat the rhythmic figure of Example 4.

After descending passages, the music returns to a quiet mood which ends this movement. In the final measures muted trumpets repeat their fanfare.

THE TREVI FOUNTAIN AT MID-DAY

"A solemn theme borne on the undulations of the orchestra" now appears in the bassoons and English horn:

Example 5

Bassoon

mp   *cresc.*

This rising figure (Example 5) is repeated in overlapping statements, rising higher and higher in pitch as the full orchestra joins in.

The orchestra builds to a climax which is marked *fff*. The combined brass, three trumpets, three trombones, and tuba, then play this bold theme accompanied by the full orchestra.

The French horns are heard over the full orchestra with a slow and sustained theme:

French Horns   *Example 6*

The French horns at the final climax sound forth a theme built on an earlier rhythmic pattern:

Example 7

The strings reach another peak in which they have quickly moving passages over a range of more than two octaves, and the combined brass boldly state the rhythmic pattern characteristic of this movement:

The orchestra quickly subsides and fades away to a *ppp,* and calmly the clarinet plays Example 7. In the final measures the piccolo imitates the theme.

THE FOUNTAIN OF THE VILLA MEDICI AT SUNSET

The flute and English horn immediately announce the first theme of this section over extremely high sustained chords in the strings marked *ppp:*

Example 8

English Horn

The Fountain of Trevi at Mid-day

The Fountain of the Villa Medici at Sunset

The chiming of the bells at sunset is heard, followed by the flute and English horn with a restatement of Example 8.

A solo violin enters with the second theme:

Example 9

Solo Violin

A counter-melody is played by a solo cello underneath this violin theme.

The second theme (Example 9) then passes to the flute with the French horn playing the counter-melody. The solo violin finishes the theme followed by the French horn and celli with it.

Above Example 9 in the low register of the violins are heard little passages played by the flutes and clarinet which suggest "the twittering of the birds."

All the violins enter in their middle register with Example 8 followed by the flutes, oboes, and clarinets with Example 8.

Gradually the music starts to fade away, the chiming of the bells is heard again; the flute repeats once more Example 8; the bell continues to toll until soft chords in the woods and strings end the symphonic poem.

CHAPTER IX

NEW MUSIC

THERE is no generally accepted term used to designate the music of the present era. *New Music* is being accepted as better than the terms *contemporary music* and *twentieth century music* since the latter could conceivably include composers such as Rachmaninoff, Sibelius, and Richard Strauss, all who lived almost to the mid-point of this century. New Music likewise better represents the "philosophy" of this era which is essentially a revolt against nineteenth century Romanticism and a search for something "new." If the term New Music is to be used, it must not become confused with earlier uses of similar terms: *Ars Nova* (Latin) which designates the music of the early fourteenth century, and *Nuove Musiche* (Italian) which designates the music of the early seventeenth century.

New Music represents a revolt against German Romanticism of the last century and all that it represented. The degree to which it is successful varies with different composers and different techniques. No universally accepted "style" has become representative of the present era as was true of Impressionism, Romanticism, or music of the Baroque era. Composers in the early part of the twentieth century branched out in many directions with many different means; composers started with one technique, then experimented and successfully used others. It is confusing to list the many names of these directions, and one is too close to this era to indicate which will be the predominant one or which will remain meaningful for future generations.

The objections to nineteenth century Romanticism centered around the use of the major and minor scale and its key feeling; the use of regularly recurring accents throughout a movement; and the use of "lush" harmonies. The revolt could first be noted in the titles of the works by Erik Satie such as *Comme un Rossignol qui a Mal du Dent* (Like a Nightingale That Has a Toothache) and *Trois Morçeaux en forme de poire* (Three Pieces in the Form of a Pear — 1903). These were reactions against the romantic titles of symphonic poems and character pieces of the last century.

525

There are many influences in the music of the twentieth century. Composers experimented with jazz influences in their music after World War I as witnessed by Stravinsky's *Ragtime* (1918), Copland's *Two Blues* (1926), and Milhaud's *Trois Rag Caprices* (1927). Means of musical communication improved with advances in science; radio brought music to thousands who had never attended a concert. Works were commissioned by radio stations for performance such as Randall Thompson's opera *Solomon and Balkis.* As sound was added to motion pictures in 1929, another field opened for serious composers. Most successful of the film scores were Prokofiev's *Lt. Kijé* and Virgil Thomson's *Louisiana Story.* Phonographs brought music to the most isolated parts of the world and left the listener complete freedom in the choice of repertoire. Roy Harris's *Four Minutes and Twenty Seconds* was composed for a phonographic recording. The most recent contribution in the electronic field is television, which among other works commissioned Menotti's *Amahl and the Night Visitors.*

The directions music took in the contemporary revolt were many. The most noticeable was the revolt against a key feeling or tonality. Several methods were used to avoid this. *Polytonality,* in which two or more keys were used at the same time, was one. Perhaps the first accepted composition using this technique was Stravinsky's *Petrouchka,* although the music of Charles Ives, hidden away on the shelf as it was, antedated Stravinsky's work. Arnold Schoenberg proceeded in a new direction which at first was called *atonality,* literally "the absence of tonality." As Schoenberg continued with his theories and experimentations, he developed a *tone row* using all twelve tones of the octave, hence its alternate name, *dodecaphonic* music. This was based on a perpetual use through variation of a chosen arrangement or series of the twelve chromatic tones. Henry Cowell used *tone clusters* or groups of adjoining notes to help dispel the feeling of a tonal center. Micro-tonal music proved impractical at first since instruments other than the unfretted stringed ones had to be rebuilt to play it. Composers such as Haba and Vyshnegradsky composed quarter-tone music, music in which the octave was divided into quarter tones instead of the traditional half-tones of western civilization. With more recent inventions in the field of electronic music, further subdivisions of the octave are more practical and are being used.

Rhythm became an important factor in New Music, perhaps first noted in the works of Stravinsky and Bartók. A freedom from the

Alois Hába playing his quarter-tone piano, constructed by August Förster about 1927

Tape recorders and electronic music are enjoying a vogue among *avant-garde* composers. Here Composer Vladimir Ussachevsky is writing a few last minute instructions to his technical assistant just prior to a concert in New York.

Martha Reker Photograph

rhythmic regularity of nineteenth century music was an important characteristic. Melodies were no longer symmetrical in length; bar lines disappeared in much of the music; music which used time signatures varied these from measure to measure. Not only did the accent change from bar to bar, but several rhythms were employed at the same time, hence the name *polyrhythmic*.

Pandiatonicism was also an avenue of investigation and experimentation. It permitted dissonances of varying degrees in music that was still tonal. The use of different modes or scales also intrigued composers. Malipiero and Creston have both used Gregorian chants as a thematic basis in composition.

After the first surge of the revolt came moderation. The so-called *eclectic* composers attempted a return to certain features of the past. The *neo-classicists* employed some of the techniques and forms of the Baroque and Classical eras: Hindemith returned to the styles of Bach, Piston turned to the formal structure of the Classical era. The *neo-romanticists* were more easily accepted by concert audiences because their music was not far removed in style from Brahms, Wagner, and Strauss. Howard Hanson boldly called his *Symphony No. 2* "The Romantic."

A German term, *Gebrauchsmusik* (literally "music for use") is usually associated with the early works of Hindemith although works of many other composers would fall in this "category." Gebrauchsmusik was an attempt to make music practical — it was composed for student use, for family singing gatherings, for specific instruments and ensembles. Actually it was a return to certain features of the past as represented by Bach and his many sacred works for his church choir, by Haydn and his compositions for his orchestra at the Esterházy estate. Since the German term is loose in its definition, all music commissioned for films, television, and specific occasions could be considered Gebrauchsmusik.

An attempt has been made by certain musical historians to denote a twentieth century *nationalism*. It is in contrast to nineteenth century nationalism in philosophy. The composer of the last century determined to make his music representative of his country as his primary objective, and in doing this relied heavily on folk melodies, peasant dance rhythms, and folk stories. The twentieth century composer attempts to create a sincere piece of music that will communicate with all musical audiences. Because he has been educated in the musical traditions of his own country, he uses folk melodies because they are beautiful and best express the musical thought he is attempting to convey. Bartók's use of Hungarian melodies might be cited as an example, as well as the use of folk melodies of France by Milhaud, of England by Vaughan Williams, of the United States by Ives and Copland.

Primitivism is a term sometimes used to designate compositions such as Stravinsky's *The Rite of Spring* and Carl Orff's *Die Kluge*. The first is so-called because of its departure from a key center, the use of polyrhythms, and the sparse harmonizations. The latter qualifies because of its reference to things past — the influence of Greek tragedy in its staging, the use of modal writing, and the frequent use of tonic-dominant harmony familiar in the early Classical age of music.

The use of percussion instruments has increased tremendously in New Music. Edgar Varèse's *Ionisation* (1931) is scored for sixteen instruments of "percussion, friction, and sibilization," the latter consisting of two sirens. In 1955 John Cage composed a work for twelve radios and two players at each. The score calls for one performer to manipulate the dial that selects the various stations, and another performer to operate the dial that regulates the dynamics. This, as in much *avant-garde* music, allows an element of chance to enter.

The mid-century mark finds experimentation centering around electronic devices. *Electronic music* uses purely musical sounds of electronic origin which may be transformed. With this technique it is possible to compose a work on paper with serial organization and using non-tempered tones. The earlier compositions of Pierre Boulez are examples of electronic music. *Musique concrète,* on the other hand, begins by recording various sounds (either musical sounds or noises of indeterminate pitch) and then speeding them up, slowing them down, filtering or inverting them on the tape recorder, and metamorphosing them into "sound objects" (*objets sonores*) whose origin is not always possible to distinguish. Karlheinz Stockhausen of Germany seems to be the leading exponent of this last category.

BIBLIOGRAPHY

Hansen, Peter S. *An Introduction to Twentieth Century Music.* Boston: Allyn and Bacon, Inc., 1961.
Machlis, Joseph. *Introduction to Contemporary Music.* New York: W. W. Norton and Co., Inc., 1961.
Salazar, Adolfo. *Music In Our Time.* New York: W. W. Norton and Co., Inc., 1946.
Slonimsky, Nicolas. *Music Since 1900.* New York: Coleman-Ross Co., Inc. (3rd ed.), 1949.

RALPH VAUGHAN WILLIAMS

BORN: October 12, 1872; Down Ampney, Gloucestershire, England.
DIED: August 26, 1958; London, England.

Vaughan Williams was not only one of Britain's great composers, but a warm-hearted, down-to-earth musician. He admonished composers not to sit in ivory towers and think about absolute art but to live with their fellow citizens and make music an expression of the life of the community. He told fellow composers to study wherever they might choose (he had studied in Berlin and Paris), but above all else to be sincere. His theory was that the roots of one's soil, its training and historical heritage, are bound to affect one's final work and make it representative of his country. Throughout his music, Vaughan Williams has proved faithful to these admonitions.

Vaughan Williams was the son of a clergyman and received his early education at the Charterhouse School in London. From this institution he went to the Royal College of Music for two years and then took his Bachelor of Music degree at Trinity College, Cambridge. He returned to the Royal College of Music for one year's work in the field of piano and pipe organ. After finishing school in his early twenties, he became organist at St. Barnabas Church, South Lambeth, for three years. Wishing to do additional work in the field of composition, he went to Berlin to study with composer Max Bruch at the Akademie der Kunste. He returned from the continent to complete his Doctor of Music degree at Cambridge in 1901.

Late in emerging as a composer, it was perhaps joining the English Folk Song Society in 1904 that gave him impetus as a composer, for he wrote one of his first notable works the same year, *In the Fen Country*. This was followed by a survey of folk music from the Norfolk area and the composition of *Three Norfolk Rhapsodies*. Feeling the need for more help in the field of composition, Vaughan Williams went to Paris for private work with Maurice Ravel. Ravel was two years younger than Vaughan Williams but had matured as a composer faster. Vaughan Williams spent eight months studying with him.

Vaughan Williams produced one of his best known compositions on his return to England, *Fantasia On a Theme of Thomas Tallis,* which was followed by *A London Symphony* (which he regarded as his Symphony No. 1). His first experience with the theater was the composition of a "ballad opera" entitled *Hugh the Drover*. World

RALPH VAUGHAN WILLIAMS

ARNOLD SCHOENBERG

Florence Homolka Photo

BÉLA BARTÓK

Photograph by the conductor Fritz Reiner

Courtesy of Boosey and Hawkes

SERGE PROKOFIEV

War I interrupted his artistic efforts and although he was over-age and exempt from war duty (he was forty-two), he enlisted and served first in Macedonia and then transferred to the Territorial Royal Army Military Corps for duty in France. Here he qualified as an officer and saw service on the field of battle.

After demobilization, Vaughan Williams became a professor at the Royal College of Music where he served for over thirty years. In 1922 he composed his *Pastoral Symphony* and in the same year made his first trip to the United States to conduct his works at a Norfolk, Connecticut festival. Ten years later he paid a second visit to this country during which he made several lecture appearances and gave a course on national music at Bryn Mawr College. In 1935 he received the Order of Merit from King George V. His book, *National Music,* was published the same year.

In 1942, during the life and death struggle against the Nazi Germans, England honored Vaughan Williams on his seventieth birthday with a series of six concerts over the BBC devoted entirely to his compositions. Vaughan Williams served the British as a civilian during World War II and managed to complete his *Symphony No. 5* during those trying days.

Vaughan Williams was a faithful conductor at various annual festivals in Great Britain. Many of his choral masterpieces were written for these festivals. In earlier days he had served as conductor of the Bach Choir and for fifty years was the conductor for the Leith Hill Festival. He conducted special festivals in London, Bournemouth, and Birmingham, also.

Vaughan Williams became known as the "grand old man" of British music (a term he abhorred). He was accorded world-wide honor on the occasion of his eightieth birthday in 1952. This celebration did not terminate his creative abilities for it was followed by the composition of his opera *Pilgrim's Progress* and *Symphony No. 8* and *Symphony No. 9,* within three years. During this period Vaughan Williams made his third tour of the United States lecturing at both Cornell and Yale.

Vaughan Williams was an honored and revered composer of his native land and had achieved international recognition for his artistic accomplishments. He passed away on the 26th of August, 1958. He left a legacy of nine symphonies; various rhapsodies and serenades; concerti for piano, violin, viola, oboe, bass tuba; much great choral music including *A Serenade to Music; Dona Nobis Pacem; Job, A Masque for Dancing;* six operas including *Pilgrim's Progress, Sir John in Love, Riders to the Sea;* and a quantity of chamber music. His ashes have been interred in Westminster Abbey alongside the great heroes of English art, history, and royalty.

BIBLIOGRAPHY

Howes, Frank. *The Music of Ralph Vaughan Williams.* London: Oxford University Press, 1954.

Pakenham, Simona. *Ralph Vaughan Williams: A Discovery of His Music.* New York: St. Martins Press, 1957.

SYMPHONY NO. 8

in D Minor

Ralph Vaughan Williams

Second Movement: Scherzo Alla Marcia (per stromenti a fiato).
Allegro alla marcia

The "per stromenti a fiato" in the title of this movement means for wind instruments alone, no strings. Vaughan Williams employs flute, piccolo, two oboes, two clarinets, three bassoons, two French horns, two trumpets, and three trombones in this movement.

The second movement opens with the first theme played by the bassoons:

Example 1

Four bars later the bassoons are answered by the flute with essentially the same theme.

The second theme, repeated, appears in the trumpets:

Example 2

The trumpets are answered by the high woodwinds: piccolo, flute, oboes, with a third theme:

Example 3

After a brief rhythmic figure played by the clarinets and solo trumpet, this theme is repeated.

The rhythmic figure then becomes the beginning of a fugato:

Example 4

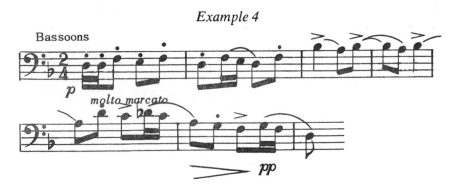

The "fugato" subject (Example 4) appears in the following order:

the bassoons
the clarinet
the flutes, piccolo, and oboes
the trumpet
the French horn
the trombones

The trio of this movement is an *Andante* in 6/8 meter. A new theme occurs in the clarinets and bassoons accompanied by staccato trumpets:

Example 5

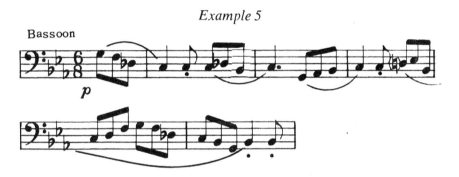

The trio theme (Example 5) occurs again, this time with a flute and two clarinets.

There is no recapitulation of the first section; instead there is a stretto of material already presented and based primarily on the subject of the "fugato" (Example 4).

FOURTH MOVEMENT: Toccata, *Maestoso*

The final movement calls for full orchestra, plus, as the composer says:

A large supply of extra percussion, including all the 'phones and 'spiels known to the composer . . . [It] commandeers all the available hitting instruments which can make noise, including the glockenspiel, celesta, xylophone, vibraphone, tubular bells, and tuned gongs.

After an initial impact by the tuned gongs, bells, cymbals, and harp, an introductory theme appears immediately in full orchestra:

Example 6

Violins

The principal theme appears in two parts (A and B), rhythmically similar, announced by the trumpet and repeated by the full orchestra. It also becomes the principal theme of the "rondo" treatment.

Example 7

Trumpet

An episode follows this in which the violins play another theme:

Violins   *Example 8*

cantabile

The principal theme (Example 7) returns in the trombones and violins, and then passes to the glockenspiel, bells, oboes, and clarinets.

The full orchestra follows with the principal theme (Example 7).

Another episode occurs with a theme in the violins:

Example 9

This theme passes through the strings and woodwinds, and eventually it is played by the harp with vibraphone accompaniment.

The principal theme (Example 7) returns in the harps, glockenspiel, bells, and clarinet.

This is followed by an episode for the xylophone doubled by the clarinet and followed by the bassoon and horns:

Example 10

The principal theme (Example 7) is repeated by full orchestra, answered by an episode for vibraphone and violins:

Example 11

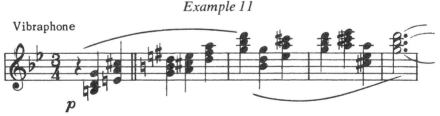

The principal theme (Example 7) next appears in the low brass and strings with glissandi for harp and bells, moving to the upper strings and woodwinds.

The full orchestra states this principal theme.

A *coda* based on the introductory figure (Example 6) ends the movement.

ARNOLD SCHOENBERG

BORN: September 13, 1874; Vienna, Austria.
DIED: July 13, 1951; Los Angeles, California.

During Schoenberg's lifetime he was known as the musician that wrote angry and bitter letters to music critics, symphony conductors, and radio commentators. He complained that they either ignored his music, that they didn't play enough of it, or else they would schedule for performance only his early works. After a performance of his *Gurre-Lieder* (Songs of Gurre) in Vienna in 1913 the audience was most enthusiastic in its ovation and friends tried to encourage Schoenberg to take a "composer's bow." He left the concert hall exclaiming, "For years these people who cheered me tonight refused to recognize me, why should I thank them for appreciating me now?"

After these early compositions in the "late-romantic" vein of Mahler and Wagner, Schoenberg developed a style based on a "tone-row." Basically, if a given octave on the keyboard were counted, there would be twelve half-steps if the starting note were not repeated at the next octave. Schoenberg's tone-row was based on using each of these twelve tones in any succession. Once this order or succession of tones had been decided upon (known as the "tone-row"), throughout any given composition they had to be used in that order, none of them appearing again until all the others in the row had been used in the arbitrary order already decided upon. Sometimes this use of twelve-tones is called *dodecaphonic* music, a form of *atonalism* because it lacks any tone center or "key feeling." Schoenberg's compositions in this later style were not well received by the public, and of this he complained bitterly. When the New York Philharmonic Orchestra celebrated Schoenberg's birthday by broadcasting parts of his *Gurre-Lieder,* he wrote the commentator, "I hope on my hundredth birthday you get around to playing one of my more recent compositions."

Accused of trying to compose music in a strictly mechanical, mathematical fashion, Schoenberg replied:

I offer incontestable proof of the fact that in following the twelve-tone scale, a composer is neither less nor more bound, hindered nor made independent. He may be as cold-hearted and unmoved as an engineer, or, as laymen imagine, may conceive in sweet dreams — in inspiration.

What can be constructed with these twelve tones depends on one's inventive faculty. The basic tones will not invent for you. Expression is limited only by the composer's creativeness and his personality. He may be original or moving, with old or modern methods. Finally, success depends only on whether we are touched, excited, made happy, enthusiastic . . . or not.

The tempest raised about my music does not rest upon my ideas, but exists because of the dissonances. Dissonances are but consonances which appear later among the overtones . . .

There is no such distinction as old and modern music, but only good music and bad. All music, in so far as it is the product of a truly creative mind, is *new* . . . Truly good things are new . . . Music without ideas is unthinkable, and people who are not willing to use their brains to understand music which cannot be grasped at first hearing are simply lazy-minded.*

Arnold Schoenberg faced great poverty in his early life in Vienna, but fortunately he was surrounded by a city full of music and musicians. During his six years in school he played some music with chamber ensembles, having received violin lessons and taught himself the cello. He had no idea until he was sixteen that he wished to become a musician. For the amateur groups he played with as a youth Schoenberg composed several chamber works. His father's death during Arnold's sixteenth year left the family in a very bad financial situation, and lessons in music were out of the question for the incipient musician.

When Schoenberg was twenty, his music aroused the interest of Alexander von Zemlinsky, a friend of Johannes Brahms. Zemlinsky took Schoenberg under his protective arm and for two years taught the lad composition, the only formal training in music that Schoenberg ever had. Schoenberg was later to marry Zemlinsky's sister. His first work to receive a public hearing was a string quartet which was received with favor (the music to this work has since been lost). His songs, however, were more daring, less academic, and aroused violent objections.

During his twenty-fifth year Schoenberg composed *Verklärte Nacht* (Transfigured Night) for string sextet. The next year his *Gurre-Lieder* (Songs of Gurre) for soli, chorus, and orchestra was completed. These were written in the late style of Wagner and Mahler and have by now been fairly well accepted by the public since they are in tonal style and with some rich romantic melodies throughout. Although *Gurre-Lieder* was almost complete in 1901 it had to wait ten years for Schoenberg to orchestrate it because he had to orchestrate operettas to earn a living — 6,000 pages of operetta music!

Schoenberg taught composition in several conservatories during his European days — Stern, Vienna, Berlin; also he guest conducted his works throughout Europe, including St. Petersburg, Amsterdam,

* Merle Armitage, *The Book of Modern Composers.* New York: Alfred A. Knopf.

and London. While in Berlin he started his *Pierrot Lunaire* at the suggestion of the actress Albertine Zehme. When it was first performed after some forty rehearsals, actual fist fights broke out in the audience and cat-calls and boos were the order of the day.

During World War I Schoenberg, already forty, served only short periods of garrison duty in Vienna. After the war, he settled near Vienna and conducted composers' seminars. In 1925 he was appointed to the staff of the Prussian Academy of Arts but resigned in 1933 when Adolf Hitler rose to power and started his crusade against Jews.

Schoenberg moved first to Paris and later that year accepted a position with a conservatory in Boston. Because of his health, a serious sinus condition, after one year in Boston Schoenberg and his family moved to southern California where he served first on the staff of the University of Southern California for one year and then was employed by the University of California at Los Angeles. He remained there for the next eight years until the state law forced him to retire at seventy. While he was on the faculty at UCLA, he had many visits from contemporary composers: Henry Cowell, Darius Milhaud, and Roger Sessions. George Gershwin was an especially good friend of Schoenberg, although neither influenced the other in style of composition. Shortly after assuming his duties at UCLA, Schoenberg moved his family to a lovely home in Brentwood that was always open on week-ends to visits from students and fellow musicians alike. He played tennis until his final illness started, and then contented himself with watching his son Ronnie practice on the court working towards a tennis championship.

While at UCLA Schoenberg composed his *Violin Concerto* which was immediately cast as unplayable, but a year later Stokowski premiered it with the Philadelphia Orchestra. Since the concert was not broadcast, Schoenberg had to wait until shortly before his death to hear it in a recording that had been made at that performance. He made many trips lecturing on modern music and composition, trips to Denver, San Diego, Kansas City, and Chicago. The *Second Chamber Symphony* was completed in 1940, and the following year he and his wife became American citizens. With the brutalities that were occurring against the Jewish people in Nazi Germany, Schoenberg became so incensed he wrote his *Ode to Napoleon Buonaparte* based on Byron's poem inspired by the announcement that Napoleon had abdicated at Fontainebleu.

Two years after Schoenberg's retirement from the university he was incapacitated by his health — heart trouble and asthma. He ventured out in public for concerts celebrating his seventy-fifth birthday. The following year a complete break-down of his heart finished his career. Simple non-sectarian services were held in a chapel and were conducted by a Rabbi. Only about forty people attended the service.

BIBLIOGRAPHY

Schoenberg, Arnold. *Style and Idea.* New York: Philosophical Library, 1950.
Leibowitz, Rene. *Schoenberg and His School: The Contemporary Stage of the Language of Music.* New York: Philosophical Library, 1949.

PIERROT LUNAIRE**
Melodrama, Opus 21

ARNOLD SCHOENBERG

Pierrot Lunaire is based on a melodrama entitled *Three Times Seven Poems* by Albert Giraud. Schoenberg employed the German translation of these poems by Otto Erich Hartleben. The work is divided as indicated by the title into three sections, each with seven subdivisions or songs.

The work is scored for a small ensemble: piano; flute interchangeable with piccolo; clarinet interchangeable with bass clarinet; violin interchangeable with viola; and cello. In addition, the composer uses a *reciter* to present the lyrics of the melodrama in a style called *Sprechstimme.* In each of the songs a different combination of instruments is used; they do not necessarily augment the meaning of the lyrics. For example, when Pierrot is described as playing on the viola in *Serenade*, the cello, not the viola, accompanies the passage.

Sprechstimme is a form of "singing speech" indicated in the music by Schoenberg's own invention of the *x*'s on the stems of the notes. This indicates that the rhythm should always be observed by the singer, that the parts spoken were to slide up and down from the indicated pitch at the singer's discretion. The scoring is such that the vocalist is a member of the chamber musicians, not a vocal soloist accompanied by an ensemble.

** Reprinted by permission of Gertrud Schoenberg and Universal Edition A. G. Vienna, original editor.

Part 1

No. 1: *Mondestrunken* (Moonstruck)

This movement is scored for piano, flute, violin, and cello. The piano opens the movement with a descending figure:

Piano

The voice enters in the Sprechstimme style.

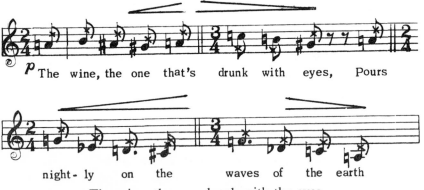

The wine, the one that's drunk with eyes, Pours

night- ly   on   the   waves of   the   earth

> The wine, the one drunk with the eyes
> Pours nightly on the waves of the earth
> And one springtide flooded the still horizon.
> Desires, dreadful and sweet,
> Flow through without number;
> The wine, the one drunk with the eyes,
> Pours nightly on the waves of the earth.

No. 2: *Colombine.*

This movement is scored for clarinet, flute, violin, and piano. It opens with the piano accompanying the voice:

The pale blos- soms of moon- light, The

won- der- ous- ly white ros- es

The pale blossoms of the moonlight,
The wondrous white of the roses,
Bloom in the July night,
I the only fallow one.

No. 3: *Der Dandy* (The Dandy).

This movement is scored for piccolo, clarinet and piano. The clarinet opens the movement with an upward phrase that is repeated by the reciter when she enters:

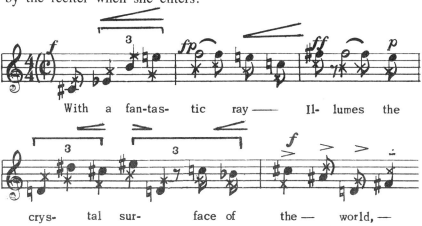

With a fan-tas- tic ray —— Il- lumes the

crys- tal sur- face of the — world, —

The dandy of Bergamo with a phantastic ray
Illuminates the crystal surface of the world,
Silently washing away the silence
Of the black heavens.

No. 4: *Eine Blasse Wäscherin* (A Pale Washerwoman).

Scored for clarinet, flute, violin, and piano, the introduction opens in triads for the first three instruments and doubled by the piano.

pale clothes;

> A pale washerwoman washes
> At nighttime her pale clothes;
> The clothes stretch in the flood
> Against her silver-white arms.

No. 5: *Valse de Chopin.*

The piano, flute, and clarinet doubling with the bass clarinet, accompany the reciter in this movement. A waltz rhythm is established by the piano; the contrapuntal style of writing vaguely suggests the idea of a Chopin waltz.

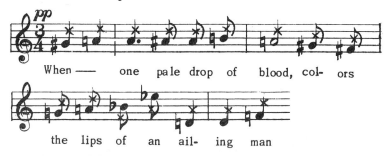

> When one pale drop of blood
> Colors the lips of an ailing man,
> So stir these tones
> Seeking charm in one's destruction.

No. 6: *Madonna.*

The reciter is accompanied by the flute, bass clarinet, and cello in this movement, the piano enters for the last two measures of the lyrics and then accompanies the other instruments in the two-measure ending. Not only are the low instruments used in this movement, the voice itself is kept on low pitches:

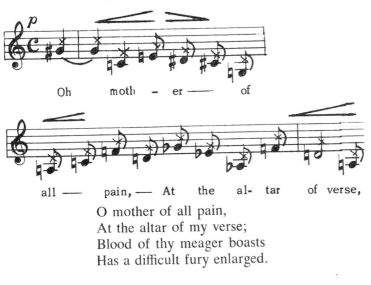

O mother of all pain,
At the altar of my verse;
Blood of thy meager boasts
Has a difficult fury enlarged.

No. 7: *Der Kranke Mond* (The Sick Moon).

The first part of *Pierrot Lunaire* ends with this short movement scored for flute and reciter only. Flute interludes separate the three divisions of the short verse.

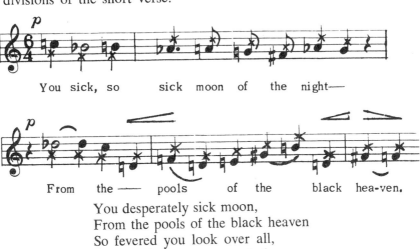

You desperately sick moon,
From the pools of the black heaven
So fevered you look over all,
Banned like a strange melody.

BÉLA BARTÓK

BORN: March 25, 1881; Nagy-szent-miklós, Hungary.
DIED: September 26, 1945; New York, New York.

Béla Bartók spent more than eight years searching for the authentic folk music of his native Hungary, digging it out from under the superimposed melodies and rhythms of the gypsies. With a crude, hand-wound phonograph of the 1905 variety he traveled through all of Transylvania, Rumania, and through the Slavic region. He recorded examples on the phonograph and later transcribed them to musical notation. In this manner Bartók collected over 6,000 folk melodies. Although as a mature composer he employed the contemporary idiom in his compositions, both his melodies and rhythms were greatly influenced by these Hungarian folk tunes.

Bartók was born in the little Hungarian community of Nagy-szent-miklós where his father was the Director of the School of Agriculture and his mother a teacher. His father's death when Béla was eight forced the family to move three times in as many years. Not only did his mother assume the responsibility for educating the family, she likewise assumed the financial burden. Although Bartók's childhood was one of poverty, through his mother's training he developed a love for music and at nine composed a set of piano pieces. A year later he made his debut as a pianist.

When he was thirteen the family settled in Pressburg and he started regular piano lessons. It was there that he met Ernst von Dohnányi who became a close friend and advisor. Dohnányi encouraged the lad to study at the Liszt Academy in Budapest, which Bartók did from 1899 to 1903. While there, he met Zoltán Kodály who became a personal friend and joined Bartók on his expeditions to collect Hungarian folk music. At the Academy, Bartók was accepted as a brilliant student in both piano and composition. His first notable work was a patriotic symphony entitled *Kossuth,* a work which showed the influence of Liszt and Richard Strauss in its style.

Bartók left the Academy the same year he finished this composition. In order to earn enough money on which to live, he played piano professionally, did some teaching, and made arrangements. In 1905 he saw his Opus 1, 2, and 3 published; Opus 1 and 2 were rhapsodies for the piano, while Opus 3 was a suite for orchestra.

Two years later Bartók was appointed professor of piano at the Liszt Academy. He encountered many criticisms there because of the

Bela Bartók collecting Hungarian folk music. The photograph was taken in 1908 (supposedly by Zoltán Kodály). The peasants line up to record their songs on the old wax cylinder phonograph operated by Bartók (without hat.)

IGOR STRAVINSKY

style his musical compositions were assuming. His first moderately successful work was *The Wooden Prince* followed shortly by *Bluebeard's Castle*. He had to wait until the performance of his *Second String Quartet* in 1918, however, before he was known as an outstanding Hungarian composer.

Bartók made his first trip to the United States in 1927 as a pianist. This was followed by trips all over Europe giving concerts as a duo-pianist with his wife. They visited Prague, Frankfurt, Belgium, Florence, and Barcelona.

In 1936 he made a trip to Turkey to investigate the music of the primitive peoples of that area whose origin he assumed had close historical ties with the Hungarians. After delivering lectures in French, German, and Hungarian at the Conservatory in Ankara, he headed for the black hills of Turkey, an area as primitive as can be found anywhere. He lived with the nomadic tribes and recorded their folk melodies. He performed this service for the Turkish government, stipulating that the only remuneration he wanted was a round-trip second-class railroad ticket. At the completion of his first work there he returned to Budapest, but since the Nazis had started their march through southern Europe, Bartók could not remain. He begged the Conservatory in Ankara, Turkey, to find him a position, but none was to be had. Bartók emigrated to the United States, leaving most of his 6,000 transcriptions behind in Europe. He worked laboriously over the few precious remnants of this collection he was able to bring with him.

Bartók served as a visiting professor at Columbia University where he was given an honorary Doctor of Music degree. He never quite acclimatized himself to the United States, and since his finances were in extremely bad condition and his health was equally poor, he spent his years in the United States under very unhappy circumstances.

Although so sick in the last three years of his life that he had a constant fever, he composed his *Concerto for Orchestra* just two years before his untimely death. It was commissioned by the Koussevitsky Foundation of Boston, and Bartók dedicated the Concerto to the memory of Koussevitsky's wife. Bartók's last work was his *Third Piano Concerto*. He was so ill during the final pages of this work that he had his son, who was home on leave from the Navy, sit at his bedside and rule the score-paper for him. It was completed just days before his death from leukemia.

Within a few months of Bartók's death, he was honored by

having his compositions played by most of the major orchestras. According to one survey made, there were forty-eight major orchestral performances of his works within the six months after his death.

BIBLIOGRAPHY

Haraszti, Emil. *Béla Bartók: His Life and Works,* trans. Dorothy Swainson and author. Paris: Lyrebird Press, 1938.
Stevens, Halsey. *The Life and Music of Béla Bartók.* New York: Oxford University Press, 1953.

CONCERTO FOR ORCHESTRA*

BÉLA BARTÓK

"The title of this symphony-like orchestral work is explained by its tendency to treat the single instrument groups in a concertant or soloistic manner," states the composer in program notes he prepared for the first performance of this work in 1944.

SECOND MOVEMENT: *Allegretto scherzando (Giuoco delle Coppie* "Game of the Couples")

To quote the composer again: "The main part of the second movement consists of a chain of independent short sections, by wind instruments consecutively introduced in five pairs (bassoons in 6ths, oboes in 3rds, clarinets in 7ths, flutes in 5ths, and muted trumpets in 2nds). Thematically, the five sections have nothing in common. A kind of 'trio' — a short chorale for brass instruments and side-drum — follows, after which the five sections are recapitulated in a more elaborate instrumentation."

An introduction is given by a solo side-drum without snares in a syncopated rhythm:

---

* *Concerto for Orchestra* — Copyright, 1946, by Hawkes & Son (London) Ltd
Reprinted by permission of Boosey & Hawkes, Inc.

The first theme is introduced by a pair of bassoons:

Example 1

A pair of oboes enter with:

Example 2

The clarinets:

Example 3

The flutes are heard next in a somewhat longer thematic passage:

Example 4

The muted trumpets complete this section of the work with a theme in seconds:

Example 5

The "trio" of brass instruments is in five voices: two trumpets, two trombones, and a tuba. The side drum, again without snares, accompanies the choral:

Example 6

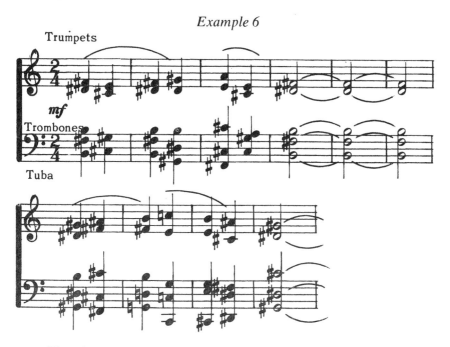

The themes of the first section then return in the same sequence. The same instruments are heard with their respective themes, although other instruments join them: the third bassoon joins the pair of bassoons; the clarinets join the oboes in their melody; the flutes join the clarinets in the third theme; the oboes join the flutes; and the harp furnishes a glissandi accompaniment to the trumpet theme.

The movement ends with a solo for the side-drum.

FOURTH MOVEMENT: Interrupted Intermezzo. *Allegretto.*

The composer states: "The form of the fourth movement . . . could be rendered by the letter symbols ABA — interruption — BA."

After a three-measure introduction by the strings, the oboe announces the "A" theme:

Example 7

Oboe

This melody is repeated by the clarinet and flute accompanied by the bassoon which plays an inversion of Example 7.

The inverted melody is heard by itself in the flute.

The horns follow with a variation in rhythm and pitch of the original Example 7.

The oboe plays Example 7 in its original form.

The *Allegretto* changes to *Calmo,* the violas play a magnificent and lyrical "B" theme:

Example 8

Violas

The violins then repeat this melody while the English horn imitates it two beats later.

At the conclusion of the English horn passage, the oboe repeats Example 7.

The interruption of the intermezzo now occurs. As the tempo accelerates, the clarinet announces the theme of the "interruption":

Example 9

After a humorous descending passage in almost mocking fashion by the woodwinds, a trombone glissando is heard twice.

Bartók then employs the woodwinds in a rhythmic section suggestive of a German band while the violins play a rhythmic variation of the "interruption" theme (Example 9).

A loud crash on the Chinese gong announces the return to the calm section and the upper strings play the lyrical "B" theme (Example 8).

The strings are followed by the English horn with Example 7.

A flute cadenza follows. A final statement of Example 7 in an inverted pattern passes from oboe to bassoon, to piccolo. The movement ends with three staccato notes for the woodwinds.

IGOR STRAVINSKY
born: June 17, 1882; Oranienbaum, Russia
died: April 6, 1971; New York, New York

Stravinsky's name is probably better known, and his works more frequently performed, than any other composer of New Music. He first shocked the musical world with three ballets created for Diaghilev, the ballet impressario, in the years 1910 to 1913. From early works strongly flavored with his Russian background, a great change took place during a fifteen year residence in Paris. Having lived for many years now in Beverly Hills, California, his latest works make use of tone rows.

Stravinsky has been accused of too many changes in style, and a decadence from his earlier works. To this criticism he has replied:

I live neither in the past nor in the future. I am in the present. I cannot know what tomorrow will bring forth. I can only know what is true for me today.

Stravinsky's father was a leading bass at the Imperial Opera in Russia and created the role of Varlaam in the first performance of *Boris Godunov*. There was much music in and around the Stravinsky household and Igor started piano lessons at nine years of age. He soon discovered the vast store of musical scores that his father kept in the house; these plus a Tchaikovsky memorial concert he heard caused him to mark this as "the beginning of a conscious life as artist and musician."

Stravinsky's father had not outlined a musical career for his son, and after completion of normal school the boy was enrolled in the University of St. Petersburg to study law. He was permitted by his family to study harmony at the University and counterpoint on his own. Almost by accident Stravinsky met Rimsky-Korsakov when they were both visiting the University of Heidelberg. The young lad played several of his original compositions for Rimsky-Korsakov. The master thought Stravinsky had possibilities but recommended that he develop his harmonic sense.

In 1905 Stravinsky completed his Opus 1, the *First Symphony*. This work was strongly influenced by Brahms' style of composition. Two years later Stravinsky quit law school and spent two years with Rimsky-Korsakov studying composition. His Opus 2, *The Faun and the Shepherdess,* became much more Russian in style than his Opus 1 had been. *The Symphony* and *The Faun* were performed the following year, and since Stravinsky was known to the public as a talented student of Rimsky-Korsakov, many ears were turned in his direction. This same year Stravinsky wrote his *Fireworks* in honor of the marriage of Rimsky-Korsakov's daughter. Rimsky-Korsakov died four days later and Stravinsky did not compose anything for a while after the loss of his friend and mentor.

In Paris Diaghilev heard the *Fantastic Scherzo* of Stravinsky at a Siloti concert and was so impressed that he asked Stravinsky to arrange

Chopin's *Valse Brilliante* and a *Nocturne* for his proposed ballet, *Les Sylphides.* Diaghilev was so pleased with the results that he commissioned Stravinsky to compose a ballet based on the Russian fairy tale of "The Firebird."

One of the most noted nights in the annals of twentieth century music was the night in 1910 when *The Firebird* was premiered. While the public continued to disagree about the merits of the work, Stravinsky started on a new one. He had been intrigued by the story of *Petrouchka, a* harlequin. Stravinsky, upon the encouragement of Diaghilev in this project, completed the score during a visit to Rome. It was presented by Diaghilev in Paris just three weeks before Stravinsky's twenty-ninth birthday. In this work Stravinsky used a chord of C major against a chord of F-sharp major, the "Petrouchka chord," and thus *polytonality* (two or more keys at the same time) was presented to the public.

The third of the three ballets of this early period was the *Rite of Spring.* No premiere had caused such a scene as this one. With audience up in arms, shouting, booing, it was followed by scandalous scenes.

Stravinsky returned to Russia for a brief visit and was not to see it again for 52 years. During World War I, he fled first to Switzerland and then settled for fifteen years in Paris, his adopted home. During this period Stravinsky composed a cantata, *Les Noces,* and the opera *Renard.* At the end of the war Stravinsky left Paris for Rome while the Russian revolution was going on. Stravinsky thought that because of the world war, the revolution, and the days of financial crisis, the era of large orchestral works was gone. He turned to smaller media and produced *L'Histoire du Soldat* for a narrator and seven instruments in 1918. Shortly before the Armistice was signed, he turned to the then popular trend in American music, jazz, and composed a work entitled *Ragtime.*

By 1923 Stravinsky turned away from Russian ideas to absolute music. One of his first works in this form was his *Octet for Wind Instruments.* His first tour of the United States took place two years later, when he appeared with several orchestras as guest conductor of his own compositions.

Both medieval and religious influences next crept into Stravinsky's music, influences which still affect him. In 1927 he had the text of *Oedipus Rex* translated from the French to Latin so that he could set it to music. Three years later he wrote the *Symphony of Psalms* for the fiftieth anniversary of the Boston Symphony Orchestra, scored for chorus and orchestra without violins or violas. In 1934, after completing his ballet *Persephone* for Ida Rubinstein, Stravinsky became a French citizen. Three years later he toured the United States again and composed his *Card Party*, a ballet in "three deals," for presentation at the Metropolitan Opera House under his baton.

After the fall of France to Hitler in 1939, Stravinsky moved to the United States where in 1940 he married the widow of the artist Soudeikine in Bedford, Massachusetts. The following year he applied for American citizenship and moved to Los Angeles. His early years in California saw some unusual commissions: a *Circus Polka* for the Ringling Brothers, Barnum & Bailey Circus (1944); *Scenes de Ballet* for Billy Rose's *Seven Lively Arts* (1944); *Ebony Concerto* for Woody Herman's band (1946); and *Praeludium*, a work of thirty-odd bars meant as a signature for a dance band.

After World War II Stravinsky completed his *Mass* which was performed in New York over radio, and at Columbia University. The Venice Festival of 1951 was dominated by the figure of Stravinsky. For the first time in about twenty-eight years he had completed an opera, *The Rake's Progress*. Having written works in Russian, French, and Latin, Stravinsky now had a work in English. Musicians, critics, and stage producers from all over the world gathered for this heralded premiere in Venice. They applauded when Stravinsky appeared at the beginning of the performance, and followed each of the nine scenes with further ovations for the composer. At the end they brought him on stage for a final round of applause. This opera was next presented in the leading opera houses of Europe: England, Denmark, Belgium, and Italy. It was presented at the Metropolitan Opera House on February 14, 1953. In this work Stravinsky uses the conventional operatic pattern: arias, duets, trios, concerted numbers, and choruses, all accompanied by a chamber orchestra.

In 1953 Stravinsky completed his *Cantata* for soprano, tenor, female chorus, and instrumental ensemble. In rondo form, it employs a great amount of polyphony, although there are harmonic sections. The following year, he finished *Three Songs from William Shakespeare*. In this he showed his investigation of styles of composition. The first of the three songs, *Musick to Heare*, was done with the tone row system; the second, *Full Fadom Five*, was developed in a "Netherlandish" style; while the final song, *When Daisies Pied*, was strophic in form and diatonic in style.

The 1956 Venice Festival was even more dominated by Stravinsky than was the earlier one of 1951. His *Canticum Sacrum* was presented at St. Mark's Cathedral in Venice and attracted both praise and criticism. The text of the *Canticum* was taken from St. Mark, John I, Song of Songs and the Psalms from the Vulgate Bible. This work for tenor, baritone, mixed chorus, and orchestra was accused of stylistic inconsistencies. Some movements were in the tone-row system, others in his own polyphonic style.

A year later Stravinsky's ballet *Agon* was presented in concert form on the eve of his seventy-fifth birthday at the University of California at Los Angeles. It had a complex score with carefully worked out details of polyphony, harmony, and sonority. The work was not entirely in the twelve-tone system. A New York festival of Stravinsky's music in 1959 witnessed the premiere of *Raoul Dufy, Memoriam* for string quartet, and *Movements for Piano and Orchestra* (a work the composer calls "anti-tonal"). Both works were well received.

Stravinsky and his wife Vera continue to live in Beverly Hills, California. One of his most recent works is a composition for television, *Noah and the Flood,* which received its first performance on that medium in the spring of 1962. This was part of a world-wide celebration of the composer's eightieth birthday. It is in the form of a fourteenth century miracle play with spoken parts and ballet.

BIBLIOGRAPHY

Stravinsky, Igor. *Igor Stravinsky: An Autobiography.* New York: M. & J. Steuer, 1958.
Vlad, Roman. *Stravinsky.* London: Oxford University Press, 1960.

PETROUCHKA

A Burlesque in Four Scenes

IGOR STRAVINSKY

Petrouchka was the second ballet which Stravinsky composed for Diaghilev. Together with the earlier *The Firebird* and the later *The Rite of Spring* it belongs to the composer's so-called "Russian" period. In *Petrouchka* Stravinsky used folk themes as well as original ones in the folk idiom. Their characteristics include narrow range, modality, and emphasis of the second degree of the scale.

Petrouchka had at first been intended as a condensed piano concerto, and the second scene contains much of the music composed with that intent. It was to be a parody of piano virtuosity. Later Stravinsky incorporated it into the music of *Petrouchka*.

The story of *Petrouchka* takes place during the Shrove Tide Fair (the last celebration before Lent) in Admiralty Square, St. Petersburg, about 1830. Three puppets — a Ballerina, Petrouchka, and a Moor — are exhibited by a Charlatan at the fair. Petrouchka "bitterly resents the Charlatan's cruelty, his own slavery . . . his ugliness and ridiculous appearance. He seeks consolation in the love of the Ballerina . . . but she is only frightened of his strange ways." The Moor "is stupid and evil, but his sumptuous clothes attract the Ballerina."

There are four scenes in the ballet; in the first the entire fair is seen with its jostling crowds in true carnival spirit. A group of drunks is seen; a carnival barker appears; and an Italian organ-grinder is heard. As the organ-grinder turns the handle of the barrel organ, a dancer accompanies herself on the triangle. To amuse the holiday crowd still further, the organ-grinder plays the trumpet with one hand and turns the organ crank with the other.

Suddenly two drummers appear in front of the Charlatan's puppet theater calling the crowd with the roll of their drums; the Charlatan takes his flute and plays it for attention. After the curtain has gone up the three puppets are brought to life by the magic of the Charlatan — the Ballerina, Petrouchka, and the Moor. They do a stiff, angular Russian dance.

The second scene of the ballet takes place in Petrouchka's room as he is kicked into the room. A frowning picture of the Charlatan hangs on the wall, and the puppet shakes his fist at it. The Ballerina enters, but she is repulsed by Petrouchka's strange actions, and flees. Petrouchka, furious that he had been rebuffed by the one he loves because of his ugliness, starts to beat his fists against the picture of the Charlatan. He knocks a hole in the wall with his violent actions and falls through it.

The Moor's room is the setting for the third scene; the Moor is seen doing a quasi-Oriental dance. The Ballerina enters and dances daintily on her tip toes to her own trumpet playing. Soon the Moor and the Ballerina are seen waltzing. Petrouchka bursts into the room, still furious with jealousy, and he and the Moor fight as the delicate Ballerina faints.

The three puppets   Margot Fonteyn as the Ballerina

The opening scene of *Petrouchka*. The charlatan (in white with top hat and wand, to the right of the "Theater") brings to life the three puppets: the Moor, the Ballerina, and Petrouchka.

The final scene is *The Grand Carnival.* It opens with a general impression of the activities at a carnival in the early evening. Soon different parts of the celebration are seen in detail: a group of nurse-maids dance; a peasant with a dancing bear crosses the scene; a drunken merchant dances with gypsies and amuses himself by throwing bank notes to the crowd; the coachmen and grooms are seen dancing and attract the attention of the nursemaids; fireworks illuminate the scene as masqueraders enter dressed as devils, goats, and pigs; the entire crowd joins in a dance.

Suddenly cries are heard from the puppet theater and Petrouchka is seen running out pursued by the Moor whom the Ballerina is unable to hold back. The Moor finally strikes Petrouchka on the head and kills him with the great sword he has been brandishing. A policeman arrives. The Charlatan picks up the little body and shakes it to show the crowd that it is only a sawdust-filled doll. As the crowd disperses, the Charlatan is left alone with the limp body of his puppet. Suddenly he sees the puppet's ghost grimacing at him from the roof of the theater. Alarmed, he drops the doll and runs away, looking back fearfully over his shoulder.

Scene 1: *The Shrove Tide Fair.*
The quotes are from the score.
The music starts with a carnival theme in the flutes:

Example 1

"A group of drunks pass, dancing" as the violins play the theme:

Example 2

Woods–Strings

"An organ player appears in the crowd with a dancer." The barrel organ is imitated rather ingeniously: the scoring is for wood-winds and glockenspiel; the clarinet finally enters with the melody:

Example 3

Clarinets

"The dancer dances, marking the measures with a triangle." The melody is played by the flute and clarinet:

Example 4

Flutes

"The organ player, continuing, turns the handle with one hand, and at the same time plays the trumpet with the other hand." The trumpet repeats Example 4 while the woodwinds continue their accompaniment.

"At the other end of the scene a music box plays and another dancer dances." Example 3 is heard again.

"The first dancer again resumes the triangle" as Example 4 is repeated by flutes and clarinets.

"The organ and the music box cease to play as the barkers renew their cries." The strings repeat chords followed by a repetition of Example 1.

"A joyous group passes by" as Example 2 is heard again, then Example 1 is repeated in an extended section.

"Two drummers advance to the front of the little theater and attract the attention of the crowd with their drums." A snare drum is heard.

"On the forestage of the little theater the Charlatan appears" as a crashing orchestral chord is heard.

After a mysterious sounding introduction, "the Charlatan plays the flute":

Example 5

"The curtain of the little theater rises and the crowd sees three puppets: Petrouchka, a Moor, a Ballerina." A short, descending motive in the strings is heard.

"The Charlatan animates them by touching them with his flute." A descending two-note motive in the flute is heard, echoed twice by the piccolo.

Russian Dance

"Petrouchka, the Moor, the Ballerina dance for the crowd to the great astonishment of the public." The woodwinds, French horns, and predominantly the piano introduce the first theme of the Russian Dance:

Example 6

Xylophone and piano glissandi punctuate the dance music. As it builds to a climax, Example 6 is heard in the full orchestra.

The oboe plays a new melody:

Example 7

The violins repeat Example 7; the piano then plays it.

Example 6 quickly passes from xylophone to clarinet, to English horn, then to the piano.

The full orchestra joins in as the Russian dance of the three puppets is brought to a colorful conclusion.

Scene 2: *Petrouchka's Room.*

"At the rise of the curtain Petrouchka's room is seen. The door opens quickly, a foot kicks him into the scene; Petrouchka falls as the door closes." Two clarinets play the famous *Petrouchka chord* in two different keys simultaneously (*polytonality*), F-sharp and C:

Example 8

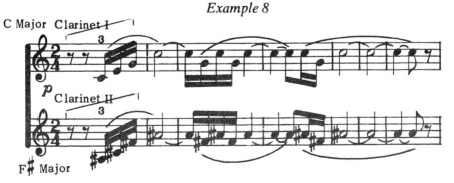

"The curses of Petrouchka" are represented by a melody in the trumpet which is derived from Example 8:

Example 9

After a piano interlude in which the flute joins, a new theme is introduced by the English horn:

Example 10

"The Ballerina enters." The piano introduces a little melodic fragment:

Example 11

After a crescendo in the orchestra and the opening part of *Petrouchka's Curse* theme, Example 9 is heard, "The Ballerina flees."

The clarinet is heard in a cadenza, followed by a piano cadenza.
"The despair of Petrouchka" is indicated by the return of Example 9.
"Darkness. Curtain." The French horns with *stopped* tones answered by the clarinets, then the *Petrouchka Chord,* Example 8, close this scene.
Scene 3: *The Moor's Room.*
After a twenty-two measure introduction, "the Moor dances" as the clarinet plays the melody of a quasi-Oriental dance.

Example 12

Clarinet

The dance continues as the bass drum and cymbals which have been prominent continue; the celli and bass viols are heard with a harsh, repeated figure. The English horn is heard over this low string accompaniment with a little thematic fragment which is followed by a series of chords in the brass.

The brass carry the melody of the Moor's dance for a few measures until the tempo returns to a tranquil pace and the trumpets, muted, play Example 12; the bassoons in thirds then play the theme.

"The Ballerina dances" with trumpet in hand. A drum cadence introduces and accompanies the trumpet melody:

Example 13

Trumpet

A short passage for strings and woodwinds, seven measures long, introduces the Waltz, "The Ballerina and the Moor Dance." A solo bassoon sets an awkward accompaniment for the melody which enters four measures later started by the trumpet and finished by a flute:

Example 14

A new waltz melody is played by the flutes and harp:

Example 15

Example 15 is repeated by the flutes and harp.

After a short motive in the horns and woodwinds, Example 14 returns to round out this little waltz in ternary form.

A variation of Example 9 (*Petrouchka's Curse*) is played by a muted trumpet which indicates that "Petrouchka appears."

"The Moor and Petrouchka quarrel. The Ballerina faints." Example 8 and ascending and descending arpeggios are played by various instruments.

The music grows in intensity with many appogiaturas as "the Moor pushes Petrouchka out."

Scene 4: *The Grand Carnival.*

The "general impression" of the carnival atmosphere at evening time is suggested in the music as orchestral bells and trumpets are heard above undulating figures played by the full orchestra.

A melodic fragment is heard in the oboe and repeated by the trumpet.

Dance of the Nursemaids

After the introduction, Figure A of Example 16 is heard first in the English horn and then in the French horn. The French horns then play all of the dance theme, Example 16:

Example 16

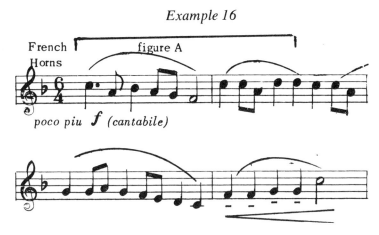

The French horns and violins repeat Example 16.

The *trio* of the Nursemaids' Dance opens with a melody in the oboes:

Example 17

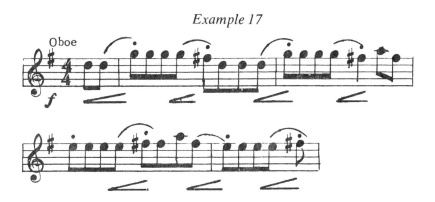

Example 17 is played by the trumpets with repeated notes; a solo trumpet then plays it. A final statement of this example is then played by the woodwinds.

The melody of the first section of this dance, Example 16, returns in the violins; the violins repeat Example 16 and Example 17 appears in counterpoint to it.

"A peasant enters with a bear. Everyone flings aside. The peasant plays his clarinet; the bear marches on his hind paws." A clumsy theme in the clarinets, an octave above the range in which they normally play, is heard:

Example 18

"There appears a merry-making merchant with two gypsies. He amuses them by throwing bank notes to the crowd." The violins introduce the theme:

Example 19

The Royal Ballet production of *Petrouchka*. Petrouchka bursts into the Moor's room as the Moor and the Ballerina are waltzing.

Dance of the Coachman in the final scene — "The Grand Carnival"

"The gypsies dance. The merchant plays his accordian." The melody is played by an oboe and English horn to the accompaniment of two harps and strings.

Example 20

The merchant and the gypsies "get together" as Example 19 is heard followed by the melody of Example 20.

A muted trumpet plays Example 20 as "the merchant and the gypsies disappear."

Dance of the Coachmen and the Grooms

A rhythmical introduction indicates that the coachmen and the grooms are about to dance. The theme, Example 21, is started by the trumpets, continued by the violins, pizzicato, and finished by the trombones:

Example 21

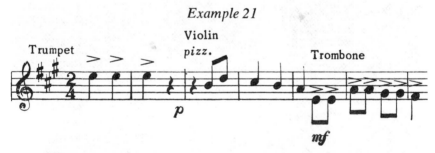

"The nursemaids dance with the coachmen and the grooms." Example 16, the Nursemaids' theme, is played by the clarinets and bassoons, then by the full orchestra. Example 21 returns.

The Disguises

The masqueraders' arrival is announced in the music by descending chromatic figures in the clarinets and strings; these are interrupted by a call sounded by horns and trumpets.

"The devil (masked) mocks the crowd." Octave figures pass back and forth between trumpets, trombones, and the tuba.

"Buffoons in disguise (goat and pig)" — trombones and low strings are predominant.

"The maskers and mummers dance." The piccolo and orchestral bells brilliantly introduce a new theme:

Example 22

The trumpet repeats Example 22.
"The rest of the crowd joins the dance" as the French horns are heard with the theme:

Example 23

"The crowd continues to dance until a cry comes from the little theater." There is a prolonged note in the trumpet which crescendos.

"The dance is interrupted. Petrouchka leaves the little theater pursued by the Moor whom the Ballerina attempts to hold back." The *Petrouchka Chord*, Example 8, is heard ascending and descending in the English horn, then in the violins.

A descending chromatic scale in the violins indicates "the Moor's furious blow . . . the strike of the saber." This culminates in a crashing orchestral chord.

"Petrouchka falls with a crushed skull."

A two-note motive played by the piccolo signals that "the crowd gathers around Petrouchka."

"He dies, complaining." A melodic variation of the *Petrouchka Curse* theme, Example 9, is played by the clarinet.

The bassoon is heard as "a policeman looks for the Charlatan."

A descending five-note chromatic scale played by the French horn indicates the Charlatan has arrived. "He raises the body of Petrouchka and shakes it."

"The crowd disperses" as the French horns are heard with parallel triads in the music.

The oboes play parallel triads as "the Charlatan rests. He drags the lifeless body towards the little theater."

"He sees Petrouchka's ghost grimacing at him from the top of the little theater." A high "D trumpet" plays *Petrouchka's Curse,* Example 9, in *retrograde* (the backward reading of a melodic line).

"The Charlatan, alarmed, drops the puppet Petrouchka and runs away, glancing back fearfully over his shoulder." Two high "D trumpets" repeat Example 8 a final time.

SERGE PROKOFIEV

BORN: April 23, 1891; Sontzovka, Russia.
DIED: March 5, 1953; Moscow, Russia.

Serge Prokofiev's creative career spanned the gap between the Russia of old, as represented in music by Rimsky-Korsakov, and the present era of the Union of Soviet Socialist Republics with its Composers' Union. Trained in the tradition of the old school, Prokofiev lived for many years outside of Russia. Shortly after he finally returned and became a Soviet citizen, he clarified his musical position by stating:

I have striven for clarity and melodious idiom, but at the same time I have by no means attempted to restrict myself to the accepted methods of harmony and melody. This is precisely what makes lucid, straight-forward music so difficult to compose — the clarity must be new, not old.

A man of great creative talents, he apparently was not able to restrain this natural urge to explore the new, for in 1948 his name was included in a denunciatory resolution drawn by the Communist party. Although he repented in a letter addressed to the party and turned to a work that more nearly followed the recommended methods, his career was so shortly to close that it is impossible to know how these restrictions might have affected him over a long period of creative activity.

Serge Prokofiev's mother was an amateur pianist, and he received his first musical training from her. At the age of five he improvised an *Indian Galop* which she set down on paper for him, and at six he composed a March, a Waltz, and a Rondo. By the age of nine he had completed the piano score of an opera called *The Giant* which was in three acts and many tableaux. It was "produced" at his uncle's summer home by a family cast. He then wrote an overture and three tableaux for an opera, *On Desert Islands.*

Prokofiev was sent to study with Glière and under his guidance wrote a symphony in G major. Two operas followed: *Feast During the Plague,* after the writings of Pushkin, and *Ondine.* The first was completed when Serge was twelve, the latter a year later.

At thirteen Prokofiev entered the St. Petersburg Conservatory and studied composition with Rimsky-Korsakov and Liadov. After ten years of work at the Conservatory, he graduated in 1914. In his final year he won the piano competition, playing his own *Piano Concerto* (the Rubinstein Prize was a Bechstein grand piano).

As a composer, Prokofiev was attracted to primitive or elemental subjects. His first important orchestral work was the *Scythian Suite* which draws for subject material on the ancient worshippers of the sun. At twenty-six he completed his *Classical Symphony* and conducted the premiere performance in the spring of 1918. He left Russia shortly after this, proceeding through Siberia and Japan to the United States where he arrived shortly after the Armistice of World War I was signed.

In the United States Prokofiev gave concerts in New York, Chicago, and other cities. In 1920 he went to Paris where he became associated with the ballet impressario Diaghilev. His first work produced there was the ballet *Chout* (a French transliteration of the Russian word for Buffoon). This was followed by *Le Pas d'Acier* (The Steel Trot) in which the progress of the "steel age" was depicted. When he toured Russia shortly after, he was accepted as a truly Soviet composer even though his work had been done in France.

In 1921 he again visited the United States, this time to witness the first production by the Chicago Opera Company of his opera, *The Love of Three Oranges.* He returned to Paris where he continued to make his home. In the French capital he completed his second, third, and fourth symphonies, and his fourth (left hand) and fifth piano concerti.

After a series of concerts in Russia in 1927, Prokofiev decided to make Russia once again his home, although he frequently made trips throughout Europe and particularly to Paris. In 1933 he established himself as a Soviet citizen, and his first project was to compose the music for a Russian film, *Lt. Kijé.* This was followed by *Peter and the Wolf,* a fairy tale for children, although it has been accepted by the adult public as part of the permanent symphonic repertoire.

During World War II he completed his *Symphony No. 5* and the opera *War and Peace* which was based on the Tolstoy novel. His status seemed to remain high in Russia in spite of the modern tendencies in his *Symphony No. 6* and *Symphony No. 7.* He never left the tonal system, although he made excursions into polytonality and atonality.

In 1948, Prokofiev along with many other Soviet composers was denounced for his modern tendencies by the Communist party. Because of poor health (he had suffered a stroke), his doctor did not allow him to appear in person for the special convocation of composers gathered in Moscow to discuss the crises. He did, however, address a letter to them in which he said:

Elements of formalism were peculiar to my music of fifteen or twenty years ago [through] the infection caught from contact with Western ideas. [I] never questioned the importance of melody and pledge to avoid the objectionable — [from the official Soviet viewpoint] — practices in my new opera I am composing.

The new opera was *A Tale of a Real Man,* the story of a Soviet pilot who remained in the service despite the loss of both legs. When it was presented publicly, he was assailed for persevering in his Western-inculcated practices of dissonance and atonality.

In the last few years of his life, there were times when the doctors forbade him to read, and allowed him to work no more than one hour a day with rests every fifteen minutes. From this period stems the oratorio *On Guard* which won the sixth award of the Stalin Prize, and two big symphonies, *Holiday Poem* and *Symphony No. 7,* both completed in 1952. His last effort was the ballet, *The Tale of the Stone Flower,* a poetic legend of the Urals, on which he had been working the day he died suddenly of a cerebral hemorrhage. He was buried in the Novodevichye Cemetery in Moscow.

BIBLIOGRAPHY

Prokofiev, Sergei. *Autobiography, Articles, Reminiscences.* London: Central Books. 1960.
Nestyev, Israel V. *Prokofiev.* Stanford, California: Stanford University Press, 1960.

LT. KIJÉ SUITE

SERGE PROKOFIEV

Serge Prokofiev's first work after he returned to Russia as a Soviet citizen was the musical score for the film a Leningrad studio was making of the "life" of Lt. Kijé. The story concerned a legend supposedly started by Czar Nicholas I. The Czar, in reviewing the accomplishments of his army and its men, misread the list of names in his hand, linking the last syllable of an officer's name (ki) with the Russian explicative *je!* The courtiers and attendants did not wish to question anything their Czar said, so they invented a soldier by the name of Kijé, a paper soldier to be sure, on the spot. All sorts of tales sprang up about the mythical "Lt. Kijé."

The orchestral suite from the film score is in five parts. Although a baritone soloist was used in the film, his place is sometimes taken in concert versions by a substitute orchestration provided by the composer.

FIRST MOVEMENT: *Birth of Kijé.*

Kijé is born with a stroke of the pen — born full of military honors. An off-stage cornet is heard heralding his birth:

Example 1

The snare drum sets the musical stage for a parade; a melody in the piccolo starts it:

Example 2

The flute plays a counter-melody to that of the piccolo:

Example 3

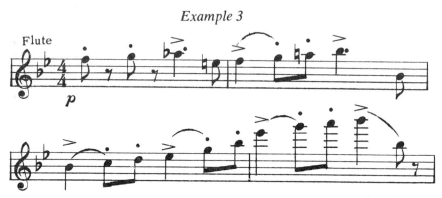

After four bars of a rhythmical, march-like figure played by the French horns, the piccolo and flute repeat their duet (Examples 2 and 3).

The march rhythm appears for two bars in the strings, then the oboe has a four measure melodic figure. Again the flute-piccolo duet is heard.

An extended rhythmical section follows in which drums and the brass instruments are predominant.

The tempo changes to an *Andante* in which a flute with the melody gives way to a bassoon:

Example 4

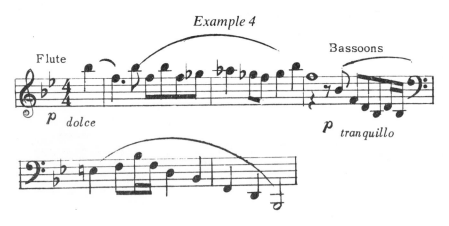

The *Andante* concludes and the flute and piccolo duet is repeated. The movement ends with the off-stage cornet playing Example 1.

SECOND MOVEMENT: *Romance.*

The *Romance* is a slow, sad lover's lament. The melody is a typical Russian one, with each phrase repeated.

After a brief chordal introduction, the soloist is heard:

Example 5

Baritone

My white dove is   full ———— of sor- row,

cry▪ - - - ing   all the day and night

My white dove is full of sorrow,
Crying all the day and night
For her dear beloved left her,
Having vanished out of sight.

A celesta is heard with the melody of Exâmple 1, and one measure later the baritone continues in counterpoint to it:

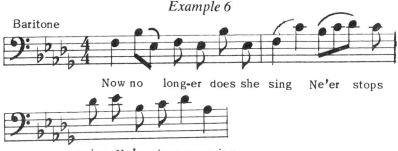

Example 6

Baritone

Now no   long-er does she sing   Ne'er   stops

cry-ing Ne'er stops moan-ing.

Now no longer does she sing;
Ne'er stops crying,
Ne'er stops moaning.

Sadly now from branch to branch
She keeps fluttering around
Looking for her dear beloved,
Hoping he will return.

Baritone   *Example 7*

To   my heart I   say: Don't flut-ter,

Don't   be   like   a   but- ter-   fly;

To my heart I say: Don't flutter,
Don't be like a butterfly;
Don't be like a butterfly.

Other pleasures lie around you;
Those who seek will surely find them.
They are yours if you desire them.
The music becomes more agitated as the soloist continues:
To my heart I say: Don't flutter,
Don't be like a butterfly.
The melody of Example 7 returns:
What, dear heart, did you decide?
Where will we in summer rest?
But her heart beats always faster,
Knowing not where she should turn.
The first melody of the movement, Example 5, returns with the same words.

THIRD MOVEMENT: *Kijé's Wedding.*

An introduction to the wedding festivities is played by the full orchestra with the trombones prominent:

Example 8

An "um-pah" accompaniment is established, then the cornet is heard with a cocky little tune:

Example 9

After an extension of this tune, the brass and woodwinds repeat it.

The tenor saxophone is heard in a more somber melody — Example 4 in extension:

Example 10

The cornet repeats Example 9.

The trombones return with Example 8, followed by the "um-pah" accompaniment.

The cornet is heard again with Example 9, followed by a repeat of it by the woodwinds.

The wedding festivities end as Example 8 is repeated.

FOURTH MOVEMENT: *Troika.*

A troika is a typically Russian sleigh drawn by three horses harnessed abreast. In this movement Prokofiev uses sleigh bells for effect and an old Russian tavern song for authenticity.

The introduction opens with the melody in the flutes and violins, succeeded by the cornet with the after-phrase:

Example 11

The rhythm of the sleigh ride is established by a tambourine, a triangle, and sleigh bells.

The baritone enters with the tavern song:

con brio   *Example 12*

Baritone

A   wo-man's heart is like an inn; All those who wish go   in.

A woman's heart is like an inn;
All those who wish go in,
And they who roam about
Day and night go in and out.

The rhythm of the sleigh bells is heard again. The voice continues:

Example 13

Baritone

And so those who are a-bout, keep go-ing in and com-ing out.

So all those who are about
Keep going in and coming out,
Night and day they roam about.

The melody of Example 12 along with its words are repeated. After a rhythmic interlude, a new melody is heard:

Example 14

Come   here I say, Come here I say, and

have no fear with me, and have no fear with me.

Come here, I say, come here, I say,
And have no fear with me.
I call you all to come here.

After another rhythmic interlude, the melody and words of Example 13 are heard again, this time in an extended section. A brass postlude completes the rowdy tavern song.

FIFTH MOVEMENT: *The Burial of Kijé.*

The burial of Kijé is no funeral dirge. Probably this paper lieutenant caused considerable consternation while he existed, and his fellow officers are probably glad to know that he is to be buried.

In this movement Prokofiev skillfully brings back the melodies of the other movements and weaves them together in an ingenious contrapuntal texture.

The off-stage cornet heralds Kijé's death as it did his birth, with Example 1.

Example 4 appears in extension as played by the clarinets in their low register.

Example 4 is repeated by the tenor saxophone with its mournful timbre.

The French horn is heard with the melody from the *Romance,* Example 5.

Example 5 returns, this time played by the tuba.

The violins take up Example 5 in a much higher register. They continue with it when, eight measures later, the cornet repeats the cocky little tune of the wedding, Example 9.

The woodwinds play Example 5 while muted trumpets play Example 9.

Example 9 is repeated by the oboes and clarinets with a string accompaniment.

After an extended interlude Example 4 is played by the clarinets and tenor saxophone.

The violins are heard with the wedding tune, Example 9, and they continue a rhythmic variation of it when, four measures later, the trumpet plays Example 5 in counterpoint to it.

Example 9 appears in the oboes and clarinets, passes to the violins, and returns to the oboes. Example 10 appears in the flute.

The suite ends as it began; the off-stage cornet is heard with Example 1.

DARIUS MILHAUD
born: September 4, 1892; Aix-en-Provence, France
died: June 22, 1974; Geneva, Switzerland

Darius Milhaud is one of the most prolific contemporary composers. By the time Milhaud was fifty, he had written fifteen ballets, fifteen operas, ten cantatas, thirty-three pieces of theater music, scores for eighteen motion pictures, fifteen sonatas, twelve concerti, six symphonies, and much vocal and piano music. He used a florist's catalogue as the vocal text for one composition! Once when he was presented with a beautiful bound volume of blank manuscript paper, he composed two string quartets that exactly filled the pages in it. Since there were eight staves per page, one quartet took the upper four and the second quartet took the lower four staves. In addition to being two separate quartets, Milhaud intended that they would form an octet when played simultaneously.

Of his joy in writing music Milhaud says:

> I love to write music. I always do it with pleasure, otherwise I just do not write it . . . The important thing is the vital element — the melody — which should be easily retained, hummed, and whistled on the street. Without this fundamental element, all the technique in the world can only be a dead letter.
>
> . . . I have never been able to understand the establishment of different categories in music: classical music and modern music; serious music and light music. It is most unjust. There is only music, and one can find it in a café opera, or work of chamber music.*

Milhaud showed his first interest in music at two years of age when he attempted to pick out street songs on the piano in the family home at Aix-en-Provence. At six he was given violin lessons and four years later gave his first public performance. From the time he was thirteen until he was sixteen, he played second violin in the string quartet of his teacher. He thus became acquainted with the seventeen string quartets of Beethoven and it was then that he made up his mind to compose eighteen quartets.

After some college work in Aix-en-Provence, Milhaud entered the Conservatory in Paris where he studied with Widor and d'Indy. He won prizes in flute, violin, counterpoint, and fugue while there. Although he was hoping to try for the Prix de Rome, his studies were cut short by the outbreak of World War I.

The French government sent Milhaud to Rio de Janiero from 1917 to 1919 as an attaché in the French Legation. During his days

* Quotation from David Ewen, *The Book of Modern Composers* (New York, 1950)

BENJAMIN BRITTEN

DARIUS MILHAUD

PAUL HINDEMITH

SIR WILLIAM WALTON

Photo by Douglas Glass

in Rio he became well acquainted with Paul Claudel, the poet-diplomat, who furnished texts for many of Milhaud's works.

At the end of the war Milhaud returned to France. He soon became associated with a group of composers who had departed from the "impressionistic" school of Debussy. These composers became known as "Les Six." The group also included Honegger, Auriac, Poulenc, Durey, and Tailleferre. Although they were united in their revolt against Impressionism, they agreed that each must find his own individual idiom.

In 1922 Milhaud made his first visit to the United States. He appeared as a piano soloist and conducted his own works. He also lectured at Harvard, Princeton, and Columbia.

Two years after his return to France, Milhaud began experimenting with the jazz idiom he had heard in the United States. He wrote a *Sonatina for Flute and Piano* in which a stylized form of the blues was presented. This was followed by his ballet, *La Création du Monde* (The Creation of the World), a jazz ballet. These works caused much controversy in France, and Milhaud was labeled a "sensationalist," a "bluffer," and "vulgar."

In 1930 his opera based on the life of Christopher Columbus was presented in Berlin, Germany. It took six years before France heard *Christophe Colomb* and then it was only a concert version. Two years later he had another opera, *Maximilien,* produced at the Paris Opéra. It was a dismal failure.

In 1937 he wrote *Suite Provençal* which seems to remain one of his most enduring orchestral works. His opera *Médée,* on a text written by his wife, was the last opera to be presented at the Paris Opéra before the Nazis occupied the city.

The following year Milhaud and his family fled to the United States and settled in a beautiful hillside home in Oakland, California, especially built for them by Mills College where he had been engaged as a composer-teacher. He spent his mornings teaching composition and in the afternoons retired to his home to work on compositions. There he composed his opera *Bolivar* (inspired by his tour of service as a diplomat in South America), two symphonies, several concerti, and chamber music.

In 1945, on commission, he wrote his *Suite Française* for high school bands. It was so successful that he soon had to rescore it for orchestra. A year later he appeared with the Boston Symphony to conduct the premiere of his *Second Symphony.*

At the end of World War II, the French people insisted that he return to France. Having just completed his *Third Symphony,* Milhaud started and completed his *Fourth Symphony* in 1947 on his way home. In Paris he was appointed by the government to a five man committee responsible for administrating French musical activities. He has since commuted between France and the United States.

In 1950 his opera *Simon Bolivar* was presented in Paris but it was immediately denounced; for one thing, it was four hours long. Later the same year his *Sabbath Morning Service* for baritone (as Cantor), chorus, and orchestra was presented in San Francisco and accepted fairly well. In 1952 the New York Philharmonic presented all of his opera *Simon Bolivar* in concert form. There was as poor a reaction from the audience at this performance as there had been in France. When one critic asked immediately after the performance to borrow from the publishers a copy of the score for review, he was told that everything had ben packed and sent back to France since "there would no longer ever be any use for this music in America."

Milhaud's most recent major work was *David,* an opera, which was commissioned by the late Serge Koussevitsky and presented for the first time in Jerusalem, the "City of David," on June 1, 1954. The opera was a mammoth work in five acts and twelve scenes lasting some three hours. Milhaud had completed the work in seven months! In 1956 it was presented in opera form at the Hollywood Bowl in California where the immense resources of the world's largest outdoor amphitheatre were used. Hundreds of people were involved in the choruses; one chorus in contemporary dress sat on either side of the stage and commented on the Biblical action. The entire hillside in back of the Bowl was used as part of the visual presentation.

Milhaud continues to be an active composer. A performance of his *String Quintet,* using a quartet plus a bass viol, was given at a meeting of the American Musicological Society in 1955. His opera *Médée* was given the same year by Brandeis University where it was well received despite the fact that it was given in an outdoor amphitheatre under a canvas roof on a very rainy night. *Symphony No. 11* was premiered in Dallas, Texas, in December of 1960.

BIBLIOGRAPHY

Milhaud, Darius. *Notes Without Music,* trans. Donald Evans. New York, 1952.

SUITE FRANÇAISE

Darius Milhaud

In the orchestral score the composer tells the origin of this composition:

The *Suite Française* was originally written for band. The parts are not difficult to play either melodically or rhythmically and use only the average ranges for the instruments. For a long time I have had the idea of writing a composition fit for high school purposes and this was the result. In the bands, orchestras and choirs of American high schools, colleges, and universities where the youth of the nation are found, it is obvious that they need music of their time, not too difficult to perform, but, nevertheless keeping the characteristic idiom of the composer.

The five parts of this *Suite* are named after French Provinces, the very ones in which the American and Allied armies fought together with the French underground for the liberation of my country: Normandy, Bretagne, Ile de France (of which Paris is the center), Alsace-Lorraine, and Provence.

I used some folk tunes of these Provinces. I wanted the young Americans to hear the popular melodies of those parts of France where their fathers and brothers fought to defeat the German invaders, who in less than seventy years have brought war, destruction, cruelty, torture and murder, three times, to the peaceful and democratic people of France.*

The *Suite* was originally introduced by the Goldman Band of New York. It was so successful that the composer re-scored it for orchestra. The first performance of the orchestral version was given by the New York Philharmonic Symphony Orchestra.

First Movement: *Normandie.*

To a dance-like rhythm, the violins introduce the first theme:

Example 1

After a variation of this theme in the woodwinds and strings, the flute and clarinet introduce a little figure:

*Quotation from David Ewen, *The Book of Modern Composers* (New York, 1950).

Example 2

Example 1 returns in the trumpet.

A variation of Example 1 is heard in the French horns and repeated by the flutes.

Example 1 appears in the trombones leading to a statement of it by full orchestra.

Just before the close of the movement, a final statement of Example 1 is made by two trumpets in unison.

SECOND MOVEMENT: *Bretagne.*

This slow movement opens with two horns introducing the principal theme:

Example 3

A variation of this theme follows immediately played by muted trumpets.

The oboes continue this theme in another variant.

The second section of this ternary form opens with a melody stated by the oboe:

Example 4

Example 4 appears as a variation in the violins who are soon joined by the flutes.

The trumpets appear with Example 3.

A final statement by the French horns of Example 3 brings the movement to a close.

THIRD MOVEMENT: *Île de France.*

A fast rhythm is immediately established by the timpani.

The flutes, oboes, trumpets, and violins introduce the spirited principal theme of the rondo:

Example 5

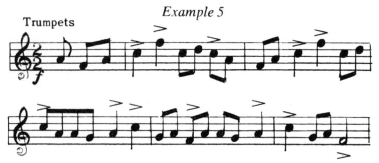

The trombones repeat Example 5.

The second theme is a lyrical one heard in the first violins:

Example 6

The violins repeat Example 6.

The principal theme of the rondo (Example 5) returns in the trumpets.

The woodwinds play Example 6.

A more spirited theme then appears in the violins:

Example 7

The violins take up the melody of Example 6 and are joined a few measures later by the flutes and clarinets.

The movement closes with the principal rondo theme (Example 5) returning in full orchestra.

FOURTH MOVEMENT: *Alsace-Lorraine.*

The fourth movement is a slow movement. The violins play the introductory theme:

Example 8

Violins

After an upward run, the violins announce the principal theme:

Example 9

Violins

A variation of Example 9 is played by the oboe and viola.

Example 8 returns.

A second variation of Example 9 is played by the first violins and clarinet.

The trumpets are heard with the last phrase of Example 8 and are answered by the violins with the last phrase of Example 9.

The violins play the last half of Example 8, followed by the trumpets playing the second half of Example 9.

A full statement of Example 9 is made by the violins.

A cymbal crash introduces the trumpet with a variation of the latter portion of Example 8.

FIFTH MOVEMENT: *Provence.*

The final movement opens in animated fashion with the trumpets boldly proclaiming Example 10:

Trumpet   *Example 10*

The flute and violins answer this trumpet melody.

Both the trumpet melody (Example 10) and its answer are presented twice more.

A dance rhythm is established by a "provençal drum," akin to our American tom-tom; over this the flutes announce a dance melody:

Example 11

Example 10 returns in the violins.

A fanfare is played by trumpets and trombones.

A melody reminiscent of a popular song is played by flutes and violins:

Example 12

Clarinets and second violins return with Example 10.

Another trumpet fanfare follows.

The music returns to Example 10.

The dance rhythm is re-established by the drum.

The flute returns with Example 11.

After chromatically descending chords, the suite ends with a return to Example 10.

PAUL HINDEMITH
born: November 16, 1895; Hanau, Germany
died: December 28, 1963; Frankfurt, Germany

When the Nazi government of Germany decided early in the 1930's that it would control the cultural as well as the political life of the country, Paul Hindemith decided to leave his native land. He had established himself as one of the great German composers of the younger generation and had an opera, *Mathis der Maler* (Matthias the Painter), ready for production. The German Cultural Office took a look at the work and decided that it was not fit for presentation since the story evolved around the defeat of the German liberals during the Peasant War. The government soon forbade the playing of any of Hindemith's music and he and his Jewish wife fled from Germany. In Switzerland, four years after it was written, *Mathis der Maler* was an overwhelming success.

Hindemith started violin lessons at eleven years of age and was said to have made a complete mastery of the violin in two years. Hindemith's parents argued against a career for him in music and finally had to forbid him to study it. So strong was the boy's desire for music, he found it necessary to run away from home in order to continue these studies. He earned enough money to support himself by playing in motion picture theaters, musical comedy houses, cafés, and with dance bands.

Hindemith eventually enrolled in the Hoch's Conservatorium in Frankfurt to learn more about music. An unpublished *String Quartet in C* which won the Mendelssohn Prize in Berlin dates from this time. Hindemith found a position playing with the Frankfurt Opera orchestra and remained there from his twentieth to twenty-eighth year, rising eventually to the position of concertmaster. While still engaged at the opera, he and his friend Licco Amar organized a string quartet in which Hindemith played the viola. This quartet, known as the Amar Quartet, toured throughout central Europe.

Hindemith's first fame outside of Frankfurt came from the performance of his chamber works at international festivals. His *Second Quartet* was played at the Donaueschingen Festival of 1921 and again the following year at the Salzburg Festival. Salzburg followed this performance two years later with his *Clarinet Quintet* and *First String Trio*. Large numbers of foreign musicians annually visited these festivals and became acquainted with Hindemith and his style of composition.

In 1925 Hindemith first experimented with the jazz idiom. His *Concerto for Piano and Twelve Instruments* was performed at the Venice Festival that year, and an opera based on the jazz idiom, *Cardillac,* was presented at the Dresden Opera a year later. In the opera Hindemith did not adhere to the traditional style, rather he employed a method usually reserved for the symphony: the first act was an exposition of thematic materials, the second a development of them, and the third act a recapitulation.

During the 1920's Hindemith composed a quantity of music for practical purposes: music for the pianola, for radio, for the theater, and for motion pictures. Since this music was written to fit a specific need, a word was created for this type of music: *Gebrauchsmusik* (music for use).

Hindemith's last major composition in Germany was his *Philharmonic Concerto* written to celebrate the fiftieth anniversary of the Berlin orchestra. He moved to Turkey where the government commissioned him to organize all music study and research there along occidental patterns. He was able to visit his old friend of string quartet days, Licco Amar, who was also in Turkey. After a year Hindemith moved temporarily to Switzerland, making two more visits to Turkey.

In 1939 Hindemith introduced his *Viola Sonata* in New York city and was appointed to the teaching staff of the Berkshire Music Academy for the following summer. In 1942 Hindemith was appointed head of the Music Department at Yale University and took up permanent residence in the United States. He applied for and received American citizenship. While at Yale he developed two books on traditional harmony which are still used widely throughout the United States as textbooks.

In 1947 Hindemith was elected to the National Institute of Art and Letters and the same year undertook an extensive tour of the United States and Europe, conducting both his own works and those of other composers. The following year he was appointed to the staff of the University of Zurich in Switzerland. In 1949 he returned to Germany for a brief visit and was greatly acclaimed by the German people. They urged him to make that country his permanent home again, but he refused.

An interesting and humorous *Concerto for Woodwinds, Harp and Orchestra* was first presented at Columbia University in 1949. Written in commemoration of his twenty-fifth wedding anniversary,

the work is based on the opening phrase of Mendelssohn's *Wedding March.*
In 1953 Hindemith again took up residence in Switzerland, and in 1955 traveled to Helsinki to receive the Sibelius Prize from the President of Finland. In 1957 his latest major work, an opera entitled *Die Harmonie der Welt,* was presented at the Munich Opera Festival. The opera is based on the life of Johannes Kepler (1608-1630) during the Thirty Years' War. A three movement symphony based on this work had been presented five years before in Basel, Switzerland. The Munich stage production was of fourteen scenes in five acts. It was presented to an international audience of leading society people, musicians, and music critics; Hindemith himself conducted the work. It was received by the audience with a moderate ovation.

His *Pittsburg Symphony* was premiered by the orchestra of that city in 1959. Infused with the spirit of Pennsylvania-Dutch music, this work received excellent reviews by the critics.

BIBLIOGRAPHY

Strobel, Heinrich: *Paul Hindemith; Testimony in Pictures.* Mainz, Germany: B. Schott's Söhne, 1961. English translation: Everett Helm, 1963.

Hindemith, Paul. *A Composer's World.* Garden City, New York: Doubleday and Company, 1961.

MATHIS DER MALER

(*Matthias the Painter*)

PAUL HINDEMITH

Mathis der Maler, a symphony, was introduced by the Berlin Philharmonic in 1934, four years before the production in Zürich of the opera from which its three movements are extracted. Both the opera and the symphony are concerned with the most ambitious and extensive creation of the German religious painter Mathis Gothart Nithart (c. 1460-1528), known as Mathis Grünewald, whose paintings for the Isenheim Altar are among the greatest achievements of late Gothic art in Germany. The opera is a partly historical, partly fictional episode in his life. The action takes place in 1524-25, during the Peasant War and the early years of the Reformation. Hindmith represents Mathis as the creative artist torn between the call of his art and the claims made upon him by political, economic, and religious upheaval. Hindemith states:

He goes to war and fights on the side of the rebellious peasants against the nobles and the church and thus against his own master, Cardinal Albrecht of Mainz. There is a gross contradiction between his imaginary ideal of a fair combat and just victory and the ugly reality of the Peasants' War.

Mathis soon sees the wide gulf separating him from his companions in arms, and when the peasants suffer a decisive defeat, he is so completely engulfed in despair that not even death by his own hand or a stranger's has mercy upon him. In an allegorical scene he experiences the temptation of St. Anthony; all the promptings of conscience within his tortured soul rise to assail and plague him and call him to account for his actions. The knowledge of being condemned to utter uselessness overwhelms him. In the subsequent stage action there is a close resemblance to the visit of St. Anthony to St. Paul in Thebald, as it is depicted on Grünewald's Isenheim altar-piece. Paul, under whose allegorical disguise Cardinal Albrecht is to be recognized, enlightens Mathis, in the likeness of Anthony, about his mistakes and instructs him as to the right road which he is to follow in the future. The conversion to conscious, supreme artistic endeavor is successful. Mathis devotes the remainder of his days to his art, which is henceforth rooted in his faith in the talent bestowed upon him by God and his attachment to his native soil.

The first movement, *Angel Concert,* is the overture to the opera and depicts the joyous spirit of the Isenheim panel showing the angels making music to celebrate the nativity. The second movement, *Entombment,* is an orchestral interlude from the last scene of the opera. It relates to the painting on the footpiece of the altar in which the internment of Jesus by John, Mary, and Mary Magdalen is depicted. The final movement, *The Temptation of St. Anthony,* portrays the heroic struggle between art and the outside world for Mathis' soul, as a battle between gods and giants in furious assault upon one another.

THIRD MOVEMENT: Versuchung des Heiligen Antonius (The Temptation of St. Anthony). *Sehr langsam, frei im Zeitmass.*
This movement is presented in three general sections. The opening or introductory section is based on two themes. The first theme is introduced immediately by the strings:

Example 1

An episode built on this theme leads to a restatement of it by the strings joined by the woodwinds.

The second theme appears in the strings with a rhythmical background provided by the woodwinds:

Example 2

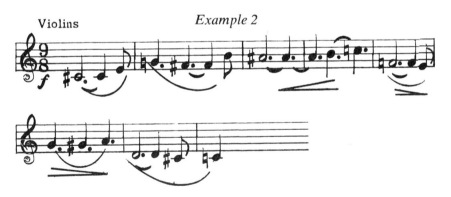

This theme then moves to the cello, followed by the woodwinds and strings over a brass accompaniment.

It appears next in the clarinet and French horn with the full orchestra accompanying it.

The brass, including bass tuba, then take up this melody.

A sustained tone by the flute, followed by two chords for full orchestra, leads to the bridge theme which in turn leads to the second section of this movement. The bridge theme is played by the oboe over a string accompaniment:

Example 3

This is then repeated by the clarinets.

A hint of Example 1 is heard in the clarinets and then in the entire woodwind section.

A statement by full orchestra of the next theme follows:

Example 4

It is repeated by the brass and woodwinds over an inversion of Example 1 in the strings.

Example 4 returns in the violins after an episodic section.

This theme is repeated by the woodwinds, but with the time values of the notes extended.

A new theme is heard in the celli:

Example 5

This moves to the violins, with the after-phrase repeated by the entire string section. This is an extended passage.

Example 4 returns in the full orchestra with the trombones predominating.

Example 4 is repeated by the oboe and clarinet.

After a development, Example 4 returns in the French horns.

The violas are heard with Example 5.

The after-phrase of Example 5 returns, this time played by the
violins.

A variant of Example 2 appears in the trumpets and horns accompanied by woodwinds and strings.

The violins appear with the last portion of Example 2, a passage
for strings only.

The score is marked *Lauda Sion Salvatorem* and the Gregorian
chant of that name appears in the flutes. Below it is compared to the
original chant which has been transposed to the key Hindemith uses:

Example 6

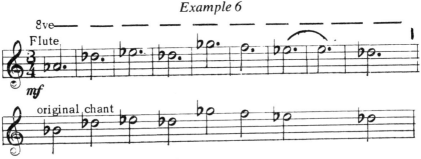

(transposed up a dim. 4th.)

The chant is repeated.

A section marked in the score *Alleluia,* a choral for brass instruments, follows:

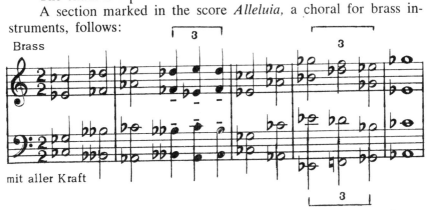

This choral in the brass section brings the symphony to a close.

WILLIAM WALTON

BORN: March 29, 1902; Oldham, England.

Probably the fame of no other composer at his age has ever rested on such few works as does that of Sir William Walton. A slow, methodical worker, intent on making each composition a true work of art, Walton was fifty-eight when his *Second Symphony* was completed.

Walton received his first musical training from his father who was a music teacher. At ten years of age William entered the Christ Church Cathedral Choir School at Oxford. Although he received academic training there as well as choral experience, he was largely self-taught in the theory of music. He did receive piano lessons, and later organ lessons, but his teachers let him go his own way, giving guidance only when necessary.

At sixteen, Walton entered Christ Church College, where again he was largely self-taught in the field of music although he received occasional advice from Busoni and Ansermet. While at college he wrote a great many compositions, mostly choral works, but he later destroyed most of them. A year after he entered this school he wrote a piano quartet which was given a Carnegie Trust Award — "a work of real achievement" stated the citation.

After graduation he went to live with his friends, the Sitwells — the famous literary family of two brothers and a sister. While living with them he completed two of his most enduring works. The most famous was *Façade* for speaking voice and six instruments, using poems of Edith Sitwell. Its novelty at first shocked the concert public, but its musical integrity has made it an enduring work, and later the composer made two different suites from it for full orchestra. The other early work dating from his residence in the Sitwell household is a *String Quartet* which was presented at the first Salzburg contemporary music festival in 1923.

A major orchestral work was written in 1923, the overture, *Portsmouth Point*. This work was full of life, with many displaced accents and changes of time signatures, characteristics which were to become typical of Walton's compositions. Six years later his *Concerto for Viola* was completed. The composer said of this work that it was written "around the key of A major." It showed influences of the jazz idiom popular at the time. The *Concerto* was premiered with Paul Hindemith as the viola soloist.

The oratorio *Belshazzar's Feast* was originally intended for a broadcast. It was commissioned by the Leeds Festival of 1931 and was an immediate success. A broadcast by the BBC shortly after the premier made it a work well-known throughout England.

After two years of work on a symphony, a performance date for it was scheduled. Although three of the movements had been completed by the performance date, it was two additional years before the symphony was complete with four movements. The *Symphony No. 1* was first heard in London in 1935.

Walton turned to some work for the motion picture industry in 1934 and has continued to provide outstanding musical scores for this medium, scoring a triumph in 1943 with the music for *Henry V* and later with *Hamlet*. For the coronation in 1937 he completed on commission from the BBC his *Crown Imperial March* which was used for the coronation ceremony in Westminster Abbey.

In 1939 Walton visited the United States, bringing with him the manuscript of his *Concerto for Violin* which had been commissioned by Jascha Heifetz, a phenomenally difficult work. The composer had made plans to do several things while in the United States but his visit was cut short by the outbreak of war in Europe. He returned to England and enlisted in the British Army; he was assigned to the Ambulance Corps in London.

Oxford University awarded Walton an honorary Doctor of Music degree in 1942. After the war he toured Scandinavia, conducting with six different orchestras. His next journeys took him to Argentina where he married Señorita Susana Gil in Buenos Aires.

Sir William was knighted in 1951 by the Queen. The opera on which he was working at this time, *Troilus and Cressida,* based on Chaucer's version of the story, was premiered three years later. Covent Garden Royal Opera, which staged this work, scheduled seven performances of it the first season.

Continuing to write slowly and methodically, Walton's *Concerto for Cello* was premiered in 1957, and his *Symphony No. 2* was first heard in the United States as performed by the Cleveland Orchestra in 1961.

BIBLIOGRAPHY

Howes, Frank. *The Music of William Walton,* 2 vols. London: Oxford University Press, 1944.

BELSHAZZAR'S FEAST

WILLIAM WALTON

The text of this oratorio relates of the wild feast of Belshazzar, and the downfall of both Belshazzar and the city of Babylon.

> Belshazzar the king made a great feast to a thousand of his lords, and drank wine before the thousands . . . They drank wine, and praised the gods of gold, and of silver, of brass, of iron, of wood, and of stone.
> In the same hour came forth fingers of a man's hand, and wrote over against the candlestick upon the plaister of the wall of the king's palace: . . . Mene, mene, tekel, upharsin. (Daniel 5:1, 4-5, 25)

The oratorio is scored for a double mixed chorus, baritone soloist, large orchestra with pipe organ, and two special brass ensembles — one to be on the conductor's left and one on his right. Each brass ensemble is composed of three trumpets, three trombones, and a tuba.

Walton has used Sir Osbert Sitwell's arrangement of passages from the Old Testament for his text. The narrative starts with Isaiah's prophecy that "the day of the Lord is at hand." The lament of the Hebrews by the waters of Babylon comes from Psalm 137, and the conclusion of the oratorio is taken from Psalm 81 (the exultant cry of triumph over the fallen city).

A trombone fanfare introduces Isaiah's prophecy, sung in harsh dissonance by male voices:

Example 1

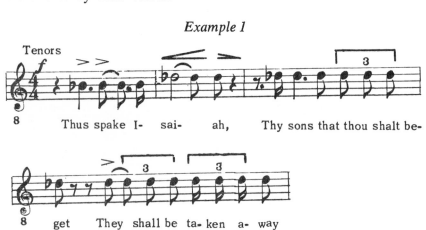

Thus spake Isaiah:
Thy sons that thou shalt beget
And be eunuchs
In the palace of the King of Babylon.
Howl ye, howl ye, therfore:
For the day of the Lord is at hand!
An eight-voice chorus enters in the sorrowful lamentations of
the Hebrews:

Example 2

By the waters of Babylon,
By the waters of Babylon
There we sat down: yea, we wept
And hanged our harps upon the willows.
The music becomes agitated as the chorus continues:
For they that wasted us
Required of us mirth;
They that carried us away captive
Required of us a song.
Sing us one of the songs of Zion.
A trumpet fanfare introduces the next section, the words of
which are repeated. The first time they are sung in a bold and forth-
right manner, the second time very softly and introspectively.
How shall we sing the Lord's song
In a strange land?
The baritone soloist carries the text of the next section, reinforced
by the double chorus:

Example 3

If I forget thee, O Jerusalem,
Let my right hand forget her cunning.
If I do not remember thee,
Let my tongue cleave to the roof of my mouth.
Yea, if I prefer not Jerusalem above my chief joy.

A return is made to the melody of Example 2 as the words are repeated by the chorus, ending slowly and very softly.

By the waters of Babylon
There we sat down: yea, we wept.

A bold chorus with sharp, rhythmic accentuations — syncopated at times — follows. The accents and the volume subside before the chorus is finished.

Example 4

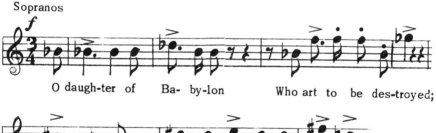

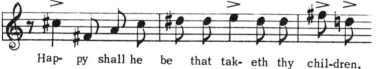

O daughter of Babylon, who art to be destroyed,
Happy shall he be that taketh thy children
And dasheth them against a stone,
For with violence shall that great city Babylon be thrown down
And shall be found no more at all.

The baritone soloist narrates in a recitative, unaccompanied. The melodic line is strongly reminiscent of Hebrew chant:

Example 5

Baritone solo

Ba- by- lon was a great —
ci- ty, her mer-chan-dise was of gold and sil-ver,

*Accidentals apply only to the notes they precede.

Babylon was a great city,
Her merchandise was of gold and silver,
Of precious stones, of pearls, of fine linen,
Of purple, silk and scarlet,
All manner vessels of ivory,
All manner vessels of most precious wood,
Of brass, iron and marble,
Cinnamon, odours and ointments,
Of frankincense, wine and oil,
Fine flour, wheat and beasts,
Sheep, horses; chariots, slaves
And the souls of men.

The chorus describes the joyous feast:

Example 6

Sopranos

In Ba- by-lon Bel-shaz-zar the king
made a feast to a thou- sand of his lords

In Babylon
Belshazzar the King
Made a great feast,
Madè a feast to a thousand of his lords,
And drank wine before the thousand.

The writing becomes more rhythmical and syncopated as the chorus describes the sacrilegious use of sacred vessels pillaged from the Temple at Jerusalem:

Belshazzar, whiles he tasted the wine,
Commanded us to bring the gold and silver vessels:
Yea! the golden vessels, which his father, Nebuchadnezzar,
Had taken out of the temple that was in Jerusalem.

He commanded us to bring the golden vessels
Of the temple of the house of God,
That the King, his Princes, his wives
And his concubines might drink therein.

A double chorus very resolutely continues the description:

Example 7

Chorus II Sopranos

Then the king com-mand-   ed us

Then the King commanded us:
Bring ye the cornet, flute, sackbut, psaltery
And all kinds of music: they drank wine again,
Yea, drank from the sacred vessels,
And then spake the King:

Trumpets and snare drums introduce Belshazzar who leads a wild song of praise to the heathen deities. The chorus passages in this section make use of contrapuntal imitation, while the orchestra responds to the end of each phrase with an appropriate instrumental sound: glockenspiel, cymbals, wood blocks, slapstick, and brass instruments.

Example 8

Praise ye
    The God of Gold
Praise ye
    The God of Silver
Praise ye
    The God of Iron
Praise ye
    The God of Wood
Praise ye
    The God of Stone
Praise ye
    The God of Brass
Praise ye the Gods!

After a muted trumpet fanfare, the last line is repeated in an extended section, starting softly and building to a climax.

A frenzied ceremonial march of crude barbarity is played by the orchestra. As it concludes, the tempo accelerates.

The chorus introduces the next section in unison, quickly breaking into a double chorus that continues to build to the final line: "Thou, O King, art King of Kings: O King, live forever."

Example 9

Thus in Babylon, the mighty city,
Belshazzar the King made a great feast,
Made a feast to a thousand of his lords
And drank wine before the thousand.

Belshazzar whiles he tasted the wine
Commanded us to bring the gold and silver vessels
That his Princes, his wives and his concubines
Might rejoice and drink therein.

After they had praised their strange gods,
The idols and the devils,
False gods who can neither see nor hear,
Called they for the timbrel and pleasant harp
To extol the glory of the King.
Then they pledged the King before the people,
Crying, Thou, O King, art King of Kings:
O King, live forever.

The baritone soloist continues, unaccompanied at first; then drums, cymbals, and gong accompany the solo.

And in that same hour, as they feasted,
Came forth fingers of a man's hand
And the King saw
The part of the hand that wrote.
And this was the writing that was written:
"MENE, MENE, TEKEL UPHARSIN."

A trumpet fanfare is heard; the male chorus interprets the Hebrew:

"THOU ART WEIGHED IN THE BALANCE
AND FOUND WANTING."

The baritone soloist continues (the chorus shouts the word "slain" as he pronounces it):

In that night was Belshazzar the King slain
And his Kingdom divided.

An orchestral prelude introduces the mighty hymn of praise which concludes the oratorio. Rhythmical accents are predominant in the orchestral prelude and continue through the choral singing. Trumpets are heard as they are mentioned in the text: "Blow up the trumpet in the new moon . . ." The music reaches a dramatic climax with its "Alleluia."

Example 10

Then —— sing, —— sing a- loud, ————

sing a- loud ————

Then sing aloud to God our strength:
Made a joyful noise unto the God of Jacob.
Take a psalm, bring hither the timbrel,
Blow up the trumpet in the new moon,
Blow up the trumpet in Zion
For Babylon the Great is fallen fallen.
Alleluia!

Then sing aloud to God our strength:
Make a joyful noise unto the God of Jacob,
While the Kings of the Earth lament
And the merchants of their Earth
Weep, wail and rend the raiment.
They cry, Alas, Alas, that great city,
In one hour is her judgment come.
The chorus continues unaccompanied:
The trumpeters and pipers are silent,
And the harpers have ceased to harp,
And the light of a candle shall shine no more.
The orchestra introduces the final, forceful *Allegro,* as the divided choir builds to a triumphant ending on the Alleluias!

Example 11

Sopranos

Then sing ———————— a-loud to God   our

strength: make a joy- ful   noise —— un- to the   God,

Then sing aloud to God our strength,
Make a joyful noise to the God of Jacob,
For Babylon the Great is fallen.
Alleluia!

BENJAMIN BRITTEN

born: November 22, 1913; Lowestoft, England
died: December 4, 1976; Aldeburgh, England

    Benjamin Britten lives in the English seacoast town of Adelburgh, Suffolk, the locale of his celebrated opera *Peter Grimes*. Britten could well be mistaken for one of the village people in the opera because he can frequently be seen wandering around the village in sloppy, baggy slacks and a loose pull-over sweater. When he is neither at work on his music nor wandering around the village on foot, he is dashing somwhere in his Rolls Royce at extremely fast speeds.

    Benjamin Britten was born in another seacoast town, Lowestoft, where his father served as a dental surgeon. His mother was an excellent amateur pianist and secretary to the local choral society. She encouraged her young son of two who kept begging to get up on the piano stool and "play the keys." Britten was at work on compositions by the time he was five years old and many village folk likened him to the precocious young Mozart. Benjamin at seven was regularly taking orchestral and opera scores to bed with him to look over.

    Britten completed his first composition in his ninth year, a string quartet, which was followed shortly by the composition of an oratorio.

When he was sixteen, Britten had to his credit a symphony, six quartets, and ten piano sonatas. As a youth he took an academic course at Gresham School and studied the viola. His early musical efforts were rewarded with a scholarship to the Royal Conservatory of Music in 1930.

After studying harmony, counterpoint, and composition at the Conservatory, Britten graduated in 1934. The same year he attracted attention with his *Fantasy Quartet* for oboe and strings which was performed at the Florence Festival in Italy. Britten then received several commissions for music from the motion picture industry, including one from the British government to write a score for a propaganda movie.

Britten gained an international reputation as his compositions were performed at the various International Society for Contemporary Music festivals: his *Suite for Violin and Piano* was performed in Barcelona in 1936; a premiere took place in Salzburg in 1937; his first important work, *Variations on a Theme of Frank Bridge*, was performed in London in 1938.

In his songs, Britten had used several of the works of the English poet, W. H. Auden, and when Auden moved to the United States and became an American citizen, Britten was inclined to follow. In 1939 he moved to the United States and considered taking out citizenship papers. Britten lived for six months in Brooklyn, during which time he became acquainted with Aaron Copland. From Brooklyn he moved to Amityville, Long Island, where he stayed for three years. While he was considering whether or not he should become an American citizen, he happened upon an article in an issue of the BBC's *The Listener.* The article discussed George Crabbe from the North Sea area of England. It reminded Britten of the English seacoast that he loved so well and he decided he would return to his homeland. He had to wait six months for transportation because of the war. This enabled him to hear Koussevitzky perform his *Sinfonia da Requiem,* which had been commissioned by the Imperial Japanese Government to celebrate the 2600th anniversary of the Imperial Japanese dynasty. The Japanse government refused the finished work since "it was too Christian in spirit." Koussevitzky was enthused by this work and tried to encourage Britten to write an opera. Britten replied that he would really enjoy composing an opera and received a direct commission from Koussevitzky for this purpose.

Britten appeared before the Tribunal of Conscientious Objectors after arriving in Great Britain and was given exemption from military service because of his pacifist views. In place of conscription, Britten worked during the balance of the war in hospitals, bomb shelters, and bombed-out villages. When not engaged in wartime activities he worked on the opera Koussevitzky had commissioned. It was started in January of 1944 to a libretto based on the poems of Crabbe whose name and association with the North Sea had hailed Britten back to England. The opera was to be a story of the sea and was named after the leading fisherman in the story, *Peter Grimes*. It was put into rehearsal after its completion in February of 1945, and was ready for presentation just after Germany had ceased hostilities. The opera was the first to be presented at the Sadler's Wells to mark the reopening of the theater after it had been closed for the five war years. It was a success and was presented over 100 times throughout Europe within a few months after its first performance.

Shortly after *Peter Grimes* went into rehearsal, Britten was commissioned to prepare some music to demonstrate the instruments of the orchestra for an educational film. Britten produced *The Young Person's Guide to the Orchestra,* sub-titled *Variations and Fugue On a Theme of Purcell,* in response to this commission. The instruments were presented in a theme and variation form so artistically that the work has entered the standard repertory of most symphony orchestras and is presented to adult audiences.

Britten turned again to the field of opera, producing *The Rape of Lucretia* in 1946, followed the next year by *Albert Herring.* During the same year that he completed *Herring,* he bought a house in the small fishing village of Aldeburgh where he now lives. In 1949 his *Spring Symphony* was presented with great success at the Holland Festival of Music.

In 1950 Britten visited Los Angeles, where an unofficial "Britten festival" took place. The composer conducted his *Saint Nicholas Cantata* at the University of Southern California, where his *Albert Herring* was also presented. On the other side of town the University of California at Los Angeles presented Britten's adaptation of the early English *Beggar's Opera.* He conducted the Los Angeles Philharmonic Orchestra in a performance of his *Serenade for Tenor, Horn, and Strings* with Peter Pears (the British tenor for whom it was written) as the soloist.

Britten's opera of 1954, *The Turn of the Screw,* was premiered in Venice, a work in which he turned to the use of the twelve-tone system for the first time. The opera did not receive a very enthusiastic reception, partially because of a poor libretto which had sixteen scenes in two acts. The public was much more receptive to his opera based on Shakespeare's play, *A Midsummer Night's Dream.* Premiered in Aldeburgh in 1960, it received its first major production at Covent Garden, London, in February of 1961. The critics' reviews were so fine and the public's reception so enthusiastic, it was soon produced on the continent in the opera houses of Hamburg and La Scala. The first performance in this country took place in October of 1961 at the San Francisco War Memorial Opera House.

BIBLIOGRAPHY

Mitchell, Donald and Hans Keller, ed. *Benjamin Britten, A Commentary on His Works From a Group of Specialists.* New York: Philosophical Library, 1952.
White, Eric Walter. *Benjamin Britten: A Sketch of His Life and Works.* London: Boosey & Hawkes, Ltd., 1948, rev. 1954.

A CEREMONY OF CAROLS

BENJAMIN BRITTEN

Composed in 1942, Benjamin Britten's suite of pieces, *A Ceremony of Carols,* for treble voices and harp reveals his deftness at setting English texts. The words of these carols are largely anonymous Middle English poems. There are nine carols sung by   treble voices, with a harp interlude following the sixth carol.

PROCESSIONAL

An unaccompanied unison melody reminiscent of the plainchants used in the early Christian churches is the musical setting for the Latin text *Hodie Christus natus est* (Today Christ is born):

Example 1

Hodie Christus natus est:	Today Christ is born,
Hodie Salvator apparuit:	Today the Saviour hath appeared,
Hodie in terra canunt angeli:	The angels sing on earth,
Laetantur archangeli:	The Archangels rejoice,
Hodie exsultant justi dicentes:	Today the just exalt, saying:
Gloria in excelsis Deo.	Glory to God in the Highest
Alleluia!	Alleluia!

WOLCUM YOLE:

Wolcum Yole! (Welcome, Yule) opens with a two-measure harp introduction followed by the women's voices in three-part harmony; the melody:

Example 2

Wol- cum,   wol-cum,   wol-cum   be thou   heve - - nè king,

Wolcum be thou hevenè king,   (*hevenè* — heavenly)
Wolcum Yole!
Wolcum, born in one morning,
Wolcum for whom we sall sing!

In the second verse the words are treated in fugal imitation, the altos entering first.

Wolcum, Thomas marter one,
Wolcum, seintes lefe and dere,
Wolcum Yole!

In sustained chords the voices sing:

Candelmesse, Quene of bliss,
Wolcum bothe to more and lesse.

The words of the next verse are set to the same music as in the first (Example 2):

Wolcum be ye that are here,
Wolcum alle and make good cheer.
Wolcum alle another yere,
Wolcum Yole. Wolcum!

THERE IS NO ROSE

In this slower carol, each line of the anonymous poem set in three-part harmony is interrupted by a Latin word or expression chanted in unison:

Example 3

There is no rose of such vertu as is the rose that bare Jesu.
Alleluia. Alleluia.
For in this rose conteined was Heaven and earth in litel space.
Resmiranda. Resmiranda.
By that rose we may well see there be one God in persons three.
Pares forma. Pares forma.
The aungels sungen the shepherd to: Gloria in excelsis Deo.
Gaudeamus. Gaudeamus.
Leave we all this werldly mirth and follow we this joyful birth.
Transeamus. Transeamus.
(*Resmiranda*—a wonderful thing. *Gaudeamus*—let us rejoice.
Pares forma—of equal beauty. *Transeamus*—let us be transformed.)

THAT YONGE CHILD

This carol is a duet for solo voice and harp, extremely difficult because the two are harmonically independent:

Example 4

That yongë child when it gan weep
With song she lulled him asleep:
That was so sweet a melody
It passed alle minstrelsy.

The nightingalë sang also:
Her song is hoarse and nought thereto:
Whoso attendeth to her song
And leaveth the first
Then doth he wrong.

BALULALOW

The text of the ancient British poets, James, John, and Robert Wedderburn (c. 1530), is used in this carol. The first verse is set for treble solo and harp:

Example 5

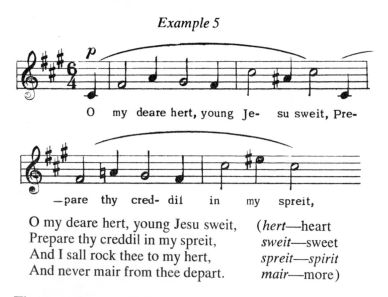

O   my deare hert, young Je-   su sweit, Pre-

—pare thy cred- dil   in   my spreit,

O my deare hert, young Jesu sweit,   (*hert*—heart
Prepare thy creddil in my spreit,   *sweit*—sweet
And I sall rock thee to my hert,   *spreit*—spirit
And never mair from thee depart.   *mair*—more)

The second verse starts one measure before the first is finished. It is a harmonic setting of the melody of Example 5:

But I sall praise thee evermoir   (*sanges*—songs
With sanges sweit unto thy gloir;   *richt*—right)
The knees of my hert sall I bow,
And sing that richt Balulalow.

As Dew in Aprille

This carol, set for three treble voices, moves very, very quickly and lightly:

Example 6

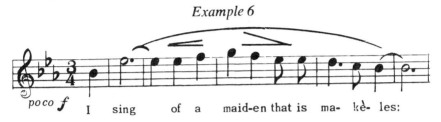

poco *f* I   sing   of   a   maid-en that is   ma- kè- les:

King of all   kings   to   her   son   she ches

I sing of a maiden that is makèles: (*makèles*—matchless
King of all kings to her son she ches.   *ches*—chose)
He came al so stille as dew in Aprille
That falleth on the grass.

He came al so stille   (*moder*—mother
To his moder's bour,   *bour*—bore)
As dew in Aprille
That falleth on the flour.

He came al so stille
There his moder lay,
As dew in Aprille
That falleth on the spray.

Moder and mayden was
Never none but she:
Well may such a lady Goddess
Moder be.

This Little Babe

A very rhythmic pattern of repeated chords in the harp introduces the vocal setting of a poem by Robert Southwell (1516?—1593).

The first verse is in unison and has strong accents that give this carol a syncopated effect:

Example 7

This lit- tle Babe so few days old, Is

come to ri-fle   Sa-tan's fold;

> This little Babe so few days old
> Is come to rifle Satan's fold;
> All hell doth at his presence quake,
> Though he himself for cold do shake;
> For in this weak unharmèd wise
> The gates of hell he will surprise.

The second verse uses the melody of the first (Example 7) but is set for two voices in canon, the altos one beat behind the sopranos.

> With tears he fights and wins the field,
> His naked breast stands for a shield,
> His battering shot are babish cries
> His arrows looks of weeping eyes,
> His martial ensigns Cold and Need,
> And feeble Flesh his warrior's steed.

The third verse uses the same melody (Example 7) for three voices in canon, each one beat apart.

> His camp is pitchèd in a stall,
> His bulwark but a broken wall;
> The crib his trench, haystalks his stakes;
> Of shepherds he his muster makes;
> And thus, as sure his foe to wound,
> The angels' trumps alarum sound.

The next verse is a three-voice harmonic setting of intensity, a variation of Example 7.

> My soul, with Christ join thou in fight;
> Stick to the tents that he hath pight.
> Within his crib is surest ward;
> This little Babe will be thy guard.

The final verse is in unison, *fortissimo*.

> If thou wilt foil thy foes with joy,
> Then flit not from this heavenly Boy.

INTERLUDE

A harp solo serves as an interlude in this "ceremony of carols." The upper voice of the harp introduces the melody:

Example 8

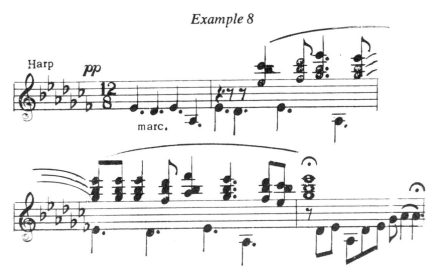

Example 8 is repeated with fuller chords.
After variations of Example 8, harp glissandi end the *Interlude*.

IN FREEZING WINTER NIGHT

The text of this carol is another poem of Robert Southwell. The second sopranos enter in canonic imitation of the first sopranos and altos:

Example 9

Be- hold, a sil- ly ten- der babe, in freez-ing win-ter night,

Behold, a silly tender babe in freezing winter night,
In homely manger trembling lies alas, a piteous sight!
The inns are full; no man will yield this little pilgrim bed.
But forced he is with silly beasts in crib to shroud his head.

The second verse is based on Example 9, this time in major mode.

This stable is a Prince's court, this crib his chair of State;
The beasts are parcel of his pomp, the wooden dish his plate.
The persons in that poor attire His royal livries wear;
The Prince himself is come from heav'n; this pomp is prizèd there.

In the final verse, a soprano sings the text as a solo accompanied by a humming chorus and harp.

With joy approach, O Christian wight,
Do homage to thy King,
And highly praise his humble pomp,
Wich he from Heav'n doth bring.

SPRING CAROL

The *Spring Carol* is essentially a trio for two solo voices and harp. The text is a poem by William Cornish:

Example 10

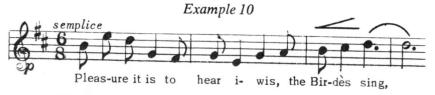

Pleas-ure it is to hear i- wis, the Bir-dès sing,

Pleasure it is to hear iwis,   (*iwis*—certainly)
The Birdès sing
   The deer in the dale,
   The sheep in the vale,
   The corn springing.
God's purvayance for sustenance,
It is for man.
Then we always to give him praise,
And thank him than.

DEO GRACIAS

The three treble voices loudly proclaim in unison:

Example 11

f De-o   grac-i - as!   De-o   grac-i - as!

In harmony, they softly sing, marked by sharp accents, the English words of the text:

Example 12

pp A-dam lay i- boun-den, boun-   den   in a   bond

Adam lay ibounden in a bond,
Four thousand winter thought he not to long.
And all was for an appil that he tok.
And clerkès finden written in their book.
Ne had the appil takè ben,
Ne haddè never our lady a ben hevenè quene.

Blessèd be the time
That appil takè was
Therefore we moun singen. Deo gracias!
(*ibounden*—bound, *appil*—apple, *tok*—took, *ne*—never, *takè*—taken, *a ben*—have been, *moun*—must).

RECESSIONAL

The *Recessional* is a duplication of the *Processional*.

THE YOUNG PERSON'S GUIDE TO THE ORCHESTRA

Variations and Fugue on a Theme of Purcell

Benjamin Britten

The *Young Person's Guide to the Orchestra* was originally commissioned to accompany a British educational film in which the instruments of the orchestra were to be demonstrated. Britten thereupon took a theme of the great English composer, Henry Purcell, and succeeded in composing a set of variations followed by a fugue that was so artistic that the entire composition, without narration, is frequently performed on regular orchestral concerts. Britten says of this work:

> The composer has written this piece of music specially to introduce you to the instruments of the orchestra. There are four teams of players; the strings, the woodwind, the brass, and the percussion. Each of these four teams uses instruments which have a family likeness. They ·make roughly the same kind of sound in the same way. The strings are played with a bow or plucked by the fingers. The woodwind are blown by the breath. The brass are blown too. The percussion are banged. First you will hear a Theme by the great English composer, Henry Purcell, played by the whole orchestra and by each of the four groups of instruments.

The "Themes and Variation" section presents two ideas: 1) the groups, families, or choirs of instruments; and, 2) individual instruments. This section is based on a theme of Henry Purcell (from the *Rondeau* of his incidental music to *Abdelazar*).

Example 1

Full orchestra

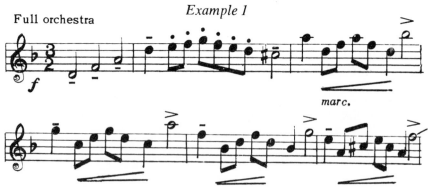

* *Young Person's Guide to the Orchestra* — Copyright, 1947, by Hawkes & Son (London) Ltd. Reprinted by permission of Boosey & Hawkes Inc.

marc.

Statements of Purcell's theme (Example 1):
Example 1 is stated by full orchestra (consisting of piccolo, two each of flutes, oboes, B-flat clarinets, and bassoons; four horns, two trumpets, three trombones, tuba, timpani, other percussion, harp, and strings).

Example 1 is stated by woodwinds in the relative major key (F), in relatively close harmony, with the bassoons playing more sustained notes than the other woodwinds.

The brass choir plays the Purcell theme in E-flat major. Horns and trombones begin, answered by trumpets. The theme is shortened by two measures.

Strings present a varied form of the theme in which measure two is extended. The four instruments take the motive of measure 3 in successive entrances, descending in pitch.

Percussion statement brings out the timpani; it plays the initial triadic figure of Example 1 (now in A major). The balance of the theme is purely rhythmic.

Example 1 is repeated by full orchestra.

The variations of the Purcell theme:
Variation 1: Flutes and piccolo. Example 1 embellished with grace notes, played staccato; two flutes play in 3rds; high range and trills on the piccolo predominate.

Variation 2: Oboes. Sustained *cantabile* style, accompanied by soft strings; second oboe has a melodic accompaniment figure.

Variation 3: Clarinets. Very fast arpeggios, scale patterns, showing virtuoso agility, wide range and different tone colors of the registers.

Variation 4: Bassoons. *Allegro alla marcia;* rhythmic accent strong; first bassoon legato, second bassoon accompanies with a rhythmic staccato figure.

Variation 5: Violins. *Brillante alla pollacca;* soaring upwards, fortissimo, showing bowing accents, division into first and second violins (second phrase) and pizzicato effect.

Variation 6: Violas. Plaintive, sustained melody.

Variation 7: Celli. Beginning on last note of the violas, but an octave higher; similar in sound and style to the violas until descent into lower range shows differences.

Variation 8: Double basses. Gradual ascent in detached, triadic figure; acceleration in tempo, ending on a climactic glissando; second part: legato style, derived from measure 2 of Example 1; then follows a descent in the triadic figure which corresponds to the first part of this variation.

Variation 9: Harp. *Maestoso;* arpeggiated figures over a string tremolo; arpeggios of connected and separated variety, glissandi.

Variation 10: Horns. Successive entrances on the rhythm ♪♩ build up to a fortissimo chord with a decrescendo following immediately; after several measures of sustained notes, a series of calls in descending order corresponds to the beginning of this variation.

Variation 11: Trumpets. *Vivace;* preceded and accompanied by constant rhythm ♩♫ ♩♫ on the snare drums; the trumpets alternate in a martial variation featuring the same rhythm as the snare drums.

Variation 12: Trombones. *Allegro pomposo;* a majestic variation in notes of even value show first the brassy power of the trombones; the tuba enters canonically in the sixth measure, after which the trombones have a soft passage of sustained chords; trombones and tuba are then combined in a canonic passage (imitation at the octave, two beats apart).

Variation 13: Percussion. Timpani plays three pitches g, c, and e,

in a rhythmic figure ♪♪♩ ♪♩ then, heard in turn: bass drum and cymbals, tambourine and triangle, snare drum and Chinese block, xylophone, castanets and gong, whip, percussion combined (timpani patter predominant. Xylophone and triangle play a codetta).

Fugue

The instruments enter in the same order as in the variations, this time playing the Subject of the fugue, Example 2.

1. piccolo. 2. flutes. 3. oboes. 4. clarinets. 5. bassoons. 6. 1st violins. 7. 2nd violins. 8. violas. 9. celli. 10. double basses. 11. harp. 12. French horns. 13. trumpets. 14. trombones and tuba. 15. percussion (xylophone, timpani, bass drum, tambourine, snare drum, cymbals).

The brass play Example 1 in augmentation while strings and woodwinds, extend Example 2, ending in a powerful tutti.

Example 2

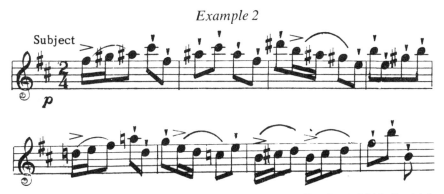

Young Person's Guide to the Orchestra, Copyright 1947 by Hawkes & Son (London) Ltd. Reprinted by permission of Boosey & Hawkes Inc.

Part of the panel depicting "The Temptation of St. Anthony" which inspired the third movement of Hindemith's *Mathis der Maler.*

First page of the conductor's score of the *Young Person's Guide to the Orchestra*.

Note that the woodwinds are listed on the upper staves of the score, followed by the brass instruments. The percussion appear just below the center of the page, the untuned ones are written on a single-line staff. The strings always appear on the lowest staves.

Courtesy Boosey and Hawkes. Music copyrighted 1946 by Hawkes and Son, London

The symphony orchestra. Although seating arrangements differ, the first violins always appear to the conductor's left. In this picture the celli are to his right and the double basses behind them. The woodwinds appear in the center of the orchestra and are backed by the brass. The percussion, except for the timpani, are out of the picture since they are to the back and left of the orchestra.

The Los Angeles Philharmonic Orchestra

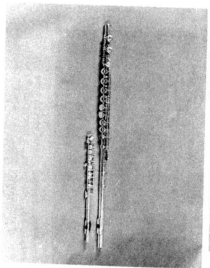

THE PICCOLO AND FLUTE

Piccolo is a contraction of the Italian term *flauto piccolo, meaning "small flute."* It is pitched an octave higher than the flute.

The player blows the flute across the side hole toward the end of the instrument.

THE OBOE

The instrument is a conical pipe made of wood to the upper end of which a double reed is fixed. The vibration of the double reed produces the tone which is nasal and "reedy" in character.

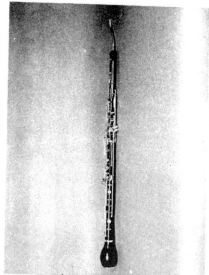

THE ENGLISH HORN

The English horn is actually neither English nor a horn. It is an alto oboe, pitched one fifth lower than the oboe.

THE CLARINET

Although at a distance the oboe and clarinet may look the same, an inspection of their *mouthpieces* will easily disclose the difference. The clarinet is a much more recent instrument and is fuller in its tone quality.

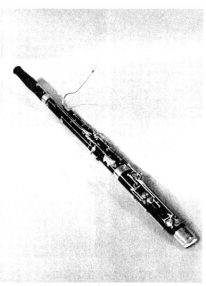

THE BASS CLARINET

It has a range an octave below that of the clarinet, with an additional semitone provided by a low E-flat key.

THE BASSOON

This is the bass member of the double-reed family; its lowest tone is two octaves below that of the oboe.

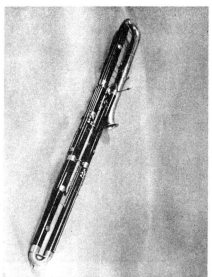

The cornet on the left, the trumpet on the right

THE CONTRABASSOON

The tube is over sixteen feet in length·and is doubled back against itself four times. Its range is one octave below the bassoon.

The cornet is similar in shape to the trumpet but is shorter and with a relatively longer conical portion of brass tubing.

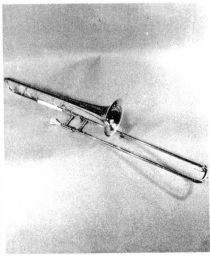

THE FRENCH HORN
It has a funnel-shaped mouthpiece. The hand inserted in the bell serves not only to support the instrument, but to "stop" tones and to mute the instrument.

THE TROMBONE
The slide of the trombone changes its pitch. There are seven positions for the slide.

THE TUBA
The bass member of the brass comes in several sizes, pitched in as many keys.

One of a pair of timpani

Ludwig Drums

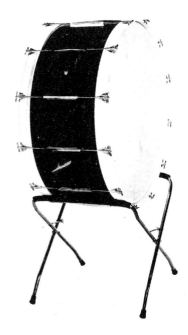

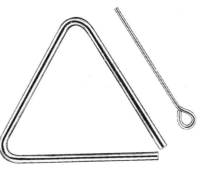

TRIANGLE

BASS DRUM

CYMBAL

SNARE DRUM

All photos from Ludwig Drums

CASTANETS (for orchestral use)

TEMPLE BLOCKS   TAMBOURINE

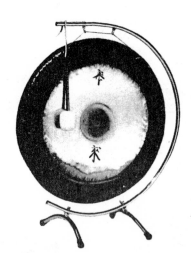

XYLOPHONE   CHINESE GONG

All photos from Ludwig Drums   THE WHIP

The violin (on the left) is the most important of the stringed instruments; the viola (on the right) is the alto member of the string choir.

The double bass (on the left) is also called *bass viol* or *contrabass;* the cello (on the right) is the tenor member of the strings.

The string family in comparison: the double bass, the cello, the viola, and the violin.

THE HARP

CHAPTER X

MUSIC OF THE UNITED STATES

IF one is to take the expression *Music of the United States* to mean music other than that of the American Indians, probably the first example would date from 1579 when it is recorded that Sir Francis Drake and his company of seamen sang psalms for the Indians on the west coast of the new continent. Most books record the Pilgrims' psalm singing of 1620 as amongst the earliest American musical performances. The first book published in the New World was a collection of psalms for singing, *The Whole Book of Psalms Faithfully Translated Into English Metre*, published in Cambridge, Massachusetts, in 1640. So important was psalm singing in the early settlements that this book went through twenty-six editions (the final edition dated some 104 years later in 1744). It is interesting to note that a first edition of this "Bay Psalm Book" (as the work was more commonly known) sold for $151,000 in New York in 1947, the highest price ever paid for a book, including the first edition of the Gutenberg Bible).

Music of the United States evolved from early psalm singing as a result of many influences. The importation of Negroes from west Africa to be sold as slaves as early as 1619 had a lasting effect on music. By 1727 over 75,000 slaves had been imported, and by 1800 there were over a million slaves in the new world, 19% of the population. In addition to the native songs they brought with them (of which we have no record) they brought a stringed instrument called a *banjar*.

Because of the nature of the early settlement of this country — the clearing of forests, the building of homes, the cultivation of farm lands — music as a profession was slow in developing. Many musical amateurs, though, were to be found among the people. Thomas Jefferson was an accomplished violinist and frequently played duets with Patrick Henry. Benjamin Franklin played both the guitar and the harp and was responsible for the invention of the glass harmonica, an instrument that for a time became quite popular.

The first composer to write music in the New World was Conrad Biessel (1690-1768) who had been a German mystic. Once in America, he founded a religious sect known as *Seventh Day Dunkers.* He was successively a baker, a violinist, a theologian. Having settled in Germantown, Pennsylvania, he composed over 1,000 hymns for four, five, six, and seven voices.

Another early religious influence on music was the establishment of the Moravian Colony in 1741. They brought from the old world many instruments and performed the new works of Haydn and Mozart. Recently there has been a renaissance of the original sacred music which they developed in those early days for their services.

The first native born composer was Francis Hopkinson (1737-1791) who had served as a Judge of the Admiralty for Pennsylvania and later signed the Declaration of Independence. In music he was only an amateur but he had talent and composed many songs and keyboard works. Probably the first name in music of this country that is still familiar today is that of William Billings (1746-1800). As a boy Billings was apprenticed to the tanners trade and apparently remained a tanner by profession all of his life. He must have presented a pitiful sight for he was short in one leg and had but one eye. Contemporary accounts report that village folk laughed at his appearance as he walked down the street. Billings was twenty-four when his first book was published, a set of religious fuguing tunes. Naïve, full of vitality and gusto, this collection broke with the English tradition of the *Bay Psalm Book;* the fuguing tunes were a new kind of hymn tune containing sections in which one voice entered at a time in polyphonic imitation, hence the name "fuguing tune." These tunes survived for seventy-five years until superseded about 1850 by the more solemn and sentimental hymns of the Victorian period.

Following the War of the Revolution professional immigrants started to arrive in the United States; singing societies were formed, concerts arranged. The oldest musical society in this country was the St. Cecilia Society founded in Charleston in 1762 with private subscription concerts. The trend of music then swung northward to New York, Boston, and Philadelphia. Philadelphia, in particular, became the leading cultural center of the young Republic and the chief center of musical activity.

Lowell Mason (1792-1872) proved to be a great influence on music in the United States. He composed many hymn tunes and his collection, *The Hallelujah,* sold over 150,000 copies, earning for the composer more than $100,000. It was Mason who was responsible for the introduction of music into the curriculum of the public schools in 1836, making it an integral part of every child's education. Likewise, he established music conventions for the dissemination of knowledge among the many teachers of music.

Music was one of the featured components of the camp meetings sponsored by traveling revivalists. The "revivalist songs" were in the more popular idiom than the older staid hymns of the church. These revivalist hymns were designed to appeal to the followers of these camp meetings and to "win them to Christ." A religious group known as the *Shakers* developed religious songs of merit. *The Gift to Be Simple*, an old Shaker melody, has been used by Aaron Copland in his ballet *Appalachian Spring*.

Negro spirituals rose to prominence after the Civil War (there are few accounts of them before then). The Negroes had originally brought with them from Africa a tradition of singing and a love for music. Toiling long hours on the plantations of the South, their only diversion from work was singing. One of the first spirituals to be published was *Roll, Jordan, Roll* in 1862. It proved to be a great favorite in the North, as did *Blow Your Trumpet, Gabriel*.

Minstrel shows were an outgrowth of several theatrical experiments in which white people donned burnt cork and imitated the music of the Negroes. Certain specific comic characters developed in these shows, establishing a tradition. One of the many composers of minstrel music was Dan Emmett who produced a tune in 1843 entitled *I Wish I Was in Dixie's Land* for one of the minstrel shows. *Dixie*, as the tune later came to be known, was the most universally accepted melody from this era.

Stephen Foster (1826-1864) wrote songs that were the "popular music" of his generation. Although these were "popular" tunes, they were more American than the music of serious musicians who composed symphonic music in the German tradition. In his songs, Foster tried to write music typical of the pattern established by the Minstrel (Ethiopian) shows. He said in a letter of May 25, 1852: "I have concluded . . . to pursue the Ethiopian business without fear or shame and . . . to establish my name as the best Ethiopian song writer."

Virtuoso pianists were in great demand in Europe in the mid-nineteenth century and an American soon joined their ranks, Louis Moreau Gottschalk (1829-1869). He was born in New Orleans and learned the piano at an early age. Original compositions of Gottschalk were based on his Creole and Caribbean background and in the

Paul Revere, an engraver by profession, made this engraving for the cover of William Billings' six-voiced canon, *Wake Ev'ry Breath*.

New York Public Library

Benjamin Franklin's musical invention, the *Armonica*

Journal of the Franklin Institute

PREPARING THE PRODUCTION OF *THE INCREDIBLE FLUTIST*

Left to right: Walter Piston, composer; Arthur Fiedler, conductor; Jan Veen, choreographer and author of the dance play; Marco Montedoro, designer of set and costumes.

virtuoso pianistic style of the period. Educated in Europe, he concertized through most of that continent after his studies and then toured the United States. For many in Europe this was their first contact with a professional musician from the United States and their first opportunity to hear music based on native melodies and rhythms of the deep south.

Native born composers finally started to establish for themselves a place in the symphonic literature of the United States. One composer of the late nineteenth century with more than average talent was John Knowles Paine (1839-1906) who started the "Boston" or "New England" group of composers which included George W. Chadwick (1854-1931) and Horatio Parker (1863-1919). Edward MacDowell (1861-1908) was the first American composer to gain fame and a reputation in Europe as well as in the United States. MacDowell received his fundamental training with the New England group and then headed for Germany for advanced study in composition. From MacDowell's time until almost World War II this was to be the pattern — composers received their fundamental training in the United States and then traveled to Europe for their advanced training and coaching by continental composers of note.

From a desire to make music of the United States "more American" and less dependent on Germanic traditions, composers turned to the melodies of the American Indians for authenticity. Because true Indian melodies were a product of another culture and tradition, not even built on the twelve tone division of the octave known to western civilization, these melodies had to be altered to fit the western scale. Compositions such as Charles Wakefield Cadman's *From the Land of the Sky Blue Water,* which he stated was based on an Indian melody, would never have been recognized by the original Indian tribe because of this change in interval relationships. The concept of rhythm also was different between the Indian and western cultures. Edward MacDowell used Indian melodies as the basis of his *Indian Suite.*

Early twentieth century composers of the United States, for the most part, clung to the tradition of late nineteenth century European Romanticism. Deems Taylor **(1885-1966)** and Howard Hanson (1896-   ) received early successes with both their instrumental compositions and with opera. (Taylor's *Peter Ibbetson* was produced at the Metropolitan Opera House in 1931; Hanson's *Merry Mount* was produced there in 1934.)

An exception to this Romantic tradition was a composer who departed radically from all accepted tradition, Charles Ives (1876-1954). As a student Ives decided against music as a profession and went into the insurance business, in which he was most successful. Ives composed at home in the evenings and on week-ends, works that he piled in cupboards and in boxes. Only in the 1950's did these compositions of the 1910's come to light, music that was bold and revolutionary for its time, music that employed polytonality, tone clusters, and strange and unusual rhythms.

Randall Thompson (1899-   ) has exhibited an unusual musical talent in his *Symphony No. 2* and in his choral composition *Alleluia*. Henry Cowell **(1897-1965)** experimented with tone clusters (groups of superimposed 2nds sounded simultaneously) and with plucked piano strings.

The 1930's saw several composers of the United States rise to international prominence: Aaron Copland (1900-   ), Roy Harris **(1898-1979)** Virgil Thomson (1896-   ), Roger Sessions (1896-   ), and Walter Piston **(1894-1976).** The next decade thoroughly established the American composer as a leader in the development of New Music. The men of this later era include Samuel Barber (1910-   ), Paul Creston (1906-   ), Gian-Carlo Menotti (1911-   ), and William Schuman (1910-   ). The youngest generation of composers includes Lukas Foss (1922-   ) and Easley Blackwood (1933-   ).

It is difficult to categorize contemporary composers, and many prefer not to be identified with a label. Some of these men change or progress from one category to another as they mature. Generally speaking, Samuel Barber (neo-Romanticist) and Walter Piston (Twentieth Century Classicist) are accepted as *traditionalists*. Eclectic composers (drawing their techniques from several areas) are Norman Dello Joio, Virgil Thomson, Randall Thompson, William Schuman, and Paul Creston. Roy Harris has been "labeled" a nationalist.

The *experimentalist* composers include Henry Cowell, George Antheil, Edgar Varèse, Charles Ives, and John Cage. Cowell was known as the *enfant terrible* (bad boy) of music when, at fifteen years of age, he shocked the San Francisco public with tone clusters and later with plucked piano strings. George Antheil wrote his *Ballet Mecanique* in 1920; it used ten pianos, an anvil, horns, and buzzers. In the same decade Edgar Varèse composed his *Hyperprism* and *Ionization* which made use in the orchestra of both a high and low siren, lion's roar, slapstick, bongos, guiro, Chinese blocks, sleigh bells, and two anvils — a total of thirty-five different instruments played by thirteen performers. John Cage has been one of the most recent experimenters, writing works in the 1940's for the *prepared piano,* novel percussion instruments including oxen bells, and tin cans. The "prepared piano" was an ordinary grand whose strings were muted at various specific points with small objects of wood, rubber, metal, glass, screws, bolts, hairpins, rubber bands, and weather stripping. Cage's *Imaginary Landscape* (1951) was written for orchestra and twelve radios.

Even though almost two-thirds of the twentieth century have elapsed, it is impossible to know the trend of composition or to list the outstanding composers for we are too close to it. It is evident, though, that the United States has established itself as one of the few centers of creativity. Our contemporary composers are ranked internationally among the finest in the world, and certainly such compositions as the Harris *Symphony No. 3,* the Barber *Adagio for Strings,* the Menotti operas, the Thompson *Alleluia* need no apology for appearing on programs alongside the works of Bach, Beethoven, and Brahms.

BIBLIOGRAPHY

Chase, Gilbert. *American Music: From the Pilgrims to the Present.* New York: McGraw-Hill Book Co., Inc., 1955.
Lang, Paul Henry (Editor). *One Hundred Years of Music in America.* New York: G. Schirmer, 1961.

CHARLES IVES

BORN: October 20, 1874; Danbury, Connecticut.
DIED: May 19, 1954; New York, New York.

Charles Ives was one of the most successful insurance men this country has ever produced, a man who made millions in the field, a man who wrote one of the most important books on the subject. In the evenings, once home from the office, he would sit at his desk and write music because he enjoyed it. As the sheets of score paper were filled, he would toss them on the floor in what resembled a pile. As these became too high, he would transport them out to the shelves in his barn.

Always planning to look over these disordered piles of manuscripts, he did, in the fall of 1949, do some rummaging around and came out with some dusty, photostatic sheets which turned out to be

CHARLES IVES
photographed in his study
Courtesy The Bridgeport Herald

CHARLES T. GRIFFES
Photo by G. D. Hackett

WALTER PISTON

HOWARD HANSON

his *Symphony No. 2* written in 1897. After the parts had been copied, it was premiered by Leonard Bernstein some fifty-four years after it had been written. Since it was one of Ives' first major works to be performed by a symphony orchestra, Bernstein invited the composer to be his guest at the premiere. When the composer declined, Bernstein offered to conduct a rehearsal of it at any hour and date that would suit Ives, and would leave the house dark so that no one would know that the composer was there. When Ives refused even this offer, the best Bernstein could do was to have Mrs. Ives as his guest of honor for the premiere. When she returned home that evening she told her husband how successful the work had been and how much the public had liked it. Ives sneaked down to the kitchen a week later and listened to a broadcast performance of it on the maid's radio. This was his only experience hearing one of his major works performed.

Charles Ives was born in Danbury, not far from where his forebears had settled shortly after the landing of the Pilgrims. His father had been a band leader in the Army during the Civil War, his mother a music teacher in Danbury. Once out of the service, the elder Ives continued his interest in music, as he played the piano for dances, was the organist for his church, led the town band, and made many of his own arrangements. Charles' father was also an experimenter, always trying out new sound relationships. He even built an instrument with twenty-four violin strings stretched over a clothes press on which he could play quarter-tone music.

As a boy, Charles attended the outdoor camp meetings and heard their revival songs. Stephen Foster had been a friend of his father, so the boy also heard the minstrel tunes and all the "tearjerkers" that were popular at the time. When Charles was eight, his father discovered him thumping out band rhythms on the family piano. Father Ives promptly took the boy down to the barber shop and turned him over to the German barber who was also the drummer in the town band.

Charles was provided with a pair of drumsticks and an empty tub on which to practice. By the time he was twelve, he was a drummer in his father's band. His father saw to it that the boy's knowledge of music was well rounded and taught him the piano, violin, cornet, sight-reading, harmony, and counterpoint. By the time he was eleven, Ives had started organ lessons and two years later was the organist at the Congregational Church of Danbury, playing two Sunday services and giving frequent recitals.

Several years earlier Charles had begun to compose, the first work being a *Dirge for Chin Chin* who was the family cat. His father's band played one of his pieces, but for that performance Charles begged out of playing in the band. As the band came down his street loudly blaring forth the melody of his composition, Charles played handball against the side of the house with his back turned toward the band.

As a high school student, Ives was active in sports. He was the captain of the high school football team, and served as a pitcher for the school baseball team the year they beat the Yale freshman team. He completed a composition entitled *Variations on America* about the time he was ready to graduate from high school, but his father suggested not to have a public performance because the composition had canons in two and three keys at once. (This was 1891!)

At twenty, Ives enrolled at Yale to study composition with Horatio Parker. As far as can be determined, Parker seems to have ignored the non-academic and daring new compositions that Ives was writing and looked only at the standard harmony exercises required of the students. Ives' *Symphony No. 1* dates from his college days, a work filled with dissonances and written in many keys at once. While at Yale he wrote music for a theater orchestra for amusement, played on the football team, and was a member of the baseball team.

After graduation Ives determined that he wanted a full and comfortable life, and although his marriage was still eight years away, he decided a musician simply didn't earn enough money to support a family. He chose a career in insurance and started work for the Mutual Life Insurance Company at $5 per week. To keep this job he had to move to New York where he roomed with several other young men in a place they called "Poverty Flat." His *Symphony No. 2* already mentioned was written here.

During these busy years at the insurance office, he wrote music every evening, works which included *Washington's Birthday* (1913), *Three Places In New England* (1914), *Sonata No. 4 for Violin* (1914), and *Concord Sonata* (1915). Almost none of his compositions were ever performed. A violinist friend had tried over a few works for that instrument and parts of two different symphonies were sent to conductors Damrosch and Mahler to look over for possible performance. Damrosch lost the symphony that had been sent to him and Mahler died before he could look over the other. Ives' only support in his musical endeavors came from his loyal and faithful wife.

About the time of World War I Ives ceased to compose. He said:

[My] things [were] done mostly in the twenty years or so between 1896 and 1916. In 1917 the War came on and I did practically nothing in music. I did not seem to feel like it. We were very busy at the office at this time with the extra Red Cross and Liberty Loan drives, and all the problems that the war brought on. As I look back [1928] I find I did almost no composing after the beginning of 1917. In October, 1918, I had a serious illness that kept me away from the office for six months.

By the end of the war the illness, diabetes, made it impossible for him to hold a pen to write. He then turned to having the unplayed music he had already written published. He paid for the printing costs himself and distributed copies free of charge to anyone that made a request. Three volumes were issued, and for many years this was all of Ives' music that was known to the public. The first major presentation of his music was in the series *Evenings On the Roof* in Los Angeles, where, in the season 1944-45, most of his chamber works and several songs were performed. His *Symphony No. 3* was premiered twenty years after he had written it, and won the 1947 Pulitzer Prize.

After his retirement in 1930, Ives lived a secluded life. Too shaky to hold a razor by that time, he grew a beard. Heart disease bothered him, and in his last few years he developed cataracts over both eyes that couldn't be removed because of his diabetic condition. He died in 1954, just four days before the biography by his friend Henry Cowell was published.

BIBLIOGRAPHY

Cowell, Henry, and Sidney. *Charles Ives and His Music.* New York: Oxford University Press, 1954.

SONATA NO. 4 FOR VIOLIN

"Children's Day at the Camp Meeting"

CHARLES IVES

In the original manuscript of this sonata, Charles Ives made many marginal notations in pencil. These were reprinted in the published score and gave the composer's views on the work. He said:

"Children's Day at the Camp Meeting" is shorter than the other violin sonatas, and a few of its parts and suggested themes were used in organ and other earlier pieces. The subject matter is a kind of reflection, remembrance, expression, etc., of the children's services at the out-door Summer camp meetings held around Danbury and in many of the farm towns in Connecticut, in the 70's, 80's, and 90's. There was usually only one Children's Day in these Summer meetings, and the children made the most of it — often the best of it. They would at times get stirred up, excited, and even boisterous, but underneath there was usually something serious, though Deacon Grey would occasionally have to "Sing a Caution."

The First Movement (which was somteimes played last and the last first) was suggested by an actual happening at one of these services. The children, especially the boys, liked to get up and join in the marching kind of hymns. And as these meetings were "out door," the "march" sometimes became a real one. One day Lowell Mason's "Work for The Night Is Coming" got the boys going and keeping on between services, when the boy who played the melodeon was practicing his "organicks of canonicks, fugatiks, harmonicks, and melodicks." In this movement, as is remembered, they — the postlude organ practise (real and improvised, sometimes both) — and the boys' fast march — got to going together, even joining in each other's sounds, and the loudest singers and also those with the best voices, as is often the case, would sing most of the wrong notes. They started this tune on "ME" so the boy organist's father made him play "SOH" hard even if sometimes it had to be in a key that the postlude was not in just then. The boys sometimes got almost as far off from Lowell M. as they did from the melodeon. The organ would be uncovering "covered 5ths" breaking "good resolutions" faster and faster and the boys' march reaching almost a "Main Street Quick-step" when Parson Hubbell would beat the "Gong" on the oaktree for the next service to begin. Or if it is growing dark, the boys' march would die away, as they marched down to their tents, the barn doors or over the "1770 Bridge" between the Stone Pillars to the Station.

The Second Movement is quieter and more serious except when Deacon Stonemason Bell and Farmer John would get up and get the boys excited. But most of the Movement moves around a rather quiet but old favorite Hymn of the children, while mostly in the accompaniment is heard something trying to reflect the out-door sounds of nature on those Summer days — the west wind in the pines and oaks, the running brook — sometimes quite loudly — and maybe towards evening the distant voices of the farmers across the hill getting in their cows and sheep.

But as usual even in the quiet services, some of the deacon-enthusiasts would get up and sing, roar, pray and shout but always fervently, seriously, reverently — perhaps not "artistically" — (perhaps the better for it). — "We're men of the fields and rocks, not artists," Farmer John would say. At times these "confurorants" would give the boys a chance to run out and throw stones down on the rocks in the brook! (Allegro conslugarocko!) — but this was only momentary and the quiet Children's Hymn is sung again, perhaps some of the evening sounds are with it — and as this Movement ends, sometimes a distant Amen is heard — if the mood of the Day calls for it. . . .

The Third Movement is more of the nature of the First. As the boys get

marching again some of the old men would join in and march as fast (sometimes) as the boys and sing what they felt, regardless — and — thanks to
Robert Lowry — "Gather at the River."

FIRST MOVEMENT: *Allegro (in a rather fast march time — most of
the time).*

A march rhythm is established in the three-measure introduction
by chords in the lower octaves of the piano. The violin enters with
the principal theme:

Example 1

The piano plays this melody canonically five measures later.

After a four-measure piano bridge, the second melodic figure
is introduced by the piano:

Example 2

The violin returns to Example 1 (one-half step higher) immediately, while the piano plays Example 2 in counterpoint to the violin.

The piano repeats Example 1, this time a full-step higher than
its initial appearance.

After an extended duet between the piano and the violin, the
violin restates Example 1. The piano accompanies this with chords
in martial rhythm.

The melodic fragment, Example 2, appears in the left hand of
the piano. The violin and piano continue an extended contrapuntal
episode that accelerates.

In a bold passage, marked *Allegro molto,* the violin introduces
a new theme in octaves:

Example 3

Violin

Allegro molto *(in octaves, ad lib.)*

When finished with this theme (Example 3), the violin returns immediately to Example 1 (*pp*) in its original tonality. There is a decrescendo to the end of the movement.

SECOND MOVEMENT: *Largo.*

The first section of this movement is without bar lines and is concerned mainly with a "recomposition" of the hymn tune *Yes, Jesus Loves Me.*

A piano introduction of chords built principally of seconds contains the melodic fragment which is the motive of the movement:

Example 4

Piano

pp (Yes, Jesus loves me)

The violin enters with the hymn tune fragment, Example 4. The piano echos it a half-step higher.

The "recomposition" of this hymn continues in a very slow and lyrical section with groups of fifths and a chordal use of the pentatonic scale.

The middle section, *Allegro (conslugarocko)*, is a piano solo. It is completely atonal and makes lavish use of seconds. The piano score is marked, in turn, *faster and with action,* then, *crescendo and gradually faster,* ending *fff.*

The violin re-enters in a section marked *Andante con spirito,* with each phrase starting legato and ending pizzicato. The figure used:

Example 5   *pizz*

Violin

After an extended passage, the tempo changes to *Largo cantabile* and the violin states in a most lyrical manner the melody, *Yes Jesus Loves Me*:

Example 6

The movement comes to a very soft conclusion at the end of the violin statement, an ending marked *pppp*.

THIRD MOVEMENT: *Allegro.*

After a piano introduction of ninth chords, the violin introduces a melody reminiscent of *Shall We Gather at the River*:

Example 7

Following an extended section, the score is marked: "At the River — Lowry," and the violin states the melody of the old hymn. In Ives' manuscript, the words appeared under the violin line and the violinist was admonished to "follow mentally" the words:

Example 8

Violin

The "recomposition" of the hymn tune continues to the end.

CHARLES T. GRIFFES

BORN: September 17, 1884; Elmira, New York.
DIED: April 8, 1920; New York, New York.

The fame of no other composer rests on such few works as does that of Charles Tomlinson Griffes; his first major work, *The Pleasure Dome of Kubla Khan,* was given its premiere less than six months before his death.

Charles Griffes had a happy home life as he grew up in Elmira, New York. He frequently took long walks through the woods with his father and was interested in both art (engravings and water colors) and photography. When he was bedridden with an attack of typhoid at eleven he heard his sister practicing some Beethoven works on the piano. These so interested him that when he recuperated he talked his sister into teaching him the piano.

When Charles was about fifteen it became evident that he needed a professional piano teacher. His first was Mary Broughton who was to play an important part in his life. Not only did she serve as his piano teacher but she corrected his speech, chose good books for him to read, and educated him in the social graces. Griffes' first public appearances as a pianist were at Sunday afternoon meetings at the local Y.M.C.A.

Having taught him all she felt she could, Mary Broughton suggested that it was time for Charles to go to Berlin and study. The family finances could not afford such a trip, so Miss Broughton furnished the money. In a "farewell recital" in 1903 the program listed besides works of Chopin, Liszt, Mendelssohn, and Brahms, two works by *Charles T. Griffes.*

In Berlin Griffes enrolled in the Stern Conservatory and found it invigorating with its concerts, lessons, the theater, and an expanding social life. He took composition lessons in addition to piano although they cost an extra $50. The late works of Wagner and Richard Strauss greatly impressed the student, and after long discussions with a close friend of his in Berlin, Griffes decided to pursue the career of a composer rather than that of a concert pianist.

Towards the end of his fourth year of study in Germany Griffes submitted some of his compositions to Humperdinck to see if the world-renowned composer would give him lessons in composition. Humperdinck was impressed by the works submitted and agreed, even waiving his usual fee when he learned the boy could not afford to pay him.

In 1907 Griffes returned to America and through a teacher-placement agency was appointed to a teaching post at the Hackley School in Tarrytown, New York, which was about an hour from New York city. He taught there the balance of his life, giving private lessons to raise money to augment his salary.

On February 4, 1910, he signed his first contract with a publisher. G. Schirmer agreed to publish his *Five German Songs;* these netted Griffes $28 in royalties the first year they were out, and $5.10 the next. The balance of his German songs were not published until many years after his death (1941).

In order to increase his income, the publishers talked Griffes into "turning out" some teaching pieces, transcriptions of American tunes. Under the name of Arthur Tomlinson he saw his *Six Familiar Songs* published; these included settings of such tunes as *Old Kentucky Home, America,* and *Yankee Doodle.*

Although most of Griffes' original piano compositions had poetic names, these were affixed after the completion of the work. An exception was *The White Peacock* which he started composing one evening after a baccalaureate service at the school. He kept Fiona MacLeod's poem of the same name on the piano all the time he worked on this composition. White peacocks had long fascinated Griffes, having seen them first in Germany and then clipping pictures of them from magazines and taking photographs of them himself.

In the summer of 1917 Griffes moved to New York city for the vacation period and worked on the production of his ballet-pantomime *Kairn of Koriden* for the Neighborhood Theater where it was produced under the sponsorship of Miss Lewisohn.

A visit with a mutual friend to the home of a Chinese minister introduced Griffes to the music of the Orient. His *Five Chinese Songs* were patterned after the native music he had heard at the minister's home. A ballet, *Sho-Jo, or The Spirit of Wine, A Symbol of Happiness* followed shortly and was presented by a Japanese dancer.

During World War I Griffes was about to enlist in the military service as an interpreter just as he learned that President Wilson had signed the armistice. The months after that were busy ones for him and in a letter to his friend, Miss Broughton, he stated:

I am rushed to death now. Everything comes with me at once. The Boston Symphony is to give the first performance of my symphonic poem *The Pleasure-Dome of Kubla Khan* on November 28th, the Philadelphia Orchestra gives the first performance of a set of four pieces for orchestra this fall, and the New York Symphony gives for the first time on November 16th a new *Poem* for solo flute and orchestra. All these things have to be put in final shape and parts prepared. Also I am finishing up my music for the Neighborhood Playhouse production in January, which is a tremendous job. Then in addition I have just signed a five years' contract with Duo-Art Reproducing Piano to make [piano rolls] only for them. I am to make six of my own pieces the first year and must start in a couple of days. . . . Now I am too busy. What a nuisance lessons are!

Shortly after this note he started missing some of these lessons because of "ill health." As he copied parts for some of the orchestral works he became so weak that he had his mother and sister copy the clef signs onto the score paper for him. He made the trip to Boston to hear the premiere of *The Pleasure-Dome of Kubla Khan*, but after his return to Hackley he was soon in bed with pleurisy which turned to pneumonia. After being moved to the hospital, doctors thought at first that he had tuberculosis, but several exploratory operations eliminated that diagnosis. His system had been weakened by the long months and years of strain and he succumbed to an "abscess of the lungs" on April 8, 1920

BIBLIOGRAPHY

Maisell, Edward M. *Charles T. Griffes: The Life of an American Composer.* New York: Alfred A. Knopf, 1943.

THE WHITE PEACOCK

Charles T. Griffes

The score of this Impressionistic work carries, at the composer's request, part of the poem by Fiona MacLeod (pen name of William Sharp) which inspired its creation:
Here where the sunlight
Floodeth the garden,
Where the pomegranate
Reareth its glory
Of gorgeous blossom;
Where the oleanders
Dream through the noontides;
. . . Where the heat lies
Pale blue in the hollows,

. . . Here where the dream-flowers
The cream-white poppies,
Silently waver,
. . . Here as the breath, as the soul of this beauty
Moveth in silence, and dreamlike, and slowly,
White as a snowdrift in mountain valleys
When softly upon it in the gold light lingers:
. . . Moves the white peacock, as tho' through the noontide
A dream of the moonlight was real for a moment.
Dim on the beautiful fan that he spreadeth
. . . Dim on the cream-white are blue adumbrations,
. . . Pale, pale as the breath of blue smoke in far woodlands,
Here, as the breath, as the soul of this beauty,
Moves the White Peacock.

Originally composed as a piano solo in a group of *Four Roman Sketches,* it was orchestrated by Griffes himself.

Over soft string chords, the oboe plays Example 1:

Example 1

The flute immediately answers the oboe with Example 2:

Example 2

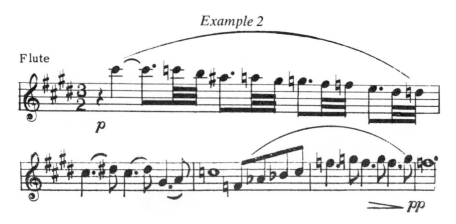

The clarinet responds with a theme that is heard frequently throughout the composition. This clarinet theme would seem to be an inversion of the flute theme with some rhythmical changes:

Example 3

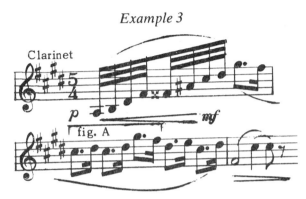

The clarinet having finished this theme, repeats it only to be echoed by the flute with it.

Rolling chords in the harp and celesta are heard introducing a duet in the flutes:

Example 4

An episode for oboe, then strings, follows with hints of several of the themes.

The oboe enters with a variation of Example 3 (Figure A) against horns, harp, and sustained strings.

Violins answer, leading to a statement by the high flutes and celesta of Example 2 over rolling arpeggios in the harp.

The oboe echoes Example 2 and passes the theme to the flute.

The oboe appears a second time with Example 2 and returns it once more to the flute.

Another episode leads to a solo violin playing Example 2 above arpeggios in the harp and a low sustained tone in the flute.

The clarinet responds with Example 3 played twice.

The flute responds with the same theme.

The opening theme (Example 1) is heard in the oboe over chords in the strings and harp, bringing *The White Peacock* to a close.

WALTER PISTON

born: January 20, 1894; Rockland, Maine
died: November 12, 1976; Belmont, Mass.

Walter Piston's name will be a familiar one in the annals of American music for many years to come, for in addition to being the composer of two Pulitzer prize-winning symphonies, he spent thirty-six years teaching composition at Harvard, and is the author of four basic music textbooks: *Harmony* (1941), *Counterpoint* (1947), *Principles of Harmonic Analysis* (1933), and *Orchestration* (1955).

Piston was born in Rockland, Maine, where his grandfather, an Italian sailor named Antonio Pistone had settled, married an American girl, and dropped the final *e* from his name. Walter's father was a bookkeeper and music was not predominant in the home. When Walter was nine, the family moved to Boston where he grew up with his three brothers. The family lived for several years in Boston before they purchased a violin for Walter and a piano for one of his brothers. Walter started violin lessons while he was a student at Mechanic Arts High School and played in the school orchestra.

Upon graduation in 1912 Piston became a draftsman for an elevated railway company. Having had a strong interest in art for some time, he enrolled in the Massachusetts School of Art where there was no tuition. He earned his board and room by playing either the violin or piano in dance halls, enlisted in the Navy as a musician, learing the saxophone out of a manual. He served during the war in a band stationed at Massachusetts Institute of Technology; his rating of "second class musician" was, according to Mr. Piston, "purely technical!"

After the war Piston worked as an artist for a time and soon was married. He felt that he did not have an adequate education, so he decided to go to college and study music. He matriculated at Harvard, earning money to support himself and his wife by playing in dance halls and cafes once again. He graduated from the University in 1924 with honors, having conducted the Harvard orchestra for three years.

Piston rebelled against, in the words of Elliot Carter, "the standardized academic routine which taught harmony and counterpoint according to outmoded and unimaginative textbooks." He determined to continue his study of composition in an atmosphere more conducive to creative writing, so he moved to Paris for two years of study with Nadia Boulanger. While he lived in France, Satie, Stravinsky, and *Les Six* were all active there.

Upon his return to the United States, Piston was appointed to the music staff of Harvard University where he continued to teach until his retirement in 1961. His first work for orchestra dates from 1929, a *Suite for Orchestra* in which he combined atonality with allusions to the popular blues. Most of his works up to 1939 were written in the Neo-Classical vein. The turning point in his career seemed to be the completion of his ballet, *The Incredible Flutist*, in 1938. This was to be his only venture into programmatic music.

His *Symphony No. 2* won the New York Music Critics' Circle Award in 1943. *Symphony No. 3*, premiered in 1948 by the Boston Symphony Orchestra, won a Pulitzer Prize. His *Violin Concerto No. 2* was premiered by the Pittsburg Symphony Orchestra in 1960, and his *Symphony No. 7* completed in 1961 won the Pulitzer Prize for that year.

Now retired from the faculty of Harvard University where he taught two generations of composers (including Leonard Bernstein), he lives with his artist wife in Belmont, Massachusetts. This New England home was designed by his wife, with two wings that branch out from the living quarters on opposite sides. On one side is Piston's studio filled with scores and books, on the other side of the house is his wife's studio where she paints.

His works, all non-programmatic except for *The Incredible Flutist*, include eight symphonies, sonatas, concerti grossi, string quartets, violin concerti, and choral music. Mr. Piston's attitudes toward musical expression are best summarized in his own words:

Ours is a big country and we are a people possessing a multitude of different origins. We already have a large literature of music by native composers. The outstanding characteristic noticeable in this music is its great diversity. If a composer desires to serve the cause of American music he will best do it by remaining true to himself as an individual and not by trying to discover musical formulas for Americanism.

THE INCREDIBLE FLUTIST

Suite from the Ballet

Walter Piston

The scene of the ballet is a Spanish village at carnival time. The siesta is over and, with a hearty yawn and a wide stretch, the village shakes off its drowsiness. Various characters of the village appear: the Apprentice opens his shop; the Merchant's Daughters demonstrate their father's wares; the Busybody and the Crank have their argument.

Suddenly, a march is heard! The Band, the Circus Band, marches in, followed by the people of the circus. They're all there: the Barker, the Jugglers, the Snake Dancer, the Monkey Trainer with her Monkeys, the Crystal Gazer, and, of course, the main attraction, the Flutist. The Flutist is a remarkable fellow, an incredible fellow. He not only charms snakes, he also charms the Snake Dancer. He is so romantic, the Incredible Flutist, he also charms the Merchant's Daughter, and they agree to meet at eight o'clock that very evening in the village square.

When the clock strikes eight, young couples are all over the place, and love is in the air. Even the prudish, rich Widow cannot resist the charged atmosphere and grants the Merchant the kiss he's been begging for well nigh two years; but they don't fare so well. Their sustained embrace is discovered, and the poor rich Widow is so embarrassed she swoons right into the arms of her bewhiskered boyfriend. The Incredible Flutist hies to the rescue. A little dancing, a little flirting, and the Widow comes out of her faint. And then the Band strikes up, the spell is broken, the Circus, Incredible Flutist and all, leave the village.

Introduction: *Lento.*

The suite is continuous, one section leading directly into the next.

An oboe solo is heard over high strings:

SCENES FROM *THE INCREDIBLE FLUTIST*

(Above) After a siesta the villagers awaken from a drowsy sleep. The Apprentice is the first to open up shop.

(Upper right) The Circus Band, followed by the villagers, marches in.

(Center) The rich widow faints into the arms of her bewhiskered boy friend.

(Lower right) The Incredible Flutist brings her to life again.

Photos by Dance Magazine

Example 1

A flute and a bassoon continue the melodic line; the strings join in.

SIESTA HOUR IN THE MARKET PLACE: ENTRANCE OF THE VENDORS.

Example 2 is introduced by the clarinets; triangle and tambourine are prominent in the accompaniment:

Example 2

Example 2 is repeated by the clarinets, joined by flute and piccolo.

The violins play an extended melodic variation of Example 2. The violins and flute are heard with Example 3:

Example 3

Example 3 is repeated immediately by the flute and violins.

As the woodwinds and strings continue the melodic line, the triangle, tambourine, and snare drum are heard.

The violins again play Example 3.

In a rhythmical section, cymbals join the percussion as the strings and woodwinds play rhythmic figures.

The violins and English horn introduce a new theme:

Example 4

The piano and the woodwinds repeat Example 4 and are followed by the strings and the woodwinds playing the same theme.

A flute cadenza is heard, followed by the oboe playing Example 1.

Entrance of the Customers (short transition).

The French horns establish a rhythmic pattern, then a trumpet fanfare is heard.

The woodwinds are heard with Example 5, the oboe tone predominating:

Example 5

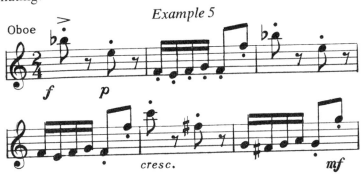

As the woodwinds repeat Example 5, a counter-melody is played by the celli, bass viols, and tuba:

Example 6

Example 5 appears in a slight melodic variation in the strings. This leads without hesitation into the Tango.

TANGO OF THE FOUR DAUGHTERS.

This is a ternary section, the first melody introduced by violins:

Example 7

The lyrical melody of Example 7 is played by the woodwinds, and then is repeated by full orchestra.

The middle section starts with a rhythmic figure established by the full percussion section. A motive is played by flute, piccolo, clarinet, and bassoon:

Example 8

The muted trumpet plays a melodic figure derived from Example 8.

After a short woodwind episode followed by a short string episode, Example 8 is heard played by the woodwinds.

The melody of the first section of the Tango, Example 7, appears after a descending figure; it is played by the violins, softly.

Example 7 is then taken up by full orchestra and builds to a powerful climax.

A bridge to the next section opens with a rhythmic pattern established by the French horns over which a trumpet is heard.

The woodwinds are heard with Example 5; as they repeat it, the counter-melody, Example 6, appears in the bass.

ARRIVAL OF THE CIRCUS, AND CIRCUS MARCH.

The arrival of the circus is announced by a snare and bass drum roll-off. A melody is heard in the trumpet:

Example 9

The trumpet melody is an extended one.

The march ends abruptly, punctuated by a dog's bark.

SOLO OF THE FLUTIST.

Against a rather slow string background, the Flutist is heard in an extended solo which starts as follows:

Example 10

MINUET — DANCE OF THE WIDOW AND THE MERCHANT.

The minuet is short, only sixteen measures in length, but is quite beautiful. The melody is introduced by the violins:

Example 11

Example 11 is repeated by the violins.

A piano cadenza is heard.

Spanish Waltz.

The waltz is based on a single melody played first by the violins and woodwinds:

Example 12

This melody (Example 12) is played, in turn, by:
the violins and woodwinds
(a woodwind interlude occurs, the woodwinds soon joined
by the strings)
the full orchestra
the clarinets
the violins

Eight O'Clock Strikes.

This is a short bridge to the next section. The French horn, piano, and cello imitate the clock striking the hour.

Siciliano — Dance of the Flutist and the Merchant's
Daughter.

There is a very high string introduction, followed by a soft string accompaniment for the clarinet melody:

Example 13

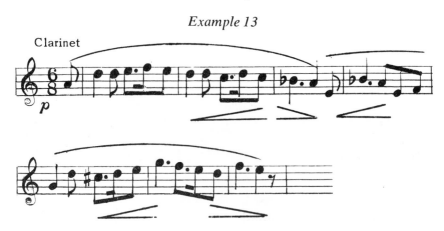

The *development* is introduced by the English horn playing the Principal Subject (Example 2).

This section treats not only the Principal and Second Subjects (Examples 2 and 4) but also the episodic theme (Example 3).

The *recapitulation* is introduced by the trumpets as the Principal Subject (Example 2) appears again in its original key.

The episodic theme (Example 3) appears first in the clarinets and then in the French horns.

A canonic imitation follows in the oboes.

The Second Subject (Example 3) returns in the strings with the counter-subject appearing above it in the French horns.

A *coda* brings the movement to an end, muted strings appearing in the final measures followed by three chords for muted French horns. The final chord in muted celli and bass viols concludes the movement.

VIRGIL THOMSON

BORN: November 25, 1896; Kansas City, Missouri.

Virgil Thomson, noted American composer and music critic of the New York *Herald Tribune* from 1940 to 1954, has had an interesting musical hobby. He has, in his own words, "made over a hundred musical portraits, all of them drawn from life, the sitter posing for me as he would an artist's portrait." Some of these have been composed for orchestra, some for unaccompanied violin, for violin and piano, for four clarinets, and for piano. Titles include *The Mayor La Guardia Waltzes, Canons for Dorothy Thompson, Bugles and Birds* (Picasso), and *Pastorale* (Aaron Copland).

Virgil Thomson's father had been a farmer, but shortly before Virgil's birth gave this up, moved to town and became a gripman on the cable car line and then an administrator in the post office. The infant's father was tone deaf and had no interest in any form of music, but his mother encouraged him as he crawled to the piano and spent considerable time at work on the keyboard. By the time he was two, Virgil was singing, and at five was given piano lessons at his own request. As the boy's interest in music became apparent, he was given singing lessons by the tenor soloist at the Baptist Church and organ lessons by the organist at the Episcopal Church. At twelve Virgil was giving recitals in both churches and schools, and served as the substitute organist for the Baptist Church. After graduation from Central High School he enrolled in the newly formed Junior College where he became a straight "A" student, acknowledged as the brightest student in the school. While there he debated between a literary career and a career in music, his abilities in both fields being in evidence.

The next twenty years of Thomson's life are succinctly stated by the composer himself:

> I . . . grew up [in Kansas City] and went to war from there. That was the other war. Then I was educated some more in Boston and Paris. In composition I was chiefly the pupil of Nadia Boulanger. While I was still young, I taught music at Harvard and played the organ at King's Chapel, Boston. Then I returned to Paris and lived there for many years, till the Germans came, in fact.

"The other war" was, of course, World War I during which Thomson enlisted in the Army and served as a second lieutenant in the Aviation Corps. His education in Boston consisted of completing his undergraduate work at Harvard University where he studied both piano and organ. On graduation he won both the Naumberg and Payne fellowships, the latter a traveling fellowship that enabled the composer to go to Paris and study with Boulanger.

In France Thomson was greatly affected by the eclectic style of Erik Satie, and it was probably the influence of Satie that caused Thomson to include a tango theme (played by clarinet and muted trumpet) in the second movement of his *Sonata da Chiesa* of 1926 (*da chiesa*, literally "of the church," see description in Music of the Baroque Era, Chapter IV). Old hymn tunes, remembered from his days as an organist, also kept appearing in his music. The *Symphony on a Hymn Tune* of 1928 used *How Firm a Foundation* as its Principal Subject, and *Yes, Jesus Loves Me* as its Second Subject.

In 1934 one of his major works was given a performance in Hartford under the auspices of the Society of Friends and Enemies of Modern Music of which Virgil Thomson served as Director from

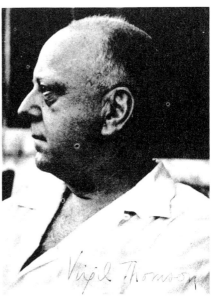

VIRGIL THOMSON

ROY HARRIS

Photo by Maurice Grosser

RANDALL THOMPSON

AARON COPLAND

Courtesy Harvard University

1934 to 1937. It was a production of his opera *Four Saints in Three Acts* to a text by his friend of Paris days, Gertrude Stein. The text actually made no sense, but was a series of sonorous sounding words; a deliberate confusion was perpetrated by the author for there were actually four acts and more than a dozen saints, one of them in duplicate. The work was performed by an all-Negro cast, not because anything in the text indicated it, but because the composer felt they would give his melodic lines a more sympathetic interpretation. Even the scenery was something different; it was made entirely of cellophane. The composer's almost solemn, hymn-like treatment created a hilarious modern *opera buffa*. It was given many performances in the United States and Europe and was revived in 1947 and again in 1952, when, after a long run on Broadway, it was taken to Paris with great success.

When Thomson returned from Paris at the start of World War II, he became music critic for the *Herald Tribune* of New York. His articles were widely read; four series of them have been published in book form: *The State of Music, The Musical Scene, The Art of Judging Music,* and *Music Right and Left.* He resigned as music critic in 1954 to devote more time to composition.

A second opera was premiered in 1947, *The Mother of Us All,* to another text by Gertrude Stein. This time, however, the text definitely made sense for it related the life story of Susan B. Anthony, the woman suffragette. The same year the French government honored Thomson by investing him as a Chevalier of the Legion of Honor.

Thomson has earned an outstanding reputation for the musical scores he has provided films. His first effort in this direction was the score for *The Plough That Broke the Plains* produced by the U.S. Government in 1936. The following year he composed the score for *The River,* another documentary for the U.S. Government. In 1948 he provided the score for Robert Flaherty's *Louisiana Story* from which two frequently played orchestral suites were made.

Three of his "landscapes" have been performed by major orchestras: *The Seine at Night* (1947); *Wheat Field at Noon* (1948); and *Sea Piece with Birds* (1952). One of his most recent compositions was *Lamentations* written for the accordion and premiered in 1961 at a meeting of the National Association for American Composers and Conductors of which Mr. Thomson is a member.

BIBLIOGRAPHY

Hoover, Kathleen and John Cage. *Virgil Thomson: His Life and Music.* New York: Thomas Yoseloff, 1959.

ACADIAN SONGS AND DANCES

from *Louisiana Story*

VIRGIL THOMSON

Two concert suites have been made by Virgil Thomson from the film score he composed for the Robert Flaherty documentary motion picture, *Louisiana Story*. The first, usually known as the *Suite from Louisiana Story,* is essentially original music; the second, known as *Acadian Songs and Dances,* is a series of folk-song settings of most original and artistic creation. In the latter suite, Thomson has used "Cajun" tunes he found in the Lomax recorded collection and in the Whitfield book, *Louisiana French Songs.*

The story of the film deals with both nature and an Acadian family into whose life an oil company intrudes. The composer determined which scenes were dominated by landscapes and provided original music for them. For those scenes that involved people, he used folk songs of the people.

There are seven movements to this suite, some depicting mood, some depicting incidents in the film. Each section is based on one or two Cajun tunes which are varied either through orchestration, harmonization, or both. A frequent change of key is a chief characteristic of many of the movements.

SADNESS

The first movement of the suite is in concise, ternary form. The first melody is introduced by the muted violins:

Example 1

The French horn repeats this melody; the harmony of the string accompanied is changed.

A solo flute plays Example 1 as the string accompaniment returns to its original harmonization.

A muted solo violin is heard with Example 1.

In the middle section, the meter changes to 3/4 as the violas introduce the second melody:

Example 2

Viola (muted)

A French horn repeats Example 2.

The return to the first section is announced by a muted trumpet playing the first half of Example 1 with a "distant effect." The last half of Example 1 is played by the muted solo violin.

Papa's Tune

With a rhythmic, pizzicato string introduction, the single tune of this movement, sixteen measures in length, appears in the English horn:

Example 3

English Horn

The pizzicato accompaniment serves as a bridge to a repetition of Example 3 by the flute and clarinet in octaves.

A Narrative

Two themes are heard in *A Narrative*. The first theme, of fourteen measures, is played by the clarinet:

Example 4

Clarinet

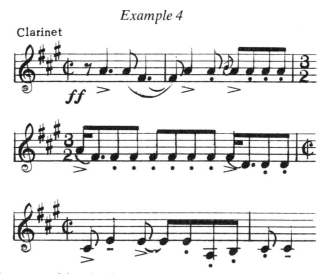

It is repeated by the flute and clarinet in octaves.
The second theme is introduced by the violas:

Example 5

Viola

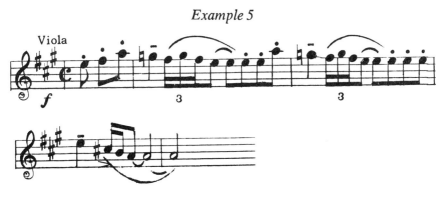

Example 5 is repeated several times as follows:
   violas accompanied by an English horn counter-melody
   violas alone
   violas with the English horn counter-melody
   violas· alone
   violas with the English horn counter-melody
A return is made to the melody of the first section, Example 4, which is again heard in the clarinet.
The flute and clarinet repeat Example 4 in octaves.

THE ALLIGATOR AND THE 'COON

Three melodic motives alternate in this movement. Every eight measures the music shifts abruptly from one key to another. The first melody is introduced by the bassoon:

Example 6

It is repeated by the violins.
Example 7 is played by the xylophone:

Example 7

The oboe repeats Example 6.
The full orchestra introduces a new motive:

Example 8

An eleven measure bridge, in which strings and woodwinds predominate, starts softly, crescendos, then fades away.

The three melodic motives are heard in quick succession as follows: Example 6 in the oboe; Example 6 in the muted trumpet; Example 7 in the flute; Example 7 in the xylophone; Example 6 in the trumpet (unmuted); Example 8 in the oboe and violins; Example 8 in full orchestra; Example 6 in the flute and clarinet; Example 8 in the woodwinds and strings; Example 8 in the oboes and violins; (there is an eight measure bridge); Example 7 in two trumpets in 2nds.

SUPER-SADNESS

A single theme is heard in this movement. Each of the three times it is heard, it is in a different key. Two French horns introduce the theme in 3rds against a low, muted string accompaniment:

Example 9

French Horn (muted)

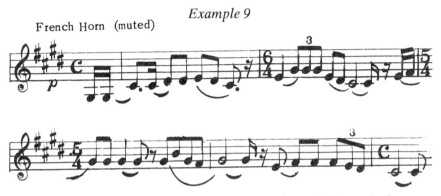

The oboe and English horn repeat the duet of Example 9.
The muted trumpets with a "distant effect" play the duet.

WALKING SONG

The Walking Song is based on one theme of two figures. Figure A is heard twice in the clarinet, the first time played loudly, the second time very softly:

Example 10 (Figure A)

Clarinet

Figure B is played twice by the clarinet:

Example 10 (Figure B)

These two figures are repeated: Figure A by the flute, softly (the glockenspiel is heard in the accompaniment); Figure B by the flute and muted trumpet; (there is a four measure bridge); Figure A by the flute and clarinet, loudly; Figure A by the flute and clarinet, very softly; Figure B by the flute and clarinet; Figure A by the strings, loudly; Figure A by woodwinds, very loudly; Figure A by the oboe, very softly; Figure B by the oboe, moderately soft.

THE SQUEEZE BOX

The composer adds an accordion to the orchestra in this section. The first melody appears in two parts; the first, played by the flutes, clarinets, and accordion, is quite rhythmical:

Example 11 (Part 1)

The after-phrase of this melody is lyrical and played by the trumpet with a *wa-wa* mute:

Example 11 (Part 2)

Scene from the documentary motion picture, *Louisiana Story*, for which Virgil Thomson composed the film score

Robert Flaherty Film Foundation, Inc.

Thomson at a recording session of his film score — The Philadelphia Orchestra conducted by Eugene Ormandy

Both parts of Example 11 are repeated.
The strings introduce a new theme:

Violins   *Example 12*

Example 12 is repeated by the full orchestra in a section of some length.

A solo violin appears with a melodic variation of Example 12 over a pizzicato string accompaniment.

Flute and clarinet take up this variation; the melody returns to the solo violin; and, finally, flute and clarinet are heard again.

The first part of Example 11 returns in the upper strings accompanied by the full orchestra. The trumpet plays the second part without a mute.

The full orchestra repeats the first part of Example 11, the trumpet responding with the second part with mute.

Papa's Tune, Example 3, appears in the English horn. It is repeated by flute and clarinet in octaves.

The woodwinds play the first part of Example 11 and are answered by the unmuted trumpet with the second part.

Flute and clarinet play the first part of Example 11 in unison, and the oboe plays the second part.

The first part of Example 11 is heard for the final time played softly by the piccolo which is answered by a clarinet (*ppp — sotto voce*) with the second part.

ROY HARRIS

BORN: Lincoln County, Oklahoma; February 12, 1898.

America could not ask for a native composer with a more typical "American" background than Roy Harris. Born in Lincoln County in a log cabin on Lincoln's birthday, Roy Harris grew up on a farm that had been homesteaded by his father. Because of a siege of malaria near their farm, his family moved to the San Gabriel Valley in California when Roy was five. At Covina High School, Roy played football so vigorously that, while on the team, he broke both his nose and an arm.

The family purchased an old upright piano shortly after moving to California, and it was on this instrument that Roy received his first lessons in piano from his mother. As he grew older he also experimented with the clarinet and the pipe organ. All his musical activities took place in spare moments when he could get away from his chores on the family farm where he helped his father till and harvest the fields. By the time he was twenty he owned a farm of his own.

World War I interrupted both Harris's farming chores and his studies. He served as a private in the army but did not see action in Europe. When he was discharged, he returned to southern California and started work at the University. During these days in the University of California at Los Angeles, he paid his way by driving a dairy truck in the daytime and attending classes at night. Actually this was to be his first serious study of music, for although he had dabbled in piano, clarinet, and organ, he played none of them well. One of his youthful compositions from University days was his *Suite for String Orchestra*. After graduation, Harris served for a time as the music critic for the Los Angeles *Daily News* and, at the same time, taught at a music school in Hollywood. In 1926 Howard Hanson played one of Harris's compositions, *Andante* for orchestra, at a concert in Rochester. Harris borrowed enough funds to travel east and hear the performance.

In this same year, the *Andante* appeared on the program of the New York Stadium Concerts. From this date, Harris's compositions were to take their place on orchestral concerts. Later that year Harris journeyed to Paris to study with Nadia Boulanger at the American Academy. While he was there he won the Guggenheim Fellowship two consecutive years, 1927 and 1928. At the end of the two years an injury to his spine caused him to be hospitalized and he eventually had to return to the United States for a successful operation. During the time he spent immobilized in bed, he discovered he could compose away from the piano. This immobilization caused him to turn from writing in pianistic style to works conceived directly in the orchestral idiom.

He returned to the United States in 1929 and won the Creative Fellowship from the Pasadena Music and Arts Association the following year. Four years later he was appointed head of the composition department at the Westminster Choir School in Princeton, New Jersey, where he served from 1934 to 1938. It was during his tenure at the Westminster School that he wrote his *Third Symphony*. Serge Koussevitzky, then director of the Boston Symphony and an authority on contemporary music, said that it was the greatest American work written so far in the twentieth century. It has since been recorded and performed more than any other American symphony of this century. Eugene Ormandy featured the work on his international tour with the Philadelphia Orchestra in 1957-58 and performed it at the World's Fair in Belgium and in Moscow.

After 1933 Harris taught at the Juilliard School of Music in the summer months, when away from the Westminster School. In 1941 he was appointed composer in residence at Cornell University to be followed by positions at Colorado College, Utah State Agricultural College, Peabody College for Teachers, Pennsylvania College for Women, and since 1957, at Indiana University at Bloomington. During World War II he obtained a leave from Cornell University and served in the Overseas Branch of the Office of War Information as head of the music section.

Although Harris has written for the motion pictures and for ballet, he has not yet attempted opera. His compositions include nine symphonies (*Symphony No. 9* was written in 1962); three string quartets, a quantity of chamber music, and numerous choral works. With the establishment of the International Institute of Music in San Juan, Puerto Rico, Roy Harris was appointed its director (1961).

BIBLIOGRAPHY

Slonimsky, Nicolas. *Roy Harris.* New York: G. Schirmer (in prep.).

SYMPHONY NO. 3
ROY HARRIS

The *Symphony No. 3* of Roy Harris is cast in one movement, although the composer has outlined five sections in this work. The sections include: *Section I* — Tragic, low string sonorities; *Section II* — Lyric, strings, horns, woodwinds; *Section III* — Pastoral, woodwinds with a polytonal string background; *Section IV* — Fugue, dramatic; and *Section V* — Dramatic, tragic.

SECTION I: Tragic; low string sonorities (2/2).

The symphony opens with the celli playing a recitative-like melody unaccompanied, a melody which eventually uses all the tones of the chromtaic scale:

Example 1

Celli

The celli are joined by the violas (divisi). As they continue, the violas play intervals of 4ths and 5ths (organum) against the celli (divisi). In this they are later joined by bassoon, string bass, and bass clarinet. Eventually a third is added to the harmonic structure.

The melody then receives a contrapuntal treatment which leads to the introduction of a second theme.

The violins enter for the first time with a sonorous melody:

Example 2

Violins

This is a long melody, twenty-nine measures in length. Example 2 like the first theme, uses all the tones of the chromatic scale.

The woodwinds repeat this theme and develop it while the strings accompany it with a counter-melody that becomes increasingly strong.

A unison passage for violins brings this section to a close with a final descending figure for solo flute.

Section II: Lyric; strings, horns, woodwinds.

The *lyric section* opens with a lyrical melody in A major in the upper strings:

Example 3

The strings and woodwinds then answer each other and alternate with this theme, punctuated first by the French horns and then by the trumpets.

A descending counter-melody is played strongly by the strings. It is based on the same melody the solo flute played when introducing this section.

An eighth-note figure appears in the clarinets and flutes and prepares the transition to the next section.

Section III: Pastoral; woodwinds with a polytonal string background.

This section opens with an undulating figure for strings, eighth-note arpeggios in contrasting motion (in a polytonal pattern).

The theme is introduced by the English horn:

Example 4

Fragments of this theme and extensions of it appear in the clarinet, then the oboe, next the flute, followed by the English horn which plays a variation of it.

This theme (Example 4) is repeated in identical or in altered form by the following instruments in succession: solo clarinet; bassoon; flutes in octaves; clarinet and bass clarinet in octaves; all woodwinds (chords in vibraphone and trumpets).

The music accelerates and against an accompaniment of strings, variations of the theme (Example 4) are played by the French horn; solo trombone; trumpet; French horn; trumpet; trumpets and trombones in octaves; horns, then trumpets, then trombones play fragments of the theme contrapuntally (during this extended passage strings gradually remove mutes).

The accompaniment figures move from strings to woodwinds.

The strings take bold pizzicato chords that bring this section to a close.

SECTION IV: Fugue; dramatic.

The subject of the fugue appears first in the strings:

Example 5

This is answered by a rhythmic figure in the timpani.

The subject of this fugue moves as follows: trombones; French horns; trumpets; (short episode); trombones followed by trumpets in canon; percussion (with rhythmic pattern of subject); French horns and trumpets in canonical repetition; trombones and trumpets in canon.

A *legato* passage in contrary motion for the woodwinds is derived from the theme of the Pastoral section (Example 4) accompanied by the horns and later the strings playing derivations of Example 5.

The fugue subject (Example 5) then appears in the trumpet and trombones, then in full brass.

A predominately rhythmic transition of sixteen measures leads to Section V.

SECTION V: Dramatic, tragic.

From Section I, Example 2 (augmented) is played by strings, followed three measures later in canon at the 5th in the woodwinds, while the brass state the rhythmical figure of the fugal section.

A repeated D on the timpani (pedal point) appears and is heard up to the closing sixteen measures.

Over the pedal point the strings play Example 2 while the horns and woodwinds suggest Example 3 from the *Lyric Section.*

Repeated rolls on the timpani lead to a final cadence ending on a g minor chord.

RANDALL THOMPSON

BORN: April 21, 1899; New York, New York.

Randall Thompson is probably best known as a choral composer although he is also a highly successful symphonic composer as proven by his *Symphony No. 2.* His choral works range in text from the humorous setting of some columns of Mencken that appeared in the *American Mercury,* titled *Americana* (1932), to the setting of the writings of Thomas Jefferson in *The Testament of Freedom* (1944). Two of his choral works seem to enjoy a popularity above his other compositions, one short and one of extended length. The shorter one is a setting of the single word of its title: *Alleluia.* The longer work is based on a text from Isaiah, *The Peaceable Kingdom.*

Randall Thompson was born in New York city where he graduated from both elementary and high school. He then enrolled in Harvard University and earned his Bachelor's degree. He remained for two more years to complete his Master's degree.

After graduation from the University, Thompson won the Prix de Rome which entitled him to spend three years in Rome. He also won a fellowship from the Guggenheim Foundation.

Having completed his tenure in Rome and his work under the Guggenheim fellowship, Thompson became an instructor in theory and organ, and a choral director for Wellesley College from 1927 until 1929. During this time he experimented with the use of the popular jazz idiom in his compositions and produced a symphonic work entitled *Jazz Poem* in 1928.

His next appointment came from the Juilliard School of Music in New York where he was in charge of choral classes for the years 1931-1932. At the same time he was also the conductor of the Dessoff Choirs of that same city. Thompson left that position to make a detailed study of the music curriculum in various schools of music throughout the country, and after completing the survey wrote a book based on his findings with suggestions for the future curricula of these schools.

Having received a commission from the League of Composers, Thompson turned to selected verses from the book of Isaiah for the text of his composition. This choral work was the result of inspiration from an eighteenth century American painting by Edward Hicks called the "Peaceable Kingdom." Thompson used the title of the picture for this extended choral work and it was introduced by the combined choral groups of Harvard and Radcliffe in 1936.

The following year Randall Thompson moved to California to spend two years teaching at the University of California. This position was succeeded by his appointment as the Director of the Curtis Institute of Music in Philadelphia in 1939 where he served for three years.

Thompson next joined the faculty of the University of Virginia. It was while he served there that the Columbia Broadcasting System commissioned him to write an opera for radio. He turned to the *Just So Stories* of Kipling for the text of his opera and called it *Solomon and Balkis*. Upon its completion in 1942, it was broadcast by CBS and repeated some seven months later. The opera was later mounted at both Harvard University and the Juilliard School of Music.

In 1943 Thompson was asked to write a choral selection to celebrate the 200th anniversary of the birth of Thomas Jefferson. From a text of selected writings by Jefferson, he wrote the *Testament of Freedom*. CBS presented this work with an all-male chorus.

Three years later Thompson became Professor of Composition at Princeton and served there until 1948. He then became professor of music at Harvard University where he has continued to serve. A year after joining the faculty at Harvard, his *Third Symphony* was presented at the Columbia University spring festival of contemporary American music. The last two movements of this symphony make use of folk-like material. In the same year Thompson was asked to write a composition honoring the 25th anniversary of Serge Koussevitzky's conductorship of the Boston Symphony Orchestra. Turning again to a Biblical text, Thompson wrote for this occasion a composition for choir and orchestra entitled *The Last Words of David*. His *Mass of the Holy Spirit* for mixed voices unaccompanied was completed in 1956 and premiered the following year.

ALLELUIA

For Unaccompanied Choir

RANDALL THOMPSON

This work, written at the request of Serge Koussevitzky for the opening exercises of the Berkshire Music Center in 1940, is based on the single word of praise, *Alleluia*.

The work ópens slowly with the four-part chorus intoning the word Alleluia:

Example 1

To the accompaniment of a moving part for altos and tenors, the sopranos introduce the main theme of the work:

Example 2

After the sopranos finish this theme, the balance of the choir returns to the melody of Example 1.

The altos then appear with Example 2, with a moving accompaniment in the soprano and tenors.

Again Example 1 returns, this time in three voices, as the altos finish their statement of Example 2.

The upper three voices join in the moving accompaniment figure that has appeared before, as the basses sustain a firm line underneath them.

Having reached a climax in this moving figure, the three lower voices return to a passage reminiscent of the opening bars as the sopranos supply a counter-melody above it.

Starting to reach a climax, the choir suddenly returns to a pianissimo and builds toward the climax again.

At the climax of the work the sopranos start the syncopated section:

Example 3

Al-le- lu-ia,   Al- le - lu-   ia, Al-   le-

lu-   ia, Al- le- lu- ia, Al- le-   lu- ia

The accents now come closer and closer together until they appear over every note and the sopranos make an octave leap as they sing "Alleluia," echoed in turn by the tenors and then the altos.

The music quickly subsides as the tenors start to introduce the final "Alleluias," answered with a moving "Alleluia" by sopranos, altos, and basses.

Three slow, sustained "Alleluias" follow for the full choir.

The altos alone intone an "Alleluia" deep in their register and are answered by the balance of the choir in an "Amen."

AARON COPLAND

BORN: November 14, 1900; Brooklyn, New York.

Aaron Copland has been a champion of American music in the twentieth century. Successful in his early compositions for orchestra, he decided that the American composers of this generation were writing good music which was not being performed very often; it was not being accepted by the general public into the permanent repertoire. Looking into his own style he tried to effect a change whereby his music would become more acceptable. Having arrived at some of the answers, his works *El Salon Mexico, Rodeo,* and *Billy the Kid* have become standard orchestral fare. In two books, *What to Listen for In Music* and *Our New Music,* Copland has further tried to explain to the audience at large how to become appreciative listeners and know what the contemporary composers are trying to accomplish in their music.

Copland was born in an old house in Brooklyn, New York, and spent the first twenty years of his life there. Around ten years of age, he first became interested in music and, at thirteen, decided to become a musician. Because the family had spent good money giving music lessons to four older children, only to have them lose all interest in music, Aaron had to plead with his parents many times before they would consent to lessons for him. He had to go on his own to find a piano instructor and arrange for the lessons when his parents finally relented. Two years after he started work on the piano, he decided he wished to become a composer. His compositions of this period include mostly two-page songs and works for the piano. One was entitled *The Cat and the Mouse* and was so modern in its structure that his teacher frankly admitted he was unable to judge it because he had been schooled in traditional harmony.

It had become a tradition for incipient composers to travel to Europe for the study of music and Copland looked forward to making such a pilgrimage. As World War I had just ended, Germany was no longer the place to go. A new school for Americans was opening in Fontainebleau, just outside of Paris, and in 1921 Copland left for a year's study at this new school. Once again he faced training in traditional harmony which he felt he already knew. He wanted something to guide him into more modern music. It was suggested that he look in on a class of Nadia Boulanger, who was then, as now, teaching there. He was so impressed with her work that he enrolled and extended his visit from one to three years. During his days in Fontainebleau, Copland wrote several motets, a *Passacaglia* for piano, and a one-act ballet called *Grohg*.

Before his return to the United States in 1924 he was asked by Nadia Boulanger to compose a work for organ and symphony orchestra since she was soon to appear with a New York orchestra in a concert. Never having tried a composition of such length before, Copland turned immediately to the writing of his *First Symphony for Orchestra and Organ* on his return to America. Copland had completed this work while playing in a hotel trio in Milford, Pennsylvania, earning enough money for board and room providing "dinner music." Nadia Boulanger performed the work with the New York Philharmonic and later repeated the work with the Boston Symphony Orchestra.

This same year the League of Composers wished to perform two of his works. They selected his early work *The Cat and the Mouse,* and the *Passacaglia* that had been written in Paris. Following the Boston orchestra's performance of his *Symphony for Orchestra and Organ,* the director of that orchestra, Serge Koussevitzky, requested a new chamber selection. Copland turned to the jazz idiom to make his work more American. This work he called *Music for the Theater* and it was performed by Koussevitzky and the Boston orchestra.

The Guggenheim Memorial Foundation had recently been established and Copland was to be the first recipient of a grant in 1925 which was renewed the following year. Copland's next work was a *Concerto for Piano and Orchestra,* his last attempt to use the jazz idiom. This work was also premiered by the Boston Symphony Orchestra. He was then commissioned by them to write a work for performance at their Fiftieth Anniversary Concert. For this occasion Copland wrote his *Symphonic Ode.*

It was at this point in his career that Copland decided that the works of his contemporaries as well as his own were not appealing to the public. He decided that his music must be simpler in style, "spare in sonority, lean in texture." His *El Salon Mexico* was the first composition in his "new" style, a work based on Mexican folk tunes. Two ballets followed written for Agnes De Mille, a dancer, *Billy the Kid* and *Rodeo,* both using some cowboy tunes.

For several years Copland had hoped to complete a ballet for his friend Martha Graham, another dancer of the modern school, and had talked to her about it, but it remained for a commission from the Coolidge Foundation to bring him actually to work on such a score.

His *Appalachian Spring,* written for Miss Graham, was first presented in Washington, D.C., in 1944. The following year the work won the Pulitzer Prize.

Copland's *Third Symphony* was performed by the Boston Symphony in 1946. Four years later the League of Composers honored his fiftieth birthday by a concert devoted to his works. The program scheduled works from 1950, *Piano Quartet,* to an early work of 1929, *As It Fell Upon A Day.*

The New York City Center presented Copland's opera, *The Tender Land,* in 1954, a two-act opera which was fairly simple in style. It received a "curiously tentative reception" despite an excellent review by critics. The following year Copland's *Canticle of Freedom* for chorus and orchestra was presented by the Symphony of the Air with Leonard Bernstein conducting. This was a semi-religious work, mystical in quality, and somewhat modal in style.

In 1958 the Juilliard School of Music commissioned Copland to write a work of major length to celebrate their fiftieth anniversary. For this he wrote a work using the twelve-tone system and called it *Piano Fantasy,* a really "virtuoso" work for piano and orchestra. Copland was the only American composer represented on the program when the Lincoln Center of the Performing Arts was dedicated on September 23, 1962.

BIBLIOGRAPHY

Berger, Arthur. *Aaron Copland.* New York: Oxford University Press, 1953.
Smith, Julia. *Aaron Copland: His Work and Contribution to American Music.* New York: E. P. Dutton and Co., 1955.

APPALACHIAN SPRING

A Ballet

AARON COPLAND

In the score for Appalachian Spring the following description of the ballet appears:

> The action of the ballet concerns a pioneer celebration in Spring around a newly-built farmhouse in the Pennsylvania hills in the early part of the last century. The bride-to-be and the young farmer-husband enact the emotions, joyful and apprehensive, their new domestic partnership invites. An older

Stewart Hodes and Martha Graham in the original production of *Appalachian Spring*

"At the end the couple are left quiet and strong in their new house."

"A revivalist . . . reminds the new householders of the strange and terrible aspects of human fate."

Photo by Arnold Eagle

neighbor suggests now and then the rocky confidence of experience. A revivalist and his followers remind the new householders of the strange and terrible aspects of human fate. At the end, the couple are left quiet and strong in their new house.

In the opening scene of the ballet the characters are introduced one by one in a suffused light, first the courageous husband, then the bride with her feminine charm, the revivalist with his zeal, and then the elders with their rock-like fortitude. The music opens with sustained notes in the second violins and celli, after which the clarinet gives the introductory theme:

Example 1

This theme is then repeated by muted trumpet, flute, and bassoon.

As the characters are introduced, the music develops this introductory theme.

The tempo changes and octave leaps in the violins, hinting of the new theme yet to come, suggest the rhythm of an old-fashioned square dance. In this new section the people assemble to wish Godspeed to the young couple.

After rising staccato and pizzicato passages in the woodwinds and strings, the violins finally announce Example 2:

Example 2

Example 3 is shortly introduced by the woodwinds and brass, a theme to be associated with the young couple, while the violins and strings repeat the "square dance" theme (Example 2) in counterpoint to it.

Example 3

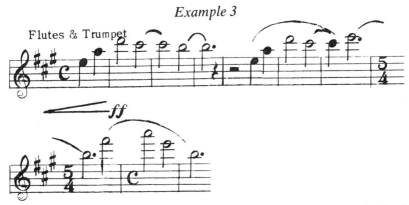

Flutes & Trumpet

A dance section follows in which Copland develops both the "square dance" theme (Example 2) and the theme of the young couple (Example 3).

After having reached a climax, the music fades away until the flute appears with the "square dance" theme (Example 2) barely audible and the violas with the theme of the young couple (Example 3).

As the harp plays chords "like a guitar," the theme of the young couple (Example 3) is suggested in the clarinet as the young couple dance a scene "of tenderness and passion."

After several repetitions of the opening phrase of Example 3, the music moves to sonorous passages for strings.

A variation of Example 3 in the oboe is answered by the clarinet.

A new theme appears in the oboe which is not finished (opening of Example 4).

The woodwinds carry on until finally the violins state the new theme in full:

Example 4

Violins

This playful theme is then answered in the unison bassoons and violas.

A development of Example 4 follows as it passes from bassoon to trumpet, thence to the oboe and finally to the flute.

The "square dance" theme (Example 2) returns in the violins as the revivalist and his flock start to dance.

Suddenly Example 5 is heard in the clarinets and French horns:

Example 5

The voice of the trumpet is heard above the orchestra as it develops Example 5.

The clarinets, oboes, and trumpets are heard with a repetition of Example 5 followed by the strings with it.

After the music has built to a climax, Example 6 appears in the strings.

Example 6

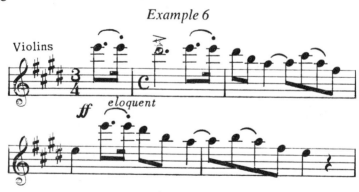

This theme passes from violins to woodwinds.

Example 7 appears as the bride dances, showing the "extremes of wonderment and fear."

Example 7

Violins

mp *non legato*

After Example 7 is developed and brought to a climax, the violins return with it and a second time it builds to a climax.

After building to a climax the third time, the oboe returns with Example 3.

Echod by clarinet, hymn-like chords follow establishing "a calm and flowing atmosphere."

The next theme was borrowed by Copland from a collection of Shaker tunes made by Edward D. Andrews. This tune is called *The Gift to Be Simple*:

Example 8

Shaker Melody, "The Gift to be Simple"
Clarinet

p

simply expressive

The text of this Shaker tune (although Copland uses only the melody in the ballet):

'Tis the gift to be simple,   And when we find ourselves
'Tis the gift to be free,   In the place just right
'Tis the gift to come down   'Twill be in the valley
Where we ought to be.   Of love and delight.

This melody introduces the bride.and groom in a scene which depicts the activities of daily living.

Example 8 passes from the clarinet to the oboe and bassoon.

The trombones and violas then take it up and are eventually imitated in canonic style by the violins and French horns.

After a passage for full orchestra, the trumpet and trombone return with Example 8, the trombone forming a counterpoint underneath the trumpet.

The strings enter after eight measures with running figures.

The French horns, oboes, and clarinets then join in, followed by running figures in the strings.

Finally the full orchestra enters with Example 8 in a bold fashion.

Immediately following this, the strings enter "like a prayer":

Example 9

Violins

This serves as a coda in which the young couple take their places among their new neighbors and are left "quiet and strong in this new house."

Twice hymn-like Example 9 is repeated.

The work closes wtih a final statement of Example 3 apppearing in the flute.

A solo violin joins the flute and they are answered by the clarinet with the opening phrase of Example 3. A chord growing from the bass of the orchestra moves steadily upward, a chord of the 14th, which is sustained as the harp plucks the last three tones.

PAUL CRESTON

BORN: October 10, 1906; New York, New York.

Paul Creston's musical career proves that composers need not depend on formal musical education to become outstanding creative artists. Creston left high school before graduation and went to work earning money for his family. To make up for this lack of education, he practiced at night and studied history, philosophy, and literature in addition to music.

SAMUEL BARBER PAUL CRESTON

GIAN-CARLO MENOTTI

WILLIAM SCHUMAN

Photo by Carl Mydans

Paul Creston was born Joseph Guttoveggio. His parents had moved to New York from near Palermo, Sicily, just one year prior to his birth. His father was a house painter and had no money to spare for music lessons. The boy's musical education was gained largely from books he borrowed from the New York Public Library, but he did study piano for six years with "a very mediocre teacher." This study consisted, principally, of piano reductions of opera scores and Waldteufel waltzes.

After Creston left school he obtained several different jobs in succession: errand boy, receptionist, bank clerk, and insurance examiner. His first position as a musician was an organist in a silent movie theater, but sound pictures soon eliminated that phase of his musical career. He turned next to playing the piano for concert dancers and to teaching piano.

Creston's future wife had been a dancer in the Martha Graham dance troupe. He met her on his first job when he was fifteen, they were "promised" the following year, and married when he was twenty. It was at the time of his marriage that he changed his name from Joseph Guttoveggio to Paul Creston, taken from his childhood nickname of "Cress."

In 1932 he decided on a career as a composer, having wavered for two years between music and literature. He said, "I decided on music when I realized that I could only write poems or essays whereas in music I had facility in any form. The encouragement I received through dancers commissioning me to write special music for them verified my decision."

Creston's career as a composer began by an arduous study of many books and works of the great masters past and present. He is entirely self-taught in the fields of harmony, counterpoint, composition, and orchestration.

An appointment as church organist at the church of St. Malachy's in 1932 has been an enduring one for he is still organist at that church. His Opus 1 was a set of dances for the piano published in 1932. A tour through the southwest in 1936 with saxophonist Cecil Leeson led to the composition of a *Concerto for Saxophone and Orchestra*. Two years later the public first began to recognize him as a composer because of the success of his two *Choric Dances*. In the same year he was awarded a Guggenheim Fellowship for the first time.

In 1941 Creston's *Symphony No. 1* was premiered by the Philadelphia Orchestra with Eugene Ormandy conducting. This work received the Music Critic Circle's Award for the best composition of the year. In ·1952 he was awarded the Paris Referendum Prize for the same work.

Four more symphonies have come from the pen of Creston, No. 2 in 1945, No. 3 commissioned by the Worcester Festival and performed there in 1950, and Symphonies No. 4 and 5 completed in 1952 and 1956 respectively. The latter work was commissioned and premiered by the National Symphony Orchestra of Washington, D.C., which has also recorded his second and third symphonies.

Busy with music, Creston has never had much time for hobbies. He counts his linguistic ability as his one hobby. The languages include Italian, French, Spanish, Turkish, Portuguese, German and Russian; the first three he speaks and writes fluently.

Creston has appeared on many university campuses as a lecturer on music and composition. In 1948 he occupied the Alchin Chair at the University of Southern California. He has served at other times on the faculty of George Peabody Teachers College, the University of Minnesota, the University of Delaware, Swarthmore College, and in 1959 he was guest conductor of the National Intercollegiate Band Festival in Tallahasee, Florida.

A book entitled *Principles of Rhythm* by Paul Creston is published by G. Ricordi and Company. Asked by this author when his interest in rhythm as a factor in musical composition began, the composer replied:

My interest in rhythm began when I first composed. However, when I began to teach composition I realized that the subject of rhythm was never even mentioned, while I felt it was just as important as the study of harmony, melody, counterpoint and form. I analyzed my own works and evolved certain principles. I checked with the works of the past and I learned that these principles always existed, although no teacher bothered with them. I started a book on composition, realized that one on rhythm was more urgent, and turned to research on the subject. The result was my book *Principles of Rhythm*.

The television film *Revolt In Hungary* which appeared in 1959 had a musical score composed by Creston. For this music Creston received the Christopher Award. In March, 1960, he traveled to Turkey where he lectured and conducted concerts as a music specialist for the United States Government's State Department. *Concerto*

No. 1 for Violin and Orchestra was premiered by the Detroit Symphony Orchestra in January, 1960, while *Concerto No. 2 for Violin and Orchestra* was premiered by the Los Angeles Philharmonic Orchestra in December of the same year.

SYMPHONY NO. 3

The Three Mysteries

PAUL CRESTON

The *Symphony No. 3* of Paul Creston is subtitled "The Three Mysteries." This refers to the division of the symphony into three movements, each with a title: "The Nativity," "The Crucifixion," and "The Resurrection." The thematic material of each movement is taken from the Gregorian chant of the Roman Catholic Church. In most cases the chant melody is used in its entirety, although, as in the second movement, only motives from the original chant are used. The titles of the Gregorian chants used are:

FIRST MOVEMENT: The Nativity
  (1) *Puer natus est nobis*
    (A Child is born to us)
  (2) *Gloria in Excelsis Deo*
    (Glory to God in the Highest)

SECOND MOVEMENT: The Crucifixion
  (1) *Pater, si non potest, hic calix*
    (Father, if it be possible, let this chalice pass from me)
  (2) *Stabat Mater*
    (There Stood the Mother)

THIRD MOVEMENT: The Resurrection
  (1) *Angelus Domini descendit de caelo*
    (The Angel of God descended from heaven)
  (2) *Christus resurgens ex mortuis*
    (Christ risen from the dead)
  (3) *Victimae paschali laudes*
    (Praise the Paschal Victim)

THIRD MOVEMENT: The Resurrection. *Lento moderato.*
A chord in the upper harmonics of the string section accompanies the opening statement of the first theme, *Angelus Domini* (Example 1) as it is played by the low strings:

Example 1 (Angelus Domini)

No sooner has this statement finished than the French horns introduce the second theme, *Christus resurgens*:

Example 2 (Christus resurgens)

The trumpet then plays a later portion of the *Angelus Domini* theme (Example 1) recitative style, which melody is finished by the flute (representing the angel's words: "Ye seek Jesus of Nazareth. He is not here. He is risen.")

The meter changes to 2/4 and the clarinet introduces the third theme, *Victimae Paschali* (Rejoicing at the news):

Example 3 (Victimae Paschali)

Clarinet

Fragments of this chant appear alternately in the woodwinds and strings until the oboe plays all of Example 3.

The opening phrase of Example 3 passes from violin to bass clarinet and then a figure taken earlier from Example 3 becomes more prominent:

Example 4

Violins

This figure moves upwards in the violins, then the flutes, and then in low woodwinds and strings.

The opening phrase of Example 3 moves from the woodwinds to strings.

Example 2 (French horns) is combined with Example 3 (low strings).

Example 2 is repeated by the trombones.

The following come in quick succession: Example 2, agitated woodwinds accompanied by low strings; Example 3, varied form, strings; Example 2, brasses, strong timpani; Example 3, strings, sharp syncopation; full orchestra, Example 3; and Example 4, horns with celli.

Fragments of Example 4 are heard in rapid sequence in: oboes, violas and celli, violins, low brasses, basses and celli.

Trombones and tuba play Example 4. A climax develops. The music softens and a trio of trombones intones the *Christus resurgens* (Example 2).

The horns then join the trombones in Example 2 and this theme takes the work to its final climax (The Ascension).

SAMUEL BARBER

BORN: March 9, 1910; West Chester, Pennsylvania.

In a rambling home called "Capricorn" which overlooks Croton Lake, New York, live two world famous composers under the same roof. In one wing there is the neat and orderly study of Samuel Barber, best known for his *Adagio for Strings, Essay for Orchestra,* and *Symphony No. 1;* in the opposite wing in a disorderly and informal study lives Gian-Carlo Menotti, famous for his chamber operas, *The Telephone, The Medium,* and *Amahl and the Night Visitors.* Between these two wings are the living quarters of these well-known gentlemen. The mountain cottage is about an hour's drive from New York, near Mt. Kisco. The two composers met when students at the Curtis Institute of Music in Philadelphia. Menotti arrived as a student from Italy, unable to speak English but having a knowledge of French. Barber was conversant in French and was asked to show Menotti around the school. A warm friendship developed, and when World War II ended, the composers turned to "Capricorn" as a retreat from busy city life, a place where they could compose in peaceful surroundings. The greatest musical outcome of this friendship was the successful production of their opera *Vanessa* at the Metropolitan Opera House in 1956 with the libretto by Menotti and the music by Barber.

Samuel Barber was born in a century-old home in the quiet Pennsylvania community of West Chester. His father was a successful doctor with little interest in music and anxious for his son also to become a doctor. Samuel's mother was a pianist and her sister, Louise Homer, was a leading singer at the Metropolitan Opera. Young Samuel started piano lessons at the age of six and tried his hand at composition a year later. One of his first attempts at opera (he was ten at the time) was the composition of one act of an opera entitled *The Rose Tree* to a libretto by the Barbers' Irish cook.

In high school Barber organized a small orchestra which he conducted in performances for local social organizations for a small fee. His hobbies included reading a great deal and taking long walks in the country, two hobbies he has never lost. The Curtis Institute of Philadelphia was just beginning during Barber's early high school days and he arranged to take lessons at the Institute on Friday mornings. By special action of the school board in West Chester (his father was chairman and had served on the board for twenty-five years), he was permitted to attend the concerts of the Philadelphia Orchestra under Leopold Stokowski on Friday afternoons.

At the Curtis Institute Barber became the first student to major in three fields: piano, composition, and voice. One day at the Institute Barber saw a notice posted on the bulletin board offering a $1200 prize (The Bearns Prize) for composition, so he submitted his *Sonata for Violin* and won the prize.

With the money Barber went to Salzburg to study. This was the first of many trips to Europe. Money from his family allowed him to spend the summers of 1929 and 1930 in Italy with the family of his friend, Gian-Carlo Menotti.

Before World War II Barber spent a great deal of time in Italy, first on a Pulitzer Traveling Scholarship of $1500 and then on a $2500 award of the Prix de Rome for study at the American Academy there. It was in Italy that Barber completed his overture to *The School for Scandal* and later his *Symphony No. 1.*

In 1936 Barber met the Italian conductor Bernardino Molinari who conducted the first performance of his *First Symphony* which later won the Pulitzer Prize. Barber journeyed to the United States to hear the first American performance of this work in Cleveland and then to Salzburg to hear it performed as the first American work at the Salzburg Festival. Arturo Toscanini was so impressed by this work at the Salzburg Festival that he approached Barber about a composition for presentation by the new NBC Symphony that was being organized for him to conduct. For this occasion Barber submitted to Toscanini his *Adagio for Strings* and his *Essay for Orchestra,* both of which Toscanini presented.

Because of the gathering war clouds in Europe, Barber returned to the United States where he assumed a position at the Curtis Institute of Music teaching orchestration and conducting a chorus. He was inducted into the Army in 1943 and soon transferred to the Air

Force for which he was asked to write some band music, producing his *Commando March*. The Army Air Force then asked him to write a symphony. When it was completed as his *Symphony No. 2* it was dedicated to the Air Force. Its first performance was conducted by Serge Koussevitzky in 1944.

After Barber was discharged from the service he moved to the mountain retreat he and Menotti had purchased in 1943. One of his first works written there was the ballet *Medea* for Martha Graham who entitled it *Cave of the Heart*. On an invitation from the London Gramophone Corporation, Barber traveled to Denmark and then to England in 1950 to conduct performances of some of his works for recording purposes. At that time he felt the American composer was being ignored by the American recording companies.

Returning from the recording session in London to his "Capricorn," he completed his work for soprano, chorus and orchestra, *Prayers of Kierkegaard*, in 1954. Then, in collaboration with Menotti as his librettist, he produced the opera *Vanessa* in 1958 at the Metropolitan Opera House. Barber was granted an honorary Doctor of Music degree in June, 1959, by Harvard University. During the 1961-62 season, the Philadelphia Orchestra premiered his *Toccata Festiva*, and the Boston Symphony *Die Natali*.

BIBLIOGRAPHY

Broder, Nathan. *Samuel Barber.* New York: G. Schirmer, Inc., 1954.

SYMPHONY NO. 1
in One Movement

SAMUEL BARBER

Although the *Symphony No. 1* of Samuel Barber is called by the composer a "symphony in one movement," it consists of four main sections which closely parallel the standard four movements of the Romantic symphony pattern. Three themes are presented in the first section, and these form the melodic material for the other three sections in which it is repeated in varied form.

The first section follows the accepted sonata-allegro form to the point where the recapitulation normally would occur. There the second section, a scherzo, begins. It is followed by a song-like section, and the final section of the symphony is a passacaglia. In a sense, the three last sections are a recapitulation of the first one since they are based respectively on the three themes of the exposition of the *opening* section.

In a passacaglia there are two things for which one should listen. First, the ground bass when it is introduced by itself, and its subsequent repetitions; second, the variations which appear above the ground bass. In most passacaglias the ground bass is eight measures in length; in this symphony, Barber uses a ground bass that is only six measures in length.

SECTION 1: *Allegro ma non troppo.*

The tonality of this symphony is strongly E minor although the one-measure introduction opens with a chord of E—B—F♯.

After this one-measure introduction, the strings and woodwinds present the Principal Subject of the exposition:

Example 1 (Principal Subject)

The trumpets are soon heard with the opening motive and then in the second bar the subject reverts to the strings.

A climax is built with the addition of brass, at the end of which the full orchestra rests on a sustained F-sharp.

The Second Subject is then played by the violas and English horn.

Example 2 (Second Subject)

Fragments of the Second Subject (Example 2) return in various instruments: English horn; oboe and violins; strings; low woodwinds with Figure B.

A rising passage of sixteenth-notes in the strings leads to the closing theme (Example 3).

The closing theme of the *exposition* is heard in the strings and woodwinds:

Example 3

It is repeated by celli, first violins in the low register, and the English horn.

The *exposition* closes with fragments of the three themes shifting among the sections of the orchestra.

The *development* opens with the Principal Subject (Example 1) in the strings in fragmentary groupings.

It then moves (*tranquillo*) to the English horn and to other woodwinds accompanied by strings and harp.

The trombones then take the Principal Subject in augmentation accompanied by agitated strings.

The French horns follow with it in augmentation. Almost immediately three trumpets play it in diminution.

In place of a *recapitulation* the composer opens with a new section reminiscent of a scherzo.

SECTION II: *Allegro molto.*

This section opens with the strings playing a diminution of the Principal Subject (Example 1):

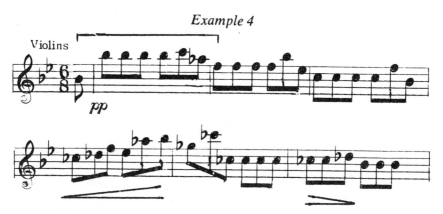

Example 4

This is then imitated and inverted, then syncopated. It passes in order to: solo clarinet; solo oboe; solo bassoon; (an episode for strings and woodwinds); celli and basses; French horns; solo trumpet; (full orchestra interlude).

Fragments of the theme appear in the following order: three flutes, two clarinets, solo bassoon, three flutes, solo bassoon, two clarinets, solo oboe, violins, solo clarinet, three muted trumpets, solo English horn, viola and celli, upper strings, full orchestra — a rather extended section marked by sharply syncopated rhythms.

The timpani appear with the theme; horns and trumpets then proclaim it; trombones have chords that move from $p < ff$. The opening motive of Example 1 is played by the trumpet, then the trombone, then the tuba.

After Example 4 has been played by a solo bassoon, then two clarinets, and again by the bassoon, this section ends with four measures of silence broken only by two timpani notes.

SECTION III: *Andante tranquillo.*

The third section is song-like, opening quietly with muted strings and harp, over which the oboe immediately plays a variation of the Second Subject (Example 2) in augmentation:

Example 5

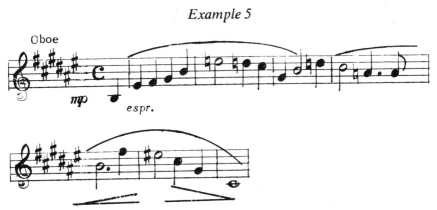

All of this section relates to this theme.

This is a long theme of twenty-four measures, after which derivations from it are heard in the strings with woodwind interjections.

The full theme is then played by strings against brass and woodwind.

This leads to an intense crescendo which is an introduction to the finale.

SECTION IV: *Con moto.*

The final section, which performs the functions of the finale of a four-movement symphony, is a passacaglia.

The ground bass of the passacaglia in the celli and double basses is derived from the opening motive of Example 1:

Example 6

Over repetitions of the ground bass, variations are heard in which the following instrumentation is predominant:

Variation 1: Oboes and bassoons.

Variation 1

Oboe

Variation 2: Oboes and bassoons.

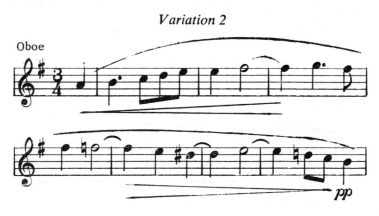

Variation 2

Oboe

Variation 3: Strings joined by woodwinds (from Example 3).
Variation 4: Strings (melody of Variation 1).
Variation 5: Strings (melody of Variation 2).
Variation 6: Strings (from Example 1).
Variation 7: Woodwinds and strings (related to Variation 1).
Variation 8: Woodwinds and strings; the trumpet plays the opening motive of Example 1 in diminution.
Variation 9: Woodwinds and strings accompany brasses which play the opening motive of Example 1 in diminution.
Variation 10: Full orchestra (Example 3).

The passacaglia section finished, the French horns play the original version of Example 3 in full while the trumpets play Example 1 in augmentation against it.

Example 3 continues in the woodwinds while the trombones take the opening motive of Example 1 in augmentation.

The tempo changes to *Largamente* and Figure A is heard in the full orchestra.

The strings sweep upward into a fragmentary variation of Example 1.

The trombones and tuba close the symphony with a figure that has the contour of the opening motive.

WILLIAM SCHUMAN

BORN: August 4, 1910; New York, New York.

William Schuman was born in New York, a city that has hundreds of symphony concerts annually, yet he did not hear a symphony concert until he was twenty years of age. Inspired by that concert, he turned to the study of serious music and crammed into a few short years of study what is frequently covered by the incipient musician in a period of a decade or more. Ten years after Schuman heard his first symphony concert he was awarded the prize of the New York Music Critics' Circle for his *Third Symphony,* and five years later he was appointed to the presidency of the Juilliard School of Music.

Since neither radio nor television had taken over the place of prominence in the living room during Schuman's childhood, the "Victrola" was the center of attraction and amusement many evenings in the Schuman home, with recordings of Caruso being played over and over. The family also gathered around the piano, singing some of the hit tunes of Victor Herbert. Although William took violin lessons, it was a struggle to talk him into practicing, for he would rather play baseball.

Schuman attended an experimental junior high school for gifted children and early showed his organizational ability. He organized a "Milray Outing Club" which charged $15 a month for boys to join, a sort of glorified "baby-sitting" project which scheduled boxing and wrestling matches and all kinds of games for the youngsters from 3:30 to 5:30 in the afternoons and all day Saturdays. At fifteen Schuman went to France for the summer under the auspices of a program of the French government. He returned to George Washington High School in New York, where he organized a jazz band. The band had several good engagements at Hunter College which were arranged through his sister, a student there. Schuman also became a leader at

Camp Cobbossee in Maine and on frequent occasions wrote music for campfire productions. After several summers at the camp he wrote music to the lyrics of one of his co-workers at the camp, Frank Loesser (known later for his *Guys and Dolls* and *Hans Christian Andersen*).

In 1928 Schuman enrolled in the New York University of Commerce. It was two years later that he was to hear his first symphony concert. His sister happened to have an extra ticket for a concert being given by the New York Philharmonic Symphony Society Orchestra and, with her mother's help, his sister was able to persuade William to go to the concert and use the extra ticket. This concert, on April 4, 1930, included the *Symphony No. 3* of Robert Schumann and the *Funeral Music* from *Die Götterdämmerung*.

The next day Schuman walked out of the lecture at the Commerce University, collected his unused tuition, went to the advertising agency for which he was working, and resigned. As he wandered around that day he saw a sign reading, "Malkin Conservatory of Music," went in, and signed up for a course in harmony. His family advised him against a career in music and were disappointed that he had given up his study at the University. In 1933 Schuman entered Teacher's College, Columbia University, and two years later earned the Bachelor of Science degree in music.

Now a college graduate with a degree, Schuman looked about for a job. Noting in the handbook of Sarah Lawrence College the emphasis upon self-education and the importance of an environment conducive to learning, Schuman applied for a teaching position. At the time of his first application there were no openings, but after a tryout on the elementary level teaching music, he again tried Sarah Lawrence College and was enabled to go there on a grant the college had received from the Rockefeller Foundation.

In preparation for his college work he spent the summer at the Mozarteum in Salzburg and returned in his twenty-fifth year to start work at the college. During his first year on the faculty he married Frances Prince. Schuman submitted his *Chorale Canons* (later published as *Four Canonic Choruses*) for a contest and failed to earn a prize. Realizing he needed additional work, he went to study with Roy Harris at Juilliard School of Music during the summer. His *First Symphony* was performed at a Composers' Forum Laboratory of the WPA in 1936. His *Second Symphony* won a prize in a contest, but unfortunately the backers of the contest did not have any money to fulfill the prize, a public performance and a recording. This *Second Symphony*, however, did enable him to meet Aaron Copland, and the symphony later was broadcast by CBS. Copland then encouraged Koussevitzky to perform it with the Boston Symphony. The *American Festival Overture* was written for an ASCAP concert of American music in 1939. Roy Harris praised the overture and took it to Koussevitzky for performance. Two years later Schuman's *Symphony No. 3* was given a good review by the Boston critics and won the Music Critics' Circle of New York prize. The following two years saw the composition of the *Symphony No. 4* and the *Symphony for Strings* as well as *A Free Song*, a choral setting based on the words of Walt Whitman. It won a Pulitzer Prize, the first for a musical composition.

In 1944 Schuman became the Director of Publications for G. Schirmer, music publishers in New York City, under a three-year contract. While in this position he wrote the ballet *Undertow* for the Antony Tudor Ballet to be performed at the Metropolitan Opera House. In the meantime, the Juilliard School of Music was looking for a president and the name of William Schuman seemed to be the answer to their search. G. Schirmer released Schuman from his contract there (although he remained an adviser on the publication of contemporary music), and he assumed the presidency of the Juilliard School of Music.

Schuman's *Symphony No. 6* was commissioned by the Dallas Symphony Orchestra League in 1949. Schuman composed an opera based on a baseball story, one of his life-long interests, entitled *The Mighty Casey* (1953). In 1955 he produced his *Credendum*, an article of faith for the U. S. National Commission for UNESCO. The following year (1956) he wrote his *New England Triptych* on a commission from Andre Kostelanetz. His *Symphony No. 7* was premiered in Boston during the fall of the 1960-61 season.

William Schuman, as president of the Juilliard School of Music, has contributed much to American music education. After assuming the presidency of that school, he revamped the entire curriculum in order to achieve a more integrated and functional approach to music. Classes in analysis and solfege were incorporated into classes on the history and performance of music. Formerly the student had learned the structure of chords in one class, form in another, and attended a third class in which recordings for "appreciation" were heard. Now all the techniques and functions of music are studied concurrently, form and harmonic structure being the logical outgrowth of every composition studied.

Schuman was appointed Director of the Lincoln Center for the

Performing Arts project in 1962. In assuming this new position —
and the responsibility for seeing the new homes for the New York
Philharmonic, the Metropolitan Opera, the Juilliard School of Music
completed — he became President Emeritus of Juilliard.

BIBLIOGRAPHY

Schreiber, Flora Rheta and Vincent Persichetti. *William Schuman*. New York:
G. Schirmer, Inc., 1954.

NEW ENGLAND TRIPTYCH

Three Pieces for Orchestra after William Billings

WILLIAM SCHUMAN

William Schuman says of Billings:

William Billings (1746-1800) is a major figure in the history of American
music. The works of this dynamic composer capture the spirit of sinewy
ruggedness, deep religiosity and patriotic fervor that we associate with the
Revolutionary period. Despite the undeniable crudities and technical shortcomings of his music, his appeal, even today, is forceful and moving. I am not
alone among American composers who feel an identity with Billings and it is
this sense of identity which accounts for my use of his music as a point of
departure. These pieces do not constitute a "fantasy" on themes of Billings,
nor "variations" on his themes, but rather a fusion of styles and musical language.

FIRST MOVEMENT: *Be Glad Then, America.*

Billings' text for this anthem includes the following lines:
Be glad then, America.
Shout and rejoice,
Fear not, O land,
Be glad and rejoice.
Hallelujah!

A timpani solo introduces the movement with a rhythmic variation of Billings' melody:

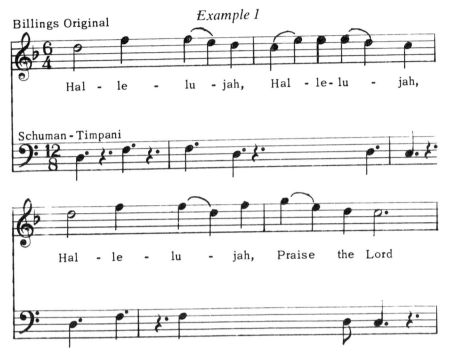

The bass clarinet, bassoon and double bass sustain a low D (lowest note possible for the bass clarinet) for thirty measures while the timpani continue.

After the timpani, the celli enter with a rhythmic variation of Billings' original melody:

The violas enter a third above the celli.

Five measures later the first and second violins enter with the melody.

Woodwinds, then horns and timpani, are added, and the music builds to a climax.

(*Allegro Vivo*)

Trumpets and trombones boldly announce the phrase: "Be glad then, America."

Example 3

Strings and woodwinds then proclaim it.

The full brass choir declaims it once more.

The full orchestra enters with a variation of the "Be glad then" theme.

The strings drop out and the brass and woodwinds play a rhythmical variation.

French horns enter with the theme (Example 3). A contrapuntal passage follows as more horns enter one measure later in stretto.

The timpani enter with the theme.

Celli and violas begin a new section with a short subject (an inversion of the contour of Example 3):

Example 4

It then appears in turn in: first violins; second violins; first violins; celli.

An extended contrapuntal development of this follows in the strings, later joined by woodwinds, trombone, and tuba.

As the full orchestra is building to a climax trumpets, then trombones, play variations of Example 4.

After a climax had been reached, the horns announce Example 3. Its rhythmic pattern descends in trombones and tuba while its first three notes in augmentation are played by trumpets and clarinets.

The piccolo and oboe play an unaccompanied duet based on the theme of Example 2.

Horns play all of Example 2, repeated immediately by the trumpets.

A *coda*, dominated by the brasses boldly playing rhythms from Example 3, concludes the movement.

SECOND MOVEMENT: *When Jesus Wept.*

When Jesus wept the falling tear
In mercy flowed beyond all bound;
When Jesus groaned, a trembling fear
Seized all the guilty world around.

Schuman says of this movement: "Here, Billings' music is used in its original form, as well as in new settings with contrapuntal embellishments and melodic extensions."

The melody of this movement is modal; specifically, it is in the Æolian mode. The Æolian mode is normally described as the pattern established by the playing of all the white keys on the piano between a and a'. Transposed to the key of g minor which Schuman uses, the scale is G—A—B-flat—C—D—E-flat—F—G.

A snare drum solo introduces the movement.

The solo bassoon presents the first half of Billings' melody; then while the bassoon sustains the tonic, the oboe finishes the melody:

Example 5

When Je- sus wept the fall- ing tear,

Bassoon

p

legato, cantabile

In mer- cy flow-ed be- yond all bound;

Oboe

legato, cantabile

An extended bassoon-oboe duet finishes the presentation of the thematic material.

Muted strings enter with sustained chords while the first violins play a variation of the melody.

After reaching a climax, the first violas then take the opening portion of the theme.

The violins are heard with fragments of the melody.

The full string choir presents the theme.

The solo bassoon returns with the opening phrase of the theme, the oboe entering with a contrapuntal melody two measures later.

The background of string chords for the oboe-bassoon duet drops out and the duet continues, accompanied by the snare drum.

The duet is finished; strings re-enter with solid, sustained chords; the drum closes the movement.

THIRD MOVEMENT: *Chester.*
Concerning the third movement, the composer states:

This music, composed as a church hymn, was subsequently adopted by the Continental Army as a marching song and enjoyed great popularity. The orchestra piece derives from the spirit both of the hymn and the marching song. The original words, with one of the verses especially written for use by the Continental Army, follow:

> Let tyrants shake their iron rods,
> And slavery clank her galling chains,
> We fear them not, we trust in God,
> New England's God forever reigns.

> The foe comes with haughty stride,
> Our troops advance with martial noise,
> Their vet'rans flee beyond our youth,
> And gen'rals yield to beardless boys.

The woodwinds present the theme in the style of a hymn as Billings originally wrote it, with the bassoons and bass clarinet playing the final line:

Example 6

The tempo changes to *Allegro Vivo;* chords in martial rhythm for pizzicato strings and muted brass accompany Billings' tune in the upper woodwinds.

A sixteenth-note passage for woodwinds leads to a bridge for agitated strings, building to a climax.

At the climax, horns and woodwinds present the theme in extension. Trombones finish it.

The woodwinds take over with a rhythmic figure, trombones refer to the theme, strings join in, and a climax is built.

The volume subsides and the snare and bass drums and cymbals provide accompaniment for the brass choir with a sustained variation of the theme (Example 6).

After the brass climax, strings and woodwinds join in a crisp, rhythmic passage.

Trumpets play the opening notes of Example 6 in extension.

The horns enter with a fragment of the theme.

At the climax, the timpani are played with hard sticks; horns, trumpets, trombones, with bells in the air; and final chords are sharply punctuated by snare and bass drums.

GIAN-CARLO MENOTTI

BORN: July 7, 1911; Cadegliano, Italy.

Two young Broadway producers thought Menotti's early opera, *The Medium,* had "box office appeal" so they rented a theater on Broadway and scheduled performances of it. The advance sale was $47. The patrons that attended the first few performances could easily be counted without the use of an adding machine, and a closing date was announced. At the last minute there was an increase in attendance so that the producers extended the run for a short period and then had to announce another closing date. By the time the second closing date arrived, a miracle had happened. Apparently by word of mouth, the success of the opera had spread and it was rescheduled to play indefinitely. *The Medium* not only played through until the following spring, but was then presented throughout the United States, in London and in Paris. Over a thousand performances were given in a few years.

Gian-Carlo Menotti was born of a wealthy family in Cadegliano, Italy, the sixth of ten children. His father was a retired exporter and his mother had some knowledge of music. She taught the peasants of the neighborhood Gregorian chant and was able to give Gian-Carlo his first music lessons. These lessons started when Gian-Carlo was four and it was not long until he was taking part in the chamber music concerts the Menottis held regularly at their home. By the time the boy was six, he had begun composing and he completed his first opera, *The Death of Pierrot*, at eleven. In the last act of this opera, every character killed himself, leaving the final scene strewn with bodies.

The Menotti family moved to Milan and subsequently Gian-Carlo had an opportunity to hear most of the opera productions at the La Scala Opera House where his family maintained a box. The boy started studying at the Milan Conservatory when he was twelve, and before he left there in his seventeenth year, he had completed his second opera. On the death of his father, his mother took him on a trip to South America to settle some financial matters which her husband had there. On the return they stopped in New York for a visit with Tullio Serafin, then conducting at the Metropolitan Opera House. The conductor was interested in some of the compositions that young Menotti had been working on and suggested the boy attend the Curtis Institute of Music in Philadelphia. He arranged for young Menotti to meet the head of the composition department who was so impressed he arranged for Gian-Carlo to attend Curtis on a scholarship.

At Curtis Institute Menotti had to learn the English language as he spoke only Italian. Visiting the motion pictures about four times a week, he soon developed a command of English. He was a good student at the Institute and completed his opera buffa, *Amelia Goes to the Ball*, while there. It was presented at Curtis under the direction of Fritz Reiner in April, 1937. Six days later it was given in New York at the New Amsterdam Theatre and proved so successful that the Metropolitan Opera House scheduled it for seven performances the following year. Menotti had written the libretto himself in Italian, and then had it translated into English for performance, a practice he followed on other occasions.

On the strength of *Amelia,* the NBC network commissioned him to write an opera for radio presentation. *The Old Maid and the Thief,* another opera buffa, was written for this commission and produced by the NBC Orchestra on April 22, 1939. The composer's next opera was a dramatic work, *The Island God,* which was presented at the Metropolitan on February 20, 1942. Both the public and the critics deemed this opera a failure.

Three years later Menotti finished his *Concerto for Piano and Orchestra* which was premiered by the Boston Symphony Orchestra. The following year he received a commission from the Ditson Fund for an opera. This time Menotti based the dramatic plot around a seance, and called the work *The Medium*. It was first produced at Columbia University in 1946 and the next year on Broadway. *The Telephone,* a second opera with a small cast and chamber orchestra, centered around a woman who loved to talk on the telephone. It was mounted off Broadway at the Heckscher Theatre along with *The Medium* on February 18, 1947. Two young theatrical producers moved the operas to a Broadway theater, the Ethel Barrymore, on May 1 of that year. As already recounted, these two operas seemed doomed from the start, but amazingly attendance picked up until eventually they were a financial success.

In 1950 Menotti produced his opera *The Consul.* It was one of the outstanding hits of the Broadway season, winning the Pulitzer Prize as well as the New York Drama Critics' Award. It was soon translated into eight different languages (including Flemish and Turkish) and presented throughout the western hemisphere. Menotti had become such a success that *Life* magazine ran a story entitled "The Wizard of Opera."

The NBC Television Network then commissioned Menotti to write an opera for that medium. On Christmas Eve, 1951, television's first opera was presented, *Amahl and the Night Visitors.* It was repeated on the stage the following year by the New York City Opera and has since become a Christmas Eve tradition on television.

Menotti's *The Saint of Bleecker Street* won a Pulitzer Prize in 1954 and was later performed at La Scala in Italy. Menotti turned to a different medium for his next work, *The Unicorn, The Gorgon, and The Manticore,* subtitled *The Three Sundays of a Poet.* This forty-minute "madrigal-fable" was presented in Washington, D.C. at the Coolidge Auditorium. The work calls for a chorus, ten dancers, and nine instruments. The chorus relates the story in twelve madrigals interrupted by instrumental interludes while the dancers mime the action.

So successful was Menotti's television opera, *Amahl,* that NBC television commissioned him to do another such opera in 1963.

Amahl tries to cheer his mother as he sings: "Don't cry, Mother dear, don't worry for me."

The Three Kings — Caspar, Balthasar, and Melchior — show Amahl their gifts.

The mother swings the door open and beholds in utter amazement the Three Kings

Photos from the NBC Television production

AMAHL AND THE NIGHT VISITORS

Gian-Carlo Menotti

The Christmas Eve story concerns a crippled little shepherd boy named Amahl, who plays the pipes and dreams of great stars with flowing tails. Nothing is left to him and his widowed mother of the little they ever had and they are now faced with hunger and cold in their empty house.

The crystal-clear winter sky is dotted with stars, the Eastern Star flaming among them. Outside the cottage not far from its door, Amahl wrapped in an over-sized cloak, sits on a rock playing his shepherd's pipe. His crudely-made crutch lies on the ground beside him. Within, his mother works at household chores in the tiny room lighted only by the dying fire and the low flame of the oil lamp.

Amahl's pipe tune is played by the oboe, a melody reminiscent of the folk tunes of the Near East and Hungary:

Example 1

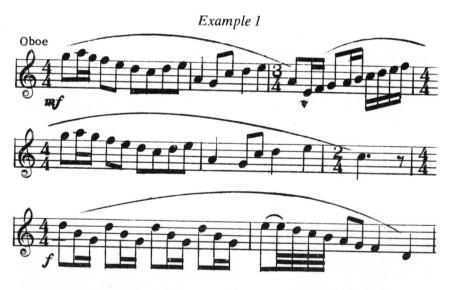

After Amahl's mother calls to him several times that it is time to go to bed, he stops his playing and hobbles into the cottage. He dreamily looks out at the beautiful sky and tells his mother that there's never been such a sky. "Damp clouds have shined it and soft winds have swept it as if to make ready for a king's ball."

His mother wearily accuses him of dreaming again. He begs her to come outside and look at the star with a tail of fire. She refuses and says, "Poor Amahl! Hunger has gone to your head." She sinks weeping onto a little stool and he comforts her by singing that he will go begging ·with his shepherd's pipe.

Example 2

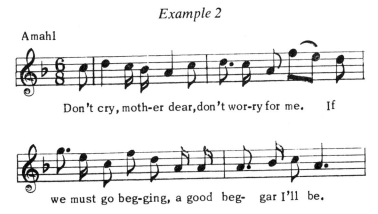

After singing "good night" to each other, Amahl goes to his pallet of straw and lies down. His mother covers him with his cloak, then she puts out the tiny oil lamp and reclines on the bench.

The voices of the Three Kings are heard very far away and Amahl raises himself on one elbow and listens with astonishment. The voices are saying, "From far away we come and farther we must go. How far, how far, my crystal star?"

Amahl throws back his cloak and hobbles on his crutch to the window.

Example 3

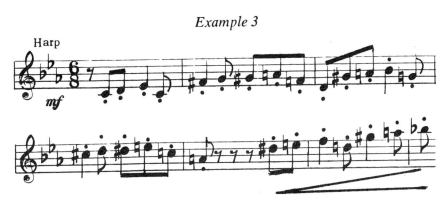

(The theme used in returning from the window utilizes diminished fifths also, this time descending.)

The singing of the Kings comes closer, ending with a knock on the door. Amahl's mother sends him to the door which he opens only a crack. He returns with the story that there is a King outside. She threatens to spank him for lying again when the knock is repeated. He repeats the scurrying trip and returns saying that there are two Kings. "What shall I do?" says his mother just as the knock is repeated a third time. "Hurry back, and don't you dare tell lies!" When he reports that there are three Kings, she threateningly goes to the door herself only to step back in utter amazement at the magnificence of the Three Kings and their Page, who ask to rest and warm themselves by her fire. The Kings say, "Good evening," and upon being assured that they may enter, they form a processional. The Page enters first with a lantern and bundles; King Kaspar, bearing a box for incense, sweeps across to the crude bench; Balthazar, bearing a chalice of myrrh, sits next to Kaspar; and Melchior follows bearing a coffer of gold.

Example 4 (The Kings' Processional March)

When Amahl's mother goes to the neighbors for food and fuel, the boy seizes the opportunity to ask questions. He learns that Balthazar lives in a black marble palace, that Kaspar is deaf and very eccentric. In fact, his box contains jewels and licorice which he shares with Amahl.

When Amahl's mother returns, she sends him to call other shepherds (as Example 3 is heard again). His mother is irresistibly drawn to the gold and wealthy gifts on the rug. She is told by Melchior that these are gifts for the Holy Child. "The Star will guide us to Him." The mother asks, "What does he look like?" and Melchior sings:

Example 5

Melchior

Have you seen a Child the col-or of wheat, the col-or of dawn?

"Have you seen a Child the color of wheat, the color of dawn?
His eyes are mild, His hands are those of a King, as the King
　　He was born.
Incense, myrrh, and gold we bring to His side.
And the Eastern Star is our guide,"

The mother says she knows a child who is sick, poor, hungry,
and cold, and names Amahl as needing their gifts. The Three Kings
continue to sing (Example 5):

"Choirs of angels hover over His roof and sing Him to sleep.
He's warmed by breath,
He's fed by Mother who is both Virgin and Queen.
Incense, myrrh, and gold we bring to His side,
And the Eastern Star is our guide."

The call of the shepherds is heard as they come down the path
to the hut. The shepherds appear first singly, then in twos and threes.
On the hills in the distance the darkness is pierced by the light of many
lanterns. The shepherds approach the hut led by a radiant Amahl.
Shyly they enter, singing:

Example 6

Shepherds

Ol-ives and quinc-es, ap-ples and rai-sins,

nut-meg and myr-tle, med-lars and chest-nuts,

"Olives and quinces, apples and raisins, nutmeg and myrtle, medlars and chestnuts, this is all we shepherds can offer you."

There follows a dance during which the shepherds forget their shyness.

Example 7

The shepherds sing, "Good-night, my good Kings, good-night and farewell. The pale stars foretell that dawn is in sight."

As the Kings fall asleep, the mother creeps closer to the gold, wondering if rich people know what to do with their gold. Finally, she convinces herself that they'll never miss it if she takes some for her child. The Page shouts "Thief!" as he grabs the mother. Amahl awakens and cries, "Don't you dare hurt my mother," and he struggles with the Page.

Example 8

At a sign from Kaspar, the Page releases the mother. Amahl staggers toward her, and letting his crutch fall, collapses, sobbing into his mother's arms.

Melchior quietly announces that she may keep the gold for the Child they seek will build His kingdom without gold. "On love, on love alone He will build His kingdom."

The mother frees herself from Amahl's embrace and throws herself on her knees before the Kings, spilling the gold she had taken onto the carpet. "Take back your gold! For such a King I've waited all my life, and if I weren't so poor I would send a gift of my own to such a child."

Amahl lifts his crutch, saying, "Let me send my crutch. Who knows, he may need one, and this I made myself." As a hush comes over the room, Amahl takes one step after another toward the Kings, holding the crutch in his outstretched arms. Realizing that he has moved without the help of his crutch, he claims, "I walk, Mother, I walk!" "It is a sign from the Holy Child," announce the Kings.

One by one the Kings pass before Amahl and lay their hands on him. They then take up their gifts for the Child, ready to depart. Amahl says, "Look, I can fight, I can work, I can play! Oh, Mother, let me go with the Kings! I want to take the crutch to the Child myself!"

Having taken his place at the head of the procession, Amahl begins to play his pipes (the melody of Example 1). The soft colors of dawn are brightening the sky; a few flakes of snow have begun to fall upon the road, as the procession disappears around the bend in the road.

The Mother, having given her most precious gift, is left alone.

INDEX

Index

INDEX